SUMMER HEAT

Linda Howard
Ann Major
Lindsay McKenna

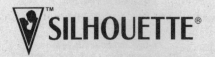

SILHOUETTE®

*First published in Great Britain 2001.
Silhouette Books, Eton House, 18-24 Paradise Road,
Richmond, Surrey TW9 1SR*

SUMMER HEAT © Harlequin Books S.A. 2001

The publisher acknowledges the copyright holders of the individual works as follows:

A GAME OF CHANCE © Linda Howington 2000
MIDNIGHT FANTASY © Ann Major 2000
HEART OF THE WARRIOR © Lindsay McKenna 2000
(This title was originally published as Morgan's Mercenaries: Heart of the Warrior)

ISBN 0 373 04719 3

81-0701

*Printed and bound in Spain
by Litografía Rosés S.A., Barcelona*

A GAME OF CHANCE

Linda Howard

Dear Reader,

When I wrote *Mackenzie's Mountain*, one of the supporting characters was Wolf's son, Joe. I fell in love with Joe, and so did everyone else. I have never received so many letters asking for a character to have his own book as I did about Joe—until Chance Mackenzie came along.

Chance was one of those characters I didn't plan. All of a sudden he was just there, without warning. He was instantly fascinating, his past mysterious and unknown, his appeal so strong he inspired literally hundreds of readers to write asking for his full story, sometimes even suggesting plot lines if I didn't have one of my own! Thank you for your suggestions, but Chance's story was in my head from the beginning.

A Game of Chance will probably be the last of the Mackenzie books. I say 'probably' because all the Mackenzie offspring are still children in my mind, and they may well stay children. I can't let them grow up without Wolf and Mary dying of old age, and I can't bear that.

There were no books on Mike and Josh, the other Mackenzie sons. Somehow I already had them settled in my mind, so their stories didn't spark for me. I wish they had.

Few readers have caught it, but all of the Mackenzie books since *Mackenzie's Mountain* have been set slightly in the future. I haven't made drastic changes, just little details here and there, to have fun and keep the time line straight. So if you catch something that doesn't seem quite right…it may be twenty years in the future!

I hope you enjoy Chance's story as much as I did!

Sincerely,

Linda Howard

For the readers

The Beginning

Coming back to Wyoming—coming home—always evoked in Chance Mackenzie such an intense mixture of emotions that he could never decide which was strongest, the pleasure or the acute discomfort. He was, by nature and nurture—not that there had been any nurturing in the first fourteen or so years of his life—a man who was more comfortable alone. If he was alone, then he could operate without having to worry about anyone but himself, and, conversely, there was no one to make him uncomfortable with concern about his own well-being. The type of work he had chosen only reinforced his own inclinations, because covert operations and anti-terrorist activities predicated he be both secretive and wary, trusting no one, letting no one close to him.

And yet… And yet, there was his family. Sprawling, brawling, ferociously overachieving, refusing to let him withdraw, not that he was at all certain he could even if they would allow it. It was always jolting, alarming, to step back into that all-enveloping embrace, to be teased and questioned—*teased,* him, whom some of the most deadly people on earth justifiably feared—hugged and kissed, fussed over and yelled at and…loved, just as if he were like everyone else. He knew he wasn't; the knowledge was always there, in the back of his mind, that he was *not* like them. But he was drawn back, again and again, by something deep inside hungering for the very things that so alarmed him. Love was scary; he had learned early and hard how little he could depend on anyone but himself.

The fact that he had survived at all was a testament to his toughness and intelligence. He didn't know how old he was, or where he had been born, what he was named as a child, or if he even had a name—nothing. He had no memory of a mother, a father, anyone who had taken care of him. A lot of people simply didn't remember their childhoods, but Chance couldn't comfort himself with that possibility, that there had been someone who had loved him and taken care of him, because he remembered too damn many other details.

He remembered stealing food when he was so small he had to stand on tiptoe to reach apples in a bin in a small-town supermarket. He had been around so many kids now that, by comparing what he remembered to the sizes they were at certain ages, he could estimate he had been no more than three years old at the time, perhaps not even that.

He remembered sleeping in ditches when it was warm, hiding in barns, stores, sheds, whatever was handy, when it was cold or raining. He remembered stealing clothes to wear, sometimes by the simple means of catching a boy playing alone in a yard, overpowering him and taking the clothes off his back. Chance had always been much stronger physically than other boys his size, because of the sheer physical difficulty of staying alive—and he had known how to fight, for the same reason.

He remembered a dog taking up with him once, a black-and-white mutt that tagged along and curled up next to him to sleep, and Chance remembered being grateful for the warmth. He also remembered that when he reached for a piece of steak he had stolen from the scraps in back of a restaurant, the dog bit him and stole the steak. Chance still had two scars on his left hand from the dog's teeth. The dog had gotten the meat, and Chance had gone one more day without food. He didn't blame the dog; it had been hungry, too. But Chance ran it off after that, because stealing enough food to keep himself alive was difficult enough, without having to steal for the dog, too. Besides, he had learned that when it came to survival, it was every dog for himself.

He might have been five years old when he learned that particular lesson, but he had learned it well.

Of course, learning how to survive in both rural and urban areas, in all conditions, was what made him so good at his job now, so he supposed his early childhood had its benefits. Even considering that, though, he wouldn't wish his childhood on a dog, not even the damn mutt that had bitten him.

His real life had begun the day Mary Mackenzie found him lying beside a road, deathly ill with a severe case of flu that had turned into pneumonia. He didn't remember much of the next few days—he had been too ill—but he had known he was in a hospital, and he had been wild with fear, because that meant he had fallen into the hands of the system, and he was now, in effect, a prisoner. He was obviously a minor, without identification, and the circumstances would warrant the child welfare services being notified. He had spent his entire life avoiding just such an event, and he had tried to make plans to escape, but his thoughts were vague, hard to get ordered, and his body was too weak to respond to his demands.

But through it all he could remember being soothed by an angel with soft blue-gray eyes and light, silvery brown hair, cool hands and a loving voice. There had also been a big, dark man, a half-breed, who calmly and repeatedly addressed his deepest fear. "We won't let them take you," the big man had said whenever Chance briefly surfaced from his fever-induced stupor.

He didn't trust them, didn't believe the big half-breed's reassurances. Chance had figured out that he himself was part American Indian, but big deal, that didn't mean he could trust these people any more than he could trust that damn thieving, ungrateful mutt. But he was too sick, too weak, to escape or even struggle, and while he was so helpless Mary Mackenzie had somehow hog-tied him with devotion, and he had never managed to break free.

He hated being touched; if someone was close enough to touch him, then they were close enough to attack him. He couldn't fight off the nurses and doctors who poked and prodded and moved him around as if he were nothing more than a mindless piece of meat. He had endured it, gritting his teeth, struggling with both his own panic and the almost overpowering urge to fight, because he knew if he fought them he would be restrained. He had to stay free, so he could run when he recovered enough to move under his own power.

But *she* had been there for what seemed like the entire time, though logically he knew she had to have left the hospital sometimes. When he burned with fever, she washed his face with a cold cloth and fed him slivers of ice. She brushed his hair, stroked his forehead when his head ached so bad he thought his skull would crack; and took over bathing him when she saw how alarmed he became when the nurses did it. Somehow he could bear it better when she bathed him, though even in his illness he had been puzzled by his own reaction.

She touched him constantly, anticipating his needs so that his pillows were fluffed before he was aware of any discomfort, the heat adjusted before he became too hot or too cold, his legs and back massaged when the fever made him ache from head to toe. He was swamped by maternal fussing, enveloped by it. It terrified him, but Mary took advantage of his weakened state and ruthlessly overwhelmed him with her mothering, as if she were determined to pack enough loving care into those few days to make up for a lifetime of nothing.

Sometime during those fever-fogged days, he began to like the feel of her cool hand on his forehead, to listen for that sweet voice even when he couldn't drag his heavy eyelids open, and the sound of it reassured him on some deep, primitive level. Once he dreamed, he didn't know what, but he woke in a panic to find her arms around him, his head pillowed on her narrow shoulder as if he were a baby, her hand gently stroking his hair while she murmured reassuringly to him—and he drifted back to sleep feeling comforted and some-how…safe.

He was always startled, even now, by how small she was. Someone so relentlessly iron-willed should have been seven feet tall and weighed three hundred pounds; at least then it would have made sense that she could bulldoze the hospital staff, even the doctors, into doing what she wanted. She had estimated his age at fourteen, but even then he was over a full head taller than the dainty woman who took over his life, but in this case size didn't matter; he was as helpless against her as was the hospital staff.

There was nothing at all he could do to fight off his growing addiction to Mary Mackenzie's mothering, even though he knew he was developing a weakness, a vulnerability, that terrified him. He had never before cared for anyone or anything, instinctively knowing that to do so would expose his emotional underbelly. But knowledge and wariness couldn't protect him now; by the time he was well enough to leave the hospital, he loved the woman who had decided she was going to be his mother, loved her with all the blind helplessness of a small child.

When he left the hospital it had been with Mary and the big man, Wolf. Because he couldn't bear to leave her just yet, he braced himself to endure her family. Just for a little while, he had promised himself, just until he was stronger.

They had taken him to Mackenzie's Mountain, into their home, their arms, their hearts. A nameless boy had died that day beside the road, and Chance Mackenzie had been born in his place. When Chance had chosen a birthday—at his new sister Maris's insistence—he chose the day Mary found him, rather than the perhaps more logical date that his adoption was final.

He had never had anything, but after that day he had been flooded with...everything. He had always been hungry, but now there was food. He had been starved, too, for learning, and now there were books everywhere, because Mary was a teacher down to her fragile bones, and she had force-fed him knowledge as fast as he could gulp it down. He was accustomed to bedding down wherever and whenever he could, but now he had his own room, his own bed, a routine. He had clothes, new ones, bought specifically for him. No one else had ever worn them, and he hadn't had to steal them.

But most of all, he had always been alone, and abruptly he was surrounded by family. Now he had a mother and a father, *four* brothers, a little sister, a sister-in-law, an infant nephew, and all of them treated him as if he had been there from the beginning. He could still barely tolerate being touched, but the Mackenzie family touched *a lot*. Mary—Mom—was constantly hugging him, tousling his hair, kissing him good-night, fussing over him. Maris, his new sister, pestered the living hell out of him just the way she did her other brothers, then would throw her skinny arms around his waist and fiercely hug him, saying, "I'm so glad you're ours!"

He was always taken aback on those occasions, and would dart a wary glance at Wolf, the big man who was the head of the Mackenzie pack and who was now Chance's dad, too. What did he think, seeing his innocent little daughter hug someone like Chance? Wolf Mackenzie was no innocent; if he didn't know exactly what experiences had molded Chance, he still recognized the dangerous vein in the half-wild boy. Chance always wondered if those knowing eyes could see clear through him, see the blood on his hands, find in his mind the memory of the man he had killed when he was about ten.

Yes, the big half-breed had known very well the type of wild animal he had taken into his family and called son, had known and, like Mary, had loved him, anyway.

His early years had taught Chance how risky life was, taught him not to trust anyone, taught him that love would only make him vulnerable and that vulnerability could cost him his life. He had known all that, and still he hadn't been able to stop himself from loving the Mackenzies. It never stopped scaring him, this weakness in his armor, and yet when he was in the family bosom was the only time he was completely relaxed, because he knew he was safe with them. He couldn't stay away, couldn't distance himself now that he was a man who was more than capable of taking care of himself, because their love for him, and his for them, fed his soul.

He had stopped even trying to limit their access to his heart and instead turned his considerable talents to doing everything he could to make their world, their lives, as safe as possible. They kept making it tougher for him; the Mackenzies constantly assaulted him with expansions: his brothers married, giving him sisters-in-law to love, because his brothers loved them and they were part of the family now. Then there were the babies. When he first came into the family there was only John, Joe and Caroline's first son, newly born. But nephew had followed nephew, and somehow Chance, along with everyone else in the Mackenzie family, found himself rocking infants, changing diapers, holding bottles, letting a dimpled little hand clutch one of his fingers while tottering first steps were made…and each one of those dimpled hands had clutched his heart, too. He had no defense against them. There were twelve nephews now, and one niece against whom he was particularly helpless, much to everyone else's amusement.

Going home was always nerve-racking, and yet he yearned for his family. He was afraid for them, afraid for himself, because he didn't know if he could live now without the warmth the Mackenzies folded about him. His mind told him he would be better off if he gradually severed the ties and isolated himself from both the pleasure and the potential for pain, but his heart always led him home again.

Chapter 1

Chance loved motorcycles. The big beast between his legs throbbed with power as he roared along the narrow winding road, the wind in his hair, leaning his body into the curves with the beast so they were one, animal and machine. No other motorcycle in the world sounded like a Harley, with that deep, coughing rumble that vibrated through his entire body. Riding a motorcycle always gave him a hard-on, and his own visceral reaction to the speed and power never failed to amuse him.

Danger was sexy. Every warrior knew it, though it wasn't something people were going to read about in their Sunday newspaper magazines. His brother Josh freely admitted that landing a fighter on a carrier deck had always turned him on. "It falls just short of orgasm," was the way Josh put it. Joe, who could fly any jet built, refrained from commenting but always smiled a slow, knowing smile.

As for both Zane and himself, Chance knew there

were times when each had emerged from certain tense situations, usually involving bullets, wanting nothing more than to have a woman beneath him. Chance's sexual need was ferocious at those times; his body was flooded with adrenaline and testosterone, he was *alive,* and he desperately needed a woman's soft body in which he could bury himself and release all the tension. Unfortunately, that need always had to wait: wait until he was in a secure position, maybe even in a different country entirely; wait until there was an available, willing woman at hand; and, most of all, wait until he had settled down enough that he could be relatively civilized in the sack.

But for now, there was only the Harley and himself, the rush of sweet mountain air on his face, and the inner mixture of joy and fear of going home. If Mom saw him riding the Harley without a helmet she would tear a strip off his hide, which was why he had the helmet with him, securely fastened behind the seat. He would put it on before sedately riding up the mountain to visit them. Dad wouldn't be fooled, but neither would he say anything, because Wolf Mackenzie knew what it was to fly high and wild.

He crested a ridge, and Zane's house came into view in the broad valley below. The house was large, with five bedrooms and four baths, but not ostentatious; Zane had instinctively built the house so it wouldn't attract undue attention. It didn't look as large as it was, because some of the rooms were underground. He had also built it to be as secure as possible, positioning it so he had an unrestricted view in all directions, but using natural formations of the land to block land access by all but the one road. The doors were steel, with state-of-the-art locks; the windows were shatterproof, and had cost a small fortune. Strategic walls had interior armor, and an emergency generator was installed in the basement. The basement also concealed another means of escape, if escape became necessary. Motion sensors were installed around the house, and as Chance wheeled the motorcycle into the driveway, he knew his arrival had already been signaled.

Zane didn't keep his family locked in a prison, but the security provisions were there if needed. Given their jobs, prudence demanded caution, and Zane had always prepared for emergencies, always had a backup plan.

Chance cut off the motor and sat for a minute, letting his senses return to normal while he ran a hand through his windswept hair. Then he kicked the stand down and leaned the Harley onto it, and dismounted much the way he would a horse. Taking a thin file from the storage compartment, he went up on the wide, shady porch.

It was a warm summer day, mid-August, and the sky was a cloudless clear blue. Horses grazed contentedly in the pasture, though a few of the more curious had come to the fence to watch with huge, liquid dark eyes as the noisy machine roared into the driveway. Bees buzzed around Barrie's flowers, and birds sang continuously in the trees. Wyoming. Home. It wasn't far away, Mackenzie's Mountain, with the sprawling house on the mountaintop where he had been given…life and everything else in this world that was important to him.

''The door's open.'' Zane's low, calm voice issued from the intercom beside the door. ''I'm in the office.''

Chance opened the door and went inside, his booted feet silent as he walked down the hall to Zane's office. With small clicks, the door locks automatically engaged behind him. The house was quiet, meaning Barrie and the kids weren't at home; if Nick was anywhere in the house she would have run squealing to him, hurling herself into his arms, chattering nonstop in her mangled English while holding his face clasped between both her little hands, making certain his attention didn't wander from her—as if he would dare look away. Nick was like a tiny package of unstable explosives; it was best to keep a weather eye on her.

The door to Zane's office was unexpectedly closed. Chance paused a moment, then opened it without knocking.

Zane was behind the desk, computer on, windows open to the warm, fresh air. He gave his brother one of his rare, warm smiles. "Watch where you step," he advised. "Munchkins on deck."

Automatically Chance looked down, checking out the floor, but he didn't see either of the twins. "Where?"

Zane leaned back in his chair a little, looking around for his offspring. Spotting them, he said, "Under the desk. When they heard me let you in, they hid."

Chance raised his eyebrows. To his knowledge, the ten-month-old twins weren't in the habit of hiding from anyone or anything. He looked more carefully and saw four plump, dimpled baby hands peeping from under the cover of Zane's desk. "They aren't very good at it," he observed. "I can see their hands."

"Give them a break, they're new at this stuff. They've only started doing it this week. They're playing Attack."

"Attack?" Fighting the urge to laugh, Chance said, "What am I supposed to do?"

"Just stand there. They'll burst from cover as fast as they can crawl and grab you by the ankles."

"Any biting involved?"

"Not yet."

"Okay. What are they going to do with me once they have me captured?"

"They haven't gotten to that part yet. For now, they just pull themselves up and stand there giggling." Zane scratched his jaw, considering. "Maybe they'll sit on your feet to hold you down, but for the most part they like standing too much to settle for sitting."

The attack erupted. Even with Zane's warning, Chance was a little surprised. They were remarkably quiet, for babies. He had to admire their precision; they launched themselves from under the desk at a rapid crawl, plump little legs pumping, and with identical triumphant crows attached themselves to his ankles. Dimpled hands clutched his jeans. The one on the left plopped down on his foot for a second, then thought better of the tactic and twisted around to begin hauling himself to an upright position. Baby arms wrapped around his knees, and the two little conquerors squealed with delight, their bubbling chuckles eliciting laughter from both men.

"Cool," Chance said admiringly. "Predator babies." He tossed the file onto Zane's desk and leaned down to scoop the little warriors into his arms, settling each diapered bottom on a muscular forearm. Cameron and Zack grinned at him, six tiny white baby teeth shining in each identical dimpled face, and immediately they began patting his face with their fat little hands, pulling his ears, delving into his shirt pockets. It was like being attacked by two squirming, remarkably heavy marshmallows.

"Good God," he said in astonishment. "They weigh a ton." He hadn't expected them to have grown so much in the two months since he had seen them.

"They're almost as big as Nick. She still outweighs

them, but I swear they feel heavier.'' The twins were
sturdy and strongly built, the little boys already showing
the size of the Mackenzie males, while Nick was as
dainty as her grandmother Mary.

''Where are Barrie and Nick?'' Chance asked, missing
his pretty sister-in-law and exuberant, cheerfully diabolic
niece.

''We had a shoe crisis. Don't ask.''

''How do you have a shoe crisis?'' Chance asked,
unable to resist. He sat down in a big, comfortable chair
across from Zane's desk, setting the babies more comfortably in his lap. They lost interest in pulling his ears
and began babbling to each other, reaching out, entwin-
ing their arms and legs as if they sought the closeness
they had known while forming in the womb. Chance
unconsciously stroked them, enjoying the softness of
their skin, the feel of squirming babies in his arms. All
the Mackenzie babies grew up accustomed to being constantly, lovingly touched by the entire extended family.

Zane laced his hands behind his head, his big, powerful body relaxed. ''First you have a three-year-old who
loves her shiny, black, patent leather Sunday shoes. Then
you make the severe tactical error of letting her watch
The Wizard of Oz.'' His stern mouth twitched, and his
pale eyes glittered with amusement.

Chance's agile mind immediately made the connection, and his acquaintance with the three-year-old in
question allowed him to make a logical assumption:
Nick had decided she had to have a pair of red shoes.
''What did she use to try to dye them?''

Zane sighed. ''Lipstick, what else?'' Each and every
young Mackenzie had had an incident with lipstick. It
was a family tradition, one John had started when, at the
age of two, he had used his mother's favorite lipstick to

recolor the impressive rows of fruit salad on Joe's dress uniform. Caroline had been impressively outraged, because the shade had been discontinued and finding a new tube had been much more difficult than replacing the small colored bars that represented medals Joe had earned and services he had performed.

"You couldn't just wipe it off?" The twins had discovered his belt buckle and zipper, and Chance moved the busy little hands that were trying to undress him. They began squirming to get down, and he leaned over to set them on the floor.

"Close the door," Zane instructed, "or they'll escape."

Leaning back, Chance stretched out a long arm and closed the door, just in time. The two diaper-clad escape artists had almost reached it. Deprived of freedom, they plopped down on their padded bottoms and considered the situation, then launched themselves in crawling patrol of the perimeters of the room.

"I *could* have wiped it off," Zane continued, his tone bland, "if I had known about it. Unfortunately, Nick cleaned the shoes herself. She put them in the dishwasher."

Chance threw back his head with a shout of laughter.

"Barrie bought her a new pair of shoes yesterday. Well, you know how Nick's always been so definite about what she wants to wear. She took one look at the shoes, said they were ugly, *even though they were just like the ones she ruined,* and refused to even try them on."

"To be accurate," Chance corrected, "what she said was that they were 'ugwy.'"

Zane conceded the point. "She's getting better with

her *L*s, though. She practices, saying the really important words, like lollipop, over and over to herself.''

"Can she say 'Chance' yet, instead of 'Dance'?" Chance asked, because Nick stubbornly refused to even acknowledge she couldn't say his name. She insisted everyone else was saying it wrong.

Zane's expression was totally deadpan. ''Not a chance.''

Chance groaned at the pun, wishing he hadn't asked. ''I gather Barrie has taken my little darling shopping, so she can pick out her own shoes.''

"Exactly.'' Zane glanced over to check on his roaming offspring. As if they had been waiting for his parental notice, first Cam and then Zack plopped down on their butts and gave brief warning cries, all the while watching their father expectantly.

"Feeding time,'' Zane said, swiveling his chair around so he could fetch two bottles from a small cooler behind the desk. He handed one to Chance. ''Grab a kid.''

"You're prepared, as always,'' Chance commented as he went over to the twins and leaned down to lift one in his arms. Holding the baby up, he peered briefly at the scowling little face to make sure he had the one he thought he had. It was Zack, all right. Chance couldn't say exactly how he knew which twin was which, how anyone in the family knew, because the babies were so identical their pediatrician had suggested putting ID anklets on them. But they each had such definite personalities, which were reflected in their expressions, that no one in the family ever confused one twin for the other.

"I have to be prepared. Barrie weaned them last month, and they don't take kindly to having to wait for dinner.''

Zack's round blue eyes were fiercely focused on the bottle in Chance's hand. "Why did she wean them so early?" Chance asked as he resumed his seat and settled the baby in the crook of his left arm. "She nursed Nick until she was a year old."

"You'll see," Zane said dryly, settling Cam on his lap.

As soon as Chance brought the bottle within reach of Zack's fat little hands the baby made a grab for it, guiding it to his rapacious, open mouth. He clamped down ferociously on the nipple. Evidently deciding to let his uncle hold the bottle, he nevertheless made certain the situation was stabilized by clutching Chance's wrist with both hands, and wrapping both chubby legs around Chance's forearm. Then he began to growl as he sucked, pausing only to swallow.

An identical growling noise came from Zane's lap. Chance looked over to see his brother's arm captured in the same manner as the two little savages held on to their meals.

Milk bubbled around Zack's rosebud mouth, and Chance blinked as six tiny white teeth gnawed on the plastic nipple.

"Hell, no wonder she weaned you!"

Zack didn't pause in his gnawing, sucking and growling, but he did flick an absurdly arrogant glance at his uncle before returning his full attention to filling his little belly.

Zane was laughing softly, and he lifted Cam enough that he could nuzzle one of the chubby legs so determinedly wrapped around his arm. Cam paused to scowl at the interruption, then changed his mind and instead favored his father with a dimpled, milky smile. The next

second the smile was gone and he attacked the bottle
again.

Zack's fuzzy black hair was as soft as silk against
Chance's arm. Babies were a pure tactile pleasure, he
thought, though he hadn't been of that opinion the first
time he'd held one. The baby in question had been John,
screaming his head off from the misery of teething.

Chance hadn't been with the Mackenzies long, only a
few months, and he had still been extremely wary of all
these people. He had managed—barely—to control his
instinct to attack whenever someone touched him, but
he still jumped like a startled wild animal. Joe and Caroline came to visit, and from the expressions on their
faces when they entered the house, it had been a very
long trip. Even Joe, normally so controlled and unflap-
pable, was frustrated by his futile efforts to calm his son,
and Caroline had been completely frazzled by a situation
she couldn't handle with her usual impeccable logic. Her
blond hair had been mussed, and her green eyes ex-
pressed an amazing mixture of concern and outrage.

As she had walked by Chance, she suddenly wheeled
and deposited the screaming baby in his arms. Startled,
alarmed, he tried to jerk back, but before he knew it he
was in sole possession of the wiggling, howling little
human. "Here," she said with relief and utmost confidence. "You get him calmed down."

Chance had panicked. It was a wonder he hadn't
dropped the baby. He'd never held one before, and he
didn't know what to do with it. Another part of him was
astounded that Caroline would entrust her adored child
to *him,* the mongrel stray Mary—Mom—had brought
home with her. Why couldn't these people see what he
was? Why couldn't they figure out he had lived wild in

a kill-or-be-killed world, and that they would be safer if
they kept their distance from him?

Instead, no one seemed to think it unusual or alarming
that he was holding the baby, even though in his panic
he held John almost at arm's length, clutched between
his two strong young hands.

But blessed quiet fell in the house. John was startled
out of his screaming. He stared interestedly at this new
person and kicked his legs. Automatically Chance
changed his grip on the baby, settling him in the cradle
of one arm as he had seen the others do. The kid was
drooling. A tiny bib was fastened around his neck, and
Chance used it to wipe away most of the slobber. John
saw this opportunity and grabbed Chance by the thumb,
immediately carrying the digit to his mouth and chomp-
ing down. Chance had jumped at the force of the hard
little gums, with two tiny, sharp teeth already breaking
the surface. He grimaced at the pain, but hung in there,
letting John use his thumb as a teething ring until Mom
rescued him by bringing a cold wet washcloth for the
baby to chew.

Chance had expected then to be relieved of baby duty,
because Mom usually couldn't wait to get her hands on
her grandson. But that day everyone had seemed content
to leave John in his hands, even the kid himself, and
after a while Chance calmed down enough to start walking around and pointing out things of interest to his little
pal, all of which John obediently studied while gnawing
on the relief-giving washcloth.

That had been his indoctrination to the ways of babies,
and from that day on he had been a sucker for the parade
of nephews his virile brothers and fertile sisters-in-law
had produced on a regular basis. He seemed to be getting

even worse, because with Zane's three he was total mush.

"By the way, Maris is pregnant."

Chance's head jerked up, and a wide grin lit his tanned face. His baby sister had been married nine whole months and had been fretting because she hadn't immediately gotten pregnant.

"When is it due?" He always ruthlessly arranged things so he could be home when a new Mackenzie arrived. Technically, this one would be a MacNeil, but that was a minor point.

"March. She says she'll be crazy before then, because Mac won't let her out of his sight."

Chance chuckled. Other than her father and brothers, Mac was the only man Maris had ever met whom she couldn't intimidate, which was one of the reasons she loved him so much. If Mac had decided he was going to ride herd on Maris during her pregnancy, she had little hope of escaping on one of those long, hard rides she so loved.

Zane nodded toward the file on his desk. "You going to tell me about it?"

Chance knew Zane was asking about more than the contents of the file. He was asking why it hadn't been transmitted by computer, instead of Chance personally bringing a hard copy. Zane knew his brother's schedule; he was the only person, other than Chance himself, who did, so he knew Chance was currently supposed to be in France. He was also asking why he hadn't been notified of Chance's change in itinerary, why his brother hadn't made a simple phone call to let him know he was coming.

"I didn't want to risk even a hint of this leaking out."

Zane's eyebrows rose. "We have security problems?"

"Nothing that I know of," Chance said. "It's what I don't know about that worries me. But, like I said, no one else can hear even a whisper of this. It's between us."

"Now you've made me curious." Zane's cool blue eyes gleamed with interest.

"Crispin Hauer has a daughter."

Zane didn't straighten from his relaxed position, but his expression hardened. Crispin Hauer had been number one on their target list for years, but the terrorist was as elusive as he was vicious. They had yet to find any way to get close to him, any vulnerability they could exploit or bait they could use to lure him into a trap. There was a record of a marriage in London some thirty-five years ago, but Hauer's wife, formerly Pamela Vickery, had disappeared, and no trace of her had ever been found. Chance, along with everyone else, had assumed the woman died soon after the marriage, either by Hauer's hand or by his enemies'.

"Who is she?" Zane asked. "*Where* is she?"

"Her name is Sonia Miller, and she's here, in America."

"I know that name," Zane said, his gaze sharpening.

Chance nodded. "Specifically, she's the courier who was supposedly robbed of her package last week in Chicago."

Zane didn't miss the "supposedly," but then, he never missed anything. "You think it was a setup?"

"I think it's a damn good possibility. I found the link when I checked into her background."

"Hauer would have known she'd be investigated after losing a package, especially one containing aerospace documents. Why take the risk?"

"He might not have thought we would find anything.

She was adopted. Hal and Eleanor Miller are listed as her parents, and they're clean as a whistle. I wouldn't have known she was adopted if I hadn't tried to pull up her birth certificate on the computer. Guess what—Hal and Eleanor never had any children. Little Sonia Miller didn't have a birth certificate. So I did some digging and found the adoption file—''

Zane's eyebrows rose. Open adoptions had caused so many problems that the trend had veered sharply back to closed files, which, coupled with electronic privacy laws and safeguards, had made it damn difficult to even locate those closed files, much less get into them. ''Did you leave any fingerprints?''

''Nothing that will lead back to us. I went through a couple of relays, then hacked into the Internal Revenue and accessed the file from their system.''

Zane grinned. If anyone did notice the electronic snooping, it likely wouldn't even be mentioned; no one messed with the tax people.

Zack had finished his bottle; his ferocious grip on it slackened, and his head lolled against Chance's arm as he briefly struggled against sleep. Automatically Chance lifted the baby to his shoulder and began patting his back. ''Ms. Miller has been employed as a courier for a little over five years. She has an apartment in Chicago, but her neighbors say she's seldom there. I have to think this is a long-term setup, that she's been working with her father from the beginning.''

Zane nodded. They had to assume the worst, because it was their job to do so. Only by anticipating the worst could they be prepared to handle it.

''Do you have anything in mind?'' he asked, taking the bottle from Cam's slackened grip and gently lifting the sleeping baby to his own shoulder.

"Getting next to her. Getting her to trust me."

"She's not going to be the trusting sort."

"I have a plan," Chance said, and grinned, because that was usually Zane's line.

Zane grinned in return, then paused as a small security console in the wall dinged a soft alarm. He glanced at the security monitor. "Brace yourself," he advised. "Barrie and Nick are home."

Seconds later the front door opened and a shriek filled the house. "Unca *Dance*! UncaDanceUncaDance-Unca*Dance*!" The chant was punctuated by the sound of tiny feet running and jumping down the hall as Nick's celebration of his visit came closer. Chance leaned back in his chair and opened the office door a bare second before Nick barreled through it, her entire little body quivering with joy and eagerness.

She hurled herself at him, and he managed to catch her with his free arm, dragging her onto his lap. She paused to bestow a big-sisterly kiss and a pat on the back of Zack's head—never mind that he was almost as big as she was—then turned all her fierce attention to Chance.

"Are you staying dis time?" she demanded, even as she lifted her face for him to kiss. He did, nuzzling her soft cheek and neck and making her giggle, inhaling the faint sweet scent of baby that still clung to her.

"Just for a few days," he said, to her disappointment. She was old enough now to notice his long and frequent absences, and whenever she saw him she tried to convince him to stay.

She scowled; then, being Nick, she decided to move on to more important matters. Her face brightened. "Den can I wide your moborcycle?"

Alarm flared through him. "No," he said firmly.

"You can't ride it, sit on it, lean on it, or put any of your toys on it *unless I'm with you.*" With Nick, it was best to close all the loopholes. She seldom disobeyed a direct order, but she was a genius at finding cracks to slip through. Another possibility occurred to him. "You can't put Cam or Zack on it, either." He doubted she could lift either of them, but he wasn't taking any risks.

"Thank you," Barrie said dryly, entering the office in time to catch his addendum. She leaned down to kiss him on the cheek, at the same time lifting Zack from his arms so he could protect himself from Nick's feet. All the Mackenzie males, at one time or another, had fallen victim to a tiny foot in the crotch.

"Mission accomplished?" Zane asked, leaning back in his chair and smiling at his wife with that lazy look in his pale eyes that said he liked what he was seeing.

"Not without some drama and convincing, but, yes, mission accomplished." She pushed a feather lock of red hair out of her eyes. As always, she looked stylish, though she was wearing nothing dressier than beige slacks and a white sleeveless blouse that set off her slim, lightly tanned arms. You could take the girl out of the finishing school, Chance thought admiringly, but you could never take the finishing school out of the girl, and Barrie had gone to the most exclusive one in the world.

Nick was still focused on negotiating riding rights on the motorcycle. She caught his face between her hands and leaned down so her nose practically touched his, insuring his complete attention. He nearly laughed aloud at the fierce intent in her expression. "I wet you wide my twicycle," she said, evidently deciding to cajole instead of demand.

"Somehow I missed that," Zane murmured in amusement, while Barrie laughed softly.

"You *offered* to let me ride your tricycle," Chance corrected. "But I'm too big to ride a tricycle, and you're too little to ride a motorcycle."

"Den when *can* I wide it?" She made her blue eyes wide and winsome.

"When you get your driver's license."

That stymied her. She had no idea what a driver's license was, or how to get it. She stuck a finger in her mouth while she pondered this situation, and Chance tried to divert her interest. "Hey! Aren't those new shoes you're wearing?"

Like magic, her face brightened again. She wriggled around so he could hold one foot up so close to his face she almost kicked him in the nose. "Dey're so *pwetty*," she crooned in delight.

He caught the little foot in his big hand, admiring the shine of the black patent leather. "Wow, that's so shiny I can see my face in it." He pretended to inspect his teeth, which set her to giggling.

Zane rose to his feet. "We'll put the boys down for their naps while you have her occupied."

Keeping Nick occupied wasn't a problem; she was never at a loss for something to say or do. He curled one silky black strand of her hair around his finger while she chattered about her new shoes, Grampa's new horses, and what Daddy had said when he hit his thumb with a hammer. She cheerfully repeated exactly what Daddy had said, making Chance choke.

"But I'm not 'posed to say dat," she said, giving him a solemn look. "Dat's a weally, weally bad word."

"Yeah," he said, his voice strained. "It is."

"I'm not 'posed to say 'damn,' or 'hell,' or 'ass,' or—"

"Then you shouldn't be saying them now." He managed to inject a note of firmness in his tone, though it was a struggle to keep from laughing.

She looked perplexed. "Den how can I tell you what dey are?"

"Does Daddy know what the bad words are?"

The little head nodded emphatically. "He knows dem *all*."

"I'll ask him to tell me, so I'll know which words not to say."

"Otay." She sighed. "But don't hit him too hard."

"Hit him?"

"Dat's de only time he says *dat* word, when he hits his dumb wid de hammer. He said so."

Chance managed to turn his laugh into a cough. Zane was an ex-SEAL; his language was as salty as the sea he was so at home in, and Chance had heard "dat word," and worse, many times from his brother. But Mom had also instilled strict courtesy in all her children, so their language was circumspect in front of women and children. Zane must not have known Nick was anywhere near him when he hit his thumb, or no amount of pain could have made him say that in her hearing. Chance only hoped she forgot it before she started kindergarten.

"Aunt Mawis is goin' to have a baby," Nick said, scrambling up to stand in his lap, her feet braced on his thighs. Chance put both hands around her to steady her, though his aid probably wasn't needed; Nick had the balance of an acrobat.

"I know. Your daddy told me."

Nick scowled at not being the first to impart the news. "She's goin' to foal in de spwing," she announced.

He couldn't hold back the laughter this time. He gathered the little darling close to him and stood, whirling her around and making her shriek with laughter as she clung to his neck. He laughed until his eyes were wet. God, he loved this child, who in the three short years of her life had taught them all to be on their toes at all times, because there was no telling what she was going to do or say. It took the entire Mackenzie family to ride herd on her.

Suddenly she heaved a sigh. "When's de spwing? Is it a wong, wong time away?"

"Very long," he said gravely. Seven months was an eternity to a three-year-old.

"Will I be old?"

He put on a sympathetic face and nodded. "You'll be four."

She looked both horrified and resigned. "Four," she said mournfully. "Whodadunkit?"

When he stopped laughing this time, he wiped his eyes and asked, "Who taught you to say *whoda-thunkit?*"

"John," she said promptly.

"Did he teach you anything else?"

She nodded.

"What? Can you remember it?"

She nodded.

"Will you tell me what they are?"

She rolled her eyes up and studied the ceiling for a moment, then gave him a narrow-eyed look. "Will you wet me wide your moborcycle?"

Damn, she was bargaining! He trembled with fear at the thought of what she would be like when she was sixteen. "No," he said firmly. "If you got hurt, your mommy and daddy would cry, Grampa and Gamma would cry, *I* would cry, Aunt Maris would cry, Mac would cry, Unca Mike would cry—"

She looked impressed at this litany of crying and interrupted before he could name everyone in the family. "I can wide a horse, Unca Dance, so why can't I wide your moborcycle?"

God, she was relentless. Where in the hell were Zane and Barrie? They'd had plenty of time to put the twins down for their naps. If he knew Zane, his brother was taking advantage of having a baby-sitter for Nick to get in some sexy time with his wife; Zane was always prepared to use a fluid situation to his advantage.

It was another ten minutes before Zane strolled back into the office, his eyes slightly heavy-lidded and his hard face subtly relaxed. Chance scowled at his brother. He'd spent the ten minutes trying to talk Nick into telling him what John had taught her, but she wasn't budging from her initial negotiation. "It's about time," he groused.

"Hey, I hurried," Zane protested mildly.

"Yeah, right."

"As much as possible," he added, smiling. He smoothed his big hand over his daughter's shining black hair. "Have you kept Uncle Chance entertained?"

She nodded. "I told him de weally, weally bad word you said when you hit your dumb."

Zane looked pained, then stern. "How did you tell him when you aren't supposed to say the word?"

She stuck her finger in her mouth and began studying the ceiling again.

"Nick." Zane plucked her from Chance's arms. "Did you say the word?"

Her lower lip stuck out a little, but she nodded, owning up to her transgression.

"Then you can't have a bedtime story tonight. You promised you wouldn't say it."

"I'm sowwy," she said, winding her arms around his neck and laying her head on his shoulder.

Gently he rubbed his hand up and down her back. "I know you are, sweetheart, but you have to keep your promises." He set her on her feet. "Go find Mommy."

When she was gone, out of curiosity Chance asked, "Why didn't you tell her that she couldn't watch television, instead of taking away the bedtime story?"

"We don't want to make television attractive by using it as a treat or a privilege. Why? Are you taking notes on being a parent?"

Appalled, Chance said, "Not in this lifetime."

"Yeah? Fate has a way of jumping up and biting you on the ass when you least expect it."

"Well, my ass is currently bite-free, and I intend to keep it that way." He nodded at the file on Zane's desk. "We have some planning to do."

Chapter 2

This whole assignment was a tribute to Murphy's Law, Sunny Miller thought in disgust as she sat in the Salt Lake City airport, waiting for her flight to be called—if it were called at all, which she was beginning to doubt. This was her fifth airport of the day, and she was still almost a thousand miles from her destination, which was Seattle. She was *supposed* to have been on a direct flight from Atlanta to Seattle, but that flight had been canceled due to mechanical problems and the passengers routed on to other flights, none of which were direct.

From Atlanta she had gone to Cincinnati, from Cincinnati to Chicago, from Chicago to Denver, and from Denver to Salt Lake City. At least she was moving west instead of backtracking, and the flight from Salt Lake City, assuming it ever started boarding, was supposed to actually land in Seattle.

The way her day had gone, she expected it to crash instead.

She was tired, she had been fed nothing but peanuts all day, and she was afraid to go get anything to eat in case her flight was called and the plane got loaded and in the air in record time, leaving her behind. When Murphy was in control, anything was possible. She made a mental note to find this Murphy guy and punch him in the nose.

Her normal good humor restored by the whimsy, she resettled herself in the plastic seat and took out the paperback book she had been reading. She was tired, she was hungry, but she wasn't going to let the stress get to her. If there was one thing she was good at, it was making the best of a situation. Some trips were smooth as silk, and some were a pain in the rear; so long as the good and the bad were balanced, she could cope.

Out of ingrained habit, she kept the strap of her soft leather briefcase looped around her neck, held across her body so it couldn't easily be jerked out of her grasp. Some couriers might handcuff the briefcase or satchel to their wrists, but her company was of the opinion that handcuffs drew unwanted attention; it was better to blend in with the horde of business travelers than to stand out. Handcuffs practically shouted "Important stuff inside!"

After what had happened in Chicago the month before, Sunny was doubly wary and also kept one hand on the briefcase. She had no idea what was in it, but that didn't matter; her job was to get the contents from point A to point B. When the briefcase had been jerked off her shoulder by a green-haired punk in Chicago last month, she had been both humiliated and furious. She was *always* careful, but evidently not careful enough, and now she had a big blotch on her record.

On a very basic level, she was alarmed that she had

been caught off guard. She had been taught from the cradle to be both prepared and cautious, to be alert to what was going on around her; if a green-haired punk could get the best of her, then she was neither as prepared nor alert as she had thought. When one slip could mean the difference between life and death, there was no room for error.

Just remembering the incident made her uneasy. She returned the book to her carry-on bag, preferring to keep her attention on the people around her.

Her stomach growled. She had food in her carry-on, but that was for emergencies, and this didn't qualify. She watched the gate, where the two airline reps were patiently answering questions from impatient passengers. From the dissatisfied expressions on the passengers' faces as they returned to their seats, the news wasn't good; logically, she should have enough time to find something to eat.

She glanced at her watch: one-forty-five p.m., local time. She had to have the contents of the briefcase in Seattle by nine p.m. Pacific time tonight, which should have been a breeze, but the way things were going, she was losing faith the assignment could be completed on time. She hated the idea of calling the office to report another failure, even one that wasn't her fault. If the airline didn't get on the ball soon, though, she would have to do something. The customer needed to know if the packet wasn't going to arrive as scheduled.

If the news on the flight delay hadn't improved by the time she returned from eating, she would see about transferring to another airline, though she had already considered that option and none of the possibilities looked encouraging; she was in flight-connection hell. If she couldn't work out something, she would have to make that phone call.

Taking a firm grip on the briefcase with one hand and her carry-on bag with the other, she set off down the concourse in search of food that didn't come from a vending machine. Arriving passengers were pouring out of a gate to her left, and she moved farther to the right to avoid the crush. The maneuver didn't work; someone jostled her left shoulder, and she instinctively looked around to see who it was.

No one was there. A split-second reaction, honed by years of looking over her shoulder, saved her. She automatically tightened her grip on the briefcase just as she felt a tug on the strap, and the leather fell limply from her shoulder.

Damn it, not again!

She ducked and spun, swinging her heavy carry-on bag at her assailant. She caught a glimpse of feral dark eyes and a mean, unshaven face; then her attention locked on his hands. The knife he had used to slice the briefcase strap was in one hand, and he already had his other hand on the briefcase, trying to jerk it away from her. The carry-on bag hit him on the shoulder, staggering him, but he didn't release his grip.

Sunny didn't even think of screaming, or of being scared; she was too angry for either reaction, and both would have splintered her concentration. Instead, she wound up for another swing, aiming the bag for the hand holding the knife.

Around her she heard raised voices, full of confused alarm as people tried to dodge around the disturbance, and jostled others instead. Few, if any, of them would have any idea what the ruckus was about. Vision was hampered; things were happening too fast. She couldn't rely on anyone coming to help, so she ignored the noise, all her attention centered on the cretin whose dirty hand clutched her briefcase.

Whap! She hit him again, but still he held on to the knife.

"Bitch," he snarled, his knife-hand darting toward her.

She jumped back, and her fingers slipped on the leather. Triumphantly he jerked it away from her. Sunny grabbed for the dangling strap and caught it, but the knife made a silver flash as he sliced downward, separating the strap from the briefcase. The abrupt release of tension sent her staggering back.

The cretin whirled and ran. Catching her balance, Sunny shouted, "Stop him!" and ran in pursuit. Her long skirt had a slit up the left side that let her reach full stride, but the cretin not only had a head start, he had longer legs. Her carry-on bag banged against her legs, further hampering her, but she didn't dare leave it behind. Doggedly she kept running, even though she knew it was useless. Despair knotted her stomach. Her only prayer was that someone in the crowd would play hero and stop him.

Her prayer was abruptly answered.

Up ahead, a tall man standing with his back to the concourse turned and glanced almost negligently in the direction of the ruckus. The cretin was almost abreast of him. Sunny drew breath to yell out another "Stop him," even though she knew the cretin would be past before the man could react. She never got the words out of her mouth.

The tall man took in with one glance what was happening, and in a movement as smooth and graceful as a ballet pirouette, he shifted, pivoted and lashed out with one booted foot. The kick landed squarely on the cretin's right knee, taking his leg out from under him. He cart-wheeled once and landed flat on his back, his arms flung over his head. The briefcase skidded across the concourse before bouncing against the wall, then back into the path of a stream of passengers. One man hopped over the briefcase, while others stepped around it.

Sunny immediately swerved in that direction, snatching up the briefcase before any other quick-fingered thief could grab it, but she kept one eye on the action.

In another of those quick, graceful movements, the tall man bent and flipped the cretin onto his stomach, then wrenched both arms up high behind his back and held them with one big hand.

"Owww!" the cretin howled. "You bastard, you're breaking my arms!"

The name-calling got his arms roughly levered even higher. He howled again, this time wordlessly and at a much higher pitch.

"Watch your language," said his captor.

Sunny skidded to a halt beside him. "Be careful," she said breathlessly. "He had a knife."

"I saw it. It landed over there when he fell." The man didn't look up but jerked his chin to the left. As he spoke he efficiently stripped the cretin's belt from its loop and wound the leather in a simple but effective snare around his captive's wrists. "Pick it up before someone grabs it and disappears. Use two fingers, and touch only the blade."

He seemed to know what he was doing, so Sunny obeyed without question. She took a tissue out of her skirt pocket and gingerly picked up the knife as he had directed, being careful not to smear any fingerprints on the handle.

"What do I do with it?"

"Hold it until Security gets here." He angled his dark head toward the nearest airline employee, a transportation escort who was hovering nervously as if unsure what to do. "Security *has* been called, hasn't it?"

"Yes, sir," said the escort, his eyes round with excitement.

Sunny squatted beside her rescuer. "Thank you," she said. She indicated the briefcase, with the two dangling pieces of its strap. "He cut the strap and grabbed it away from me."

"Any time," he said, turning his head to smile at her and giving her her first good look at him.

Her first look was almost her last. Her stomach fluttered. Her heart leaped. Her lungs seized. *Wow,* she thought, and tried to take a deep breath without being obvious about it.

He was probably the best-looking man she had ever seen, without being pretty in any sense of the word. *Drop-dead handsome* was the phrase that came to mind. Slightly dazed, she took in the details: black hair, a little too long and a little too shaggy, brushing the collar at the back of his battered brown leather jacket; smooth, honey-tanned skin; eyes of such a clear, light brown that they looked golden, framed by thick black lashes. As if that wasn't enough, he had also been blessed with a thin, straight nose, high cheekbones, and such clearly delineated, well-shaped lips that she had the wild impulse to simply lean forward and kiss him.

She already knew he was tall, and now she had the time to notice the broad shoulders, flat belly and lean hips. Mother Nature had been in a *really* good mood when he was made. He should have been too perfect and pretty to be real, but there was a toughness in his expression that was purely masculine, and a thin, crescent-shaped scar on his left cheekbone only added to the impression. Looking down, she saw another scar slashing across the back of his right hand, a raised line that was white against his tanned skin.

The scars in no way detracted from his attractiveness; the evidence of rough living only accentuated it, stating unequivocally that this was a *man.*

She was so bemused that it took her several seconds to realize he was watching her with mingled amusement and interest. She felt her cheeks heat in embarrassment at being caught giving him a blatant once-over. Okay, twice-over.

But she didn't have time to waste in admiration, so she forced her attention back to more pressing concerns. The cretin was grunting and making noises designed to show he was in agony, but she doubted he was in any great pain, despite his bound hands and the way her hero had a knee pressed into the small of his back. She had the briefcase back, but the cretin still presented her with a dilemma: It was her civic duty to stay and press charges against him, but if her flight left any time soon, she might very well miss it while she was answering questions and filling out forms.

"Jerk," she muttered at him. "If I miss my flight…"

"When is it?" asked her hero.

"I don't know. It's been delayed, but they could begin boarding at any time. I'll check at the gate and be right back."

He nodded with approval. "I'll hold your friend here and deal with Security until you get back."

"I'll only be a minute," she said, and walked swiftly back to her gate. The counter was now jammed with angry or upset travelers, their mood far more agitated than when she had left just a few moments before. Swiftly she glanced at the board, where CANCELED had been posted in place of the DELAYED sign.

"Damn," she said, under her breath. "Damn, damn, damn." There went her last hope for getting to Seattle in time to complete her assignment, unless there was another miracle waiting for her. Two miracles in one day was probably too much to ask for, though.

She needed to call in, she thought wearily, but first she could deal with the cretin and airport security. She retraced her steps and found that the little drama was now mobile; the cretin was on his feet, being frog-marched under the control of two airport policemen into an office where they would be out of the view of curious passersby.

Her hero was waiting for her, and when he spotted her, he said something to the security guys, then began walking to meet her.

Her heart gave a little flutter of purely feminine appreciation. My, he was good to look at. His clothes were nothing special: a black T-shirt under the old leather jacket, faded jeans and scuffed boots, but he wore them with a confidence and grace that said he was utterly comfortable. Sunny allowed herself a moment of regret that she would never see him again after this little contretemps was handled, but then she pushed it away. She couldn't take the chance of letting anything develop into a relationship—assuming there was anything there to develop—with him or anyone else. She never even let anything start, because it wouldn't be fair to the guy, and she didn't need the emotional wear and tear, either. Maybe one day she would be able to settle down, date, eventually find someone to love and marry and maybe have kids, but not now. It was too dangerous.

When he reached her, he took her arm with old-fashioned courtesy. "Everything okay with your flight?"

"In a way. It's been canceled," she said ruefully. "I have to be in Seattle tonight, but I don't think I'm going to make it. Every flight I've had today has either been delayed or rerouted, and now there's no other flight that would get me there in time."

"Charter a plane," he said as they walked toward the office where the cretin had been taken.

She chuckled. "I don't know if my boss will spring for that kind of money, but it's an idea. I have to call in, anyway, when we're finished here."

"If it makes any difference to him, I'm available right now. I was supposed to meet a customer on that last flight in from Dallas, but he wasn't on the plane, and he hasn't contacted me, so I'm free."

"You're a charter pilot?" She couldn't believe it. It—*he*—was too good to be true. Maybe she did qualify for two miracles in one day after all.

He looked down at her and smiled, making a tiny dimple dance in his cheek. God, he had a dimple, too! Talk about overkill! He held out his hand. "Chance McCall—pilot, thief-catcher, jack-of-all-trades—at your service, ma'am."

She laughed and shook his hand, noticing that he was careful not to grip her fingers too hard. Considering the strength she could feel in that tough hand, she was grateful for his restraint. Some men weren't as considerate. "Sunny Miller, tardy courier and target of thieves. It's nice to meet you, Mr. McCall."

"Chance," he said easily. "Let's get this little problem taken care of, then you can call your boss and see if he thinks a charter flight is just what the doctor ordered."

He opened the door of the unmarked office for her, and she stepped inside to find the two security officers, a woman dressed in a severe gray suit and the cretin, who had been handcuffed to his chair. The cretin glared at her when she came in, as if all this were her fault instead of his.

"You lyin' bitch—" the cretin began.

Chance McCall reached out and gripped the cretin's shoulder. "Maybe you didn't get the message before," he said in that easy way of his that in no way disguised the iron behind it, "but I don't care for your language. Clean it up." He didn't issue a threat, just an order—and his grip on the cretin's shoulder didn't look gentle.

The cretin flinched and gave him an uneasy look, perhaps remembering how effortlessly this man had manhandled him before. Then he looked at the two airport policemen, as if expecting them to step in. The two men crossed their arms and grinned. Deprived of allies, the cretin opted for silence.

The gray-suited woman looked as if she wanted to protest the rough treatment of her prisoner, but she evidently decided to get on with the business at hand. "I'm Margaret Fayne, director of airport security. I assume you're going to file charges?"

"Yes," Sunny said.

"Good," Ms. Fayne said in approval. "I'll need statements from both of you."

"Any idea how long this will take?" Chance asked. "Ms. Miller and I are pressed for time."

"We'll try to hurry things along," Ms. Fayne assured him.

Whether Ms. Fayne was super-efficient or yet another small miracle took place, the paperwork was completed in what Sunny considered to be record time. Not much more than half an hour passed before the cretin was taken away in handcuffs, all the paperwork was prepared and signed, and Sunny and Chance McCall were free to go, having done their civic duty.

He waited beside her while she called the office and explained the situation. The supervisor, Wayne Beesham, wasn't happy, but bowed to reality.

"What's this pilot's name again?" he asked.

"Chance McCall."

"Hold on, let me check him out."

Sunny waited. Their computers held a vast database of information on both commercial airlines and private charters. There were some unsavory characters in the charter business, dealing more in drugs than in passengers, and a courier company couldn't afford to be careless.

"Where's his home base?"

Sunny repeated the question to Chance.

"Phoenix," he said, and once again she relayed the information.

"Okay, got it. He looks okay. How much is his fee?" Sunny asked.

Mr. Beesham grunted at the reply. "That's a bit high."

"He's here, and he's ready to go."

"What kind of plane is it? I don't want to pay this price for a crop-duster that still won't get you there in time."

Sunny sighed. "Why don't I just put him on the line? It'll save time." She handed the receiver to Chance. "He wants to know about your plane."

Chance took the receiver. "McCall." He listened a moment. "It's a Cessna Skylane. The range is about eight hundred miles at seventy-five percent power, six hours flying time. I'll have to refuel, so I'd rather it be around the midway point, say at Roberts Field in Redmond, Oregon. I can radio ahead and have everything rolling so we won't spend much time on the ground.'' He glanced at his wristwatch. ''With the hour we gain when we cross into the Pacific time zone, she can make it—barely.''

He listened for another moment, then handed the receiver back to Sunny. ''What's the verdict?'' she asked.

''I'm authorizing it. For God's sake, get going.''

She hung up and grinned at Chance, her blood pumping at the challenge. ''It's a go! How long will it take to get airborne?''

''If you let me carry that bag, and we run...fifteen minutes.''

Sunny never let the bag out of her possession. She hated to repay his courtesy with a refusal, but caution was so ingrained in her that she couldn't bring herself to take the risk. ''It isn't heavy,'' she lied, tightening her grip on it. ''You lead, I'll follow.''

One dark eyebrow went up at her reply, but he didn't argue, just led the way through the busy concourse. The private planes were in a different area of the airport, away from the commercial traffic. After several turns and a flight of stairs, they left the terminal and walked across the concrete, the hot afternoon sun beating down on their heads and making her squint. Chance slipped on a pair of sunglasses, then shrugged out of the jacket and carried it in his left hand.

Sunny allowed herself a moment of appreciation at the way his broad shoulders and muscled back filled out the black T-shirt he wore. She might not indulge, but she could certainly admire. If only things were different—but they weren't, she thought, reining in her thoughts. She had to deal with reality, not wishful thinking.

He stopped beside a single-engine airplane, white with gray-and-red striping. After storing her bag and briefcase and securing them with a net, he helped her into the co-pilot's seat. Sunny buckled herself in and looked around with interest. She'd never been in a private plane before, or flown in anything this small. It was surprisingly comfortable. The seats were gray leather, and behind her was a bench seat with individual backs. Carpet covered the metal floor.

There were two sun visors, just like in a car. Amused, she flipped down the one in front of her and laughed aloud when she saw the small mirror attached to it.

Chance walked around the plane, checking details one last time before climbing into the seat to her left and buckling himself in. He put on a set of headphones and began flipping switches while he talked to the air traffic control tower. The engine coughed, then caught, and the propeller on the nose began to spin, slowly at first, then gaining speed until it was an almost invisible blur.

He pointed to another set of headphones, and Sunny put them on. "It's easier to talk using the headphones," came his voice in her ear, "but be quiet until we get airborne."

"Yes, sir," she said, amused, and he flashed a quick grin at her.

They were airborne within minutes, faster than she had ever experienced on a commercial carrier. Being in the small plane gave her a sense of speed that she had never before felt, and when the wheels left the ground the lift was incredible, as if she had sprouted wings and jumped into the air. The ground quickly fell away below, and the vast, glistening blue lake spread out before her, with the jagged mountains straight ahead.

"Wow," she breathed, and brought one hand up to shield her eyes from the sun.

"There's an extra pair of sunglasses in the glove box," he said, indicating the compartment in front of her. She opened it and dug out a pair of inexpensive but stylish Foster Grants with dark red frames. They were obviously some woman's sunglasses, and abruptly she wondered if he was married. He would have a girlfriend, of course; not only was he very nice to look at, he seemed to be a nice person. It was a combination that was hard to find and impossible to beat.

"Your wife's?" she asked as she put on the glasses and breathed a sigh of relief as the uncomfortable glare disappeared.

"No, a passenger left them in the plane."

Well, that hadn't told her anything. She decided to be blunt, even while she wondered why she was bothering, since she would never see him again after they arrived in Seattle. "Are you married?"

Again she got that quick grin. "Nope." He glanced at her, and though she couldn't see his eyes through the dark glasses, she got the impression his gaze was intense. "Are you?"

"No."

"Good," he said.

Chapter 3

Chance watched her from behind the dark lenses of his sunglasses, gauging her reaction to his verbal opening. The plan was working better than he'd hoped; she was attracted to him and hadn't been trying very hard to hide it. All he had to do was take advantage of that attraction and win her trust, which normally might take some doing, but what he had planned would throw her into a situation that wasn't *normal* in any sense of the word. Her life and safety would depend on him.

To his faint surprise, she faced forward and pretended she hadn't heard him. Wryly, he wondered if he'd misread her and she wasn't attracted to him after all. No, she had been watching him pretty blatantly, and in his experience, a woman didn't stare at a man unless she found him attractive.

What was *really* surprising was how attractive he found *her*. He hadn't expected that, but sexual chemistry was an unruly demon that operated outside logic. He had known she was pretty, with brilliant gray eyes and golden-blond hair that swung smoothly to her shoulders, from the photographs in the file he had assembled on her. He just hadn't realized how damn *fetching* she was.

He slanted another glance at her, this time one of pure male assessment. She was of average height, maybe, though a little more slender than he liked, almost delicate. Almost. The muscles of her bare arms, revealed by a white sleeveless blouse, were well-toned and lightly tanned, as if she worked out. A good agent always stayed in good physical condition, so he had to expect her to be stronger than she looked. Her delicate appearance probably took a lot of people off guard.

She sure as hell had taken Wilkins off guard. Chance had to smother a smile. While Sunny had gone back to her gate to check on the status of her flight, which Chance had arranged to be cancelled, Wilkins had told him how she had swung her carry-on bag at him, one-armed, and that the damn thing had to weigh a ton, because it had almost knocked him off his feet.

By now, Wilkins and the other three, "Ms. Fayne" and the two security "policemen," would have vanished from the airport. The real airport security had been briefed to stay out of the way, and everything had worked like a charm, though Wilkins had groused at being taken down so roughly. "First that little witch damn near breaks my arm with that bag, then you try to break my back," he'd growled, while they all laughed at him.

Just what was in that bag, anyway? She had held on to it as if it contained the crown jewels, not letting him carry it even when she was right there with him, and only reluctantly letting him take it to stow in the luggage compartment behind them. He'd been surprised at how heavy it was, too heavy to contain the single change of clothes required by an overnight trip, even with a vast array of makeup and a hairdryer thrown in for good measure. The bag had to weigh a good fifty pounds, maybe more. Well, he would find out soon enough what was in it.

"What were you going to do with that guy if you'd caught him?" he asked in a lazy tone, partly to keep her talking, establishing a link between them, and partly because he was curious. She had been chasing after Wilkins with a fiercely determined expression on her face, so determined that, if Wilkins were still running, she would probably still be chasing him.

"I don't know," she said darkly. "I just knew I couldn't let it happen again."

"Again?" Damn, was she going to tell him about Chicago?

"Last month, a green-haired cretin snatched my briefcase in the airport in Chicago." She slapped the arm of the seat. "That's the first time anything like that has ever happened on one of my jobs, then to have it happen again just a month later—I'd have been fired. Heck, *I* would fire me, if I were the boss."

"You didn't catch the guy in Chicago?"

"No. I was in Baggage Claims, and he just grabbed the briefcase, zipped out the door and was gone."

"What about security? They didn't try to catch him?"

She peered at him over the top of the oversize sunglasses. "You're kidding, right?"

He laughed. "I guess I am."

"Losing another briefcase would have been a catastrophe, at least to me, and it wouldn't have done the company any good, either."

"Do you ever know what's in the briefcases?"

"No, and I don't want to. It doesn't matter. Someone could be sending a pound of salami to their dying uncle Fred, or it could be a billion dollars worth of diamonds—not that I think anyone would ever ship diamonds by a courier service, but you get the idea."

"What happened when you lost the briefcase in Chicago?"

"My company was out a lot of money—rather, the insurance company was. The customer will probably never use us again, or recommend us."

"What happened to you? Any disciplinary action?" He knew there hadn't been.

"No. In a way, I would have felt better if they had at least fined me."

Damn, she was good, he thought in admiration—either that, or she was telling the truth and hadn't had anything to do with the incident in Chicago last month. It was possible, he supposed, but irrelevant. Whether or not she'd had anything to do with losing that briefcase, he was grateful it had happened, because otherwise she would never have come to his notice, and he wouldn't have this lead on Crispin Hauer.

But he didn't think she was innocent; he thought she was in this up to her pretty neck. She was better than he had expected, an actress worthy of an Oscar—so good he might have believed she didn't know anything about her father, if it wasn't for the mystery bag and her deceptive strength. He was trained to put together seemingly insignificant details and come up with a coherent picture, and experience had made him doubly cynical. Few people were as honest as they wanted you to believe, and the people who put on the best show were often the ones with the most to hide. He should know—he was an expert at hiding the black secrets of his soul.

He wondered briefly what it said about him that he was willing to sleep with her as part of his plan to gain her trust, but maybe it was better not to think about it. Someone had to be willing to work in the muck, to do things from which ordinary people would shrink, just to protect those ordinary people. Sex was…just sex. Part of the job. He could even divorce his emotions to the point that he actually looked forward to the task.

Task? Who was he kidding? He couldn't wait to slide into her. She intrigued him, with her toned, tight body and the twinkle that so often lit her clear gray eyes, as if she was often amused at both herself and the world around her. He was fascinated by her eyes, by the white striations that made her eyes look almost faceted, like the palest of blue diamonds. Most people thought of gray eyes as a pale blue, but when he was close to her, he could see that they were, very definitely, brilliantly gray. But most of all he was intrigued by her expression, which was so open and good-humored she could almost trademark the term "Miss Congeniality." How could she look like that, as sweet as apple pie, when she was working hand in glove with the most-wanted terrorist in his files?

Part of him, the biggest part, despised her for what she was. The animal core of him, however, was excited by the dangerous edge of the game he was playing, by the challenge of getting her into bed with him and convincing her to trust him. When he was inside her, he wouldn't be thinking about the hundreds of innocent people her father had killed, only about the linking of their bodies. He wouldn't let himself think of anything else, lest he give himself away with some nuance of expression that women were so good at reading. No, he would make love to her as if he had found his soul mate, because that was the only way he could be certain of fooling her.

But he was good at that, at making a woman feel as if he desired her more than anything else in the world. He knew just how to make her aware of him, how to push hard without panicking her—which brought him back to the fact that she had totally ignored his first opening. He smiled slightly to himself. Did she really think that would work?

"Will you have dinner with me tonight?"

She actually jumped, as if she had been lost in her thoughts. "What?"

"Dinner. Tonight. After you deliver your package."

"Oh. But—I'm supposed to deliver it at nine. It'll be late, and—"

"And you'll be alone, and I'll be alone, and you have to eat. I promise not to bite. I may lick, but I won't bite."

She surprised him by bursting into laughter.

Of all the reactions he had anticipated, laughter wasn't one of them. Still, her laugh was so free and genuine, her head tilted back against the seat, that he found himself smiling in response.

"'I may lick, but I won't bite.' That was good. I'll have to remember it," she said, chuckling.

After a moment, when she said nothing else, he realized that she was ignoring him again. He shook his head. "Does that work with most men?"

"Does what work?"

"Ignoring them when they ask you out. Do they slink away with their tails tucked between their legs?"

"Not that I've ever noticed." She grinned. "You make me sound like a femme fatale, breaking hearts left and right."

"You probably are. We guys are tough, though. We can be bleeding to death on the inside and we'll put up such a good front that no one ever knows." He smiled at her. "Have dinner with me."

"You're persistent, aren't you?"

"You still haven't answered me."

"All right—no. There, I've answered you."

"Wrong answer. Try again." More gently, he said, "I know you're tired, and with the time difference, nine o'clock is really midnight to you. It's just a meal, Sunny, not an evening of dancing. That can wait until our second date."

She laughed again. "Persistent *and* confident." She paused, made a wry little face. "The answer is still no. I don't date."

This time he was more than surprised, he was stunned. Of all the things he had expected to come out of her mouth, that particular statement had never crossed his mind. Damn, had he so badly miscalculated? "At all? Or just men?"

"At all." She gestured helplessly. "See, this is why I tried to ignore you, because I didn't want to go into an explanation that you wouldn't accept, anyway. No, I'm not gay, I like men very much, but I don't date. End of explanation."

His relief was so intense, he felt a little dizzy. "If you like men, why don't you date?"

"See?" she demanded on a frustrated rush of air. "You didn't accept it. You immediately started asking questions."

"Damn it, did you think I'd just let it drop? There's something between us, Sunny. I know it, and you know it. Or are you going to ignore that, too?"

"That's exactly what I'm going to do."

He wondered if she realized what she had just admitted. "Were you raped?"

"No!" she half shouted, goaded out of control. "I just…don't…date."

She was well on her way to losing her temper, he thought, amused. He grinned. "You're pretty when you're mad."

She sputtered, then began laughing. "How am I supposed to stay mad when you say things like that?"

"You aren't. That's the whole idea."

"Well, it worked. What it didn't do was change my mind. I'm sorry," she said gently, sobering. "It's just…I have my reasons. Let it drop. Please."

"Okay." He paused. "For now."

She gave an exaggerated groan that had him smiling again. "Why don't you try to take a nap?" he suggested. "You have to be tired, and we still have a long flight ahead of us."

"That's a good idea. You can't badger me if I'm asleep."

With that wry shot, she leaned her head back against the seat. Chance reached behind her seat and produced a folded blanket. "Here. Use this as a pillow, or you'll get a stiff neck."

"Thanks." She took off the headset and tucked the blanket between her head and shoulder, then shifted around in her seat to get more comfortable.

Chance let silence fall, occasionally glancing at her to see if she really fell asleep. About fifteen minutes later, her breathing deepened and evened out into a slow rhythm. He waited a few minutes longer, then eased the plane into a more westerly direction, straight into the setting sun.

Chapter 4

"Sunny." The voice was insistent, a little difficult to hear, and accompanied by a hand on her shoulder, shaking her. "Sunny, wake up."

She stirred and opened her eyes, stretching a little to relieve the kinks in her back and shoulders. "Are we there?"

Chance indicated the headset in her lap, and she slipped it on. "We have a problem," he said quietly.

The bottom dropped out of her stomach, and her heartbeat skittered. No other words, she thought, could be quite as terrifying when one was in an airplane. She took a deep breath, trying to control the surge of panic. "What's wrong?" Her voice was surprisingly steady. She looked around, trying to spot the problem in the cluster of dials in the cockpit, though she had no idea what any of them meant. Then she looked out of the window at the rugged landscape below them, painted in stark reds and blacks as the setting sun threw shadows over jagged rock. ''Where are we?''

''Southeastern Oregon.''

The engine coughed and sputtered. Her heart felt as if it did, too. As soon as she heard the break in the rhythm, she became aware that the steady background whine of the motor had been interrupted several times while she slept. Her subconscious had registered the change in sound but not put it in any context. Now the context was all too clear.

''I think it's the fuel pump,'' he added, in answer to her first question.

Calm. She had to stay calm. She pulled in a deep breath, though her lungs felt as if they had shrunk in size. ''What do we do?''

He smiled grimly. ''Find a place to set it down before it falls down.''

''I'll take setting over falling any day.'' She looked out the side window, studying the ground below. Jagged mountain ridges, enormous boulders and sharp-cut arroyos slicing through the earth were all she could see. ''Uh-oh.''

''Yea. I've been looking for a place to land for the past half hour.''

This was not good, not good at all. In the balance of good and bad, this weighed heavily on the bad side.

The engine sputtered again. The whole frame of the aircraft shook. So did her voice, when she said, ''Have you radioed a Mayday?''

Again that grim smile. ''We're in the middle of a great big empty area, between navigational beacons. I've tried a couple of times to raise someone, but there haven't been any answers.''

The scale tipped even more out of balance. ''I knew

it,'' she muttered. ''The way today has gone, I *knew* I'd crash if I got on another plane.''

The grouchiness in her voice made him chuckle, despite the urgency of their situation. He reached over and gently squeezed the back of her neck, startling her with his touch, his big hand warm and hard on her sensitive nape. ''We haven't crashed yet, and I'm going to try damn hard to make sure we don't. The landing may be rough, though.''

She wasn't used to being touched. She had accustomed herself to doing without the physical contact that it was human nature to crave, to keep people at a certain distance. Chance McCall had touched her more in one afternoon than she had been touched in the past five years. The shock of pleasure almost distracted her from their situation—almost. She looked down at the unforgiving landscape again. ''How rough does a landing have to get before it qualifies as a crash?''

''If we walk away from it, then it was a landing.'' He put his hand back on the controls, and she silently mourned that lost connection.

The vast mountain range spread out around them as far as she could see in any direction. Their chances of walking away from this weren't good. How long would it be before their bodies were found, if ever? Sunny clenched her hands, thinking of Margreta. Her sister, not knowing what had happened, would assume the worst— and dying in an airplane crash was *not* the worst. In her grief, she might well abandon her refuge and do something stupid that would get her killed, too.

She watched Chance's strong hands, so deft and sure on the controls. His clear, classic profile was limned against the pearl and vermillion sky, the sort of sunset one saw only in the western states, and likely the last sunset she would ever see. He would be the last person she ever saw, or touched, and she was suddenly, bitterly angry that she had never been able to live the life most women took for granted, that she hadn't been free to accept his offer of dinner and spend the trip in a glow of anticipation, free to flirt with him and maybe see the glow of desire in his golden-brown eyes.

She had been denied a lot, but most of all she had been denied opportunity, and she would never, never forgive her father for that.

The engine sputtered, caught, sputtered again. This time the reassuring rhythm didn't return. The bottom dropped out of her stomach. God, oh God, they were going to crash. Her nails dug into her palms as she fought to contain her panic. She had never before felt so small and helpless, so fragile, with soft flesh and slender bones that couldn't withstand such battering force. She was going to die, and she had yet to live.

The plane jerked and shuddered, bucking under the stress of spasmodic power. It pitched to the right, throwing Sunny against the door so hard her right arm went numb.

"That's it," Chance said between gritted teeth, his knuckles white as he fought to control the pitching aircraft. He brought the wings level again. "I have to take it down now, while I have a little control. Look for the best place."

Best place? There *was* no best place. They needed somewhere that was relatively flat and relatively clear; the last location she had seen that fit that description had been in Utah.

He raised the right wingtip, tilting the plane so he had a better side view.

"See anything?" Sunny asked, her voice shaking just a little.

"Nothing. Damn."

"Damn is the wrong word. Pilots are supposed to say something else just before they crash." Humor wasn't much of a weapon with which to face death, but it was how she had always gotten herself through the hard times.

Unbelievably, he grinned. "But I haven't crashed yet, sweetheart. Have a little faith. I promise I'll say the right word if I don't find a good-looking spot pretty soon."

"If you don't find a good-looking spot, I'll say it for you," she promised fervently.

They crossed a jagged, boulder-strewn ridge, and a long, narrow black pit yawned beneath them like a doorway to hell. "There!" Chance said, nosing the plane down.

"What? Where?" She sat erect, desperate hope flaring inside her, but all she could see was that black pit.

"The canyon. That's our best bet."

The black pit was a canyon? Weren't canyons supposed to be big? That looked like an arroyo. How on earth would the plane ever fit inside it? And what difference did it make, when this was their only chance? Her heart lodged itself in her throat, and she gripped the edge of the seat as Chance eased the pitching aircraft lower and lower.

The engine stopped.

For a moment all she heard was the awful silence, more deafening than any roar.

Then she became aware of the air rushing past the metal skin of the plane, air that no longer supported them. She heard her own heart beating, fast and heavy, heard the whisper of her breath. She heard everything except what she most wanted to hear, the sweet sound of an airplane engine.

Chance didn't say anything. He concentrated fiercely on keeping the plane level, riding the air currents down, down, aiming for that long, narrow slit in the earth. The plane spiraled like a leaf, coming so close to the jagged mountainside on the left that she could see the pits in the dark red rock.

Sunny bit her lip until blood welled in her mouth, fighting back the terror and panic that threatened to erupt in screams. She couldn't distract him now, no matter what. She wanted to close her eyes, but resolutely kept them open. If she died now, she didn't want to do it in craven fear. She couldn't help the fear, but she didn't have to be craven. She would watch death come at her, watch Chance as he fought to bring them down safely and cheat the grim horseman.

They slipped below the sunshine, into the black shadows, deeper and deeper. It was colder in the shadows, a chill that immediately seeped through the windows into her bones. She couldn't see a thing. Quickly she snatched off the sunglasses and saw that Chance had done the same. His eyes were narrowed, his expression hard and intent as he studied the terrain below.

The ground was rushing at them now, a ground that was pocked and scored with rivulets, and dotted with boulders. It was flat enough, but not a nice, clear landing spot at all. She braced her feet against the floor, her body rigid as if she could force the airplane to stay aloft.

"Hold on." His voice was cool. "I'm going to try to make it to the stream bed. The sand will help slow us down before we hit one of those rocks."

A stream bed? He was evidently much better at reading the ground than she was. She tried to see a ribbon of water, but finally realized the stream was dry; the bed was that thin, twisting line that looked about as wide as the average car.

She started to say "Good luck," but it didn't seem appropriate. Neither did "It was nice knowing you." In the end, all she could manage was "Okay."

It happened fast. Suddenly they were no longer skimming above the earth. The ground was *there,* and they hit it hard, so hard she pitched forward against the seat belt, then snapped back. They went briefly airborne again as the wheels bounced, then hit again even harder. She heard metal screeching in protest; then her head banged against the side window, and for a chaotic moment she didn't see or hear anything, just felt the tossing and bouncing of the plane. She was boneless, unable to hold on, flopping like a shirt in a clothes dryer.

Then there came the hardest bounce of all, jarring her teeth. The plane spun sideways in a sickening motion, then lurched to a stop. Time and reality splintered, broke apart, and for a long moment nothing made any sense; she had no grasp on where she was or what had happened.

She heard a voice, and the world jolted back into place.

"Sunny? Sunny, are you all right?" Chance was asking urgently.

She tried to gather her senses, tried to answer him. Dazed, battered, she realized that the force of the landing had turned her inside the confines of the seat belt, and she was facing the side window, her back to Chance. She felt his hands on her, heard his low swearing as he unclipped the seat belt and eased her back against his chest, supporting her with his body.

She swallowed, and managed to find her voice. "I'm

okay.'' The words weren't much more than a croak, but if she could talk at all that meant she was alive. They were both alive. Joyful disbelief swelled in her chest. He had actually managed to land the plane!

"We have to get out. There may be a fuel leak." Even as he spoke, he shoved open the door and jumped out, dragging her with him as if she was a sack of flour. She felt rather sacklike, her limbs limp and trembling.

A fuel leak. The engine had been dead when they landed, but there was still the battery, and wiring that could short out and spark. If a spark got to any fuel, the plane and everything in it would go up in a fireball.

Everything in it. The words rattled in her brain, like marbles in a can, and with dawning horror she realized what that meant. Her bag was still in the plane.

"Wait!" she shrieked, panic sending a renewed surge of adrenaline through her system, restoring the bones to her legs, the strength to her muscles. She twisted in his grasp, grabbing the door handle and hanging on. "My bag!"

"Damn it, Sunny!" he roared, trying to break her grip on the handle. "Forget the damn bag!"

"No!"

She jerked away from him and began to climb back into the plane. With a smothered curse he grabbed her around the waist and bodily lifted her away from the plane. "I'll get the damn bag! Go on—get out of here! Run!"

She was appalled that he would risk his life retrieving her bag, while sending her to safety. "I'll get it," she said fiercely, grabbing him by the belt and tugging. "*You* run!"

For a split second he literally froze, staring at her in shock. Then he gave his head a little shake, reached in for the bag and effortlessly hefted it out. Wordlessly Sunny tried to take it, but he only gave her an incendiary look and she didn't have time to argue. Carrying the bag in his left hand and gripping her upper arm with his right, he towed her at a run away from the plane. Her shoes sank into the soft grit, and sand and scrub brush bit at her ankles, but she scrambled to stay upright and keep pace with him.

They were a good fifty yards away before he judged it safe. He dropped the bag and turned on her like a panther pouncing on fresh meat, gripping her upper arms with both hands as if he wanted to shake her. "What the hell are you thinking?" he began in a tone of barely leashed violence, then cut himself off, staring at her face. His expression altered, his golden-brown eyes darkening.

"You're bleeding," he said harshly. He grabbed his handkerchief out of his pocket and pressed it to her chin. Despite the roughness of his tone, his touch was incredibly gentle. "You said you weren't hurt."

"I'm not." She raised her trembling hand and took the handkerchief, dabbing it at her chin and mouth. There wasn't much blood, and the bleeding seemed to have stopped. "I bit my lip," she confessed. "Before you landed, I mean. To keep from screaming."

He stared down at her with an expression like flint. "Why didn't you just scream?"

"I didn't want to distract you." The trembling was growing worse by the second; she tried to hold herself steady, but every limb shook as if her bones had turned to gelatin.

He tilted up her face, staring down at her for a moment in the deepening twilight. He breathed a low, savage curse, then slowly leaned down and pressed his lips to her mouth. Despite the violence she sensed in him, the kiss was light, gentle, more of a salute than a kiss. She caught her breath, beguiled by the softness of his lips, the warm smell of his skin, the hint of his taste. She fisted her hands in his T-shirt, clinging to his strength, trying to sink into his warmth.

He lifted his head. "That's for being so brave," he murmured. "I couldn't have asked for a better partner in a plane crash."

"Landing," she corrected shakily. "It was a landing."

That earned her another soft kiss, this time on the temple. She made a strangled sound and leaned into him, a different sort of trembling beginning to take hold of her. He framed her face with his hands, his thumbs gently stroking the corners of her mouth as he studied her. She felt her lips tremble a little, but then, all of her was shaking. He touched the small sore spot her teeth had made in her lower lip; then he was kissing her again, and this time there was nothing gentle about it.

This kiss rocked her to her foundation. It was hungry, rough, deep. There were reasons why she shouldn't respond to him, but she couldn't think what they were. Instead, she gripped his wrists and went on tiptoe to slant her parted lips against his, opening her mouth for the thrust of his tongue. He tasted like man, and sex, a potent mixture that went to her head faster than hundred-proof whiskey. Heat bloomed in her loins and breasts, a desperate, needy heat that brought a low moan from her throat.

He wrapped one arm around her and pulled her against him, molding her to him from knee to breast while his kisses became even deeper, even harder. She locked her arms around his neck and arched into him, wanting the feel of his hard-muscled body against her with an urgency that swept away reason. Instinctively she pushed her hips against his, and the hard length of his erection bulged into the notch of her thighs. This time she cried out in want, in need, in a desire that burned through every cell of her body. His hand closed roughly around her breast, kneading, rubbing her nipple through the layers of blouse and bra, both easing and intensifying the ache that made them swell toward his touch.

Suddenly he jerked his head back. "I don't believe this," he muttered. Reaching up, he prised her arms from around his neck and set her away from him. He looked even more savage than he had a moment before, the veins standing out in his neck. "Stay here," he barked. "Don't move an inch. I have to check the plane."

He left her standing there in the sand, in the growing twilight, suddenly cold all the way down to the bone. Deprived of his warmth, his strength, her legs slowly collapsed, and she sank to the ground.

Chance swore to himself, steadily and with blistering heat, as he checked the plane for fuel leaks and other damage. He had deliberately made the landing rougher than necessary, and the plane had a reinforced landing gear as well as extra protection for the fuel lines and tank, but a smart pilot didn't take anything for granted. He had to check the plane, had to stay in character.

He didn't want to stay in character. He wanted to back her against one of those big boulders and lift her skirt. Damn! What was wrong with him? In the past fifteen years he'd held a lot of beautiful, deadly women in his arms, and even though he let his body respond, his mind had always remained cool. Sunny Miller wasn't the most beautiful, not by a long shot; she was more gamine than goddess, with bright eyes that invited laughter rather than seduction. So why was he so hot to get into her pants?

"Why" didn't matter, he angrily reminded himself. Okay, so his attraction to her was unexpected; it was an advantage, something to be used. He wouldn't have to fake anything, which meant there was even less chance of her sensing anything off-kilter.

Danger heightened the emotions, destroying inhibitions. They had lived through a life-threatening situation together, they were alone, and there was a definite physical attraction between them. He had arranged the first two circumstances; the third was a bonus. It was a textbook situation; studies in human nature had shown that, if a man and a woman were thrown together in a dangerous situation and they had only each other to rely on, they quickly formed both sexual and emotional bonds. Chance had the advantage, in that he knew the plane hadn't been in any danger of crashing, and that they weren't in a life-and-death situation. Sunny would think they were stranded, while he knew better. Whenever he signaled Zane, they would promptly be "rescued," but he wouldn't send that signal until Sunny took him into her confidence about her father.

Everything was under control. They weren't even in Oregon, as he'd told her. They were in Nevada, in a narrow box canyon he and Zane had scouted out and selected because it was possible to land a plane in it, and, unless one had the equipment to scale vertical rock walls, impossible to escape. They weren't close to any commercial flight pattern, he had disabled the transponder so no search plane would pick up a signal, and they were far off their route. They wouldn't be found.

Sunny was totally under his control; she just didn't know it.

The growing dusk made it impossible to see very much, and it was obvious that if the plane was going to explode in flames, it would already have done so. Chance strode back to where Sunny was sitting on the ground, her knees pulled up and her arms wrapped around her legs, and that damn bag close by her side. She scrambled to her feet as he approached. "All clear?"

"All clear. No fuel leaks."

"That's good." She managed a smile. "It wouldn't do us any good for you to fix the fuel pump if there wasn't any fuel left."

"Sunny…if it's a clogged line, I can fix it. If the fuel pump has gone out, I can't."

He decided to let her know right away that they might not be flying out of here in the morning.

She absorbed that in silence, rubbing her bare arms to ward off the chill of the desert air. The temperature dropped like a rock when the sun went down, which was one of the reasons he had chosen this site. They would have to share their body heat at night to survive.

He leaned down and hefted the bag, marveling anew at its weight, then took her arm to walk with her back to the plane. "I hope you have a coat in this damn bag, since you thought it was important enough to risk your life getting it," he growled.

"A sweater," she said absently, looking up at the crystal clear sky with its dusting of stars. The black walls of the canyon loomed on either side of them, making it obvious they were in a hole in the earth. A big hole, but still a hole. She shook herself, as if dragging her thoughts back to the problem at hand. "We'll be all right," she said. "I have some food, and—"

"Food? You're carrying food in here?" He indicated the bag.

"Just some emergency stuff."

Of all the things he'd expected, food was at the bottom of the list. Hell, food wasn't even *on* the list. Why would a woman on an overnight trip put food in her suitcase?

They reached the plane, and he set the bag down in the dirt. "Let me get some things, and we'll find a place to camp for the night. Can you get anything else in there, or is it full?"

"It's full," she said positively, but then, he hadn't expected her to open it so easily.

He shrugged and dragged out his own small duffel, packed with the things a man could be expected to take on a charter flight: toiletries, a change of clothes. The duffel was unimportant, but it wouldn't look right if he left it behind.

"Why can't we camp here?" she asked.

"This is a stream bed. It's dry now, but if it rains anywhere in the mountains, we could be caught in the runoff."

As he spoke, he got a flashlight out of the dash, the blanket from the back, and a pistol from the pocket in the pilot's side door. He stuck the pistol in his belt, and draped the blanket around her shoulders. "I have some water," he said, taking out a plastic gallon milk jug that he'd refilled with water. "We'll be all right tonight." Water had been the toughest thing to locate. He and Zane had found several box canyons in which he could have landed the plane, but this was the only one with water. The source wasn't much, just a thin trickle running out of the rock at the far end of the canyon, but it was enough. He would "find" the water tomorrow.

He handed her the flashlight and picked up both bags.

"Lead the way," he instructed, and indicated the direction he wanted. The floor of the canyon sloped upward on one side; the stream bed was the only smooth ground. The going was rough, and Sunny carefully picked her way over rocks and gullies. She was conscientious about shining the light so he could see where he was going, since he was hampered by both bags.

Damn, he wished she had complained at least a little, or gotten upset. He wished she wasn't so easy to like. Most people would have been half-hysterical, or asking endless questions about their chances of being rescued if he couldn't get the plane repaired. Not Sunny. She coped, just as she had coped at the airport, with a minimum of fuss. Without *any* fuss, actually; she had bitten the blood out of her lip to keep from distracting him while he was bringing the plane down.

The canyon was so narrow it didn't take them long to reach the vertical wall. Chance chose a fairly flat section of sandy gray dirt, with a pile of huge boulders that formed a rough semi-circle. "This will give us some protection from the wind tonight."

"What about snakes?" she asked, eyeing the boulders.

"Possible," he said, as he set down the bags. Had he found a weakness he could use to bring her closer to him? "Are you afraid of them?"

"Only the human kind." She looked around as if taking stock of their situation, then kind of braced her shoulders. It was a minute movement, one he wouldn't have noticed if he hadn't been studying her so keenly. With an almost cheerful note she said, "Let's get this camp set up so we can eat. I'm hungry."

She squatted beside her bag and spun the combination dial of the rather substantial lock on her bag. With a quiet *snick* the lock opened, and she unzipped the bag.

Chance was a bit taken aback at finding out what was in the bag this easily, but he squatted beside her. "What do you have? Candy bars?"

She chuckled. "Nothing so tasty."

He took the flashlight from her and shone it into the bag as she began taking out items. The bag was as neatly packed as a salesman's sample case, and she hadn't been lying about not having any room in there for anything else. She placed a sealed plastic bag on the ground between them. "Here we go. Nutrition bars." She slanted a look at him. "They taste like you'd expect a nutrition bar to taste, but they're concentrated. One bar a day will give us all we need to stay alive. I have a dozen of them."

The next item was a tiny cell phone. She stared at it, frozen, for a moment, then looked up at him with fragile hope in her eyes as she turned it on. Chance knew there wasn't a signal here, but he let her go through the motions, something inside him aching at the disappointment he knew she would feel.

Her shoulders slumped. "Nothing," she said, and turned the phone off. Without another word she returned to her unpacking.

A white plastic box with a familiar red cross on the top came out next. "First aid kit," she murmured, reaching back into the bag. "Water purification tablets. A couple of bottles of water, ditto orange juice. Light sticks. Matches." She listed each item as she set it on the ground. "Hairspray, deodorant, toothpaste, premoistened towelettes, hairbrush, curling iron, blow dryer, two space blankets—" she paused as she reached the bottom of the bag and began hauling on something bigger than any of the other items. "—and a tent."

Chapter 5

A tent. Chance stared down at it, recognizing the type. This was survivalist stuff, what people stored in underground shelters in case of war or natural disaster—or what someone who expected to spend a lot of time in the wilderness would pack.

"It's small," she said apologetically. "Really just a one-man tent, but I had to get something light enough for me to carry. There will be enough room for both of us to sleep in it, though, if you don't mind being a little crowded."

Why would she carry a *tent* on board a plane, when she expected to spend one night in Seattle—in a hotel—then fly back to Atlanta? Why would anyone carry that heavy a bag around when she could have checked it? The answer was that she hadn't wanted it out of her possession, but he still wanted an explanation of why she was carrying it at all.

Something didn't add up here.

* * *

His silence was unnerving. Sunny looked down at her incongruous pile of possessions and automatically emptied out the bag, removing her sweater and slipping it on, sitting down to pull on a pair of socks, then stuffing her change of clothes and her grooming items back into the bag. Her mind was racing. There was something about his expression that made a chill go down her spine, a hardness that she hadn't glimpsed before. Belatedly, she remembered how easily he had caught the cretin in the airport, the deadly grace and speed with which he moved. This was no ordinary charter pilot, and she was marooned with him.

She had been attracted to him from the first moment she saw him, but she couldn't afford to let that blind her to the danger of letting down her guard. She was accustomed to living with danger, but this was a different sort of danger, and she had no idea what form it could, or would, take. Chance could simply be one of those men who packed more punch than others, a man very capable of taking care of himself.

Or he could be in her father's pay.

The thought chilled her even more, the cold going down to her bones before common sense reasserted itself. No, there was no way her father could have arranged for everything that had happened today, no way he could have known she would be in the Salt Lake City airport. Being there had been pure bad luck, the result of a fouled-up flight schedule. *She* hadn't known she would be in Salt Lake City. If her father had been involved, he would have tried to grab her in either Atlanta or Seattle. All the zig-zagging across the country she had done today had made it impossible for her father to be involved.

As her mind cleared of that silent panic, she remembered how Chance had dragged her bodily from the plane, the way he had draped the blanket around her, even the courtesy with which he had treated her in the airport. He was a strong man, accustomed to being in the lead and taking the risks. *Military training,* she thought with a sudden flash of clarity, and wondered how she had missed it before. Her life, and Margreta's, depended on how well she could read people, how prepared she was, how alert. With Chance, she had been so taken off guard by the strength of her attraction to him, and the shock of finding that interest returned, that she hadn't been thinking.

"What's this about?" he asked quietly, squatting down beside her and indicating the tent. "And don't tell me you were going to camp out in the hotel lobby."

She couldn't help it. The thought of setting up the tent in a hotel lobby was so ludicrous that she chuckled. Seeing the funny side of things was what had kept her sane all these years.

One big hand closed gently on the nape of her neck. "Sunny," he said warningly. "Tell me."

She shook her head, still smiling. "We're stranded here tonight, but essentially we're strangers. After we get out of here we'll never see each other again, so there's no point in spilling our guts to each other. You keep your secrets, and I'll keep mine."

The flashlight beam sharpened the angles of his face. He exhaled a long, exasperated breath. "Okay—for now. I don't know why it matters, anyway. Unless I can get the plane fixed, we're going to be here a long time, and the reason why you have the tent will be irrelevant."

She searched his face, trying to read his impassive expression. "That isn't reassuring."

"It's the truth."

"When we don't show up in Seattle, someone will search for us. The Civil Air Patrol, someone. Doesn't your plane have one of those beacon things?"

"We're in a canyon."

He didn't have to say more than that. Any signal would be blocked by the canyon walls, except for directly overhead. They were in a deep, narrow slit in the earth, the narrowness of the canyon limiting even more their chances of anyone picking up the signal.

"Well, darn," she said forcefully.

This time he was the one who laughed, and he shook his head as he released her neck and stood up. "Is that the worst you can say?"

"We're alive. That outcome is so good considering what *could* have happened that, in comparison, being stranded here only rates a 'darn.' You may be able to fix the plane." She shrugged. "No point in wasting the really nasty words until we know more."

He leaned down and helped her to her feet. "If I can't get us going again, I'll help you with those words. For now, let's get this tent set up before the temperature drops even more."

"What about a fire?"

"I'll look for firewood tomorrow—*if* we need it. We can get by tonight without a fire, and I don't want to waste the flashlight batteries. If we're here for any length of time, we'll need the flashlight."

"I have the lightsticks."

"We'll save those, too. Just in case."

Working together, they set up the tent. She could have done it herself; it was made for one person to handle, and she had practiced until she knew she could do it with a minimum of fuss, but with two people the job took only moments. Brushing away the rocks so they would have a smooth surface beneath the tent floor took longer, but even so, they weren't going to have a comfortable bed for the night.

When they were finished, she eyed the tent with misgivings. It was long enough for Chance, but... She visually measured the width of his shoulders, then the width of the tent. She was either going to have to sleep on her side all night long—or on top of him.

The heat that shot through her told her which option her body preferred. Her heart beat a little faster in anticipation of their enforced intimacy during the coming night, of lying against his strong, warm body, maybe even sleeping in his arms.

To his credit, he didn't make any insinuating remarks, even though when he looked at the tent he must have drawn the same conclusion as she had. Instead, he bent down to pick up the bag of nutrition bars and said smugly, "I knew you'd have dinner with me tonight."

She began laughing again, charmed by both his tact and his sense of humor, and fell a little in love with him right then.

She should have been alarmed, but she wasn't. Yes, letting herself care for him made her emotionally vulnerable, but they had lived through a terrifying experience together, and she *needed* an emotional anchor right now. So far she hadn't found a single thing about the man that she didn't like, not even that hint of danger she kept sensing. In this situation, a man with an edge to him was an asset, not a hindrance.

She allowed herself to luxuriate in this unaccustomed feeling as they each ate a nutrition bar—which was edible, but definitely not tasty—and drank some water. Then they packed everything except the two space blankets back in the bag, to protect their supplies from snakes and insects and other scavengers. They didn't have to worry about bears, not in this desertlike part of the country, but coyotes were possible. Her bag was supposedly indestructible; if any coyotes showed up, she supposed she would find out if the claim about the bag was true, because there wasn't room in the tent for both them and the bag.

Chance checked the luminous dial of his watch. "It's still early, but we should get in the tent to save our body heat, and not burn up calories trying to stay warm out here. I'll spread this blanket down, and we'll use your two blankets for cover."

For the first time, she realized he was in his T-shirt. "Shouldn't you get your jacket from the plane?"

"It's too bulky to wear in the tent. Besides, I don't feel the cold as much as you do. I'll be fine without it." He sat down and pulled off his boots, tossed them inside the tent, then crawled in with the blanket. Sunny slipped off her own shoes, glad she had the socks to keep her feet warm.

"Okay, come on in," Chance said. "Feet first."

She gave him her shoes, then sat down and worked herself feetfirst into the tent. He was lying on his side, which gave her room to maneuver, but it was still a chore keeping her skirt down and trying not to bunch up the blanket as she wiggled into place. Chance zipped the tent flaps shut, then pulled his pistol out of his waistband and placed it beside his head. Sunny eyed the big black automatic; she wasn't an expert on pistols, but she knew it was one of the heavier calibers, either a .45 or a 9mm. She had tried them, but the bigger pistols were too heavy for her to handle with ease, so she had opted for a smaller caliber.

He had already unfolded the space blankets and had them ready to pull in place. She could already feel his body heat in the small space, so she didn't need a blanket yet, but as the night grew colder, they would need all the covering they could get.

They both moved around, trying to get comfortable. Because he was so big, Sunny tried to give him as much room as possible. She turned on her side and curled her arm under her head, but they still bumped and brushed against each other.

"Ready?" he asked.

"Ready."

He turned off the flashlight. The darkness was complete, like being deep in a cave. "Thank God I'm not claustrophobic," she said, taking a deep breath. His scent filled her lungs, warm and...different, not musky, exactly, but earthy, and very much the way a man should smell.

"Just think of it as being safe," he murmured. "Darkness can feel secure."

She did feel safe, she realized. For the first time in her memory, she was certain no one except the man beside her knew where she was. She didn't have to check locks, scout out an alternate exit, or sleep so lightly she sometimes felt as if she hadn't slept at all. She didn't have to worry about being followed, or her phone being tapped, or any of the other things that could happen. She did worry about Margreta, but she had to think positively. Tomorrow Chance would find the problem was a clogged fuel line, he would get it cleared, and they would finish their trip. She would be too late to deliver the package in Seattle, but considering they had landed safely instead of crashing, she didn't really care about the package. The day's outcome could have been

so much worse that she was profoundly grateful they
were all in one piece and relatively comfortable—"relatively" being the key word, she thought, as she tried
to find a better position. The ground was as hard as a
rock. For all she knew the ground *was* a rock, covered
by a thin layer of dirt.

She was suddenly exhausted. The events of the day—
the long flight and fouled-up connections, the lack of
food, the stress of being mugged, then the almost unbearable tension of those last minutes in the plane—
finally took their toll on her. She yawned and unconsciously tried yet again to find a comfortable position,
turning over to pillow her head on her other arm. Her
elbow collided with something very solid, and he
grunted.

"I'm sorry," she mumbled. She squirmed a little
more, inadvertently bumping him with her knee. "This
is so crowded I may have to sleep on top."

She heard the words and in shock realized that she
had actually said them aloud. She opened her mouth to
apologize again.

"Or I could be the one on top."

His words stopped her apology cold. Her breath tangled in her lungs and didn't escape. His deep voice
seemed to echo in the darkness, that single sentence re-
verberating through her consciousness. She was suddenly, acutely, aware of every inch of him, of the sensual
promise in his tone. The kiss—the kiss she could write
off as reaction; danger was supposed to be an aphrodisiac, and evidently that was true. But this wasn't reaction; this was desire, warm and curious, seeking.

"Is that a 'no' I'm hearing?"

Her lungs started working again, and she sucked in a
breath. "I haven't said anything."

"That's my point." He sounded faintly amused. "I guess I'm not going to get lucky tonight."

Feeling more certain of herself with his teasing, she said dryly, "I guess not. You've already used up your quota of luck for the day."

"I'll try again tomorrow."

She stifled a laugh.

"Does that snicker mean I haven't scared you?"

She should be scared, she thought, or at least wary. She had no idea why she wasn't. The fact was, she felt tempted. Very tempted. "No, I'm not scared."

"Good." He yawned. "Then why don't you pull off that sweater and let me use it as a pillow, and you can use my shoulder. We'll both be more comfortable."

Common sense said he was right. Common sense also said she was asking for trouble if she slept in his arms. She trusted him to behave, but she wasn't that certain of herself. He was sexy, with a capital SEX. He made her laugh. He was strong and capable, with a faintly wicked edge to him. He was even a little dangerous. What more could a woman want?

That was perhaps the most dangerous thing about him, that he made her want him. She had easily resisted other men, walking away without a backward look or a second thought. Chance made her long for all the things she had denied herself, made her aware of how lonely and alone she was.

"Are you sure you can trust me to behave?" she asked, only half joking. "I didn't mean to say that about being on top. I was half-asleep, and it just slipped out."

"I think I can handle you if you get fresh. For one thing, you'll be sound asleep as soon as you stop talking."

She yawned. "I know. I'm crashing hard, if you'll pardon the terminology."

"We didn't crash, we landed. Come on, let's get that sweater off, then you can sleep."

There wasn't room to fully sit up, so he helped her struggle out of the garment. He rolled it up and tucked it under his head, then gently, as if worried he might frighten her, drew her against his right side. His right arm curled around her, and she nestled close, settling her head in the hollow of his shoulder.

The position was surprisingly comfortable, and comforting. She draped her right arm across his chest, because there didn't seem to be any other place to put it. Well, there were other places, but none that seemed as safe. Besides, she liked feeling his heartbeat under her hand. The strong, even thumping satisfied some primitive instinct in her, the desire not to be alone in the night.

"Comfortable?" he asked in a low, soothing tone.

"Um-hmm."

With his left arm he snagged one of the space blankets and pulled it up to cover her to the shoulders, keeping the chill from her bare arms. Cocooned in warmth and darkness, she gave in to the sheer pleasure of lying so close to him. Sleepy desire hummed just below the surface, warming her, softening her. Her breasts, crushed against his side, tightened in delight, and her nipples felt achy, telling her they had hardened. Could he feel them? she wondered. She wanted to rub herself against him like a cat, intensifying the sensation, but she lay very still and concentrated on the rhythm of his heartbeat.

He had touched her breasts when he kissed her. She wanted to feel that again, feel his hard hand on her bare flesh. She wanted him, wanted his touch and his taste and the feel of him inside her. The force of her physical yearning was so strong that she actually ached from the emptiness.

If we don't get out of here tomorrow, she thought in faint despair just before she went to sleep, I'll be under him before the sun goes down again.

Sunny was accustomed to waking immediately when anything disturbed her; once, a car had backfired out in the street and she had grabbed the pistol from under the pillow and rolled off the bed before the noise had completely faded. She had learned how to nap on demand, because she never knew when she might have to run for her life. She could count on one hand the number of nights since she had stopped being a child that she had slept through undisturbed.

But she woke in Chance's arms aware that she had slept all night long, that not only had lying next to him not disturbed her, in a very basic way his presence had been reassuring. She was safe here, safe and warm and unutterably relaxed. His hand was stroking slowly down her back, and that was what had awakened her.

Her skirt had ridden up during the night, of course, and was twisted at midthigh. Their legs were tangled together, her right leg thrown over his; his jeans were old and soft, but the denim was still slightly rough against the inside of her thigh. She wasn't lying completely on top of him, but it was a near thing. Her head lay pillowed on his chest instead of his shoulder, with the steady thumping of his heart under her ear.

The slow motion of his hand continued. "Good morning," he said, his deep voice raspy from sleep.

"Good morning." She didn't want to get up, she realized, though she knew she should. It was after dawn; the morning light seeped through the brown fabric of the tent, washing them with a dull gold color. Chance should get started on the fuel pump, so they could get airborne and in radio contact with someone as soon as possible, to let the FAA know they hadn't crashed. She knew what she should do, but instead she continued to lie there, content with the moment.

He touched her hair, lifting one strand and watching it drift back down. "I could get used to this," he murmured.

"You've slept with women before."

"I haven't slept with *you* before."

She wanted to ask how she was different, but she was better off not knowing. Nothing could come of this fast-deepening attraction, because she couldn't let it. She had to believe that he could repair the plane, that in a matter of hours they would be separating and she would never see him again. That was the only thing that gave her the strength, finally, to pull away from him and straighten her clothes, push her hair out of her face and unzip the tent.

The chill morning air rushed into their small cocoon. "Wow," she said, ignoring his comment. "Some hot coffee would be good, wouldn't it? I don't suppose you have a jar of instant in the plane?"

"You mean you don't have coffee packed in that survival bag of yours?" Taking his cue from her, he didn't push her to continue their provocative conversation.

"Nope, just water." She crawled out of the tent, and he handed her shoes and sweater out through the opening. Quickly she slipped them on, glad she had brought a heavy cardigan instead of a summer-weight one.

Chance's boots came out next, then him. He sat on the ground and pulled on his boots. "Damn, it's cold. I'm going to get my jacket from the plane. I'll take care of business there, and you go on the other side of these boulders. There shouldn't be any snakes stirring around this early, but keep an eye out.''

Sunny dug some tissues out of her skirt pocket and set off around the boulders. Ten minutes later, nature's call having been answered, she washed her face and hands with one of the pre-moistened towelettes, then brushed her teeth and hair. Feeling much more human and able to handle the world, she took a moment to look around at their life-saving little canyon.

It was truly a slit in the earth, no more than fifty yards wide where he had landed the plane. About a quarter of a mile farther down it widened some, but the going was much rougher. The stream bed was literally the only place they could have safely landed. Just beyond the widest point, the canyon made a dog leg to the left, so she had no idea how long it was. The canyon floor was littered with rocks big and small, and a variety of scrub brush. Deep grooves were cut into the ground where rain had sluiced down the steep canyon walls and arrowed toward the stream.

All the different shades of red were represented in the dirt and rock, from rust to vermillion to a sandy pink. The scrub brush wasn't a lush green; the color was dry, as if it had been bleached by the sun. Some of it was silvery, a bright contrast against the monochromatic tones of the earth.

They seemed to be the only two living things there. She didn't hear any birds chirping, or insects rustling. There had to be small wildlife such as lizards and snakes, she knew, which meant there had to be something for them to eat, but at the moment the immense solitude was almost overwhelming.

Looking at the plane, she saw that Chance was already

poking around in its innards. Shoving her cold hands into the sweater pockets, she walked down to him.

"Don't you want to eat something?"

"I'd rather save the food until I see what the problem is." He gave her a crooked grin. "No offense, but I don't want to eat another one of those nutrition bars unless I absolutely have to."

"And if you can fly us out of here, you figure you can hold out until we get to an airport."

"Bingo."

She grinned as she changed positions so she could see what he was doing. "I didn't eat one, either," she confessed.

He was checking the fuel lines, his face set in that intent expression men got when they were doing anything mechanical. Sunny felt useless; she could have helped if he was working on a car, but she didn't know anything about airplanes. "Is there anything I can do to help?" she finally asked.

"No, it's just a matter of taking off the fuel lines and checking them for clogs."

She waited a few more minutes, but the process looked tedious rather than interesting, and she began getting restless. "I think I'll walk around, explore a bit."

"Stay within yelling distance," he said absently.

The morning, though still cool, was getting warmer by the minute as the sun heated the dry desert air. She walked carefully, watching where she placed each step, because a sprained ankle could mean the difference between life and death if she had to run for it. Someday, she thought, a sprain would be an inconvenience, nothing more. One day she would be free.

She looked up at the clear blue sky and inhaled the clean, crisp air. She had worked hard to retain her enjoyment of life, the way she had learned to rely on a sense of humor to keep her sane. Margreta didn't handle things nearly as well, but she already had to deal with a heart condition that, while it could be controlled with medication, nevertheless meant that she had to take certain precautions. If she were ever found, Margrēta lacked Sunny's ability to just drop out of sight. She had to have her medication refilled, which meant she had to occasionally see her doctor so he could write a new prescription. If she had to find a new doctor, that would mean being retested, which would mean a lot more money.

Which meant that Sunny never saw her sister. It was safer if they weren't together, in case anyone was looking for sisters. She didn't even have Margreta's phone number. Margreta called Sunny's cell phone once a week at a set time, always from a different pay phone. That way, if Sunny was captured, she had no information her captors could get by any means, not even drugs.

She had four days until Margreta called, Sunny thought. If she didn't answer the phone, or if Margreta didn't call, then each had to assume the other had been caught. If Sunny didn't answer the phone, Margreta would bolt from her safe hiding place, because with the phone records her location could be narrowed down to the correct city. Sunny couldn't bear to think what would happen then; Margreta, in her grief and rage, might well throw caution to the wind in favor of revenge.

Four days. The problem *had* to be a clogged fuel line. It just had to be.

Chapter 6

Mindful of Chance's warning, Sunny didn't wander far. In truth, there wasn't much to look at, just grit and rocks and scraggly bushes, and those vertical rock walls. The desert had a wild, lonely beauty, but she was more appreciative when she wasn't stranded in it. When rain filled the stream this sheltered place probably bloomed with color, but how often did it rain here? Once a year?

As the day warmed, the reptiles began to stir. She saw a brown lizard dart into a crevice as she approached. A bird she didn't recognize swooped down for a tasty insect, then flew back off to freedom. The steep canyon walls didn't mean anything to a bird, while the hundred feet or so were unscalable to her.

She began to get hungry, and a glance at her watch told her she had been meandering through the canyon for over an hour. What was taking Chance so long? If there was a clog in the lines he should have found it by now.

She began retracing her steps to the plane. She could see Chance still poking around the engine, which meant he probably hadn't found anything. A chilly finger of fear prodded her, and she pushed it away. She refused to anticipate trouble. She would deal with things as they happened, and if Chance couldn't repair the plane, then they would have to find some other way out of the canyon. She hadn't explored far; perhaps the other end was open, and they could simply walk out. She didn't know how far they were from a town, but she was willing to make the effort. Anything was better than sitting and doing nothing.

As she approached, Chance lifted his hand to show he saw her, then turned back to the engine. Sunny let her gaze linger, admiring the way his T-shirt clung to the muscles of his back and shoulders. The fit of his jeans wasn't bad, either, she thought, eyeing his butt and long legs.

Something moved in the sand near his feet.

She thought she would faint. Her vision dimmed and narrowed until all she saw was the snake, perilously close to his left boot. Her heart leaped, pounding against her ribcage so hard she felt the thuds.

She had no sensation or knowledge of moving; time took on the viscosity of syrup. All she knew was that the snake was getting bigger and bigger, closer and closer. Chance looked around at her and stepped back from the plane, almost on the coiling length. The snake's head drew back and her hand closed on a coil, surprisingly warm and smooth, and she threw the awful thing as far as she could. It was briefly outlined against the stark rock, then sailed beyond a bush and dropped from sight.

"Are you all right? Did it bite you? Are you hurt?"

She couldn't stop babbling as she went down on her knees and began patting his legs, looking for droplets of blood, a small tear in his jeans, anything that would show if he had been bitten.

"I'm all right. I'm all right. Sunny! It didn't bite me." His voice overrode hers, and he hauled her to her feet, shaking her a little to get her attention. "Look at me!" The force of his tone snagged her gaze with his and he said more quietly, "I'm okay."

"Are you sure?" She couldn't seem to stop touching him, patting his chest, stroking his face, though logically she knew there was no way the snake could have bitten him up there. Neither could she stop trembling. "I hate snakes," she said in a shaking voice. "They terrify me. I saw it—it was right under your feet. You almost *stepped* on it."

"Shh," he murmured, pulling her against him and rocking her slowly back and forth. "It's all right. Nothing happened."

She clutched his shirt and buried her head against his chest. His smell, already so familiar and now with the faint odor of grease added, was comforting. His heartbeat was steady, as if he hadn't almost been snakebitten. *He* was steady, rock solid, his body supporting hers.

"Oh my God," she whispered. "That was awful." She raised her head and stared at him, an appalled expression on her face. "Yuk! I *touched* it!" She snatched her hand away from him and held it at arm's length. "Let me go, I have to wash my hand. Now!"

He released her, and she bolted up the slope to the tent, where the towelettes were. Grabbing one, she scrubbed furiously at her palm and fingers.

Chance was laughing softly as he came up behind her.

"What's the matter? Snakes don't have cooties. Besides, yesterday you said you weren't afraid of them."

"I lied. And I don't care what they have, I don't want one anywhere near me." Satisfied that no snake germs lingered on her hand, she blew out a long, calming breath.

"Instead of swooping down like a hawk," he said mildly, "why didn't you just yell out a warning?"

She gave him a blank look. "I couldn't." Yelling had never entered her mind. She had been taught her entire life not to yell in moments of tension or danger, because to do so would give away her position. Normal people could scream and yell, but she had never been allowed to be normal.

He put one finger under her chin, lifting her face to the sun. He studied her for a long moment, something dark moving in his eyes; then he tugged her to him and bent his head.

His mouth was fierce and hungry, his tongue probing. She sank weakly against him, clinging to his shoulders and kissing him in return just as fiercely, with just as much hunger. More. She felt as if she had always hungered, and never been fed. She drank life itself from his mouth, and sought more.

His hands were all over her, on her breasts, her bottom, lifting her into the hard bulge of his loins. The knowledge that he wanted her filled her with a deep need to know more, to feel everything she had always denied herself. She didn't know if she could have brought herself to pull away, but he was the one who broke the kiss, lifting his head and standing there with his eyes closed and a grim expression on his face.

"Chance?" she asked hesitantly.

He growled a lurid word under his breath. Then he

opened his eyes and glared down at her. "I can't believe I'm stopping this a second time," he said with a raw, furious frustration. "Just for the record, I'm *not* that noble. Damn it all to hell and back—" He broke off, breathing hard. "It isn't a clogged fuel line. It must be the pump. We have other things we need to do. We can't afford to waste any daylight."

Margreta. Sunny bit her lip to hold back a moan of dismay. She stared up at him, the knowledge of the danger of their situation lying like a stark shadow between them.

She wasn't licked yet. She had four days. "Can we walk out?"

"In the desert? In August?" He looked up at the rim of the canyon. "Assuming we can even get out of here, we'd have to walk at night and try to find shelter during the day. By afternoon, the temperature will be over a hundred."

The temperature was probably already well into the seventies, she thought; she was dying of heat inside her heavy sweater, or maybe that was just frustrated lust, since she hadn't noticed how hot it was until now. She peeled off the sweater and dropped it on top of her bag. "What do we need to do?"

His eyes gleamed golden with admiration, and he squeezed her waist. "I'll reconnoiter. We can't get out on this end of the canyon, but maybe there's a way farther down."

"What do you want me to do?"

"Look for sticks, leaves, anything that will burn. Gather as much as you can in a pile."

He set off in the direction she had gone earlier, and she went in the opposite direction. The scrub brush grew heavier at that end of the canyon, and she would find more wood there. She didn't like to think about how limited the supply would be, or that they might be here for a long, long time. If they couldn't get out of the canyon, they would eventually use up their meager resources and die.

He hated lying to her. Chance's expression was grim as he stalked along the canyon floor. He had lied to terrorists, hoodlums and heads of state alike without a twinge of conscience, but it was getting harder and harder to lie to Sunny. He fiercely protected a hard core of honesty deep inside, the part of him that he shared only with his family, but Sunny was getting to him. She wasn't what he had expected. More and more he was beginning to suspect she wasn't working with her father. She was too…*gallant* was the word that sprang to mind. Terrorists weren't gallant. In his opinion, they were either mad or amoral. Sunny was neither.

He was more shaken by the episode with the snake than he had let her realize. Not by the snake itself—he had on boots, and since he hadn't heard rattles he suspected the snake hadn't been poisonous—but by her reaction. He would never forget the way she had looked, rushing in like an avenging angel, her face paper-white and utterly focused. By her own admission she was terrified of snakes, yet she hadn't hesitated. What kind of courage had it taken for her to pick up the snake with her bare hand?

Then there was the way she had patted him, looking for a bite. Except with certain people, or during sex, he had to struggle to tolerate being touched. He had learned how to accept affection in his family, because Mom and Maris would *not* leave him alone. He unabashedly loved playing with all his nephews—and niece—but his family had been the only exception. Until now. Until Sunny. He not only hadn't minded, he had, for a moment, allowed himself the pure luxury of enjoying the feel of her hands on his legs, his chest. And that didn't even begin to compare to how much he had enjoyed sleeping with her, feeling those sweet curves all along his side. His hand clenched as he remembered the feel of her breast in his palm, the wonderful resilience that was both soft and firm. He ached to feel her bare skin, to taste her. He wanted to strip her naked and pull her beneath him for a long hard ride, and he wanted to do it in broad daylight so he could watch her brilliant eyes glaze with pleasure.

If she wasn't who she was he would take her to the south of France, maybe, or a Caribbean island, any place where they could lie naked on the beach and make love in the sunshine, or in a shaded room with fingers of sunlight slipping through closed blinds. Instead, he had to keep lying to her, because whether or not she was working with her father didn't change the fact that she was the key to locating him.

He couldn't change the plan now. He couldn't suddenly ''repair'' the plane. He thanked God she didn't know anything about planes, because otherwise she would never have fallen for the fuel pump excuse; a Skylane had a backup fuel pump, for just such an emergency. No, he had to play out the game as he had planned it, because the goal was too damned important to abandon, and he couldn't take the risk that she was involved up to her pretty ears, after all.

He and Zane had walked a fine line in planning this out. The situation had to be survivable but grim, so nothing would arouse her suspicion. There was food to be had, but not easily. There was water, but not a lot. He hadn't brought any provisions that might make her wonder why he had them, meaning he had limited himself to the blanket, the water and the pistol, plus the expected items in the plane, such as flares. Hell, she was a lot more prepared than he was, and that made him wary. She wasn't exactly forthcoming about her reason for toting a damn tent around, either. The lady had secrets of her own.

He reached the far end of the canyon and checked to make certain nothing had changed since he and Zane had been here. No unexpected landslide had caved in a wall, allowing a way out. The thin trickle of water still ran down the rock. He saw rabbit tracks, birds, things they could eat. Shooting them would be the easy way, though; he would have to build some traps, to save his ammunition for emergencies.

Everything was just as he had left it. The plan was working. The physical attraction between them was strong; she wouldn't resist him much longer, maybe not at all. She certainly hadn't done anything to call a halt earlier. And after he was her lover—well, women were easily beguiled by sexual pleasure, the bonds of the flesh. He knew the power of sex, knew how to use it to make her trust him. He wished he could trust *her*—this would be a lot easier if he could—but he knew too much about the human soul's capability of evil, and that a pretty face didn't necessarily mean a pretty person was behind it.

When he judged enough time had passed for him to completely reconnoiter the canyon, he walked back. She was still gathering sticks, he saw, going back and forth between the bushes and the growing pile next to the tent. She looked up when he got closer, hope blazing in her expression.

He shook his head. "It's a box canyon. There's no way out," he said flatly. "The good news is, there's water at the far end."

She swallowed. Her eyes were huge with distress, almost eclipsing her face. "We can't climb out, either?"

"It's sheer rock." He put his hands on his hips, looking around. "We need to move closer to the water, for convenience. There's an overhang that will give us shade from the sun, and the ground underneath is sandier, so it'll be more comfortable."

Or as comfortable as they could get, sleeping in that small tent.

Wordlessly she nodded and began folding the tent. She did it briskly, without wasted movement, but he saw she was fighting for control. He stroked her upper arm, feeling her smooth, pliant skin, warm and slightly moist from her exertion. "We'll be okay," he reassured her. "We just have to hold out until someone sees our smoke and comes to investigate."

"We're in the middle of nowhere," she said shakily. "You said so yourself. And I only have four days until—"

"Until what?" he asked, when she stopped.

"Nothing. It doesn't matter." She stared blindly at the sky, at the clear blue expanse that was turning whiter as the hot sun climbed upward.

Four days until what? he wondered. What was going to happen? Was she supposed to do something? Was a terrorist attack planned? Would it go forward without her?

The dogleg of the canyon was about half a mile long, and the angle gave it more shade than where they had landed. They worked steadily, moving their camp, with

Chance hauling the heaviest stuff. Sunny tried to keep her mind blank, to not think about Margreta, to focus totally on the task at hand.

It was noon, the white sun directly overhead. The heat was searing, the shade beneath the overhang so welcome she sighed with relief when they gained its shelter. The overhang was larger than she had expected, about twelve feet wide and deep enough, maybe eight feet, that the sunshine would never penetrate its depths. The rock sloped to a height of about four feet at the back, but the opening was high enough that Chance could stand up without bumping his head.

"I'll wait until it's cooler to get the rest," he said. "I don't know about you, but I'm starving. Let's have half of one of your nutrition bars now, and I'll try to get a rabbit for dinner."

She rallied enough to give him a look of mock dismay. "You'd eat Peter Cottontail?"

"I'd eat the Easter Bunny right now, if I could catch him."

He was trying to make her laugh. She appreciated his effort, but she couldn't quite shake off the depression that had seized her when her last hope of getting out of here quickly had evaporated.

She had lost her appetite, but she dug out one of the nutrition bars and halved it, though she hid the fact that Chance's "half" was bigger than hers. He was bigger; he needed more. They ate their spartan little meal standing up, staring out at the bleached tones of the canyon. "Drink all the water you want," he urged. "The heat dehydrates you even in the shade."

Obediently she drank a bottle of water; she needed it to get the nutrition bar down. Each bite felt as if it was getting bigger and bigger in her mouth, making it difficult to swallow. She resorted to taking only nibbles, and got it down that way.

After they ate, Chance made a small circle of rocks, piled in some sticks and leaves, both fresh and dead, and built a fire. Soon a thin column of smoke was floating out of the canyon. It took him no more than five minutes to accomplish, but when he came back under the over-hang his shirt was damp with sweat.

She handed him a bottle of water, and he drank deeply, at the same time reaching out a strong arm and hooking it around her waist. He drew her close and pressed a light kiss to her forehead, nothing more, just held her comfortingly. She put her arms around him and clung, desperately needing his strength right now. She hadn't had anyone to lean on in a long time; she had always had to be the strong one. She had tried so hard to stay on top of things, to plan for every conceivable glitch, but she hadn't thought to plan for this, and now she had no idea what to do.

"I have to think of something," she said aloud.

"Shh. All we have to do is stay alive. That's the most important thing."

He was right, of course. She couldn't do anything about Margreta now. This damn canyon had saved their lives yesterday, but it had become a prison from which she couldn't escape. She had to play the hand with the cards that had been dealt to her and not let depression sap her strength. She had to hope Margreta wouldn't do anything foolish, just go to ground somewhere. How she would ever find her again she didn't know, but she could deal with that if she just knew her sister was alive and safe somewhere.

"Do you have family who will worry?" he asked.

God, that went to the bone! She shook her head. She

had family, but Margreta wouldn't worry; she would simply assume the worst.

"What about you?" she asked, realizing she had fallen halfway in love with the man and didn't know a thing about him.

He shook his head. "C'mon, let's sit down." With nothing to use for a seat, they simply sat on the ground. "I'll take two of the seats out of the plane this afternoon, so we'll be more comfortable," he said. "In answer to your question, no, I don't have anyone. My folks are dead, and I don't have any brothers or sisters. There's an uncle somewhere, on my dad's side, and my mom had some cousins, but we never kept in touch."

"That's sad. Family should stay together." *If they could,* she added silently. "Where did you grow up?"

"All over. Dad wasn't exactly known for his ability to keep a job. What about your folks?"

She was silent for a moment, then sighed. "I was adopted. They were good people. I still miss them." She drew a design in the dirt with her finger. "When we didn't show up in Seattle last night, would someone have notified the FAA?"

"They're probably already searching. The problem is, first they'll search the area I should have been over when I filed my flight plan."

"We were off course?" she asked faintly. It just kept getting worse and worse.

"We went off course looking for a place to land. But if anyone is searching this area, eventually he'll see our smoke. We just have to keep the fire going during the day."

"How long will they look? Before they call off the search?"

He was silent, his golden eyes narrowed as he

searched the sky. "They'll look as long as they think we might be alive."

"But if they think we've crashed—"

"Eventually they'll stop looking," he said softly. "It might be a week, a little longer, but they'll stop."

"So if no one finds us within, say, ten days—" She couldn't go on.

"We don't give up. There's always the possibility a private plane will fly over."

He didn't say that the possibility was slight, but he didn't have to. She had seen for herself the kind of terrain they'd flown over, and she knew how narrow and easily missed this canyon was.

She drew up her knees and wrapped her arms around her legs, staring wistfully at the languid curls of gray smoke. "I used to wish I could go someplace where no one could find me. I didn't realize there wouldn't be room service."

He chuckled as he leaned back on one elbow and stretched out his long legs. "Nothing gets you down for long, does it?"

"I try not to let it. Our situation isn't great, but we're alive. We have food, water and shelter. Things could be worse."

"We also have entertainment. I have a deck of cards in the plane. We can play poker."

"Do you cheat?"

"Don't need to," he drawled.

"Well, I do, so I'm giving you fair warning."

"Warning taken. You know what happens to cheaters, don't you?"

"They win?"

"Not if they get caught."

"If they're any good, they don't get caught."

He twirled a finger in her hair and lightly tugged. "Yeah, but if they get caught they're in big trouble. You can take that as my warning."

"I'll be careful," she promised. A yawn took her by surprise. "How can I be sleepy? I got plenty of sleep last night."

"It's the heat. Why don't you take a nap? I'll watch the fire."

"Why aren't you sleepy?"

He shrugged. "I'm used to it."

She really was sleepy, and there was nothing else to do. She didn't feel like setting up the tent, so she dragged her bag into position behind her and leaned back on it. Silently Chance tossed her sweater into her lap. Following his example, she rolled up the sweater and stuffed it under her head. She dozed within minutes. It wasn't a restful sleep, being one of those light naps in which she was aware of the heat, of Chance moving around, of her worry about Margreta. Her muscles felt heavy and limp, though, and completely waking up was just too much trouble.

The problem with afternoon naps was that one woke feeling both groggy and grungy. Her clothes were sticking to her, which wasn't surprising considering the heat. When she finally yawned and sat up, she saw that the sun was beginning to take on a red glow as it sank, and though the temperature was still high, the heat had lost its searing edge.

Chance was sitting cross-legged, his long, tanned fingers deftly weaving sticks and string into a cage. There was something about the way he looked there in the shadow of the overhang, his attention totally focused on the trap he was building while the light reflected off the sand outside danced along his high cheekbones, that made recognition click in her brain. "You're part Native American, aren't you?"

"American Indian," he corrected absently. "Everyone born here is a native American, or so Dad always told me." He looked up and gave her a quick grin. "Of course, 'Indian' isn't very accurate, either. Most labels aren't. But, yeah, I'm a mixed breed."

"And ex-military." She didn't know why she said that. Maybe it was his deftness in building the trap. She wasn't foolish enough to attribute that to any so-called Native American skills, not in this day and age, but there was something in the way he worked that bespoke survival training.

He gave her a surprised glance. "How did you know?"

She shook her head. "Just a guess. The way you handled the pistol, as if you were very comfortable with it. What you're doing now. And you used the word 'reconnoiter.'"

"A lot of people are familiar with weapons, especially outdoorsmen, who would also know how to build traps."

"Done in by your vocabulary," she said, and smirked. "You said 'weapons' instead of just 'guns,' the way most people—even outdoorsmen—would have."

Again she was rewarded with that flashing grin. "Okay, so I've spent some time in a uniform."

"What branch?"

"Army. Rangers."

Well, that certainly explained the survival skills. She didn't know a lot about the Rangers, or any military group, but she did know they were an elite corps.

He set the finished trap aside and began work on another one. Sunny watched him for a moment, feeling useless. She would be more hindrance than help in building traps. She sighed as she brushed the dirt from her skirt. Darn, stranded only one day and here she was, smack in the middle of the old sexual stereotypes.

She surrendered with good grace. "Is there enough water for me to wash out our clothes? I've lived in these for two days, and that's long enough."

"There's enough water, just nothing to collect it in." He unfolded his legs and stood with easy grace. "I'll show you."

He led the way out of the overhang. She clambered over rocks in his wake, feeling the heat burn through the sides of her shoes and trying not to touch the rocks with her hands. When they reached more shade, the relief was almost tangible.

"Here." He indicated a thin trickle of water running down the face of the wall. The bushes were heavier here, because of the water, and the temperature felt a good twenty degrees cooler. Part of it was illusion, because of the contrast, but the extra greenery did have a cooling effect.

Sunny sighed as she looked at the trickle. Filling their water bottles would be a snap. Washing off would be easy. But washing clothes—well, that was a different proposition. There wasn't a pool in which she could soak them, not even a puddle. The water was soaked immediately into the dry, thirsty earth. The ground was damp, but not saturated.

The only thing she could do was fill a water bottle over and over, and rinse the dust out. "This will take forever," she groused.

An irritating masculine smirk was on his face as he peeled his T-shirt off over his head and handed it to her. "We aren't exactly pressed for time, are we?"

She almost thrust the shirt back at him and demanded he put it on, but not because of his comment. She wasn't a silly prude, she had seen naked chests more times than she could count, but she had never before seen *his* naked chest. He was smoothly, powerfully muscled, with pectorals that looked like flesh-covered steel and a hard, six-pack abdomen. A light patch of black hair stretched from one small brown nipple to the other. She wanted to touch him. Her hand actually ached for the feel of his skin, and she clenched her fingers hard on his shirt.

The smirk faded, his eyes darkening. He touched her face, curving his fingers under her chin and lifting it. His expression was hard with pure male desire. "You know what's going to happen between us, don't you?" His voice was low and rough.

"Yes." She could barely manage a whisper. Her throat had tightened, her body responding to his touch, his intent.

"Do you want it?"

So much she ached with it, she thought. She looked up into those golden-brown eyes and trembled from the enormity of the step she was taking.

"Yes," she said.

Chapter 7

She had lived her entire life without ever having lived at all, Sunny thought as she mechanically rinsed out his clothes and draped them over the hot rocks to dry. She and Chance might never get out of this canyon alive, and even if they did, it could take a long time. Weeks, perhaps months, or longer. Whatever Margreta did, she would long since have done it, and there wasn't a damn thing Sunny could do about the situation. For the first time in her life, she had to think only about herself and what *she* wanted. That was simple; what she wanted was Chance.

She had to face facts. She was good at it; she had been doing it her entire life. The fact that had been glaring her in the face was that they could very well die here in this little canyon. If they didn't survive, she didn't want to die still clinging to the reasons for not getting involved that, while good and valid in civilization, didn't mean spit here. She already *was* involved with him, in a battle for their very lives. She certainly didn't want to die without having known what it was like to be loved by him, to feel him inside her and hold him close, and to tell him that she loved him. She had a whole world of love dammed up inside her, drying up because she hadn't had anyone to whom she could give it, but now she had this opportunity, and she wasn't going to waste it.

A psych analyst would say this was just propinquity: the "any port in a storm" type of attraction, or the Adam and Eve syndrome. That might be part of it, for him. If she had to guess, Sunny would say that Chance was used to having sex whenever he wanted it. He had that look about him, a bone-deep sexual confidence that would draw women like flies. She was currently the only fly available.

But it wasn't just that. He had been attracted to her before, just as she had been to him. If they had made it to Seattle without trouble, she would have been strong enough to refuse his invitation and walk away from him. She would never have allowed herself to get to know him. Maybe they had met only twenty-four hours before, but those hours had been more intense than anything else she had ever known. She imagined it was as if they had gone into battle together; the danger they had faced, and were still facing, had forged a bond between them like soldiers in a war. She had learned things about him that it would have taken her weeks to learn in a normal situation, weeks that she would never have given herself.

Of all the things she had learned about him in those twenty-four hours, there wasn't one she didn't like. He was a man willing to step forward and take a risk, get involved, otherwise he wouldn't have stopped the cretin in the airport. He was calm in a crisis, self-sufficient and capable, and he was more considerate of her than anyone else she had ever known. On top of all that, he was so sexy he made her mouth water.

Most men, after hearing something like what she had told him, would have immediately gone for the sex. Chance hadn't. Instead, he had kissed her very sweetly and said, ''I'll get the rest of the things from the plane, so I can change clothes and give you my dirty ones to wash.''

''Gee, thanks,'' she had managed to say.

He had winked at her. ''Any time.''

He was a man who could put off his personal pleasure in order to take care of business. So here she was, scrubbing his underwear. Not the most romantic thing in the world to be doing, yet it was an intimate chore that strengthened the link forming between them. He was working to feed her; she was working to keep their clothes clean.

So far, Chance was everything that was steadfast and reliable. So why did she keep sensing that edge of danger in him? Was it something his army training had given him that was just *there* no matter what he was doing? She had never met anyone else who had been a ranger, so she had no means of comparison. She was just glad of that training, if it helped keep them alive.

After his clothes were as clean as she could get them, she hesitated barely a second before stripping out of her own, down to her skin. She couldn't tolerate her grimy clothes another minute. The hot desert air washed over her bare skin, a warm, fresh caress on the backs of her knees, the small of her back, that made her nipples pinch into erect little nubs. She had never before been outside in the nude, and she felt positively decadent.

What if Chance saw her? If he was overcome with

lust by the sight of her naked body, nothing would happen that hadn't been going to happen, anyway. Not that it was likely he would be overcome, she thought wryly, smiling to herself, her curves were a long way from voluptuous. Still, if a man was faced with a naked, available woman—it could happen.

She poured a bottle of water over herself, then scooped up a handful of sand and began scrubbing. Rinsing off the sand was a matter of refilling the bottle several times. When she was finished she felt considerably refreshed and her skin was baby smooth. Maybe the skin-care industry should stop grinding up shells and rock for body scrubs, she thought, and just go for the sand.

Naked and wet, she could feel a slight breeze stirring the hot air, cooling her until she was actually comfortable. She didn't have a towel, so she let herself dry naturally while she washed her own clothes, then quickly dressed in the beige jeans and green T-shirt that she always carried. They were earth colors, colors that blended in well with vegetation and would make her more difficult to see if she had to disappear into the countryside. She would have opted for actual camouflage-patterned clothing, if that wouldn't have made her more noticeable in public. Her bra was wet from its scrubbing, so she hadn't put it back on, and the soft cotton of the T-shirt clung to her breasts, clearly revealing their shape and their soft jiggle when she walked, and the small peaks of her nipples. She wondered if Chance would notice.

"Hey," he said from behind her, his voice low and soft.

Startled, she whirled to face him. It was as if she had conjured him from her thoughts. He stood motionless about ten yards away, his eyes narrowed, his expression focused. His whiskey-coloured gaze went straight to her breasts. Oh, he noticed all right.

Her nipples got even harder, as if he had touched them.

She swallowed, trying to control a ridiculous twinge of her nerves. After all, he had already touched her breasts, and she had given him permission to do more. "How long have you been there?"

"A while." His eyelids were heavy, his voice a little rough. "I kept waiting for you to turn around, but you never did. I enjoyed the view, anyway."

Her breath hitched. "Thank you."

"You have the sweetest little ass I've ever seen."

Liquid heat moved through her. "You sweet talker, you," she said, not even half kidding. "When do I get a peep show?"

"Any time, honey." His tone was dark with sensual promise. "Any time." Then he smiled ruefully. "Any time except now. We need to move these clothes so I can set the trap up here. Since this is where the water is, this is where the game will come. I'll set the traps now and try to catch something for supper, then wash up after I clean whatever we catch—if we catch anything at all."

He wasn't exactly swept away with lust, but there was that reassuring steadfastness again, the ability to keep his priorities straight. In this situation, she didn't want Gonad the Barbarian; she wanted a man on whom she could depend to do the smart thing.

He began gathering the wet clothes off the rocks, and Sunny moved to help him. "Let me guess," she said. "The clothes still smell like humans."

"There's that, plus they're something different. Wild

animals are skittish whenever something new invades their territory."

As they walked back to the overhang she asked, "How long does it normally take to catch something in a trap?"

He shrugged. "There's no 'normal' to it. I've caught game before within ten minutes of putting out the trap. Sometimes it takes days."

She wasn't exactly looking forward to eating Peter Cottontail, but neither did she want another nutrition bar. It would be nice if some big fat chicken had gotten lost in the desert and just happened to wander into their trap. She wouldn't mind eating a chicken. After a moment of wishful thinking she resigned herself to rabbit—if they were lucky, that is. They would have to eat whatever Chance could catch.

When they reached "home," which the overhang had become, they spread their clothes out on another assortment of hot rocks. The first items she had washed were already almost dry; the dry heat of the desert was almost as efficient as an electric clothes dryer.

When they had finished, Chance collected his two handmade traps and examined them one last time. Sunny watched him, seeing the same intensity in his eyes and body that she had noticed before. "You're enjoying this, aren't you?" she asked, only mildly surprised. This was, after all, the ultimate in primitive guy stuff.

He didn't look at her, but a tiny smile twitched the corners of his mouth. "I guess I'm not all that upset. We're alive. We have food, water and shelter. I'm alone with a woman I've wanted from the first minute I saw her." He produced a badly crushed Baby Ruth candy bar from his hip pocket and opened the wrapper, then pinched off small pieces of it and put them in the traps.

Sunny was instantly diverted. "You're using a candy bar as bait?" she demanded in outraged tones. "Give me that! You can use my nutrition bar in the traps."

He grinned and evaded her as she tried to swipe the remainder of the candy bar. "The nutrition bar wouldn't be a good bait. No self-respecting rabbit would touch it."

"How long have you been hiding that Baby Ruth?"

"I haven't been hiding it. I found it in the plane when I got the rest of the stuff. Besides, it's melted from being in the plane all day."

"Melted, schmelted," she scoffed. "That doesn't affect chocolate."

"Ah." He nodded, still grinning. "You're one of those."

"One of those *what?*"

"Chocoholics."

"I am not," she protested, lifting her chin at him. "I'm a sweetaholic."

"Then why didn't you pack something sweet in that damn survival bag of yours, instead of something that tastes like dried grass?"

She scowled at him. "Because the idea is to stay alive. If I had a stash of candy, I'd eat it all the first day, then I'd be in trouble."

The golden-brown gaze flicked at her, lashing like the tip of a whip. "When are you going to tell me why you packed survival gear for an overnight plane trip to Seattle?" He kept his tone light, but she felt the change of mood. He was dead serious about this, and she wondered why. What did it matter to him why she lugged that stuff everywhere she went? She could understand why he would be curious, but not insistent.

"I'm paranoid," she said, matching his tone in lightness. "I'm always certain there will be some sort of emergency, and I'm terrified of being unprepared."

His eyes went dark and flat. "Bull. Don't try to blow me off with lies."

Sunny might be good-natured almost to a fault, but she didn't back down. "I was actually trying to be polite and avoid telling you it's none of your business."

To her surprise, he relaxed. "That's more like it."

"What? Being rude?"

"Honest," he corrected. "If there are things you don't want to tell me, fine. I don't like it, but at least it was the truth. Considering our situation, we need to be able to totally rely on each other, and that demands trust. We have to be up front with each other, even when the truth isn't all sweetness and light."

She crossed her arms and narrowed her eyes, giving him an "I'm not buying this" look. "Even when you're just being nosy? I don't think so." She sniffed. "You're trying to psych me into spilling my guts."

"Is it working?"

"I felt a momentary twinge of guilt, but then logic kicked in."

She sensed he tried to fight it, but a smile crinkled his eyes, then moved down to curl the corners of that beautifully cut mouth. He shook his head. "You're going to cause me a lot of trouble," he said companionably as he picked up the traps and started back to their little water hole, if a trickle could be called a hole.

"Why's that?" she called to his back.

"Because I'm afraid I'm going to fall in love with you," he said over his shoulder as he walked around a jutting curve of the canyon wall and disappeared from sight.

Sunny's legs felt suddenly weak; her knees actually

wobbled, and she reached out to brace her hand on the wall. Had he really said that? Did he mean it? Would a man admit to something like that if he wasn't already emotionally involved?

Her heart was pounding as if she had been running. She could handle a lot of things most people never even thought of having to do, such as running for her life, but when it came to a romantic relationship she was a babe in the woods—or in the desert, to be accurate. She had never let a man get close enough to her to matter, because she had to be free to disappear without a moment's notice or regret. But this time she couldn't disappear; she couldn't go anywhere. This time she was in a lot more trouble than Chance was, because she was already in love—fully, falling-down-a-mine-shaft, terrifyingly in love.

The feeling was a stomach-tightening mixture of ecstasy and horror. The last thing she wanted to do was love him, but it was way too late to worry about that now. What had already begun had blossomed into full flower when he *didn't* make love to her after she had said he could. Something very basic and primal had recognized him then as her mate. He was everything she had ever wanted in a man, everything she had ever dreamed about in those half-formed thoughts she had never let fully surface into her consciousness, because she had always known that life wasn't for her.

But those circumstances held sway up in the world, not down here in this sunlit hole where they were the only two people alive. She felt raw inside, as if all her nerve endings and emotions had been stripped of their protective coverings, leaving her vulnerable to feelings she had always before been able to keep at bay. Those emotions kept sweeping over her in exhilarating waves, washing her into unknown territory. She wanted very much to protect herself, yet all the shields she had used over the years were suddenly useless.

Tonight they would become lovers, and one last protective wall would be irrevocably breached. Sex wasn't just sex to her; it was a commitment, a dedication of self, that would be part of her for the rest of her life.

She wasn't naive about what else making love with him could mean. She wasn't on any form of birth control, and while he might have a few condoms with him, they would quickly be used. The bell couldn't be unrung, and once they had made love they couldn't go back to a chaste relationship. What would she do if she got pregnant and they weren't rescued? She had to hold out hope that they wouldn't be down here forever, yet a small kernel of logic told her that it was possible they wouldn't be found. What would she do if she got pregnant even if they *were* rescued? A baby would be a major complication. How would she protect it? Somehow she couldn't see herself and Chance and a baby making a normal little all-American family; she would still be running, because that was the only way to be safe.

Keeping him at a distance, remaining platonic, was the only safe, sane thing to do. Unfortunately, she didn't seem to have a good grip on her sanity any longer. She felt as if those waves had carried her too far from shore for her to make it back now. For better or worse, all she could do was ride the current where it would take her.

Nevertheless, she tried. She tried to tell herself how stupidly irresponsible it was to risk getting pregnant under any circumstances, but particularly in *this* circumstance. Yes, women all over the world conceived and gave birth in primitive conditions, but for whatever reasons, cultural, economic or lack of brain power, they didn't have a choice. She did. All she had to do was say "no" and ignore all her feminine instincts shrieking "yes, yes."

When Chance returned she was still standing in the same spot she had been when he left, her expression stricken. He was instantly alert, reaching for the pistol tucked into his waistband at the small of his back. "What's wrong?"

"What if I get pregnant?" she asked baldly, indicating their surroundings with a sweep of her hand. "That would be stupid."

He looked surprised. "Aren't you on birth control?"

"No, and even if I was, I wouldn't have an unlimited supply of pills."

Chance rubbed his jaw, trying to think of a way around this one without tipping his hand. He knew they wouldn't be here for long, only until she gave him the information he needed on her father, but he couldn't tell her that. And why in the hell wasn't she on some form of birth control? All of the female agents he knew were on long-term birth control, and Sunny's circumstances weren't that different. "I have some condoms," he finally said.

She gave him a wry smile. "How many? And what will we do when they're gone?"

The last thing he wanted to do now was make her hostile. Deciding to gamble a little, to risk not being able to make love to her in exchange for keeping her trust, he put his arms around her and cradled her against his chest. She felt good in his arms, he thought, firm with muscle and yet soft in all the right places. He hadn't been able to stop thinking about the way she looked naked: her slender, graceful back and small waist, and

the tight, heart-shaped—and heart-stopping—curve of
her butt. Her legs were as slim and sleekly muscled as
he had expected, and the thought of them wrapping
around his waist brought him to full, instant arousal. He
held her so close there was no way she could miss his
condition, but he didn't thrust himself at her; let her
think he was a gentleman. *He* knew better, but it was
essential she didn't.

He kissed the top of hcr head and took that gamble.
"We'll do whatever you want," he said gently. "I want
you—you know that. I have about three dozen condoms—"

She jerked back, glaring at him. *"Three dozen?"* she
asked, horrified. "You carry around three dozen condoms?"

There it was again, that urge to laugh. She could get
to him faster than any other woman he knew. "I had
just stocked up," he explained, keeping his tone mild.

"They have an expiration date, you know!"

He bit the inside of his jaw—hard. "Yeah, but they
don't go bad as fast as milk. They're good for a couple
of years."

She gave him a suspicious look. "How long will
thirty-six condoms keep you supplied?"

He sighed. "Longer than you evidently think."

"Six months?"

He did some quick math. Six months, thirty-six condoms...he would have to have sex more than once a
week. If he were in a monogamous relationship, that
would be nothing, but for an unattached bachelor...

"Look," he said, letting frustration creep into both
his voice and his expression, "with you, three dozen
might last a week."

She looked startled, and he could see her doing some

quick math now. As she arrived at the answer and her eyes widened, he thrust his hand into her hair, cupping the back of her head and holding her still while he kissed her, ruthlessly using all his skill to arouse her. Her hands fluttered against his chest as if she wanted to push him away, but her hands wouldn't obey. He stroked his tongue into her mouth, slow and deep, feeling the answering touch of her tongue and the pressure of her lips. She tasted sweet, and the fresh smell of her was pure woman. He felt her nipples peak under the thin fabric of her T-shirt, and abruptly he had to touch them, feel them stabbing into his palm. He had his hand under her shirt almost before the thought formed. Her breasts were firm and round, her skin cool silk that warmed under his touch. Her nipples were hard little nubs that puckered even tighter when he touched them. She arched in his arms, her eyes closed, a low moan humming in her throat.

He had intended only to kiss her out of her sudden attack of responsibility. Instead, the pleasure of touching her went to his head like old whiskey, and suddenly he had to see her, taste her. With one swift motion he pulled her shirt up, baring her breasts, and tilted her back over his arm so the firm mounds were offered up to him in a sensual feast. He bent his dark head and closed his mouth over one tight, reddening nipple, rasping his tongue over it before pressing it against the roof of his mouth and sucking. He heard the sound she made this time, the cry of a sharply aroused woman, a wild, keening sound that went straight to his loins. He was dimly aware of her nails biting into his shoulders, but the pain was small, and nothing in comparison with the urgency that had seized him. Blood thundered in his ears, roared through his veins. He wanted her with a savage intensity that rode him with sharp spurs, urging him to take instead of seduce.

Grimly he reached for his strangely elusive self-control. Only the experience and training of his entire adulthood, spent in the trenches of a dirty, covert, ongoing war, gave him the strength to rein himself in. Reluctantly he eased his clamp on her nipple, giving the turgid little bud an apologetic lick. She quivered in his arms, whimpering, her golden hair spilling back as she hung helplessly in his grasp, and he almost lost it again.

Damn it all, he couldn't wait.

Swiftly he dipped down and snagged the blanket from the ground, then hooked his right arm under her knees and lifted her off her feet, carrying her out into the sunlight. The golden glow of the lowering sun kissed her skin with a subtle sheen, deepened the glitter of her hair. Her breasts were creamy, with the delicate blue tracery of her veins showing through the pale skin, and her small nipples were a sweet rosy color, shining wetly, standing out in hard peaks. "God, you're beautiful," he said in a low, rough voice.

He set her on her feet; she swayed, her lovely eyes dazed with need. He spread out the blanket and reached for her before that need began to cool. He wanted her scorching hot, so ready for him that she would fight him for completion.

He stripped the T-shirt off over her head, dropped it on the blanket, and hooked his fingers in the waistband of her jeans. A quick pop of the snap, a jerk on the tab of the zipper, and the jeans slid down her thighs.

Her hands gripped his forearms. "Chance?" She sounded strangely uncertain, a little hesitant. If she changed her mind now—

He kissed her, slow and deep, and thumbed her nipples. She made that little humming sound again, rising on her toes to press against him. He pushed her jeans down to her ankles, wrapped both arms around her and carried her down to the blanket.

She gasped, her head arching back. "Here? Now?"

"I can't wait." That was nothing more than the hard truth. He couldn't wait until dark, until they had politely crawled into the tent together as if they were following some script. He wanted her now, in the sunlight, naked and warm and totally spontaneous. He stripped her panties down and freed her ankles from the tangle of jeans and underwear.

It seemed she didn't want to wait, either. She tugged at his shirt, pushing it up. Impatiently he gripped the hem and wrenched the garment off over his head, then spread her legs and eased his weight down on her, settling into the notch of her open thighs.

She went very still, her eyes widening as she stared up at him. He fished in his pocket for the condom he'd put there earlier, then lifted himself enough to unfasten his jeans and shove them down. He donned the condom with an abrupt, practiced motion. When he came back down to her, she braced her hands against his shoulders as if she wanted to preserve some small distance between them. But any distance was too much; he grasped her hands in one of his and pulled them over her head, pinning them to the blanket and arching her breasts against him. With his free hand he reached between them and guided his hard length to the soft, wet entrance of her body.

Sunny quivered, helpless in his grasp. She had never before felt so vulnerable, or so alive. His passion wasn't controlled and gentle, the way she had expected; it was fierce and tumultuous, buffeting her with its force. He held her down, dwarfed her with his big muscular body, and she trembled as she waited for the hard thrust of penetration. She was ready for him, oh, so ready. She ached with need; she burned with it. She wanted to beg him to hurry, but she couldn't make her lungs work. He reached down, and she felt the brush of his knuckles between her legs, then the stiff, hot length of him pushing against her opening.

Everything in her seemed to tighten, coiling, focusing on that intimate intrusion. The soft flesh between her legs began to burn and sting as the blunt pressure stretched her. He pushed harder, and the pressure became pain. Wild frustration filled her. She wanted him *now,* inside her, easing the ache and tension, stroking her back into feverish pleasure.

He started to draw back, but she couldn't let him, couldn't bear losing what his touch had promised. She had denied herself so many things, but not this, not now. She locked her legs around his and lifted her hips, fiercely impaling herself, thrusting past the resistance of her body.

She couldn't hold back the thin cry that tore from her throat. Shock robbed her muscles of strength, and she went limp on the blanket.

Chance moved over her, his broad shoulders blotting out the sun. He was a dark, massive silhouette, his shape blurred by her tears. He murmured a soft reassurance even as he probed deeper, and deeper still, until his full length was inside her.

He released her hands to cradle her in both arms. Sunny clung to his shoulders, holding as tight as she could, because without his strength she thought she might fly apart. She hadn't realized this would hurt so much, that he would feel so thick and hot inside her, or go so deep. He was invading all of her, taking over her body and commanding its responses, even her breathing, her heartbeat, the flow of blood through her veins.

He moved gently at first, slowly, angling his body so he applied pressure where she needed it most. He did things to her with his hands, stroking her into a return of pleasure. He kissed her, leisurely exploring her with his tongue. He touched her nipples, sucked them, nibbled on the side of her neck. His tender attention gradually coaxed her into response, into an instinctive motion as her hips rose and fell in time with his thrusts. She still clung to his shoulders, but in need rather than desperation. An overwhelming heat swept over her, and she heard herself panting.

·He pushed her legs farther apart and thrust deeper, harder, faster. Sensation exploded in her, abruptly convulsing her flesh. She writhed beneath him, unable to hold back the short, sharp cries that surged upward, past her constricted throat. The pounding rhythm wouldn't let the spasms abate; they kept shuddering through her until she was sobbing, fighting him, wanting release, wanting more, and finally—when his hard body stiffened and began shuddering—wanting nothing.

Chapter 8

A virgin. Sunny Miller had been a *virgin*. He tried to think, when he could think at all, what the possible ramifications were, but none of that seemed important right now. Of far more immediate urgency was how to comfort a woman whose first time had been on a blanket spread over the rough ground, in broad daylight, with a man who hadn't even taken off his boots.

He lay sprawled on his back beside her on the blanket. She had turned on her side away from him, curling in on herself while visible tremors shook her slender, naked body. Moving was an effort—*breathing* was an effort—as he pulled off the condom and tossed it away. He had climaxed so violently that he felt dazed. And if it affected him so strongly, with his experience, what was she thinking? Feeling? Had she anticipated the pain, or been shocked by it?

He knew she had climaxed. She had been as aroused as he; when he had started to pull back in stunned realization, she had hooked her legs around his and forced the entry herself. He had seen the shock in her eyes as he penetrated her, felt the reverberations in her flesh. And he had watched her face as he carefully aroused her, holding himself back with ruthless control until he felt the wild clenching of her loins. Then nothing had been able to hold him back, and he had exploded in his own gut-wrenching release.

For a woman of twenty-nine to remain a virgin, she had to have some strongly held reason for doing so. Sunny had willingly, but not lightly, surrendered her chastity to him. He felt humbled, and honored, and he was scared as hell. He hadn't been easy with her, either in the process or the culmination. At first glance the fact that she had climaxed might make everything all right with her, but he knew better. She didn't have the experience to handle the sensual violence her body and emotions had endured. She needed holding, and reassuring, until she stopped shaking and regained her equilibrium.

He put his hand on her arm and tugged her over onto her back. She didn't actively resist, but she was stiff, uncoordinated. She was pale, her eyes unusually brilliant, as if she fought tears. He cradled her head on his arm and leaned over her, giving her the attention and the contact he knew she needed. She glanced quickly up at him, then away, and a surge of color pinkened her cheeks.

He was charmed by the blush. Gently he smoothed his hand up her bare torso, stroking her belly, trailing his fingers over her breasts. The lower curves of her breasts bore the marks of his beard stubble. He soothed them with his tongue, taking care not to add more abrasions, and made a mental note to shave when he washed.

Something needed to be said, but he didn't know what. He had talked his way into strongholds, drug dens and government offices; he had an uncanny knack for making a lightning assessment of any given person and situation, and then saying exactly the right thing to get the reaction he wanted. But from the moment he had seen Sunny, lust had gotten in the way of his usual expertise. No amount of prep work could have prepared him for the impact of her sparkling eyes and bright smile, or told him he could be so disarmed by a sense of humor. "Sunny" was a very apt nickname for her.

Just now his sunshine was very quiet, almost stricken, as if she regretted their intimacy. And he couldn't bear it. He had lost count, over the years, of the women who had tried to cling to him after the sex act was finished and he slipped away, both physically and mentally, but he couldn't bear it that this one woman wasn't trying to hold him. For some reason, whether this was simply too much too soon or for some deeper reason, she was trying to hold her distance from him. She wasn't curling in his arms, sighing with repletion; she was retreating behind an invisible wall, the one that had been there from the beginning.

Everything in him rejected the idea. A primitive, possessive rage swept over him. She was his, and he would not let her go. His muscles tightened in a renewed surge of lust, and he mounted her, sliding into the tight, swollen clasp of her sheath. She inhaled sharply, the shock of his entry jarring her out of her malaise. She wedged her hands between them and sank her nails into his chest, but she didn't try to push him away. Her legs came up almost automatically, wrapping around his hips. He caught her thighs and adjusted them higher, around his waist. "Get used to it," he said, more harshly than he'd intended. "To me. To this. To us. Because I won't let you pull away from me."

Her lips trembled, but he had her full attention now. "Even for your own sake?" she whispered, distress leaching the blue undertones from her eyes and leaving them an empty gray.

He paused for a fraction of a second, wondering if she was referring to her father. "Especially for that," he replied, and set himself to the sweet task of arousing her. This time was totally for her; he wooed her with a skill that went beyond sexual experience. His extensive training in the martial arts had taught him how to cripple with a touch, kill with a single blow, but it had also taught him all the places on the human body that were exquisitely sensitive to pleasure. The backs of her knees and thighs, the delicate arches of her feet, the lower curve of her buttocks, all received their due attention. Slowly she came alive under him, a growing inner wetness easing his way. She began to move in time with his leisurely thrusts, rising up to meet him. He stroked the cluster of nerves in the small of her back and was rewarded by the reflexive arch that took him deeper into her.

She sighed, her lips parted, her eyes closed. Her cheeks glowed; her lips were puffy and red. He saw all the signs of her arousal and whispered encouragement. Her head tossed to the side, and her hardened nipples stabbed against his chest. Gently, so gently, he bit the tender curve where her neck met her shoulder.

She cried out and began climaxing, her peak catching him by surprise. So did his own. He hadn't meant to climax, but the delicate inner clench and release of her body sent pleasure roaring through him, bursting out of control.

He tried to stop, tried to withdraw; his body simply wouldn't obey. Instead, he thrust deep and shuddered wildly as his seed spurted from him into the hot, moist depths of her. He heard his own deep, rough cry; then both time and thought stopped, and all that was left of him sank down on her in a heavy sprawl.

Shadow had crept across the canyon floor when he wrapped her in the blanket and carried her back to the sheltering overhang. The surrounding rock blocked the sun during the day, but it also absorbed its heat so that at night, when the temperature dropped, it was noticeably warmer in their snug little niche than it was outside. Sunny yawned, drowsy with satisfaction, and rested her head on his shoulder. "I can walk," she said mildly, though she made no effort to slide her feet to the ground.

"Hey, I'm doing my macho act here," he protested. "Don't ruin it."

She tilted her head back to look at him. "You aren't acting, though, are you?"

"No," he admitted, and earned a chuckle from her.

Time had gotten away from him while they drifted in the sleepy aftermath of passion. The sun was so far down in the sky that only the upper rim of the canyon was lit, the reds and golds and purples of the rock catching fire in the sunset, while the sky had taken on a deep violet hue.

"I'm going to check the traps while there's still a few minutes of light left," he said as he deposited her on the ground. "Sit tight. I won't be long."

Sunny sat tight for about two seconds after he disappeared from view, then bounced to her feet. Quickly she washed and dressed, needing the protection of her clothing. She had the uneasy feeling that nothing was the same as it had been before Chance carried her out into the sunlight. She had been prepared for the lovemaking, but not for that overwhelming assault on her senses. She had hoped for pleasure, and instead found something so much more powerful that she couldn't control it.

And most of all, Chance had revealed himself for the marauder he was.

She had seen glimpses of it before, in moments when the force of his personality broke through his control. She should have realized then; one didn't bolt a steel gate on an empty room. His control had given her the rare, luxurious feeling of safety, and she had been so beguiled that she had ignored the power that gate held constrained, or what would happen if it ever broke loose. This afternoon, she had found out.

He had said he'd been in the Army Rangers. That should have told her everything she needed to know about the kind of man he was. She could only think she'd let the stress of the situation, and her worry about Margreta, blind her to his true nature.

A shiver rippled down her spine, a totally sensual reaction as she remembered the tumultuous hour—or hours—on the blanket. She had been helpless, totally blindsided by the force of her reaction. She had known from the beginning that she responded to him as she never had before to any man, but she still hadn't been prepared for such a complete upheaval of her senses. He wasn't the only one accustomed to control; her very life had depended on her control of any given situation, and with Chance, she had found that she couldn't control either him or herself.

She had never been more terrified in her life.

The way she had felt about him before was nothing compared to now. It wasn't just the sex, which had been so much more intense and harsh than she had ever imagined. No, it was the part of his character he had revealed, the part that he had tried to keep hidden, that called to her so strongly she knew only her own death would end the love she felt for him. Chance was one of a very special breed of men, a warrior. All the little pieces of him she had sensed were now settled into place, forming the picture of a man who would always have something wild and ruthless inside him, a man willing to put himself at risk, step into the line of fire, to protect what he loved. He was the complete antithesis of her father, whose life was devoted wholly to destruction.

Sunny hadn't had a choice in a lot of the sacrifices of her life. Their mother had given her and Margreta away in an effort to save them, but hadn't been able to completely sever herself from her daughters' lives. Instead, she had taught them all her hard-learned skills, taught them how to hide, to disappear—and, if necessary, how to fight. By necessity, Pamela Vickery Hauer had become an expert in her own brand of guerrilla warfare. Whenever she thought it safe she would visit, and the kindly Millers would go out of their way to give her time with her girls.

When Sunny was sixteen, Pamela's luck had finally run out. Their father's network was extensive, and he had many more resources at his disposal than his fugitive wife could command. Logically, it had been only a matter of time before he found her. And when she was finally run to ground, Pamela had killed herself rather than take the chance he would, by either torture or drugs, be able to wring their location from her.

That was Sunny's legacy, a life living in shadows, and a courageous mother who had killed herself in order to protect her children. No one had asked her if this was the life she wanted; it was the life she had, so she had made the best of it she could.

Nor had it been her choice to live apart from Margreta; that had been her sister's decision. Margreta was older; she had her own demons to fight, her own battles to wage, and she had never been as adept at the survival skills taught by their mother as Sunny had been. So Sunny had lost her sister, and when the Millers died, first Hal and then Eleanor, she had been totally alone. The calls on her cell phone from Margreta were the only contact she had, and she knew Margreta was content to leave it at that.

She didn't think she had the strength to give up Chance, too. That was why she was terrified to the point of panic, because her very presence endangered his life. Her only solace was that because he was the man he was, he was very tough and capable, more able to look after himself.

She took a deep breath, trying not to anticipate trouble. If and when they got out of this canyon, then she would decide what to do.

Because she was too nervous to sit still, she checked the clothes she had washed out and found they were already dry. She gathered them off the various rocks where they had spread them, and though the little chore had taken only minutes, by the time she walked back to the overhang there was barely enough light for her to see.

Chance hadn't taken the flashlight with him, she remembered. It was a moonless night; if he didn't get back within the next few minutes, he wouldn't be able to see.

The fire had been kept smoldering all day, to maximize the smoke and conserve their precious store of wood, but now she quickly added more sticks to bring

up a good blaze, both for her own sake and so he would
have the fire as a beacon. The flickering firelight penetrated the darkness of the overhang, sending patterns
dancing against the rock wall. She searched through their
belongings until she found the flashlight, to have it at
hand in case she had to search for him.

Total blackness came suddenly, as if Mother Nature
had dropped her petticoats over the land. Sunny stepped
to the front of the overhang. "Chance!" she called, then
paused to listen.

The night wasn't silent. There were rustlings, the
whispers of the night things as they crept about their
business. A faint breeze stirred the scrub brush, sounding
like dry bones rattling together. She listened carefully,
but didn't hear an answering call.

"Chance!" She tried again, louder this time. Nothing.
"Damn it," she muttered, and flashlight in hand set off
for the deep end of the canyon where their life-giving
water trickled out of a crack in the rock.

She walked carefully, checking where she put her feet.
A second encounter with a snake was more than she
could handle in one day. As she walked she periodically
called his name, growing more irritated by the moment.
Why didn't he answer her? Surely he could hear her by
now; sound carried in the thin, dry air.

A hard arm caught her around the waist and swung
her up against an equally hard body. She shrieked in
alarm, the sound cut off by a warm, forceful mouth. Her
head tilted back under the pressure, and she grabbed his
shoulders for support. He took his time, teasing her with
his tongue, kissing her until the tension left her body
and she was moving fluidly against him.

When he lifted his head his breathing was a little ragged. Sunny felt obliged to complain about his treatment

of her. "You scared me," she accused, though her voice sounded more sultry than sulky.

"You got what you deserved. I told you to sit tight." He kissed her again, as if he couldn't help himself.

"Is this part of the punishment?" she murmured when he came up for air.

"Yeah," he said, and she felt him smile against her temple.

"Do it some more."

He obliged, and she felt the magic fever begin burning again deep inside her. She ached all over from his previous lovemaking; she shouldn't feel even a glimmer of desire so soon, and yet she did. She wanted to feel all the power of his superbly conditioned body, take him inside her and hold him close, feel him shake as the pleasure overwhelmed him just as it did her.

Finally he tore his mouth from hers, but she could feel his heart pounding against her, feel the hard ridge in his jeans. "Have mercy," he muttered. "I won't have a chance to starve to death. I'm going to die of exhaustion."

Starving reminded her of the traps, because she was very hungry. "Did you catch a rabbit?" she asked, her tone full of hope.

"No rabbit, just a scrawny bird." He held up his free hand, and she saw that he held the plucked carcass of a bird that was quite a bit smaller than the average chicken.

"That isn't the Roadrunner, is it?"

"What's this thing you have with imaginary animals? No, it isn't a roadrunner. Try to be a little more grateful."

"Then what is it?"

"Bird," he said succinctly. "After I spit it and turn

it over the flames for a while, it'll be roasted bird. That's all that matters."

Her stomach growled. "Well, okay. As long as it isn't the Roadrunner. He's my favorite cartoon character. After Bullwinkle."

He began laughing. "When did you see those old cartoons? I didn't think they were on anywhere now."

"They're all on disk," she said. "I rented them from my local video store."

He took her arm, and they began walking back to camp, chatting and laughing about their favorite cartoons. They both agreed that the slick animated productions now couldn't match the older cartoons for sheer comedy, no matter how realistic the modern ones were. Sunny played the flashlight beam across their path as they walked, watching for snakes.

"By the way, why were you calling me?" Chance asked suddenly.

"It's dark, in case you didn't notice. You didn't carry the flashlight with you."

He made a soft, incredulous sound. "You were coming to *rescue* me?"

She felt a little embarrassed. Of course, a former ranger could find his way back to camp in the dark. "I wasn't thinking," she admitted.

"You were thinking too much," he corrected, and hugged her to his side.

They reached their little camp. The fire she had built up was still sending little tongues of flame licking around the remnants of the sticks. Chance laid the bird on a rock, swiftly fashioned a rough spit from the sticks, and sharpened the end of another stick with his pocket knife. He skewered the bird with that stick, and set it in the notches of the spit, then added some small sticks to the fire. Soon the bird was dripping sizzling juice into the flames, which leaped higher in response. The delicious smell of cooking meat made her mouth water.

She shoved a flat rock closer to the fire and sat down, watching him turn the bird. She was close enough to feel the heat on her arms; as chilly as the night was already, it was difficult to remember that just a few short hours ago the heat had been scorching. She had camped out only once before, but the circumstances had been nothing like this. For one thing, she had been alone.

The amber glow of the flames lit the hard angles of his face. He had washed up while he was gone, she saw; his hair was still a little damp. He had shaved, too. She smiled to herself.

He looked up and saw her watching him, and a wealth of knowledge, of sensual awareness, flashed between them. "Are you all right?" he asked softly.

"I'm fine." She had no idea how her face glowed as she wrapped her arms around her legs and rested her chin on her drawn-up knees.

"Are you bleeding?"

"Not now. And it was only a little, at first," she added hastily when his eyes narrowed in concern.

He returned his gaze to the bird, watching as he carefully turned it. "I wish I had known."

She wished he didn't know now. The reasons for her recently lost virginity weren't something she wanted to dissect. "Why?" she asked, injecting a light note into her tone. "Would you have been noble and stopped?"

"Hell, no," he said. "I'd have gone about it a little differently, is all."

Now, that was interesting. "What would have been different?"

"How rough I was. How long I took."

"You took long enough," she assured him, smiling. "Both times."

"I could have made it better for you."

"How about for you?"

His dark gaze flashed upward, and he gave a rueful smile. "Sweetheart, if it had been any better for me, my heart would have given out."

"Ditto."

He turned the bird again. "I didn't wear a condom the second time."

"I know." The evidence had been impossible to miss.

Their gazes met and locked again, and again they were linked by that silent communication. He might have made her pregnant. He knew it, and she knew it.

"How's the timing?"

She rocked her hand back and forth. "Borderline." The odds were in their favor, she figured, but it wasn't a risk she wanted to take again.

"If we weren't stuck here—" he began, then shrugged.

"What?"

"I wouldn't mind."

Desire surged through her, and she almost jumped his bones right then. She got a tight grip on herself, literally, and fought to stay seated. Hormones were sneaky devils, she thought, ready to undermine her common sense just because he mentioned wanting to make her pregnant.

"Neither would I," she admitted, and watched to see if he had the same reaction. Color flared high on his carved cheekbones, and a muscle in his jaw flexed. His hand tightened on the spit until his knuckles were white. Yep, it went both ways, she thought, fascinated by his battle to remain where he was.

When he judged the bird was done, he took the skewer

off the spit and kicked another rock over to rest beside hers, then sat down on it. With his pocket knife he cut a strip of meat and held it out to her. "Careful, don't burn yourself," he warned as she reached eagerly for the meat.

She juggled the strip back and forth in her hands, blowing on it to cool it. When she could hold it, she took her first tentative bite. Her taste buds exploded with the taste of wood and smoke and roasted fowl. "Oh, that's good," she moaned, chewing slowly to get every ounce of flavor.

Chance cut off a strip for himself and took his first bite, looking as satisfied as she with their meal. They chewed in silence for a while. He was careful to divide the meat equally, until she was forced to stop eating way before she was satisfied. He was so much bigger than she was that if they each ate the same amount, he would be short-changed.

He knew what she was doing, of course. "You're taking care of me again," he observed. "You're hell on my image, you know that? I'm supposed to be taking care of you."

"You're a lot bigger than I am. You need larger portions."

"Let me worry about the food, sweetheart. We won't starve. There's more game to catch, and tomorrow I'll look for some edible plants to round out our diet."

"Bird and bush," she said lightly. "What all the trendy people are eating these days."

Her quip made him grin. He persuaded her to eat a little more of the meat, then they finished off one of the remaining nutrition bars. Their hunger appeased, they began getting ready to turn in for the night.

He banked the fire while she got the tent ready. They

brushed their teeth and made one last nature call, just like old married folks, she thought in amusement. Their "home" wasn't much, really nothing more than a niche in the rock, but their preparations for the night struck her as very domestic—until he said, "Do you want to wear my shirt tonight? It would be more like a nightgown on you than the shirt you're wearing."

There was nothing the least bit tamed in the way he was looking at her. Her heartbeat picked up in speed, and the now familiar heat began spreading through her. That was all he had to do, she thought; one look and she was aroused. He had taught her body well during the short time she had been sprawled beneath him on the blanket. Now that she knew exactly how it felt to take his hard length inside her, she craved the sensation. She wanted that convulsive peak of pleasure, even though it had frightened her with its intensity. She hadn't realized she would feel as if she were flying apart, as if her soul was being wrenched from her body. In a blinding, paralyzing moment of clarity, she knew that no other man in the world would be able to do that for her, to her. He was the One for her, capital *O,* big letter, underlined and italicized. The *One*. She would never again be whole without him.

She must have looked stricken, because suddenly he was by her side, supporting her with an arm around her waist as he gently but inexorably guided her to the tent. He would be considerate, she realized, but he didn't intend to be refused.

She cleared her throat, searching for her equilibrium. "You'll need your shirt to keep warm—"

"You're joking, right?" He smiled down at her, the corners of his eyes crinkling. "Or did you think we were through for the night?"

She couldn't help smiling back. "That never crossed my mind. I just thought you'd need it *afterward.*"

"I don't think so," he said, his hands busy unsnapping her jeans.

They were both naked and inside the tent in record time. He switched off the flashlight to save the batteries, and the total darkness closed around them, just as it had the night before. Making love when one was going totally by feel somehow heightened the other senses, she found. She was aware of the calluses on his hands as he stroked her, of the heady male scent of his skin, of the powerful muscles that bunched under her own exploring hands. His taste filled her; his kisses were a feast. She reveled in the smooth firmness of his lips, the sharp edges of his teeth; she rubbed his nipples and felt them contract under her fingers. She loved the harsh groan he gave when she cupped the soft, heavy sacs between his legs, and the way they tightened even as she held them.

She was shocked when she closed her hand around his pulsing erection. How on earth had she ever taken him inside her? The long, thick column ended in a smooth, bulbous flare, the tip of which was wet with fluid. Entranced, she curled down until she could take the tip in her mouth and lick the fluid away.

He let out an explosive curse and tumbled her on her back, reversing their positions. The confines of the small tent restricted their movement, but he managed the shift with his usual powerful grace.

She laughed, full of wonder at the magic between them, and draped her arms around his neck as he settled on top of her. "Didn't you like it?"

"I almost came," he growled. "What do you think?"

"I think I'll have my way with you yet. I may have

to overpower you and tie you up, but I think I can handle the job.''

''I'm positive of it. Let me know when you're going to overpower me, so I can have my clothes off.''

That afternoon, caught in the whirlpool of his love-making, she wouldn't have believed she would be so at ease with him now, that they could indulge in this sensual teasing. She wouldn't have believed how naturally her thighs parted to accommodate his hips, or how comfortable it was, as if nature had designed them to fit together just so. Actually nature had; she just hadn't realized it until now.

He gave her a taste of her own medicine, kissing his way down her body until his hair brushed the insides of her thighs and she discovered a torture so sweet she shattered. When she could breathe again, when the colored pinpoints of light stopped flashing against her closed eyelids, he kissed her belly and laid his head on the pillowing softness. ''My God, you're easy,'' he whispered.

She managed a strangled sound that was almost a laugh. ''I guess I am. For you, anyway.''

''Just for me.'' The dark tones of masculine possessiveness and triumph underlaid the words.

''Just for you,'' she whispered in agreement.

He put on a condom and slid into place between her thighs. She fought back a cry; she was sore and swollen, and he was big. He moved gently back and forth until she accepted him more easily and the discomfort faded, but gradually his thrusts quickened, became harder. Even then she sensed he was holding himself back to keep from hurting her. When he climaxed, he pulled back so only half his length was inside her, and held himself there while shudders racked his strong body.

Afterward, he tugged his T-shirt on over her head, immediately enveloping her in his scent. The roomy garment came halfway to her knees—or it would have if he hadn't bunched it around her waist. He cradled her in his arms, one big hand on her bare bottom to keep her firmly against him. He used her rolled-up cardigan for a pillow, and she used him. Oh, this was wonderful.

"Is Sunny your real name, or is it a nickname?" he asked sleepily, his lips brushing her hair.

Even as relaxed as she was, as sated, a twinge of caution made her hesitate. She never told anyone her real name. It took her a moment to remember that none of that made any difference here now. "It's a nickname," she murmured. "My real name is Sonia, but I've never used it. Sonia Ophelia Gabrielle."

"Good God." He kissed her. "Sunny suits you. So you're saddled with four names, huh?"

"Yep. I never use the middle ones, though. What about you? What's your middle name?"

"I don't have one. It's just Chance."

"Really? You aren't lying to me because it's something awful, like Eustace?"

"Cross my heart."

She settled herself more comfortably against him. "I suppose it balances out. I have four names, you have two—together, we average three."

"How about that."

She could hear a smile in his voice now. She rewarded him with a small, sneaky pinch that made him jump. His retaliation ended, a long time later, in the use of another condom.

Sunny went to sleep to the knowledge that she was happier now, with Chance, than she had ever before been in her life.

Chapter 9

The next morning the traps were empty. Sunny struggled with her disappointment. After such an idyllic, pleasure-filled night, the day should have been just as wonderful. A nice hot, filling breakfast would have been perfect.

"Could you shoot something?" she asked as she chewed half of one of the tasteless nutrition bars. "We have eight of these bars left." If they each ate a bar a day, that meant they would be out of food in four days.

In three days, Margreta would call.

Sunny pushed that thought away. Whether or not they got out of here in time for her to answer Margreta's call was something she couldn't control. Food was a more immediate problem.

Chance narrowed his eyes as he scanned the rim of the canyon, as if looking for a way out. "I have fifteen rounds in the pistol, and no extra cartridges. I'd rather save them for emergencies, since there's no telling how long we'll be here. Besides, a 9mm bullet would tear a rabbit to pieces and wouldn't leave enough left of a bird for us to eat. Assuming I could hit a bird with a pistol shot, that is.''

She wasn't worried about his marksmanship. He was probably much better with a rifle, but with his military background, he would be more than competent with the pistol. She looked down at her hands. ''Would a .38 be better?''

''It isn't as powerful, so for small game, yeah, it would be better. Not great, but better—but I have a 9mm, so it's a moot point.''

''I have one,'' she said softly.

His head whipped around. Something dangerous flashed in his eyes. ''What did you say?''

She nodded toward her bag. ''I have a .38.''

He looked in the direction of her gaze, then back at her. His expression was like flint. ''Would you like to tell me,'' he said very deliberately, ''just how you happen to have a pistol of any kind with you? You were on a commercial flight. How did you get past the scanners?''

She didn't like giving away all her secrets, not even to Chance. A lifetime on the run had ingrained caution into her very bones, and she had already given him more of herself than she ever had anyone else. Still, they were in this together. ''I have some special containers.''

''Where?'' he snapped. ''I saw you unpack everything in your bag and there weren't any—ah, hell. The hair spray can, right?''

Unease skittered along her spine. Why was he angry? Even if he was a stickler for rules and regulations, which she doubted, he should be glad they had an extra weapon, no matter how they came by it. She straightened her shoulders. "And the blow-dryer."

He stood over her like an avenging angel, his jaw set. "How long have you been smuggling weapons on board airplanes?"

"Every time I've flown," she said coolly, standing up. She was damned if she would let him tower over her as if she was a recalcitrant child. He still towered over, just not as much. "I was sixteen the first time."

She walked over to the bag and removed the pertinent items. Chance leaned down and snagged the can of spray from her hands. He took the cap off and examined the nozzle, then pointed it away from him and depressed it. A powder-fine mist of spray shot out.

"It's really hair spray," she said. "Just not much of it." She took the can and deftly unscrewed the bottom. A short barrel slid out of the can into her hands. Putting it aside, she lifted the hair-dryer and took it apart with the same deft twist, yielding the remaining parts of the pistol. She assembled it with the ease of someone who had done the task so often she could do it in her sleep, then fed the cartridges into the magazine, snapped it into place, reversed the pistol and presented it to him butt-first.

He took it, his big hand almost swallowing the small weapon. "What in *hell* are you doing with a weapon?" he bit out.

"The same thing you are, I imagine." She walked away from him and missed the look of shock that crossed his face. With her back to him she said, "I carry it for self-protection. Why do you carry yours?"

"I charter my plane to a lot of different people, most of whom I don't know. I fly into some isolated areas sometimes. And my weapon is licensed." He hurled the words at her like rocks. "Is yours?"

"No," she said, unwilling to lie. "But I'm a single woman who travels alone, carrying packages valuable enough that a courier service is hired to deliver them. The people I deliver the packages to are strangers. Think about it. I'd have to be a fool not to carry some means of protection." That was the truth, as far as it went.

"If your reason for carrying is legitimate, then why don't you have a license?"

She felt as if she were being interrogated, and she didn't like it. The tender, teasing lover of the night was gone, and in his place was someone who sounded like a prosecutor.

She had never applied for a license to carry a concealed weapon because she didn't want any background checks in the national data system, didn't want to bring herself to the notice of anyone in officialdom.

"I have my reasons," she retorted, keeping her tone very deliberate.

"And you aren't going to tell me what they are, right?" He threw her a look that was almost sulfuric in its fury and stalked off in the direction of the traps. His stalking, like everything else he did, was utterly graceful—and completely silent.

"Good riddance, Mr. Sunshine," she hurled at his back. It was a childish jab, but she felt better afterward. Sometimes a little childishness was just what the doctor ordered.

With nothing better to do, she set off in the opposite direction, toward the plane, to gather more sticks and twigs for the all-important fire. If he tried to keep her pistol when they got out of here—and they *would* get out, she had to keep hoping—then it would be war.

*   *   *

Chance examined the compact pistol in his hand. It
was unlike any he had ever seen before, for the simple
reason that it hadn't come from any manufacturer. A
gunsmith, a skilled one, had made this weapon. It bore
no serial number, no name, no indication of where or
when it was made. It was completely untraceable.

He couldn't think of any good reason for Sunny to
have it, but he could think of several bad ones.

After yesterday, he had been more than halfway convinced she was innocent, that she was in no way involved with her father. Stupid of him, but he had equated
chastity with honor. Just because a woman didn't sleep
around didn't mean she was a fine, upstanding citizen.
All it meant was that, for whatever reason, she hadn't
had sex.

He knew better. He was far better acquainted with the
blackness of the human soul than with its goodness, because he had chosen to live in the sewers. Hell, he came
from the sewers; he should be right at home there, and
most of the time he was. The blackness of his own soul
was always there, hidden just a few layers deep, and he
was always aware of it. He used to make his way in the
dangerous world he had chosen, shaped it into a weapon
to be used in defense of his country and, ultimately, his
family. And being on such intimate terms with hell, with
the twisted evil humans could visit on one another, he
should know that golden hair and bright, sparkling eyes
didn't necessarily belong on an angel. Shakespeare had
hit the nail on the head when he warned the world
against smiling villains.

It was just—*damn* it, Sunny got to him. She had
slipped right past defenses he would have sworn were
impregnable, and she had done it so easily they might

as well not have been there at all. He wanted her, and so he had almost convinced himself that she was innocent.

Almost. There was just too much about her that didn't add up, and now there was this untraceable pistol that she smuggled on board airplanes, concealed in some very effective but simple containers. Airport scanners would show metal, but if a security guard was suspicious enough to check, he or she would find only the normal female styling aids. The hair spray can actually sprayed, and he didn't doubt the blow-dryer would work, too.

If Sunny could get a pistol on board a plane, then others could, too. He went cold at the thought of how many weapons must be flying around at any given time. Airport security wasn't his line of work, but damn if he wasn't going to make it a point to kick some asses over this.

He shoved his anger aside so he could concentrate on this assignment. He hoped he hadn't blown it by losing his temper with her, but his disillusionment had been too sharp for him to contain. The pleasure of the night they had just spent together should more than outweigh their first argument. Her inexperience with men worked against her; she would be easy to manipulate, where a seasoned veteran of the mattress wars would be more wary and blasé about their lovemaking. He still held all the trump cards, and soon he would be playing them.

He reached a particular point in the canyon and positioned himself so he was in the deepest morning shadows. Sunny couldn't catch him unawares here, and he had a clear line of sight to a certain rock on the rim of the canyon. He took a laser light from his pocket, a pencil-thin tube about two inches long that, when clicked, emitted an extraordinarily bright finger of light.

He aimed it at the rock on the rim and began clicking, sending dashes of light in the code he and Zane had agreed on at the beginning of the plan. Every day he signalled Zane, both to let him know that everything was all right and that they shouldn't be rescued yet.

There was an answering flash, message received. No matter how closely he watched that rock, he never saw any movement, though he knew Zane would have immediately pulled back. He himself was damn good at moving around undetected, but Zane was extraordinary even for a SEAL. There was no one else on this earth Chance would rather have beside him in a fight than Zane.

That mission accomplished, Chance settled down in some cover where he could watch the trickle of water. Since the traps hadn't been productive overnight, he really did need to shoot something for supper. He was willing to starve to achieve his ends—but only if he had to. If a bunny rabbit showed its face, it was history.

As Sunny walked the canyon floor, picking up what sticks she could find, she studied the rock walls, looking for a fissure that might have escaped notice, an animal trail, anything that might point the way to freedom. If they only had some rock-climbing gear, she thought wistfully. A rope, cleats, anything. She had tried to anticipate any possible need when she packed her bag, but somehow being trapped in a box canyon hadn't occurred to her.

For the most part, the walls were perpendicular. Even when they slanted a little, the angle wasn't much off ninety degrees. Erosion from wind and rain had, over millions of years, cut grooves in the rock that looked like ripples in water. The only sign the canyon wasn't impregnable was the occasional little heap of rubble where smaller rocks had crumbled and fallen.

She had passed several of those small heaps before the light went on.

A fragile stirring of hope made her stomach tighten as she investigated one scattered pile of rock. It looked as if a larger boulder had fallen from the rim and shattered on impact. She picked up a fist-sized rock and rubbed her thumb over the surface, finding it gritty, the texture of sandpaper. Sandstone, she thought. It was a lovely pink color. It was also soft.

Just to be certain, she banged the rock down on a larger rock, and it broke into several pieces.

This site was no good; it was too steep. She walked along the wall, looking up at the rim and trying to find a place where the wall slanted back just a little. That was all she asked; just a little slant, enough that the angle wasn't so extreme.

There. One of the ripples curved backward, and when she picked her way through rocks and bushes to investigate she saw the opportunity for which she had been looking. She ran her hand over the rock, exulting in the sandpaper texture of it under her palm. Maybe, just maybe...

She ran back to the camp and grabbed the curling iron out of the bag. Chance hadn't asked, but the pistol wasn't the only weapon she carried. Quickly she unscrewed the metal barrel from the handle and removed a knife from the interior. It was a slender blade, made for slicing rather than hacking, but sharp and almost indestructible.

Her idea registered somewhere between being a long shot and just plain crazy, but it was the only idea she'd had that was even remotely possible. At least she would be doing *something,* rather than just waiting around for a rescue that might never happen.

She needed gloves to protect her hands, but she didn't have any. Hastily she opened the first-aid box and took out the roll of gauze. She wrapped the gauze around her palms and wove it in and around her fingers, then taped the loose ends. The result was crude but workable, she thought. She had seen the gloves rock climbers wore, with their fingers and thumbs left free; this makeshift approximation would have to do. She might wear blisters on her hands, anyway, but that was a small price to pay if they could get out of here.

Knife in hand, she went back to her chosen point of attack and tried to figure out the best way to do this. She needed another rock, she realized, one that wasn't soft. Anything that crumbled would be useless. She scouted around and finally found a pitted, dark gray rock that was about the size of a grapefruit, heavy enough to do the job.

Digging the point of the knife into the soft sandstone of the wall, she gripped the rock with her right hand and pounded it against the knife, driving the blade deeper. She jerked the blade out, moved it a little to the right, and pounded it in again. The next time she drove the knife in at a right angle to the original gouge, and hammered it downward. A chunk of sandstone broke loose, leaving a nice little gouge in the rock.

"This just might work," Sunny said aloud, and set herself to the task. She didn't let herself think how long it would take to carve handholds out of the rock all the way to the top, or if it was even possible. She was going to try; she owed it to Margreta, and to herself, to do everything she could to get out of this canyon.

Almost two hours later, the sharp crack of a pistol

shot reverberated through the canyon, startling her so much that she nearly fell. She clung to the rock, her cheek pressed against the rough surface. Her heart pounded from the close call. She wasn't that high, only about ten feet, but the canyon floor was jagged with rock, and any fall was certain to cause injuries.

She wiped the sweat from her face. The temperature was rising by the minute, and the rock was getting hotter and hotter. Standing with her toes wedged into the gouges she had hammered out of the rock, she had to lean inward against the rock to brace herself, because she had to have both hands free to wield the knife and the rock. She couldn't put nearly as much effort into it now, or the impact would jar her from her perch.

Panting, she reached over her head and blindly swung the rock. Because she had to press herself to the rock to keep her balance, she couldn't see to aim. Sometimes she hit the target and the knife bit into the rock; sometimes she hit her own hand. There had to be a better way to do this, but she couldn't think of one. She was an expert at working with what she had; she could do it this time, too. All she had to do was be careful, and patient.

"I can do this," she whispered.

Chance carried the skinned and cleaned rabbit back to the camp. He had also found a prickly pear cactus and cut off two of the stems, sticking himself several times as he removed the spines. The prickle pear was both edible and nutritious; it was usually fried, but he figured roasting would do just as well.

His temper had cooled. All right, so she had taken him in. He hadn't blown the plan; everything was still on track. All he had to do was remember not to be fooled

by that oh-so-charming face she presented to the world
and the plan would work just as he had expected. Maybe
he couldn't make her love him, but he could make her
think she did, and that was all he needed. A little trust,
a little information, and he was in business.

He stepped beneath the overhang, grateful for the relief the shade afforded, and took off his sunglasses.
Sunny wasn't here. He turned around and surveyed what
he could see of the canyon but couldn't spot her. Her
green T-shirt and beige jeans didn't exactly stand out in
the terrain, he thought, and abruptly realized what effective camouflage her clothing was. Had she chosen it for
that exact purpose? She must have; everything she carried in that bag had been geared toward survival, so why
should her clothing be any different?

"Sunny!" he called. His voice echoed, then died. He
listened, but there was no answer.

Damn it, where was she?

The fire had died down, which meant she hadn't
tended it in quite a while. He bent down and added more
sticks, then skewered the rabbit and set it on the spit,
more to keep it away from insects than anything else.
The fire was too low to cook it, but the smoke wafting
over the meat would give it a good flavor. He wrapped
the prickly pear stems in his handkerchief and walked
back under the overhang to keep them out of the sun
until he was ready to cook them.

The first thing he saw was the open first aid kit.

Alarm punched him in the gut. The paper wrapping
had been torn off the roll of gauze; the tape was lying
in the lid of the box, and it had also been used, because
the end had been left free rather than stuck back to the
roll.

Another detail caught his eyes. The curling iron had been taken apart; the two halves of it lay in the sand.

He swore viciously. Damn it, he should have remembered the curling iron and not assumed the pistol was the only weapon she had. She couldn't have hidden another pistol in the curling iron, but a knife would fit.

He didn't see any blood, but she must have injured herself somehow. Where in the hell was she?

"Sunny!" he roared as he stepped back out into the sun. Only silence answered him.

He studied the ground. Her footprints were everywhere, of course, but he saw where she had walked to her bag, presumably to get the first aid kit; then the prints led back out into the canyon. She was headed toward the plane.

He wasn't aware of reaching for his pistol. He was so accustomed to it that he didn't notice the weight of it in his hand as he followed her tracks, everything in him focusing on finding her.

If it hadn't been for the tracks, he would have missed her. She was almost at the far end of the canyon, past where the plane sat baking in the sun. The rock walls were scored with hundreds of cuts, and she was tucked inside one of them, clinging to the rock about a dozen feet off the ground.

Astonishment, anxiety, relief and anger all balled together in his gut. In speechless fury he watched her reach over her head and stab a wicked-looking blade into the soft rock, then, still keeping her face pressed against the hot stone, use another rock to try to pound the knife deeper. She hit her hand instead of the knife handle, and the curse she muttered made his eyebrows rise.

Strips of gauze were wound around her hands. He didn't know if she had wrapped her hands because she had hurt them, or if the gauze was an effort to keep them from being hurt. All he knew was that if she fell she would likely maim herself on the rocks, and that he really, *really* wanted to spank her.

He ruthlessly restrained the urge to yell at her. The last thing he wanted to do was startle her off her precarious perch. Instead, he stuck the pistol in his waistband at the small of his back and worked his way over until he was standing beneath her, so he could catch her if she fell.

He forced himself to sound calm. "Sunny, I'm right beneath you. Can you get down?"

She stopped with her right hand drawn back to deliver another blow with the rock. She didn't look down at him. "Probably," she said. "It has to be easier than getting up here."

He was fairly certain what she was doing, but the sheer magnitude of the task, the physical impossibility of it, left him stunned. Just for confirmation he asked, "What are you doing?"

"I'm cutting handholds in the rock, so we can climb out of here." She sounded grim, as if she also realized the odds against success.

His hands clenched into fists as he fought for control. He looked up at the towering wall, at the expanse stretching above her. The dozen feet she had climbed was only about one tenth of the distance needed—and it was the easiest tenth.

He put his hand on the rock and almost jerked back at the heat radiating from it. A new concern gnawed at him. He didn't yell at her that this was the stupidest idea he'd ever heard of, the way he wanted. Instead, he said, "Sweetheart, the rock's too hot. Come down before you're burned."

She laughed, but without her usual humor. "It's too late."

To hell with cajoling. "Throw the knife down and get off that damn rock," he barked in sharp command.

To his surprise, she dropped the knife, then the rock she held in her right hand, tossing both to the side so they wouldn't land near him. Every muscle in her body was taut with strain as she reached for the handholds she had cut and began to work her way down, feeling with her toes for the gouges. He stood directly beneath her, reaching up for her in case she fell. The muscles in her slender arms flexed, and he realized anew just how strong she was. One didn't get that kind of strength with a once-in-a-while jog or the occasional workout in a gym. It took dedication and time; he knew, because he kept himself in top physical condition. Her normal routine would be at least an hour of work, maybe two, every day. For all he knew, while he had been checking the traps she had been doing pushups.

For all the gut-deep burn of his anger, it was overridden by his concern as he watched her inch her way down the face of the rock. She was careful and took her time, despite the fact that he knew the rock was scorching her fingers. He didn't speak again, not wanting to distract her; he simply waited, not very patiently, for her to get within his reach.

When she did, he caught her feet and guided them to the next gouges. "Thanks," she panted, and worked her way down another foot.

That was enough. He caught her around the knees and scooped her off the rock. She shrieked, fighting for her balance, but now that he had her in his grip he wasn't about to let her go. Before she could catch her breath, he turned her and tossed her face down over his shoulder.

"Hey!" The indignant protest was muffled against his back.

"Just shut up," he said between his teeth as he dipped down to pick up her knife, then set off for the camp. "You scared the hell out of me."

"Good. You had too much hell in you, anyway." She clutched him around the waist to steady herself. He just hoped she didn't grab the pistol out of his waistband and shoot him, since it was so close to hand.

"Damn it, don't you dare joke about it!" Her upturned bottom was very close to his hand. Temptation gnawed at him. Now that he had her down, he was shaking, and he wanted some retribution for having been put through that kind of anxiety. He put his hand on her butt and indulged in a few moments of fantasy, which involved her jeans around her knees and her bent over his lap.

He realized he was stroking his palm over the round curves of her buttocks and regretfully gave up on his fantasy. Some things weren't going to happen. After he tended her hands and got through raising hell with her for taking such a risk, he fully intended to burn off his fright and anger with an hour or two on the blanket with her.

How could he still want her so much? This wasn't part of the job; he could live with it, if it had been. This was obsession, deep and burning and gut-twisting. He had tried to put a light face on it, for her benefit, but if she had been more experienced, she would have known a man didn't make love to a woman five times during the night just because she was available. At this rate, those three dozen condoms wouldn't last even a week.

He had already used six, and it might take two or three more to get him settled down after the scare she had given him.

The hard fact of it was, a man didn't make love to a woman that often unless he was putting his brand on her.

This wouldn't work. Couldn't work. He had to get himself under control, stay focused on the job.

He heard her sniffing as they neared the camp. "Are you *crying?*" he demanded incredulously.

She sniffed again. "Don't be silly. What's that smell?" She inhaled deeply. "It smells like…food."

Despite himself, a smile quirked the corners of his mouth. "I shot a rabbit."

There was a small disruption on his shoulder as she twisted around so she could see the fire. Her squeal of delight almost punctured his eardrums, and his smile grew. He couldn't stop himself from enjoying her; he had never before met anyone who took such joy in life, who was so vibrantly alive herself. How she could be a part of a network devoted to taking lives was beyond his understanding.

He dumped her on the ground under the overhang and squatted beside her, taking both her hands in his and turning them up for his inspection. He barely controlled a wince. Her fingers were not only scorched from the hot rock, they were scraped raw and bleeding.

Fury erupted in him again, a flash fire of temper at seeing the damage she had done to herself. He surged to his feet. "Of all the stupid, lame-brained…! What in hell were you thinking? You weren't thinking at all, from the looks of it! Damn it, Sunny, you risked your life pulling this stupid stunt—"

"It wasn't stupid," she shouted, shooting to her feet

to face him, her brilliant eyes narrowed. She clenched her bleeding hands into fists. "I know the risks. I also know it's my only hope of getting out of this damn canyon before it's too late!"

"Too late for what?" he yelled back. "Do you have a date this weekend or something?" The words were heavy with sarcasm.

"Yeah! It just so happens I do!" Breathing hard, she glared at him. "My sister is supposed to call."

Chapter 10

A sister? Chance stared at her. His investigation hadn't turned up any information about a sister. The Millers hadn't had any children of their own, and he had found adoption papers only on Sunny. His mind raced. "You said you didn't have any family."

She gave him a stony look. "Well, I have a sister."

Yeah, right. "You'd risk your life for a phone call?" Some terrorist act was being planned after all, he thought with a cold feeling in the pit of his stomach. That was why she'd been lugging the tent around. He didn't know how the tent fit into the scheme, but evidently she had been planning to drop out of sight.

"I would for this one." She wheeled away, every line of her body tense. "I have to try. Margreta calls my cell phone every week at the same time. It's how we know the other is still alive." She turned back to him and shouted, "If I don't answer that call, she'll think I'm dead!"

Whoa. Once again, the pieces of the puzzle that was Sunny had been scattered. Margreta? Was that a code name? He searched his memory, which was extensive, but couldn't find anything or anyone named Margreta. Sunny was so damned convincing....

"Why would she think you're dead?" he demanded. "You might just be in a place that doesn't have a signal—like here. What is she, some kind of nutcase?"

"I make certain I'm always somewhere that has a signal. And, no, she isn't a *nutcase!*" She threw the words back at him like bullets, her mouth twisted with fury at him, at the situation, at her own helplessness. "Her problem is the same as mine—we're our father's daughters!"

His pulse leaped. There it was, out in the open, just like that. He hadn't needed seduction; anger had done the job. "Your father?" he asked carefully.

Tears glittered in her eyes, dripped down her cheeks. She dashed them away with a furious gesture. "Our father," she said bitterly. "We've been running from him all our lives."

The pieces of the puzzle jumped about a little more, as if a fist had slammed down and jarred them. Easy, he cautioned himself. Don't seem too interested. Find out exactly what she means; she could be referring to his influence. "What do you mean, running?"

"I mean running. Hiding." She wiped away more tears. "Father dear is a terrorist. He'll kill us if he ever finds us."

Chance gently cleaned her hands with the alcohol wipes from the first aid kit, soothed the red places with burn ointment and the raw spots with antibiotic cream. The gauze she'd wrapped around her hands had protected her palms, but her fingers were a mess. Sunny felt a little bewildered. One minute they had been yelling at each other, the next she had been locked against him, his arms like a vise around her. His heart had been pounding like a runaway horse.

Since then he had been as tender as a mother with a child, rocking her in comfort, cuddling her, drying her tears. The emotional firestorm that had burned through her had left her feeling numb and disoriented; she let him do whatever he wanted without offering a protest, not that she had any reason to protest. It felt good to lean on him.

Satisfied with the care he had given her hands, he left her sitting on the rock while he added some fuel to the fire and turned the rabbit on the spit. Coming back under the overhang, he spread the blanket against the wall, scooped her into his arms, and settled on the blanket with her cradled against him. He propped his back against the wall, arranged her so she was draped half across his lap and lifted her face for a light kiss.

She managed a shaky smile. "What was that? A kiss to make it better?"

He rubbed his thumb over her bottom lip, his expression strangely intent as if studying her. "Something like that."

"I'm sorry for crying all over you. I usually handle things better than this."

"Tell me what's going on," he said quietly. "What's this about your father?"

She leaned her head on his shoulder, grateful for his strength. "Hard to believe, isn't it? But he's the leader of a terrorist group that has done some awful things. His name is Crispin Hauer."

"I've never heard of him," Chance lied.

"He operates mostly in Europe, but his network extends to the States. He even has someone planted in the FBI." She was unable to keep the raw bitterness out of her voice. "Why do you think I don't have a license for that pistol? I don't know who the plant is, how high he ranks, but I do know he's in a position to learn if the FBI gets any information Hauer wants. I didn't want to be in any database, in case he found out who adopted me and what name I'm using."

"So he doesn't know who you are?"

She shook her head. She had spent a lifetime keeping all her fear and worry bottled up inside her, and now she couldn't seem to stop it from spewing out. "My mother took Margreta and left him before I was born. I've never met him. She was five months pregnant with me when she ran."

"What did she do?"

"She managed to lose herself. America's a big place. She stayed on the move, changing her name, paying with cash she had taken from his safe. When I was born, she intended to have me by herself, in the motel room she'd taken for the night. But I wouldn't come, the labor just kept on and on, and she knew something was wrong. Margreta was hungry and scared, crying. So she called 911."

He wound a strand of golden hair around his finger. "And was there something wrong?"

"I was breech. She had a C-section. While she was groggy from the drugs, they asked her the father's name and she didn't think to make up a name, just blurted out *his*. So that's how I got into the system, and how he knows about me."

"How do you know he knows?"

"I was almost caught, once." She shivered against

him, and he held her closer. "He sent three men. We were in...Indianapolis, I think. I was five. Mom had bought an old car and we were going somewhere. We were always on the move. We got boxed in, in traffic. She saw them get out of their cars. She had taught us what to do if she ever told us to run. She dragged us out of the car and screamed 'Run!' I did, but Margreta started crying and grabbed Mom. So Mom took off running with Margreta. Two men went after them, and one came after me." She began shuddering. "I hid in an alley, under some garbage. I could hear him calling me, his voice soft like he was singing. 'Sonia, Sonia.' Over and over. They knew my name. I waited forever, and finally he went away."

"How did your mother find you again? Or was she caught?"

"No, she and Margreta got away, too. Mom taught herself street smarts, and she never went anywhere that she wasn't always checking out ways to escape."

He knew what that was like, Chance thought.

"I stayed in my hiding place. Mom had told us that sometimes, after we thought they were gone, the bad men would still be there watching, waiting to see if we came out. So I thought the bad men might be watching, and I stayed as still as I could. I don't think it was winter, because I wasn't wearing a coat, but when night fell I got cold. I was scared and hungry and didn't know if I'd ever see Mom again. I didn't leave, though, and finally I heard her calling me. She must have noticed where I ran and worked her way back when she thought it was safe. All I knew was that she'd found me. After that was when she decided it wasn't safe to keep us with her anymore, so she began looking for someone to adopt us."

Chance frowned. He hadn't found a record of any adoption but hers. "The same family took both of you?"

"Yes, but I was the only one adopted. Margreta wouldn't." Her voice was soft. "Margreta...remembers things. She had lost everything except Mom, so I guess she clung more than I did. She had a hard time adapting." She shrugged. "Having grown up the way I did, I can adjust to pretty much anything."

Meaning she had taught herself not to cling. Instead, with her sunny personality, she had found joy and beauty wherever she could. He held her closer, letting her cling to him. "But...you said he was trying to kill you. It sounds as if he was trying very hard to get you back."

She shook her head. "He was trying to get *Margreta* back. He didn't know me. I was just a means he could have used to force Mom to give Margreta back to him. That's all he would want with me now, to find Margreta. If I was caught, when he found out I don't know where she is, I'd be worthless to him."

"You don't know?" he asked, startled.

"It's safer that way. I haven't seen her in years." Unconscious longing for her sister was in her voice. "She has my cell phone number, and she calls me once a week. So long as I answer the call, she knows everything is all right."

"But you don't know how to get in touch with her?"

"No. I can't tell them what I don't know. I move around a lot, so a cell phone was the best way for us. I keep an apartment in Chicago, the tiniest, cheapest place I could find, but I don't live there. It's more of a decoy than anything else. I suppose if I live anywhere it's in Atlanta, but I take all the assignments I can get. I seldom spend more than one night at a time in one place."

"How would he find you now, since your name has

been changed? Unless he knows who adopted you, but how could he find that out?'' Chance himself had found her only because of the incident in Chicago, when her courier package was stolen and he checked her out. As soon as he said it, though, he knew that the mole in the FBI—and he would damn sure find out who *that* was— had probably done the same checking. Had he gone as deep in the layers of bureaucracy as Chance had, to the point of hacking into those sealed adoption records? Sunny's cover might have been blown. He wondered if she realized it yet.

"I don't know. I just know I can't afford to assume I'm safe until I hear he's dead."

"What about your mom? And Margreta?"

"Mom's dead." Sunny paused, and he felt her inhale as if bracing herself. "They caught her. She committed suicide rather than give up any information on us. She had told us she would—and she did."

She stopped, and Chance gave her time to deal with the bleakness he heard in her voice. Finally she said, "Margreta is using another name, I just don't know what it is. She has a heart condition, so it's better if she stays in one location."

Margreta was living a fairly normal life, he thought, while Sunny was on the move, always looking over her shoulder. That was what she had known since birth, the way she had been taught to handle the situation. But what about the years they had spent with the Millers? Had her life been normal then?

She answered those questions herself. "I miss having a home," she said wistfully. "But if you stay in one place you get to know people, form relationships. I couldn't risk someone else's life that way. God forbid I should get married, have children. If Hauer ever found me—'' She broke off, shuddering at the thought of what Hauer was capable of doing to someone she loved in order to get the answers he wanted.

One thing didn't make sense, Chance thought. Hauer was vicious and crazy and cunning, and would go to any lengths to recover his daughter. But why Margreta, and not Sunny, too? ''Why is he so fixated on your sister?''

''Can't you guess?'' she asked rawly, and began shuddering again. ''That's why Mom took Margreta and ran. She found him with her, doing…things. Margreta was only four. He had evidently been abusing her for quite a while, maybe even most of her life. By then Mom had already found out some of what he was, but she hadn't worked up the nerve to leave. After she found him with Margreta, she didn't have a choice.'' Her voice dropped to an agonized whisper. ''Margreta remembers.''

Chance felt sick to his stomach. So in addition to being a vicious, murdering bastard, Hauer was also a pervert, a child molester. Killing was too good for him; he deserved to be dismembered—slowly.

Worn out by both physical labor and her emotional storm, Sunny drifted to sleep. Chance held her, content to let her rest. The fire needed more fuel, but so what? Holding her was more important. Thinking his way through this was more important.

First and foremost, he believed every word she'd said. Her emotions had been too raw and honest for any of it to have been faked. For the first time, all the pieces of the puzzle fit together, and his relief was staggering. Sunny was innocent. She had nothing to do with her father, had never seen him, had spent her entire life running from him. That was why she lugged around a tent, with basic survival provisions; she was ready to disappear at any given moment, to literally go to ground and live out in the forest somewhere until she thought it was safe to surface and rebuild her life yet again.

She had no way of contacting Hauer. The only way to get to him, then, was to use her as bait. And considering how she felt about her father, she would never, under any circumstances, agree to any plan that brought her to his attention.

He would have to do it without her agreement, Chance thought grimly. He didn't like using her, but the stakes were too high to abandon. Hauer couldn't be left free to continue wreaking his destruction on the world. How many innocent people would die this year alone if he wasn't caught?

There was no point in staying here any longer; he'd found out what he needed to know. Zane wouldn't check in again, though, until tomorrow morning, so they were stuck until then. He adjusted Sunny in his arms and rested his face against the top of her head. He would use the time to formulate his game plan—and to use as many of those condoms as possible.

"Get away from me," Sunny grumbled the next morning, turning her head away from his kiss. She pried his hand off her breast. "Don't touch me, you—you *mink.*"

Chance snorted with laughter.

She pulled his chest hair.

"Ouch!" He drew back as far as he could in the small confines of the tent. "That hurt."

"Good! I don't think I can walk." Quick as a snake, her hand darted out and pulled his chest hair again. "This way, you can have as much fun as I'm having."

"Sunny," he said in a cajoling tone.

"Don't 'Sunny' me," she warned, fighting her way

into her clothes. Since they barely had room to move, he began dodging elbows and knees, and his hands slipped over some very interesting places. "Stop it! I mean it, Chance! I'm too sore for any more monkey business."

More to tease her than anything else, he zeroed in on an interesting place that had her squealing. She shot out of the tent, and he collapsed on his back, laughing—until she raised the tent flap and dashed some cold water on him.

"There," she said, hugely satisfied by his yelp. "One cold shower, just what you needed." Then she ran.

If she thought the fact that he was naked would hamper his pursuit, she found out differently. He snatched up a bottle of water as he passed by their cache of supplies and caught her before she had gone fifty yards. She was laughing like a maniac, otherwise she might have gotten away. He held her with one arm and poured the water over her head. It was ice-cold from having been left out all night, and she shrieked and sputtered and giggled, clinging to him when her legs went weak from so much laughter.

"Too sore to walk, huh?" he demanded.

"I w-wasn't walking," she said, giggling as she pushed her wet hair out of her face. Cold droplets splattered on him, and he shivered.

"Damn, it's cold," he said. The sun was barely up, so the temperature was probably in the forties.

She slapped his butt. "Then get some clothes on. What do you think this is, a nudist colony?"

He draped his arm around her shoulders, and they walked back to the camp. Her playfulness delighted him; hell, everything about her delighted him, from her wit to her willingness to laugh. And the sex—God, the sex was unbelievable. He didn't doubt she was sore, because *he* was. Last night had been a night to remember.

When she awakened yesterday afternoon she had been naturally melancholy, the normal aftermath of intense emotions. He hadn't talked much, letting her relax. She went with him to check the traps, which were still empty, and they had bathed together. After a quiet supper of rabbit and cactus they went to bed, and he had devoted the rest of the night to raising her spirits. His efforts had worked.

"How are your hands?" he asked. If she could pull his chest hairs and slap his butt, the antibiotic cream must have worked wonders.

She held them out, palms up, so he could see. The redness from the burns was gone, and her raw fingertips looked slick and shiny. "I'll wrap Band-Aids around them before I get started," she said.

"Get started doing what?"

She gave him a startled look. "Cutting handholds in the rock, of course."

He was stunned. He stared at her, unable to believe what he was hearing. "You're not climbing back on that damn wall!" he snapped.

Her eyebrows rose in what he now recognized as her "the-hell-you-say" look. "Yes, I am."

He ground his teeth. He couldn't tell her they would be "rescued" today, but no way was he letting her wear herself out hacking holes in rock or put herself at that kind of risk.

"I'll do it," he growled.

"I'm smaller," she immediately objected. "It's safer for me."

She was trying to protect him again. He felt like beating his head against a rock in frustration.

"No, it isn't," he barked. "Look, there's no way you can cut enough handholds for us to climb out of here in the next two days. You got, what, twelve feet yesterday? If you managed twelve feet a day—and you wouldn't get that much done today, with your hands the way they are—it would take you over a week to reach the top. That's if—*if*— you didn't fall and kill yourself."

"So what am I supposed to do?" she shot back. "Just give up?"

"Today you aren't going to do a damn thing. You're going to let your hands heal if I have to tie you to a rock, is that clear?"

She looked as if she wanted to argue, but he was a lot bigger than she was, and maybe she could tell by his expression that he meant exactly what he said. "All right," she muttered. "Just for today."

He hoped she would keep her word, because he would have to leave her alone while he went to the spot where he signaled Zane. He would just have to risk it, but there would be hell to pay if he came back to find her on that rock.

He quickly dressed, shivering, and they ate another cold breakfast of water and nutrition bar, since there wasn't anything left of the rabbit from the night before. Tomorrow morning, he promised himself, breakfast would be bacon and eggs, with a mountain of hash browns and a pot of hot coffee.

"I'm going to check the traps," he said, though he knew there wouldn't be anything in them. When he'd checked them the afternoon before, knowing they would be leaving here today, he had quietly released them so they couldn't be sprung. "Just tend to the fire and keep it smoking. You take it easy today, and I'll wash our clothes this afternoon.'' That was a safe promise to make.

"It's a deal,'' she said, but he could tell she was thinking about Margreta.

He left her sitting by the fire. It was a good ten-minute walk to the designated spot, but he hurried, unwilling to leave her to her own devices for so long. Taking the laser light from his pocket, he aimed it toward the rock on the rim and began flashing the pickup signal. Immediately Zane flashed back asking for confirmation, to make certain there wasn't an error. After all, they hadn't expected this to happen so fast. Chance flashed the signal again and this time received an okay.

He dropped the light back in his pocket. He didn't know how long it would take for Zane to arrange the pickup, but probably not long. Knowing Zane, everything was already in place.

He was walking back to the camp when the small twin-engine plane flew over. A grin spread across his face. That was Zane for you!

He began running, knowing Sunny would be beside herself. He heard her shrieking before he could see her; then she came into view, jumping in her glee as she came to meet him. "He saw me!'' she screamed, laughing and crying at the same time. "He waggled the wings! He'll come back for us, won't he?''

He caught her as she hurled herself into his arms and couldn't stop himself from planting a long, hard kiss on that laughing mouth. "He'll come back,'' he said. "Unless he thought you were just waving hello at him.'' The opportunity to tease her was too great to resist, considering she had pulled his chest hair and poured cold water on him. He'd retaliated for the cold water; this was for the hair-pulling.

She looked stricken, the laughter wiped from her face as if it had never been. "Oh, no," she whispered.

He didn't have the heart to keep up the pretense. "Of course he'll come back," he chided. "Waggling the wings was the signal that he saw you and would send help."

"Are you sure?" she asked, blinking back tears.

"I promise."

"I'll get you for this."

He had to kiss her again, and he didn't stop until she had melted against him, her arms locked around his neck. He hadn't thought he would be interested in sex for quite a while, not after last night, but she proved him wrong.

He huffed out a breath and released her. "Stop manhandling me, you hussy. We have to get packed."

The smile she gave him was brilliant, like the sun rising, and it warmed him all the way through.

They gathered their belongings. Chance returned her pistol to her, and watched her break it down and store the pieces in their hiding places. Then they walked back to the plane and waited.

Rescue came in the form of a helicopter, the blades beating a thumping rhythm in the desert air, the canyon echoing with the sound. It hovered briefly over them, then lowered itself like a giant mosquito. Sand whipped into their air, stinging them, and Sunny hid her face against his shirt.

A sixtyish man with a friendly face and graying beard hopped out of the bird. "You folks need some help?" he called.

"Sure do," Chance answered.

When he was closer, the man stuck out his hand. "Charlie Jones, Civil Air Patrol. We've been looking for you for a couple of days. Didn't expect to find you this far south."

"I veered off course looking for a place to land. Fuel pump went out."

"In that case, you're mighty lucky. That's rough territory out there. This might be the only spot in a hundred miles when you could have landed. Come on. I expect you folks are ready for a shower and some food."

Chance held out his hand to Sunny, and she gave him that brilliant smile again as she put her hand in his and they walked to the helicopter.

Chapter 11

Sunny was almost dizzy with mingled relief and regret; relief because she wouldn't miss Margreta's call, regret because this time with Chance, even under such trying conditions, had been the happiest, most fulfilling few days of her life and they were now over. She had known from the beginning that their time together was limited; once they were back in the regular world, all the old rules came back into play.

She couldn't, wouldn't risk his life by letting him be a part of hers. He had given her two nights of bliss, and a lifetime of memories. That would have to be enough, no matter how much she was already aching at the thought of walking away from him and never seeing him again. At least now she knew what it was to love a man, to revel in his existence, and she was richer for it. She wouldn't have traded these few days with him for any amount of money, no matter the price in loneliness she would have to pay.

So she held his hand all during the helicopter flight to a small, ramshackle air field. The only building was made of corrugated metal, rounded at the top like a Quonset hut, with a wooden addition, housing the office, added to one side. If the addition had ever seen a coat of paint, the evidence of it had long since been blasted off by the wind-driven sand. After living under a rock for three days, Sunny thought the little field looked like heaven.

Seven airplanes, of various makes and vintage, were parked with almost military precision along one side of the air strip. Charlie Jones landed his helicopter on a concrete pad behind the corrugated building. Three men, one wiping his greasy hands on a stained red rag, left the building by the back door and walked toward them, ducking their heads against the turbulence of the rotor blades.

Charlie took off his headset and hopped out of the chopper, smiling. "Found 'em," he called cheerfully to the approaching trio. To Chance and Sunny he said, "The two on the left fly CAP with me. Saul Osgood, far left, is the one who spotted your smoke this morning and radioed in your position. Ed Lynch is the one in the middle. The one with the greasy hands is Rabbit Warren, the mechanic here. His real name's Jerome, but he'll fight you if you call him that."

Sunny almost laughed aloud. She controlled the urge, but she was careful not to look at Chance as they shook hands with the three men and introduced themselves.

"I couldn't believe it when I saw your bird in that little bitty narrow canyon," Saul Osgood said, shaking his head after Chance told them what had happened. "How you ever found it is a miracle. And to make a

dead stick landing—'' He shook his head again. ''Someone was sure looking out for you, is all I can say.''

''So you think it was your fuel pump went out, huh?''
Rabbit Warren asked as they walked into the hangar.

''Everything else checked out.''

''It's a Skylane, right?''

''Yeah.'' Chance told him the model, and Rabbit
stroked his lean jaw.

''I might have a pump for that. There was a feller in
here last year flying a Skylane. He ordered some parts
for it, then left and never did come back for 'em. I'll
check while you folks are refreshing yourselves.''

If ''refreshing'' themselves had anything to do with a
bathroom, Sunny was more than ready. Chance gave her
the first turn, and she almost crooned with delight at the
copious water that gushed from the faucet at a turn of
the handle. And a flush toilet! She was in heaven.

After Chance had his turn, they indulged in ice-cold
soft drinks from a battered vending machine. A snack
machine stood beside it, and Sunny surveyed the offer-
ings with an eager eye. ''How much change do you
have?'' she asked Chance.

He delved his hand into his front pocket and pulled
out his change, holding it out for Sunny to see. She
picked out two quarters and fed them into the machine,
punched a button, and a pack of cheese and crackers fell
to the tray.

''I thought you'd go for a candy bar,'' Chance said
as he fed more quarters into the machine and got a pack
of peanuts.

''That's next.'' She raised her eyebrows. ''You didn't
think I was going to stop with cheese and crackers, did
you?''

Ed Lynch opened the door to the office. ''Is there

anyone you need to call? We've notified the FAA and called off the search, but if you have family you want to talk to, feel free to use the phone.''

"I need to call the office," Sunny said, pulling a wry face. She had a good excuse—a very good one—for not making her delivery, but the bottom line was that a customer was unhappy.

Chance waited until she was on the phone, then strolled over to where Rabbit was making a show of looking for a fuel pump. His men were good, Chance thought; they had played this so naturally they should have been on the stage. Of course, subterfuge was their lives, just as it was his.

"Everything's good," Chance said quietly. "You guys can clear out after Charlie takes us back to the canyon with the fuel pump."

Rabbit pulled a greasy box from a makeshift shelf that was piled with an assortment of parts and tools. Over Chance's shoulder he eyed Sunny through the windowed door to the office. "You pulled a real hardship assignment this time, boss," he said admiringly. "That's the sweetest face I've seen in a while."

"There's a sweet person behind it, too," Chance said as he took the box. "She's not part of the organization."

Rabbit's eyebrows went up. "So all this was for nothing."

"No, everything is still a go. The only thing that's changed is her role. Instead of being the key, she's the bait. She's been on the run from Hauer her entire life. If he knows where she is, he'll come out of hiding." He glanced around to make certain she was still on the phone. "Spread the word that we're going to be extra careful with her, make sure she doesn't get hurt. Hauer has already caused enough damage in her life."

And he himself was going to cause more, Chance thought bleakly. As terrified as she was of Hauer, when she learned Chance had deliberately leaked her location to the man she was going to go ballistic. That would definitely be the end of *this* relationship, but he'd known from the beginning this was only temporary. Like her, he wasn't in any position for permanent ties. Sunny's circumstances would change when her father was gone, but Chance's wouldn't; he would move on to another crisis, another security threat.

Just because he was her first lover didn't mean he would be her last.

The idea shot a bolt of pure rage through him. Damn it, she was *his*—he caught the possessive thought and strangled it. Sunny wasn't his; she was her own person, and if she found happiness in her life with some other man, he should be happy for her. She more than deserved anything good that came her way.

He wasn't happy. Her laughter, her passion—he wanted it all for himself. Knowing he couldn't have her was already eating a huge hole out of his insides, but she deserved far better than a mongrel with blood on his hands. He had chosen his world, and he was well-suited for it. He was accustomed to living a lie, to pretending to be someone he wasn't, to always staying in the shadows. Sunny was…sunny, both by name and by nature. He would enjoy her while he had her—by God, he'd enjoy her—but in the end he knew he would have to walk away.

Sunny ended the call and left the office. Hearing the door close, he turned to watch her approach, and he let himself savor the pleasure of just watching her.

She wrinkled her nose. ''Everyone's glad the plane didn't crash, that I'm alive—but the fact that I didn't die makes it a little less forgivable that I didn't deliver the package on time. The customer still wants it, though, so I still have to go to Seattle.''

She came to him as naturally as if they had been together for years, and just as naturally he found himself slipping his arm around her slender waist. ''Screw 'em,'' he said dismissively. He lifted the box. ''Guess what I have.''

She beamed. ''The keys to the kingdom.''

''Close enough. Charlie's going to take me back to the plane so I can swap out the fuel pump. Do you want to go with me, or stay here and rest until I get back?''

''Go with you,'' she said promptly. ''I don't know anything about airplanes, but I can keep you company while you work. Are we coming back here, anyway?''

''Sure. This is as good a place to refuel as any.'' Plus she wouldn't find out they weren't in Oregon as he'd told her.

''Then I'll leave my bag here, if that's all right with Rabbit.'' She looked inquiringly at Rabbit, who nodded his head.

''That'll be just fine, ma'am. Put it in the office and it'll be as safe as a baby in the womb.''

Sunny walked away to get the bag. She felt safe, Chance realized, otherwise she would never let the bag out of her possession. Except for her worry for Margreta, these last few days she must have felt free, unburdened by the need to constantly look over her shoulder.

He had enjoyed their little adventure, too, every minute of it, because he had known they weren't in any danger. Sunny made him feel more alive than he ever had before, even when he was angry at her because she had just scared him half to death. And when he was inside her—then he was as close to heaven as he was ever likely to get. The pleasure of making love to her was so intense it was almost blinding.

He grinned to himself as he hefted his own overnight bag. No way was he leaving it here; after all, the condoms were in it. No telling what might happen when he and Sunny were alone.

The afternoon was wearing on when Charlie set the helicopter down in the canyon again. He looked up at the light with an experienced pilot's eye. "You think you have enough time to get that fuel pump put on before dark?"

"No problem," Chance said. After all, as he and Charlie both knew, there was nothing wrong with the fuel pump, anyway. He would tinker around for a while, make it look realistic. Sunny wasn't likely to stand at his elbow the entire time, and if she did he would distract her.

He and Sunny jumped out of the helicopter, and he leaned in to get his bag. "See you in a few hours."

"If you don't make it back to the airfield, we know where you are," Charlie said, saluting.

They ducked away from the turbulence as the helicopter lifted away. Sunny pushed her hair away from her face and looked around the canyon, smiling. "Home again," she said, and laughed. "Funny how it looks a lot more inviting now that I know we aren't stuck here."

"I'm going to miss it," he said, winking at her. He carried his bag and the box containing the fuel pump over to the plane. "But we'll find out tonight if a bed is more fun than a tent."

To his surprise, sadness flashed in her eyes. "Chance...once we're away from here..." She shook her head. "It won't be safe."

He checked for a moment, then very deliberately put

down the bag and box. Turning back to her, he put his hands on his hips. "If you're saying what I think you're saying, you can just forget about it. You aren't dumping me."

"You know what the situation is! I don't have a choice."

"*I* do. You're not just a fun screw who was available while we were here. I care about you, Sunny," he said softly. "When you look over your shoulder, you're going to see my face. Get used to it."

Tears welled in her brilliant eyes, filling them with diamonds. "I can't," she whispered. "Because I love you. Don't ask me to risk your life, because I can't handle it."

His stomach muscles tightened. He had set out to make her love him, or at least get involved in a torrid affair with him. He had succeeded at doing both. He felt humbled, and exhilarated—and sick, because he was going to betray her.

He had her in his arms before he was aware of moving, and his mouth was on hers. He felt desperate for the taste of her, as if it had been days since he'd kissed her instead of just hours. Her response was immediate and wholehearted, as she rose on her tiptoes to fit her hips more intimately to his. He tasted the salt of her tears and drew back, rubbing his thumbs across her wet cheeks.

He rested his forehead against hers. "You're forgetting something," he murmured.

She sniffed. "What?"

"I was a ranger, sweetheart. I'm a little harder to kill than your average guy. You need someone watching your back, and I can do it. Think about it. We probably made the news. When we get to Seattle, don't be surprised if there's a television camera crew there. Both our faces will be on television. Besides that, we were reported missing to the FAA, which is federal. Information would have been dug up on both of us. Our names our linked. If the mole in the FBI tumbles to who you are, your father's goons will be after me, anyway—especially if they can't find you.''

She went white. "Television?" She looked a lot like her mother; Chance had seen old photos of Pamela Vickery Hauer. Anyone familiar with Pamela would immediately notice the resemblance. As sharp as she was, Sunny also knew the danger of being on television, even a local newscast.

"We're in this together." He lifted her hand to his mouth and kissed her knuckles, then grinned down at her. "Lucky for you, I'm one mean son of a bitch when I need to be—lucky for you, unlucky for them."

Nothing she said would sway him, Sunny thought with despair late that night as she showered in the hotel suite he had booked them into for the night—a suite because it had more than one exit. He had been exactly right about the television news crew. Crews, she corrected herself. News had been slow that day, so every station in Seattle had jumped on the human-interest story. The problem was, so had both national news channels.

She had evaded the cameras as much as possible, but the reporters had seemed fixated on her, shouting questions at her instead of Chance. She would have thought the female reporters, at least, would be all over Chance, but he'd worn such a forbidding expression that no one had approached him. She hadn't answered any questions on camera, though at Chance's whispered suggestion she had given them a quick comment off-camera, for them to use as a filler on their broadcast.

Her one break was that, since it had been so late when they landed, the story didn't make even the late news. But unless something more newsworthy happened soon, the story would air in just a few hours over millions of breakfast tables countrywide.

She had to assume her cover had been blown. That meant leaving the courier service, moving—not that she had much to move; she had never accumulated many possessions—even changing her name. She would have to build a new identity.

She had always known it could happen, and she had prepared for it, both mentally and with actual paperwork. Changing her name wouldn't change who she was; it was just a tool to use to escape her father.

The real problem was Chance. She couldn't shake him, no matter how she tried, and she knew she was good at that kind of thing. She had tried to lose him at the airport, ducking into a cab when his back was turned. But he seemed to have a sixth sense where she was concerned, and he was sliding in the other door before she could give the driver the address where she had to deliver the courier package. He had remained within touching distance of her until they walked into the hotel room, and she had no doubt that, if she opened the bathroom door, she would find him sprawled across the bed, watching her.

In that, she underestimated him. Just as she began lathering her hair, the shower curtain slid back and he stepped naked into the tub with her. "I thought I'd conserve water and shower with you," he said easily.

"Hah! You're just afraid I'll leave if you shower by yourself," she said, turning her back on him.

A big hand patted her bottom. "You know me so well."

She fought a smile. Damn him, why did he have to be so well-matched to her in every way? She could, and had, run rings around most people, but not Chance.

She hogged the spray, turning the nozzle down to rinse her hair. He waited until she was finished with that, at least, then adjusted the nozzle upward so the water hit him in the chest. It also hit her full in the face. She sputtered and elbowed him. "This is *my* shower, and I didn't invite you. I get control of the nozzle, not you."

She knew challenging him was a mistake. He said, "Oh, yeah?" and the tussle was on. Before she knew it she was giggling, he was laughing, and the bathroom was splattered with water. She had played more with Chance than she had since she'd been a little girl; she felt lighthearted with him, despite her problems. Their wet, naked bodies slid against each other, and neither of them could get a good grasp on any body part. At least, she couldn't. She suspected he could have won the tussle at any time simply by using his size and strength and wrapping his arms around her, but he held back and played at her level, as if he were used to restraining his strength to accommodate someone weaker than himself.

His hands were everywhere: on her breasts, her bottom, sliding between her legs while she laughed and batted them away. One long finger worked its way inside her and she squealed, trying to twist away while excitement spiraled wildly through her veins. Their naked wrestling match was having a predictable effect on both of them. She grabbed for the nozzle and aimed the blast of water at his face, and while he was trying to deflect the spray she made her escape, hopping out of the tub and snatching up a towel to wrap around her.

He vaulted out of the tub and slammed the door shut just as she reached for it. "You left the shower running," she accused, trying to sidetrack him.

"I'm not the one who turned it on." He grinned and hooked the towel away from her.

"Water's getting all over the floor." She tried to sound disapproving.

"It needed mopping, anyway."

"It did not!" She pushed a strand of dripping wet hair out of her eyes. "We're going to be kicked out. Water will drip through the floor into the room below and we'll be kicked out."

He grabbed her and swung her around so she was facing the shower. "Turn it off, then, if you're worried."

She did, because she hated to waste the water, and it was making such a mess. "There, I hope you're satisfied."

"Not by a long shot." He turned her to face him, holding her lips against his and angling her torso away from him, so he could look his fill at her. "Have I told you today how damn sexy you are?"

"Today? You've never told me at all!"

"Have so."

"Have not. When?"

"Last night. Several times."

She tried not to be entranced by the way water droplets were clinging to his thick dark lashes. "That doesn't count. Everyone knows you can't believe anything a man says when he's in...uh—"

"You?" he supplied, grinning.

She managed a haughty look. "I was going to say 'extremis,' but I think that applies only to dying."

"Close enough." He looked down at her breasts, his expression altering and the laughter fading. Still holding her anchored to him with one arm, he smoothed a hand up her torso to cup her breasts, and they both watched his long brown fingers curve around the pale globes. "You're sexy," he murmured, a slow, dark note entering his voice. She knew that note well, having heard it many times over the past two nights. "And beautiful. Your breasts are all cream-and-rose colored, until I kiss your nipples. Then they pucker up and turn red like they're begging me to suck them."

Her nipples tightened at his words, the puckered tips flushing with color. He groaned and bent his dark head, water dripping from his hair onto her skin as he kissed both breasts. She was leaning far back over his arm, supported by his arm around her hips and her own desperate grasp on his shoulders. She didn't know how much longer she would be able to stand at all. Her loins throbbed, and she gasped for breath.

"And your ass," he growled. "You have the sweetest little ass." He turned her around so he could stroke the aforementioned buttocks, shaping his palms to the full, cool curves. Sunny's legs trembled, and she grabbed the edge of the vanity for support. The cultured marble slab was a good six feet long, and a mirror covered the entire wall behind it. Sunny barely recognized herself in the naked woman reflected there, a woman whose wet hair dripped water down her back and onto the floor. Her expression was etched with desire, her face flushed and her eyes heavy-lidded.

Chance looked up, and his gaze met hers in the mirror. Electricity sparked between them. "And here," he whispered, sliding one hand around her belly and between her legs. His muscled forearm looked unbelievably powerful against her pale belly, and his big hand totally covered her mound. She felt his fingers sliding between her folds, rubbing her just as she liked. She moaned and collapsed against him, her legs going limp.

"You're so soft and tight," the erotic litany continued in her ear. "I can barely get inside you. But once I do— my heart stops. And I can't breathe. I think I'm going to die, but I can't, because it feels too good to stop." His fingers slid farther, and he pressed two of them inside her.

She arched under the lash of sensation, soaring close to climax as his fingers stretched her. She heard herself cry out, a strained cry that told him exactly how near she was to fulfillment.

"Not yet, not yet," he said urgently, sliding his fingers out of her and bending her forward. He braced her hands on the vanity. "Hold on, sweetheart."

She didn't know if he meant to the vanity, or to her control. Both were impossible. "I can't," she moaned. Her hips moved, undulating, searching for relief. "Chance, I can't—please!"

"I'm here," he said, and he was, dipping down and pushing his muscled thighs between her legs, spreading them. She felt his lower belly against her buttocks, then the smooth, hard entry of his sex. Instinctively she bent forward to aid his penetration, taking all of him deep within her. He began driving, and on the second hard thrust she convulsed, crying out her pleasure. His climax erupted a moment later, and he collapsed over her back, holding himself as deep as he could while he groaned and shook.

Sunny closed her eyes, fighting for breath. Oh God, she loved him so much she ached with it. She wasn't strong enough to send him away, not even for his own protection. If she had been really trying, she could have gotten away from him, but deep down she knew she couldn't give him up. Not yet. Soon. She would have to, to keep him safe.

Just one more day, she thought as tears welled. One more. Then she would go.

Chapter 12

Ten days later, Sunny still hadn't managed to shake him. She didn't know if she was losing her touch or if army rangers, even ex ones, were very, very good at not being shaken.

They had left Seattle early the next morning. Sunny was too cautious to fly back to Atlanta; as she had feared, the morning newscasts had been splashed with the "real-life romantic adventure" she and Chance had shared. His name was mentioned, but by some perverse quirk his face was never clearly shown; the camera would catch the back of his head, or while he was in a quarter profile, while hers was broadcast from coast to coast.

One of the a.m. news shows even tracked them down at the hotel, awakening them at three in the morning to ask if they would go to the local affiliate studios for a live interview.

"Hell, no," Chance had growled into the phone before he slammed it down into the cradle.

After that, it had seemed best they remove themselves from the reach of the media. They checked out of the hotel and took a taxi to the airport before dawn. The plane was refueled and ready to go. By the time the sun peeked over the Cascades they were in the air. Chance didn't file a flight plan, so no one had any way of finding out where they were going. Sunny didn't know herself until they landed in Boise, Idaho, where they refurbished their wardrobes. She always carried a lot of cash, for just such a situation, and Chance seemed to have plenty, too. He still had to use his credit card for refueling, so she knew they were leaving a trail, but those records would show only where they had last been, not where they were going.

Chance's presence threw her off her plan. She knew how to disappear by herself; Chance and his airplane complicated things.

From a pay phone in Boise, she called Atlanta and resigned her job, with instructions to deposit her last paycheck into her bank. She would have the money wired to her when she needed it. Sometimes, adrift from the familiar life she had fashioned for herself, she wondered if she was overreacting to the possibility anyone would recognize her. Her mother had been dead for over ten years; there were few people in the world able to see the resemblance. The odds had to be astronomical against one of those few people seeing that brief human-interest story that had been shown for only one day.

But she was still alive because her mother had taught her that any odds at all were unacceptable. So she ran, as she had learned how to do in the first five years of her life. After all, the odds were also against her getting pregnant, yet here she was, waiting for a period that hadn't materialized. They had slipped up twice, only twice: once in the canyon, and in the hotel bathroom in Seattle. The timing hadn't been great for her to get pregnant even if they hadn't used protection at all, so why hadn't her period started? It was due two days ago, and her cycle was relentlessly regular.

She didn't mention it to Chance. She might just be late, for one of the few times in her life since she'd starting having menstrual periods. She had been terrified when she thought they were going to crash; maybe her emotions had disrupted her hormones. It happened.

She might sprout wings and fly, too, she thought in quiet desperation. She was pregnant. There were no signs other than a late period, but she knew it deep down in her bones, as if on some level her body was communicating with the microscopic embryo it harbored.

It would be so easy just to let Chance handle everything. He was good at this, and she had too much on her mind to be effective. She didn't think he'd noticed how easily distracted she'd been these past few days, but then, he didn't know when her period had been due, either.

She had talked to Margreta twice, and told her she was going underground. She would have to arrange for a new cellular account under a different name, with a new number, and do it before the service she now had was disconnected. She had tried to tell Margreta everything that was going on, but her sister, as usual, kept the calls short. Sunny understood. It was difficult for Margreta to handle anything having to do with their father. Maybe one day they would be able to live normal lives, have a normal sisterly relationship; maybe one day Margreta would be able to get past what he had done to her and find some happiness despite him.

Then there was Chance. He had brought sunshine into her life when she hadn't even known she was living in shadows. She had thought she managed quite well, but it was as if B.C., Before Chance, had been in monochrome. Now, A.C., was in vivid technicolor. She slept in his arms every night. She ate her meals with him, quarreled with him, joked with him, made plans with him—nothing long term, but plans nevertheless. Every day she fell more and more in love with him, when she hadn't thought it possible.

Sometimes she actually pinched herself, because he was too good to be true. Men like him didn't come along every day; most women lived their entire lives without meeting a man who could turn their worlds upside down with a glance.

This state of affairs couldn't last much longer, this aimless drifting. For one thing, it was expensive. Chance wasn't earning any money while they were flying from one remote airfield in the country to another, and neither was she. She needed to get the paperwork for her new name, get a job, get a new cellular number—and get an obstetrician, which would cost money. She wondered how her mother had managed, with one frightened, traumatized child in tow, pregnant with another, and without any of the survival skills Sunny possessed. Pamela must have spent years in a state of terror, yet Sunny remembered her mother laughing, playing games with them, and making life fun even while she taught them how to survive. She only hoped she could be half as strong as her mother had been.

She was full of wild hopes these days. She hoped she hadn't been recognized. She hoped her baby would be healthy and happy. Most of all, she hoped she and Chance could build a life together, that he would be thrilled about the baby even though it was unplanned, that he truly cared about her as much as he appeared to. He never actually said he loved her, but it was there in his voice, in his actions, in his eyes and his touch as he made love to her.

Everything had to be all right. It had to. There was too much at stake now.

Sunny slept through the landing as Chance set the plane down in Des Moines. He glanced at her, but she was soundly asleep, like a child, her breathing deep and her cheeks flushed. He let her sleep, knowing what was coming to a head.

The plan was working beautifully. He had arranged for Sunny's face to be broadcast worldwide, and the bait had been taken immediately. His people had tracked two of Hauer's men into the country and maintained discreet but constant surveillance on them. Chance hadn't made it easy for anyone to follow him and Sunny; that would have been too obvious. But he had left a faint trail that, if the bloodhounds were good, they would be able to follow. Hauer's bloodhounds were good. They had been about a day behind them for about a week now, but until Hauer himself showed up, Chance made sure the hounds never caught up with him.

The news he'd been waiting for had finally come yesterday. Word in the underground of terrorist organizations was that Hauer had disappeared. He hadn't been seen in a few days, and there was a rumor he was in the States planning something big.

Somehow Hauer had slipped out of Europe and into America without being spotted, but now that Chance knew there was a mole in the FBI helping Hauer, he wasn't surprised.

Hauer was too smart to openly join his men, but he would be nearby. He was the type who, when Sunny was captured, would want to interrogate this rebellious daughter himself.

Chance would take him apart with his bare hands before he let that happen.

But he would have to let them think they had her, not knowing they were surrounded at all times, at a distance, by his men. Chance just hoped he himself wasn't shot at the beginning, to get him out of the way. If Hauer's men were smart, they would realize they could use threats to Chance to keep Sunny in line, and they had proven they were smart. This was the risky part, but he had taken all the safeguards he could without tipping his hand.

His interlude with Sunny would end tonight, one way or another. If all went well, they would both live through it, and she would be free to live her life out in the open. He just hoped that one day she wouldn't hate him, that she would realize he had done what he had to do in order to capture Hauer. Who knows? Maybe one day he would meet her again.

He guided the Cessna to a stop in its designated spot and killed the engine. Sunny slept on, despite the sudden silence. Maybe he'd cost her too much sleep and it had finally caught up with her, he thought, smiling despite his inner tension. He had glutted himself with sex for the past two weeks, as if subconsciously he had been trying to stockpile memories and sensations for the time when she was no longer there. But as often as he'd had her, he still wanted her. Again. More. He was half hard right now, just thinking about her.

Gently he shook her, and she opened her sleepy eyes with a look of such trust and love that his heart leaped. She sat up, stretching and looking around. "Where are we?"

"Des Moines." Puzzled, he said, "I told you where we were going."

"I remember," she said around a yawn. "I'm just groggy. Wow! That was some nap. I don't usually sleep during the daytime. I must not be getting enough sleep at night." She batted her eyelashes at him. "I wonder why."

"I have no idea," he said, all innocence. He opened the door and climbed out, turning around to hold his hands up for her. She clambered out, and he lifted her to the ground. Looking up at the wide, cerulean-blue sky, he stretched, too, twisting his back to get out the kinks. "It's a pretty day. Want to have a picnic?"

"A what?" She looked at him as if he were speaking a foreign language.

"A picnic. You know, where you sit on the ground and eat with your hands, and fight wild animals for your food."

"Sounds like fun. But haven't we already done that?"

He laughed. "This time we'll do it right—checkered tablecloth, fried chicken, the works."

"All right, I'm game. Where are we going to have this picnic? Beside the runway?"

"Smart-ass. We'll rent a car and go for a drive."

Her eyes began to sparkle as she realized he meant it. That was what he loved best about Sunny, her ability to have fun. "How much time do we have? What time are we leaving?"

"Let's stay for a couple of days. Iowa's a nice place,

and my tail could use some time away from that airplane seat.''

He handled his business with the airport, then went to a rental car desk and walked away with the keys to a sport utility.

''You rented a *truck?*'' Sunny teased when she saw the green Ford Explorer. ''Why didn't you get something with style, like a red sports car?''

''Because I'm six-three,'' he retorted. ''My legs don't fit in sports cars.''

She had bought a small backpack that she carried instead of the bulky carry-on she had been lugging around. She could get her toiletries and a change of clothes into the backpack, and that was enough for the single night they usually spent in a place. That meant her pistol was always with her, fully assembled when they weren't having to go through x-ray scanners, and he didn't protest. He always carried his own pistol with him, too, tucked into his waistband under his loose shirt. She put the backpack on the floorboard and climbed into the passenger seat, and began pushing buttons and turning knobs, every one she could reach.

Chance got behind the wheel. ''I'm afraid to start this thing now. There's no telling what's going to happen.''

''Chicken,'' she said. ''What's the worst that could happen?''

''I'm just thankful Explorers don't have ejection seats,'' he muttered as he turned the key in the ignition. The engine caught immediately. The radio blared, the windshield wipers flopped back and forth at high speed, and the emergency lights began blinking. Sunny laughed as Chance dived for the radio controls and turned the volume down to an acceptable level. She buckled herself into the seat, smiling a very self-satisfied smile.

He had a map from the rental car company, though he already knew exactly where he was going. He had gotten very specific directions from the clerk at the rental agency, so the clerk would remember where they had gone when Hauer's men asked. He had personally scouted out the location before putting the plan into motion. It was in the country, to cut the risk of collateral damage to innocent civilians. There was cover for his men, who would be in place before he and Sunny arrived. And, most important, Hauer and his men couldn't move in without being observed. Chance had enough men in place that an ant couldn't attend this picnic unless he wanted it there. Best of all, he knew Zane was out there somewhere. Zane didn't usually do fieldwork, but in this instance he was here guarding his brother's back. Chance would rather have Zane looking out for him than an entire army; the man was unbelievable, he was so good.

They stopped at a supermarket deli for their picnic supplies. There was even a red-checkered plastic cloth to go on the ground. They bought fried chicken, potato salad, rolls, cole slaw, an apple pie, and some green stuff Sunny called pistachio salad. He knew he wasn't about to touch it. Then he had to buy a small cooler and ice, and some soft drinks to go in it. By the time he got Sunny out of the supermarket, over an hour had passed and he was almost seventy bucks lighter in the wallet.

"We have apple pie," he complained. "Why do we need apples?"

"I'm going to throw them at you," she said. "Or better yet, shoot them off your head."

"If you come near me with an apple, I'll scream," he warned. "And pickled beets? Excuse me, but who eats pickled beets?"

She shrugged. "Someone does, or they wouldn't be on the shelves."

"Have *you* ever eaten pickled beets?" he asked suspiciously.

"Once. They were nasty." She wrinkled her nose at him.

"Then why in hell did you buy them?" he shouted.

"I wanted you to try them."

He should be used to it by now, he thought, but sometimes she still left him speechless. Muttering to himself, he stowed the groceries—including the pickled beets—in the back of the Explorer.

God, he was going to miss her.

She rolled down the window and let the wind blow through her bright hair. She had a happy smile on her face as she looked at everything they passed. Even service stations seemed to interest her, as did the old lady walking a Chihuahua that was so fat its belly almost kept its feet from touching the ground. Sunny giggled about the fat little dog for five minutes.

If it made her laugh like that, he thought, he would eat the damn pickled beets. But he'd damn sure eat something else afterward, because if he got shot, he didn't want pickled beets to be the last thing he tasted.

The late August afternoon was hot when he pulled off the road. A tree-studded field stretched before them. "Let's walk to those trees over there," he said, nodding to a line of trees about a hundred yards away. "See how they're growing, in a line like that? There might be a little creek there."

She looked around. "Shouldn't we ask permission?"

He raised his eyebrows. "Do you see a house anywhere? Who do we ask?"

"Well, all right, but if we get in trouble, it's your fault."

He carried the cooler and most of the food. Sunny slung her backpack on her shoulders, then took charge of the ground cloth and the jar of pickled beets. "I'd better carry these," she said. "You might drop them."

"You could take something else, too," he grunted. This stuff was heavy.

She stretched up to peek in the grocery bag. The apple pie was perched on top of the other stuff. "Nah, you won't drop the pie."

He grumbled all the way to their picnic site, more because she enjoyed it than any other reason. This was the last day she would ever tease him, or he would see that smile, hear that laugh.

"Oh, there *is* a creek!" she exclaimed when they reached the trees. She carefully set the jar of beets down and unfolded the ground cloth, snapping it open in that brisk, economical movement all women seemed to have, and letting it settle on the thick, overgrown grass. A light breeze was blowing, so she anchored the cloth with her backpack on one corner and the jar of beets on the another.

Chance set the cooler and food down and sprawled out on the cloth. "I'm too tired now to enjoy myself," he complained.

She leaned over and kissed him. "You think I don't know what you're up to? Next thing I know you'll get something in your eye, and I'll have to get really, really close to see it. Then your back will need scratching, and you'll have to take off your shirt. Before I know it, we'll both be naked and it'll be time to leave, and we won't have had a bite to eat."

He gave her a quizzical look. "You have this all planned out, don't you?"

"Down to the last detail."

"Suits me." He reached for her, but with a spurt of laughter she scooted out of reach. She picked up the jar of beets and looked at him expectantly.

He flopped back with a groan. "Oh, man. Don't tell me you expect me to try them *now*."

"No, I want you to open the jar so *I* can eat them."

"I thought you said they were nasty."

"They are. I want to see if they're as nasty as I remember." She handed him the jar. "If you'll open them for me, I'll let you eat fried chicken and potato salad to build up your strength before I wring you out and hang you up to dry."

He sat up and took the jar. "In your dreams, little miss 'don't-touch-me-again-you-lech.'" He put some muscle behind the effort, twisting the lid free.

"I've been sandbagging," she said. "This time, don't even bother begging for mercy."

She reached for the jar. The loosened lid came off, and the jar slipped from her hands. He dived for it, not wanting beets all over everything. Just as he moved, the tree beside him exploded, and a millisecond later he heard the blast of the shot.

He twisted in midair, throwing himself on top of Sunny and rolling with her behind the cover of the tree.

Chapter 13

"Stay down!" Chance barked, shoving her face into the grass.

Sunny couldn't have moved even if she had wanted to, even if his two hundred-plus pounds hadn't been lying on top of her. She was paralyzed, terror freezing in her veins as she realized her worst nightmare had come true; her father had found them, and Chance was nothing more than an obstacle to be destroyed. That bullet hadn't been aimed at *her*. If she hadn't dropped the jar of beets, if Chance hadn't lunged for it, the slug that blew chunks of wood out of the tree would have blown off half his head.

"Son of a bitch," he muttered above her, his breath stirring her hair. "Sniper."

The earth exploded two inches from her head, clods of dirt flying in her face, tiny pieces of gravel stinging her like bees. Chance literally threw her to the side, rolling with her again; the ground dropped out from beneath her, and her stomach gave a sickening lurch. As suddenly as the fall began, it stopped. She landed hard in three inches of sluggish water.

He had rolled them into the creek, where the banks afforded them more cover. A twist of his powerful body and he was off her, his big pistol in his hand as he flattened himself against the shallow bank. Sunny managed to get to her knees, slipped on the slimy creek bottom, and clambered on her hands and knees to a spot beside him. She felt numb, as if her arms and legs didn't belong to her, yet they were working, moving.

This wasn't real. It couldn't be. How had he found them?

She closed her eyes, fighting the terror. She was a liability to Chance unless she got herself under control. She'd had close calls before and handled herself just fine, but she had never before seen the man she loved almost get killed in front of her. She had never before been pregnant, with so much to lose.

Her teeth were chattering. She clamped her jaw together.

Silence fell over the field. She heard a car drive by on the road, and for a wild moment she wondered why it didn't stop. But why would it? There was nothing the average passerby would notice, no bodies lying around on the highway, no haze of gun smoke hanging over the green grass. There was only silence, as if even the insects had frozen in place, the birds stopped singing; even the breeze had stopped rustling the leaves. It was as if nature held its breath, shocked by the sudden violence.

The shot had come from the direction of the road, but she hadn't seen anyone drive up. They had only just arrived themselves; it was as if whoever had shot at them had already been here, waiting. But that was impossible, wasn't it? The picnic was an impulse, and the location sheer chance; they could just as well have stopped at a park.

The only other explanation that occurred to her was if the shooter had nothing to do with her father. Maybe it was a crazy landowner who shot at trespassers.

If only she had brought her cell phone! But Margreta wasn't due to call her for several more days, and even if she had brought the phone, it would be in her backpack, which was still lying on the ground cloth. The distance of a few yards might as well be a mile. Her pistol was also in the pack; though a pistol was useless against a sniper, she would feel better if she had some means of protection.

Chance hadn't fired; he knew the futility of it even more than she did. His dark gold eyes were scanning the countryside, looking for anything that would give away the assailant's position: a glint of sunlight on the barrel, the color of his clothing, a movement. The extreme angle of the late afternoon sun picked out incredible detail in the trees and bushes, but nothing that would help them.

Only nightfall would help, she thought. If they could just hold out for…how long? Another hour? Two hours, at most. When it was dark, then they could belly down in the little creek and work their way to safety, either upstream or down, it didn't matter.

If they lived that long. The sniper had the advantage. All they had was the cover of a shallow creek bank.

She became aware that her teeth were chattering again. Again she clamped her jaw together to still the movement. Chance spared a glance at her, a split-second assessment before he returned to once again scanning the trees for the sniper. "Are you all right?" he asked, though he obviously knew she was all in one piece. He wasn't asking about her physical condition.

"S-scared spitless," she managed to say.

"Yeah. Me, too."

He didn't look scared, she thought. He looked coldly furious.

He reached out and rubbed her arm, a brief gesture of comfort. "Thank God for those beets," he said.

She almost cried. The beets. She had thoroughly enjoyed teasing him about the beets, but the truth was, when she saw them in the supermarket she had been overcome by an almost violent craving for them. She wanted those beets. She felt as if she could eat the entire jar of them. Could cravings start this early in a pregnancy? If so, then he should thank God not for the beets, but for the beginnings of life forming inside her.

She wished she had told him immediately when her period didn't come. She couldn't tell him now; the news would be too distracting.

If they lived through this, she thought fervently, she wouldn't keep the secret to herself a minute longer.

"It can't be Hauer's men," she blurted. "It's impossible. They couldn't be here ahead of us, because we didn't know we were coming here. It has to be a crazy farmer, or a—a jerk who thought it would be funny to shoot at someone."

"Sweetheart." He touched her arm again, and she realized she was babbling. "It isn't a crazy farmer, or a trigger-happy jerk."

"How do you know? It could be!"

"The sniper's too professional."

Just four words, but they made her heart sink. Chance would know; he had training in this sort of thing.

She pressed her forehead against the grassy bank,

fighting for the courage to do what she had to do. Her mother had died protecting her and Margreta; surely she could be as brave? She couldn't tell Hauer anything about Margreta, so her sister was safe, and if she could save Chance, then dying would be worth it....

Her child would die with her.

Don't make me choose, she silently prayed. *The child or the father.*

If it were just her, she wouldn't hesitate. In the short time she had known Chance—was it really just two weeks?—he had given her a lifetime of happiness and the richness of love. She would gladly give her life in exchange for his.

The life inside her wasn't really a child yet; it was still just a rapidly dividing cluster of cells. No organs or bones had formed, nothing recognizable as a human. It was maybe the size of a pin head. But the potential...oh, the potential. She loved that tiny ball of cells with a fierceness that burned through every fiber of her being, had loved it from the first startled awareness that her period was late. It was as if she had blinked and said, "Oh. Hello," because one second she had been totally unaware of its existence, and the next she had somehow known.

The child or the father. The father or the child.

The words writhed in her brain, echoing, bouncing. She loved them both. How could she choose? She couldn't choose; no woman should have to make such a decision. She hated her father even more for forcing her into this situation. She hated the chromosomes, the DNA, that he had contributed to her existence. He wasn't a father, he had never been a father. He was a monster.

"Give me your pistol." She heard the words, but the voice didn't sound at all like hers.

His head snapped around. "What?" He stared at her as if she had lost her mind.

"Give me the pistol," she repeated. "He—they—don't know we have it. You haven't fired back. I'll tuck it in the back of my jeans and walk out there—"

"The hell you will!" He glared at her. "If you think I—"

"No, listen!" she said urgently. "They won't shoot me. He wants me alive. When they get close enough for me to use the pistol I—"

"No!" He grabbed her by the shirt and hauled her close so they were almost nose to nose. His eyes were almost shooting sparks. "If you make one move to stand up, I swear I'll knock you out. Do you understand me? *I will not let you walk out there.*"

He released her, and Sunny sank back against the creek bank. She couldn't overpower him, she thought bleakly. He was too strong, and too alert to be taken by surprise.

"We have to do something," she whispered.

He didn't look at her again. "We wait," he said flatly. "That's what we do. Sooner or later, the bastard will show himself."

Wait. That was the first idea she'd had, to wait until dark and slip away. But if Hauer had more than one man here, the sniper could keep them pinned down while the other worked his way around behind them—

"Can we move?" she asked. "Up the creek, down the creek—it doesn't matter."

He shook his head. "It's too risky. The creek's shallow. The only place we have enough cover is flat against the bank on this side. If we try to move, we expose ourselves to fire.''

''What if there's more than one?''

''There is.'' He sounded positive. A feral grin moved his lips in a frightening expression. ''At least four, maybe five. I hope it's five.''

She shook her head, trying to understand. Five to two were deadly odds. ''That makes you happy?''

''Very happy. The more the merrier.''

Nausea hit the back of her throat, and she closed her eyes, fighting the urge to vomit. Did he think sheer guts and fighting spirit would keep them alive?

His lean, powerful hand touched her face in a gentle caress. ''Chin up, sweetheart. Time's on our side.''

Now wasn't the time for explanations, Chance thought. The questions would be too angry, the answers too long and complicated. Their situation was delicately balanced between success and catastrophe; he couldn't relax his guard. If he was correct and there were five men out there hunting them—and that was the only explanation, that one of his own men was a traitor and had given Hauer the location of their supposedly impromptu picnic—then they could, at any time, decide to catch him in a pincer movement. With only one pistol, and Sunny to one side of him, he couldn't handle an attack from more than two directions. The third one would get him— and probably Sunny, too. In a fire fight, bullets flew like angry hornets, and most of them didn't hit their target. If a bullet didn't hit its target, that meant it hit something—or someone—else.

His own men would have been stood down, or sent to a bogus location. That was why there hadn't been any return fire when he and Sunny were fired on—no one was there. For that to have happened, the traitor had to be someone in a position of authority, a team leader or higher. He would find out. Oh, yeah, he'd find out. There had been several betrayals over the years, but they hadn't been traceable. One such breach had almost cost Barrie, Zane's wife, her life. Chance had been trying to identify the bastard for four years now, but he'd been too smart. But this time it was traceable. This time, his men would know who had changed their orders.

The traitor must have thought it was worth blowing his cover, to have this opportunity to kill Chance Mackenzie himself. And he should be here in person, to see the job done. Hauer's two men would bring the count to three. Hauer made it four. The only way Hauer could have gotten into the country and moved about as freely and undetected as he had was with inside help—the FBI mole. If Chance were really lucky, the mole was here, too, bringing the count to five.

But they'd made a big mistake. They didn't know about his ace in the hole: Zane. They didn't know he was out there; that was an arrangement Chance had made totally off the record. If Zane wasn't needed, no one would ever know he was there. Chance's men were damn good, world class, but they weren't in Zane's class. No one was.

Zane was a superb strategist; he always had a plan, and a plan to back up his plan. He would have seen in an instant what was going down and been on the phone calling the men back into position from wherever they'd been sent. How long it took them to get here depended on how far away they were, assuming they could get here at all. And after the call Zane would have started moving, ghosting around, searching out Hauer and his men. Every minute that passed increased the odds in Chance's favor.

He couldn't explain any of that to Sunny, not now, not even to ease the white, pinched expression that made him ache to hold her close and reassure her. Her eyes were haunted, their sparkle gone. She had worked her entire life to make certain she was never caught off guard, and yet she had been; he himself had seen to it.

The knowledge was bitter in his mouth. She was terrified of the monster who had relentlessly hunted her all her life, yet she had been willing to walk out there and offer herself as a sacrifice. How many times in the short two weeks he'd known her had she put herself on the line for him? The first time had been when she barely knew him, when she swooped down to grab the snake coiled so close to his feet. She was terrified of snakes, but she'd done it. She was shaking with fear now, but he knew that if he let her, she would do exactly what she'd offered. That kind of courage amazed him, and humbled him.

His head swiveled restlessly as he tried to keep watch in all directions. The minutes trickled past. The sun slid below the horizon, but there was still plenty of light; twilight wouldn't begin deepening for another fifteen, twenty minutes. The darker it was, the more Zane was in his element. By now, he should have taken out at least one, maybe two—

A man stepped out from behind the tree under which Chance and Sunny had intended to have their picnic and aimed a black 9mm automatic at Sunny's head. He didn't say "Drop it" or anything else. He just smiled, his gaze locked with Chance's.

Carefully Chance placed his pistol on the grass. If the gun had been aimed at his own head, he would have taken the risk that his reflexes were faster. He wouldn't risk Sunny's life. As soon as he moved his hand away from the pistol, the black hole in the man's weapon centered between his eyes.

"Surprised?" the man asked softly. At his voice Sunny gasped and whirled, her feet sliding on the slippery creek bottom. Chance reached out and steadied her without taking his gaze from a man he knew very well.

"Not really," he said. "I knew there was someone."

Sunny looked back and forth between them. "Do you *know* him?" she asked faintly.

"Yeah." He should have been prepared for this, he thought. Knowing one of his own men was involved, he should have realized the traitor would have the skill to approach silently, using the same tree that helped shield them as his own cover. Doing so took patience and nerve, because if Chance had happened to move even a few inches to one side, he would have seen the man's approach.

"H-how?" she stammered.

"We've worked together for years," Melvin Darnell said, still smiling. Mel the Man. That was what the others called him, because he would volunteer for any mission, no matter how dangerous. What better way to get inside information? Chance thought.

"You sold out to Hauer," Chance said, shaking his head. "That's low."

"No, that's lucrative. He has men everywhere. The FBI, the Justice Department, the CIA…even here, right under your nose." Mel shrugged. "What can I say? He pays well."

"I misjudged you. I never thought you'd be the type to get a kick out of torture. Or are you chickening out and leaving as soon as he gets his hands on her?'' Chance nodded his head toward Sunny.

"Nice try, Mackenzie, but it won't work. He's her father. All he wants is his little girl." Mel smirked at Sunny.

Chance snorted. "Get a clue. Do you think she'd be so terrified if all he wanted was to get to know her?"

Mel spared another brief glance in her direction. She was absolutely colorless, even her lips. There was no mistaking her fear. He shrugged. "So I was wrong. I don't care what he does with her."

"Do you care that he's a child molester?" Keep him talking. Buy time. Give Zane time to work.

"Give it up," Mel said cheerfully. "He could be Hitler's reincarnation and it still wouldn't change the color of his money. If you think I'm going to develop a conscience—well, you're the one who needs to get a clue."

There was movement behind Mel. Three men approaching, walking openly now, as if they had nothing to fear. Two were dressed in suits, one in slacks and an open-necked shirt. The one in slacks and one of the suits carried hand guns. The suit would be the FBI informant, the one in slacks one of Hauer's bloodhounds. The man in the middle, the one wearing the double-breasted Italian silk suit, his skin tanned, his light brown hair brushed straight back—that was Hauer. He was smiling.

"My dear," he said jovially when he reached them. He stepped carefully around the spilled beets, his nose wrinkling in distaste. "It is so good to finally meet you. A father should know his children, don't you think?"

Sunny didn't speak for a moment. She stared at her father with unconcealed horror and loathing. Beside her, Chance felt the fear drain out of her, felt her subtly relax. Extreme terror was like that, sometimes. When one feared that something would happen, it was the dread and anxiety, the anticipation, that was so crippling. Once the thing actually happened, there was nothing left to fear. He took a firm grip on her arm, wishing she had remained petrified. Sunny was valiant enough when she was frightened; when she thought she had nothing left to lose, there was no telling what she would do.

"I thought you'd be taller," she finally said, looking at him rather dismissively.

Crispin Hauer flushed angrily. He wasn't a large man, about five-eight, and slender. The two men flanking him were both taller. Chance wondered how Sunny had known unerringly how to prick his ego. "Please get out of the mud—if you can bring yourself to leave your lover's side, that is. I recommend it. Head shots can be nasty. You wouldn't want his brains on you, would you? I hear the stain never comes out of one's clothes."

Sunny didn't move. "I don't know where Margreta is," she said. "You might as well kill me now, because I can't tell you anything."

He shook his head in mock sympathy. "As if I believe that." He held out his hand. "You may climb out by yourself, or my men will assist you."

There wasn't much light left, Chance thought. If Sunny could keep delaying her father without provoking him into violence, Zane should be here soon. With Hauer out in the open, Zane must be positioning himself so he could get all four men in his sights.

"Where's the other guy?" he asked, to distract them. "There *are* five of you, aren't there?"

The FBI man and the bloodhound looked around, in the direction of the trees on the opposite side of the road. They seemed vaguely surprised that no one was behind them.

Mel didn't take his attention from Chance. "Don't let him spook you," he said sharply. "Keep your mind on business."

"Don't you wonder where he is?" Chance asked softly.

"I don't give a damn. He's nothing to me. Maybe he fell out of the tree and broke his neck," Mel said.

"Enough," Hauer said, distaste for this squabbling evident in his tone. "Sonia, come out now. I promise you won't like it if my men have to fetch you."

Sunny's contemptuous gaze swept him from head to foot. Unbelievably, she began singing. And the ditty she sang was a cruel little song of the sort gradeschoolers sang to make fun of a classmate they didn't like. "Monkey man, monkey man, itty bitty monkey man. He's so ugly, he's so short, he needs a ladder to reach his butt."

It didn't rhyme, Chance thought in stunned bemusement. Children, crude little beasts that they were, didn't care about niceties such as that. All they cared about was the effectiveness of their taunt.

It was effective beyond his wildest expectation.

Mel Darnell smothered a laugh. The two other men froze, their expressions going carefully blank. Crispin Hauer flushed a dark, purplish red and his eyes bulged until white showed all around the irises. "You bitch!" he screamed, spittle flying, and he grabbed for the gun in the FBI mole's hand.

A giant red flower bloomed on Hauer's chest, accompanied by a strange, dull splat. Hauer stopped as if he had run into a glass wall, his expression going blank.

Mel had excellent reflexes, and excellent training. In that nanosecond before the sound of the shot reached them, Chance saw Mel's finger begin tightening on the trigger, and he grabbed for his own weapon, knowing

he wouldn't be fast enough. Then Sunny hit him full
force, her entire body crashing into him and knocking
him sideways, her scream almost drowning out the thun-
derous boom of Mel's big-caliber pistol. She clambered
off him almost as fast as she had hit him, trying to
scramble up the grassy bank to get to Mel before he
could fire another round, but Mel never had another opportunity to pull the trigger. Mel never had anything
else, not even a second, because Zane's second shot took
him dead center of the chest just as his first had taken
Hauer.

Then all hell broke loose. Chance's men, finally back
in position and with the threat to Chance and Sunny
taken care of, opened fire on the remaining two men.
Chance grabbed Sunny and flattened her in the creek
again, covering her with his own body, holding her there
until Zane roared a cease fire and the night was silent.

Sunny sat off to the side of the nightmarish scene,
brightly lit now with battery-operated spotlights that
picked out garish detail and left stark black shadows.
From somewhere, one of the small army of men who
suddenly swarmed the field had produced a bucket that
he turned upside down for her, providing her with a seat.
She was wet and almost unbearably cold, despite the
warmth of the late August night. Her muddy clothes
were clammy, so the blanket she clutched around her
with nerveless fingers didn't do much to help, but she
didn't release it.

She hurt, with an all-consuming agony that threatened
to topple her off the bucket, but she grimly forced herself
to stay upright. Sheer willpower kept her on that bucket.

The men around her were professionals. They were
quiet and competent as they dealt with the five bodies

that were laid out on the ground in a neat row. They were courteous with the local law enforcement officers who arrived *en force,* sirens blasting, blue lights strobing the night, though there was never any doubt who held jurisdiction.

And Chance was their leader.

That man, the one who had first held a gun on them, had called him "Mackenzie." And several times one or another of the locals had referred to him as Mr. Mackenzie; he had answered, so she knew there was no mistake in the name.

The events of the night were a chaotic blur in her mind, but one fact stood out: this entire scene was a setup, a trap—and she had been the bait.

She didn't want to believe it, but logic wouldn't let her deny it. He was obviously in charge here. He had a lot of men on site, men he commanded, men who could be here only if he had arranged it in advance.

Viewed in the light of that knowledge, everything that had happened since she met him took on a different meaning. She even thought she recognized the cretin who had stolen her briefcase in the Salt Lake City airport. He was cleaned up now, with the same quiet, competent air as the others, but she was fairly certain he was the same man.

Everything had been a setup. Everything. She didn't know how he'd done it, her mind couldn't quite grasp the sphere of influence needed to bring all of this off, but somehow he had manipulated her flights so that she was in the Salt Lake City airport at a certain time, for the cretin to grab her briefcase and Chance to intercept him. It was a hugely elaborate play, one that took skill and money and more resources than she could imagine.

He must have thought she was in cahoots with her

father, she thought with a flash of intuition. This had all happened after the incident in Chicago, which was undoubtedly what had brought her to Chance's notice. What had his plan been? To make her fall in love with him and use her to infiltrate her father's organization? Only it hadn't worked out that way. Not only was she not involved with her father, she desperately feared and hated him. So Chance, knowing why Hauer really wanted her, had adjusted his plan and used her as bait.

What a masterful strategy. And what a superb actor he was; he should get an Oscar.

There hadn't been anything wrong with the plane at all. She didn't miss the significance of the timing of their "rescue." Charlie Jones had just happened to find them first thing in the morning after she spilled her guts about her father to Chance the night before. He must have signaled Charlie somehow.

How easy she had been for him. She had been completely duped, completely taken in by his lovemaking and charm. He had been a bright light to her, a comet blazing into her lonely world, and she had fallen for him with scarcely a whisper of resistance. He must think her the most gullible fool in the world. The worst of it was, she was an even bigger fool than he knew, because she was pregnant with his child.

She looked across the field at him, standing tall in the glaring spotlights as he talked with another tall, powerful man who exuded the deadliest air she had ever seen, and the pain inside her spread until she could barely contain it.

Her bright light had gone out.

Chance looked around at Sunny, as he had been doing periodically since the moment she sank down on the

overturned bucket and huddled deep in the blanket
someone had draped around her. She was frighteningly
white, her face drawn and stark. He couldn't take the
time to comfort her, not now. There was too much to
do, local authorities to soothe at the same time that he
let them know he was the one in control, not they, the
bodies to be handled, sweeps initiated at the agencies
Mel had listed as having Hauer's moles employed there.

She wasn't stupid; far from it. He had watched her
watching the activity around her, watched her expression
become even more drawn as she inevitably reached the
only conclusion she *could* reach. She had noticed when
people called him Mackenzie instead of McCall.

Their gazes met, and locked. She stared at him across
the ten yards that separated them, thirty feet of unbridge-
able gulf. He kept his face impassive. There was no excuse he could give her that she wouldn't already have
considered. His reasons were good; he knew that. But
he had used her and risked her life. Being the person
she was, she would easily forgive him for risking her
life; it was the rest of it, the way he had used her, that
would strike her to the core.

As he watched, he saw the light die in her eyes, draining away as if it had never been. She turned her head
away from him—

And gutted him with the gesture.

Shaken, pierced through with regret, he turned back
to Zane and found his brother watching him with a world
of knowledge in those pale eyes. "If you want her,"
Zane said, "then don't let her go."

It was that simple, and that difficult. Don't let her go.
How could he not, when she deserved so much better
than what he was?

But the idea was there now. Don't let her go. He

couldn't resist looking at her again, to see if she was still watching him.

She wasn't there. The bucket still sat there, but Sunny was gone.

Chance strode rapidly across to where she had been, scanning the knots of men who stood about, some working, some just observing. He didn't see that bright hair. Damn it, she was just here; how could she disappear so fast?

Easily, he thought. She had spent a lifetime practicing.

Zane was beside him, his head up, alert. The damn spotlights blinded them to whatever was behind them. She could have gone in any direction, and they wouldn't be able to see her.

He looked down to see if he could pick up any tracks, though the grass was so trampled by now that he doubted he would find anything. The bucket gleamed dark and wet in the spotlight.

Wet?

Chance leaned down and swiped his hand over the bucket. He stared at the dark red stain on his fingers and palm. Blood. Sunny's blood.

He felt as if his own blood was draining from his body. My God, she'd been shot, and she hadn't said a word. In the darkness, the blood hadn't been noticeable on her wet clothing. But that had been…how long ago? She had sat there all that time, bleeding, and not told anyone.

Why?

Because she wanted to get away from him. If they had known she was wounded, she would have to be bundled up and taken to a hospital, and she wouldn't be able to escape without having to see him again. When

Sunny walked, she did it clean. No scenes, no excuses, no explanations. She just disappeared.

If he had thought it hurt when she turned away from him, that was nothing to the way he felt now. Desperate fear seized his heart, froze his blood in his veins. "Listen up!" he boomed, and a score of faces, trained to obey his every command, turned his way. "Did anyone see where Sunny went?"

Heads shook, and men began looking around. She was nowhere in sight.

Chance began spitting out orders. "Everyone drop what you're doing and fan out. Find her. She's bleeding. She was shot and didn't tell anyone." As he talked, he was striding out of the glare of the spotlights, his heart in his mouth. She couldn't have gone far, not in that length of time. He would find her. He couldn't bear the alternative.

Chapter 14

Chance blindly paced the corridor outside the surgical waiting room. He couldn't sit down, though the room was empty and he could have had any chair he wanted. If he stopped walking, he thought, he might very well fall down and not be able to stand again. He hadn't known such crippling fear existed. He had never felt it for himself, not even when he looked down the barrel of a weapon pointed at his face—and Mel's hadn't been the first—but he felt it for Sunny. He'd been gripped by it since he found her lying facedown in the grassy field, unconscious, her pulse thready from blood loss.

Thank God there were medics on hand in the field, or she would have died before he could get her to a hospital. They hadn't managed to stop the bleeding, but they had slowed it, started an IV saline push to pump fluid back into her body and raise her plummeting blood pressure, and gotten her to the hospital still alive.

He had been shouldered aside then, by a whole team

of gowned emergency personnel. "Are you any relation to her, sir?" a nurse had asked briskly as she all but manhandled him out of the treatment room.

"I'm her husband," he'd heard himself say. There was no way he was going to allow the decisions for her care to be taken out of his hands. Zane, who had been beside him the entire time, hadn't revealed even a flicker of surprise.

"Do you know her blood type, sir?"

Of course he didn't. Nor did he know the answers to any of the other questions posed by the woman they handed him off to, but he was so numb, his attention so focused on the cubicle where about ten people were working on her, that he barely knew anyone was asking the questions, and the woman hadn't pushed it. Instead, she had patted his hand and said she would come back in a little while when his wife was stabilized. He had been grateful for her optimism. In the meantime, Zane, as ruthlessly competent as usual, had requested that a copy of their file on Sunny be downloaded to his wireless Pocket Pro, so Chance would have all the necessary information when the woman returned with her million and one questions. He was indifferent to the bureaucratic snafu he was causing; the organization would pay for everything.

But the shocks had kept arriving, one piling on top of the other. The surgeon came out of the cubicle, his green paper gown stained red with her blood. "Your wife regained consciousness briefly," he'd said. "She wasn't completely lucid, but she asked about the baby. Do you know how far along she is?"

Chance had literally staggered and braced his hand against the wall for support. "She's pregnant?" he asked hoarsely.

"I see." The surgeon immediately switched gears. "I think she must have just found out. We'll do some tests and take all the precautions we can. We're taking her up to surgery now. A nurse will show you where to wait." He strode away, paper gown flapping.

Zane had turned to Chance, his pale blue eyes laser sharp. "Yours?" he asked briefly.

"Yes."

Zane didn't ask if he was certain, for which Chance was grateful. Zane took it for granted Chance wouldn't be mistaken about something that important.

Pregnant? How? He pinched the bridge of his nose, between his eyes. He knew how. He remembered with excruciating clarity how it felt to climax inside her without the protective sheath of a condom dulling the sensation. It had happened twice—just twice—but once was enough.

A couple of little details clicked into place. He'd been around pregnant women most of his life, with first one sister-in-law and then another producing a little Mackenzie. He knew the symptoms well. He remembered Sunny's sleepiness this afternoon, and her insistence on buying the beets. Those damn pickled beets, he thought; her craving for them—for he was certain now that was why she'd wanted them—had saved his life. Sometimes the weird cravings started almost immediately. He could remember when Shea, Michael's wife, had practically wiped that section of Wyoming clean of canned tuna, a full week before she missed her first period. The sleepiness began soon in a pregnancy, too.

He knew the exact day when he'd gotten her pregnant. It had been the second time he'd made love to her, lying on the blanket in the late afternoon heat. The baby would be born about the middle of May...if Sunny lived.

She had to live. He couldn't face the alternative. He loved her too damn much to even think it. But he had seen the bullet wound in her right side, and he was terrified.

"Do you want me to call Mom and Dad?" Zane asked.

They would drop everything and come immediately if he said yes, Chance knew. The whole family would; the hospital would be inundated with Mackenzies. Their support was total, and unquestioning.

He shook his head. "No. Not yet." His voice was raw, as if he had been screaming, though he would have sworn all his screams had been held inside. If Sunny…if the worst happened, he would need them then. Right now he was still holding together. Just.

So he walked, and Zane walked with him. Zane had seen a lot of bullet wounds, too; he'd taken his share. Chance was the lucky one; he'd been cut a few times, but never shot.

God, there had been so much blood. How had she stayed upright for so long? She had answered questions, said she was all right, even walked around a little before one of the men had found that bucket for her to sit on. It was dark, she had a blanket wrapped around her—that was why no one had noticed. But she should have been on the ground, screaming in pain.

Zane's thoughts were running along the same path. "I'm always amazed," he said, "at what some people can do after being shot."

Contrary to what most people thought, a bullet wound, even a fatal one, didn't necessarily knock the victim down. All cops knew that even someone whose heart had been virtually destroyed by a bullet could still attack and kill *them*, and die only when his oxygen-starved brain died. Someone crazed on drugs could absorb a truly astonishing amount of damage and keep on fighting. On the other side of the spectrum were those who suffered relatively minor wounds and went down as if they had been poleaxed, then screamed unceasingly until they reached the hospital and were given enough drugs to quiet them. It was pure mind over matter, and Sunny had a will like titanium. He only hoped she applied that will to surviving.

It was almost six hours before the tired surgeon approached, the six longest hours of Chance's life. The surgeon looked haggard, and Chance felt the icy claw of dread. No. No—

"I think she's going to make it," the surgeon said, and smiled a smile of such pure personal triumph that Chance knew there had been a real battle in the O.R. "I had to remove part of the liver and resection her small intestine. The wound to the liver is what caused the extensive hemorrhage. We had to replace almost her complete blood volume before we got things under control." He rubbed his hand over his face. "It was touch and go for a while. Her blood pressure bottomed out and she went into cardiac arrest, but we got her right back. Her pupil response is normal, and her vitals are satisfactory. She was lucky."

"Lucky," Chance echoed, still dazed by the combination of good news and the litany of damage.

"It was only a fragment of a bullet that hit her. There must have been a ricochet."

Chance knew she hadn't been hit while he'd had her flattened in the creek. It had to have happened when she knocked him aside and Darnell fired. Evidently Darnell had missed, and the bullet must have struck a rock in the creek and fragmented.

She had been protecting him. Again.

"She'll be in ICU for at least twenty-four hours, maybe forty-eight, until we see if there's a secondary infection. I really think we have things under control, though." He grinned. "She'll be out of here in a week."

Chance sagged against the wall, bending over to clasp his knees. His head swam. Zane's hard hand gripped his shoulder, lending his support. "Thank you," Chance said to the doctor, angling his head so he could see him.

"Do you need to lie down?" the doctor asked.

"No, I'm all right. God! I'm great. She's going to be okay!"

"Yeah," said the doctor, and grinned again.

Sunny kept surfacing to consciousness, like a float bobbing up and down in the water. At first her awareness was fragmented. She could hear voices in the distance, though she couldn't make out any words, and a soft beeping noise. She was also aware of something in her throat, though she didn't realize it was a tube. She had no concept of where she was, or even that she was lying down.

The next time she bobbed up, she could feel smooth cotton beneath her and recognized the fabric as sheets.

The next time she managed to open her eyes a slit, but her vision was blurry and what seemed like a mountain of machinery made no sense to her.

At some point she realized she was in a hospital. There was pain, but it was at a distance. The tube was gone from her throat now. She vaguely remembered it being removed, which hadn't been pleasant, but her sense of time was so confused that she thought she remembered the tube being there after it was removed. People kept coming into the small space that was hers, turning on bright lights, talking and touching her and doing intimate things to her.

Gradually her dominion over her body began to return, as she fought off the effects of anesthesia and drugs. She managed to make a weak gesture toward her belly, and croak out a single word. "Baby?"

The intensive care nurse understood. "Your baby's fine," he said, giving her a comforting pat, and she was content.

She was horribly thirsty. Her next word was "Water," and slivers of ice were put in her mouth.

With the return of consciousness, though, came the pain. It crept ever nearer as the fog of drugs receded. The pain was bad, but Sunny almost welcomed it, because it meant she was alive, and for a while she had thought she might not be.

She saw the nurse named Jerry the most often. He came into the cubicle, smiling as usual, and said, "There's someone here to see you."

Sunny violently shook her head, which was a mistake. It set off waves of agony that swamped the drugs holding them at bay. "No visitors," she managed to say.

It seemed as if she spent days, eons, in the intensive care unit, but when she asked Jerry he said, "Oh, about thirty-six hours. We'll be moving you to a private room soon. It's being readied now."

When they moved her, she was clearheaded enough to watch the ceiling tiles and lights pass by overhead. She caught a glimpse of a tall, black-haired man and quickly looked away.

Settling her into a private room was quite an operation, requiring two orderlies, three nurses and half an hour. She was exhausted when everything, including herself, had been transferred and arranged. The fresh bed was nice and cool; the head had been elevated and a pillow tucked under her head. Sitting up even that much made her feel a hundred percent more normal and in control.

There were flowers in the room. Roses, peach ones, with a hint of blush along the edges of their petals, dispensed a spicy, peppery scent that overcame the hospital scents of antiseptics and cleaning fluids. Sunny stared at them but didn't ask who they were from.

"I don't want any visitors," she told the nurses. "I just want to rest."

She was allowed to eat Jell-O, and drink weak tea. On the second day in the private room she drank some broth, and she was placed in the bedside chair for fifteen minutes. It felt good to stand on her own two feet, even for the few seconds it took them to move her from bed to chair. It felt even better when they moved her back to the bed.

That night, she got out of bed herself, though the process was slow and unhappy, and walked the length of the bed. She had to hold on to the bed for support, but her legs remained under her.

The third day, there was another delivery from a florist. This was a bromeliad, with thick, grayish green leaves and a beautiful pink flower blooming in its center. She had never had houseplants for the same reason she had never had a pet, because she was constantly on the move and couldn't take care of them. She stared at the bromeliad, trying to come to grips with the fact that she could have all the houseplants she wanted now. Everything was changed. Crispin Hauer was dead, and she and Margreta were free.

The thought of her sister sent alarm racing through

her. What day was it? When was Margreta due to call? For that matter, where was her cell phone?

On the afternoon of the fourth day, the door opened and Chance walked in.

She turned her head to look out the window. In truth, she was surprised he had given her this long to recover. She had held him off as long as she could, but she supposed there had to be a closing act before the curtain could fall.

She had held her inner pain at bay by focusing on her physical pain, but now it rushed to the forefront. She fought it down, reaching for control. There was nothing to be gained by causing a scene, only her self-respect to lose.

"I've kept your cell phone with me," he said, walking around to place himself between her and the windows, so she had to either look at him or turn her head away again. His conversational opening had guaranteed she wouldn't turn away. "Margreta called yesterday."

Sunny clenched her fists, then quickly relaxed her right hand as the motion flexed the IV needle taped to the back of it. Margreta would have panicked when she heard a man's voice answer instead of Sunny's.

"I talked fast," Chance said. "I told her you'd been shot but would be okay, and that Hauer was dead. I told her I'd bring the phone to you today, and she could call again tonight to verify everything I said. She didn't say anything, but she didn't hang up on me, either."

"Thank you," Sunny said. He had handled the situation in the best possible way.

He was subtly different, she realized. It wasn't just his clothing, though he was now dressed in black slacks and a white silk shirt, while he had worn only jeans, boots, and casual shirts and T-shirts before. His whole demeanor was different. Of course, he wasn't playing a raffish, charming charter pilot any longer. He was himself now, and the reality was what she had always sensed beneath the surface of his charm. He was the man who led some sort of commando team, who exerted enormous influence in getting things done his way. The dangerous edge she had only glimpsed before was in full view now, in his eyes and the authority with which he spoke.

He moved closer to the side of the bed, so close he was leaning against the rail. Very gently, the touch as light as gossamer, he placed his fingertips on her belly. "Our baby is all right," he said.

He knew. Shocked, she stared at him, though she realized she should have known the doctor would tell him.

"Were you going to tell me?" he asked, his golden-brown eyes intent on her face, as if he wanted to catch every nuance of expression.

"I hadn't thought about it one way or the other," she said honestly. She had just been coming to terms with the knowledge herself; she hadn't gotten around to forming any plans.

"This changes things."

"Does it really," she said, and it wasn't a question. "Was *anything* you told me the truth?"

He hesitated. "No."

"There was nothing wrong with the fuel pump."

"No."

"You could have flown us out of the canyon at any time."

"Yes."

"Your name isn't Chance McCall."

"Mackenzie," he said. "Chance Mackenzie."

"Well, that's one thing," she said bitterly. "At least your first name was really your own."

"Sunny…don't."

"Don't what? Don't try to find out how big a fool I am? Were you really an army ranger?"

He sighed, his expression grim. "Navy. Naval Intelligence."

"You arranged for all of my flights to be fouled up that day."

He shrugged an admittance.

"The cretin was really one of your men."

"A good one. The airport security people were mine, too."

She creased the sheet with her left hand. "You knew my father would be there. You had it set up."

"We knew two of his men were trailing us, had been since the television newscast about you aired."

"You arranged that, too."

He didn't say anything.

"Why did we fly all over the country? Why didn't we just stay in Seattle? That would have been less wear and tear on the plane."

"I had to make it look good."

She swallowed. "That day…the picnic. Would you have made love—I mean, had sex—with me with your men watching? Just to make it look good?"

"No. Having an affair with you was necessary, but…private."

"I suppose I should thank you for that, at least. Thank you. Now get out."

"I'm not going anywhere." He sat down in the bedside chair. "If you've finished with the dissection, we need to make some decisions."

"I've already made one. I don't want to see you again."

"Sorry about that, but you aren't getting your wish. You're stuck with me, sweetheart, because that baby inside you is mine."

Chapter 15

Sunny was released from the hospital eight days after the shooting. She could walk, gingerly, but her strength was almost negligible, and she had to wear the nightgown and robe Chance had bought her, because she couldn't stand any clothing around her middle. She had no idea what she was going to do. She wasn't in any condition to catch a flight to Atlanta, not to mention that she would have to travel in her nightgown, but she had to find somewhere to stay. Once she knew she was being released, she got the phone book and called a hotel, made certain the hotel had room service, and booked herself a room there. The hotel had room service; until she was able to take care of herself again, a hotel was the best she could do.

In the hospital she had, at first, entertained a fragile hope that Margreta would come to stay with her and help her until she was recovered. With their father dead, they didn't have to hide any longer. But though Margreta had sounded happy and relieved, she had resisted Sunny's suggestion that she come to Des Moines. They had exchanged telephone numbers, but that was all—and Margreta hadn't called back.

Sunny understood. Margreta would always have problems relating to people, forming relationships with them. She was probably very comfortable with the long-distance contact she had with Sunny, and wanted nothing more. Sunny tried to fight her sadness as she realized she would never have the sister she had wanted, but melancholy too easily overwhelmed her these days.

Part of it was the hormonal chaos of early pregnancy, she knew. She found herself tearing up at the most ridiculous things, such as a gardening show she watched on television one day. She lay in her hospital bed and began thinking how she had always wanted a flower garden but had never been able to have one, and presto, all of a sudden she was feeling sorry for herself and sitting there like an idiot with tears rolling down her face.

Depression went hand in glove with physical recovery, too, one of the nurses told her. It would pass as she got stronger and could do more.

But the biggest part of her depression was Chance. He visited every day, and once even brought along the tall, lethal-looking man she had noticed him talking to the night she was injured. To her surprise, Chance introduced the man as his brother, Zane. Zane had shaken her hand with exquisite gentleness, shown her photos of his pretty wife and three adorable children, and spent half an hour telling her yarns about the exploits of his daughter, Nick. If even half of what he said about the child was true, the world had better brace itself for when she was older.

After Zane left, Sunny was even more depressed. Zane

had what she had always wanted: a family he loved, and who loved him in return.

When he visited, Chance always avoided the subject that lay between them like a coiled snake. He had done what he had done, and no amount of talking would change reality. She had to respect, reluctantly, his lack of any attempt to make excuses. Instead, he talked about his family in Wyoming, and the mountain they all still called home, even though only his parents lived there now. He had four brothers and one sister, a dozen nephews—and one niece, the notorious Nick, whom he obviously adored. His sister was a horse trainer who was married to one of his agents; one brother was a rancher who had married the granddaughter of an old family enemy; another brother was an ex-fighter pilot who was married to an orthopedic surgeon; Zane was married to the daughter of an ambassador; and Joe, his oldest brother, was General Joseph Mackenzie, chairman of the Joint Chiefs of Staff.

That couldn't all be true, she thought, yet the tales had a ring of truth to them. Then she remembered that Chance was a consummate actor, and bitterness would swamp her again.

She couldn't seem to pull herself out of the dismals. She had always been able to laugh, but now she found it difficult to even smile. No matter how she tried to distract herself, the knowledge was always there, engraved on her heart like a curse that robbed her life of joy: Chance didn't love her. It had all been an act.

It was as if part of her had died. She felt cold inside, and empty. She tried to hide it, tried to tell herself the depression would go away if she just ignored it and concentrated on getting better, but every day the grayness inside her seemed to spread and deepen.

The day she was released, the escort finally arrived with a wheelchair and Sunny called a taxi to meet them at the entrance in fifteen minutes. She gingerly lowered herself into the wheelchair, and the escort obligingly placed the small bag containing her few articles of clothing and her backpack on her lap, then balanced the bromeliad on top.

"I'm sure I have to sign some papers before I'm released," Sunny said.

"No, I don't think so," the woman said, checking her orders. "According to this, you're all ready to go. Your husband probably handled it for you."

Sunny bit back the urge to snap that she wasn't married. He hadn't mentioned it, and in truth she hadn't given a thought to how she would pay for her hospital care, but now that she thought about it, she realized Chance had indeed handled all of that. Maybe he thought the least he could do was pick up her tab.

She was surprised he wasn't here, since he'd been so adamant about being a part of the baby's life, and persistent in visiting. For all she knew, she thought, he had been called away on some mysterious spy stuff.

She underestimated him. When the escort rolled her to the doors of the patient discharge area, she saw a familiar dark green Ford Explorer parked under the covered entrance. Chance unfolded his long length from behind the steering wheel and came to meet her.

"I've already called a taxi," she said, though she knew it was a waste of breath.

"Tough," he said succinctly. He took her clothes and the bromeliad and put them in the back of the Explorer, then opened the passenger door.

Sunny began to inch herself forward in the wheelchair seat, preparatory to standing; she had mastered the art when seated in a regular chair, but a wheelchair was trickier. Chance gave her an exasperated look, then leaned down and scooped her up in his powerful arms, handling her weight with ease as he deposited her in the Explorer.

"Thank you," she said politely. She would at least be civil, and his method had been much less painful and time-consuming than hers.

"You're welcome." He buckled the seat belt around her, making certain the straps didn't rub against the surgical incision, then closed the door and walked around to slide under the steering wheel.

"I've booked a room in a hotel," she said. "But I don't know where it is, so I can't give you directions."

"You aren't going to a hotel," he growled.

"I have to go somewhere," she pointed out. "I'm not able to drive, and I can't handle negotiating an airport, so a hotel with room service is the only logical solution."

"No it isn't. I'm taking you home with me."

"No!" she said violently, everything in her rejecting the idea of spending days in his company.

His jaw set. "You don't have a choice," he said grimly. "You're going—even if you kick and scream the whole way."

It was tempting. Oh, it was tempting. Only the thought of how badly kicking would pull at the incision made her resist the idea.

The dime didn't drop until she noticed he was driving to the airport. "Where are we going?"

He gave her an impatient glance. "I told you. Hell, Sunny, you know I don't live in Des Moines."

"All right, so I know where you don't live. But I *don't* know where you *do* live." She couldn't resist adding, "And even if you had told me, it would probably be a lie."

This time his glance was sulfuric. "Wyoming," he said through gritted teeth. "I'm taking you home to Wyoming."

She was silent during the flight, speaking only when necessary and then only in monosyllables. Chance studied her when her attention was on the landscape below, his sunglasses hiding his eyes. They had flown around so much during the time they'd been together that it felt natural to once again be in the plane with her, as if they were where they belonged. She had settled in with a minimum of fussing and no complaints, though he knew she had to be exhausted and uncomfortable.

She looked so frail, as if a good wind would blow her away. There wasn't any color in her cheeks or lips, and she had dropped a good ten pounds that she didn't need to lose. The doctor had assured him that she was recovering nicely, right on schedule, and that while her pregnancy was still too new for any test to tell them anything about the baby's condition, they had taken all precautions and he had every confidence the baby would be fine.

As thrilled as he was about the baby, Chance was more worried that the pregnancy would sap her strength and slow her recovery. She needed all the resources she could muster now, but nature would ensure that the developing child got what it needed first. The only way he could be confident she was getting what *she* needed was if he arranged for her to be watched every minute, and coddled and spoiled within an inch of her life. The best place for that was Mackenzie's Mountain.

He had called and told them he was bringing Sunny

there, of course. He had told them the entire situation, that she was pregnant and he intended to marry her, but that she was still mad as hell at him and hadn't forgiven him. He had set quite a task for himself, getting back in Sunny's good graces. But once he had her on the Mountain, he thought, he could take his time wearing her down.

Mary, typically, was ecstatic. She took it for granted Sunny would forgive him, and since she had been prodding him about getting married and giving her more grandchildren, she probably thought she was getting everything she wanted.

Chance was going to do everything he could to see that she did, because what she wanted was exactly what he wanted. He'd always sworn he would never get married and have children, but fate had stepped in and arranged things otherwise. The prospect of getting married scared him—no, it terrified the hell out of him, so much so that he hadn't even broached the subject to Sunny. He didn't know how to tell her what she needed to know about him, and he didn't know what she would do when she found out, if she would accept his proposal or tell him to drop dead.

The only thing that gave him hope was that she'd said she loved him. She hadn't said it since she found out how he'd set her up, but Sunny wasn't a woman who loved lightly. If there was a spark of love left in her, if he hadn't totally extinguished it, he would find a way to fan it to life.

He landed at the airstrip on Zane's property, and his heart gave a hard thump when he saw what was waiting for them. Even Sunny's interest was sparked. She sat up straighter, and for the first time since she'd been shot he saw a hint of that lively interest in her face. "What's going on?" she asked.

His spirits lifting, he grinned. "Looks like a welcoming party."

The entire Mackenzie clan was gathered by the airstrip. Everyone. Josh and Loren were there from Seattle with their three sons. Mike and Shea and their two boys. Zane and Barrie, each holding one of the twins. And there was Joe, decked out in his Air Force uniform with more rows of fruit salad on it than should be allowed. How he had carved time out of his schedule to come here, Chance didn't know—but then, Joe could do damn near anything he wanted, since he was the highest ranking military officer in the nation. Caroline, standing beside him and looking positively chic in turquoise capri pants and white sandals—and also looking damn good for her age—had probably had a harder time getting free. She was one of the top-ranked physicists in the world. Their five sons were with him, and John, the oldest, wasn't the only one this time who had a girlfriend with him. Maris and Mac stood together; Mac had his arm draped protectively around Maris's slight frame. And Mom and Dad were in the middle of the whole gang, with Nick perched happily in Wolf's arms.

Every last one of them, even the babies, held a balloon.

"Oh, my," Sunny murmured. The corners of her pale mouth moved upwards in the first smile he had seen in eight days.

He cut the motor and got out, then went to the other door and carefully lifted Sunny out. She was so bemused by the gathering that she put her arm around his neck.

That must have been the signal. Wolf leaned down and set Nick on her feet. She took off toward Chance like a shot, running and skipping and shrieking his name in the usual litany. "UncaDance, UncaDance, Unca-*Dance!*" The balloon she was holding bobbed like a mad thing. The whole crowd started forward in her wake.

In seconds they were surrounded. He tried to introduce everyone to Sunny, but there was too much of a hubbub for him to complete a sentence. His sisters-in-law, bless them, were laughing and chattering as if they had known her for years; the men were flirting; Mary was beaming; and Nick's piping voice could be heard above everyone. "Dat's a weally, weally pwetty dwess." She fingered the silk robe and beamed up at Sunny.

John leaned down and whispered something in Nick's ear. *"Dress,"* she said, emphasizing the *r.* "Dat's a weally, weally pwetty *dress."*

Everyone cheered, and Nick glowed.

Sunny laughed.

Chance's heart jumped at the sound. His throat got tight, and he squeezed his eyes shut for a second. When he opened them, Mary had taken control.

"You must be exhausted," she was saying to Sunny in her sweet, Southern-accented voice. "You don't have to worry about a thing, dear. I have a bed all ready for you at the house, and you can sleep as long as you want. Chance, carry her along to the car, and be careful with her."

"Yes, ma'am," he said.

"Wait!" Nick wailed suddenly. "I fordot de sign!"

"What sign?" Chance asked, gently shifting Sunny so he could look down at his niece.

She fished in the pocket of her little red shorts and pulled out a very crumpled piece of paper. She stretched up on her tiptoes to hand it to Sunny. "I did it all by myself," she said proudly. "Gamma helped."

Sunny unfolded the piece of paper.

"I used a wed cwayon," Nick informed her. "Because it's de pwettiest."

"It certainly is," Sunny agreed. She swallowed audibly. Chance looked down to see the paper shaking in her hand.

The letters were misshapen and wobbly and all different sizes. The little girl must have labored over them for a long time, with Mary's expert and patient aid, because the words were legible. "'Welcome home Sunny,'" Sunny read aloud. Her face began to crumple. "That's the most beautiful sign I've ever seen," she said, then buried her face against Chance's neck and burst into tears.

"Yep," Michael said. "She's pregnant, all right."

It was difficult to say who fell more in love with whom, Sunny with the Mackenzies, or the Mackenzies with her. Once Chance placed her in the middle of the king-sized bed Mary had made up for her—he didn't tell her it was his old bedroom—Sunny settled in like a queen holding court. Instead of lying down to sleep, she propped herself up on pillows, and soon all of the women and most of the younger kids were in there, sitting on the bed and on the floor, some even in chairs. The twins were working their way from one side of the bed to the other and back again, clutching the covers for support and babbling away to each other in what Barrie called their "twin talk." Shea had Benjy down on the floor, tickling him, and every time she stopped he would shriek, "More! More!" Nick sat cross-legged on the bed, her "wed cwayon" in hand as she studiously worked on another sign. Since the first one had been such a resounding success, this one was for Barrie, and she was embellishing it with lopsided stars. Loren, being a doctor, wanted the details of Sunny's wound and present condition. Caroline was doing an impromptu fashion consultation, brushing Sunny's hair and swirling it on top of her head, with some very sexy tendrils curling loose on her slender neck. Maris, her dark eyes glowing, was telling Sunny all about her own pregnancy, and Mary was overseeing it all.

Leaving his family to do what they did best, weave a magic spell of warmth and belonging, Chance walked down to the barn. He felt edgy and worried and a little panicked, and he needed some peace and quiet. When everything quieted down tonight, he had to talk to Sunny. He couldn't put it off any longer. He prayed desperately that she could forgive him, that what he had to tell her didn't completely turn her against him, because he loved her so much he wasn't certain he could live without her. When she had buried her face against him and cried, his heart had almost stopped because she had turned *to* him instead of away from him.

She had laughed again. That sound was the sweetest sound he'd ever heard, and it had almost unmanned him. He couldn't imagine living without being able to hear her laugh.

He folded his arms across the top of a stall door and rested his head on them. She had to forgive him. She had to.

"It's tough, isn't it?" Wolf said in his deep voice, coming up to stand beside Chance and rest his arms on top of the stall door, too. "Loving a woman. And it's the best thing in the world."

"I never thought it would happen," Chance said, the

words strained. "I was so careful. No marriage, no kids. It was going to end with me. But she blindsided me. I fell for her so fast I didn't have time to run."

Wolf straightened, his black eyes narrowed. "What do you mean, 'end with you'? Why don't you want kids? You love them."

"Yeah," Chance said softly. "But they're Mackenzies."

"You're a Mackenzie." There was steel in the deep voice.

Tiredly, Chance rubbed the back of his neck. "That's the problem. I'm not a real Mackenzie."

"Do you want to walk in the house and tell that little woman in there that you're not her son?" Wolf demanded sharply.

"*Hell*, no!" No way would he hurt her like that.

"You're my son. In all the ways that matter, you're mine."

The truth of that humbled Chance. He rested his head on his arms again. "I never could understand how you could take me in as easily as you did. You know what kind of life I led. You may not know the details, but you have a good general idea. I wasn't much more than a wild animal. Mom had no idea, but you did. And you still brought me into your home, trusted me to be around both Mom and Maris—"

"And that trust was justified, wasn't it?" Wolf asked.

"But it might not have been. You had no way of knowing." Chance paused, looking inward at the darkness inside him. "I killed a man when I was about ten, maybe eleven," he said flatly. "That's the wild kid you brought home with you. I stole, I lied, I attacked other kids and beat them up, then took whatever it was they had that I wanted. That's the kind of person I am. That kid will always live inside me.''

Wolf gave him a sharp look. "If you had to kill a man when you were ten, I suspect the bastard deserved killing."

"Yeah, he deserved it. Kids who live in the street are fair game to perverts like that." He clenched his hands. "I have to tell Sunny. I can't ask her to marry me without her knowing what she'll be getting, what kind of genes I'll be passing on to her children." He gave a harsh laugh. "Except I don't know what kind of genes they are. I don't know what's in my background. For all I know my mother was a drugged-out whore and—"

"Stop right there," Wolf said, steel in his voice.

Chance looked up at him, the only father he had ever known, and the man he respected most in the world.

"I don't know who gave birth to you," Wolf said. "But I do know bloodlines, son, and you're a thoroughbred. Do you know what I regret most in my life? Not finding you until you were fourteen. Not feeling your hand holding my finger when you took your first step. Not getting up with you in the night when you were teething, or when you were sick. Not being able to hold you the way you needed holding, the way all kids need holding. By the time we got you I couldn't do any of that, because you were as skittish as a wild colt. You didn't like for us to touch you, and I tried to respect that.

"But one thing you need to know. I'm more proud of you than I've ever been of anything in my life, because you're one of the finest men I've ever known, and you had to work a lot harder than most to get to where you are. If I could have had my pick of all the kids in the world to adopt, I still would have chosen you."

Chance stared at his father, his eyes wet. Wolf Mackenzie put his arms around his grown son and hugged him close, the way he had wanted to do all these years. "I would have chosen you," he said again.

Chance entered the bedroom and quietly closed the door behind him. The crowd had long since dispersed, most to their respective homes, some spending the night here or at Zane's or Michael's. Sunny looked tired, but there was a little color in her cheeks.

"How do you feel?" he asked softly.

"Exhausted," she said. She looked away from him. "Better."

He sat down beside her on the bed, taking care not to jostle her. "I have some things I need to tell you," he said.

"If it's an explanation, don't bother," she shot back. "You used me. Fine. But *damn* you, you didn't have to take it as far as you did! Do you know how it makes me feel that I was such a fool to fall in love with you, when all you were doing was playing a game? Did it stroke your ego—"

He put his hand across her mouth. Above his tanned fingers, her gray eyes sparked pure rage at him. He took a deep breath. "First and most important thing is: I love you. That wasn't a game. I started falling the minute I saw you. I tried to stop it but—" He shrugged that away and got back to the important part. "I love you so much I ache inside. I'm not good enough for you, and I know it—"

She swatted his hand aside, scowling at him. "What? I mean, I agree, after what you did, but—what do you mean?"

He took her hand and was relieved when she didn't pull away from him. "I'm adopted," he said. "That part's fine. It's the best. But I don't know who my biological parents are or anything about them. They—she—tossed me into the street and forgot about me. I grew up wild in the streets, and I mean literally in the streets. I don't remember ever having a home until I was about fourteen, when I was adopted. I could come from the trashiest people on the planet, and probably do, otherwise they wouldn't have left me to starve to death in the gutter. I want to spend the rest of my life with you, but if you marry me, you have to know what you'll be getting.''

''What?'' she said again, as if she couldn't understand what he was telling her.

''I should have asked you to marry me before,'' he said, getting it all out. ''But—hell, how could I ask anyone to marry me? I'm a wild card. You don't know what you're getting with me. I was going to let you go, but then I found out about the baby and I couldn't do it. I'm selfish, Sunny. I want it all, you and our baby. If you think you can take the risk—''

She drew back, such an incredulous, outraged look on her face that he almost couldn't bear it. ''I don't believe this,'' she sputtered, and slapped him across the face.

She wasn't back to full strength, but she still packed a wallop. Chance sat there, not even rubbing his stinging jaw. His heart was shriveling inside him. If she wanted to hit him again, he figured he deserved it.

''You fool!'' she shouted. ''For God's sake, my father was a *terrorist!* That's the heritage *I'm* carrying around, and you're worried because you *don't know who your parents were?* I wish to hell I didn't know who my father was! I don't believe this! I thought you didn't love me! Everything would have been all right if I'd known you love me!''

Chance uttered a startled, profound curse, one of Nick's really, really bad words. Put in those terms, it did sound incredibly trivial. He stared at her lovely, outraged face, and the weight lifted off his chest as if it had never been. Suddenly he wanted to laugh. "I love you so much I'm half crazy with it. So, will you marry me?"

"I have to," she said grumpily. "You need a keeper. And let me tell you one thing, Chance Mackenzie, if you think you're still going to be jetting all over the world getting stabbed and shot at while you get your adrenaline high, then you'd better think again. You're going to stay home with me and this baby. Is that understood?"

"Understood," he said. After all, the Mackenzie men always did whatever it took to keep their women happy.

Epilogue

Sunny was asleep, exhausted from her long labor and then the fright and stress of having surgery when the baby wouldn't come. Her eyes were circled with fatigue, but Chance thought she had never been more beautiful. Her face, when he laid the baby in her arms, had been exalted. Until he died, he would never forget that moment. The medical personnel in the room had faded away to nothing, and it had been just him and his wife and their child.

He looked down at the wrinkled, equally exhausted little face of his son. The baby slept as if he had run a marathon, his plump hands squeezed into fierce little fists. He had downy black hair, and though it was difficult to judge a newborn's eye color, he thought they might turn the same brilliant gray as Sunny's.

Zane poked his head in the door. "Hi," he said softly. "I've been sent to reconnoiter. She's still asleep, huh?"

Chance looked at his wife, as sound asleep as the baby. "She had a rough time."

"Well, hell, he weighs ten pounds and change. No wonder she needed help." Zane came completely into the room, smiling as he examined the unconscious little face. "Here, let me hold him. He needs to start meeting the family." He took the baby from Chance, expertly cradling him to his chest. "I'm your uncle Zane. You'll see me around a lot. I have two little boys who are just itching to play with you, and your aunt Maris—you'll meet her in a minute—has one who's just a little older than you are. You'll have plenty of playmates, if you ever open your eyes and look around."

The baby's eyelids didn't flicker open, even when Zane rocked him. His pink lips moved in an unconscious sucking motion.

"You forget fast how little they are," Zane said softly as he smoothed his big hand over the baby's small round skull. He glanced up at Chance and grinned. "Looks like I'm still the only one who knows how to make a little girl."

"Yeah, well, this is just my first try."

"It'll be your last one, too, if they're all going to weigh ten pounds," came a voice from the bed. Sunny sighed and pushed her hair out of her eyes, and a smile spread across her face as she spied her son. "Let me have him," she said, holding out her arms.

There was a protocol to this sort of thing. Zane passed the baby to Chance, and Chance carried him to Sunny, settling him in her arms. No matter how often he saw it, he was always touched by the communion between mother and new baby, that absorbed look they both got as if they recognized each other on some basic, primal level.

"Are you feeling well enough for company?" Zane asked. "Mom's champing at the bit, wanting to get her hands on this little guy."

"I feel fine," Sunny said, though Chance knew she didn't. He had to kiss her, and even now there was that flash of heat between them, even though their son was only a few hours old. She pulled back, laughing a little and blushing. "Get away from me, you lech," she said, teasing him, and he laughed.

"What are you going to name him?" Zane demanded. "We've been asking for months, but you never would say. It can't stay a secret much longer."

Chance trailed his finger down the baby's downy cheek, then he put his arms around both Sunny and the baby and held them close. Life couldn't get much better than this.

"Wolf," he said. "He's little Wolf."

* * * * *

MIDNIGHT FANTASY
Ann Major

To Aaron Clark, my late cousin, and his widow,
Glenda Clark. There are lessons in life,
both dark and bright. Sometimes the dark ones teach
us what we most need to know.

Aaron, you have blazed bright with love.
You have taught me about courage. You have taught
me that it is never too late to begin anew. You have
become everything and more than you ever dreamed.
You are one of my real-life heroes.

To Glenda, who taught me more about real love
than almost anyone I know.

Prologue

Get the hell out of here, you half-wild, no-good bastard!

The van swerved off the asphalt. A rumble of bumps and rattles jolted the prisoner on the floorboards back to queasy consciousness. Murky, gray light filtered through his blindfold.

He saw his father's face, mottled with rage.

You're damn sure no son of mine!

He'd turned away, knowing what he'd always felt deep down, that he was nothing. He'd gotten his start in the gutter. That's where he should have stayed.

The stench of dank air made him shudder.

God, he was scared. So scared.

They were in the swamp now, in that eerie, primeval kingdom of cypress trees, stagnant brown bayous, knobby-headed gators and mud deep enough to swallow a man whole.

Cajun music whined through bursts of static. He was

bound hand and foot, sprawled on top of smelly fast-food boxes, Styrofoam cups and candy wrappers.

The waxy-faced driver with the spider tattoo was driving faster than he had in New Orleans. "You're gonna be gator food, boy."

A surge of fresh fear shook the captive.

Another voice. "You know what gators do, don't you, no?"

A boot nudged the prisoner's hip. "They'll drag you to some underground hole, stuff you inside, yes, and tear off little bits of you for days."

A *strange terror* gripped the blindfolded man. When he shifted on top of the garbage, something squished against his clean-shaven face. Only yesterday he'd sat with his father in the best restaurant in the French Quarter. He swallowed carefully against the gag, fighting not to choke on the oily rag in his mouth and the coppery flavor of his own blood. He tried not to breathe because every tortured breath made weird, gargling noises in his broken nose.

His assailants' mood was quiet, tense, electric.

The road got bumpier, wetter; the pungent odor of still, dark waters and rotting vegetation stronger.

Big tires sloshed to a standstill.

"Let's dump him. Sack him up, throw those concrete blocks in. Haul him out deep so he sinks."

The back doors were thrown open. His fine Italian loafers came off when they grasped him around the ankles and pulled him roughly over garbage, tools, and bits of wood. They flung him onto the muddy ground, and his head struck a rotten log. When he regained consciousness, they were waist deep, pushing him under.

He fought to stand up in the gummy mud, but a boot sent him reeling in the warm, soupy water. Panic surged through him when big hands clamped around his shoulders and pressed him deeper.

He fought. His lungs burned with the fierce will to breathe. He pushed harder and was stunned when their grip on his neck miraculously loosened. His head broke the surface, and he choked on watery breaths as a shell was racked into a chamber. A shotgun blast exploded. Then everything got quiet.

He reeled backwards, flopping helplessly as the weights pulled him under. Strangely, as he began to sink, dying, his terror subsided.

All was peace and darkness.

Was this how she'd felt when her alarm went off and she couldn't get up?

Again he was a frightened, guilt-stricken boy shivering in wet pajamas. Bear tucked under his arm, he'd padded into his mother's dark bedroom. Bright sunshine lit her black, tangled hair. Lost in shadows her body was a slovenly heap, half on, half off the bed.

Her alarm kept ringing. He'd lain for hours, listening to that ringing till it had become a roar in his head. She was mean most mornings. Mean every night. How he lived for those rare moments when she tried to be nice, when she read to him from the books Miss Ancil loaned him from the library.

As always her bedroom stank of booze and cigarettes.

"Mommy! I—I's sorry, so sorry…I wet…."

He'd called her name after this confession and promised the way he did every morning never ever to do it again.

Only she hadn't cussed him. Nor had she gathered him into her arms and clung to him as if he were very dear which she sometimes did. She'd just lain there.

Finally, he'd gone to her and shaken her. "Open your eyes. Please, Mommy." He'd touched her cheek. She'd felt so stiff and cold…like his frosted windowpane in winter. Her alarm clock kept ringing.

He hadn't thought of that morning in years. Then here it was, his last thought on earth.

After her funeral his aunts had marched him over to his father's house. A man with black hair and blazing silver eyes had thrown open the door. His aunts had pushed him forward just as the door had slammed.

He'd been shuffled among distant kinfolk who had too many kids of their own. He'd done time in foster homes with other throwaways like himself, gotten in trouble at school. Then, miraculously, his father had had a change of heart and adopted him. He'd done everything in the world to please his father, eventually, even going into business with him.

Then one night he'd worked late and without warning opened the wrong file on a computer.

A gush of water soaked his gag, slid down his throat, up his nostrils, burning, strangling. He was dying when brutal hands manacled his waist, maneuvered his head forcefully to the surface, dragged him out of the water and flung him onto the muddy bank.

A rough voice cursed him in Cajun French. Gnarled fingers tore off his soggy blindfold, ripped at the duct tape over his mouth, then yanked the gag out.

"Jesus." His rescuer's breath stank of gin and tobacco as he pounded his back. Water trickled out of the drowning man's lips in spurts.

"Damn it," he pleaded.

The hard palm froze. "Ha! So! You're alive!"

He was rolled over and a flashlight jammed under his chin. "You don't look too good."

"Damn it!" He grabbed the light and shone it at his rescuer.

The stranger had wrinkled brown skin, white hair, and soulless black eyes. "You don't look so good yourself."

Yellow teeth flashed in an irreverent grin. "The name's

Frenchy." Frenchy seized his long black flashlight and turned it off. "Frenchy LeBlanc. I was just helping my brother check his trotlines. We fell out…. He's kinda cranky."

"Not like you…sweet as sugarcane."

With a grin, Frenchy ripped off the tape at the prisoner's ankles along with a wad of dark body hair.

"Ouch!"

"You need a ride home? A hospital? Or the police station?"

"I'm okay."

"You're beat up pretty bad—" When he said nothing, Frenchy held out his hand and helped him to his feet. "You gotta name, boy?"

He hesitated. Then, just like that, a name popped up from his childhood. But his voice sounded rusty when he used it. "Tag…"

The older man eyed him. "Tag. Tag what?"

Right. Right. Last name. "Campbell… Tag…Campbell."

"Like hell!" The yellow grin brightened. "You been to Texas…*Tag?*"

Tag shook his head.

The older man's gaze appraised his tall, muscular body. "You got soft hands for a big guy…and a hard face…and eyes that don't quite match it. That suit, even trashed, looks like it set you back some."

Tag said nothing.

"Real work might do you good—"

"Damn it…if you're going to insult me—"

"I fish. I could use a deckhand."

Tag turned away helplessly, and stared at the lurid shadows the cypress trees with their draperies of moss made. *A deckhand. Minimum wage.* For years he'd been on the fast track. His education. His career. His high-flying plans for his father's company. He'd been good, really really good at one thing.

But he couldn't go back.

"I've always worked in an office, but I lift weights in my gym every afternoon. I've never had time to fish," he said. *Never wanted to.* But he didn't say that.

Frenchy nodded, taking in more than was said. "I don't blame you for saying no to such hard, thankless work."

"I didn't say no, old man.... You'd have to teach me."

Frenchy patted his shoulder. "You gotta job."

"Thanks." Tag's voice was hoarse. He was disgusted that it might betray eagerness and gratitude. He knew better than to believe that this crude stranger or his casual offer and his kindness tonight meant anything.

He was through with ambition, through with dreams, through with false hopes that led nowhere. Again he was staring into his father's cold gray eyes. He was through with family and dreams of real love, too.

A deckhand. A trashy job working for a crude, trashy guy.

Get the hell out of here, you half-wild, no-good bastard.

"Thanks, Frenchy," Tag repeated in a colder, darker tone.

One

Five years later...

Stay with me, Frenchy. I need you.

That's as close as Tag had come to telling the best friend he'd ever had, he loved him.

But maybe Frenchy had known.

Tag had clasped him in his arms long after Frenchy's eyes had gone as glassy as the still bay, long after his skin had grown as cool as his dead mother's that awful morning when the alarm clock had kept ringing.

Stay with me, Frenchy.

He'd lashed the wheel of the shrimp boat to starboard with a nylon sheet...his makeshift autopilot...and headed home, cradling Frenchy's limp, grizzled head in his lap.

Stay with me, Frenchy.

But Frenchy's eyes had remained closed.

The deck had rolled under them.

*   *   *

It was midnight. The full moon shone through the twisted live oaks and tall grasses, casting eerie shadows across Frenchy's tombstone. Tag was all alone in that small, picturesque, historical cemetery located on a mound of higher earth that overlooked Rockport's moonwashed bay. Come morning, this time of year, the graves would be ablaze with wildflowers. Funny, how death could make you see the truth you didn't want to see. Tag had been living so hard and fast for so long, he hadn't admitted he'd loved the old bastard, till he'd held his friend's limp body and begun to weep.

"This wasn't supposed to happen! Damn your hide, Frenchy, for leaving me like everybody else.... But most of all I damn you for making me give a damn. It should be me who's dead."

They'd buried Frenchy beside his son, the son he'd lost right before Frenchy had saved Tag's life.

Tag was glad the cemetery was deserted. He didn't want anybody to see how profoundly Frenchy's death had upset him.

Sunken black circles ringed Tag's bloodshot eyes; his jaw was shadowed with several days of dark stubble. His stomach rumbled painfully from too much liquor and too little food.

The moon shone high in a cloudless, bright sky. The salt-laden sea air smelled of dry earth and newly mown grass. Frenchy's favorite kind of night. The shrimp would be running. Not that Tag could bear the thought of shrimping under a full moon without Frenchy.

Tag's big black bike was parked a little way from Frenchy's tombstone under a live oak tree that had been sculpted by the southeasterly prevailing winds that blew off the gulf, cooling its protected bays and low-lying coastal prairies.

Tag was kneeling before the pink tombstone. Soft as a prayer, his deep voice whispered. "Haunt me, Frenchy. Damn you, haunt me. Stay with me."

"You don't need an old man past his prime. You need a woman, kids," Frenchy had pointed out, in that maddening know-it-all way of his, a few nights ago.

"Strange advice coming from a man who's failed at marriage four times."

"Nothing like a pretty woman to make a man old enough to know better hope for the best. Life's a circle, constantly repeating itself."

God, I hope not.

"You're young. But you'll get old. You'll die. Life's short. You gotta fall in love, get married, spawn kids, repeat the circle."

"There's places in my circle I don't want to revisit."

"You're not the tough guy you pretend. You're the marrying kind."

"Where'd you get a damn fool notion like that?"

"You're either sulkin' or ragin' mad."

"Which is why you think I'd make a delightful husband."

"You don't fit in here. Your heart's not in bars or fights or gambling...or even in fishing. Or even in getting laid by those rich, wild girls who come to Shorty's looking for a fast tumble in the back seat of their car with a tough guy like you."

"What if I said I like what they do to me? And what if I said I can do without a heart, old man?"

"You're a liar. You got a heart, a big one, whether you want it or not. It's just busted all to pieces same as your pretty, sissy-boy face. Only the right woman can fix what ails you."

"You're getting mighty mushy, old man."

"You think you can stay dead forever?"

The wind drifting through moss and honeysuckle brought the scent of the sea, reminding him of the long hours of brutal work on a shrimp boat. The work numbed him. The beauty of the sea and its wildlife comforted him, made this hellish exile in an alien world somehow more endurable. Just as those women and what they did to him in their cars gave him a taste of what he'd once had, so that he could endure this life. But always after the women left, he felt darker, as if everything that was good in him had been used up. Which was what he wanted. Maybe if they used him long enough, he wouldn't feel anything.

Tag knelt in the soft earth and studied the snapshot of a younger Frenchy framed in cracked plastic in the center of the pink stone.

"You're a coward to run from who you are and what you want, Tag Campbell—a coward, pure and simple."

Tag had sprung out of his chair so fast, he'd knocked it over. "You lowdown, ignorant cuss! Every time you drink, your jaw pops like that loose shutter."

Frenchy laughed. "What's the point of wisdom, if I can't pass it on to a blockhead like you? Life's a circle…."

"Don't start that circle garbage."

Tag had slammed out of the beach house, taken the boat out, stayed gone the rest of the night on that glassy, moonlit sea. He hadn't apologized when he saw Frenchy waiting for him on the dock.

Then Frenchy had collapsed on the boat a few hours later when they were setting their nets.

Guilt swamped Tag. He'd never thanked the old man for anything he'd done.

The wind roared up from the bay, murmuring in the oak trees, mocking Tag as his empty silver eyes studied the grave. It was difficult to imagine the hard-living, advice-giving meddler lying still and quiet, to imagine him inside that box, dead. Emotions built inside Tag—guilt, grief—

but he bottled them, the way he always did when he wasn't driving fast, fighting, chasing women, or drinking.

The dangerous-looking man who knelt at his friend's grave bore little resemblance to the younger man whose life Frenchy had saved in a Louisiana swamp. That man had been elegantly handsome before the beating, his smooth features classically designed, the aquiline nose straight, his trusting silver eyes warm and friendly.

That man was dead. As dead as Frenchy.

The powerfully-built man beside the grave was burned dark from the sun. On the inside his heart had charred an even blacker shade. Fists had smashed and rearranged his once handsome features into a ruggedly-brutal composition. The broken nose had been flattened. There was a narrow, white ridge above one brow. Despite these changes, or perhaps because of them, an aura of violence clung to him. Maybe it was this reckless, outlaw attitude that made him so lethally attractive, at least to women of a certain class. Such women cared little about his inner wounds. They came on strong, wanting nothing from him except to use his body for quick, uncomplicated sex.

His guarded silver eyes beneath black arcing brows missed nothing, trusted no one. Especially not such women—women who made him burn, but left him feeling even colder and lonelier when they were done with him and drove off in their fancy cars to their big houses and safe men.

His muscles were heavy from hard, manual labor. He wore scuffed black cowboy boots, tight jeans, a worn white T-shirt, and a black leather jacket.

Frenchy.

Death triggered deep, primal needs.

Death. Violence. Sex. Somehow they went together.

Alone with his demons, without Frenchy to irritate and distract him, Tag needed a bar fight or a woman—bad. So bad, he almost wished he'd gone to the funeral and wrestled some shrimper for a topless waitress. So bad, he almost wished he was in jail nursing a hellish hangover with the rest of Frenchy's wild bunch.

Instead he'd driven his motorcycle—too fast and over such rough roads, he'd almost rolled. He'd scared himself. Which was a sign that cold as he was in his lonely life, he wasn't ready to end it. When he'd calmed down, he'd come to the cemetery to pay his last respects.

The silvery night was warm and lovely.

Perfect kind of weather to hang out in a cemetery perfumed by wild flowers and glistening with moonlight.

If you could stand cemeteries.

Which Tag couldn't. Any more than he could stand funerals. Especially the funeral of his best friend. Not when his own mood was as brittle and hopeless as the morning his mother had died, as the afternoon his father had slammed the door in his face.

Frenchy's funeral had been a blowout brawl at Shorty's. The cocktail waitresses, even Mabel, had danced topless on the pool tables. Some of the shrimpers had found their dance inspiring, and since there weren't ever enough women to go around in Shorty's, the "funeral" had gotten so wild, two of Frenchy's ex-wives had called the cops who hauled the shrimpers and barmaids to jail.

It had been just the sort of uproar that gave shrimpers and the industry a bad name.

Then Frenchy's will had been read. Everybody really got mad when they found out that, fool that he was, Frenchy had left that black dog, Tag Campbell, everything.

Everything. Boats. Restaurant. Fishhouses. Wharves. Even the beach house which was practically an historic landmark. *Everything.*

Campbell.

That snobby bastard! He didn't even like to fish! Still,

he was the best fisherman any of them had ever seen. Just as he was way too popular with *their* women even though he secretly despised them. The bastard preferred books to beer even though he could drink any one of them under the table. Tag Campbell was too proud and high-and-mighty to hang out with the likes of them at Shorty's. How in the hell had he outsmarted them all—even Frenchy?

Everything was his.

There was lots of angry muttering.

"It isn't right! Frenchy dead on that boat with just that lying Tag Campbell to tell the tale."

"If you ask me, the bastard killed him."

"You heard the coroner. Autopsy report says massive coronary. Says Frenchy smoked and drank too much. Says it's a miracle Frenchy lived as long as he did."

"I say it was murder. Frenchy was fit as a fiddle. Why just two nights ago he was drunker than a skunk dancing on that table with Mabel."

Rusty and Hank, two of the rougher prisoners, deckhands Tag had fired for laziness and pure meanness, vowed that as soon as they got loose, they'd see their friend, Frenchy, avenged.

Frenchy had a lot more money than the shrimpers suspected. The sheriff paid Tag a visit just to tell him he'd be smart to leave town, at least till Rusty and Hank cooled off.

At the sight of the sheriff's car in his drive and Trousers, his Border collie, slinking off to the woods, Tag grimaced. No wonder Trousers was scared. The big man cut an impressive figure in his uniform and silvered sunglasses. He had heavy features, squared off shoulders, and a big black gun hanging from his thick belt.

Tag had dealt with more than his share of armed bullies in uniforms. The law, they called themselves.

Self-righteous bullies, strutting around in their shiny

boots like they owned the world. They'd boarded his boats, slashed his nets, kicked his ice chests over and swept his catch overboard, fined his captains. No sooner had Sheriff Jeffries slammed his meaty fist against his screen door and bellowed Tag's name, than sweat started trickling under his collar. A lot of his cats scurried under the house or after the cowardly Trousers. Others hunkered low behind pot plants to watch the suspicious character stomping down their breezeway.

"I just let Rusty and Hank out. They're calling you a murderer."

You half-wild, no-good bastard.

His own father had wrongly accused him of embezzlement and grand larceny. Anger burned in Tag's throat, but he smiled as if he didn't give a damn and saluted the man with a whiskey bottle. "You got a warrant—"

"Sometimes, Campbell, the smart thing is to walk away."

Tag stared at his own reflection in the silver glasses and then pushed the door wider. "I ain't runnin'."

The sheriff planted himself on his thick legs and then leaned against the doorway.

"Jeffries, those guys talk big when they're safe in jail, but they're like dogs barking from inside a fence. You let 'em out, and they'll lick my hand like puppies."

"Just a friendly warning, Campbell."

"Thanks, amigo."

Still, Tag had opened a drawer, loaded his automatic and stuffed it in the waistband of his jeans before setting out on his bike alone.

Numbly Tag studied his friend's tombstone. Frenchy had been mighty proud of the pink stone. He'd chosen it himself on a lark five years earlier right after he'd brought Tag home. Frenchy was known for cheating at cards, and had won the plot off one of Rockport's most respectable citizens in a drunken poker game at Shorty's.

"You cheated him," the man's indignant wife had ranted, and the whole town, at least the women, had believed her. "You got him drunk, so you could cheat him."

Now Frenchy was as ashamed of his lack of talent at cards which made cheating a necessity as he was proud of his drinking skills. He might have gallantly returned the plot had she not accused him of cheating.

"We wuz drinking his whiskey, I'll have you know, and I was even drunker than he was, lady," Frenchy had declared almost proudly. "Could be *he* cheated *me.*"

The lady sued, but the judge, a poker player, had sided with Frenchy.

Tag studied Frenchy's name and the date of his birth and the single line etched in caps on the bottom of the stone— IT WAS FUN WHILE IT LASTED.

Slowly Tag lowered his gaze. Instead of flowers, a mountain of beer cans and baseball caps were piled high on the mound of clods. Indeed, every baseball cap that had been nailed to the ceiling of Shorty's had been enthusiastically ripped off and reverently placed on his grave.

Tag's eyes stung. Frenchy would've been mighty proud.

Grief tore a hole in Tag's wide chest as he slowly rose and stalked over to his bike. He pulled on his black leather jacket, zipped it. Next came his gloves, his black helmet. Straddling the big black monster, jumping down hard, revving the engine, he made enough noise to wake the dead.

But then maybe that was his intention.

Not that it did any good.

Frenchy wasn't coming back.

Tag roared to the gate, skidding to a stop in a pool of brilliant gold that spilled over him from the streetlight.

He turned and looked back at the cemetery.

Stay with me, Frenchy.

Suddenly, time as Tag knew it did a tailspin. Or maybe the world just turned topsy-turvy. Whatever. The moon got bigger. Then it flattened itself into the shape of a huge pink egg in that inky sky. Stars popped like fireworks. For a second or two Tag felt there really might be a mastermind up there.

Tag got all warm and tingly inside. The wind sped up and the silvery night pulsed bluish-pink. A couple of beer cans came loose from the grave and started to roll straight toward Tag.

He shut his eyes, but the same pulsating, vivid rosy-blue fog swirled behind his eyelids, too. He blinked. Open or shut, the otherworldly, blue-pink radiance pulsed.

After a while, somebody, maybe Frenchy, switched off the pink light, and the moon settled down. The streetlamp came back on, gold and bright as ever. The night beyond was silvery dark. The can didn't stop rolling till it hit the toe of Tag's boot. He picked it up, noticed it was Frenchy's favorite brand. Tag flattened the can, stuffed it in his back pocket.

What the hell had that been about? Had the streetlight malfunctioned? Or was it just him?

As he stared at the moon he felt different somehow, not so tight and morose. The hole in his chest seemed to have closed. And the night, like his future, beckoned with amazing possibilities.

Had Frenchy done this? Had he actually haunted him? Had he given him this strange sensation of peace? Of new opportunities?

Hell no. The grief and the booze he'd drunk earlier, coupled with not eating, was getting to him. He was hallucinating.

He'd better make it a short night, grab a burger and go to bed. Warily, he looked both ways before pulling out.

Two cars zoomed recklessly toward him from his right.

Kids, playing chase. Where the hell was Jeffries when there was real work for a big bully with a gun to do?

Impatiently, Tag waited for the juvenile delinquents to pass.

When he caught that first glimpse of long blond hair, the back of his neck began to tingle. She was a rich tart on the prowl for a cheap thrill.

Happy to oblige, pretty lady.

Then *she* came into clearer focus the way a terrified deer does in your headlight.

He didn't notice the make of her late-model, flashy red sports car. He was too busy noticing her. She looked nervous and scared.

He felt her—deep inside. She touched a raw place he hadn't known was still alive. She made him ache and hurt and crave things he'd thought he'd given up for good. What would it be like to have a woman like her waiting at the door with a smile every night when he came home?

In the space of a microsecond he memorized that pale pampered face; those classy, even features she'd painted with way too much makeup, probably to make herself look older and more sophisticated. Pert, shapely breasts spilled above a low-cut white bodice. The style was overly sophisticated for her, too.

He caught a glimpse of something sparkly around her throat. Diamonds? Rich, too?

He knew her type. She was the kind of woman who wanted her real man to be a money machine but found "nice" men too tame in bed. So, she came looking for a guy like him at Shorty's. He'd gone with plenty to motels. Some preferred backseats of cars, but once they got their kicks, they rearranged their skirts and drove off. They never asked his name, and he always felt depressed and cheapened, less than nothing when they were done with him.

Other men envied him his popularity. What the hell was the matter with him? What did he want really?

He couldn't tear his gaze from this one. With her long blond hair streaming behind her, she looked like an angel riding the wind.

He willed her to look at him, to really see him.

Suddenly she tossed her head toward him. Her eyes grew huge the instant she saw him—as if she were equally fascinated and yet scared, too. Again, he thought her different than the others. He had the strangest feeling that if he stared into her eyes long enough, he would rediscover his own soul—which was a crazy feeling, if ever there was one.

Something dangerous and fatal connected them. Unwanted longings and painful needs bubbled too near the surface. His pulse raced out of control.

How could he feel so much in the space of a few heartbeats? She was a baby, younger than her voluptuous body, while he was far older than his years.

"Do you hold yourself as cheap underneath as all the others, baby?" he growled.

The minx flirtily tooted her horn and sped up. As if she wasn't already driving fast, way too fast.

Her little car careened onto the shoulder, pinging his bike and long, denim-clad legs with gravel, but she regained control. The beat-up sedan behind her raced past Tag in hot pursuit. Gravel sprayed his boots and his bike like bullets. Only he didn't get any hormonal bang from these punks.

Damn. He knew that junk heap. Rusty and Hank. Not kids. Two mean guys who were mad at the world in general and out for vengeance against him tonight. What if they took it out on her?

He'd lied to Jeffries. Those guys were bad news. As bad as the thugs who'd almost killed him in the swamp. After he'd fired them, they'd sprayed paint all over the cars in the parking lot out back of Frenchy's restaurant. Painted the outer walls of the kitchen in purple graffiti.

Correction. *His* restaurant now.

He had a score to settle. A damsel as a trophy only upped the stakes.

Tag whipped his big bike onto the asphalt road, gunned it.

The cars raced north at double the speed limit, flying over the lighted bridge, veering left on screaming tires, onto Fulton Beach Road. The moonlit bay glittered to the east of them. The mansions on pilings that lined the canals loomed tall and dark to the west.

The quaint road along the beach, with its cottages, historic Fulton Mansion and motels, narrowed, roughened, but the girl and her pursuers kept driving like maniacs. Just as she got to the wharves and warehouses that lined the waterfront near his own restaurant, a black shadow raced from the water side into the road.

Her brake lights flashed.

Adrenaline pumped through Tag's veins.

Had she hit whatever it was…killed it—

Animals touched a soft spot, especially strays. He had a collection of mongrel dogs and cats that lived out back in the woods behind his house.

Her car spun off to the right, bounced over something on the shoulder, and rolled to a crooked stop in front of the alley that ran between two abandoned fish houses. A long shadowy tail disappeared into the tall reedy grasses of the marshy wetlands on the other side of the road.

The junk heap came to a stop right behind her car, ramming her.

The woman in skintight white stumbled out of her sports car.

Rusty and Hank fell on top of her.

Party time.

Tag ripped his bike off road, stopping so fast, he nearly rolled. His right boot hit white shell, and he skidded in a geyser of white dust.

Party time.

Not their party.

His.

He'd been spoiling for a fight...and a woman.

Looks like he had his own personal wish fairy looking out for him up there in heaven.

Frenchy?

Stay with me, Frenchy.

A girl's terrified scream went through Tag like a knife. He was off his bike—running.

Two

Tonight should have been the happiest night of Claire Woods's life. Instead, tears of disillusionment stung her eyes. North had let her drive off. So, now here she was, forty miles from home, her blond hair whipping her face like a mop, and two unsavory goons honking on her tail.

She hit the accelerator. Nothing was turning out the way she'd planned. She had so wanted her wedding to be a fairy tale, but as the big day approached Claire Woods, who everybody thought spoiled and pampered, was feeling bereft and hollow.

If only Melody, her quirky, irrepressible, unpredictable sister, hadn't come home to spoil everything!

It was just like Melody to helicopter off that freighter bound for China and fly home—tonight! Just like her to stage that provocative dance for North's benefit and steal Claire's show and maybe *her* man.

Claire had wanted to shout, "I'm the bride! North loves

me now! Not you!'' But, of course, she'd only stood there with a frozen smile while Melody hummed and did her cute routine.

And North…

''It's not North's fault!''

He hadn't known Melody would pull one of her stunts. Who but Melody would fly in from China just to crash their party? From the second Melody had waltzed into the yacht club ballroom in those tight pants and shimmery blouse, looking like she owned the place, everybody had been electrified. Nobody could stop talking about that buffoon, Merle somebody, a fly-by-night P.I. their daddy had sent to find her six months ago. Melody had laughingly explained how she'd lured Merle on board her China-bound freighter and then tricked him into walking the plank, so to speak.

''Why did you come home?'' North had demanded of Melody. ''Why now?''

''I…I couldn't miss your wedding.''

''You sure missed the last one.'' North's low voice was rapier-sharp.

If North truly loved Claire, he would be chasing Claire right now instead of the two hoods flashing their highbeams and honking behind her.

Instead, her fiancé and her sister were still at the party, probably making eyes at each other this very minute, while she was driving around alone.

No…. No….

A vision of Melody humming softly, Melody, in those skintight black jeans and a white silk shirt, eyes aglow, her honey-gold hair streaming down her slim back took shape in Claire's too-vivid imagination. Her sister's dance had been so enthusiastic, so spontaneous, and so original that everybody had stopped dancing and started clapping the moment she kicked off her shoes and threw them to North. Everyone except North who'd gripped those sparkly high heels in a stranglehold. Not that he hadn't watched her dance, his expression darkening when the other men had started clapping.

How much of her childhood had Claire spent curled up with a book or in her room alone with her dreams while bubbly Melody was out in the yard putting on a show that had all the neighborhood children, especially the boys, spellbound?

Applause and love and sheer sexiness came so easily to the uninhibited Melody.

All her life Claire had wanted to be first with somebody.

"Don't think about Melody," Claire whispered to herself. "Don't think about the pain in North's eyes when he'd watched her dance."

"But I can't stop."

Claire had never outgrown the childish habit of talking to herself, especially when she was in her car alone or primping in front of her mirror.

"Chase me then!" she'd laughingly challenged North a little while after Melody's dance.

The memory made her blush, made her eyes burn. What a brazen fool she was. When would she ever learn North was too cool and mature to play what he called her childish games?

Or was that really it? Did he love her, really love her as once he had loved...

He had told her once, "I can never love you as I loved Melody. But I believe what we'll have will be better and stronger than what I felt for her."

Claire was sick of driving around. More than a little scared, too, and not just of losing North. The jerks behind her were persistent. Her parents' warnings played like tapes in the back of her mind.

A woman alone on the road is prey, Claire. This in a shrill tone from her bossy mother, Dee Dee.

When a man sees a woman alone, he takes it as an invitation. This from Sam, her all-knowing doctor father.

Maybe the old folks were smarter than she'd thought. Her legs had been jelly ever since these two goons had almost sideswiped her, forcing her onto the shoulder a while ago.

The humid wind that battered her face and tangled her butter-colored hair stank with the pungent fragrance of a plankton-laced bay. When their car speeded up, attempting to pass her again, Claire shakily pushed a sticky strand of hair out of her eyes.

Her front wheels skidded. Her heart skittered.

"I'm not scared!"

When the car in her rearview mirror rushed forward and she could no longer see it, she yanked her steering wheel to the left and cut them off. Honking, they eased off the accelerator and veered back into the right lane behind her. So did she. They slowed, and she relaxed enough to rehash the humiliating little scene at the country club with North and Melody, which was the reason she was in this mess.

North never wanted to discuss wedding details, maybe because his first wedding had ended in such disaster.

"We'll all be happier when you grow up!" North had thundered distractedly a few minutes after Melody's dance had ended. Claire had been trying to discuss some of the difficulties with wedding costs. "So, scale back. Compromise!"

North could hold onto his cowboy cool a whole lot longer than most guys, so his uncustomary show of temper should have warned her.

"But I can't. It's our wedding day. If your family would just—"

"You know what your problem is?" North had waved one of Melody's shoes at her. "You're spoiled, Claire."

"Me? Spoiled? You're the big multimillionaire rancher."

Men. At first she hadn't been able to believe that North, whose wealth was legendary, had joined forces with the wedding consultant, caterers, her parents, and his family to attack her. Why couldn't he understand how unsure she felt with Melody home and everybody else pulling her to pieces?

"Darling, Mother keeps saying she just wants our wedding day to be fairy-tale perfect," she'd whispered, "something special we'll remember forever. We're doing this for you...to make up for..." Claire stopped, staring at the sparkly shoes he still held because she couldn't say, *my sister jilting you at the altar.*

"I wish you two would worry a little more about what comes after that day—our marriage."

"Oh, that— That's the happily-ever-after part."

"Damn it." North had shrugged wearily. "I'm beginning to wonder about that."

Finally, she'd said what was really on her mind. "Is this about Melody?"

"Hell, no." But he'd reddened, and the sparkly shoes had glinted. "Life's not lived like the glossy pictures of those bridal and home magazines you and your mother pore over all the time. I wish to hell we'd eloped."

Suddenly she'd realized everyone, especially Melody, had begun watching them when North had raised his voice in annoyance. Claire had felt frightened and guilty when North's gaze had drifted back to her blushing sister.

"I'm sorry," Claire had said. "So sorry. I shouldn't have said anything." When he'd scowled at her and then at the shoes and hadn't apologized, she hadn't known what to do. Suddenly she'd realized she shouldn't have upset him with wedding details right after Melody's dance. "Dance with me, darling,'' she'd pleaded, realizing he hadn't said one word about how beautiful she was in her white sheath.

Again his black gaze had drifted to Melody. ''I'm really not in the mood to put on a show!''

''But we're supposed to be madly in love.''

''Claire, your sister's show is a hard act to follow. And now you've got me all worked up, too. I can't just... You're always pressuring me, chasing me—''

'''Cause you never chase me.''

His black eyes left Melody and flicked over Claire with a strange look of pity that startled them both. When he pressed his handsome lips together and continued to regard her thoughtfully, she was terrified.

''How will it look to everybody if we just stand around, not dancing, not talking?'' Claire pleaded. ''And holding my sister's shoes?''

''Frankly, I don't much give a damn.''

''You'd better be careful,'' Melody had quipped, gliding up to them. ''That sounds a lot like Rhett Butler's exit line.''

A look had passed between Melody and North. Then North's face had hardened and he slammed the shoes into her open palms. ''And you're just the girl to appreciate a good exit line.''

Melody had gone as pale as death.

Claire had felt a burst of sympathy for North.

Would he ever get over her sister?

Of course, he would. He was. She had just been immature to push him.

Would he ever be over her sister?

People were turning to stare. Not knowing what to do, Claire had flown out of the club and gone to her car.

North would follow. He would leave the stuffy party where all anybody ever did was try to impress each other. He would chase her. He had to.

Nobody had been more upset than Dee Dee when Claire's wacky, unconventional sister had broken North's heart. Just as nobody had been more elated when he'd found consolation first in Claire's friendship, and then in her love.

Claire banged her hands on her steering wheel and listened to the band. Even out here the throbbing music was loud, almost loud enough to drown out the loneliness in her young aching heart, almost.

"Go back inside."

"No, any minute North will march out those polished mahogany doors with the shiny brass handles and prove his love for me—to everyone."

But the doors didn't open, and the brass handles began to swim in a sea of hot tears. North stayed at the club.

And even though Claire had known deep down that she was, at least, partly in the wrong—she hadn't had the guts to go back inside, face Melody and meekly apologize to North.

Her mother, Dee Dee, who'd all but engineered this marriage after Melody had jilted North, was, once again, planning the wedding of the year. Only Dee Dee was determined that Claire's wedding would be so magnificent everybody would forget and forgive what Melody had done. But the financial burden of marrying great wealth for the second time was a strain on their upper-middle-class budget, a fact her father never let Dee Dee forget, which was why Claire had asked North to help.

"Have a wedding your family can afford," he'd said. "After what Melody pulled, all that matters is a sacred ceremony."

Mother said the wedding had to be perfect…perfect. Just the event to reestablish Dee Dee Woods as a Texas hostess to be reckoned with after having been made the laughingstock of the town last year by Melody. The effort and pressure to impress the right people had her mother in bed with what she called "heat" headaches.

Bridal nerves. Maybe that's what had Claire so uptight and jittery lately...even before Melody's return.

The moon lit a path from the horizon to the shoreline. Not that she noticed when the jerks behind her honked loudly.

Their bumper slammed into hers. A sickening chill of fear shivered up her spine.

She had driven forty miles on this fool's errand to regain her pride. Halfway to Rockport where her parents had a condo on the bay, the punks had forced her onto the shoulder.

They honked flirtily again. Somehow she had to get back to North and apologize, really apologize. But first she had to shake these juvenile delinquents before she left Rockport.

When the hoods flashed their high beams, she stomped down on the accelerator of her sports car.

It was now or never.

As the cars raced, she began to practice her apology.

"Oh, North, I'm sorry. You were right and I was wrong. You're my best friend." She would close her long lashes, let them drift open slowly. "Of course, I love you just as I know you love me. Seeing Melody... Those shoes... That dance... I just wanted you to chase me... To excite me... To thrill me... To act like a caveman for once."

The way Loverboy does.

"You can't say that to North Black!" an irreverent masculine voice in her head drawled.

"I know that, silly." She couldn't ever let North...or anyone else know about her embarrassing, secret, fantasy life with...with Loverboy.

The trouble had started innocently, the way most bad things do. A lonely little girl, Claire hadn't ever been able to make friends as easily as Melody. And if she had made a friend, Melody had quickly charmed her or him.

Claire had worn lace dresses when Melody and the other girls wore jeans. Claire had read books, while Melody and her friends had made mud pies and climbed trees. Finally, Claire had invented an imaginary friend, Hal, who was just as lonely and shy as she was. Everybody had thought it was so cute the way she included him in every conversation, set a special place for him, even bought presents for him. Somehow over the years, Hal had grown up and gotten way too sexy for her to handle. She was a virgin…but only technically. In her imagination, Hal and she got up to wanton mischief in all sorts of dark and inappropriate locations, on kitchen tables and the hood of her car. Hal was tall with black hair…like North.

And yet not like North at all.

North didn't have all that much time for her. He kept much of himself hidden from her. He was steady and predictable when it came to his work, too tied to the responsibilities of his ranching empire and his duties to his legendary family.

Hal was wild and dangerous and free, insidiously attentive, and as faceless as an outlaw's shadow.

North could give her the kind of safe, secure life her upper-middle-class mother could brag about.

Mostly her imaginary lover was a pirate on a ship who carried her off to sea. Sometimes he was a bandit or a highwayman who carried her to his hideout and robbed her of more than her gold.

Strip, my lady. Slowly. And every time she took something off, he would toss a gold coin at her feet.

Mostly she dreamed about him at night, but lately she'd been having the most lurid daydreams. The oversexed phantom was becoming terribly distracting. One reason she was so anxious to get married was to send Loverboy packing. Once North made love to her, she would have a husband to dream about. What sane woman would chase a dream, when she had a man like North in her bed? Everybody, simply everybody told her North was the sexiest, hottest, richest cowboy prince in all of Texas.

North could have chosen any woman. He had chosen her.

"That's not the way it was, *Sugar-Baby,*" purred Loverboy.

She hated to be called that. "Shut up, Hal!"

"I was there! *And Melody was first!*"

"Go away and leave me alone!"

"Never. I am not abandoning you till I find a more suitable companion for you."

"Stay out of my love life!"

Suddenly a strange thing happened. The black sky turned pink, and she saw a lone black figure on a motorcycle off to her left silhouetted in a white cone of light. Pinkish-blue light pulsated around him. He was wearing a helmet, but the heat of his gaze was a visceral, physical connection. Even in that blurred, peripheral glimpse, she sensed that such a man in the flesh might prove wilder and more chaotically thrilling than any secret interior existence with Loverboy.

She knew better than to look at the biker, but some dark and dangerous force compelled her.

Curiosity kills more than cats.

The forbidden—especially in the tame, pampered life of a woman like Claire, who lived her life by rules the way some people paint by numbers—was the most powerful temptation. Besides, Melody's dance and North's dark mood had opened a crack in her heart and self-esteem.

She was on the brink of marriage to the most desirable of men. Never had she felt less sexually attractive, nor more afraid or vulnerable. What was the biker doing alone in a dark cemetery?

Jauntily, she turned toward him. For the space of a heart-beat her long-lashed eyes fixed on the black helmet that hid his face with an avidity that should have shamed her. Then with a will all its own, her glossily tipped fingernail tooted her horn.

He nodded. Her lips parted coquettishly. But when the biker skidded out onto the road after her, her heart jumped into her throat.

The thunder of his big bike racing to catch up to her was a fuse that lit a primal heat in every nerve in her body.

The biker left asphalt, caught up with her pursuers, spewing gravel on them before braking and then falling in behind them.

She knew he was bad.

Bad to the bone.

Why did she suddenly feel she was on a collision course with destiny? She turned her three-carat engagement ring backwards.

North was in Corpus, but the chase was on.

Three

————

"**Y**ou're driving too fast!" Claire's voice sounded panicky as she raced past the entrance to her parents' condo. Not that she had any intention of leading the pack straight to her door.

She didn't know what to do, how to get away from the hoods or the biker. Why weren't there any other cars on the road? Fulton was deserted, the restaurants shut down, the warehouses locked up.

Suddenly a black cat dashed out from under a pile of construction rubbish right in front of her.

"Oh, my God!"

She honked, slammed on the brakes, swerving off the pavement, careening toward two shadowy buildings surrounded by scaffolding.

"Stupid!"

Then she bounced over a pile of discarded roof shingles. Her front left tire blew on a nail and she bumped to a stop.

The jerks rolled right up behind her and nudged her back bumper.

"Oh, no!"

They gunned their engine, then killed it.

She was caught in the dark tunnel between two buildings with a fence at one end and them behind her. Scaffolding cast eerie bars of light and shadow.

"Oh, dear." Claire's shaking hands fumbled in her overstuffed purse. A package of tissues, her change purse, and her keys fell out.

Behind her, car doors banged open. Glowing cigarette butts were pitched onto the shell drive and ground into pulp beneath bootheels. Like a pair of raptors, they eyed her edgily, their hostile faces framed for a second or two in her rearview mirror.

One glance had her heart beating like a jungle drum, her fingers shaking so hard their tips went numb.

Where was it?

Headlights rushed by.

"Help me! Somebody help me!"

The sedan's red taillights vanished into the dark.

Her trembling fingertips closed over her cell phone. Peering over her door, she got a glimpse of a dirty T-shirt and black tank top, slashed jeans before she began backing down the alley.

"Well, looky, looky, Rusty." The dark, skinny guy with the mean, narrow face lit a cigarette, took a drag.

Rusty, a greasy blonde built like a tank, snatched the cigarette, inhaling deeply.

Gripping her phone, she got out of her car, stumbling down the dark alley between the two white-washed buildings. Rusty followed, laughing, his heavy heels crunching shell, his long shadow curling around her like a black snake.

No! No!

Before she could punch in in the numbers 9-1-1, they had her cornered against a springy, cyclone fence topped with razorwire. She clawed. Chain-link chimed.

The greasy blonde's thick fist snatched the phone and threw it on the ground. His face loomed. His blue irises blazed scarily brighter. "We wuz looking for somebody."

Throaty male laughter.

"Looks like you're our consolation prize."

She broke into an icy sweat. She made little low sounds deep in her throat.

The large freckled hand reached for her diamond necklace. Paralyzed, she endured his touch. He stroked her lip, brushed her cheek, his dirty fingers obscenely gentle, his leering smile horrible. She squeezed her eyes shut as that unbearable hand explored, but she couldn't stop the tears that slowly beaded her long black lashes and leaked silently down her cheeks.

Rusty's hand traced the shape of her mouth.

She opened her eyes. With a deceptive smile, she bravely met his feral blue stare. His tongue lolled as he unzipped his jeans and moved in for the kill. Quick as a turtle, she bit his filthy, thick finger.

On a yelp of pain, he jumped back.

She screamed and ran.

The skinny one jumped her and knocked her to the ground. Her head struck a brick. Stars spun in a white sky above the palm trees. They fell on top of her, grabbed her wrists, pinning her body with knees that dug hard into her belly. The last thing she saw was those overbright white eyes. The last thing she felt was the pain in her head, in her neck, in her shoulders. The last thing she heard was their voices, telling her how much she wanted them.

Dimly she heard her silk sheath ripping, then their belt buckles unsnapping, leather sliding through denim loops. But when they knelt over her again, there was a monstrous roar from the other end of the alley. Fantails of white shell and powdery dust spewed above her.

"Rusty! Hank! She's mine!" thundered a deep male voice from the end of the alley.

Loverboy? she wondered woozily.

"Holy damn! It's him!"

"Frenchy's murderer!" Hank spat. A switchblade snapped, flashing silver.

"Get, before I send you to hell along with Frenchy!" A black barrel flashed. She saw a dark hand. Then the black hole at the end of an automatic. "Get—out of my town—permanently."

She saw flame, heard a pop.

"You heard me. Get off her. She's mine."

Pop. Pop. Pop. Loose shells pinged when the bullets hit dirt. Miraculously, she wasn't hurt. The cruel hands on her body loosened.

She opened her eyes and saw two figures furtively scuffling past her on bloody hands and knees, their lank hair falling forward. Car doors slammed as the other man's shadow fell over her.

"This ain't a free peep show. Get!"

The pair cursed, started their engine, and roared away, leaving her alone—with *him.*

Maybe she should've felt afraid. But she was too numb.

All was silent save for the palm trees rustling above her. She swallowed. Vaguely she tasted shell dust and that awful tobacco-stained finger.

Shell crunched under a man's heavy boots. Then his low, hard voice cracked. "You gonna get up? Or are you really out for a good time?"

Her eyes snapped open and shot fire.

Wide-spread black boots were planted mere inches from her face. Her gaze climbed a virile, masculine body packed into denim so tight the cloth looked painted on.

He had a lean waist, a shapely torso, and a linebacker's squared-off, wide shoulders. A bright halo backlighted a well-shaped ebony head. His untamed hair was longish, and like a pirate, he sported a silver earring. They must've hurt him because he was pressing a white handkerchief against his cheek, sopping blood.

She couldn't see the fierce face that went with this diabolical individual, but his bold, stripping gaze made her shiver.

Was this over-sexed caveman with the massive biceps a figment of her maddeningly-fertile imagination? She shut her eyes, willing him to disappear. When she opened them, the scuffed black boots were an inch closer.

The biker jammed the black automatic into his waistband, his bloody handkerchief into his pocket and kneeled down.

"They...they called you a murderer."

"You gonna believe scum...or the man who just saved you?"

She didn't know how to answer this beast.

"Do you know how to say thank you, pretty lady?"

His hard gaze knocked the breath out of her.

"Because you owe me—big time," he murmured, "and I can think of any number of ways for a woman like you to thank a man like me. The night is young—"

A woman like you? "You have some nerve."

"So do you...running around at this hour...in that car. In that body. Where were you going? What were you looking for?" He laughed derisively. "I know your type."

"I don't want to know yours!"

His blazing eyes settled on her face, moved lower with an overabundance of feral sensuality. "You wanna bet?"

"Just go!"

"You're too weak to get up, too rude to say thank you, too much of a liar to admit what you are.... You have a flat tire which you probably don't know how to change. You're half-naked and lying flat on your good-looking tush in a most seductive pose—'' There was no mistaking the sexually-charged innuendo in his low tone. "I don't blame you for wanting something wild. I was on the prowl for the same thing myself."

"Half-naked?" Her brain stalled. Alarm bells jangled. "What—?"

She shut up when the biker wrapped his arms around her in the darkness. When he touched her, she got the sexual charge she'd been waiting for her whole life.

From him.

She was too shocked to resist as he began to check for bruises and other injuries. His fingers on her skin just got hotter and hotter.

Instantaneous man-woman combustion.

Waves of erotic heat lapped her like a turbulent wake.

He tensed.

She froze.

"See! I was right about you," he said.

"Take your hands off me!"

He laughed and then jerked her unceremoniously from the ground. Strands of her torn white silk skirt tickled her bare thighs as he pulled her to her feet. When she collapsed against him, his large, sure hands caught her.

More dizzying heat.

Blood from the cut on his cheek smeared the right half of his face. There was a dark stain on his white T-shirt, too. He had gotten hurt because of her. Her expression softened as she studied his rich black hair, his mouth, and then the cut.

"It's a scratch," he muttered.

"Maybe you should put something on it."

His eyes went dark with dislike. "Don't act like you give a damn."

"Are you always this rude? Or are you just showing off for me?"

His brows slanted. He studied her and then suddenly he laughed again.

She smiled. That broke the ice a bit. Then the air between them began to thicken again a little like sauce left to simmer over a fire. He was gorgeous, if a girl went for all male...and lethal. Which she certainly didn't.

Nonetheless, she couldn't stop looking at him. And that made her blush.

"Who are you?" she whispered, trying to push him away even though some part of her wanted to be locked in those warm muscular arms forever.

"You don't care who I am."

"Were you friends...with them?"

"No." He didn't explain.

"I hit my head when I fell," she said. "I'm a little woozy. Not...not myself. This feels like a bad dream."

His hands combed tangled, golden hair and found the blood-crusted bump on the back of her head.

She jerked away. "Ouch!"

"You have a lump the size of a hen's egg there. You need a doctor—"

"No doctor!"

Black eyebrows arched. "You're in no position to give me orders, princess."

"Nobody can know about this."

"About me, you mean." His gaze slid over her hips, down her legs.

Her legs! She experienced a full-body blush. Their entire length was exposed to his view. Her silk skirt was shredded. Strips of the gauzy stuff were curling high above her thighs. Why, he could probably see her panties!

Panties!

Melody and her little jokes!

Claire wasn't wearing pant—

Frantic fingers tugged modestly at the remnants of white silk to cover panties that simply didn't exist.

"Don't bother." His eyes had narrowed, the intimacy in his gaze and raw whisper shaming her. "Black lace. Thong. And your voluptuous body to pull it off."

She recoiled, her blush reheating.

"Very becoming," he said.

Melody had given her the thong panties as a joke tonight. When she'd tried them on in the ladies' room, Melody had dared her to wear them.

"Thong-bikini," he jeered softly. "A deliberate turn-on."

"For a man like you maybe."

"Careful! You're the one in the naughty underwear— Like I said—you were asking for it."

"Your jeans are two sizes too tight!"

His handsome mouth quirked. "A nice girl wouldn't notice."

That was the sort of teasing boast Loverboy was always making…when she got undressed…when she was scrubbing herself between her legs in intimate places with a washcloth beneath foaming bubbles in her bathtub.

"Shut up, Loverboy!"

His avid grin was white against his sun-darkened skin. "What did you call me?"

"Nothing!"

He dazzled her with another smile. "You talk to yourself then?"

"Mind your own business!" Her drop-dead glare made that smile of his broaden, gentling those rugged features; she found his smile so charming it almost undid her fierce resolve to dislike him.

If his jeans were tight, his white shirt was equally tight, revealing way too much muscle and black furred chest.

"You shouldn't strip a guy with those big baby blues...'cause he might take you up on that invitation."

She couldn't quit looking at him. The light seemed better, or she was more accustomed to the gloom. His tense, carved features held a powerful fascination for her. Suddenly she was studying the tiny white scar above his brow, the nose that had been broken. With a moan, she reached up and feathered a fingertip across the jagged white mark above his arcing brow.

Velvet fingertip against his warm, tanned forehead. Her unexpected touch and the inexplicable tenderness in her gaze brought wary turbulence to his silver eyes.

A shadow swept his face, and she saw naked vulnerability. He wrenched her hand away so fast she cried out. With a wordless scowl, he strode toward her car.

"What did I do?" she cried, running to catch up to him.

He whirled. "You don't give a damn about me any more than I give a damn about you!"

"So...you're scared, too."

His panicky eyes grew colder.

She was sure she'd seen his softer side. Ignoring his sudden tension, she smilingly moved toward him. The urge to cup his chin in her soft fingers sent a chill through her.

"Women like you want only one thing," he said.

"Really?" This time she laughed.

"Open your trunk," he growled. "Show me your spare."

When she didn't budge, he strode past her, back down the alley. In the darkness he leaned down and picked up her cell phone. When he brought it back and handed it to her, his fingers accidentally grazed hers. He tore his hand away, but not in time. Jolted by the same charge, the phone slid through her fingers.

"Hey..." With lightning-fast reflexes he caught it and jammed it into her open palm, closing each of her fingers, one at a time, around the black plastic. He wasn't exactly caressing her, but her knees felt shaky.

The savage downward flick of his dark brow, told her she disturbed him, too. His glinting eyes swept her from head to toe, lingering on her breasts where she clasped her phone.

"Is every damn thing you do deliberately sexy?" he rasped.

"What?" Parting her lips, she leaned forward.

"Did you tease those guys for the hell of it too?" He caught her to him. "You rich girls are all alike. You make us dream, lust, and you don't even see us...except when you want *this*."

She struggled, but he didn't let her go.

That got her mad and scared. But it was too late for both of them.

He didn't want to kiss her.

She didn't want to be kissed.

But faster than either of them could blink or think, his hard mouth was on hers, and her lips opened as his tongue met hers with a needy desire that under ordinary circumstances would have humiliated her.

"You can't get this in your safe little world. That's why you came looking for it tonight. Well, baby, you're gonna get what you were looking for after all."

In the next instant, he slammed her against the wall of the warehouse, and she loved it. His eyes flamed. His dark, carved face lowered to hers again.

She should have fought.

Melting into him, she surrendered to his devouring kisses. One hard hand yanked her zipper down, moved under her white silk bodice, inside it, his long fingers shaping and caressing her satin throat, her breasts, stroking her pink, pearly nipples till they peaked. Then she felt his warm tongue there, laving those tender tips as she arched against his mouth.

He knew how to touch, where to touch to set her on fire. When she wiggled closer, his other hand tore her thong bikini down and slid his hand into the wetness there.

"This is wrong," she managed in a hoarse whisper.

"You started it," he taunted.

With a groan, he cupped her bottom, pulled her legs up, wrapping them around his hips, holding her up easily. Her heart rushed, slowed, rushed again. Never ever had she done anything like this before. But then this wasn't real. This had to be fantasy.

Her fingertips explored his sandpaper rough jaw, combed through his coarse black hair. His mouth and hands and body were so hot, so hard...and yet so infinitely gentle. Never, ever had she felt so flamingly, completely, sensually alive. So close to such a vitally explosive edge. Her whole world was a molten whirlpool with him at the center.

She yanked his leather jacket down over his shoulders, smothering kisses against his throat, tasting his skin, even the caked blood there, all the while murmuring, "Yes...yes...."

A car roared by, the white glare of headlights exposing them.

His kiss stopped instantly.

"Do you want it like this? In a back alley? With a man whose name you don't even know? I'm game if you are."

He was real. This was real.

Outraged, she stared at him. He was low-class and barbaric. What was *her* excuse? One kiss and she'd sunk to his level.

Shock made her cheeks flame. Shame made her shiver. What had gotten into her?

Shaking, she collapsed against the rough wooden wall.

Abruptly his hands on her hips fell away, and he lowered her body to the ground.

"Now that was a thank-you," he whispered hoarsely.

She fell back against the unpainted boards. As she rubbed her eyes, her pulse thudded violently. Her skin was drenched with perspiration.

Five-hundred wedding invitations had been mailed. Wedding gifts were stacked to the ceiling in her mother's den. North, who'd already been jilted once, would be devastated if she publicly humiliated him a second time. And her mother...

After Melody had vanished, the constantly-busy, gregarious Dee Dee had sat in a dark corner of her living room for days, not bothering to put on her makeup, lunch with her friends, or run her house.

The wedding was three weeks away. Claire had made irrevocable choices. Her mother had invested months in this project.

Her rescuer—if that was what he was—was furious. His silver eyes blazed with lethally fierce emotion.

He is so beautiful, she thought.

"Let's get your trunk open," he whispered. When she didn't move: "Move!" he roared.

"Okay... okay...." Quickly she scampered toward her car, clumsily yanking at the clump of keys dangling from her ignition. Instead of handing the keys to him, self-consciously she lifted her hand above his, dropping them into his open palm, careful not to touch so much as a callused fingertip.

Suddenly their not touching was almost worse than touching. His silver eyes studied her too knowingly, reminding her that a moment ago she'd melted against him. Body and soul, she'd been his for the taking.

When she began to shake, he tore off his leather jacket.

"Cover yourself! I'm a beast," he murmured viciously, "driven mad by lust for you. Trash."

Her thoughts to a *T*. She reddened, felt shamed.

Again she had to ask herself—what was she?

Her fingers closed around soft leather. "Thanks," she whispered. When she slid into the garment that held his heat and male scent, her womb contracted so violently, she almost ripped the jacket off.

Quickly he had her trunk open and her jack and tire thrown out on the ground. He worked fast, furiously loosening the lug nuts, jacking the car. She stood over him, trying not to think of the kiss, admiring his skill with the heavy work. Focusing on him made her wonder who he was and what had happened to him.

"You must have been very handsome before…"

When he tilted his black head at her, his hard gaze sent an embarrassed trill of sensation through her lower belly.

She gasped self-consciously. "Before…before the accident," she continued.

"What accident?" The bleakness in his dark tone scared her.

After that he worked in silence. Ten minutes later he was done.

He slammed her trunk shut, dusted his broad, brown palms together, and ensnared her in another hot glance.

"Thanks," she whispered, heat spreading through her. She started to shrug out of his jacket, but he stopped her.

"Keep it. Get in." Like a well-bred gentleman, he opened her door. "I'll follow you home."

Manners. *Where had he learned manners?*

"No."

"Where do you live?"

"I'd rather not say."

"You're not driving home alone till we get your tire fixed then."

"I'll be fine."

"You rich girls too spoiled to compromise, princess?"

She resented his sharp tone. "As if you've known so many."

"Too many."

"I—I…I'm not spoiled!"

"Prove it." He tossed her her keys and slung a long leg over his bike.

"But—"

"I know a mechanic who works late."

She sank back against her leather seat. "But—"

"His shop. Or I follow you home. Right to your doorstep. It's your choice, princess."

"Don't call me princess!"

At the garage, the biker did not relinquish command. At first his retro behavior made her feel awkward. Then it really got under her skin.

It was *her* tire; *her* car.

When she had taken all the domination and arrogance she could take, she went up to him and thumped him on his wide shoulder. "You can go."

He cocked a dark brow.

"I'm an adult," she said.

"You're also a woman. A woman who's gotten into more than her share of trouble for one night."

"You have no right to tell me what to do."

"Well, you're not getting into any more— Not on my shift—*princess*."

The mechanic, a skinny guy with a skimpy goatee, smiled at the conclusion of this humiliating exchange. To make matters worse, he kept peeping at her from underneath her car, his eyes almost popping out of his head every time he got a glimpse of her legs.

The biker circled her car, barking orders. He insisted that all the fluid levels be checked as well as the air pressure in all her tires. When her car was nearly done, he joined her on the shabby automobile backseat where she sat in a shadowy corner of the garage.

"Since we're all done, you really can go," she whispered. "I can pay him and—"

"I'm not leaving you here alone...in the middle of the night."

"I can take care of myself." Her voice sounded surer than she felt.

His rugged face was implacable. "The way you did in the alley?"

Her gaze fell. She didn't want to remember her feelings of utter helplessness when those thugs had knocked her to the ground.

She began to shake, her eyes to glisten.

"Anybody would've been scared," he said.

"I—I don't want you to see me...like this, but I don't want you to go, either. I want— I want—" Suddenly she was too overwhelmed by her emotions to go on.

When he bent closer, her hands reached out for him, blindly clutching at his sleeves, then tugging him closer, gripping his muscled arms. When he lifted her and pulled her against him, settling her closer, her hands wound around his neck, and she clung, holding onto him with a fierce incomprehensible need, her breath slicing in short gasps.

"I thought they..." She broke off shudderingly.

His fingers brushed her cheek. "*They* didn't."

"I—I hate the way you think I'm an idiot."

His arms pressed her against the long, hard length of him, and he began to rock back and forth, his compassion so genuine she was moved. "Don't. Hush."

"All done," rang a tinny, too curious voice behind them.

When the biker tried to ease her out of his arms, she was

too shaken in some deep fathomless way to let him go. She began to cry and to tremble all over.

"Why don't we get some coffee somewhere? You're in no condition to drive," he said. "I could call someone—"

"No! Nobody must know…about this!"

"About me, you mean." His silver eyes hardened. But his voice softened. "Why don't we go to my place…just till you feel better?"

Only after he uttered this absurdity, did she relax and let him go. Dimly she was aware of him paying, of him negotiating with the mechanic to leave his bike there for the night.

"Come on," he whispered.

Her tears had drained her. Her legs felt like leaden weights.

He took her hands in his. "Sweetheart, he's closing."

Vaguely, she watched his lips move. She tried to concentrate, but his words ran together like jibberish.

Instead of obeying him, she reached up to touch the bloody place on his face.

"We have to get you home," he said.

Home. As if it were a place they shared.

Almost, almost she wished it was.

She remembered the alley, the shells tearing her silk sheath, the brutal hands on her bare skin.

Her head throbbed. Then a belated wave of dizzying blackness crashed over her.

"Oh, baby," she heard him say right before he caught her.

When she woke up, it was as if she were in a dream. Her clothes were gone. Somebody had bathed all the white dust and blood from her scratched skin. She was in a rustic house that smelled of wet grasses and the sea as well as the nearby marshes. She lay between sheets scented with laundry soap. She heard crickets and cicadas and night frogs. Unlike most houses in Texas, his was on the water, and not air-conditioned. The windows were screened to let in cool, salt-scented breezes. Banana leaves rustled against the screens and beyond she could hear the lap of waves. The natural smells and humid air brought back her childhood when she'd spent more time outside running free in backyards...on wet sandy beaches.

Then *his* black head stirred on her pillow and she made out his harsh features in the shimmering moonlight.

She was in *his* bed. Underneath *his* cotton sheet, snuggled companionably against his long, male body.

When she opened her mouth to scream, his predatory silver eyes burned into hers. Then a big hand clamped down on her lips.

When she fought to twist away, he held her frightened glance wordlessly.

"No, no," she whispered, pushing at him.

He rolled on top of her, his big body pinning her to the soft mattress. "I won't hurt you."

He stroked her cheek until she stilled. When she closed her eyes, he loosened his hold. But she remained in his arms and reveled in his velvet touch as she listened to the night sounds.

His fingertips burned her up, tracing the shape of her eyelashes and brows, caressing her lips and the curve of her nose. His exquisite gentleness made her quiver.

But his gentleness mixed with her own physical needs was not what drew her into the vortex. It was more, much more. Some part of her remembered him carrying her inside, holding her close, comforting her.

His touch was so soothing, his eyes intense. He made her feel so special, so cared for, so loved—*his*. Which was odd. She had North, who was her dear friend...her family. But this man was touched by her vulnerability as they weren't.

Why hadn't she ever felt like this before? So complete? Like she mattered for herself? She'd always had to jump through hoops for love. She'd had to make good grades. She'd had to be beautiful, dutiful. Perfect. She'd had to prove that she was better than the son her father had wanted. Had to prove herself to North's family. She'd had to follow her bossy mother's orders. And always Melody had been there. Melody, with her sunny disposition and impish sense of humor. Melody, the show-off, who was so effortlessly, so easily loved.

With this man Claire could be herself. She could simply be.

Your daddy cried when the nurse told him you were a girl.

All her life Claire had had to prove to her father that she was even better than precious Harry who had died. Harry who would have been perfect if he had lived.

But no matter what she'd done, she'd never measured up to her family's expectations or to her own.

When the biker withdrew his hand from her face, she felt infinitely calmed. She took his long, lean fingers in hers, manipulating them, kissing them one by one, thanking him for his unique gift which was acceptance.

When she was done, his gray eyes stared straight into hers.

"How can this be?" she whispered. "How can we be?"

"You came looking for this."

"No."

"Admit it."

Their gazes clashed. Then a powerful gust slapped the banana leaves against the house. A shutter came loose and began to bang. He got up, padded out of the room on bare feet, then down the breezeway to secure it. When he came back, he lay beside her once again.

She was too afraid to move, to speak. Too afraid of her intense, inexplicable needs.

Afraid of his, too.

And yet she was more afraid of the loneliness in her real life, of the loneliness she would return to when this dream with him had spun its course.

She closed her eyes and pretended she was asleep. He let her pretend, and soon, all too soon, she really was.

Her childhood nightmare came back to her.

She was lost. All alone in the dark. Cut off from her family and love.

Terrified.

Four

Claire was lost and running. It was so dark she couldn't see. Then someone called her name.

"Sugar-Baby."

She shot bolt upright to moonlight flowing in a slant across an immense bed. A ceiling fan crouched, undulating above her like a giant black spider. She shuddered, trying to make sense of weird groupings of shadows and shapes in the unfamiliar room. A monstrous ladderback chair draped with a man's black leather jacket stood out like a frieze against the white wooden wall.

"It was just a bad dream," rumbled a deep, sleepy voice beside her. "No more bad guys. You're safe in bed…with me—*Sugar-Baby.*"

Sugar-Baby. Loverboy's pet nickname.

His silver earring glinted wickedly from the dark.

The biker!

"You kept saying Sugar-Baby and Loverboy in your sleep."

Slowly the incredible man beside her came into focus. She saw amused, gray eyes and heavy, black brows. A crop of untidy, blue-black hair toppled over his wide forehead. His features, even his long nose that had been broken, his stubborn chin, all seemed carved of some polished, dark wood. His shoulders were dangerously broad. If he wasn't exactly handsome, he was smolderingly masculine. Strangely, she wasn't scared of him at all.

Yawning lazily, he rolled away from her, carrying the sheet off her.

Naked, she hugged her breasts and then yanked the sheet back.

He laughed, unashamed that she'd stripped him of all but his tough, brown hide. "You were sweeter asleep."

She shot him a dirty look only to gasp when she saw how much of his rampant male form was sprawled beside her.

Hastily she lowered her gaze, but not before the impression of his muscular frame and black-furred chest had burned an indelible image into her brain.

"Where are your clothes?"

"You swiped the sheet, my lady!"

"Oh…" Quickly she tugged the bottom end loose from the massive bed frame and threw it at his middle.

"Thanks." He covered the essentials and lay back, pillowing his head in the crook of his dark arms.

His stare brought a self-conscious blush. Or was it the awareness of his well-shaped, dusky body lying right next to her under the sheet that had her so rattled?

Primly she bunched her end of the sheet at her throat. "I've got to go."

"Not till the sun comes up, pretty lady."

"Who made you my jailer?"

"Your keeper, my pet. Think of me as your knight in

shining armor...er...who risked his life fighting to save your honor.''

''I don't see any armor.''

''It's uncomfortable in bed.''

''And as for saving my honor— You didn't have the slightest intention—''

''I thought you were looking for a man who turned you on. Forgive me for offering my services.''

His coarse whisper and quick, irreverent grin caught her off guard. Tangible need raced like quicksilver through her veins. But when a brown arm reached for her, she scooted to the edge of the bed. Scooping up the chenile spread, she wrapped herself up like an outraged mummy.

''Where's your bathroom?''

''Sugar-Baby, I prefer to snuggle when I first wake up.''

''Don't call me that! Where—''

Grinning, he nodded toward a door, and she bolted.

Whiskers leaned into the brush, bit at it, slapped at it and then hurled himself onto the kitchen throw rug, enthusiastically rolling, purring as Tag stroked his fat black tummy.

''You're hooked on this, aren't you, old fella?''

Whiskers slapped the brush out of his hand and arrogantly padded over to his empty bowl.

The first time Tag saw Whiskers, he'd been a puny, half-starved kitten eating garbage in a culvert pipe.

''Had enough, old fella?''

Tag pitched the brush under the sink. He'd been grooming the cat while he waited on her.

Hell.

Sipping from a mug of coffee, Tag strode from the kitchen to the bathroom door for the third time since she'd locked herself inside.

She'd cracked the door, and he could see inside. She was

looking at herself, making dramatic faces, whispering to the mirror.

A big diamond flashed when she waved her left hand. She must've seen it when he did because she gasped. Quickly she removed the ring and stuffed it into a small bag that she put in her purse.

A few minutes later she tiptoed out.

"What took you so long?" he demanded.

At the sound of his voice, she froze.

"You look good in my clothes, pretty lady. Sexy!"

Startled, she ran her hand down his shirt. Her fingers smoothed the soft, black cotton over her lush breasts so that her nipples peaked. She was engaged to another man. Yet she'd showered in his bathroom and was standing in his bedroom looking flushed and fresh and too alluring to believe.

"They're way too big," she said.

"Yes." The baggy, black shirt and jeans left a lot to his imagination. But since he already knew what a terrific body she had, keeping it hidden tantalized him. And that hair— Tangled as it was in that awful ponytail that made her look like a smart-ass thirteen-year-old, those golden tresses were the rarest shade of yellow silk. He'd touched them, wrapped his fingers round and round in the soft masses when she'd trustingly laid her head on his chest in her sleep. Her eyes were a dark and luminous blue-blue. And yet innocent. So charmingly, sweetly innocent.

When she slept, she hadn't been afraid of him.

"Black is definitely your color," he muttered.

Against that dark hue, her skin seemed paler and yet incandescent in the moonlight. Even without makeup, her kissable lips were ruby-red. To look at her was a sensual feast.

It felt good having her in his house. She fit. Belonged.

The ring.

She was engaged. Like the rich women who came to Shorty's, she had a safe, rich man on the string.

He wanted to grab her now, to have it done with, to lose himself in her flesh, get her out of his system, to prove she was like all the others. Yet he didn't want to spoil it.

"I watched you through the crack…primping…."

"How dare—"

"When you put on my shirt, you spun round and round…like a little girl playing dress-up."

She tossed her ponytail and pointed her nose in the air.

His eyes fell to her lips and then to her breasts. "Only not like a little girl at all."

Her flush deepened.

"Who were you talking to in there?"

She swallowed. "Nobody."

He smiled. "You have quite an imagination."

"Mother says it's a failing."

"Do you want a cup of coffee?"

When she nodded, smiling at this safer topic of conversation, he led her to the kitchen.

As he poured the strong, black, steaming gourmet brew, he couldn't stop staring at the creamy curve of her neck which was revealed because she hadn't buttoned the top two buttons of his shirt. He wondered if she'd left them that way just to tempt him. Whatever. Her skin glowed like honey against his black shirt.

It was a crazy, dangerous feeling, but for an instant he felt like he was back in New Orleans when his father had first adopted him. He felt like he could be happy with this woman, that he would do anything to win her respect and admiration.

"Are you hungry?" he whispered roughly, resenting the way she stirred long-abandoned hopes and dreams.

She nodded too vigorously. He suspected that she just

wanted to keep him busy at something she deemed harmless.

"How about an omelette?"

"Anything."

Her breathy answer hung in his imagination as he put his heavy frying pan on a gas burner, lit the jet, cracked eggs into the pan with a splatter. *Anything.* In no time he was beside her at the table sharing a fluffy omelette and toast.

"You're a good cook," she said.

"A sensitive cook. I like my guests to eat every bite and brag on me."

She smiled impishly. "This is the best omelette I've ever eaten in my whole life."

He hated himself for basking in her praise, for waiting for more.

"Every single bite is pure rapture."

"Ah, rapture." Another word to hang there in his imagination. He'd show her rapture. He wanted to lick her golden hairline. To slide his hand beneath black cotton and cup her breasts. To rip those jeans she was wearing off. To brand her as his.

"Rapture. I like the sound of that. Keep talking, pretty lady."

She laughed between bites. "You could be a chef...." She shot him a megawatt smile.

I'd rather be your lover. He grinned sheepishly, ashamed of the egotistical pleasure he found in her compliments. "Okay. Okay."

"And you're a good host."

That surprised him. He'd never had a single conversation with any of the women he'd brought here. Only sex. Which he could have already had with her—if he'd pushed it.

"Am I?"

She went still beneath his silent stare. Her voice lowered

to a scratchy whisper. "Too good. You make me feel like I belong…like I'm special."

Her compliment stung, maybe because that's the way she made him feel.

"Maybe you are."

She got up stiffly and took her plate to the sink. When she sat back down and sipped her coffee, she seemed pale. The banana leaves were still now, the wind outside having died. The tiny kitchen got so quiet all he could hear was his own heart.

She was a stranger, but her sensual, feminine presence charged him. His uneasiness grew. Maybe that was why he got up and washed dishes with such a boisterous clatter. When he was done, he grabbed a bottle of whiskey and sat down, splashing a shot into his coffee. "Want some?"

She caught her lower lip nervously in her teeth, then shook her head.

Small talk. What to say when he couldn't think. When he was too damned conscious of *that* body, of the warmth of that silky skin, of the softness and sweetness of those red lips. His desire for her was a pulsing, tangible want. Not like what he'd felt for the others.

Small talk. With a woman he'd seen naked but whose mind was a stranger to him. "So, how come you talk to your mirror, pretty lady?"

"You shouldn't have spied on me."

He swallowed his whiskey, not liking the way it burned going down. "That's beside the point. Why do you talk to yourself?"

"You don't give up."

He stared at her ruby-red lips as she sipped from her cup and then set it crookedly in its saucer.

"I shouldn't tell," she began, hypnotizing him with her gaze.

"Oh, go ahead. We're both living dangerously tonight," he said.

"I was a shy, unpopular child. I used to read…all the time…and the things that happened in my books were so exciting. When I was a little girl I used to sit in front of my mirror and drape myself with scarves. I'd put on makeup…preen. My sister used to accuse me of being vain and conceited. But I was pretending I was in some exotic locale like the ones I read about. I was always with a pirate or a bandit…doing forbidden, adventurous things."

"So you like pirates?" He poured more whiskey into his cup.

Her lips pursed as she stared at the cup. At him. Then she got up so fast she nearly knocked her chair over.

"Hey…hey…."

Recovering, she walked away from him down the long hallway that led to his den. She eyed his bookshelves with a maddening nonchalance that challenged him, fingering his books, the stacks of real estate and investment magazines, learning about him without asking, when he didn't know a damn thing about her.

"I don't know any pirates," she finally said.

"You know me."

"I don't want to talk about this. Not to you." Deftly she changed the subject. "Your house is surprisingly neat."

His mouth twisted. "You mean for a low-life like me."

"I didn't say that." She paused and straightened the frame of a wild seascape that included a shrimp boat and a stormy sky swirling with gulls. "I like this painting."

"There's a lot of local talent here."

"Everything fits somehow. I mean your house. It's simple and comfortable. Classy…not overdone."

"What'd you expect?"

"Not this." She sounded a little disappointed. "I thought you'd be wild."

"Hey, I'm not all that neat…or tame." He threw back his head and drained his cup. Then almost angrily he flung the empty cup into a corner, smashing it to bits.

She gazed at him, her face shocked. "What'd you go and do that for?"

He grabbed for her, but she jumped, eluding him.

"Simmer down," he whispered. "That was just to prove…I've got a wild side. As for my neat house," he began, still on the defensive. "I have some help. A lady and her kid live in the house out back. Cute kid. Kinda nosey sometimes. But cute."

She ran down the length of the hall, vanishing into his den. "More bookshelves. You must read an awful lot."

He followed her. "Lots of lonely people read. It was a habit I started as a kid. There was a nice lady at the school library. I didn't know many nice ladies."

She was staring at him again, making him breathe too hard.

"So," he continued, "you dreamed about pirates because they…were exciting?"

"I'd rather talk about you."

"Fine," he said.

"What's your favorite book?"

"Whatever book I'm currently reading. I read nonfiction, mainly biographies. I don't like novels. They're…"

"Too emotional," she finished.

"Maybe. Now it's your turn. What's your favorite book?"

"*Frenchman's Creek.* It's a novel."

"About pirates?"

"How—" She blushed. "A married lady does have an adventure with a pirate."

"Does she choose the pirate or her husband?"

She was standing by the screen door, watching him.

"Her heart chooses the pirate, but she stays with her husband."

He moved toward her, closing in, cornering her. "That's not very romantic." He kept walking till he had her backed against the door.

"Oh, it was…in the book," she breathed, clutching the door.

He was so close he could feel the heat of her body and catch her sweet, feminine scent. "So, she had a fling?"

Her gaze seized on his carved face with fear and silent longing. "Your eyes are the coolest gray and yet…they burn…like no other eyes I've ever seen." She shuddered. "I bet no pirate ever had hotter eyes…."

He assumed a hard, insolent expression. *Girl, don't you be thinking what you're thinking. Fantasies are dangerous in real life.*

Shaking her head, she pushed the screen door open behind her and stepped out onto the breezeway. He followed close on her heels, the door clapping shut behind him, the sound that of summers and childhoods and memories buried deep but never forgotten. When she stepped onto the porch and climbed down to the lawn, he was right behind her. The night smelled of wet grass and salt air, and he could hear the gentle lapping of the surf beyond.

Not far from the house, she stopped and stared out at his hammock beneath the trees, at the wharf where his favorite shrimp boat was docked and then at the bay that stretched toward a moon-bright horizon.

"It's pretty out here…. I like the way your oak trees bent almost double from the wind. I like the way moonlight sparkles all the way across the bay."

"I don't think there's any other place quite like Rockport, but I never realized how gorgeous it all was before." He wasn't one for views, so he didn't stare at the familiar bay that hid sunken oyster reefs or the sculpted trees all the local artists painted so often; his devouring gaze raked the length of her.

Shakily she began to button the collar of her shirt. She was so golden and slender and lush and lovely. So uncertain and at the same time, so blatantly seductive.

"Black's damn sure your color, sweetheart," he drawled, repeating himself. His eyes shone. He wanted to seize her, to hold her, to crush her into his body, to taste her again, but she stiffened and backed away.

Music drifted toward them from Shorty's, Frenchy's favorite honky-tonk down the road.

"I like that song," she said.

Frenchy? Was he still meddling?

"I feel like dancing," Tag murmured gently. "How about you, pretty lady?"

"What? Here?"

"Play like I'm your fantasy pirate." He held out his hand and bowed low, inviting her to dance on his lawn beneath twisted oaks and silvery moonlight. Her soft gaze locked on his outstretched hand, then on his rugged, dark face, and last of all, she was drawn to his eyes that were aglow with passionate tenderness.

He hardly dared hope that the scene would appeal to that wild romantic imagination of hers and was stunned when her expression became drowsy and voluptuous. Then her cheeks reddened, but she laid her warm fingers over his. He slid his arm around her waist and drew her close.

Soon they were swaying in perfect harmony to the beat of the music. When she laid her cheek against his shoulder, his heart raced.

"So...what's your name?" he asked lightly.

"No names."

"We've shared violence, a bed, a meal, coffee...." He could feel her heartbeats quickening. "You're in my arms—"

"No names," she insisted, drawing a long breath. "They're too personal. This is a dream. Only a dream."

"Miss *X?*" He tipped his head back and stared thoughtfully at her pink face. "I guess that makes me Captain *X*. Same last name. Sounds like we're married."

She shivered and fought to pull away, but the music grew louder. And his arms tightened around her, holding her closer, so close that every time he moved, her legs and thighs burned his so intimately, waves of heat lit every nerve.

Hesitantly, shyly, she laughed.

"No way could you end up married to a guy like me in real life," he whispered into her hair, kissing her scalp again.

Her voice was low and sad. "No way."

"But in your imagination you fall for bandits and pirates."

"I shouldn't have told you that."

"Doesn't anybody know who you really are and what turns you on?"

"Nice girls don't talk about such things."

"Not even to their boyfriends?"

She was silent.

Tag stopped dancing and pulled her deeper into the shadows. "How come you're telling them to me tonight, instead of to him?" he demanded.

"We quarreled." She tossed her head. "It was silly really."

"But it changed everything."

"What do you mean?"

"I mean Rusty…Hank. That alley. I mean your torn dress, that lump on your head. I mean…. Tonight. Fate. You. Me. *Us.*"

"There is no…*us—*"

"So you'll go home and pretend you never met me."

She pressed her cheek to his chest again. "I have to. My life is perfect."

His eyes blazed, intent on her lips. "On the surface maybe."

He moved so swiftly she had no chance to evade him. The first thing she felt was the warmth of his breath against her cheek. Then his mouth covered hers. Almost instantly her eyelids closed and her breath caught expectantly.

Before she could surrender, he released her shoulders and pulled back. "How come you melt every time I touch you?"

"Don't— Please—"

"Sweetheart, it's real easy to think a life that measures up outwardly is the life you want. It's what everybody in this country thinks. You can have the great husband, the great house, the great car, but if those images are false, they won't matter any more than a new toy to a spoiled child. Someday, I swear to you, you'll find yourself out in the cold—alone…feeling empty…and all used up. I know—" He caught himself. "Sorry. I got carried away."

"Don't apologize." She turned her face fully toward him. Her eyes had softened with some intense emotion. "What is it about you…." There was awe in her voice. She drew a long, agonized breath that held pure feeling. "Why, oh, why…why do I feel…" She broke off, almost hurled herself back into his arms. "Just dance with me. Hold me," she begged. "Do you want to hear something crazy? I know I should run. Right now. This very minute. At the same time I wish this night could last forever."

"I learned you can't count on anything, and there's no such thing as forever. There's only now. This instant. You. Me. If it's good—go for it." Her heat consumed him. Her innocent smell was dizzying.

He pulled her close, whirled her across the lawn. She

glided, laughing now. He wanted to crush her to him, to kiss her, carry her into his bedroom.

He felt the heat of her body, the softness of her breasts. Then she stumbled, fell against him. He caught her and held her, his hands moving down her shoulders to her waist. He pressed her tighter. When the song ended, the mood between them was electric.

The sea breezes ruffled the leaves in the oak trees. Strands of her hair came loose and flew against his cheek. An odd shiver went through them both.

"Kiss me," she whispered, hardly breathing.

"What about your real life? Tomorrow?"

"What am I going to do? I have this thing for pirates who carry me away to a desert isle." Her eyes were startlingly blue, drinking in his soul. "You said I couldn't leave…not till the sun comes up. You said— Never mind what you said. Just kiss me…."

Intending a swift, light kiss, Tag cupped her face in his hands. Maybe she was inexperienced, but she was starving. Looping her arms around his neck, she nudged her tongue inside the moist aperture of his lips, kissing him back too hungrily for a tender peck to do.

Her hands. Her burning hands were all over him. She was an innocent, untutored, but her fumbling explorations, her natural wantonness stirred him more than all his previous, more experienced lovers had. And yet there was something clean and pure and true in every thing she did. She was everything he'd dreamed of that could be good in life and more.

Liquid heat spiraled through him. A low moan rose from his throat. She pulled back, moonlight streaming across her pale, stunned face. Her cheeks were flushed, her mouth swollen as she began to unbutton her black shirt.

He ran his fingers through his hair, gulped in air as she

stripped. Whipping his shirt off, she stood before him, her opulent breasts gleaming in the silver light.

"Tell me who you are," he whispered.

"No names."

So—she was…like the others.

She tossed him the shirt and ran. He chased her through the high grasses, into the deepening shadows of the trees.

He pounced when she came out of the thicket at the back of the house. Picking her up, he carried her to the house. Inside, he pressed her against the wall. With his free hand, he slowly stroked her warm neck, her shoulders, her breasts. "Don't make me stop," he growled.

"Oh…oh," she whispered in a small, frightened voice when his fingers rubbed her nipples till they hardened. Then he suckled first one and then the other.

Her eyes were torpid and unfocused. "Please…oh… please…."

"Please…what?"

"I…I…I'm too ashamed to ask."

He lifted his head.

"And too filled with delight not to ask." A sheen of tears glazed her eyes. "Would you pretend—"

"Anything—" he murmured hoarsely, recklessly.

"Would you be…my midnight fantasy? Would you play the pirate I sometimes dream about?"

"Loverboy?" he whispered.

There was something so needy and vulnerable, so imploring in her guilt-stricken blue gaze when she nodded. She made him burn and ache as no woman ever had before.

His large hands plunged into her hair. He tugged the rubberband loose, and yellow hair spilled to her shoulders. She cried out in pain at first but then began to shiver when he ran his fingers through the long perfumed masses before burying his hot mouth beneath them, first hungrily kissing her throat and then lowering his mouth to taste again her nipples that were still wet and taut from his previous kisses. His hands parted the zipper of her jeans, but her hands rushed to stop him. He got down on his knees, cupped her buttocks, pulled her pelvis against his face. His warm breath teased denim that covered that most erogenous of feminine places. Instantly her hands were in his black hair and she was shuddering.

"So, my pretty, nameless virgin, you want to be ravished, do you?" he whispered.

Five

Ravished?

Claire's blue eyes darkened with incredulity and disgust as she stared at the trampy looking girl with the frizzy blond hair and the purple hickey on her neck in *his* bathroom mirror. She could still taste him thrillingly on her swollen lips just as she could taste, smell, and sense disaster awaiting her in his house.

Her fists clenched as she eyed her reflection. "I don't know you! I don't want to know you!"

You want it. You need it—bad.

Loverboy's silken, silent taunt in her head.

"No!"

"I hear you," Loverboy's real-life, virile counterpart thundered from the other side of the thin, bathroom door. "You're talking to yourself again, Sugar-Baby!"

Sugar-Baby. Loverboy. They weren't real.

But he was.

Head throbbing, she sagged against the wall. How could this be happening? She couldn't hurt North after what he'd been through. She and North were the perfect couple. Everybody said so. He was the catch of south Texas. She was madly, madly in love with him.

Wasn't she? When she tried to think of North's dear, handsome face, instead, the image of a battered warrior's transfixed her. Merciless gray eyes, eyes as pale as the silver moon pinned her, claimed her soul, made every nerve buzz with sweet longing. The dream they shared was all-powerful.

How deliciously warm *his* long body had felt next to hers under his sheet. His mouth on her breasts had sent jolts of blind, carnal sensation through every part of her. And she was still on fire and aching for more of the same. Why did she feel her whole life had meant nothing till him?

A wave of dizziness swamped her. The lump on her head. That had to be why. Why she wasn't herself. Why she was in this mess. Spellbound.

She had to get out of here! Away from him! She had to break this blasted connection to a man who was utterly and completely wrong! Before he destroyed her whole life!

She touched the telltale bruises on her throat. They would be impossible to explain to North or her mother. This man had kissed her so deeply, consumed her almost…made her knees go so weak, he'd had to pick her up. After he'd carried her inside, he'd put on music that matched his mood. They'd danced and danced, their bodies moving as if they were one.

Now the CD thrummed faster than the wildest voodoo drums, and her own heart was pounding even faster.

Something crashed against his bedroom wall. What was he doing? On a shudder she backed against the door.

How could she get away from him? When every time she looked at him, she sensed his inner pain, his masculine need of her and was thrilled on some primal, female level. He turned her on, made her melt, made her feel utterly new and whole, made her feel that she belonged with him forever. Which was crazy. It was as if he were everything, and her real life, all her ambitions, her friends, her family, were nothing. As if this dream was real and lasting.

She had to get out of here. Make some excuse. No. She didn't dare talk to him.

Then what?

His bike was still at the mechanic's. If she could just get to her car, get it started, before he realized she was gone.... Maybe she'd have a chance.

When his hard knuckles rapped impatiently on the door, she nearly jumped out of her skin.

"I need to come in there."

"What for?" When he hesitated, she said, "Don't you have another bathroom?"

"Okay. But I'm done with the costume. I wanted you to see it."

"I'm sure it's great," she whispered.

"I even painted on a moustache."

"I...I can't wait...."

"Hurry." His retreating footsteps thudded heavily down the hall. A door slammed at the other end of the house.

This was her chance! When she tried to push the door open and peer out, hinges groaned loud enough to wake a corpse. Which sent her rushing noisily down the hall, careening down the steps of the porch, flying toward the garage and carport. She leapt into her car, slammed the door, and grabbed wildly for the keys.

They weren't there!

She almost wept. "Where?" she sobbed. "Where?" She fumbled under the floormat. Then she looked up and the constellation Scorpio danced above her.

"Where?"

"Right here, Sugar-Baby." His deep, gravelly voice made the skin on the back of her neck prickle. Keys jingled high above her head. She blanched when they disappeared in the high grasses behind his house. She'd never find them, never get away. She kept a spare set chained under her bumper, but there was no way she could get them now.

He yanked her door open and bowed low. "I thought you wanted to play pirate," he jeered, holding out his hand to help her alight.

She studied those long, lean fingers with the shading of hair at the center and felt her stomach go weightless. She swallowed. "Not anymore."

"You mean…not with me." His silken voice turned her blood to ice.

Moonlight streamed across his dark skin, across the carved angles of his brutal face, across the evil-looking moustache he had painted on. He ripped off the black patch that covered one eye and threw it to the ground. "Nobody plays me for a fool. Not even you—Miss *X*."

A strong blue vein throbbed in his throat. His gray eyes glittered. He was furious, close to some sheer edge.

"I'm sorry," she said thickly. "You obviously took a lot of pains with your costume."

His black gaze skewered her. "To please you, damn it."

He wore a loose, long-sleeved, white cotton shirt that was unbuttoned from his neck to his lean waist. Skin-tight denim molded his powerful, muscular legs. He'd even slashed the bottom edges of his jeans to look like pirate garb, and his brown feet were bare. From somewhere he'd found a red sash and tied it around his waist. A gold chain and coin glittered against the mat of black curling hair that shadowed his broad chest. His silver earring glinted from beneath the red kerchief that bound his ebony hair.

Loverboy. The pirate lover of her dreams. In warm, sun-bronzed flesh. With blazing silver eyes. Somehow he was more handsome than she'd ever imagined, more compelling, too.

She knelt and picked up the black patch. "I am sorry I put you to so much trouble."

"The prize I intend to claim makes it worth it." Erotic danger put a roughness in his low tone, added more fire to the intense silver eyes that raked her.

"I underestimated you."

"Likewise," he replied.

"You're angry. I know you feel rejected."

"You don't know me at all."

"Which is the problem—"

"Why did I think you were different? You want to play the same tired game. You wanted a fling…with the forbidden…with some rough-cut, low-class stranger the real you despises…before you tie yourself to your fancy, boring life and statusy man forever. You were using me."

"I'm-m s-sorry," she stammered

"You started this, sweetheart. But do you have the guts to finish it?" He seized her, his lips smothering hers almost violently.

Why was it so impossible to fight him? Her arms twined around his neck. When his tongue dipped inside her mouth, her tongue met his so eagerly he groaned aloud and then threw her from him.

"Go," he muttered, his voice savage, his eyes dark, almost agonized. "Go…before I change my mind."

But his kiss had started something that had to be finished.

"Don't be hurt—"

"To hell with you! Go home. Quickly. To your fancy boyfriend…. Go… before…something happens tonight we both regret."

She licked her lips, tasted him, and that only made her want him more. "You would regret it, too?"

"Does that surprise you?" he demanded. "That I'm not

all animal? That I might feel something? That I might attach some emotion other than lust to our little sexual encounter? You think you're so superior to me. I know your kind. Go home. Leave me be. I'm sick and tired of women like you—women who come looking for cheap thrills but who could care less about…'' He stopped abruptly.

Why did he sound almost injured…almost jealous…and angry, too? Even more angry at himself than he was at her? And so desolate and lonely?

Pirate costume or no, he was a real human being. Not some fantasy of her own imagination. Not somebody to use or tease for a night's pleasure. He wasn't a dream. He was real….

He'd dressed up for her.

Because he'd wanted to please her.

He made her feel special. For the first time in her life.

Don't listen to him. He did it for sex. He couldn't care about her…any more than she could let herself care about him.

North hadn't followed her from the party. This man had followed her into a dark alley and fought two thugs for her. It had been one against two. They could've been armed, but he'd fought for her anyway, had saved her life, risked his own life to do it. Then he'd seen to the repairs of her car, comforted her when she wept with belated hysteria, taken her home, protected her. She'd been so scared. He was tough, but nobody had ever made her feel so gently protected, so precious, so tenderly cared for as he did. And even angry, he did look darling in that costume.

Beneath his temper, there was genuine concern. He was scowling, yet she felt a melting sweetness inside her. She longed for more of his kisses, for his touch. For everything.

Which was insane.

Dazed, she stared at his dark, angry face in confusion, not knowing what to do.

He shrugged in disgust. Then he turned his back on her and walked away.

If he'd slapped her, he couldn't have made her feel more rejected.

Her heart and soul leapt with lightning speed. Then a still quiet voice inside her told her what to do.

Claire had no idea her life had changed course. Tomorrow the voices of family, duty, and grave self-doubt would scream louder than her heart. Tonight that still, quiet part of her knew that from the moment she'd met this man, he'd become everything.

Now he was walking away, and she couldn't bear it.

"No," she cried.

He kept walking.

Without knowing what she did or why, she started after him, slowly at first. Then she was running, hurling herself after his broad-shouldered form. Arms wrapping around him, she hugged him, pressing her face into his spine.

He turned slowly, read her beautiful face. In his eyes, did she only imagine she saw hope and joy as well as profound self-doubt and melting pain?

Breathless, her heart beating thunderously, she stood very still. Their gazes burned.

After a long moment his slow grin lit her whole being. "Make up your mind, sweetheart," he commanded in that low, hard voice she already loved.

When she flung her arms around him, he buried his face in her neck, his breath warm against her satin skin.

"This is scary for me, too," he whispered thickly against her hair. "Everybody I've ever cared for has left me. Even I...left me. I've been dead. I wanted to be dead. But you... *You. Why?*"

He began to kiss her, his lips, loving and gentle and yet hard, too.

Everything he did, everything he said, filled her with

yearning and made her forget all thoughts of wrong. Then he picked her up, swirled her round and round so that her golden hair was flying. Slowing, he stopped spinning and held her high above his black head. Just as slowly he lowered her so that every delicious inch of her body slid against his face, his lips.

Adrift in pleasure, her fingers curved around his neck, curled into the long, thick black hair at his nape.

"You're sure? Very sure?" he demanded in a raw, urgent tone.

She nodded.

He ran the back of his knuckles down her cheek. "You are beautiful. Exquisite. You make me come alive."

His next kiss was different, harder, more insistent with purpose and yet softer, holding infinite wonder. His hands moved over her, caressing her hair, her throat, every part of her. They slid under her shirt. Then he buried his face in her breasts, hugged her close, and sighed as if releasing some deep, bitter pain.

"Time to play pirate," he teased a long time later. More kisses followed, but these were playful. When they were both breathless, he dragged her eagerly across the grasses, to the wharf, to his boat.

He lifted her on board and began casting off lines. Soon the boat was drifting away from the dock, out into the moonlit bay.

"What are you doing?"

He ducked inside the pilothouse. "I'm a pirate abducting my pretty lady."

"This is a shrimp boat. You're a shrimper."

"...among other trades...." His voice had darkened. "You might be surprised.... But who are you—underneath?"

"I...I don't want to talk about myself."

"You want to play dangerous games. Let me guess. Soft

hands. Soft skin. Silky hair. Life's been very good to you. Money. Class. You don't have to work."

"I work very, very hard."

"Book work which is easy for you because you're smart."

"How would you know?"

"You're a reader."

"When I have time," she admitted. "You've probably been to good schools."

"The best," she said quietly.

"And you think me a poor, illiterate shrimper."

"You read."

His eyes held secrets. "You think I'm beneath you. Not good enough for a lady like you." He touched her, ran his hands boldly down her breasts, staking his claim before yanking her close. "Except for this," he said, his lethal gaze disconcertingly direct. "Sex. I'm good enough for *this.*"

"*This?*"

His rough hands were inside her shirt, all over her breasts. Her spine went taut as one hand flowed downward. "Us." His mouth was on hers. "Tonight. You and me."

"I don't understand."

"You don't want to. Lots of girls go slumming for thrills."

"Not me."

"Guys do the same thing." He made some quick adjustment with the engine and put the boat on autopilot. "But who am I to judge? You want to hear something funny? I want you to be different. Me to be different. *This* to be special."

What he said scared her, but before she could protest, he seized her, tossing her over his wide shoulder.

Kicking, her head lightly bouncing upside down against his spine, she screamed.

"Put me down!"

"You started this game."

Stomping swiftly down the stairs, he flung her gently onto his narrow bunk. She was scrambling to escape him when he grabbed her ankle and yanked her back.

"Me illiterate pirate. You fair, civilized lady." He thumped his chest which was as hard as iron. "Maybe tomorrow night we'll swing from the oak trees and play Tarzan and Jane." At her look of shock, he laughed. "Oh, I know, I know. There won't be a tomorrow. You want me to kiss you, get it over with—"

She squeezed her eyes shut and took a deep breath. That wasn't really what she wanted—

He seized her, kissed her, his heavy body tumbling on top of her, his dominant position making it easy to hold her down. She wanted to explain, so she kicked and squirmed as he unzipped her jeans, shoved them down her thighs.

Then his hand dipped into her.

Whatever she would have said to defend herself died on her lips. She went still in shock, but then began to tremble with pleasure. She squeezed her eyes shut, twisting away from him shyly and yet clasping him, too.

"You're so tight."

"I—I'm a virgin."

He hesitated. "There has to be a first time," he said quietly. "Do you want it to be me?"

She looked at him. Strangely, she did.

Why? She studied his dark face. Then she nodded. She didn't know why. She didn't care why. It simply was.

When his fingers encountered resistance, he pushed, stroking gently until she grew wetter and began to moan. In seconds he was past the barrier and he had her gasping and arching up to his palm, writhing, crying out, begging him to take her.

His fingers plunged. Deeply. Inside.

"Us."

She cried out at the exquisite pressure and yet felt a completion to be touched there.

He stopped and waited. Only when she begged him, did he continue. It wasn't long till pain became pleasure, and she went up in flames.

He grinned. "Me. You."

All too soon his low voice and caressing, expert fingers were too erotic for words. He sensed every nuance of response in her, stopping time and again, taking her just to the edge of satiation. *"Us."*

His eyes held hers. His finger stayed inside her. "Say it," he commanded. "Say *us*."

"Us," she repeated weakly, reveling in the intimacy of his touch and words.

His mouth stretched into a slow, triumphant grin. With a deft flick, his hand moved, and she exploded.

He let her rest. Then he ripped off his sash and blindfolded her.

She fingered the red silk that covered her eyes. "Why?" she whispered, afraid.

"Trust me."

She felt shaky, shy, unsure.

"Trust yourself. You've wanted this for years," he said. "If you hadn't met me, you might have lived your whole life without it."

No. She didn't want it. Or just sex. It was him she wanted.

"Now imagine you're on a pirate ship, its hold full of gold. I'm the pirate captain, and my sheets are red satin. You're my captive, my slave, part of my booty, and you have to please me or I'll give you to my men. Not really, for I have a jealous nature, and I covet you too much to ever follow through...but you don't know that. You think you must please me, or I'll sell you to the highest bidder.''

Her stomach knotted on a strange thrill.

''Strip, my lady.'' His low-pitched, hard voice made her shiver and go hot all over. ''Slowly.''

Loverboy's words.

''Strip, I said.''

A helpless feeling of inevitability possessed her. Somehow this man knew all her secret and most wanton desires.

She swallowed against the dry, hot lump in her throat and clumsily began unbuttoning the black cotton shirt he had loaned her. She heard his low groan of pleasure when she eased it over her shoulders, off her breasts and let it fall. For an instant or two she just lay there blushing because she didn't know where his eyes were and yet she could sense his excitement as they burned down her throat, her nipples, her navel.

Hurriedly, because she felt shy and unsure, she began pushing her jeans further down, and then curled into a fetal ball, trying to hide herself.

''No,'' he growled. ''Go slower. Stretch out...full length...like a cat in heat. Purr. Beg. Seduce...but make me wait.''

''I...I can't.''

''Tantalize me.''

''How?''

''You're a woman. And beautiful. Move. Undulate. Run your hand down your body. Open your legs.''

Shyly she curled her body into his and then bent one knee.

''Take my hand, sweetheart. Put it where you most want to be touched. Use it as you would...to pleasure yourself.''

''I...''

''Sex is more fun than anything else...if you let yourself go.''

If you're with the right man.

Some other force outside herself took his hand and put it beneath her knee so that he could run his hands up the inside of her thigh. Soon she was arching up to meet his caresses as he trailed lips and fingers everywhere.

"Kiss me," she whispered.

With his tongue, he suckled her breasts. Then he hooked his thumbs around the elastic of her thong bikini panties and peeled them down her long legs. "Now strip me, pretty lady," he said in that playful, harsh tone.

Because she couldn't see him, this was much more difficult. Blindly, she climbed on top him, straddling his lean waist. She swayed over him, her golden hair swinging loosely over his chest. He caught her wrist, blew a warm kiss into her palm that sent a tremor through her.

For no reason, the urge to trace her fingertips along his nose and brow seized her. Blindly she used both hands to learn with her fingertips the dark, carved beauty of his male features. It was a long time before she scooted her pelvis lower. Then her trembling hands trailed down his neck, down his torso to grasp the bottom edges of his shirt.

"Peel it off. Kiss me," he whispered, his breathing ragged now. Inch by inch, she pushed the white cotton back, trailing her lips upward over his lean, naked torso, then his furry chest.

"Unzip me."

She hesitated.

"Don't think. Just do it." He grabbed her hand, and she obeyed helplessly, not because he forced her, but because she wanted to. When she had him unzipped, he urged her to reach inside and touch him as he had touched her earlier, and when she did, that started everything.

In a microsecond he was on fire; in the next so was she. He paused just long enough to dig a condom out of a drawer and put it on. Then he rolled over, covering her completely. He pressed his tongue inside her mouth at the same moment his hips thrust deeply. She would have cried out, but his mouth smothered hers with kisses. He undid the blindfold. He began to move, thrusting again and again inside her, and each time he did, she felt more intimately joined, more completely, thrillingly his. He took her higher and higher into their dark whirling fantasy that was so much more wonderful and meaningful than her wildest dream. Crushed beneath him, she felt his arms wrapped tightly around her. Time and again he plunged, until finally he lost himself and all the dark desperation in his soul shattered on a tidal wave of desire for her.

When it was over, she lay in his arms, too shaken to move.

Sex.

Not just sex.

"Us," he had said.

He had claimed every part of her.

She regarded him shyly.

His dark gaze was even warier than hers, and his voice was infinitely changed. "I told you these are dangerous games, my lady."

"Why did this happen?"

He fingered the damp tendrils that were glued to her brow. "It's easy to become addicted to such pleasurable experiences. One or both of us might not want them to end."

"Every game has to end."

"If indeed, it's a game." He paused. "Love's a wild-card."

"Love?" she whispered softly.

"Sex then. Lust. Cupid's mischievous arrow. This. Us. Call it what you like. A night like tonight can change everything. Winner take all."

She turned her face away. "Lust and love—they're the same to you?"

He stroked his knuckles down the length of her spine. "When a man gets lucky."

"Like tonight?" she whispered.

His voice was suddenly dark, lost. "I thought I was playing a bad hand tonight. Then you came along."

"What do you mean?"

"Once I was good at games. The stakes were high—like tonight. But I was a winner—always…till the last hand. When I lost, I lost big. You're not the only one with secrets, my love."

My love. The endearment lit her soul.

He began to kiss her, and all too soon she was trembling, protesting, sighing, and then succumbing to the magic again.

The second session was sweeter, wilder. It lasted longer.

When it was over, they were too awed for words. But he stayed inside her and held her until she fell sound asleep.

She awoke some time in the night, every muscle in her body aching, but her heart more joyous than ever before. The beach house was awash in moonlight. Their bodies were joined, their arms and legs tangled in boneless contentment.

She had been dreaming her recurring dream of being wrapped in colored banners of silk.

"Unwrap me, Loverboy," she'd teased.

On their way back from the boat, they'd waded in warm, ankle-deep water, picked up feathers and shells. In his bed, she'd run a feather over his torso while his pale eyes raked her hotly as she drove him wild. He'd returned the favor, only he'd used it with far more skill than she.

Flushing in embarrassment, she relived everything she'd done, everything he'd done, every look, every wanton touch they'd shared. At the end, she'd been moved to tears,

tears of joy and tears of the loss she felt at the thought of not seeing him again. He made promises, such sweet promises, promises she couldn't let him keep.

When she glanced down at the floor, his pirate costume, the clothes he'd loaned her, as well as the feathers and silver shells littered the floor. Her soulful eyes studied him.

If he woke up, what would he say? Do? Want?

She was afraid of all she might want, so she forced herself to thoughts that cheapened what they'd shared.

What did a night like that make her? Was he right when he'd said she was no better than other girls seeking a fleeting thrill from a rough guy who was good in bed?

What did it matter what he thought? She had to put this incredible, this inexplicable night, *him,* all her longings, his passionate promises and understanding of her, behind her.

Only this morning she had her whole life figured out. She was getting married, going to medical school.... There was North. And her mother. She couldn't hurt them the way Melody had.

But, if she didn't get out of here and fast, she would. Some deep instinct told her, this man wanted her on a level more profound than anyone would ever want her, that all he might have to do was touch her to keep her.

Still, for a while she lay in his arms, savoring the warmth of his steady breath in her hair. Tears formed on her lashes. It was so pleasant lying here with him. So dangerously pleasant to recall all the strange and wonderful intimacies they'd shared.

Then he murmured an endearment, reminding her she couldn't risk his waking and finding her. Easing herself out of his arms, she dressed hurriedly.

But at the door she made the fatal mistake of turning to look at him. His male beauty stopped her dead. That final glance at his rumpled dark head, his lithe, bronze body, was all it took to make her heartbeats accelerate with fresh stabs of pain.

When she saw the feathers and shells and his black eye patch on the floor, she started shaking. With a muffled sniffle, she leaned down, picked up his eye patch, one feather and a seashell. Each treasure, she pressed to her lips.

When she stood up to go, tears began to cascade down her cheeks. Maybe that was why she didn't notice her change purse falling out of her handbag.

He made a sound, reached for her, and she fled swiftly down the hall.

Six

———

Tag awoke to the jaunty roar of her sports car and the squeal of tires bouncing off the curb of his driveway. Queasily, he shot to a sitting position just as a red car zoomed out of his carport and vanished down the road.

The cotton sheet he yanked back was cool to his touch. Her side of the bed was empty.

Her absence struck him like a blow. For a moment he couldn't breathe.

Good. He forced that thought. *She was gone!*

Like his mother. Like his father. Like the women who came to the bar and used him for sex.

For no particular reason his heart thudded so violently he thought it might implode.

Which was absurd. He hardly knew her. The last thing he'd expected or wanted was a fairy tale.

But she'd been so sweet. The sheets he'd brought home from his boat were spotted with her blood. He remembered how she'd clung to him at the end, how she'd wept, great wrenching sobs…because she'd explained, threading her hands through his hair, pulling his face down to hers. Because she'd loved what they'd done together more than she could ever express in words.

"I'm crying because it was so beautiful, so perfect…. Because I adore you."

Adore. That word, the sweet way she'd said it, with that look of utter vulnerability softening her fragile features had set off a furor inside him.

She wasn't like the others.

"Because you make me whole," she'd whispered, her luminous eyes burning him. "Because I can't ever see you again."

Words said during sex weren't to be believed. Still, he couldn't forget what she'd said. He'd said equally tender things to her.

"It doesn't have to be like that." He'd cradled her against himself, his arms wrapping her, believing in that moment he could protect her from all pain. "I care about you."

Her tear-glazed eyes had held his with a fervor so fierce, she'd mesmerized him. "If only—"

That was then—before the white-heat of their passion had slowed to a simmer. This was now—in the cold light of a new sun that blazed on the flat sea beyond his house.

"I'm not what you think," he'd whispered in that same nighttime voice and mood. "Tell me who you are."

"Shhh." She cupped his carved face as if he were very dear, put a finger to his lips. Then she'd kissed the edges of his mouth, the tip of his nose, his brow. Finally, she'd laid her soft cheek against his and snuggled so close to his body, he'd been totally enveloped by the perfumed warmth of her legs and arms.

Exhausted, not wanting to let her go, he'd fallen asleep in her arms.

But she was gone. Nameless like all the others.

They were adults. They would pick up and go on as if last night hadn't happened. She'd given him something to brag about the next time he got drunk.

As if he'd share her, in any way, with those bastards at Shorty's.

She'd been a virgin.

He'd been her first.

Which meant nothing.

Which did.

Tag combed his hands through his mussed black hair. He told himself he wasn't straining to hear her car long after it was gone. He told himself he wasn't listening to the gulls soaring beyond the trees.

Trousers nudged the door open with his nose, padded across the floor and laid his head on the bed and stared at him with hungry, glowing eyes. Which meant it was time for breakfast.

"Damn it!" Tag felt too lethargic to get up and get on with his day. He laid a hand on the warm fur. Trousers whined and began to lick his hand.

Old hurts rushed back, sharpened by the wisdom of his years. Tag remembered the wonder he'd felt when his father's wife had first led him into his charmingly furnished blue bedroom with its models of ships and armies of tin soldiers in New Orleans.

"Your father had me fix it up for you."

It had seemed like a dream. A dream he hadn't wanted to end even though he'd felt like a fraud.

Last night when she'd worn his clothes, praised his omelette, asked him to play pirate, he'd experienced that same young-again, bittersweet wonder that life could feel so good.

He hadn't wanted it to end.

"Who the hell was she, Trousers?"

Tail flicking, Trousers lay down on the floor to wait.

Wrap me. Unwrap me.

Blue eyes sparkling in the dark as she eagerly twirled round and round with the excitement of a playful little girl, pressing those pink shells over her breasts.

Strip, my lady. Slowly.

Tear-streaked eyes, a woman's eyes, memorizing his face right before she fell asleep in his arms.

Who the hell was this fantasy girl with the yellow hair who liked to dance and strip and make love with feathers? Who'd made him feel young again.

Who made him care. Who made him want to be a different man.

He'd wanted her. He'd taken her.

She'd willingly let him. End of story.

Despite her aura of class and money, she was no better than all his other cheap one-night stands.

She'd been a virgin.

It was over. So, forget her.

She'd gone back to her family.

When he saw the red scarf he'd used as a blindfold lying across the foot of the bed, he picked it up. The instant he touched it, he remembered undoing the knot, staring deeply into her eyes when he'd been inside her. And the memory of her sweet eagerness was a claw in his chest, tearing his heart out.

He felt nothing.

But he couldn't control his mind. Again he was in the cemetery on his bike, watching a girl with golden hair ride the wind. He saw her in the alley, half-naked...her eyes wide, terrified.... Those legs of hers that went for-damn-forever.

When Rusty had cut him, he'd been scared when blood

had gushed through his fingers. Scared they'd overpower him and hurt her. Scared they'd make her feel helpless and all alone, like he'd felt as a kid when the bullies had gotten him in back alleys behind his foster homes, when those thugs had nearly drowned him outside New Orleans.

But he'd kept her safe.

She'd been so beautiful. The way she'd looked at him. She'd been spooked…but spunky enough to stand up to him, too.

She was highbred, high-strung, ambitious. She was just like every other snob, who despised people who weren't like them. She'd made it painfully clear he couldn't be part of her life.

As he was going over every logical reason why he had to put her out of his mind, he saw her little black change purse on the floor a few feet from his bed. Groggily, he leaned down and snatched it.

The velvet was soft and elegant and sweet smelling…like the woman. Maybe her name or address was inside. Unzipping it, he shook out its contents.

A chill shot through him when a three-carat diamond engagement ring in a white gold, antique setting hit his palm. Eyes narrowing, he held the stone to the light in such a way that it seemed a faceted beacon emitting dazzling, fluttering bursts of white. She must've taken her ring off.

The brightness made him squint and caused hard lines to bracket his mouth. Sucking in a savage breath, Tag saw her in the arms of another, tamer man. This ring was a symbol of her attachment to that bright world that would never accept him.

His hand clenched on the rock so hard, a softer stone would have shattered.

What games would she play to get her diamond back? *Strip, my lady. Slowly.*

* * *

"Guilty conscience?" Melody's knowing smile was annoyingly cheerful when Claire stumbled into their mother's too-perfect kitchen in her trailing white nightgown and plopped wearily down on the stool opposite her sister.

"Guilty? About what?" Deliberately Claire kept her eyes downcast.

"What's with the ever-so-proper, Victorian nightgown? You look like you belong in another century with that high lace collar buttoned tight enough to choke you."

Claire pushed the prim lace ruffle higher. She'd worn the gown to hide her neck and because she knew the gown made her look virginal.

Which she never would be again.

Melody stared at Claire's pale features. Then she began to hum as was sometimes her habit. For some reason Melody reminded Claire of an unremorseful cat who'd swallowed a whole cage of canaries. Something was up with her.

Claire picked up a bridal magazine and began leafing through the glossy pages. White gowns. Wedding bouquets. She felt a drowning sorrow in her heart.

What had happened to the girl who'd believed—and not long ago—that such beautiful gowns were indeed magical, that her own wedding day would be wonderful, that she would make North and her mother very, very happy?

That girl had come blazingly alive in a forbidden stranger's arms. After that cornucopia of carnal pleasures, she might never be the same.

Claire forced herself to visualize herself frothily gowned in white lace, her train trailing the length of the sanctuary. But her imagination played a cruel trick on her, for it was the biker who dazzled her from the altar with a slow, heart-stopping grin—not North. She saw herself flying down the aisle, straight into her fantasy man's arms.

Dreams.

All her dreams had turned to dust.

A tear stung her lashes. She slammed the magazine shut. She looked up to sunlight filtering through massive French doors and brightening tile floors and chamois-colored walls and her mother's copper pots.

Dee Dee's elegant, fashionable kitchen seemed surreal. Claire shut her eyes, but that only made her conscious of the warring voices in her head.

"He means nothing."

"Liar."

"You won't forget him."

"I have."

"You're crazy about him."

"It was the bump on the head."

"Shouldn't you see him again...to make sure?"

"No."

"Afraid you'd change your mind—Sugar-Baby?"

Shut up. Shut up.

When the patio door slammed, Claire toppled from her stool. *"It's Mother!"* she squeaked

"So?" Melody whispered, watching Claire scramble back onto her stool.

"Hello!" Dee Dee's shrill voice rang from the hall. "Hello? Anybody up?"

Dee Dee had to be the perfect mother, the perfect hostess, the perfect wife. She had to have the perfect house. Thus, she arose early, especially when her girls were home for a visit. Even on such days, she was compulsive about walking and swimming before it got too warm or before her busy day got away from her.

Melody set her coffee mug down squarely on top of her mother's catalogues, house and garden magazines, bills and checkbook. "Seven-thirty." With an impish smile, Melody tossed her long honey-gold hair. "On the dot. Nothing's changed since we left home. You can set your watch by

Mother. And she's already got a half-dozen trucks in the front yard. Those men with the spiders are here. They're out there putting them in the trees. Yuck.''

Claire's heart wasn't in her smile. Only yesterday the thought of spiders and decorating for her wedding would have thrilled her.

The sisters were amazingly alike, and yet completely different. Both were slim, blond, and leggy. Both were bright overachievers. But while Claire was logical and reliable, Melody was intuitive and zanily impulsive. Claire was a dresser because she wanted to be admired. Melody reveled in the grunge look. This morning she wore a tattered, red football jersey that showcased her long, tawny legs. She wasn't wearing makeup, either. Still, in her own natural way, she was as beautiful as her stylish sister. Her sparkling smile made up for the lack of artifice and feminine wiles. And except for Dee Dee, who found Melody's flakiness unnerving, she was everybody's favorite, which was why, until last night, Claire had tried so hard.

Wearing a tight black swimsuit, Dee Dee whirled toward them like a human tornado. Her delicate blond looks and angelic smile masked a fierce will and temper. Baby, her devoted, snaggle-toothed Himalayan, was a fluffy white shadow chasing right behind her.

As always Dee Dee did at least three things at once. This morning while listening to a motivational tape, she'd watered her flower beds, completed her routine workout in her home gym, made lists for her maid and yard people, and then swum her usual number of laps in her swimming pool. Not to mention, she'd set in motion a project that was of uppermost importance to her—the spiders who were to spin webs in her trees.

Dee Dee had grown up in a crumbling plantation in Louisiana where tales were still told of a plantation wedding a hundred years ago. The father of the bride had imported spiders to spin webs in his oak trees. On the wedding day, he'd had gold glitter sprinkled into the trees, so that his trees had seemed to be draped in canopies of gold.

Dee Dee toweled herself off, unfurled the morning newspaper, set two new bridal magazines in front of Claire, eyed her to-do list, put out some fresh tuna for Baby, poured herself a cup of coffee, all while regarding both her daughters, especially Claire, avidly. Thanks to surgery, clothes, diet, genes, and an indulgent husband, Dee Dee hardly looked a day older than her girls.

Dee Dee frowned at Claire. "So, what's up with you two?"

Claire's tenuous smile fluttered. She pushed her high collar higher. "Nothing. I'm fine." Her voice sounded robotic, not hers at all.

Soon…soon she would regain her senses, and that little interlude with a nameless biker would make her even surer that her real world—her upper-middle-class parents, her sister, her acceptable friends, her academic record, her acceptances to top medical schools, even North—were the only things that could ever matter.

"You don't look well!"

"Bridal jitters," blurted Melody, who was her usual off-the-beam, intuitive self.

Claire swallowed. "Those spider men came so early. I'm…just a little tired."

Her heart wasn't threatening to explode, her burning eyes to flood. She didn't feel trapped or doomed in her mother's too-perfect house that somehow made all its occupants so edgy. She was thrilled to be home with her family again. Thrilled to be safe. Thrilled to be marrying North.

"But you're so pale, dear. There are dark shadows under your eyes. Have you been crying? You're not upset because your sister had that long talk with North last night, are you?"

"Melody? North?"

"I think it's wonderful they finally discussed—" Dee Dee noticed Claire's pallor and went quiet. "You're not jealous—"

"Mother!" said Melody.

"Melody was with North?" whispered Claire.

"When you ran out of the club," Melody explained. "North and I went looking for you."

"Where were you, Claire?" Dee Dee asked.

"Just…er…riding around."

"Where?"

"Please…please…don't meddle, Mother," Melody pleaded.

"Meddle?"

"Just don't, Mother—" Melody begged.

When Melody had jilted North, Dee Dee had been devastated. What had snapped her out of her depression had been having him to dinner when Claire was home for spring break. She had advised Claire to be sweet to him and had encouraged their friendship.

"Melody and North were in the living room till two, but I didn't hear you come in last night, dear," Dee Dee persisted. "You know how I worry when you don't come in and kiss me." She skimmed the newspaper headlines. "Oh dear…. Another one of those silly wars…"

"It was late. I didn't want to bother you."

"So, have you talked to North this morning?" Dee Dee demanded, setting her paper down and picking up the stack of bills.

Melody's gaze was strangely *alight*.

"Not yet," Claire said.

Oddly enough, she didn't care that he hadn't called. For no reason at all, Claire forgot Melody and North and her mother. Again she saw *him* standing in the pilothouse of his shrimp boat, barefoot, in nothing but his ragged jeans, the wheel sliding through his long tanned fingers, his hair rumpled and dark, his painted mustache and silver gaze more disturbingly attractive than ever. He'd caught her to him, placed her between himself and the wheel. She'd leaned against him and placed the black patch over his eye again.

He'd laughed, held her close, sheltering her in his arms. She'd felt so safe, so complete.

Forget him. It was a dream. Only a dream.

Then why did he seem so real?

"Your ring—" Dee Dee said.

"My...my what...?" Claire looked down at her hand. *Where was it?*

Then she remembered.

She fumbled for words. "I—I put it in my purse."

"Oh...dear...dear," Melody said. "You took his ring off. You *were* mad at North."

Claire closed her ringless left hand, thrust it under her hip to hide it. Then realizing the gesture was suspicious, pulled it out, held it up, flexed her fingers with an air of too-studied innocence. "Maybe for a little while."

"As long as you know where it is, dear," said Dee Dee, relaxing. She glanced at her watch and gathered up her checkbook.

Melody's curious gaze was fixed on her sister's white face.

"It's very expensive, dear," Dee Dee said.

"It's a priceless family heirloom. It was North's grandmother's to be exact," Melody murmured. "He told me all about it...a long time ago, of course...when he slipped it..."

Dee Dee blanched.

"What did you talk about last night?" Claire asked as she got up.

"You, of course," Melody said.

Nightgown billowing, Claire went to the fridge and pretended delight in the accumulation of snapshots, newspaper clippings of wedding festivities, and the tattered copy of the present month from Dee Dee's wall calendar.

In every photograph Claire was perfectly dressed and posed while the pictures of Melody were more offbeat. In one, Claire lounged on a towel in a white bikini and matching, see-through cover-up. Everybody had said she was so beautiful that day. Beside her, Melody, who'd had her friends bury her, was covered to her neck in wet sand. Even her honey-gold hair was caked with gooey sand. Everybody had laughed at Melody. Ignoring the glamorous Claire, the boys had heaped more sand on her fun-loving sister.

Claire read Dee Dee's calendar page that listed meetings, lunch, and the supper party tonight. Number three said, Claire. Bridesmaids. Luncheon. Nana. Country Club.

"Oh, my—" Claire gasped and then smiled. "I'd better wash my hair."

"I'll be in my office trying to scrape up enough money to pay for some of these. Hang your pink dress on your doorknob…so Lucia can press it. And don't forget to pick up your black sheath at the cleaners," Dee Dee said.

"Black? I'm not into fashion…but a bride…in black?" Melody asked.

"It has a designer label. It has a lacy collar that's white," Dee Dee retorted. "It was very expensive."

Black's your color, taunted an all-too-familiar, pirate voice in the back of Claire's mind.

Strip, my lady. Slowly.

Claire smiled a little too brightly. "I…I can't wait to wear it."

Oh, how she wished she could undo what she'd done. Oh, how she wished she'd never met the biker. In the past, lots of her friends had bragged to her about impulsive, one-night trysts. Alarmed and amazed, she'd listened to their whispered confessions about men who brought out their wild side.

But they'd all gone on with their lives.

Somehow, she would too.

Strip, my lady. Slowly.

Color crept up behind the high collar of her nightgown. For no reason at all her fingertips began to massage the bruised place on her neck where his lips had marked her.

Her friends hadn't been consumed with guilt and embarrassment. They hadn't hurt their families, thrown their whole lives away.

His name. She didn't even know his name.

Suddenly Claire was running from the kitchen, through the dining room, past the swirling stairs, down the long hall that led to her room on the far side of the house.

"Claire?" Dee Dee stepped out of her office. "Claire!"

Claire stopped. "What—"

"Why don't you borrow some of my concealer for those shadows under your eyes."

And for your neck, teased Loverboy.

"Shut up!"

"What dear?"

"Nothing, Mother."

Safe in her room, Claire fell across her bed and lay staring at her ringless finger as if her blood was sluggish and she lacked the energy to even rise.

Strangely what she wanted far more than North's ring was to know her fantasy pirate's real name.

Seven

Lush red bougainvillea dripped charmingly from the trellis above Claire's patio, adding just the right touch to her feminine bedroom with the antique canopy bed that had belonged to Aunt Sister, the aunt who had raised her mother. The bed had a pink bedspread that matched her overstuffed chairs and their floral slipcovers. Usually her perfect room was a refuge.

Not today.

Wet hair hanging over her face like a mop, wrapped in a towel, Claire was on her hands and knees on her floor. With trembling fingers she shook out her purse and then searched through the empty bag and the contents on her white carpet, her heart racing in panic.

She picked up the shell, the feather, the black satin eye patch. No ring!

Her change purse must have fallen out in his bedroom. Had he found it?

What would he do when he did?

What could she do?

Dear God.

Then she heard Melody singing in the hall, and her sister's voice was getting louder as she came closer.

Claire couldn't let on how upset she was; somehow she had to act calm and poised.

As fast as lightning, Claire shoved her purse and all its contents under her bed. Then she raced to her vanity and turned her hair-dryer full blast and began blow-drying her hair.

Melody came up close and shouted in her ear.

"So, where is it?"

Claire's skin went hot and clammy.

Melody pointed to her ringless finger. "Your three-carat wonder!"

Claire's heart thudded. "I-I don't want to talk about it."

"I bet you don't want to talk about where you went last night, either."

Claire sucked in a breath.

"North and I waited for you for hours," Melody continued. "Don't get mad. When you didn't come in last night, I covered for you."

"What?"

"Didn't you wonder who stuffed all those pillows under your sheets? I threw some of your clothes and hair rollers all over the place, and shut your door, so she'd think you were asleep if she checked on you this morning as usual."

"Thank you."

"I...I saw how upset you were when you left the party."

Melody's smile was so endearingly warm, it touched a soft place in Claire's heart. There had been a strain between them for too long.

"Oh, Mel— This wedding. It's got me so crazy. You wouldn't believe."

"Oh, yes, I would. Why do you think I ran? All those wedding parties! Having to live up to North's family's expectations…knowing I couldn't…. I was always wearing the wrong dresses, saying the wrong things. Do you remember how furious his grandmother got when I wore tennis shoes under my formal because I'd hurt my foot running? I was just completely overwhelmed. At least…last night…North and I talked it out."

"Why did you come home without telling us?"

"Have you ever done anything impulsive in your whole life?"

Oh, yes.

"I was afraid to call," Melody said. "I guess because I didn't know if you'd want me here."

"Oh, Mel… Mel…"

"I never felt so lonely and weird in my whole life as I did on that freighter to China. All I could think of was you and North getting married. I was afraid to call. I hurt…I hurt so many people. So, I just came home. I felt so guilty…like such a failure…and that just made me madder at all of you. Especially you…the perfect daughter…. Why couldn't I ever be perfect like you?"

"Me? Perfect? Everybody adores *you.*"

"They adore the clown. That's not me. I've always been afraid to play the straight guy, to be serious, to let anybody close enough to really know who I am. Even North. Not that he's important." She hesitated. "Even you. Everybody's proud of you. They respect you."

Respect.

If they only knew.

Strip, my lady.

"I…I can't believe…."

Swiftly they were in each other's arms. Their hug was brief, and afterward they shared a long quiet look.

"Thanks," Claire said. "Thanks for coming home. I—I think we're more alike…than we know."

"I owe you," Melody whispered, her eyes and cheeks aglow in a way they had not been for a very long time. "Maybe more than I can ever repay. I had to come home. I had no choice about that. But I'm sorry…about dancing like that last night. You ran out because of me. I—I felt so unsure of my welcome…. When I feel scared, I act crazy, so people will clap or laugh. Whatever happened, wherever you went, last night was my fault."

"I lost North's ring, Melody," Claire confided.

"Then I'll help you get it back."

Immediately, Claire regretted her confession. "No. No. Forget we had this conversation. Last night's our secret."

Claire looked at the red bougainvillea dripping onto her patio, so she didn't see her sister's gaze go to the mark a certain pirate's mouth had left on her throat.

"You know, Claire, I don't think anybody ever forgets anything. Especially not secrets or mysteries or anything having to do with sex."

"Sex! For goodness sake, Melody. You have the wildest imagination."

At just that moment Melody saw a length of black ribbon under Claire's dust ruffle. She knelt and picked up what turned out to be a black silk eye patch.

"Hmmm?"

Melody's curious gaze rose to her sister's flaming face. When she put the eye patch over one eye, Claire's heart thundered.

Carefully, she hid her panic. "Give me that," she said quietly.

Melody dropped the eye patch in her sister's open palm.

Claire closed her fingers, but just the feel of the warm black silk made her ache.

"Wild imaginations run in this family," Melody said softly. "Sometimes they're our downfall."

The swimming pool was the centerpiece of Dee Dee's flower bejeweled backyard that contained acres of well-manicured lawn and flowerbeds, terraces, a hot tub and a playhouse that was a perfect replica of the larger mansion. Winding gravel drives ran through thick clumps of yellow daisies to the various outhouses.

Still wet from their afternoon swim Claire and Melody, their eyes closed, lay side by side, not speaking, their paperback books face down on matching little wicker tables beside their chaise lounges. Yet, the sisters were very preoccupied with each other.

Even though Claire had to wear a high-collared dress, she'd played the happy bride to perfection at Nana's luncheon. She'd chatted easily with everyone, and had laughed constantly. She'd been so good that she'd fooled everyone, even herself…for a time.

But Melody had played the clown, stolen the show, entertained the crowd. All the old sibling rivalries had been revived. The minute the luncheon was over, Claire had felt completely drained. When she'd come out for a swim, Melody had followed her.

"I guess you and North plan to build a house like this."

Claire didn't want to talk about North to Melody. "Do you remember all the fights Mother and Daddy had over it?"

"Only bigger," Melody persisted, "because North is so much richer than Daddy."

Dee Dee had trained them both from birth that marrying a lowly doctor would never, ever do. Their mother knew this because she'd made that very mistake. In south Texas, a girl with social aspirations had to marry big money or old money. Oil money and the big ranch were the ultimate status symbols. Sam had a habit of digging in his heels when it came to spending the kind of money it took to impress the people Dee Dee wanted to impress.

Which was why Dee Dee thought North was so perfect. He had acres and acres of money, and all those cows and horses and oil wells to sweeten his legendary name.

Melody sighed. "Did you find North's ring?"

Claire's still face gave her away.

"Where *did* you go last night?"

Claire said nothing.

"Why do I feel like I'm playing Twenty Questions?"

That brought a fleeting smile.

"Who put that mark on your throat?"

Claire's hand rushed to her neck. But it was covered. She was wearing a high-collared shirt over her swimsuit. She'd even swum in it. Where, when, how had Melody seen the bruise?

Again Claire felt that damp, salt-laden breeze caressing her. Again, she saw a dark hand tracing her belly with a white feather until she shivered and pulled him on top of her.

"Did he dress up like a pirate?"

"I—I can't talk about it."

"But we have to get North's ring back."

"That's not so easy. Someone…someone I can't possibly see again…has it."

"This someone…in a black eye patch, who kissed you?" Melody's tone brightened. "Why do I imagine this someone tall and dark…and…and gorgeous…male, of course."

"Too male," Claire admitted on a breathy note. "And awful. Except…except he did save my life."

"And you repaid him with a torrid kiss—"

"No!"

"Then he stole it?"

"Don't tease. Not about this."

"Did he steal the ring, too?"

He stole a far more precious jewel, taunted Loverboy.

"What's his name?"

With a cry, Claire buried her face in her hands.

"Could I go get it for you—"

Claire flushed hotly. "Stay away from him."

"Claire, you have to get it back."

"Nobody must know about him. There are reasons, good reasons, why I don't want to see him again."

"I'm sure." Melody chewed on a fingernail which was how she always did her best thinking. "Look, do you remember that awful P.I.? That patient of Daddy's who didn't pay his surgery bill? The guy Daddy hired to find me when I ran out on North?"

"The guy you made walk the plank."

Melody laughed. "Him!"

"Why would he help you?"

"He couldn't swim, and I threw him a life raft. He's like a bloodhound. He'll get your ring back. When you have it on your finger again, you can relax and go on with your life."

Which was exactly what Claire wanted to do. "Why are you helping me?"

"You're my sister."

"What about North?"

"We worked out our differences last night. But our romance and North's love for me ended a long time ago." Melody fell silent. "I—I can tell you're upset about the ring...and about what happened last night, that's all," she whispered, her gaze drifting to her sister's high, white collar. "Some kiss, huh?"

Claire shuddered. Instead of the ring, she thought of a man who was tall and dark and slim, yet powerfully built. A man in a pirate costume with a jeering white smile, a man who'd slung her over his wide shoulder and carried her to bed. She thought of all the bold kisses he'd given her as well as the other intimacies they'd shared.

"I'm not nearly as upset about the ring as…as I am about him," she breathed, little chills darting up her arms. "That's why I—I can't hire your P.I. to go over there. I—I don't even know his name."

"Do you know where *he* lives?"

Claire rubbed her arms. "Rockport. Not far from our condo." Nervously she answered a few of Melody's questions and then stopped, immediately wishing she'd never discussed this with her unpredictable sister. "Melody, it's very important you don't do something rash. I have to be very, very careful. He's got a temper…and…and powerful feelings. If he finds out who I am…or where I live…if I make him angry…I… I…don't know what he might do."

Just thinking about him stripped her soul bare of all but a single truth.

A truth she did not want to see.

Melody's eyes measured her, and a dangerous flutter of emotion danced inside Claire.

Claire jumped up, grabbed her towel. "Forget what I told you, Melody. Just forget it. Forget him."

Melody rose and very gently flipped her sister's collar down. "What if I can't?" She studied the bruise. "What if you can't forget the man who kissed you like that?"

"Whatever you do, don't hire that P.I."

"At least then…you'd know *his* name."

Eight

The sleaze with the crowbar hacking at Tag's back door was a bowlegged runt on the wrong side of forty.

"That son-of-a...a..." Because of the thin, black boy beside him, Tag bit back a string of curses.

"Son-of-a-dachshund," Ricky Navarro, Tag's young friend, supplied with a mischievous grin. Ricky was eleven and atremble with excitement.

Too furious to smile back, Tag hugged Ricky reassuringly just as Whiskers plopped in the grass at his feet. Next Trousers, Tag's Border collie slunk by, his tail between his legs.

"Some watchdog you are," Tag muttered.

"He only barks at friends," said Ricky.

Several of his other stray cats and dogs moved through the grass with equal stealth. The group watched the incompetent intruder.

Crooks came in all shapes and sizes. This one working

on Tag's door had thinning hair and wire-rimmed glasses. He had a florid complexion and a spare tire around the middle section of his slight frame. He wore a black Stetson and black silver-tipped boots that matched his jeans. He was huffing hard and drenched in sweat. The guy was in lousy shape.

Tag's eyes glittered. His fingers tightened on the boy's shoulder.

This was about her.

For the past few nights he'd lain in bed dreaming about her coming back and the games he'd make her play before he gave her back the ring.

She'd had her fill of him, so she'd sent a hired hand to do her dirty work.

Tag hunkered beside Ricky in the high grass at the edge of the wood.

"Told you it wasn't a woman, huh?" Ricky's black eyes shone with their usual hero worship.

"You did good. Real good."

He'd been repairing a net on the dock when Ricky's skinny black legs had come pounding down the dock, shouting that there was a man breaking into his house.

"You gonna buy me another Millennium 2000?" Ricky whispered, black eyes aglow.

A Millennium 2000 was long for yo-yo.

"If it doesn't set me back more than twenty bucks."

"It won't!"

The boy began to fidget in the high brown grass near the twisted oaks with acute discomfort. "Hey, there's stickers."

"You should've worn shoes."

Wood splintered. The door fell off its hinges with a crash, bouncing down the steps. Then the bastard was inside.

"Ricky, you stay put."

"But I wanna see you kick some dachshund butt."

"Your Mama says you aren't supposed to talk like that."

"She talks like that every time she watches the Cowboys play and the other team makes a touchdown."

"What women tell us we should do and what they do themselves is different."

Tag crawled toward his house.

"What are you gonna do without your gun?" Ricky whispered.

"Shhh."

"Just in case he whups you or finds your gun before you do, I stuck an icepick in his front tire, so he won't drive off real fast the way that blonde did. She sure was pretty. Prettier than all the others…"

"You been spying on my house?"

"She had a shell and a feather. She kissed them. She was crying when she got in her car."

Tag hated the way his heart hurt.

"You gonna marry her—"

"I said shhh."

Stray cats scattered as Tag scrambled on his knees down the length of his breezeway. Curses and dishes exploded from the kitchen. As Tag raced down the hall, he noted that his usually tidy house was a shambles. Sofa, tables, chairs—everything had been turned over.

In the kitchen the man was bent over. Breathing hard, he slid an open palm across the dark insides of a cabinet. A single lunge from the doorway and Tag and the man were sprawled on the floor. Tag yanked his hair, got him by the throat. The son-of-a-dachshund's bulging eyes darted wildly. His arms flayed helplessly.

"What'd ya bet a pretty girl from Corpus Christi sent you?"

Their eyes clashed. When the man didn't answer, Tag dug in his back pocket and yanked out a wallet.

"Merle Mello. P.I." Tag snorted. "What's her name?"

When he didn't answer, Tag shook him. Then he leaned down and spoke very softly against his ear. "I want her name, Merle."

"You give me the ring you stole, and I'll give you the money she paid me."

"I'm not for sale, you lousy bastard. I'll give her ring back—but on my terms."

"Which are?" The man's voice held a tinge of nervousness.

"First, her name."

"I ain't ever gonna tell."

Tag laughed. "You wanna bet?"

A tangerine sky and a reddening sea bathed Claire in a pink glow. In her white shorts, with her hair swept away from her face in a headband, she made a pretty picture on her daddy's yacht, *Fanta-Sea,* as she scrubbed a stanchion. Claire had decided it was time, way past time to make up with North. Since *that* night, they'd talked once. He was busy at the ranch, he said, working some nights till midnight, trying to get ahead before their wedding. She'd said she'd let him work, that she would concentrate on the wedding. Their brief conversation had been cool and strangely stilted as if each of them were holding something back.

Tonight she was going to change all that.

The preacher was coming over to talk about the ceremony tonight. North was supposed to have called to find out what time an hour ago. So, why hadn't he?

Claire wasn't concentrating on her handiwork nearly as hard as she was polishing. She was too aware of seconds ticking by, of the orange light behind the skyline deepening and darkening. Too aware that she really didn't care if North ever called. These last few days with him out of the picture hadn't bothered her nearly as much as they should have. What bothered her were memories of a man she had to forget.

It was a funny thing about the people who owned yachts. They might have maids for such menial chores at home, but they performed these same tasks on their boats themselves. Sam Woods, who wouldn't even reach down to put a dirty sock in his hamper, loved cleaning his boat. When he wasn't onboard polishing teak or chrome, he could usually talk his wife or a daughter into doing it.

She had used polishing as an excuse to get away from the house, away from all the perfection and pretense of her life. She needed to prepare for the preacher and North, time to think more positively about her future.

Strangely, the salt-laden air and the lapping of the water made her remember those same sights and sounds from the night she'd spent with the biker. She still didn't have a clue as to how she could get her ring back. Melody kept begging her to let her hire that detective, but she kept telling her no.

When her cell phone finally buzzed, Claire dropped the toothbrush and dug frantically in her purse for her phone.

"North?" she breathed. With an effort she put more excitement in her tone. "Darling, I thought you'd never call—"

"Hello, Claire." The hard voice shook her to the core. Her feet felt leaden. Her heart raced. She sank to her knees, pressed the phone against her ear.

Dear God—

When she could breathe, she whispered, "Who...who is this?"

But she knew.

"You little liar. You know damn well who—" His voice was deeper, gruffer. "Captain *X.*"

The name and the memories that went with it sent a shiver through her.

"But maybe it's time you had a real name to go with the motorcycle and the pirate costume...and your fantasy lover, Captain *X*. It's Tag Campbell."

Tag Campbell.

Just his name stung her heart.

Oh, God, he'd found her.

She began to tremble.

"I have something you want," he purred. "Something valuable."

"Oh, yes.... Yes, you do." Her words were barely audible.

"What price are you willing to pay...to get it back?"

He sounded so cruel, so changed.

"I...I'm through playing games."

"You shouldn't have started this one then, pretty lady."

Why was he so angry? "No—"

"Yes!" he rasped. "Think of this as a simple business proposition. I have something you want. You have something I want. You give me what I want. I give you what you want. It's real simple—sweetheart."

"But I don't know what you want!"

In the lengthening silence she began to shiver.

His deep, dark voice bit. "Was I so easy to forget?"

His question brought tumult. Guilt crept over her. Pain seared her.

No way could she tell him that every night she'd lain in bed for hours, unable to sleep, remembering how scared she'd been, remembering he'd saved her from those thugs and been so sweet afterwards. No way could she admit that all her dreams were of him now.

"You were very easy to forget," she said.

"Maybe it's time I made more of an impression," he muttered thickly.

Seething sexual tension charged the silence. Before she could reply, he hung up.

She sucked in huge gulps of air.

The phone rang again.

"He-hello," she stammered, her voice strange and hollow and yet…and yet eager, too.

"You sound excited," North said matter-of-factly. "Sorry I'm so late calling you. What time do you want me to come tonight?"

Nine

Tag picked up his straight razor and then threw it into the lavatory. He was going to Corpus—to see her.

The thought both angered and excited him. Just as her soft voice had angered and excited him when she'd called him darling, thinking he was her fiancé.

She'd slept with him, but she called another man darling.

Tag strode into his bathroom and turned on the shower. Then he caught a glimpse of his dark, unshaven reflection in the mirror and frowned. His black shirt was dirty. So were his jeans. He'd worked hard on the boat for nearly twenty-four hours, driven his captains hard, too. He'd worked long hours in the restaurant. Much of his drive came from an effort to quit thinking about her. It hadn't succeeded. Nothing had. Still, the catches had been good. His captains had done well, too. Business at the restaurant had never been better.

Money. He'd always been good at making money. Too good.

"It's your gift," Frenchy had said.

A gift that had nearly destroyed him once.

"You're like a money machine," his father had said.

His father had used him, ruined him, despised him—
betrayed him.

You're damn sure no son of mine

*I didn't do it. Hugh couldn't have. You did. Nobody
knows as much about the business as you.*

Except you.

You're not taking me down.

You were born in the gutter.

Whose fault is that?

You've got her bad blood.

Yours, too.

Salt crusted his skin and black hair. He stank of sweat,
saltwater, and dead sea things. He craved a shower, clean
clothes, a hot meal. No, he craved her and despised himself
for the hunger.

He turned off the shower.

For any other woman he would've showered and
primped.

Not for her.

Not tonight.

And he'd smell worse by the time he got to Corpus.

He could almost feel the warm clean water splashing his
skin, soothing his nerves; almost feel freshly pressed
denim.

Not for her.

His life had been hellish ever since she'd left.

For himself he washed his face and brushed his teeth.
But that was all. When Trousers barked and bounded into
the bathroom, soft brown eyes aglow with love, tail thumping against his leg, Tag knelt and embraced his wet dog,
knowing full well the dog smell would cling. Let it.

Since she'd shared his bed, Claire Woods had rarely been

off his mind. He remembered her taste, the silkiness of her hair, the sleek texture of her skin as he'd entered her.

You were very easy to forget, she'd whispered in that sexy, scared tone that tore his heart out.

When he finished roughing Trousers's ears, he didn't bother to comb his own hair. Halfway out the back door, he stopped, then stomped back inside, opened a cabinet and grabbed a bottle of cheap gin. This he splashed all over his grimy T-shirt. Then he hopped on his bike and gunned it.

''We're playin' by my rules tonight, pretty lady.''

An hour later he was in Corpus Christi. The evening sea breezes were cooler against Tag's sunburned face as he braked his big bike in sun-dappled shade. From there, he studied the numbers on the houses.

Her tall white mansion was like a punch in the gut. The white pillars reminded him of his father's home, of his own former life. Like his father's, this mansion could have been in a photograph in one of those glossy home and garden magazines. Her street was a wide, tree-lined avenue with large houses built to impress and set back on spacious lawns.

A young red-haired mother pushing a stroller with a plump toddler glanced his way. Ducking her head, the woman hurriedly changed sides of the street and raced away from him.

Lady, you didn't even get close enough to get a whiff.

Suddenly he regretted the gin and not showering and changing. What was he trying to prove? He felt as ashamed as when he was a kid and the son of the town's drunken cocktail waitress who slept around. People used to avoid his mother and him. The kids at school had despised him, never seeing him as human.

Then his father had taught him how to dress, taught him what it took to make people admire him. And for what?

Frenchy and the other shrimpers he knew were a rough

bunch. They didn't care much about following other people's rules. Tag had been hiding in their midst so long he'd nearly forgotten who he was. But this house and this street and this woman made him remember who he'd been and all that he'd wanted.

He studied her front door so long that his throat closed up. Then he swallowed against the dryness, removed his helmet, and swung a long leg over the leather seat.

Maybe he would've lost his nerve, but her front door swung open. A woman with a beautiful smile and thick masses of straight, honey-colored hair held out her hand to him.

Not Claire. Not as pretty as Claire. But nice in her own sparkly way.

When he clasped her hand, she puckered her nose the way a kitten sniffs the air. "Dog," she murmured. "And?"

He smiled. "Gin."

"Shrimp, too." She pinched her nose and then laughed, looking him over. "My. My. You and my sister?"

"Is Claire here?"

"She's around…somewhere. I'm Melody."

Instantly charmed, he smiled. "Tag Campbell. I should've showered—"

"But you're like me—impulsive. Not like Claire—who isn't."

"People can fool you."

Again, she smiled. "So you met my sister that night when she was driving around—"

"Is that what she said?"

Again Melody smiled. "She hasn't been too talkative lately."

"Stress," he whispered. "Brides are under lots of stress."

"Especially brides that don't want to be brides. How well I know." Her smile grew warier when she led him into the foyer. "You be quiet now, and we'll try to find Claire without stirring the rest of the pack up."

"Thanks."

Except for the voluptuous wallpaper, the mansion was amazingly like his father's on the inside. There were the same gleaming oak floors, the usual antiques, the glittering silver-framed photographs of family and celebrities on the grand piano, the same crystal rose bowls with their warmly glowing candles.

The wallpaper was really something, though. Lush, boldly colored flowers seemed to grow out of every wall, to race across the high ceilings above him so that he almost felt he'd stepped into an exotic garden.

From some nearby room he heard the clink of silver and china as well as subdued voices.

Where was Claire?

Melody attempted to lead him swiftly by the partially closed doors of the formal dining room, but a woman's sharp, curious voice stopped them.

"Darling… Melody?" The shrill voice went higher. "What's that smell?"

"He's come to see Claire."

The woman got up. She was beautiful, golden, thin. Like her daughters.

"I thought North—" The blond woman pushed the doors further apart. She wrinkled her elegant nose in disgust. "What is that awful smell?"

"Me," Tag said.

"Gin," the older woman corrected.

"You do know your liquor," he said.

"Cheap gin," she declared.

A plump man in wire-rimmed glasses and a clerical collar stared in outrage.

The rumpled bear with a thatch of silver hair slouching in his chair, turned. He knew trouble when he saw it. One look at Tag, and he bolted his red wine. "And just how would you know our Claire?" Claire's father demanded.

"She had car trouble. I helped her."

"Then why hasn't she once mentioned you?" the mother demanded, her tone shrill.

"Because she had too good a time and she's no dummy," Melody suggested, slinging gasoline onto the flames.

Whoof!

Mr. Woods shoved his chair back from the table. "I've told her and told her not to ride around in that car at night. That she could meet the wrong sort—"

"Let me handle this," his wife commanded.

Mr. Woods poured himself more wine. "You must've scared some sense into her. She's sure been underfoot a lot more. She won't even go out with North."

"Maybe we shouldn't speculate," said Melody. "Maybe we should go straight to the source."

Tag heard light, nervous footsteps and pivoted.

Claire.

Tag sucked in a breath when he saw her. So did she.

Silence.

Breathless, her cheeks pink, a tiny pulse pounding in her throat, she was incredibly sexy in tight jeans and a snug, white T-shirt that molded her slim curves. She looked clean and lovely and fresh as he was foul and stale. So lovely, his anger lessened, and he wished he'd showered and changed for her. All he wanted to do was wrap his arms around her.

"I've been working on the boat with my men," he said as an excuse.

Her huge, blue eyes fastened on his face and didn't let go. She went paper-white, took a step back, faltered and stood still.

"Where's North?" demanded her father.

Silence.

"I thought North was coming," her mother pressed.

Claire's cheeks flamed. "He is."

"Well, this...this man is here to see you."

"He won't be long." Claire's tone was clear and cool, and so dismissive it made Tag's stomach knot. And yet her eyes and the bright fire in her face made him burn.

"Can I fix you a drink?" Melody offered, her sympathetic voice so light it cut the tension. "Gin your special poison?"

"Scotch and water," Tag said.

"Claire?"

"Nothing. Thank you."

Ice cubes clinked. Melody handed him the drink, and Claire quickly said, "Let's go out back...to the pool."

He smiled. "I could use a swim."

Her lips barely moved. "Don't make this harder."

She turned abruptly and fled across the living room, about to slip through a pair of tall, double doors. Beyond those doors stretched a vast expense of greenery, terraces and a swimming pool.

He raced to catch her at the door. Holding it open, he bowed low, as he had the night he'd made love to her.

"Please...." she begged.

He downed his drink and might have set it on an antique table had not Dee Dee, who was right behind him, said, "I'll take that."

"Thank you, Mother," Claire said.

"Claire?!? Don't be a fool. Are you really going out there—alone? With him?"

He turned to catch the mother mouthing frantic entreaties to Claire who was waving goodbye by fluttering her fingertips.

"I'll be fine, Mother," Claire said. "He won't hurt me."

Tag shut the door, and after another long exchange of

glances and fingertip fluttering between mother and daughter, the older woman marched off in a huff.

"Alone at last," he whispered.

"You stink like a brewery."

"Gin," he corrected. "Among other things."

"Did you drive your motorcycle all the way from Rockport drunk?"

"Would you give a damn?"

"Answer my question first." Underneath her anger, she was pleading with him somehow.

"I haven't had a drink for days. Not till the one Melody just gave me. I've been working too hard. Falling into bed every night with a book. Not that I can concentrate on what I read. I pass out with exhaustion, the book still open on my chest." He didn't say he'd done all these things in a futile attempt to forget a woman with long golden hair who reminded him of an angel riding the wind.

In the quiet evening afterglow, Claire was as incandescent and fragile and lovely as the most exquisite white orchid. She smelled sweet, too.

"It's your turn," he whispered, moving closer.

"What?" Instinctively she backed away from him into the shadows.

"Would you give a damn if I drove drunk?"

"Naturally, I wouldn't want you to hit an innocent person...."

"But you don't care what happens to me?"

He let his gaze drop from her pale face—to her mouth, her neck, her breasts—then for good measure, he reversed the order.

"You look good, Claire."

She wet her dry lips.

"Too good."

A hot dangerous spark lit the air between them.

"Do you have the ring?" she whispered.

"You don't care?" he repeated in a hoarse voice. "That's why you want this exchange to be quick and easy?"

"Why torture ourselves—"

"Is that what we're doing?"

"You don't fit into my life. I told you that."

"What if I was different?"

"You're even wilder than you were the first night."

A primal awareness fluttered between them.

"You liked me that night," he reminded her.

Her voice was softer, hesitant. "You're a shrimper. I'm going to be a doctor."

"Do you give people labels? Is that the only way you can think? I've been other things besides a shrimper. I could be more." His voice was darker, deeper. "I'm a man and you're a woman."

"Don't—"

His lips scarcely moved. "You think you're so superior to me. You sent that man to tear up my house, like I'm nothing, like my house is nothing—"

"I don't know what you're talking about."

"Merle. The P.I. you hired."

"But I didn't—"

"You didn't give a damn what he did as long as you got what you wanted. You wanted to play pirate. You wanted sex. Now you want to forget me. You want your ring back. You're used to getting what you want effortlessly."

"Not...not everything."

"Name one thing you want and don't have."

She stared at his mouth. Then she touched her own lips with her fingers. "Please...please just give me the ring and go."

"Maybe I've missed you. Maybe I'm curious as to how you've really been, too."

"I told you I'm fine."

"You don't look fine. You look upset. Scared."

She whirled angrily. "Because you're here."

"You don't really want to marry him."

"I do."

"How come you slept with me when you're engaged to him?"

"I...I wasn't myself. That...that bump on the head... those guys.... I was so scared.... Temporary insanity."

"You were a virgin. You'd never slept with him. Don't tell me you couldn't have if you'd wanted to."

"North isn't like you. He never pushes himself on me sexually."

"That's mighty suspicious behavior."

"To a man...with...with your low instincts maybe."

"The girl who wanted to play games with a pirate has no low instincts?" he mocked.

Her face burned. Her voice shook. "North would never come over here...filthy...to deliberately humiliate me."

"You wanted me."

"This is all Melody's fault."

"Charming girl. At least I know who to thank."

"She danced for North the night I met you. She used to be in love with him, you see, engaged even. I didn't like the way he watched her. I ran out because I was...jealous. When I met you, after those guys in the alley, I didn't know what I was doing."

"This isn't about Melody. You knew exactly what you were doing. You wanted me. You still do."

"I want my ring."

"You can have it." He paused. "But for a price."

"W-what...what do you want?"

"A kiss."

"That's insane." But her soft, slightly breathy gasp warmed him.

He smiled. "I know."

"One kiss?"

He nodded.

"Just one?" She drew another quick breath. "And you'll give me the ring?"

A smile brushed his mouth. "That's what I said."

"Okay," she said quickly, closing her eyes, tilting her chin up to his, and puckering her lips.

He was tempted, mighty tempted by her beauty, by her sweet, soft scent, most of all by her lips. But unlike her, he wanted to prolong the moment.

When all he did was brush her hair back from her face, she jumped, her eyes snapping open.

"Uh-uh." He grinned down at her. "You have to kiss me."

"I can't believe you're making me do this."

"Believe it."

She reached up, and he felt her lips peck the side of his throat, just under his left ear. A single flutter of breath and fire, and it was over.

"On my lips," he ordered.

"You didn't say—"

"That's what I meant."

Even before she did it, he felt his blood race like a heat wave and his heart pound like he'd been running hard. Only he hadn't moved. Once she settled her mouth on his, once she started, he wasn't about to let her stop.

Cautiously her lips settled on his, and he felt a rush of pure, sweet sensation. His chest tightened. He opened his mouth, answered her kiss. And was stunned she let him.

When he wrapped her in his arms, she clung, shuddering.

After all the lonely days and nights, holding her was heaven. She closed her eyes. Kissing her was ecstasy.

"I want more than one kiss," he whispered, his eyes burning into hers. "You know that, don't you?"

She swallowed, but she didn't pull away. Instead she pressed herself against him, put her arms around his neck, caressed his face with her light fingertips. Then her mouth found his again.

The second kiss was sweeter and lasted longer and told him how much she'd missed him. He caressed her face, and the longing that cut through him cut through her, too. They began to shake.

"You have the softest lips, and the hardest body," she murmured.

"Claire, is everything all right?"

Her mother's voice cracked them like a whip.

Claire stiffened, pushed him angrily away. "You got what you wanted," she whispered. "So, give me the ring." Then in a louder voice, she called to her mother. "Yes…everything's all right, Mother."

"North's here."

"I'll just be a minute, Mother."

When Tag tried to pull Claire back into his arms, she drew a quivering breath before pushing him away. "He's here. You've got to give me the ring and go."

"You don't love him."

"I will. I swear I will."

"But you don't now. And you never will. And deep down you're afraid I'm right."

Impulsively, she feathered protesting fingertips against his lips. Just as impulsively, he began to kiss those fingers.

"Please…. I'm begging you."

"The road to hell is paved with good intentions," he said, a desperate tone tinging his voice. "I can't get you out of my mind. I thought I'd die if I didn't see you again. Only now that I've seen you, I feel even worse."

"So do I. I'm marrying North Black. I want my ring. If I'd met you under different circumstances…but I didn't. If you were different…"

If he wasn't a low, filthy shrimper.

"All right. You win." He yanked the ring out of his pocket, but instead of giving it to her, he knelt before her like a besotted suitor.

"Hand it to me!"

"And I thought you were a romantic." He took her hand in his, and the minute he stroked her fingers, felt how they shook, some of the anger left him. He pressed his lips against her fingers, held on to them tightly when she tried to tug them away.

"Do hurry," she whispered.

"Did North hurry that night?" he rasped. "Or did he get on his knees like this when he proposed?"

"Don't—"

On his knees, in an attitude of lover-like worship, Tag pressed her hand to his lips again. Only this time he kissed each finger, sliding his warm tongue between them, causing her to shiver.

"Don't you dare do that again!"

"Did he dare? Do you drive him wild the way you do me?" His low voice was savaged by emotion. "Claire, I can't forget you. No matter how I try. I lie awake and think I can't live without you beside me in that bed. I've never felt so alone. I'll quit shrimping. I wasn't always a shrimper. I can be what you want. I can make money. Lots of money. It's easy for me. There's nothing, Claire, nothing I wouldn't do for you or give you. Did he say these things to you?"

Claire was ill-prepared to deal with the ferocity of his mock proposal, and the passion in his voice brought a sigh to her lips, for North had proposed in a brightly-lit restaurant. He'd been on the run because he had to get back to the ranch. In separate cars, she'd driven back to school, and he'd driven back to his ranch.

"Just give me the ring," she said, refusing to dwell on the disappointment of North's proposal.

Tag slid the ring over her knuckle ever so carefully. "You have beautiful hands. Did he tell you that?"

"Be quiet about North, do you understand?"

"Don't marry him."

"I have to."

"The night I met you, I was at the cemetery. I'd just buried my best friend."

"I'm sorry."

"I hadn't known what a friend he was till... I was scared. God, I was scared. Then you were there. Like a magical being, lighting something inside me that had been dead for years. A comfort in a dark hour."

She ran a finger lightly over his eyebrow, down his rough cheek, over his smooth high cheekbone. "I'm sorry about your friend." Her voice died away. "Most of all I'm sorry about—"

"Claire, are you still out there?" Her mother's voice slicing the darkness again.

"Coming—"

"Be happy," Tag said.

He didn't know if she heard him because she was already running away, past her mother, into the house.

"Show him out the back way," the mother snapped out coldly to a silent figure behind her. The door slammed, and he felt diminished.

Again, he was that lost little boy outside his father's house in the dark.

Ten

Melody glided toward him through silvery light and gray shadow. "Let's go, Tag."

Numbly, he felt her take his arm as she led him around to the back gate.

Back gates were for servants and other undesirables.

For little boys not worth keeping.

For smelly shrimpers in rough, work clothes. But long before they reached that gate, a liquid movement in a ground-floor bedroom jolted Tag out of his self-pitying mood.

Hair flying behind her like a golden banner, a slim girl ran inside.

Claire. His angel riding the wind.

She flung a wild, lost look around the room and then hurled herself onto her bed. There she buried her head in a wadded pillow and lay still. Her phone rang, but she ignored it. Her fluffy white cat bounded up to her patio door, stretched full length, and began pawing the glass.

"That Claire's bedroom?"

"I shouldn't tell a man like you a thing like that." But her smile said yes.

They stood in the shadows together and watched Claire's slender shoulders heave and her fingers claw her bedspread.

"She's been like that…since the night she met you."

"Hasn't she been with *him?*"

"North? Not once. Tonight's the first time. He's in with Mother and Daddy and the preacher. Nobody but you and me know what's really going on."

"And what's that?"

"Claire and I… We're all mixed up. We've got to get straight."

Melody pointed toward another square of light that was partially obscured by lush climbing roses. Like players, the three figures framed in that glowing cubicle kept mouthing cues, looking toward the door, waiting for the lead actress to come on stage.

"Why don't you go in there and keep that bunch entertained for a spell?"

"You mean you want me to run interference for you?"

Somehow he knew Melody was on his side. "Maybe it's me, who's running interference for you. How come you came back and danced for your sister's man?"

"Sometimes a girl's a fool and she throws away the only thing she really wants."

"The trait must run in the family."

She smiled. "What makes you think you're what my sister wants?"

He pulled Melody close and whispered something into her ear.

She grinned. "I'll do it. It's so dumb it just might work. I'm a little jealous I didn't think of it."

She vanished into the house.

Claire. He was a fool to stay, a fool to scheme. But he couldn't stop watching the way light sparked from the fall of butter-gold hair that hid Claire's features. He ached from watching her slender body quiver on every sob.

This beautiful, special girl had gone to bed with him. He'd been her first man. But she'd been first with him in other ways. She'd pulled feelings out of him, thoughts too, along with secrets that had been festering inside him way too long. He'd been in hiding—from the world, from himself. Frenchy had tried to tell him, but he hadn't cared enough to do anything about it. Not till her.

Like an angel riding the wind, she led him out of his dark cave and set him free. She'd given him comfort, shown him what it was to have feelings for a woman that were good and clean instead of shameful.

He stood in the dark and watched her cat paw the glass. Claire never looked up.

What was that black ribbon she was holding, kissing?

When Melody pranced into the dining room, her mother's face flashed with annoyance. Worse, the tall, tanned rancher turned to stone.

His and Claire's lives weren't the only knots in this tangle.

Tag stepped toward her cat and let it sniff his boot. Then he picked the curious animal up and rapped on her door.

Claire looked up. With glistening eyes she stared straight into his heart.

Chemistry. Neither of them could stop staring once they started.

The cat meowed and began to lick. He felt like a fool in his dirty clothes, holding her sissy cat. Hell, her fiancé was here with the preacher.

But she stepped toward him. As if in a dream, she opened the doors, and took the fluffy, purring bundle of fur clinging to his awful shirt. Her cat had a flat, white face, pale blue eyes and a snaggle tooth that made it charmingly ridiculous.

"She likes you," Claire whispered.

"And she's no mongrel…like my pets."

"But they have pure, gentle hearts."

"Indeed." He paused. "Did it ever occur to you…maybe I do, too?"

"Yes." Her hoarse whisper sounded torn.

She collapsed against his filthy shirt, and he folded her nearer. "Don't cry, baby." Holding her so that her head was tucked under his chin, he sank with her to his knees. "I can't go. Not till you stop crying," he soothed.

"I have to marry him. It's what girls like me are supposed to do."

"Says who?" His voice was soft, almost fatherly.

"You don't know my family. What they expect—" In a few choked words she sobbed out the whole story, about Melody jilting North at the altar, about her mother's smashed hopes and social ambitions, about having to be the perfect daughter to make up for the son who'd died before she was born.

"I don't care what your reasons are. You can't build a life on a lie. I know. I tried."

"I have to make my family happy. You and me—we just met."

He stroked her hair out of her face. "We started something that's bigger than both of us."

"We'll get over it."

His hand froze on her cheek. "How?" The ache in his heart made it hard to breathe. "Are you so young that you really believe that? Do you really think you can make yourself have feelings you don't have?"

"Yes. Mother says—"

"You're a woman now, Claire. You may be young, but it's time you made your own choices. You can't make anybody happy if you don't do that, least of all yourself. Come away with me. We'll go somewhere. For coffee maybe. Just to talk.''

''I have a date with North.''

''Your first—since me.''

''I've…been too busy.''

''Or preoccupied with dreams of me.'' He opened her hand, and his eye patch fluttered to the floor.

She flushed guiltily.

''We are good together,'' he said. ''It wasn't just a game. That's why you don't want to see him.''

''I couldn't sleep with you…and then…just start up with him like nothing happened.''

''That's reassuring.''

''I'm serious.''

''So am I.''

''He's my fiancé.''

Tag scowled.

''Tonight, I really need to talk to him—to try to get to where we were before—''

''Before *us*.''

''There is no us.''

''Make it an early date, and come out with me.''

''No. This…'' She caught her breath. ''This, *us*, whatever it is, has to end.''

''What if we can't end it?''

''We can.''

''If it's so easy, then prove it. Prove it yourself.''

''How?''

''I'm going home. Come to me there.''

''Alone?''

''Then meet me at Shorty's.''

''Shorty's?''

''You remember that bar that played the music we danced to? If you don't show, I'll be drinking to your future happiness. To your wedded bliss. If you come, if you can dance one dance, maybe play a game of pool, have some fun with me…and then walk away…then I'd know for sure you don't want me.''

''I could do it.''

''Prove it.''

''I have a date.''

The thought of her with another man filled him with panic. So Tag blurted what he had to say, quick and fast. ''That didn't stop you before.''

''I'm not like you think.''

''Neither am I.''

Claire's eyes widened as the flat countryside swept past in a frightening blur. Her fingernails dug into her armrest. Not that she dared ask North to slow down.

He was in one of his moods, his dark hands fisted around the steering wheel. He hadn't said one word about her tight, red dress. She might as well be invisible. He hadn't once looked at her.

What had she expected?

Claire watched the speedometer needle inch upward. North was a careful man who rarely speeded.

She shot him another worried glance. Beneath the brim of his Stetson, his dark face was deathly still. He was driving fast, as if something was eating him up on the inside.

''Did the preacher say something that bothered you?'' Claire whispered in a demure tone that did not match her dress.

''It isn't *him*.''

''But something's bothering you?''

''I'm a little tired.''

''You're scaring me.''

He lifted his foot off the gas. ''What do you feel like doing tonight? How about a movie?''

They usually went to movies when North got like this. She suspected he preferred sitting in the dark, not talking, to a more intimate date.

"I'm not exactly dressed for a movie," she said a little flirtatiously.

A muscle tensed in his hard jawline. He did look at her then. If he were pleased at all the effort she'd gone to to make herself beautiful for him, he didn't show it. His eyes flared wildly with the look of a wild creature caught in a trap.

"Let's go to Rockport," she urged too gaily. "I—I need to pick up something at the condo for Mother." Just the thought of Rockport got her a little breathless.

"Fine," he said. "Whatever you want, Claire."

He lapsed into a heavy silence that made her increasingly uneasy as flying center stripes vanished too rapidly beneath the car. His grim silence was unnerving her. Did he suspect? The fingers she pressed against her window shook. She flipped on the radio and hummed along to the tunes the way Melody sometimes did.

North pushed a button and turned the radio off. "Don't hum!"

North barely said five words at the condo, but one of them was yes when she asked if he'd take her to Shorty's.

They braked in Shorty's garishly lit, crowded parking lot. When she opened her own door and jumped out, a rough-looking bunch of bikers whistled.

"That dress…" North blurted.

"You finally noticed."

He stared.

The offshore breeze ruffled her hair. This same, prevailing breeze had made all those leaning sculptures out of live oak trees around *his* beach house.

The breeze's salty caress brought memories of a man she couldn't forget.

Music thrummed in the parking lot, the same sort of music they'd danced to outside the beach house.

She was here to prove to *him* she could forget him.

She tossed her head defiantly. The wind rippled through her hair and made her feel wilder.

"You sure about this place?" North asked.

"Very sure," she said. "I've heard the band is good."

"How exactly did you hear that, Claire?"

Without answering, she flung the door open and stepped inside to howls and more whistles.

"You got a date tonight, honey," a soft, silky voice purred behind Tag's ear.

He turned and through a blur of smoke, he saw yellow hair and a shapely figure in a tight red dress. For a second or two his heart raced, just till he realized she wasn't Claire.

God, just thinking *she* might show tonight had him wired.

"I'm waiting for a particular lady." His fingers moved up and down the icy beer bottle.

"Do I know you?" she whispered.

She should, but she didn't.

His silver eyes glazed. "Not really," he replied.

"Your face. Your body. You seem familiar."

He stared past her toward the door.

When she went back to the bar, Tag slouched lower in his shadowy corner table. He'd showered, changed. Dressed in jeans and a black shirt.

A dull pain had settled in his gut. The thought of Claire coming here, to this place, to him, to prove anything, was pretty far-fetched. The girl who'd wept in his arms wasn't about to risk awakening that shadow-sister inside herself again—the one who craved him for her midnight pirate fantasy.

Maybe he was better off. If he'd unleashed her, she'd

done the same for him. Since he was a kid, he'd always wanted a better life, a real family. But every time he'd reached for the stars, doors had slammed shut.

The dimly-lit, crowded bar throbbed with music, women, voices, smoke, and laughter. Men slouched over pool cues and green tables and sent balls clicking and flying.

Except for the blonde, people were mostly leaving him alone. They weren't as angry as they'd been right after Frenchy's death about Frenchy leaving him everything. Rusty and Hank had disappeared. Most people believed the coroner. Some were even beginning to admire the way he'd gotten a tight handle on Frenchy's empire so quickly. He had plans to expand, create jobs and pay solid wages.

The door opened.

The shrimpers at the bar kicked and stomped in time to the music. Wolf whistles. Shouts. Applause.

Tag's gaze jerked back to the door.

Claire, standing in a pink pool of neon light, her pale face frozen in the garish glare as it had been that first night. The music speeded up. Everything and everybody blurred but her.

She wore a tight red dress and her hair fell wildly about her shoulders.

No bright angel tonight.

Tonight her shadow-self had come alive. The gorgeous woman in red pulsed with a wild, dark energy that turned his blood to lava.

When she saw him, she flicked her tongue wetly across her lips and locked her blue gaze on his mouth.

More wolf whistles.

What the hell was she trying to do?

In that dress, with her body, she was setting more fires than she or he could ever put out.

Somebody put a few quarters in the jukebox. The fast beat charged him and gave an edge to the atmosphere. Tag got up slowly, intending to hurry her outside as fast as possible.

But a tall man in a Stetson stomped through the door, assessed the crowd's response to Claire and circled her shoulder with a muscled, proprietary arm.

North looked fierce enough to give even this wild bunch a run for their money.

North—the man she belonged to.

You cheated, Claire.

A feeling of inevitability thrilled Claire at Tag's volcanic expression when North put his hands on her.

"Let's go, Claire," North said.

She shook him off and rushed deeper into the bar, choosing a table as far from the door as possible. North caught her. He yanked back his chair so fast he nearly knocked their table over.

"What's gotten into you? You're acting like *her.*"

"Who? Melody? You don't even see me."

"Well, you've sure got the attention of every other man in this room! Their tongues are mopping the floor."

"Maybe I need a little admiration."

Their waitress arrived. North seethed. Claire ordered two beers.

The door opened again, and a slim figure slipped inside. North shot halfway out of his seat and then fell back heavily. "What's *she* doing here?"

Passion! Livid, pure passion vibrated in North's molten, dark tone now. But he wasn't looking at her.

Melody had captured the spotlight, captured North's full attention. Again, Melody wore tight black jeans and that silky white blouse that caressed her breasts.

When she oozed by him, North sprang out of his chair again.

Slim hips undulating, Melody walked past him without

so much as a glance. Shrimpers hooted. Her smile was sexy, but for the most part, she ignored them all and headed straight for Tag.

Not Tag.

Please, not Tag.

It never took Melody long to steal her friends.

Sure enough, in the next breath Melody was leaning over him. Her arm had wound around his waist, and she was whispering in his ear. With that white grin that lit a fire in Claire's heart and made her eyes sting, he signaled the guy by the jukebox. In the next instant North's favorite song, the same husky melody Melody had danced to at the party filled the room.

Blushing and grinning, Melody broke into her madcap routine. Inspired, she raised her hands above her head and began that same quirky dance that had left North so cold.

But Melody wasn't dancing for North. She was strutting to the music like a rock star on stage. Tag leaned back in his chair like a sultan watching a favorite harem girl. With an appreciative grin, Tag egged her on with suggestive comments. Meanwhile, the shrimpers were stomping and clapping.

Shock filled Claire's throat with a salty taste. She couldn't bear watching her sister captivate Tag as all her special friends had been captivated.

The music got louder. "Get her!" a man said.

Claire heard North's snarled curse.

Melody's terrified cry cut the brittle air.

North sprang out of his chair and shoved the big man who'd grabbed Melody out of the way.

"Don't you dare touch her, you bastard!"

Then he had Melody in his arms, Melody who was protesting every step of the way as he half-dragged, half-carried her from the bar, leaving Claire inside alone.

Claire rose dizzily to her feet. She had to get out of here.

"Claire!" said a husky voice behind her.

Tag's heavy hand fell on her shoulder, spun her around. His haunted, silver eyes burned through her to the bone. Then she remembered Melody and the way he'd looked at her sister. Claire backed away from him in confusion.

"I didn't think you'd come," he said.

"What about Melody? What am I—your consolation prize?"

"No. I asked her to dance for me the way she had for North—to get to you."

Everything but his stark, dark face blurred.

"That was a low-down, dirty trick you pulled," she choked.

"It was so rotten, I thought it might work," he replied tenderly.

As usual his slow, irreverent grin worked a spell. It was crazy. But somehow she believed him.

"You want to dance?" he whispered.

She nodded. "Why not?"

He shot the shrimpers a look that made them turn back to the bar, resume their conversations. His glare toward the pool tables caused a mad scramble for pool cues. Balls began to fly. Somebody put on a slow song as Tag pulled Claire close.

Snugged against his powerful body, she put one hand around his neck. He brought the other to his warm lips in a sweet, loving gesture. Her response was so involuntary she shut out everything except him. It was as if he and she were the only man and woman on earth. As if she'd come home.

He released his hold a little, dancing with her as if she were a virgin at her first prom and he her shy, awed date. "I'm glad you came, Claire." His expression was infinitely gentle.

She hadn't expected to dance like this, to dance sweetly,

tenderly in her wild red dress in this wild, bad place. She had come looking for something else. Maybe he had, too. She had thought to prove he was bad. To prove that only the bad in her could want him.

But he was both passion and tenderness. He made her feel as pure and cared for as he had that other night when she'd been so scared. Her fears and jealousies dissolved. She felt loved and cherished.

He was more than she'd bargained for. As she was for him. Not that she was ready to accept this truth.

She pressed her head against his chest, heard his heart.

He caught his breath and laughed a little. "I never thought I'd find anything like this...in a place like Shorty's."

Neither had she.

Then the door swung open. North loomed in the doorway, his black eyes bleak and dark, his expression harsh.

"You coming home with me, Claire?"

A flutter of panic went through her when she heard the finality in his voice.

"I have to go," she whispered.

"You have to choose," Tag said, tightening his grip on her. "Me or him." His gaze seared her.

"I want you. You proved that. But that doesn't change this. I have to go home with him tonight."

"Choose."

When he saw she already had, Tag's hands fell. His whole body was tense and coiled. Not so much as a muscle in his dark face flickered. "A lot of doors have slammed in my face. If you go, we're done for."

North hurled himself back outside. Without knowing what she did, she flew after him.

Tag felt the door slam behind her in every cell in his being. He sank down into a chair, his face as still and white as bleached stone. He ordered a beer and stared at the door.

"You're losing your touch, Campbell," the bartender said.

Everybody laughed.

Not that Tag gave a damn. Another door had slammed in his face.

Claire was gone.

He'd offered his heart to her, and she'd turned him down flat.

Several beers later, the crowd had begun to thin.

Tag studied the handful of men playing pool. Shrimpers. Men who hadn't had much school. Stubborn men who didn't like to be pushed around. Tag respected these men, but—

But he wasn't one of them. He had a college education. This life, their life—wasn't enough.

There was nothing wrong with being a shrimper. But the life fit men like Frenchy, not Tag. It wasn't his game. Running Frenchy's little empire couldn't thrill him. Not with his experience. Once he'd invested millions of dollars, his father's money, other people's money, and his own.

He belonged in a fancy office. He'd been an investment banker, buying risky businesses, turning them around and then selling them. He'd dealt in big numbers, the same way his father had. He'd been an expert on all kinds of real estate and businesses, all over the country. He'd been a developer, too. There were fat bank accounts in New Orleans that still had his name on them.

He had to go back.

He had to face his father and everything else he'd run from.

"Feeling lonesome?" purred the blonde who'd hit on him earlier. Again, her face blurred. All he saw was golden hair and her tight red dress.

Damn, he wanted Claire.

He'd spent long nights dreaming of her. His body still

ached from their dance. He smiled slowly. "You parked outside?"

Her car was at the edge of the lot, almost hidden in the shadows. When he opened her door, she threw her arms around him, but her slow, hot kisses left him cold.

He hungered for something else entirely—for sweetness, not experience.

For love.

Not this cheap imitation.

For Claire.

This woman tasted of beer and cigarettes and too many other men. Suddenly he felt sick to his stomach.

"Sorry," he said, pulling away.

"Sorry?" She began to laugh. "I'm the one who's sorry. Sorry for wasting my time on a pathetic joke like you. *She* doesn't want you. She thinks you're trash."

"Maybe. But she made me want to be a better man."

She slid inside her car and slammed her door. "A better man? Ha! You're a loser."

Tag stepped into the shadows and watched her drive away.

That's when he saw Claire in North's car.

Eleven

North's arms were folded across the steering wheel. The windows were down. Salty air and the music drifting out of Shorty's filled the car.

"I dreaded telling you this, Claire."

"I'm glad we finally talked," she said gently as she slid his large engagement ring over her knuckle.

"You're ambitious, reliable, respectable—"

She cringed. "Respectable?"

"What I'm trying to say is you really ought to be the perfect girl for me." He fingered the ring, held it up to the light so that it winked at them before he slipped it into his pocket.

"You don't love me. Melody was always between us, even when she was gone," Claire said.

"I don't love her either!" he lashed. "She's just a bad habit I can't seem to kick."

"You sure that's all she is?"

"Melody and me?" He laughed harshly. "You think I'm ever going to forget how she came up to me in that church full of our friends and family? How she took off my ring, handed me that big white bouquet like I was a bridesmaid or something. She looked so sad. When I touched her face to try to calm her, she jumped like I'd shot her and said, 'I can't.' Then she hiked her skirts and ran back down that aisle like a high-stepping French dancing girl."

"She cried her heart out later."

"Melody is like some actress, only it's her real life she lives on stage. I'm tired of it."

"You galloped off after her that day. So did everybody else."

"I made one helluva fool of myself." He gritted his teeth. "Nobody ever made me so crazy. I ran till I passed out. When I came to, I was still holding that damn bouquet. She was gone, and everybody was laughing. Everybody but you."

"She sure stirred you up tonight."

"Me and that whole bar full of men. What was she thinking of?"

"Maybe she still loves you."

"So what if she does? Do you think I want a wife like that? She's too wild. I'm too tame."

"Tame? You should have seen yourself carrying her out of Shorty's."

"My family's way too conservative. Melody says I put her in a cage. And that's what I want to do half the time. The other half I want to strangle her."

"You never once looked at me the way you looked at her tonight."

"What would any man do with a woman like that? China, for God's sake. She took a freighter to China! She was the only woman on that ship. Anything could've happened to her."

"And she made that P.I. Daddy sent walk the plank!"

"Don't remind me. I want to forget her."

"Oh, North." Claire hugged him. "Good luck."

"What about your mother? How's she—"

"I'll handle mother."

North started the car. "I'd better get you home."

As he backed down the drive, the door to Shorty's swung open and Tag stepped outside, his arms around a clingy blonde in a dress a size or two too small for her. The woman's hands were all over Tag.

Suddenly Claire couldn't breathe.

"Isn't that the guy you were dancing with?"

A lump thickened in Claire's throat. She couldn't speak. All she could do was watch them glide together toward a sleek dark car in the shadows. Instead of getting in, they began to neck. Mouth to mouth. Body to body. Claire couldn't believe he let that woman kiss him like that.

But she did believe. He'd mentioned others before her. Classy women on the prowl. She'd been a fool to think what they had was so special.

The couple stopped kissing. The woman got into her car and drove away. That's when Tag saw her.

"Take me home, North," she pleaded. "I'm tired. So tired."

For once North read her. "Maybe it's not as bad as you think."

"It's probably worse."

"Then how come she drove off alone?"

His alarm buzzed. The bright glare of a new sun spilled across Tag. Tag blinked. He'd been dreaming of a slender girl, gold spilling down her back. They'd been dancing.

Awake, all he remembered was how hollow he'd felt when she'd run after North and slammed that door.

He flung a muscular brown arm over his eyes.

Whiskers, a plump roll of purring black fur at the foot of his bed, yawned.

God, his head ached. Had he really drunk that much?

He didn't want to get up, face another day without her.

A shadow flitted across him.

Then somebody slammed a fist on his alarm button. Tag sprang to a sitting position so fast sheets and a fat black cat went flying.

Ricky Navarro stood frowning at him from a pool of white light near the window.

"Hell, kid! Haven't I told you not to sneak up on me like that?" His thick voice was blurry with sleepy confusion.

Ricky shrugged and then spun his yo-yo in a defiant arc, caught it, and tossed it out again. But for all the flash, his timing was off. "You don't look so hot," Ricky attacked, his mood defensive. "How come you're still asleep?"

"I don't feel so hot."

Ricky stared moodily out the window.

"How come you're not in school?"

The yo-yo spun out furiously, wobbled and went limp at the end of the string like a dead thing. Something was definitely up. Tag grabbed the string and used it to pull the kid closer.

"Hey, fella, what's wrong?"

Ricky wouldn't look at him. "This…this mean guy Terry said something I didn't like. Pushed me down when I was running to the bus. Made the other kids laugh. Then the bus doors slammed and the bus took off. Without me."

"So? What are we going to do about it?"

"I don't like Terry. He's big and white. I don't like school much, either. Everybody's white and rich but me."

"No. Sometimes it just seems that way."

"I feel all alone."

"Hey." He pulled the string, brought Ricky even closer.

"Other kids. They've got problems, too. But I gotta meet this kid, Terry. I'm gonna drive you to school."

"But I'm scared."

"I'm scared, too. Everybody's scared on the inside, kid. It's something we've all got to lick or hide. You might as well start with this Terry."

"You got a Terry?"

"My Terry isn't just one person. It's my whole, messed up life. The kind of life I want. I just lost something I really wanted, or rather somebody I don't deserve 'cause… 'Cause… It's complicated. I've got to go home, go back where I came from, find myself, face something…deal with *my* Terry, I suppose. If I can do that, you can do this."

"Do you really think so?"

"You need to dream big dreams, kid. That's the only way to turn your life around. But it's not enough to dream. You gotta start makin' 'em happen."

"You're not marrying North?" Dee Dee's whisper was ragged.

"No, Mother." Claire's voice broke. "No…"

For once in her life, Dee Dee wasn't doing three things at once. "I feel like I'm dying," she said weakly.

"So do I, Mother. Why don't we sit down…together?"

Dee Dee had just stepped out of the shower. Still dripping, not bothering to dry herself, she stood stiff and still in her white terry cloth bathrobe. "I…I need to make my bed."

"I'm not going to medical school, either. I—I was just doing that to please you and Daddy."

Blood pounded in Claire's temples. The room felt stuffy.

"I don't believe this."

"It's time I figured out who I am, what I want."

"Way past time, Claire." Dee Dee dropped the quilted

coverlet and sank back down onto her bed. "The wedding is almost here."

"I thought I made it clear. North broke up with me last night. There isn't going to be any wedding."

"But you two talked to Reverend Bob. We all did," Dee Dee said disbelievingly.

Claire shook her head in despair.

"What will everybody say?" Dee Dee asked quietly.

"Tell them I'm sorry, or that it's better we found out now...."

"Better? I'll never be able to hold my head up in this town again. Better? This is all your fault." She pressed her hands against her head. Something ugly flickered in her expression. Her pretty mouth thinned. "It's because of *him*, isn't it?"

"I don't know what you're talking about."

"Don't start lying now. No wedding. No medical school. Next, you'll tell me you're in love with that drunk shrimper and that you're going to move into some trashy trailer with him."

"Tag. His name's Tag Campbell. And...and... He wasn't drunk, Mother."

"I know cheap gin when I smell it! He reeked!"

"He poured a whole bottle on himself because he was mad at me."

"What kind of lout would even think up a trick like that?"

"And...and he doesn't live in a trailer. Not that I'd care if he did. He has a beach house."

"You've been there—"

"I...I didn't want to tell you like this...but I—"

"Oh, Claire, you're such a little fool. A man like that, a man who doesn't even bathe—"

"Usually, he does. He's a hard worker and he gets dirty."

Dee Dee's unsmiling mouth hung ajar as she looked up at her daughter. "And how would you know his habits? Oh, God— Rough men like that only want one thing from a young girl like you. He probably thinks you're rich. Oh.... You've been too sheltered. You have no idea. Tell me you haven't slept with him—"

Claire's face caught fire. She ducked her head, so her mother wouldn't see.

"Oh... Oh.... He forced you then? We'll hire lawyers. No. No. Then everybody, all my friends would— We'll—"

Claire swallowed.

Dee Dee buried her head in her hands. "I don't believe this. This is a nightmare."

"Did you ever love Daddy?"

"That's a ridiculous question."

"Is it? Did you just marry him for..."

"What?" Dee Dee pressed her fingertips to her forehead. "How dare you insult *me?* Don't you dare compare my marriage, my life, to the mess you're making of yours. Oh, my head. My aching head. I thought you were different. Not like Melody. I was so proud of you. You were my easy, perfect daughter." She lay down slowly. "Pull the shades." Her voice was weak, fading. "The sun is making my head worse. I—I can feel one of my heat headaches coming on."

"I—If it makes you feel any better, Mother, the shrimper is through with me, too."

"Thank God." Dee Dee pulled a coverlet up to her chin. "Now...now go."

It was nearly eleven o'clock before Tag roared home on his bike. The session in the principal's office had gone well. Like all bullies, Terry was more chicken than tough guy.

Inside his beach house, Tag felt almost as scared as

Ricky when he sat down by his bed and picked up the phone.

Claire. The last time he'd seen her, she'd watched another woman kiss him.

He had to call her. Just on the faint chance…he'd been wrong about her and she would listen to his explanation. He set the phone down, lifted it again, at least half a dozen times. But every time he punched out her number, he got all sweaty, same as that bully Terry had under fire.

What the hell was he so scared of?

He punched the numbers again.

"Hel-lo," a woman said, as if from a deep well.

"Is Claire there?"

"Who is this?" The pained voice perked up a little.

"I said I want to speak to Claire."

"I won't get her unless I can say who is calling."

"Tag Campbell."

"You!" Dee Dee's voice screeched. "She just told me you two were through! Leave her alone. She's a young, innocent girl. A man like you can offer her nothing but trouble. Do we understand each other?"

"You said if I told you who I was you'd get her, Mrs. Woods."

"I lied." She hung up.

He slammed the phone down. Then he sat hunched over in silence for a long while, fuming, brooding.

To hell with Claire and her mother. Claire wanted North, her nice safe life, and there wasn't a damn thing he could do about it.

With grim dread he picked up the phone again. This time he called his father.

The old man took his time coming to the phone. He didn't sound much like himself either. His voice was thin, thready, far weaker than Dee Dee's had been when she'd first answered.

"You're alive," the old man whispered. "Thank God." There was a long incredulous, joyous silence. "I thought— You don't give a damn what I thought. Just come home— son."

Son.

The word resonated inside Tag long after his father spoke it. There was a labored pause.

"We have a lot to talk over," continued his father. "I'm afraid there's not much time."

Melody was throwing tangles of clothes into a huge purple duffel bag that had big yellow butterflies all over it.

"Where are you going this time?" Claire asked.

"I know somebody in India." Melody's voice was brittle.

Melody had friends everywhere.

"What about North?"

Melody's pain-filled eyes locked on hers for a brief moment. Then she grabbed a pair of her thong panties defiantly. "You sure you don't want these?"

Claire shook her head. "You and he—"

Melody looked down. With shaking hands she began to fold a blouse. "He made it very clear in the parking lot last night that he hates me."

"Did he kiss you?"

"Such a kiss. I think he hates me. Really hates me. My lips and arms are still bruised. He said awful, awful things. Every time I think about—"

"He broke up with me. He loves you."

"Whatever he feels, he makes me feel awful. Trapped. Why did I ever like him so much? I don't want to ever see that stuffy, bossy, impossible individual again. He had no right to…to…to hold me against that wall and…overpower me."

"North did that? Your little dance must've—"

"I don't want to talk about it." Melody drew a deep, indignant breath. "So...you and Tag—"

"He left Shorty's with another woman."

"Maybe you didn't see what you think you saw."

"He kissed her."

"Maybe it wasn't like you thought."

"You give him the benefit of the doubt, but not North."

"When a man isn't your guy, you can see clearly. Tag loves you. He's good for you, too. You're not just going through the paces, living somebody else's programmed life. Dee Dee's programmed life." She picked up another pair of thong bikinis. "Trust me. I'm your sister."

They fell into one another's arms, but quickly grew embarrassed and let each other go.

"I don't want you to leave."

"I'll be back," Melody said.

"When?"

"When I feel like it."

Twelve

The shrimper had called, for God's sake.

Dee Dee lay in the dark. If only she could sleep. But her head throbbed, and her heart ached.

Children. Daughters. Maybe Sam had been right to want sons so much.

None of her grand plans for the girls had panned out. How did other mothers raise children who did what they were supposed to do? She was chewing on this puzzling problem when she heard Sam's diesel Mercedes chug up their drive.

Dear God. What was he doing home at this hour? She had no time for him right now. He would fuss about something trivial that had gone wrong at the office. Some patient threatening to sue him, a case gone wrong, or a diagnosis he was clueless about. Worse, he might be hungry. If she didn't fix him something, he'd cook, and the kitchen would look like he'd set off a bomb.

He stomped through the front door, yelling her name. "Dee! Where the hell are my golf clubs? Dee?"

She pressed her temples. Why couldn't he ever find anything?

When she didn't answer, his footsteps trudged up the stairs. The bedroom door was thrown open. He flipped switches. Lights blazed.

He was so thoughtless. She was dying. Not that he who lavished sympathy for a living on strangers, would care.

Even from under her pillow she could hear him rummaging through one of his drawers in that maddening way of his, rooting out mismatched socks, underwear like a giant hamster on the warpath. As usual he dumped an entire drawer onto the floor.

She groaned.

His bulky torso whirled. His quick smile was both thrilled and surprised.

She frowned at the paper cup he'd set on their chest of drawers.

"Why didn't you answer? Why are you in bed?" he demanded, his tone miffed.

She rose, dragged her robe around her aching body, and went to him. "You barge in here, and in the space of one minute, you've turned this side of the room into a garbage bin. And what is that—" She jabbed a manicured nail at his cup.

"My milkshake, damn it!"

She snatched it off the wood. "You're on a diet! You're supposed to snack on that vegetable soup in the fridge I made just for you."

"If I eat one more veggie, I'll become a celery stalk."

She began to cry. Baffled, his arms came around her. The robe slipped off one shoulder, exposing bare skin, and suddenly he got interested, albeit, not in her tears. With a groan, he drew her close, kissing her gently and then not so gently.

"Why are you home?" she whispered, pushing him away.

"It's Wednesday, my afternoon off. I was going to play golf. I was going to dress, find my clubs...but...this is way more interesting."

"This?"

He winked. *"Us."*

Sex was the last thing she wanted, but suddenly, she didn't want him to go.

"Claire's not getting married," she whispered.

"North told me." He kissed her forehead.

"I'm not in the mood," she said stiffly, turning away from him.

"When did that ever stop us?"

"Not now, Sam."

He pulled the robe off. "You look so damn sexy."

"You can't be serious."

"I know how to get that way." He laughed. "Sex at our age is sort of like turning all the lights on the Christmas tree on, but one at a time."

He knew if he pressed her, she wouldn't say no.

He was out the door, back in a jiffy with a bottle of wine, two glasses and a dangerous gleam in his eye. He unlocked a drawer, pulled out a video and handed her her naughty book that had that well-thumbed scene about a virgin being captured by two pirates that shamed her but made her shiver.

It was a ritual. They both knew the moves.

Soon they lay beside each other, sipping wine. She read; he watched his video. Their hands drifted languidly over each other. It wasn't long before quite a few of the lights on their "Christmas tree" began to glow.

Their gazes locked.

She snapped her book shut.

He aimed the remote at the television set, and the screen darkened.

They began to kiss. Ten minutes before she'd had a headache. Now it was gone.

Dark passion drew them out of themselves. They did it twice. On the bed. Then the floor.

When it was over, Dee Dee lay in the crook of his arm, her impossible girls forgotten.

"Sex is so weird," she said.

"I remember how every guy in town wanted you. Hell, you just get better and better."

"So do you," she whispered.

Sam had started out on the wrong side of the tracks. But he'd been smart and ambitious. His wildness had secretly appealed to her.

He got out of bed. "Dee, have you seen my golf clubs? They aren't in the hall—"

She smiled indulgently. "Yes, dear. They're in your trunk."

"The girls will be fine," he promised reassuringly on his way out.

But she didn't want to think about the girls or the wildness in them that made them so impossibly difficult or wonder where they'd gotten it. Instead she fell asleep with a smile on her lips.

Claire didn't drive all the way up to the beach house at the end of the drive off Fulton Road. She got out of the car and studied the charming house tucked under the protective oak trees that the wind had bent and twisted. The swallows that nested under the eaves were riding the wind, soaring up into bright blue and then diving back into their nests. Cats and dogs lay curled in lazy heaps all over his front porch. High grasses waved like shoots of gold beneath a slanting sun. Tag's bike was chained in a shed out back. His boat was tied at the dock. Yet somehow the place wore an abandoned air. As she did. The windows were shut, the storm shutters closed.

Even before she knocked, she knew he was gone and wasn't coming back. Still, she rapped against the screen door till her heart beat against her ribs and her knuckles ached.

Hollow with disappointment, she went around back and let herself inside the breezeway. There she sat, remembering the magic of their first night. An hour passed, and she laid her head wearily against a weathered wall. Soon she was asleep. Which was why she didn't hear the boy until his yo-yo slammed against the wall behind her head.

She jumped.

"Oops!" he said. "Sorry."

He was thin as a wire and as dark as mahogany and too adorably shy to look up from the green yo-yo that he was deftly rewinding with long, agile fingers.

"I'm Claire."

"Ricky." His tone was muffled. "I feed Tag's animals."

"He's gone?"

"New Orleans."

She flinched. "So far?"

"His father was real sick. So he left in a hurry."

"I didn't realize he had a father."

"He don't."

"What?"

"Not no more anyhow. He called this morning. Said he died. Said there's a lot to do there. Said he ain't ever coming back."

"But—" The word was torn out of her. "His house—"

"He's got people here to take care of his stuff. Me."

Desperation was closing over her. "Do you have a phone number? An address?"

"Sure I do. Only I ain't 'sposed to give it to no stranger. You aren't his friend. I know about you. I seen you come out of his house that morning. You were crying. Then you sent that man that tore up his house."

"No, I didn't," she whispered.

"Then who did?"

"It's a long story," she began wearily.

"I got time."

Grief washed Tag in its dark wave. The drapes in his father's office were drawn, so he couldn't see the sluggish curl of the Mississippi beneath him. Tag sat in the shadows, his fists knotted on the massive mahogany desk. All he saw was his father, small and thin, a shadow of the man he'd remembered. How still and white he'd lain against the stiff satin in his coffin.

His huge, indomitable father—gone.

He should've come home a long time ago. His father was dead because he'd passed judgment too readily. Blinded by rage and self-pity and fear, too damn stubborn and insecure to think he might be wrong, he'd hated the wrong man.

Guilt and anguished heartbreak spread through Tag. Had the two of them been put on earth just to hurt each other? He'd gotten off to a bad start with his mother, his aunts, and then his father. Was he doomed to always fail at relationships that mattered? Maybe he should quit trying. Maybe he should stick to what he knew—making money.

His gaze wandered about the room. Damn. His father's presence spoke in every item in his hushed office. The priceless oil and magna on canvas by one of the world's leading painters had been his dad's favorite. But it was the insignificant sculpture of stainless steel that really grabbed Tag's heart and shook him. His father hadn't liked the piece that much, but it had been Tag's first expensive gift to him.

Now the sculpture stood in a pool of light in the center of the room.

Had his father really loved him as he'd professed on his deathbed, grieved over his loss, regretted their quarrel as much as, no, maybe far more than Tag had?

I was wrong about you. It was Hugh. Who would've thought the lazy bastard was smart enough or had it in him?

Hugh, a minor partner, had stolen everything, cheated their clients, tarnished their company's name, cost them millions in lawsuits. Realizing father and son didn't quite trust one another, Hugh had covered his tracks in such a way as to make it look like only Tag or his father could have done it, hoping they would blame each other. When Tag had discovered something was wrong, accused his father and been thrown out, Hugh had sent those goons to finish him. When Tag had vanished, the goons had reported him dead. Hugh must've thought he was home free. But somehow he'd overplayed his hand. His father, never one to trust easily, had set a trap. Then Hugh had run. He'd been caught in Switzerland with very little of the stolen fortune, most of it having been squandered in bad deals.

You were gone. I thought you were dead. It was too late. I couldn't take back the things I said.

I should've stood up for myself. I should've fought too. I was too quick to believe the worst about you.

They had held one another quietly. His father had expired in his arms. The old man had let out that final breath and then had seemed to shrivel like a balloon losing the last of its air. Tag had gone on holding him for a while.

So many lost years.

So much regret. On both sides.

Broken in spirit, his father had never recovered financially. His father had needed him, had searched for him, had become too ill to work as hard as before.

The business wasn't what it had been. Tag was going to have to work very hard.

Funny, how his life had changed instantly, irrevocably. He'd been exonerated and he was rich. His father had left him everything. Only his name wasn't Tag Campbell. It was Scott Duval.

But what did it mean now with his father dead?

It meant everything. Yes, he was grieving. Yes, there was loss. But he had his good name, money, the opportunity to start over, to prove himself. Strangely, those last few precious hours with his father at the end were his most prized legacy.

He had everything he'd ever wanted and more.

Everything except—

His mouth hardened. Forget her.

Nobody could stop him now.

Never again would people slam doors in his face.

Never would women want him just for sex. The Dee Dee's of the world were already telling their ambitious daughters he was quite a catch. Several had been by to check him out. They'd brought cakes, cookies, flowers, notes of sympathy.

To hell with them. He was through with such women and their games. They hadn't ever believed in him. Now he didn't believe in them.

In this mood of bitter grief and triumph, Miriam, his father's secretary, no, *his* secretary now, marched audaciously through the heavy doors.

"I told you to hold my calls, cancel my appointments and leave me alone."

"But there's someone here to see you, sir," Miriam said quietly. "*She* says she's a friend. She doesn't have an appointment."

Miriam was thin and small, but she was no pushover. Her soft voice, sweet smile and impeccable manners concealed a determined will. Tag would put her up against a dozen tanks any day.

So, another pretty little jackal was here to get her licks in when he was at his most vulnerable.

"I don't have any women friends. I don't have time. Not with the funeral…"

"But Miss Woods says she knows you from Texas. She's come all this way to offer her condolences. She's different from…the others."

"Miss Woods?"

His heart clamored with a wild hurt and white-hot rage at his complete vulnerability.

Claire, his angel riding the wind.

Claire, who'd slept with him but hadn't given him her name. Claire, who'd wanted to forget him and marry money. Claire, who'd chased another man out of Shorty's and slammed that door in his face.

"She sure as hell didn't waste time." Tag's voice tightened in an effort to leash his emotions. "You tell that witch to go back where she came from. I never want to see her again."

Miriam stiffened. "You're making a mistake."

"I'll be the judge of that." He stared her down.

Big-eyed with outrage, she withdrew. "Very well, *sir.*" When she closed the doors a little too loudly, the purple shadows swallowed him.

He didn't bother to look up when a metal latch clicked and a wedge of bright light spilled across the immense room.

"You're not getting rid of me that easy," said a muted voice across the darkness.

A wary prickling ran the length of his spine.

"Get out," he lashed.

"I'm sorry about your father," she persisted in that soft, sweet voice that shredded his heart.

She stepped into the light. Golden hair spilled to her shoulders. Her eyes were the deepest, darkest shade of blue and yet luminous with shimmering passion. God, why did she have to be so damn beautiful?

He let out a harsh, ragged breath. "Who the hell do you think you're kidding?"

Like a vulture she had seized on this vulnerable moment when he felt lost and alone. Seized on the fact that he would take one look at those moist ruby lips, at her, and want her.

She was right. All his pent-up longings seemed to burst inside him. How many nights had he dreamed of her? One look into those eyes, at that incandescent face, and he felt he would die if he couldn't have her again.

When she stood her ground, he got up and strode across the room. Brutally, he yanked her into his arms. "You gambled I'd want this too much, that I'd remember how it was that night...."

"*Us,*" she whispered, her tone strangled.

"Don't!"

He wound his hands in her hair, turned her face up to his, held her near, so near their lips nearly touched, so near her warm breath fell against his mouth. A rush of desire thrummed in his blood.

He loved her.

"You're just here 'cause I'm rich now. You think I'm weak because my father just died. You're worse than all those other women who came on to me in Shorty's."

The shock of his words leveled her like a blow. She went white. Her eyes glazed with pain. So much stark pain. Her knees buckled, but when she started sinking to the floor, his grip tightened. She gave a broken cry and tried to jerk away, but he held her fast.

Damn her. He loved her. He wanted to go home every night and find her there. He wanted to sleep with her, to wake in the dark and know she was there, alive and warm in his bed. He wanted to make love to her, to enjoy the simple pleasures of living with her, his woman, to watch sunsets together and moonrises together. To have children with golden hair and eager bright blue eyes.

Her perfume alone drove him crazy.

"You're just here because you found out I'm even richer than your fiancé," he accused again.

"No..." Her whisper died away in the shadows.

"You didn't want me when you thought I was nothing."

"I did. But..." She swallowed. "Oh, Tag, I'm so sorry. I see now it's too late for us. You've turned cold, set your will against me. You're too prejudiced to listen. I was wrong...then...and so wrong to come here now. But you're wrong, too. I would give anything not to remember you like this. Have you ever...in your whole life...made a mistake about someone...and regretted it?"

"You're good," he snarled. "But why are you really here then? Did your rich, boring cowboy figure out he's really in love with Melody and dump you? Did you come here to save your crushed ego?"

A hot guilty flush climbed her throat, but the color faded long before it reached her pale cheeks. "I'll go."

He yanked her closer. "So, that's it. Well, for your information, I don't want North Black's leftovers. Not for keeps anyway." He felt wild with love for her but dark and lost because she couldn't feel the same. He had to end this. He wanted all or nothing. "I'll give you the name of my favorite bar. It's classier than Shorty's." He scribbled the name on a card and pressed it into her hand. "Drop by tonight if you're still in town, if you've still got the hots for me. I'll play pirate or whatever other fantasy you want to indulge in. Come every night if you like. I want you in bed, but nowhere else."

"Don't," she pleaded. "*I came because I love you.*

And…and, oh, I don't know why I'm telling you that…when it's over.''

"Shut up!" His voice was achingly hard.

"There's nothing I can say to make you believe me. You're so cold, so remote. It's no use. You've made up your mind. You're not going to believe me. I was wrong, Tag, not to see the truth sooner. But I see it now. I love you. I love you poor or rich. I love you even when you're like this.''

Her blue eyes sparkled with tears.

A tight band closed around his chest. Every breath cut like a knife. She was killing him with her beauty and softness.

Her choked voice was almost inaudible now. "I don't blame you for not believing me.''

She turned and ran.

Thirteen

The sky was a dark dove-gray. A thickness hovered over the tight little crowd clustered around Tag who sniffled as he stood at his father's grave. A clergyman in black read from the Bible about a man being both good and bad, about a life never being all of either, about the next life being a better one, about the folly of making judgments, about the need to forgive both the living and the dead. But Tag's heart was too choked with grief to make sense of any of it.

His father was gone.

So was Claire.

Inside Tag, his heart and soul had turned to stone.

All he saw was the gleaming wood of the closed coffin upon which lay lush, blood-red roses. All he felt was the end of everything.

True, a willowy blonde held onto the dark, expensive cloth of his well-cut sleeve. The model was being well paid.

She was window decoration, a pretty lie to keep the press happy.

A brutal one, to keep Claire away.

When the preacher finished, it began to rain. Everybody scurried back to their cars except Tag. While rain pattered on vinyl, he hunkered under the tent and stared gloomily at the coffin.

Tomorrow he would work.

Today he would grieve.

Tears filled his eyes. Or was it only a few stray raindrops hitting his face? After a while the downpour slowed. He wiped his eyes just as a yellow taxi drove through the far gate.

He got up and went to the coffin, picked a red rose from the spray, and turned to go.

The sun came out and a wisp of sunshine caught a slim girl as she got out of the taxi and ran through the drizzle toward him.

Claire. Looking even more scared now than she had that first night on the edge of that other cemetery.

He straightened, threw the rose to the ground, crushed it into the wet grasses with his polished, black shoe.

Slowly, she walked toward him.

"Will you be all right?" she whispered.

As if she cared.

He nodded, touched beyond words by her presence. His face frozen into an icy mask.

She reached a hand toward him, and he wanted her touch more than anything even though he knew he would be lost then. But the willowy model had precise instructions. The sum he was paying for her performance was generous.

The door of the long white limo opened, and the beautiful girl spoke silkily, sexily. "Are you coming—darling?"

Anguish ripped his heart, but he forced a slow, dazzling smile, his bedroom smile.

Claire stared from the girl to him wordlessly, and then her stark face drove a final nail through his chest. Claire's coming here meant too much when he felt so lost and alone. This had to be a deliberate, calculated act on her part. And yet her white face looked as grief-stricken as he felt.

"I'm glad you came, Claire," he muttered. The rough, honest words were torn from him.

She didn't hear the love in his voice or see the tumult of emotion in his tortured eyes because she was already running through the wet green grass.

Then he was running after her, his long strides stalking her.

She got in the cab and sped away.

"Claire!"

Thunder crashed; the sky turned black. It started to pour again. He raced after her till his custom-made suit was soaked, his Italian shoes ruined and his heart pounding so hard he thought it would explode.

Still panting, he collapsed inside his limo beside the model a few minutes later.

"Did I do okay?" she asked worriedly.

Rain dripped through his long black hair, down his face in cold rivulets. He was shaking so hard all he could do was nod.

The model smiled.

He sank against rich black leather. "Turn on the heater," he ordered the driver. "Take us home."

Claire was gone for good.

Tag told himself it was for the best.

Tag didn't like reporters much. This one was cute though, with her red hair and bright blue eyes.

Blue eyes.

Forget *her*.

The reporter was young, a little shy, and too easily impressed. Which made the interview more fun.

Ads were expensive. Articles about his projects cost nothing and were far more readily believed.

"From rags to riches," she gushed. "Wow! Nobody in this city can stop talking about you, Mr. Duval. You've only been back two months—"

"Two and a half," he corrected in a hard voice. *Seventy-seven days, four hours.*

It felt like a lifetime since he'd seen Claire.

Forget her.

"How does it feel—to have the best of everything?"

"I'd rather talk about my projects—"

"All those beautiful women, your yacht, plane. Mr. Duval, you certainly live the fantasy life."

Fantasy. He could tell her a thing or two about fantasy.

"Do I?" he murmured.

Strip, my lady. Slowly.

He saw a slim girl winding silk around herself and a pirate holding her close in a moondark bay.

"You have it all, Mr. Duval. Everything a man could possibly want. We'll want to get shots of your house, your buildings, of you out on a date or two with women, your yacht...."

He got up, went to the long window and stared out at the cranes above Duval Towers. He'd granted this interview to publicize that project.

Success. He had it in spades. He had everything he'd ever wanted.

So, why was he counting the days, the hours?

And the nights? Oh, the nights. When he slept he fantazied about ruby lips, pink-tipped breasts and golden hair. He woke every hour, feeling hot and tight, ready to explode.

And every waking hour he remembered her white, grief-stricken face when he'd smiled at the model in the cemetery.

Why was life so hard without her?

Claire stared at the pictures of Scott Duval and the willowy model. His picture brought both pain as well as the shock of physical arousal.

So, he was still dating that same girl. She was in every picture. Claire devoured the celebrity issue of the magazine that had done a lengthy profile on him.

Did Tag…Scott ever even think of her?

Almost, almost, she felt desperate enough to run back to New Orleans. She still remembered the name of that bar. But the cost of such a night, if he still wanted her that way, knowing she loved him, would be too much to bear.

The summer had been slow and hot—endless. Loverboy never taunted her now. She'd stopped talking to herself in the mirror, stopped dreaming.

Maybe that meant she'd grown up at last. She'd been interviewing for teaching jobs in the fall. She didn't know what she wanted to do with her life. She couldn't really think when the days were so long and hot, when her future seemed to stretch before her endlessly, without meaning. But she had to do something.

"You've got to think about your future," Dee Dee was always pressuring.

"That's hard, knowing I threw away the one thing I can't live without."

"Life goes on, Claire."

"Have you ever been in love, Mother? Really, madly, passionately in love?"

"You know how much I love your father."

But she didn't. "That's not what I mean, Mother."

"Young love…is only the beginning." Her mother

picked up the magazine, flipped through the pictures that so tormented Claire. "I was wrong about Tag. About you. Will you ever forgive me?"

"Oh, yes. If I've learned anything out of this, it's to forgive."

If only he could have forgiven her.

Fanta-Sea's shrouds sang as Claire furiously scrubbed brightwork that didn't need polishing.

Nothing mattered to her now. The summer was nearly over. Two principals, one in Orange, the other in El Paso, towns at opposite ends of Texas, each colorful locales, had offered her jobs. But she didn't want either one.

"What you want, you can't have."

Go home. It's getting too dark to see.

But when she set her rag down and went below, a low wolf whistle made her spine tingle.

Startled, she whirled.

Nobody was there, so she enjoyed the last of the light fading from the magenta sky as well as the lap of purple wavelets.

She remembered another night. Another boat.

Don't remember him.

A shadow fell across her.

"Strip, my lady. Slowly," said a husky voice.

"Don't tease me, Loverboy," she pleaded. "Not now."

Still thinking it was only her imagination, she whirled.

Fierce silver eyes burned to her soul. Or, rather one very irreverent eye. The other was hidden by a black satin patch.

Excitement pierced her like an electric shock. She made an incoherent little cry when she saw the tall figure in a flowing white shirt and tight black jeans. Again, he was dressed like a pirate. Only this costume was sexier. He stood with his legs set widely apart, an earring sparked from the dark.

Lean and bronze, too unholy and wild for words, shadows dominating his dusky bone structure, her midnight fantasy had come to life.

"Nice shirt," she whispered, her heart hammering in her throat.

"Strip, my lady." His languid grin lit every part of her. "Slowly."

"You've got to be out of your mind." She felt the thrill of being driven once more by ungovernable impulses and heady emotions.

His voice was tender. "Or maybe I've come to my senses."

"What about that woman…in that fancy magazine?" she croaked. "The blonde?"

"There haven't been any women. Not a single one. No blonde. She was a paid employee. A human scarecrow…to scare you away."

"That's such a ridiculous… But…you're here. And I… I…I'm such a little fool…I believe you."

He climbed down the stairs and picked her up.

"Put me down," she whispered.

But he stomped back up on deck and held her over the side.

"Put me down—now."

"Anything to please a pretty lady." With that same slow grin, he dropped her into the water.

She started to scream and ended on a gurgle of saltwater. Under water, angry bubbles spewed to the surface. Furious, she kicked her way upward.

He was in the water, too. His arms came around her.

"I love you, Claire."

"You ruined my hair."

He pointed to a shrimp boat. "Swim for it," he ordered.

Her arms sliced through the water. She kicked off her shoes and swam quickly. Once on board, inside the pilothouse, he held her so close, his hot body burned her through their wet clothes.

"You're so beautiful," he said. "I don't even have a picture of you."

She traced his stubborn, cleanly-shaved jaw, ran her hands through the heavy black hair glued to his brow. "I...I can't believe you're really here." She began to shiver.

"We've got to get you out of these wet clothes."

Her pulse thrummed. "Kiss me first," she whispered. "Love me...."

"Always. Forever."

"Marry me," she whispered.

"Not so fast. That's my line."

"All right. Go on. Ask me."

"Why? I already know you will."

"You weren't this conceited when you were a shrimper."

"Money does things to people."

"I don't care about the money. I love you. I have never loved anybody else."

"I don't want anybody else but you either," he finally said.

"When I read that article I thought you had everything in the world you ever wanted."

"Not if I don't have you. I don't care where I live, or how much money I make, I want you. You're everything."

"That's exactly how I feel about you."

"Claire, I've been mixed up for a long time. When you didn't choose me at Shorty's, it opened old wounds that are just now beginning to heal. When you came to New Orleans, you were sweet to me, but I wouldn't let myself trust you...or anybody else, for that matter. I don't want to live like that anymore. All the money in the world isn't worth it. I was a jerk to you in my father's office...and at the cemetery. Can you ever forgive me?''

"Of course. Love doesn't hold on to wrongs. I behaved badly, too."

Then his mouth found hers, and as with all lovers, something more than words was needed. His breath was warm, his arms tight around her waist, his muscular body flooding her with heat but with tenderness too.

Their kiss told them both everything they needed to know, erased all doubts, forgave all wrongs. Most of all it showed them both how much they yearned.

"I love you," she said.

His arms wrapped tighter around her waist. Then he pulled her down below to a bed with red silk sheets. But she got up and began to whirl slowly, stripping with an expertise that made his eyes darken with wildness.

"You've been practicing," he said appreciatively, a smile curving his mouth.

They kissed. They made love. Wrapped in thin cotton blankets, they shared the sunset. And the sunrise. The first of many, she hoped.

Epilogue

With a shudder the helicopter rose into the sparkling air above the wedding party. Higher and higher, till the golden bride in her swirling veil and her handsome dark groom inside the cockpit soared above the island that winked to them like a pine-covered emerald in an aqua sea.

Their wedding had been written up in all the national magazines. Melody had caught the bouquet, and Dee Dee had been in her element. Sam hadn't minded the third wedding at all even though it was more lavish than the first two he was still paying for. Because the groom had paid for everything.

"Where are we going? I hope it's not far," Claire yelled above the noise of the rotors.

Tag pointed down.

She saw a ship with furled sails at anchor in a cove. White surf lapped against sugary beaches.

The pilot began his descent.

The flutter of a skull and crossbones against black at the top of the highest mast on the ship caught her attention.

Claire clapped her hands and laughed in delight. "Why...why it's a pirate ship."

"I hoped that come midnight, it would inspire you."

"Long before midnight," she teased. "The wedding was perfect. You are perfect. The ship is perfect."

"I love you, darling," he whispered. "More than I can ever say."

And she was inspired long before midnight.

They were below in the lavish captain's quarters.

Alone together.

She smiled. "Strip, my lord. Slowly."

He laughed. "That's my line, Mrs. Duval."

"Mrs. Duval," she repeated the name.

His brown hand found a white satin covered button.

"You were my first virgin. My first bride. My first love. And this is the first wedding dress I ever took off a woman."

"And the last, I hope," she murmured.

"For sure," he agreed.

An amazing sense of completeness filled her as he began undoing the long line of buttons that ran the length of her slim spine.

Happily ever after was no longer a dream but her reality. She had found everything she ever fantasized about and more.

With him.

"I love you," he said.

"Then prove it."

"What do you have in mind?"

"Ravish me. Be my midnight fantasy."

*   *   *   *   *

HEART OF THE WARRIOR
Lindsay McKenna

To Karen David, a real, live warrioress and healer.
And a good role model for the rest of us!

Chapter 1

"No...!"

Roan Storm Walker's cry reverberated around the small, dark log cabin. Outside, the rain dripped monotonously off the steep, rusty tin roof. Breathing harshly, Roan pressed his hands to his face, dug his fingers frantically into his skull as he felt his heart pounding relentlessly in his chest. His flesh was beaded with sweat. Lips tightly compressed to halt another scream, another cry of grief and loss, he groaned instead, like a wounded cougar.

Lifting his head, Roan turned the dampened pillow over and dropped back down onto the small, creaking bed. He had to sleep. *Great Spirit, let me sleep.* Shutting his eyes tightly, his black lashes thick and spiky against his copper-colored skin, he released a ragged sigh.

Sarah...how he missed her. Brave, confident, foolhardy Sarah. It had been two years and he still missed her. How badly he wanted to touch her firm, warm shoulder or to smell that jasmine scent that always lingered tantalizingly in the strands of her short red hair. Gone...everything was gone.

Swept from his life like litter before some invisible broom. Sarah, his wife, was dead, and his heart had died, too, on that fateful day. Even now, as he lay listening to the rain splattering against the roof of his cabin high in the Montana Rockies, he felt the force of his aching grief. The waves of agony moved through him like waves crashing in from the ocean and spilling their foamy, bubbling essence on the hard, golden sand.

Unconsciously, he rubbed his fingers across the blue stone hanging around his neck—his medicine piece. He'd worn the amulet continually since his mother, a Lakota medicine woman, gave it to him—before her death many years ago. Composed of two cougar claws representing the cougar spirit that was his protector, and two small golden eagle feathers, it hung from a thick, black, sweat-stained leather thong around his neck. The center of the medicine piece was an opalescent blue stone, roughly fashioned in a trapezoid shape. The bezel around the stone was of beaten brass that had long ago turned dark with age. No one knew what the stone was, or where it came from. He'd never seen another one like it in all his travels. His mother had told him it came from their ancestors, passed on to the medicine person in each succeeding generation of the family. He always touched this piece when he was feeling bad. In a way, it was like sending a prayer to his mother and her line of ancestors for help with the heavy emotions he wrestled with. Roan never took off his medicine piece; it was as much a part of him as his heart beating in his chest.

He closed his eyes once more. He was good at forcing himself to go back to sleep. His mother, a Lakota Yuwipi medicine woman, had taught him how to lucid dream. He could walk out of one harsh reality into the more amorphous world beyond the veil of normal human reach. More than likely he was able to do this because he had the genes of that long line of medicine people coursing richly through his bloodstream. His father was an Anglo, a white man—a physics teacher. Between both parents, Roan found it easy to surrender over to a power higher than himself, give himself back to the night owl's wings of sleep, which almost instantly embraced him again.

As he moved from the pain of the past, which continued to dog his heels like a relentless hound on the scent of the cougar spirit that protected him, his grief began to recede. In lucid dream and sleep, he could escape the sadness that was etched in his heart. This time, as he slipped into sleep, Walker heard the distant growl of thunder. Yes, a Wakan Wakinyan, a mighty thunder being who created the storms that roved across the Rockies, was now stalking his humble cabin hidden deep in the thick Douglas firs on a Montana slope.

A slight, one-cornered smile curved Roan's mouth as he felt his mood lightening, like a feather caught in a breeze and being wafted gently into the invisible realm of the Great Spirit. Yes, in dreaming there was safety. In dreaming there was relief from the pain of living in human form. Roan expected to see Sarah again, as he always did whenever this shift in his consciousness occurred. The Lakota called the state dreaming "beneath the wings of the owl," referring to the bird they considered the eagle of the night. Within the wings of this night protector, the world of dreams unfolded to those who knew how to access this realm. Reaching this altered state had been taught to Roan at a very young age and he had found it an incredible gift, a means of healing himself, really, over the last twenty-eight years of his life.

Sarah? He looked for his red-haired Sarah, those flashing Celtic blue eyes of hers, and that twisted Irish grin across her full, soft lips. Where was she? Always, she would meet him while in the embrace of the owl. Full of anticipation, he spied a glowing light coming out of the darkness toward him. Yes, it had to be Sarah. As he waited impatiently within the darkness, the golden, sunny light grew ever closer, larger, pulsating with brilliant life of its own.

His cougar spirit's senses told him this wasn't Sarah. Then who? Even as he felt his disappointment, something strange happened. His cougar, a female spirit guardian with huge, sun-gold eyes, appeared out of the darkness to stand in front of him. He could see that her attention was focused fully on the throbbing, vital orb of light drawing closer. Walker felt no fear, simply curiosity, despite the fact that it was unlike Anna, his cougar spirit guide, to appear like this unless there was danger to him. Yet he felt no danger.

The mists surrounding the oblong light reminded him of thickly moving mist on a foggy morning at the lake below his cabin, where he often fished for a breakfast trout. Anna gave a low growl. Roan's heart rate picked up. The golden oval of light halted no more than six feet away from him. Slowly, it began to congeal into a body, two very long legs, slender arms, a head and…

Walker felt his heart thundering in his chest. His cougar guardian was on full alert now, her tail stiff, the hackles on her neck ruffled and the fur raised all the way down her lean, supple spine. Roan was mesmerized as he watched the person—a woman?—appear. What the hell? He wasn't sure what or who he was looking at.

Huge, willow-green eyes with large black pupils stared fiercely back at him.

Swallowing hard, Walker felt every cell in his body respond to this unknown woman who now stood before him. Although the golden light had faded to a degree, so he could see her clearly, it still shone around her form like rays of brilliant sunlight. She warily watched him as the tension built and silence strung tautly between them.

This was no ordinary human being. Walker sensed her incredible power. Few humans he'd ever known had an aura of energy like hers. It was so brilliant that he felt like squinting or raising his hand to shield his eyes from the glow. Her eyes drew him. They were magnetic, commanding, fierce, vulnerable and magical all at the same time.

He tried to shift his consciousness; it was impossible. She held him fully within her powerful presence. She was tall, at least six feet. Her skin was a golden color. What she wore confounded him. She was dressed in army camouflage fatigues and black, shiny military jump boots. On her proud torso she wore an olive-green, sleeveless T-shirt crisscrossed with two bandoliers containing bullets. Slung across her left shoulder was a rifle. Around her slender waist was a web belt with a black leather holster and pistol, several grenades and a wicked looking K-bar knife. Down her back, resting between her shoulder blades, hung a huge leather sheath, knicked and scarred, that held a machete with a pearl handle. She was obviously a warrior. An Amazon. A soldier used to fighting.

Roan could see and sense all these things about her. Despite her dynamic presence, the threat she presented in the armament she wore, the way her hand curled around the thick leather strap that bit into her shoulder as it held the rifle in place, she was beautiful. Roan could not tear his gaze from her full, square face, those high, proud cheekbones. From her narrowing, willow-green eyes, that fine thin nose that flared like the nostrils of a wary wild horse, or those compressed, full lips.

Her hair was thick and black and hung in one long braid over her right shoulder and down between her breasts, which were hidden by the bandoliers of ammunition. There was such pride and absolute confidence in her stance, in the way her shoulders were thrown back. As she lifted her chin imperiously, Roan wanted to simply absorb the sight of her and the feeling of that incredible energy swirling around her. He wondered if she was a figment of his imagination, a hybrid between Sarah and some kind of superhuman woman.

The instant he thought that, her eyes snapped with rage and utter indignation.

"Do not waste precious energy and time on such speculations!" she growled at him. "You were born into a med-

icine family. You know better!'' She jabbed a finger at the
amulet he wore around his neck. ''You carry the stone of
the Jaguar Clan. You are one of us! I am Inca. I am asking
for your help, Roan Storm Walker. Well, will you give it?
I do not beg. This will be the only time I stand before you.
Answer me quickly, for many will die without you here by
my side to fight the fight of your life and mine. I am in a
death spiral dance. I invite you into it.''

Walker felt her outrage at the very thought that he might
say no to her request. *Inca.* A mysterious name. The name
of a woman from…where? Perhaps from the Inca empire in
Peru? Her accent was thick, reminding him of Spanish. He
touched the blue stone that lay at the base of his throat. It
felt hot, and throbbing sensations moved through his fingertips. The amulet he wore was powerful; his mother had told
him so, and Roan had often experienced strange phenomena
regarding it. But he'd never before felt the level of energy
that was emanating from it now. He glanced down and saw
a strange turquoise-white-and-gold light pulsating around it,
like a beacon.

''Where do you come from, Inca?'' he demanded in an
equally fierce voice. He was not afraid of her, but he respected her power. Where he came from, women were equal
to any man.

''I come from the south, Storm Walker. The stone you
wear around your neck tells me of your heritage. The spirits
of your ancestors led me to you. You are needed in my
country. Time is short. Many lives are at stake. My guardian
says you are the one.'' The woman's green gaze grew de-
manding. ''Are you? the *one?*''

''I don't know. How can I help you?''

''You will know that when you see me the second time.''

He searched her shadowed features. She had the face of
an Indian, all right—most probably of Incan heritage if she
was from the south. Her stance was uncompromising. This
woman feared nothing and no one. So why was she ap-

proaching him? He looked around, feeling another, invisible presence near her.

"Your guardian?" he asked.

A sour smile twisted her mouth and she gazed down at his gold cougar, which stood guard. "Watch," she commanded. "I run out of patience with you."

In moments the golden light enveloped Inca once more. Roan watched with fascination as the woman disappeared within spiraling bands that moved like a slow-motion tornado around her. But what walked out of the light moments later made him gasp. It was a huge stocky, black-and-gold male jaguar.

Roan vaguely heard Anna growl. In response the male jaguar hissed and showed his long, curved fangs. His golden eyes were huge, with large, shining black pupils. As the animal stalked around them, his tail whipping impatiently from side to side, his thick body strong and sensuous as he moved, Walker watched in awe. Anna remained on alert at his side, but did not attack the slowly circling jaguar.

The coat on the cat was a bright gold color, patterned with black crescent moons. To Roan, the massive jaguar seemed formidable, invulnerable. His mind churned with more questions than answers. A woman who turned into a male jaguar? She was a shape-shifter—a medicine person from South America who had the power to change shape from human to animal, and then back into human form at will. That in itself was a feat that few could manage successfully. He recalled that his mother, who worked with the Yaqui Indians of Mexico, had possessed shape-shifting abilities herself. One never knew, seeing a bird, a reptile or a four-footed, if it was in fact human or not. Walker had been taught never to kill anything that approached him in such a bold, fearless manner.

As he watched the male jaguar make one complete circle, Roan was wildly aware of the throbbing power around the animal…around this mysterious woman called Inca. As he stared, he felt an intense, searing telepathic message being impressed upon him, body and soul.

I cannot control the tides of the ocean. I cannot change the course of the winds. I cannot control what is free and yearns to roam. I can only bend and surrender to a higher power through my heart, which rules me. I bend to the will of the Great Goddess, and to the Jaguar Clan. I ask you to willingly, with pure heart and single-minded purpose, to work with me. My people need your help. I ask in their name…

To Walker's surprise, he felt hot, scalding tears stinging his eyes. The impassioned plea made him blink rapidly. Tears! Of all things! He hadn't cried since…since Sarah had died so unexpectedly and tragically. Trying to halt the tumult of feelings radiating through his chest and around his heart, he watched the jaguar through blurred vision. What the hell was going on? This was no lucid dream. This was some kind of phenomenal, otherworldly meeting of the highest, purest kind. He'd heard his mother speak in hushed tones of those times when the gods and goddesses of her people would come to her in her dreams. She had often described rare meetings just like the one he was having now.

Was Inca really a human being? A shape-shifting medicine woman? A shaman who lived in South America? What was the Jaguar Clan? All questions and no answers. The stone at his throat seemed like it was burning a hole in his flesh. He felt it with his fingertips; it was scalding hot. This was the first time it had ever activated to this extent. His mother had said that the stone possessed powers beyond anyone's imagination, and that at the right time, he would be introduced to them. Rubbing his throat region, he understood this was no ordinary meeting. This had something to do with the stone's origin and purpose.

The jaguar stopped. He stared up at Roan with those huge eyes that were now thin crescents of gold on a field of black.

Walker felt the inquiry of the massive jaguar. His heart

was beating hard in his chest, adrenaline pumping violently through him. Fight or flight? Run or stay and face combat? She was a warrior for something. What? Who? *Who does she represent? The light or the dark?* Walker knew she wasn't of the darkness. No. Everything within him shouted that she was of the light, working on the side of goodness. Yet she was a combat soldier. A modern-day Amazon.

Roan felt his cougar rub against his thigh, and he draped his fingers across the female animal's skull. She was purring and watching the jaguar with interest. Looking down, Roan saw Anna was once again relaxed, no longer on guard or in her protective stance. *That* was his answer.

Lifting his head, Walker looked over at the male jaguar. "Yes, I'll come. I'll be there for your people."

Within seconds, the jaguar disappeared into the cloud of brilliant, swirling light. And in the blink of an eye, the light was also gone. *She* was gone. Inca…

The drip, drip, drip of the rain off the tin roof slowly eased Walker out of his altered state. This time, as he opened his eyes, the grayness of dawn through the thick fir trees caught his attention. Twisting his head to one side, he looked groggily at the clock on the bedstand: 0600. It was time to get up, make a quick breakfast, drive down the mountain to Philipsburg, fifty miles away, and meet with his boss, Morgan Trayhern, leader of the super secret government group known as Perseus. A messenger had been sent up the mountain two days ago to tell him to be at the Perseus office in the small mining town at 0900 for a meeting with him and Major Mike Houston.

As Roan swung his naked body upward and tossed off the sheet, his feet hitting the cool pine floor, he sighed. Hands curling around the edges of the mattress, he sat there in the grayish light of dawn and wondered who the hell Inca was. This lucid dream was no dream at all, he was sure. He'd never had an experience like this before. The stone against his upper chest still burned and throbbed. Rubbing the area, he slowly rose to his full six foot six inches of height, then padded effortlessly toward the couch, where a pair of clean jeans, a long-sleeved white Western-style shirt, socks and underwear were draped. *First, make the coffee, then get dressed.* He pivoted to the right and made his way to the small, dimly lit kitchen. Without coffee, no day ever went right for him. He grinned a little at that thought, although his mind, and his heart, were centered on Inca. Who was she? What had he agreed to? First, he had to see what Morgan Trayhern and Major Mike Houston had up their sleeves. Roan knew Houston had worked down in South America for a decade, and he might be the right person to share this experience with. Maybe…

"What the hell are we supposed to do?" Morgan Trayhern growled at Mike Houston from his place behind the huge dark maple desk in his office.

Army Special Forces Major Mike Houston turned slowly away from the window where he stood and faced his boss. "Inca *must* lead that Brazilian contingent into the Amazon basin or Colonel Jaime Marcellino and company will be destroyed by the drug lords. Without her, they're dead," he said flatly. Then his eyes snapped with humor. "They just don't know it yet, that's all."

Rubbing his square jaw, Morgan dropped the opened file labeled Inca on his desk. "Damn…she's a lone wolf."

"More like a lone jaguar."

"What?" Disgruntled, Morgan gave Mike a dark look.

"Jaguars," Mike said in a calm tone, "always hunt alone. The only time they get together is to mate, and after that, they split. The cubs are raised by the mother only."

Glaring down at the colored photo of a woman in a sleeveless, olive-green T-shirt, bandoliers across her shoulders, a rifle across her knees as she sat on a moss-covered log, Morgan shook his head. "You vaguely mention in your report that Inca's a member of the Jaguar Clan."

"Well," Mike hedged, "kind of…"

"What is that? A secret paramilitary organization down in Brazil?"

Mike maintained a dour look on his face. He unwound from his at-ease position and slowly crossed the room. "You could say that, but they don't work with governments, exactly. Not formally…" Mike wasn't about to get into the metaphysical attributes of the clan with Morgan. He tip-toed around it with his boss because Mike felt Morgan would not believe him about the clan's mysterious abilities.

"But you're insisting that Inca work with the Brazilian government on this plan of ours to coordinate the capture of major drug lords in several South American countries."

"Morgan, the Amazon basin is a big place." Mike stabbed his finger at the file on the desk as he halted in front of his boss. "Inca was born near Manaus. She knows the Amazon like the back of her hand. The major drug activity is in the Juma and Yanomami Indian reservation around Manaus. You can't put army troops into something like this without experts who know the terrain intimately. Only one person, someone who's been waging a nonstop war against the drug lords in that area, knows it—Inca."

With a heavy shake of his head, Morgan muttered, "She's barely a child! She's only twenty-five years old!"

Mike smiled a little. "Inca is hardly a child. I've known her since she saved my life when she was eighteen years old."

"She's so young."

Mike nodded, the smile on his mouth dissolving. "Listen to me. In a few minutes you've got to go into that war room with emissaries from those South American countries that are capable of raising coca to produce cocaine, and sell them on this idea. Inca has a reputation—not a good one, I'll grant you—but she gets the job done. It ain't pretty, Morgan. She's a Green Warrior. That's slang for a tree hugger or environmentalist. Down there in Brazil, that carries a lot of weight with the Indian people. She's their protector. They worship her. They would go to hell and back for her if she asked it of them. If that Brazilian army is going to make this mission a success they need the support of the locals. And if Inca is there, leading the troops, the Indians will fight and die at her side on behalf of the Brazilian government. Without her, they'll turn a deaf ear to the government's needs.''

"I read in your report that they call her the jaguar goddess."

Raising one eyebrow, Houston said, "Those that love her call her that."

"And her enemies?"

"A Green Warrior—" Houston grimaced "—or worse. I think you ought to prepare yourself for Colonel Marcellino's reaction to her. He won't have anything good to say when he hears we're going to pair him up with Inca."

Studying Houston, Morgan slowly closed the file and stood up. "Mike, I'm counting on you to help carry the day in there. You're my South American expert. You've been fighting drug lords in all those countries, especially in Peru and Brazil. No one knows that turf better than you."

"That's why Inca is so important to this operation," he said as he walked with Morgan toward an inner door that led to an elevator to the top secret, underground war room. "She knows the turf even better than I do."

Morgan halted at the door. He rearranged the red silk tie at the throat of his white shirt. Buttoning up his pinstripe suit, he sighed. "Did you ever find anyone in our merc database who could work—or would want to work—with the infamous Inca?"

Grinning a little, Houston said, "Yeah, I think I did. Roan Storm Walker. He's got Native American blood in him. Inca will respect him for that, at least."

Morgan raised his brows. "Translated, that means she

won't just outright flatten him like she does every other male who gets into her line of fire?''

Chuckling, Mike put his hand on Morgan's broad shoulder. The silver at the temples of his boss's black hair was getting more and more pronounced, making Mike realize that running Perseus, a worldwide mercenary operation, would put gray hairs on just about anyone. ''She'll respect him.''

''What does that mean? She'll ask questions first and shoot later?''

''You could say that, yes.''

''Great,'' Morgan muttered. ''And Walker's in the war room already?''

''Yes. I told him to stay in the shadows and keep a low profile. I don't want him agreeing to this mission you've laid out for him without him realizing he has to work directly with Colonel Marcellino. And—'' Mike scowled, looking even more worried ''—he needs to understand that the ongoing war between Marcellino and Inca will put him between a rock and a hard place.''

Snorting, Morgan opened the door, heading for the elevator that would take them three stories down into the earth. ''Sounds like I need a damned diplomat between the colonel and Inca, not a merc. Roan's always taken oddball assignments, though. Things I could never talk anyone else into taking—and he's always pulled them off.''

''Good,'' Mike murmured, hope in his voice as he followed Morgan into the elevator, ''because Walker is gonna need that kind of attitude to survive.''

''Survive who?'' Morgan demanded, ''Marcellino or Inca?''

The doors whooshed closed. Mike wrapped his arms around his chest as his stomach tightened with tension. The elevator plummeted rapidly toward their destination.

"Both," he said grimly. "There won't be any love lost between Marcellino and Inca, believe me. They're like a dog and cat embroiled in a fight to the death. Only this time it's a dog and a jaguar...."

Chapter 2

What in the hell am I doing here with all this fruit salad?
Roan wondered as he slowly eased his bulk down into a
chair in the shadows of the huge, rectangular room. Fruit
salad was military slang for the ribbons personnel wore on
their uniforms. Ribbons that spoke of various campaigns and
wars that they served in, and medals they'd earned when
they'd survived them. His own time in the Marine Corps as
a Recon came back to him as he scanned the assembled
group of ten men. Roan recognized two of them: Morgan
Trayhern, who sat at the head of the large, oval table in a
dapper gray pinstripe suit, and Major Mike Houston, who
was a U.S. Army advisor to the Peruvian military. Roan
amended his observation. Mike was retired. Now he was
working for Perseus and for Morgan.

Roan was the only other person besides Morgan and Mike
wearing civilian attire. In his white cotton Western shirt, the
sleeves rolled up haphazardly to just below his elbows, his
well-worn jean's and a pair of dusty, scarred cowboy boots,
he knew he stuck out like a sore thumb in this assemblage,

members of which were now scrutinizing him closely. Let them. Roan really couldn't care less. At twenty-eight he was already a widower, and the dark looks of some colonels and generals were nothing in comparison to what he'd already endured.

"Gentlemen, this is Roan Storm Walker," Morgan began. "He's an ex-Recon Marine. I've asked him to sit in on this important briefing because he will be working directly with the Brazilian detachment."

Roan noticed a tall, thin man in a dark green Brazilian Army uniform snap a cold, measuring look in his direction. The name card in front of him read Marcellino, Jaime, Colonel, Brazil. The man had hard, black, unforgiving eyes that reminded Roan of obsidian, an ebony rock, similar to glass in its chemical makeup, which was created out of the belching fire of a violent volcano. Instinctively Roan felt the controlled and contained violence around the Brazilian colonel. It showed in his thinned mouth and his long, angular features that hinted of an aristocratic heritage. Everything about the good colonel spoke of his formal training; he had that military rigidity and look of expectation that said his orders would be carried out to the letter once he gave them.

Maybe it was the intelligence Roan saw in Marcellino's restless, probing eyes that made him feel a tad better about the man. Roan knew he would have to work with him, and his instincts warned him that Marcellino was a soldier with a helluva lotta baggage that he was dragging around with him like an old friend. People like that made Roan antsy because they tended to take their misery and unconscious rage out on others without ever realizing it. And Roan wouldn't join in that kind of dance with anyone. It was one of the reasons why he'd quit the Marine Corps; the games, the politics choked him, and he withered within the world of the military. His gut told him Marcellino was a man who excelled at those bonds of politics.

Clearing his throat, Morgan buttonholed everyone seated

around the oval table. One by one he introduced each man present. Roan noted there was either a colonel or a general from each of the South American countries represented at the table. In front of him was a file folder marked Top Secret. Roan resisted opening it up before being asked to. When Morgan got to his corner, Roan lowered his eyes and looked down at the well-polished table.

"I've already introduced Roan Storm Walker, but let me give you some of his background. As I mentioned, he was a Recon Marine for six years. A trained paramedic on his team, he saw action in Desert Storm. His team was responsible for doing a lot of damage over in Iraq. His specialty is jungle and desert warfare situations. He holds a degree in psychology. He speaks five languages fluently—Spanish, German, French and Portuguese, plus his own Native American language, of the Lakota Sioux nation. He will be working with Colonel Jaime Marcellino, from Brazil. But more on that later."

Roan was glad once the spotlight moved away from him. He didn't like being out front. People out front got shot at and hit. He had learned to be a shadow, because shadows could quietly steal away to live and fight another day. As he sat there, vaguely listening to the other introductions, Roan admitted to himself that the fight had gone out of him. When Sarah died two years ago, his life had been shattered. He had no more desire to take on the world. With her his reason for living had died. If it hadn't been for Morgan nudging him to get back into the stream of life, he'd probably have drunk himself to death in his cabin up in the mountains.

Morgan would visit him about once a month, toss a small mercenary job with little danger to it his way, to keep Roan from hitting the bottle in his despair. Trayhern was astute about people, about their grief and how it affected them. Roan knew a lot about grief now. He knew what loss was. The worst kind. He tried to imagine a loss that would be greater than losing a wife or husband, and figured that would probably be losing a child. It was lucky, he supposed morbidly, that he and Sarah never had children. But in truth he wished that they had. Sarah would live on through that child, and Roan wouldn't feel as devastated or alone as he did now. But that was a selfish thought, he knew.

Still, he felt that losing a loved one, whether spouse or child, was the hardest thing in the world to endure. How could one do it and survive? As a psychologist, he knew the profound scarring that took place on the psyche. He knew firsthand the terrible, wrenching grief of losing a woman he loved as well as life itself. And Roan swore he'd never, ever fall in love again, because he could not afford to go through that again. Not ever. His spirit would not survive it.

"Gentlemen, I'm turning this briefing over to Major Mike Houston. You all know him well. He was a U.S. Army advisor up until very recently." Morgan allowed a hint of a smile on his face. "Mike is now working for Perseus, my organization. He is our South American specialist. One of the reasons you have been handpicked to represent your country is because you have all worked with him in some capacity or another. Major Houston is a known quantity to you. You know he's good at his word, that he knows the terrain and the problems with the drug trade in South America. You know he can be trusted." Morgan turned to Mike. "Major Houston?"

Mike nodded and stood up. He, too, was in civilian attire—a pair of tan trousers, a white cotton shirt and a dark brown blazer. When he turned on the overhead, a map of Brazil flashed on the screen in front of the group.

"The government of Brazil has asked this administration for help in ridding the Amazon basin of two very powerful drug lords—the Valentino Brothers." Mike moved to the front and flicked on his laser pen. A small red dot appeared on the map. "We know from intelligence sources in the basin that the brothers have at least six areas of operation.

Their business consists of growing and manufacturing cocaine. They have factories, huge ones, that are positioned in narrow, steep and well-guarded valleys deep in the interior of the rain forest.

"The Valentino Brothers capture Indians from the surrounding areas and basically enslave them, turn them into forced laborers. If the Indians don't work, they are shot in the head. If they try to escape, they are killed. What few have escaped and lived to tell us about their captivity, relate being fed very little food while working sixteen hours a day, seven days a week. If they don't work fast enough, the overseer whips them. There is no medical help for them. No help at all."

Mike looked out at the shadowy faces turned raptly toward him. "All of you know I'm part Quechua Indian, from Peru. I have a personal stake in this large, ongoing mission. We have drug lords enslaving Indians in every country in South America in order to produce large quantities of cocaine for world distribution. If the Indians do not do the work, they are murdered. The captured women are raped. After working all day they become unwilling pawns to the drug dealers at night. Children who are captured are forced to work the same hours as an adult. They suffer the same fate as an adult." His mouth became set. "Clearly, we need to make a statement to these drug lords. The head honchos aren't stupid. They use the rain forests and jungles to hide in. Even our satellite tracking cannot find them under the dense canopy. What we need, in each country, is someone who knows the territory where these factories are located, to act as a guide, to bring the army forces in to destroy them."

Mike grimaced. "This is no easy task. The Amazon basin is huge and the military must march in on foot. The only way units can be resupplied is by helicopter. When they get farther in, helicopters are out of range—they can't reach them without refueling—so we must rely on cargo plane airdrops. The troops' medical needs aren't going to be met. If there is an emergency, a sick or wounded soldier will have to be carried out to a place where a helicopter can pick him up and transport him back to the nearest hospital. As you all are aware, I'm sure, there are a lot of deadly things out in the Amazon. Piranhas in the rivers, channels and pools. Bushmaster snakes that will literally chase you until they sink their fangs into you. Mosquitoes carrying malaria, yellow fever and dengue. There's always the threat of unknown hemorrhagic viruses, victims of which can bleed out before we can get them proper medical help. There are insects that with one bite can kill you in as little as forty-eight hours if you are without medical intervention.''

Mike paused, then moved on. ''Colonel Jaime Marcellino has been chosen to lead the Brazilian Army contingent, a company of their best soldiers—roughly one hundred and eighty men. He is their rain forest specialist. He has knowledge of the problems inherit in that environment.''

Jaime bowed slightly to Houston.

Mike went on. ''We all agree that Colonel Marcellino's experiment with a company of men in Brazil will teach us a lot about how to organize military attacks against drug strongholds in other countries. What we learn from his mission will help all of you in preparation for yours. He will be our guinea pig, so to speak. Mistakes made there we will learn from. What works will be passed on in an after-action report to all of you.''

Moving toward the front of the room, Mike tapped the map projected on the huge screen. ''We have it on good authority where six factories, in six different valleys, are located. We have a guide who will lead the colonel's company to the nearest one, which is about ten hours southeast of Manaus, up in a mountainous region known as Sector 5. The colonel's company will disembark at Manaus, motor down the Amazon and, at a predestined spot, off-load and meet their guide. The guide will then take them through a lot of grueling hilly and swampy terrain to reach the valley where the factory is located. Once there, Colonel Marcellino will deploy his troops for a strategic attack on the facility.'' Mike shrugged. ''It is our hope that the Indians who are captive will be freed. We don't want them killed in the cross fire. The Valentino Brothers have heavily fortified operations. Their drug soldiers are men who live in the rain forest and know it intimately. They will be a constant threat.''

Jaime held up a long, narrow hand with closely clipped carefully manicured nails. ''Major Houston, I am sure my men will be able to take this factory. Do not look so worried.'' He smiled slightly.

''Colonel, I wish I could share your optimism,'' Mike said heavily. ''I don't question your willingness and passion for this mission. But it's going to be hard. No army in South America has tried such a thing before. There's bound to be a steep learning curve on this.''

''We are prepared,'' Marcellino answered in his soothing well-modulated tone. He looked at Morgan. ''My men are trained for rain forest warfare.''

Morgan nodded. ''We realize that, Colonel. That's why you're being asked to lead this mission. Even though your men have trained for it, that doesn't mean they've actually undertaken missions in the basin, however. There's a big difference between training and real-time experience.''

Jaime nodded. ''Of course, Mr. Trayhern. I'm confident we can do this.''

Mike Houston cleared his throat. ''For this mission, we are sending Roan Storm Walker with you, Colonel. He'll be your advisor, your translator, and will work directly between you and the guide. He will answer only to you and to Morgan Trayhern at Perseus, which has the backing of this administration to undertake this plan of attack. Even though Storm Walker has no military designation, his judgment will be equal to your own.'' Houston drilled Marcellino with an incisive look. ''Do you understand that?''

Jaime shrugged thin, sharp shoulders beneath a uniform resplendent with shining brass buttons and thick, gold braid and epaulets. On his chest were at least twenty ribbons. "Yes, yes, of course. I will order my officers to acknowledge that he has full authority to override their decisions in the field." Frowning, he turned and looked down the table at Storm Walker. "However, he must check with me first before any action is taken."

"Of course," Mike assured him. "Roan knows chain of command. He recognizes you as the ultimate authority over your men."

Nodding, Jaime raised his thin, graying brows. "And what of this guide? What is his status with me?"

Mike sent a brief, flickering glance in Morgan's direction and kept his voice low and deep as he answered. "The guide knows the terrain, Colonel. You should listen to the advice given to you. This is a person who has lived in the basin all her life. Storm Walker will be her liaison with you, and she'll be your point man—woman—on this mission. You'd best heed whatever advice she gives you because she knows the territory. She's had a number of skirmishes with the Valentino Brothers and has every reason for wanting them out of the basin."

Curious, Jaime straightened, his hand resting lightly on the table. "Excuse me, Major. Am I hearing you correctly? You said 'she'? I thought our guide would be a man. What woman has knowledge of the basin?" He laughed briefly and waved his hand. "Women stay at home and have our children. They are wives and mothers—that is all. No, you must have meant 'he'. *Sim?*"

Mike girded himself internally. He flashed a look of warning in Roan's direction. Now the muck was going to hit the fan. "No," he began slowly, "I meant *she*. This is a woman who was born and raised in the basin. She knows at least fifteen Indian languages, knows the territory like the back of her hand. No one is better suited for this assignment than she is. Roan Storm Walker will interface directly with her, Colonel. You will not have to if you don't want to.''

Though he frowned, Jaime said laughingly, ''And why would I not want to meet this woman and hear her words directly? If she is Indian and knows Portuguese, there should not be a language problem, eh?''

Biting down on his lower lip for a moment, Mike said quietly, ''She is known as the jaguar goddess, Colonel. Her real name is Inca.'' He saw the colonel's eyes widen enormously, as if he'd just been hit in the chest with an artillery shell. Before the Brazilian could protest, Mike added quickly, ''We know the past history between Inca and yourself. That is why Roan Storm Walker is going along. He'll relay any information or opinions from Inca to you. We know you won't want to interface with her directly due to…circumstances….''

Marcellino uttered a sharp cry of surprise. He shot up so quickly that his chair tipped over. His voice was ragged with utter disbelief. ''No! No! A thousand times no!'' He swung toward Morgan, who sat tensely.

''You cannot do this! I will not allow it! She's a ruthless killer! She murdered my eldest son, Rafael, in cold blood!'' He slammed his fist down on the table, causing the wood to vibrate. ''I will not permit this godless woman anywhere near me or my troops!'' His voice cracked. Tears came to his eyes, though he instantly forced them back. ''I lost my eldest son to that murdering, thieving traitor! She's a sorceress! She kills without rhyme or reason.''

Choking, he suddenly realized how much of his military bearing he'd lost in front of his fellow officers. His face turned a dull red. He opened his hands and held them up. ''I apologize,'' he whispered unsteadily. ''Many of you do not know me, know of my background. My eldest son, the light of my life…the son who was to carry on my name, who was to marry and someday give me grandchildren…was senselessly and brutally murdered by this woman named Inca. She is wanted in Brazil for thirteen murders. Thirteen," he growled. Straightening up, his heart pounding, he again apologized. "I had no idea you would suggest her," he told Morgan in a hoarse tone.

Morgan slowly rose and offered a hand in peace to him. "Please, Colonel, come and sit down."

An aide scrambled from near the door to pick up the colonel's fallen chair and place it upright so that he could sit down. Hands shaking, Jaime pulled the chair, which was on rollers, beneath him. "I am sorry for my outburst. I am not sorry what I said about this sorceress." Sitting down, he glared across the table at Morgan and Mike Houston. "You know of her. You know she's a murderer. How can you ask me to tolerate the sight of her, much less work with her, when she has the blood of my son on her hands?" His voice cracked. "How?"

Houston looked to his boss. This was Morgan's battle to win, not his. Sitting down, he watched Morgan's face carefully as he rose to his full height to address the emotionally distraught colonel.

"Jaime…" Morgan began softly, opening his hand in a pleading gesture, "I have four children. I almost lost my oldest son, Jason, in a kidnapping and I know of your grief. I'm deeply sorry for your loss. I truly am." Morgan cleared his throat and glanced down at Mike who sat looking grim. "I have it on good authority that Inca did *not* kill your son Rafael. She said she was on the other side of the basin when he and his squad surprised a drug-running operation in a village. Inca denies killing your son. The person in this room who knows her well is Mike Houston. Mike, do you have anything to add to this, to help the colonel realize that Rafael was not murdered by Inca?"

Mike leaned forward, his gaze fixed on Jaime's grief-filled face. The colonel had lost his hard military expression, and his dark eyes were wild with suffering and barely checked rage. Mike knew that in most Latin American countries, the firstborn male child was the darling of the family. In the patriarchal cultures in South America, to lose the eldest son was, to the father of that family, to lose everything. The eldest was doted upon, raised from infancy to take over the family business, the family responsibilities, and carry on their long heritage. Mike knew the people in Jaime's social strata were highly educated. Jaime himself, descended from Portuguese aristocracy of the 1700s, had a proud lineage that few others in Brazil possessed. Rafael had been trained, coaxed, nurtured and lovingly molded according to this prominent family's expectations. Mike knew even as he spoke just how devastating the loss was for the colonel.

"Colonel Marcellino. Inca is my blood sister." He held up his hand and pointed to a small scar on the palm of his hand. "I met her when she was eighteen years old. She saved my life, quite literally. She almost died in the process. The Inca I know is not a murderer. She is a member of the Jaguar Clan of Peru, a group that teaches their people to defend, never attack. If someone fires on Inca, or someone attacks her, she will defend herself. But she will never fire first. She will not ever needlessly take a life."

Marcellino glared across the table at him. "Do not paint a pretty picture of this murdering sorceress. The men in Rafael's squad saw her. They saw her put a rifle to her shoulder and shoot my son cold-bloodedly in the head!"

"Listen to me," Mike rasped. "Inca was two hundred miles away from the place where your son was killed. She was with an old Catholic priest, Father Titus, at an Indian mission on the Amazon River. I can prove it." Mike pulled out a paper from the open file in front of him. "Here, this is an affidavit signed by the priest. Please, look at it. Read it."

Belligerently, Jaime jerked the paper from Mike's hand. He saw the sweat stains on the document and the barely legible signature of the old priest. Throwing it back, he barked, "This proves nothing!"

Mike placed the paper back into the file. Keeping his voice low and quashing his feelings, he said, "No one in your son's squad survived the attack by the drug lord and his men. I saw the report on it, Colonel. All you have is one person's word—a man who was later captured and who is suspected of working with the same local drug lord who indicted Inca. He said Inca was there. You have a drug runner's word. Are you going to believe him? He has every reason to lie to you on this. He wants to save his hide and do only a little bit of prison time and get released. How convenient to lay the blame at Inca's feet. Especially since she wasn't there to defend herself." Houston tapped the file beneath his hand. "I know Father Titus personally. The old priest is almost ninety. He's lived in the basin and has helped the Indians at his mission for nearly seventy of those years. At one time he helped raise Inca, who was orphaned."

"Then all the more reason for the old priest to lie!" Jaime retorted. "No! I do not believe you. The blood of thirteen men lays on Inca's head. There is a huge reward, worth six million cruzeiros, or one million dollars, U.S., for her capture, dead or alive, in Brazil. If I see her, I will kill her myself. Personally. And with pleasure. My son's life will finally be avenged."

Roan shifted slightly in his chair. The atmosphere in the room was cold and hostile. Not one man moved; all eyes were riveted on the colonel and Mike Houston. Roan saw the hatred in the colonel's face, heard the venom that dripped from every stilted English word he spoke. The colonel's black eyes were a quagmire of grief and rage. Part of Roan's heart went out to the man. Jaime had made the worst sacrifice of all; he'd lost a beloved child. Well, Roan had something in common with the colonel—he'd lost someone he'd loved deeply, too. But who was Inca? The woman he'd seen in his dream earlier? She sounded like a hellion of the first order. Warrioress, madwoman—who knew? Roan looked to Mike Houston, who was laboring to get the colonel to see reason.

"Inca's only responsibility is as a Green Warrior for Mother Earth," Mike said quietly. "She has taken a vow to protect the Amazon Basin from encroachment and destruction by anyone. Twelve of these so-called murders were really self-defense situations. Plus, the twelve men who are dead are all drug dealers. Inca does not deny killing them, but she didn't fire first. She shot back only to save herself and other innocent lives." Mike held out a thick folder toward Jaime. "Here is the proof, colonel. I haven't understood yet why the government of Brazil has not absolved Inca of those trumped up charges. I'd think Brazil would be happy to see those men gone." He laid the file down. "But I don't want to get off track here. You can read her sworn statements on each charge when you want."

"It is well known she hates white men!" Marcellino snapped, his anger flaring.

"Not all," Mike countered. "She's my blood sister by ceremony. She respects men and women alike. Now, if someone wants to destroy, rip up, start cutting down timber, hurt the Indians or make them into slaves, then Inca will be there to stop him. She will try many ways to stop the destruction, but murdering a person is not one of them. And as I said, she will fire in defense, she will never fire the first shot."

"And I suppose," Marcellino rattled angrily, "that the thirteen men she killed fired on her *first?*"

"That's exactly what happened in twelve cases," Houston said gravely. "Your son is the thirteenth to her count, he shouldn't have been added. Members of the Jaguar Clan can be kicked out of it by firing first or attacking first. She can only defend herself. So twelve men fired *first* on her, Colonel. And she shot back. And she didn't miss."

"She murdered my son! He's one of the thirteen."

"Inca was not there. She did not shoot your son."

Morgan appealed to Marcellino. "Colonel, would you, as an officer, lead your entire company of men into an unknown area without proper help and guidance?"

"Of course not!"

"Inca knows the basin better than anyone," Morgan said soothingly. He lifted a hand toward Roan at the end of the table. "This man will be standing between you and Inca. You won't have to face her. You won't have to see that much of her. He's your liaison. Your spokesman, if you will. Inca can lead you and your men safely to this valley in the mountains. I know much is being asked of you, and that is why Roan is here—to assist and help you as much as he can. Anything she tells him, Roan will relay on to you or your officers. I realize the pain of your loss, and we tried to come up with a plan that would somehow protect you and her both during this mission."

"I will kill her if I see her."

"No," Morgan said, his voice hard and uncompromising, "you won't. If you really want to take this mission, you will promise to leave her alone."

"And you will not order one of your men to shoot her, either," Houston growled. "Any attempt on Inca's life, and she'll leave you and your company wherever you are. And if you're in the middle of the rain forest, Colonel, without a guide, you'll be in jeopardy."

"Then I will hire an Indian guide to lead us."

Houston shook his head. "There isn't an Indian willing to lead you into the area, Colonel. If the drug lords find out that they did, they'd move into their village and murder everyone in retribution."

Jaime tried to take a breath. It hurt to breathe. His heart was wild with grief. Rafael had been murdered two years ago, but it felt like only yesterday. Rubbing his chest savagely, Jaime snarled, "You cannot ask this of me. You cannot."

Morgan moved around the table and faced him squarely.

"Colonel, if I thought for a heartbeat that Inca had killed your son, I would not have asked you to head this mission. Nor would I have asked Inca to be your guide. I believe Mike Houston. I've never met her, I only know of her reputation in Brazil. I know that if a person becomes a legend, many times the truth gets tattered and distorted. I believe the old priest's affidavit. He has no reason to lie to protect her. Priests don't lie about something like this. I've also read her sworn statements on each charge. I believe she's innocent in such charges." Morgan eased his bulk down on the table next to Marcellino's chair.

"Colonel, you are a man of consummate honor. Your family's heritage stretches back to the kings and queens of Portugal. You were the only person we wanted for this mission. You are a brave and resourceful man. You are someone who is good at his word. Your love of your country has been obvious in the twenty years you've served in her military. You are one of the most decorated men in your country." Morgan held the officer's dark gaze. "I believe, Colonel, that if you will give me your word that you will not harm Inca for the duration of the mission, that you can be trusted. Look beyond her. Look at what you will accomplish for all the people of Brazil. You will be a hero."

Morgan raised his hand and swept it toward the rest of the men sitting around the table. "And think of the glory you will receive, the recognition, for going in first to strike a blow for freedom from these drug runners. Your name will be on the lips of people around the globe. Is that not a credit to your son? Could this mission be undertaken in his name? In his memory?"

Morgan saw Marcellino sink back into the chair. He knew the officer's ego and pride were tremendous. And typical of South American aristocracy, fame and power would appeal strongly to the colonel. Morgan was hoping it would break the logjam on this mission. He tried to sit there appearing at ease, even though his gut was knotted while he waited for the man's answer.

Roan watched the proceedings with rapt attention. So, he was to be a bridge, a liaison between this wild woman from Amazonia and the colonel who wanted to kill her in the name of his lost son. Roan realized the immensity of his mission. Was this woman, Inca, sane? Was she manageable? Would she respect him enough to stay out of Marcellino's way so they could successfully complete the assigned task? Roan wasn't sure, and he had a helluva lot of questions to ask Houston when the time was right.

All eyes were on Marcellino as he sat back, deep in thought over Morgan's softly spoken words. No one moved. The Brazilian finally looked at Houston. "What makes you think she will work with Storm Walker?"

"He's Indian like she is. Inca respects Indians."

"He's a man." Marcellino's voice dripped with sarcasm.

"Inca doesn't hate men. She respects men who have honor, who have morals and who aren't destroying Mother Earth. Roan, here, comes from a similar background. He'll be able to understand her, and vice versa. I believe it is a good match, and I believe Inca will get along well with him."

"And what if she doesn't?"

"Then," Mike said, "the mission is off. Morgan and I realize your loss, Colonel. We've worked hard to put the right people in key positions to help you get through this mission successfully. If Roan can't forge the bond of trust we need with Inca, in order to work with you, then this mission is scrubbed."

Nodding, Marcellino glared up at Morgan. "If it had been anyone but you asking this of me, I would tell him to burn in hell."

Relief shuddered through Morgan, though he kept his face expressionless. Reaching out, he placed his hand on the colonel's proud shoulder. "Jaime, I share your grief and your loss. But I'm convinced Inca is innocent of your son's death. She is the only person we know who can give you success on your mission. I know I'm asking a lot from you in begging you to rise above personal hurt, grief and rage, and look at the larger picture. You can be the deliverer of hundreds of people. The name Marcellino will be revered in many Indian villages because you had the courage to come and eradicate the drug lords from the basin. I know you can do this. And I don't deny it will be difficult…''

The colonel slumped slightly. He felt Morgan's grip on his shoulder, heard the sincerity in his rumbling voice. "Very well," he whispered raggedly, "you have my word, Morgan. I will reluctantly work with Inca. But only through this man." He pointed at Roan. "I don't know what I'll do if I see her. I want to kill her—I won't deny it. He had best make sure that she never meets me face-to-face.…''

Morgan nodded and swallowed hard. "I know Roan will do everything in his power to convey that message to Inca. She will be your scout, your point person, so the chances of seeing her are pretty slim. But I'll make sure he tells her that. I have no wish to hurt you any more than you've already been hurt by your son's loss."

Eyes misting, Jaime forced back tears. He looked up at Morgan. "And do you know the terrible twist in all of this?"

"No, what?"

"My youngest son, Julian, who is a lieutenant, will be leading one of the squads under my command on this mission."

Morgan closed his eyes for a moment. When he opened them, he rasped, "Colonel, your son is safe. Inca is not going after him—or any of your men. She is on *your* side of this fight."

"This time," Marcellino said bitterly. "And for how long? She is infamous for turning on people when it suits her whims and wiles."

"Roan will see that things go smoothly," Morgan promised heavily, shooting him a glance down the table.

Roan waited patiently until the room cleared of all but him, Morgan and Mike. When the door shut, he slowly unwound from his chair.

"I didn't realize what I'd be doing."

Mike nodded. "I'm sorry I couldn't brief you beforehand, Roan."

Morgan moved toward the end of the table, where Roan stood. "More importantly, do you *want* to take this assignment?"

With a shrug, Roan said, "I wasn't doing much of anything else."

Morgan nodded and wiped his perspiring brow with a white linen handkerchief, then returned it to his back pocket. "I've never met Inca. Mike has. I think you should direct your questions to him. In the meantime, I'm going to join the officers at a banquet we've set up in their honor in the dining room. See me there when you're done here?"

Roan nodded, then waited expectantly as the door closed behind Morgan. Silence settled over them, and Roan discovered Mike Houston's expression became more readable once they were alone. Roan opened his hand.

"Well? Is she a killer or a saint in disguise?

Grinning, Mike said, "Not a killer and not a saint."

"What then?"

"A twenty-five-year-old woman who was orphaned at birth, and who is responsible for protecting the Indian people of the Amazon."

"Why her?"

"She's a member of the Jaguar Clan," Mike said, sitting down and relaxing. "You're Native American. You have your societies up here in the north. Down in South America, they're known as clans. One and the same."

"Okay," Roan said, "like a hunters' society? Or a warriors' society?"

"Yes, specialists. Which is why the societies were created—to honor those who had skills in a specific area of need for their community. The welfare and continuing survival of their families and way of life depends on it."

"So, the Jaguar Clan is…what?"

"What kind of society?" Mike sighed. "A highly complex one. It's not easy to define. Your mother, I understand, was a Yuwipi medicine woman of the Lakota people. She was also known as a shape-shifter?"

Roan nodded. "That's right."

"The Jaguar Clan is a group of people from around the world who possess jaguar medicine. They come from all walks of life. Their calling is to learn about their jaguar medicine—what it is and what it is capable of doing. It is basically a healers' clan. That is why Inca would never fire first. That is why she defends well, but never attacks. Her calling is one of healing—in her case, to help heal Mother Earth. She does this by being a Green Warrior in Brazil, where she was born."

"The colonel called her a sorceress."

"Inca has many different powers. She is not your normal young woman," Mike warned him. "Combine that with her passion for protecting the people of the Amazon, the mission she is charged with, and her confidence and high intelligence, and you have a powerful woman on your hands. She doesn't suffer fools lightly or gladly. She speaks her mind." Mike grinned. "I love her like a sister, Roan. I don't have a problem with her strength, her moxie or her vow of healing Mother Earth and protecting the weak from drug runners. Most men do. I figured you wouldn't because, originally, Native American nations were all matriarchal, and most still have a healthy respect for what women have brought to the table."

"Right, I do."

"Good. Hold that perspective. Inca can be hardheaded, she's a visionary, and she can scare the living hell out of you with some of her skills. They call her the jaguar goddess in the basin because people have seen her heal those who were dying."

"And do you trust Marcellino not to try and kill her?"

"No," Mike said slowly, "and that is why you'll have to be there like a rock wall between them. You'll need to watch out for Inca getting shot in the back by him or one of his men. You're going to be in a helluva fix between two warring parties. Inca has a real dislike for the military. According to her, they're soft. They don't train hard. They don't listen to the locals who know the land because they are so damned arrogant and think they know everything, when in reality they know nothing."

"So I'm a diplomat and a bodyguard on this trip."

"Yes. You're at the fulcrum point, Roan. It's a messy place to be. I don't envy you." He smiled a little. "If my wife and child didn't need me, and vice versa, I'd be taking on this mission myself. Morgan wanted someone without family to take it, because the level of risk, the chance of dying, is high. And I know you understand that."

Nodding, Roan ran his long index finger across the highly polished surface of the conference table enjoying the feel of the warm wood. "Is Inca capable of killing me?"

Chuckling, Mike said, "Oh, she can have some thunderstorm-and-lightning temper tantrums when you don't agree with her, or things don't go the way she wants them to, but hurt you? No. She wouldn't do that. If anything, she'll probably see you as one more person under her umbrella of protection."

"Will she listen to me, though? When it counts?"

Shrugging, Mike said, "If you gain her respect and trust, the answer is yes. But you don't have much time to do either."

"Where am I to meet her? Hopefully, it will be without Marcellino and his company."

"On the riverfront, near Manaus, where the two great rivers combine to create the Amazon."

"How will you get in touch with her?"

Houston gave him a lazy smile. "I'll touch base with her in my dream state."

Roan stood there for a second absorbing Houston's statement. "You're a member of the Jaguar Clan, too?"

"Yes, I am."

Roan nodded. He vividly recalled the experience he'd had earlier—the dream of the woman with willow-green eyes. "What color are Inca's eyes?" he asked.

Mike gave him a probing look. He opened his mouth to inquire why Roan was asking such a question, and then decided against it. "Green."

"What shade?"

"Ever seen a willow tree in the spring just after the leaves have popped out?"

"Many times."

"That color of green. A very beautiful, unique color. That's the color of Inca's eyes."

"I thought so...." Roan said, his own eyes narrowing thoughtfully as he realized he and Inca might have already met....

Chapter 3

Inca was lonely. Frowning, she shifted on the large stack of wooden crates where she sat, her booted feet dangling and barely touching the dry red soil of the Amazon's bank. Her fine, delicately arched brows knitted as she studied the ground. In Peru, they called the earth *Pachamama,* or Mother Earth. Stretching slightly, she gently patted the surface with the sole of her military boot. The dirt was Mother Earth's skin, and in her own way, Inca was giving her real and only mother a gentle pat of love.

Sighing, she looked around at the humid mid-afternoon haze that hung above the wide, muddy river. The sun was behind the ever-present hazy clouds that hugged the land like a lover. Making a strangled sound, Inca admitted sourly to herself she didn't know what it was to feel like a lover. The only thing she knew of romantic love was what she'd read about it from the great poets while growing up under Father Titus's tutelage.

Did she want a lover? Was that why she was feeling lonely? Ordinarily, Inca didn't have to deal with such an odd assortment of unusual emotions. She was so busy that she could block out the tender feelers that wound through the heart like a vine, and ignore them completely. Not today. No, she had to rendezvous with this man that her blood brother, Michael Houston, had asked her to meet. Not only that, but she had to work with him! Michael had visited her in the dream state several nights earlier and had carefully gone over everything with her. In the end, he'd left it up to Inca as to whether or not she would work as a guide for Colonel Marcellino—the man who wanted to kill her.

Her lips, full and soft, moved into a grimace. Always alert, with her invisible jaguar spirit guide always on guard, she felt no danger nearby. Her rifle was leaning against the crates, which were stacked and ready to take down the Amazon, part of the supplies Colonel Marcellino would utilize once they met up with him and his company downriver.

She was about to take on a mission, so why was she feeling so alone? So lonely? Rubbing her chest, the olive-green, sleeveless tank top soaked with her perspiration from the high humidity and temperature, Inca lifted her stubborn chin.

She had a mild curiosity about this man called Roan Storm Walker. For one thing, he possessed an interesting name. The fact that he was part Indian made her feel better about this upcoming mission. Indians shared a common blood, a common heritage here in South America. Inca wondered if the blood that pumped through Walker's veins was similar to hers, to the Indians who called the Amazon basin home. She hoped so.

Her hair, wrapped in one thick, long braid, hung limply across her right shoulder with tendrils curling about her face. Inca looked up expectantly toward the asphalt road to Manaus. From the wooden wharves around her, tugs and scows ceaselessly took cargo up and down the Amazon. Right now, at midday, it was siesta time, and no one was in the wharf area, which was lined with rickety wooden docks that stuck

fifty or so feet off the red soil bank into the turbid, muddy
Amazon. Everyone was asleep now, and that was good. For
Inca, it meant less chance of being attacked. She was always
mindful of the bounty on her head. Wanted dead or alive by
the Brazilian government, she rarely came this close to any
city. Only because she was to meet this man, at Michael's
request, had she left her rain forest home, where she was
relatively safe.

Bored by sitting so long, Inca lifted her right arm and
unsnapped one of the small pouches from the dark green
nylon web belt she always wore around her slender waist.
On the other side hung a large canteen filled with water and
a knife in a black leather sheath. On the right, next to the
pouch, was a black leather holster with a pistol in it. In her
business, in her life, she was at war all the time. And even
though she possessed the skills of the Jaguar Clan, good old
guns, pistols and knives were part and parcel of her trade as
well.

Easing a plastic bag out of the pouch, Inca gently opened
it. Inside was a color photo of Michael and Ann Houston.
In Ann's arms was six-month-old Catherine. Inca hungrily
studied the photo, its edges frayed and well worn from being
lovingly looked at so many times, in moments of quiet. She
was godmother to Catherine Inca Houston. She finally had
a family. Pain throbbed briefly through her heart. Abandoned
at birth, unwanted, Inca had bits and pieces of memories of
being passed from village to village, from one jaguar priestess to another. In the first sixteen years of her life, she'd had
many mothers and fathers. Why had her real parents abandoned her? Had she cried a lot? Been a bad baby? What had
she done to be discarded? Looking at the photo of Catherine,
who was a chubby-cheeked, wide-eyed, happy little tyke,
Inca wondered if she'd been ugly at birth, and if that was
why her parents had left her out in the rain forest to die of
starvation.

The pain of abandonment was always with her. Wiping

her damp fingers on the material of the brown-green-and-tan military fatigues she wore, she skimmed the photo lightly with her index finger. She must have been ugly and noisy for her mother and father to throw her away. Eyes blurring with the tears of old pain, Inca absorbed the smiling faces of Michael and Ann. Oh, how happy they were! When Inca saw Mike and Ann together she got some idea of what real love was. She'd been privileged to be around these two courageous people. She'd seen them hold hands, give each other soft, tender looks, and had even seen them kissing heatedly once, when she'd unexpectedly showed up at their camp.

He's coming.

Instantly, Inca placed the photo back into the protective plastic covering and into the pouch at her side, snapping it shut. Her guardian, a normally invisible male jaguar called Topazio, had sent her a mental warning that the man known as Storm Walker was arriving shortly. Standing, Inca felt her heart pound a little in anticipation. Michael had assured her that she would get along with Roan. Inca rarely got along with anyone, so when her blood brother had said that she had eyed him skeptically. Her role in the world was acting as a catalyst, and few people liked a catalyst throwing chaos into their lives. Inca could count on one hand the people who genuinely liked her.

The slight rise of the hill above her blocked her view, so she couldn't see the approach of the taxi that would drop this stranger off in her care. Michael had given her a physical description of him, saying that Roan was tall with black hair, blue eyes and a build like a swimmer. Mike had described his face as square with some lines in it, as if he'd been carved out of the rocks of the Andes. Inca had smiled at that. To say that Roan's face was rough-hewn like the craggy, towering mountains that formed the backbone of South America was an interesting metaphor. She was curious to see if this man indeed had a rugged face.

Inca felt the brush of Topazio against her left thigh. It was a reassuring touch, much like a housecat that brushed lovingly against its owner. He sat down and waited patiently. As Inca stared into the distance, the midday heat made curtains where heat waves undulated in a mirage at the top of the hill.

Anticipation arced through her when she saw the yellow-and-black taxi roar over the crest of the hill on the two-lane, poorly marked road. She worried about the driver recognizing her. Although there were only a few rough sketches of her posted, artists for the government of Brazil had rendered her likeness closely enough for someone to identify her. Once Storm Walker got out of the cab, it would mean a fast exit on the tug. Inca would have to wake the captain, Ernesto, who was asleep in the shade of the boat, haphazardly docked at the nearby wharf, and get him to load the crates on board pronto.

The taxi was blowing blue smoke from its exhaust pipe as it rolled down the long hill toward Inca. Eyes narrowing, she saw the shape of a large man in the back seat. She wrapped her arms against her chest and tensely waited. Her rifle was nearby in case things went sour. Inca trusted no one except Mike Houston and his wife, Rafe Antonio, a backwoodsman who worked with her to protect the Indians, Grandmother Alaria and Father Titus. That was all. Otherwise, she suspected everyone of wanting her head on a platter. Inca's distrust of people had proved itself out consistently. She had no reason to trust the cab driver or this stranger entering her life.

The cab screeched to a halt, the brakes old and worn. Inca watched as a man, a very tall, well-built man, emerged from the back of the vehicle. As he straightened up, Inca's heartbeat soared. He looked directly at her across the distance that separated them. Her lips parted. She felt the intense heat of his cursory inspection of her. The meeting of their eyes was brief, and yet it branded her. Because she was clairvoyant, her senses were honed to an excruciatingly high degree.

She could read someone else's thoughts if she put her mind to it. But rather than making the effort to mind read, she kept her sensitivity to others wide open, like an all-terrain radar system, in order to pick up feelings, sensations and nuances from anyone approaching. Her intuition, which was keenly honed, worked to protect her and keep her safe.

As the man leaned over to pay the driver, Inca felt a warm sheet of energy wrapping around her. Startled, she shook off the feeling. What was that? Guardedly, she realized it had come from *him*. The stranger. Storm Walker. A frisson of panic moved through her gut. What was this? Inca afraid? Oh, yes, fear lived in her, alive and thriving. Fear was always with her. But Inca didn't let fear stop her from doing what had to be done. After all, being a member of the Jaguar Clan, she had to walk through whatever fears she had and move on to accomplish her purpose. Fear was not a reason to quit.

The cab turned around and roared back up the hill. Inca watched as the man leaned down and captured two canvas bags—his luggage—and then straightened up to face her. Five hundred feet separated them. Her guard was up. She felt Topazio get to his feet, his nose to the air, as if checking out the stranger.

The man was tall, much taller than Inca had expected. He was probably around six foot five or six. To her, he was like a giant. She was six foot in height, and few men in the Amazon stood as tall as she did. Automatically, Inca lifted her strong chin, met his assessing cobalt-colored eyes and stood her ground. His face was broad, with the hooked nose of an eagle, and his mouth generous, with many lines around it as well as the corners of his eyes. His hair was black with blue highlights, close-cropped to his head—typical of the military style, she supposed. He wasn't wearing military clothing, however, just a threadbare pair of jean's, waterproof hiking boots and a dark maroon polo shirt that showed off his barrel chest to distinct advantage. This was not the lazy, *norte americano* that Inca was used to seeing. No, this man was hard-bodied from strenuous work. The muscles in his upper arms were thick, the cords of his forearms distinct. His hands were large, the fingers long and large knuckled. There was a tight, coiled energy around him as he moved slowly toward her, their gazes locked together. Inca dug mercilessly into his eyes, studied the huge, black pupils to find his weaknesses, for that was what she had to do in order to survive—find an enemy's weakness and use it against him.

She reminded herself that this man was not her enemy, but her radarlike assessment of him was something she just did naturally. She liked how he moved with a boneless kind of grace. Clairvoyantly, Inca saw a female cougar walking near his left side, looking at her to size *her* up! Smiling to herself, Inca wondered if this man was a medicine person. Michael had said he was Lakota, and that his mother was a medicine woman of great power and fame. His face was rough-hewn, just as her blood brother had described. Storm Walker was not a handsome man. No, he looked as if his large, square face had been carved from the granite of the Andes. She spotted a scar on his left cheek, and another on the right side of his forehead. His brows were thick and slightly arched and emphasized his large, intelligent eyes as they held hers. Few men could hold Inca's stare. But he did—with ease.

Her pulse elevated as he stopped, dropped the luggage and straightened. When his hardened mouth softened temporarily and the corners hooked upward, her heart pounded. Her response to him unnerved Inca, for she'd never responded to a man this way before. The sensations were new to her, confounding her and making her feel slightly breathless as a result. When he extended his large, callused hand toward her, and Inca saw a wand of white sage in it, she relaxed slightly. Among her people, when one clan or nation visited another, sacred sage, ceremonially wrapped, was always given as a token of respect before any words of greeting were spoken.

Just this simple acknowledgment by him, the sacred sage extended in his hand, made Inca feel a deep sense of relief. Only Indians knew this protocol. Something wonderful flittered through Inca's heart as she reached out and took the gift. If the sage was accepted, it was a sign of mutual respect between the two parties, and talk could begin. She waited. The dried sage's fragrance drifted to her flaring nostrils. It was a strong, medicinelike scent, one that made her want to inhale deeply.

"I'm Roan Storm Walker," he said in a quiet tone. "I've been sent here by Mike Houston."

"I am called Inca," she said, her voice husky. He was powerful, and Inca wanted to back away from him to assess the situation more closely. Ordinarily, men she encountered were not this powerful. "I was not expecting a medicine person. I do not have a gift of our sacred sage to give you in return."

Roan nodded. "It's not a problem. Don't worry about it." His pulse was racing. He wondered if she could hear his heart beating like a thundering drum in his chest. Roan had realized for certain as he got out of the cab that Inca was the same woman who had entered his vision state that morning at his cabin. It was definitely her. Did she remember talking to him? Asking him to come down here to help her? If she did, she gave no hint to him. He decided not to ask, for it would be considered disrespectful.

She was incredibly beautiful in his eyes. There was a wildness to her—a raw, primal power as she stood confidently before him dressed in her military attire. Even though she wore jungle fatigues, black GI boots, a web belt around her waist and an olive drab T-shirt, she could not hide her femininity from him in the least. She wore no bra, and her small breasts were upturned and proud against the damp shirt that provocatively outlined them, despite the bandoliers of ammunition criss-crossing her chest. Her face was oval, with a strong chin, high cheekbones and slightly tilted eyes. The color of her eyes made him hold his breath for a moment. Just as Mike Houston had said, they were a delicious willow-green color, with huge, black pupils. Her black lashes were thick and full, and emphasized her incredible eyes like a dark frame. Her hair was black with a slightly reddish tint when the sun peeked out between the sluggishly moving clouds and shined on it. The tendrils curling around her face gave Inca an air of vulnerability in spite of her formidable presence. He rocked internally from the power that surrounded her.

Roan had spotted the rifle leaning up against the crates, and he sensed her distrust of him. He saw it in the guarded look of her eyes. Her mouth was full and soft, yet, as she turned her attention to him, he watched it thin and compress. Mike was right: he'd have to earn her trust, inch by inch. Did he have the necessary time to do it? To protect her? To work as a liaison between her and Marcellino's troops?

"Why do you worry about me?" Inca growled. She turned and put the sage into a small, coarsely woven sack that sat on top of the crates. "I would worry more for you."

Frowning, Roan wondered if she'd read his mind. Mike had warned him that she had many clairvoyant talents. He watched as she shouldered the rifle, butt up, the muzzle pointed toward the ground. Any good soldier out in a rain forest or jungle situation would do that. Water down the barrel of one's weapon would create rust. Clearly Inca was a professional soldier.

"Come," she ordered as she strode quickly to the dock.

"*Olá!* Hello. Ernesto! Get up!" Inca called in Portuguese to the tug captain. The middle-aged, balding man roused himself from his siesta on the deck of his tug.

"Eh?"

Inca waved toward the crates. "Come, load our things. We must go, pronto."

Scrambling to his feet, the captain nodded and quickly rubbed his eyes. His face was round, and he hadn't shaved in days. Dressed only in a pair of khaki cutoffs that had seen better days, he leaped to the wharf.

Inca turned to Storm Walker, who stood waiting and watching. "We need to get these crates on board. Why don't you stow your gear on the tug and help him?"

"Of course." Roan moved past her and made his way from wharf to tug. The boat was old, unpainted, and the deck splintered from lack of sanding and paint to protect it from the relentless heat and humidity of Amazonia. Dropping his luggage at the bow, he watched as Inca moved to the stern of the tug. Her face was guarded and she was looking around, as if sensing something. He briefly saw the crescent-shaped moon on her left shoulder though it was mostly hidden beneath the tank top she wore. Mike Houston had warned him ahead of time that the thin crescent of gold and black fur was a sign her membership in the Jaguar Clan.

Inca barely gave notice to the two men placing the supplies on board. Topazio was restless, an indication that there was a disturbance in the energy of the immediate area. A warning that there was trouble coming.

"Hurry!" she snapped in Portuguese. And then Inca switched to her English, which was not that good. "Hurry."

"I speak Portuguese," Roan stated as he hefted a crate on board.

Grunting, Inca kept her gaze on the hill. Nothing moved in the humid, hot heat of the afternoon. Everything was still. Too still for her liking. She moved restlessly and shifted her position from the end of the wharf to where the asphalt crumbled and stopped. Someone was coming. And it wasn't a good feeling.

Roan looked up. He saw Inca standing almost rigidly, facing the hill and watching. What was up? He almost mouthed the query, but instead hurried from the tug to the shore to retrieve the last wooden crate. The tug captain started up the rusty old engine. Black-and-blue smoke belched from behind the vessel, the engine sputtered, coughed like a hacking person with advanced emphysema, and then caught and roared noisily to life.

"Inca?" Roan called as he placed the crate on the deck.

His voice carried sluggishly through the silence of the damp afternoon air. The hair on his neck stood on end. *Damn!* Leaping off the tug and running along the dock, Roan ordered the captain to cast off. He had just gotten to the end when he saw two cars, a white one and a black one, careening down off the hill toward them. His breath jammed in his throat. He could see rifles hanging out the open windows of both vehicles.

"Inca!"

Inca heard Storm Walker's warning, but she was already on top of the situation. In one smooth movement, she released her rifle and flipped it up, her hand gripping the trigger housing area and moving the barrel upward. She saw the guns stuck out of the windows. She felt the hatred of the men behind them. Turning on her heel, she sprinted toward the tug. It was going to be close!

To her surprise, she saw Storm Walker running toward her, his hand outstretched as if to grab her. Shaken by his protective gesture, she waved him away.

"You have no weapons!" she cried as she ran up to him. "Get back to the tug!"

Roan turned on his heel. He heard the screech of brakes. The first shots shattered the humid stillness. Bits of red dirt spurted into the air very near his feet. *Damn!* More shouts in Portuguese erupted behind them. Inca was following swiftly behind him. He didn't want her to get shot. Slowing, he reached out and shoved her in front of him. He would be the wall between her and the attackers. Who the hell were they, anyway? Digging the toes of his boots into the red dirt, Roan sprinted for the wharf. Already the tug was easing away from the dock. The captain's eyes were huge. He wanted out of here. Pronto!

More gunfire erupted. Inca cursed softly beneath her breath. She halted at the end of the wharf and shouldered her rifle. With cool precision, with wood exploding all around her, she squeezed off five shots in succession. She saw Storm Walker leap to the tug, which was sliding past her. Turning, she jumped from the wharf onto the deck of the vessel herself. It was a long jump, almost five feet. Landing on her hands and knees, she felt Roan's large hands on her arm drawing her upward. He was pushing her behind the cockpit of the tug in order to protect her.

Growling at him, she jerked her arm free. "Release me!" she snarled, and then ran to the side of the cockpit closest to the riverbank. The men were tumbling out of the cars—six of them. They were heavily armed. Inca dropped to one knee, drew the leather sling around her arm and steadied the butt of the rifle against her shoulder and cheek. She got the first man in the crosshairs and squeezed off a shot. She watched as the bullet struck him in the knee. He screamed, threw up his weapon and fell to the earth, writhing in pain.

Rifle fire rained heavily around them. The captain was swearing in Portuguese as he labored hard to get the tug turned around and heading out to the middle of the mile-wide river. Pieces of wood exploded and flew like splinters of shrapnel everywhere. He ducked behind the housing of the cockpit, one shaking hand on the old, dilapidated wooden wheel.

Crouching, Roan moved up alongside Inca. He reached out. "Let me borrow your pistol," he rasped, and leaned over her to unsnap the holster at her side.

Inca nodded and kept her concentration on the enemy. Ordinarily, she'd never let anyone use her weapons, but Roan was different. There was no time for talk. He took her black Beretta, eased away from her and steadied his gun arm on top of the cockpit. She heard the slow pop at each squeeze of the trigger. Two more men fell. He was a good shot.

Those left on the shore fell on their bellies, thrust their weapons out in front of them and continued to send a hail of fire into the tug. They made poor targets, and Inca worked to wound, not kill them. It wasn't in her nature to kill. It never had been. To wound them was to put them out of commission, and that was all she strove to do. Wood erupted next to her. She felt the red-hot pain of a thick splinter entering her upper arm. Instantly, the area went numb. Disregarding her slight injury, Inca continued to squeeze off careful shots.

Finally the tug was out of range. Inca was the first to stop firing. She sat down, her back against the cockpit, the rifle across her lap as she pulled another clip from her web belt and jammed it into the rifle. Looking up, she saw Storm Walker's glistening features as he stopped firing. This man was a cool-headed warrior. Michael had been right about him being a benefit to her, and not a chain around her neck. That was good. His face was immobile, his eyes thundercloud dark as he glanced down to see how she was doing.

"You're hurt...."

Roan's words feathered across Inca. She glanced down at her left arm. There was a bright red trail of blood down her left biceps dripping slowly off her elbow onto the deck.

Without thinking, Roan stepped across her, knelt down and placed his hand near the wound. A large splinter of wood, almost two inches long and a quarter inch in diameter, was sticking out of her upper arm. Her flesh was smooth and damp as he ran his fingers upward to probe the extent and seriousness of her wound.

"Do not touch me!" Inca jerked away from him. Her nostrils flared. "No man touches me without my permission."

Shocked by her violent response, Roan instantly released

her. He sat back on his heels. The anger in her eyes was very real. "I'm a paramedic.... I'm trained—"

"You do not presume anything with me, *norteamericano*," she spat. Scrambling to her knees, Inca made sure there was at least six feet between them. He was too close to her and she felt panic. Why? His touch had been gentle, almost tender. Why had she behaved so snottily toward him? She saw the worry in his eyes, the way his mouth was drawn in with anxiousness.

Holding up his hands in a sign of peace, Roan rasped, "You're right. I presumed. And I apologize." He saw the mixture of outrage, defiance and something else in her narrowed eyes in that moment. When he'd first touched her, he'd seen her eyes go wide with astonishment. And then, seconds later, he saw something else—something so heartwrenchingly sad that it had blown his heart wide open. And within a fraction of a second, the windows to her soul had closed and he saw righteous fury replace that mysterious emotion in her eyes.

Shaken by his concern and care for her, Inca got to her feet, despite the fact that she felt some pain in the region of the wound. They were a mile away from the dock now, the little tug chugging valiantly along on the currents. For now, they were safe. Placing the rifle on top of the cockpit, she turned her attention to the captain.

"Captain, I need a clean cloth and some good water."

The grizzled old man nodded from the cockpit. "In there, *senhorinha*." He pointed down the ladder that led below.

"Do you want some help removing that splinter?" Roan was behind her, but a respectful distance away. As Inca turned she was forced to look up at him. He was sweating profusely now, the underarms and center of his polo shirt dampened. His eyes were not guarded, but alive with genuine concern—for her. Inca was so unused to anyone caring about her—her pain, her needs—that she felt confused by his offer.

"No, I will take care of it in my own way." She spun around and headed down the stairs.

Great, Roan, you just screwed up with her. He stood there on the deck, the humid air riffling around him, cooling him as he placed his hands on his narrow hips. Looking back toward shore, he saw the men leaving. Who were they? Who had sent them? Was Marcellino behind this? No one knew Roan's itinerary except the good colonel. Worried about Inca, Roan stood there and compressed his lips. He'd forgotten Native American protocol with her. In his experience and training, Indians did not like to be touched by strangers. It was considered invasive. A sign of disrespect. Only after a long time, when respect and trust were developed, would touching be permitted.

Running his fingers through his short hair, Roan realized that he had to think in those terms with her. He was too used to being in the Anglo world, and in order to gain her trust, he must go back to the customs he'd grown up with in his own nation—the Native American way of doing things.

Still, he couldn't get the feel of her skin beneath his fingers out of his mind or heart. Inca was firm and tightly muscled. She was in superb athletic condition. There wasn't an ounce of spare flesh on her tall, slender frame. Not many women were in such great shape, except, perhaps, some in the military. Rubbing his chin, he moved back to the cockpit.

Ernesto was mopping his forehead, a worried look in his eyes. He obviously hadn't expected such an attack, and his hands still shook in the aftermath. He offered Roan a bottle of water. Roan took it and thanked him. Tipping his head back, he drank deeply.

Inca reemerged at that moment. She saw Roan, his head tipped back, his Adam's apple bobbing with each gulp he took. Again, fear rippled through her as she made her way up the stairs. A soft breeze cooled her sweaty flesh as she moved topside. Wanting to keep distance between them, she took another bottle of water that Ernesto proffered to her. She thanked him and drank deeply of it.

Roan finished off the water. He'd felt Inca's return. The sense of her power, of her being nearby, was clear to him. As he put the plastic bottle back into the box near the wheel, he glanced up at her. His mouth dropped open. And then he snapped it shut. Roan straightened. He stared at her—not a polite thing to do, but he couldn't help himself.

The injury on her upper left arm was now completely healed. No trace of swelling, no trace of blood marred her beautiful skin. As she capped the bottle of water and gave him a glaring look, he shifted his gaze. What had happened to her wound? It looked as if she hadn't even been injured. But she *had* been and Roan knew it. The captain, too, was staring with a look of disbelief on his face. He was afraid of Inca, so he quickly averted his eyes and stuck to the task of guiding the tug.

Roan had a *lot* of questions. But asking questions was a sign of disrespect, too. If Inca wanted to tell him what she'd done to heal herself, she would in her own good time. Mike Houston had told him that she was a healer. Well, Roan had just gotten a firsthand glimpse of her powerful talents.

"How far do we go downriver?" Inca demanded of him. Despite the tone she used, she was enjoying his company. Normally, men managed to irritate her with their arrogant male attitude, but he did not. Most men could not think like a woman; they were out to lunch instinctually and jammed their feelings so far down inside themselves that they were out of touch completely. Inca found the company of women far preferable. But Roan was different. She could see the remnants of his worry and concern over her wounding. He didn't try to hide or fix a mask on his feelings, she was discovering. The only other man she knew who was similar was her blood brother, Michael. Inca liked to know where a person stood with her, and when that person showed his feelings, whether they were for or against her, Inca appreciated it.

Roan smiled a one-cornered smile. At least she was still talking to him. He saw the frosty look in her eyes, the way she held herself, as if afraid he was going to touch her again. Remaining where he was, he said, "Let me get the map out of my luggage." He brightened a little. "And there's a gift in there for you from Mike and Ann, too. I think things have calmed down enough that we can sit and talk over the mission while you open it."

Inca nodded. "Very well. We will sit on the shady side of the boat, here." She pointed to the starboard side of the tug. Suddenly, she found herself wanting to talk to Roan. Why did he have the name he did? How had he earned it? She watched as he moved to the bow of the tug to retrieve his luggage.

Settling her back against the splintery wall of the cockpit, Inca waited for him. Roan placed the canvas bag, which was tubular in shape, between them and slowly sat down, his legs crossed beneath him. As he unzipped the bag, she watched his deft, sure movements and recalled his touch.

Men did not realize their touch was stronger and therefore potentially hurtful to a woman or a child. Mentally, she corrected herself. Not all men hurt women, but she'd seen too much of it in South America, and it angered her to her soul. No one had the right to hurt someone frailer or weaker.

"Here," Roan said, digging out a foil-wrapped gift tied with red ribbon. "Mike said this was special for you." And he grinned.

Inca scowled as she took the gift. She made sure their fingers did not touch this time. Oh, she wanted to touch Roan again, but a large part of her was afraid of it, afraid of what other wild, unbidden reactions would be released in her body because of it.

"Thank you."

Well, at least Inca could be civil when she wanted to be,

Roan thought, laughing to himself. He was discovering it was all about respecting boundaries with her. He watched covertly, pretending to search for the map, as she tore enthusiastically into the foil wrapping. She was like a child, her face alight with eagerness, her eyes wide with expectation. The wrapping and ribbon fluttered around her.

"Oh!"

Roan grinned as she held up smoked salmon encased in protective foil. "Mike said you had a love of salmon."

For the first time, Inca smiled. She held up the precious gift and studied it intently. "My blood brother knows my weaknesses."

"I doubt you have many," Roan said dryly, and caught her surprised look. Just as quickly, she jerked her gaze away from him.

"Do not be blinded by the legend that follows me. I have many weaknesses," she corrected him throatily. Laying the package in her lap, she took out her knife and quickly slit it open. The orange smoked fish lay before her like a feast. Her fingers hovered over it. She glanced at him. "Do you want some?"

"No, thank you. You go ahead, though, and enjoy it." Roan was pleased with her willingness to share. Among his people, it was always protocol to offer food first to those around you, and lastly, help yourself.

She stared at him through hooded eyes. "Are you sure?" How could he resist smoked salmon?

She was reading his mind. He could feel her there in his head, like a gentle wind on a summer day. For whatever reason, Roan felt no sense of intrusion, no need to protect his thoughts from her. He grinned belatedly as he pulled the map from the plastic case. "I'm sure. The salmon is your gift. Mike and Ann said you love it. I don't want to take a single bite of it away from you. Salmon's a little tough to come by down here," he joked, "and where I come from, there's plenty of it. So, no, you go ahead and enjoy."

Inca studied him. He was a generous and unselfish person. Not only that, he was sensitive and thoughtful to others' needs. Her heart warmed to him strongly. Few men had such honorable traits. "Very well." She got to her feet and went over to the tug captain. Roan watched with interest. Ernesto, his chest sunken, his flesh burned almost tobacco brown by the equatorial sun, reached eagerly for part of the salmon. He took only a little, and thanked Inca profusely for her generosity. She nodded, smiled, and then came and sat back down. Lifting a flake of the meat to her lips, she closed her eyes, rested her head against the cockpit wall and slid it into her mouth.

Roan felt Inca's undiluted pleasure over each morsel of the salmon. In no time, the fish was gone and only the foil package remained on her lap. There was a satiated look in her eyes as she stuck each of her fingers in her mouth to savor the taste of salmon there.

Sighing, Inca lifted her head and looked directly at him. "Your name. It has meaning, yes?"

Shocked at her friendly tone, Roan was taken aback. Maybe his manners had earned him further access to her. He hoped so. Clearing his throat, he said, "Yes, it does."

"Among our people, names carry energy and skills." Inca lifted her hand. "I was named Inca by a jaguar priestess who found me when I was one year old and living with a mother jaguar and her two cubs. She had been given a dream the night before as to where to find me. She kept me for one year and then took me to another village, where another priestess cared for me. When I was five years old I learned that my name meant I was tied to the Inca nation of Peru. Each year, I was passed to another priest or priestess in another village. At each stop, I was taught what each one knew. Each had different skills and talents. I learned English from one. I learned reading from another. Math from another. When I was ten, I was sent to Peru, up to Machu Picchu, to study with an Andean priest name Juan Nunez del Prado. He lived in Aqua Caliente and ran a hostel there for tourists. We would take the bus up to the temples of Machu Picchu and he would teach me many things. He told me the whole story, of what my name meant, and what it was possible to do with such a name.'' She lifted her hand in a graceful motion. ''What my name means, what my destiny is, is secret and known only to me and him. To speak of it is wrong.''

Roan understood. ''Yes, we have a similar belief, but about our vision quest, not about our name. I honor your sacredness, having such a beautiful name.'' Roan saw her fine, thin brows knit. ''With such an impressive history behind your name, I think you were destined for fame. For doing something special for Mother Earth and all her relations. The Incas were in power for a thousand years, and their base of operation was Cuzco, which is near Machu Picchu. In that time, they built an empire stretching the whole breadth and length of South America.'' Roan smiled at her. He saw that each time he met her gaze or shared a smile with her, she appeared uneasy. He wondered why. ''From what I understand from Mike, you have a name here in Amazonia that stretches the length and breadth of it, too.''

''I have lived up to my name and I continue to live the destiny of it every day,'' she agreed. Eyeing him, her head tilting slightly, Inca asked, ''Have you lived up to yours?''

Inca would never directly ask why he had been given his name, and Roan smiled to himself. She wanted to know about him, and he was more than willing to share in order to get her trust. They didn't have much time to create that bond.

''My family's name is Storm Walker. A long time ago, when my great-great-grandfather rode the plains as a Lakota medicine man, he acquired storm medicine. He had been struck by lightning while riding his horse. The horse died, and as he lay there on the plain afterward, he had a powerful vision. He woke up hours later with the name Storm Walker.

He was a great healer. People said lightning would leap from his fingers when he touched someone to heal them of their ills or wounds.''

"Yes?" Inca leaned forward raptly. She liked his low, modulated tone. She knew he spoke quietly so that the captain could not overhear their conversation, for what they spoke of was sacred.

"One member of each succeeding generation on my mother's side of the family inherited this gift of lightning medicine. When our people were put on a reservation, the white men forced us to adopt a first and last name. So we chose Storm Walker in honor of my great-great-grandfather."

"And what of Roan? What is a roan? It is a name I have never heard before."

He quelled his immediate reaction to her sudden warm and animated look. Her face was alive with curiosity, her eyes wide and beautiful. Roan had one helluva time keeping his hands to himself. He wanted to see Inca like this all the time. This was the real her, he understood instinctively. Not the tough, don't-you-dare-touch-me warrior woman, although that was part and parcel of her, too. When there wasn't danger around, she was wide-open, vulnerable and childlike. It was innocence, he realized humbly. And the Great Spirit knew, he wanted to treat that part of her with the greatest of care.

"Roan is the color of a horse," he explained. "Out on the plains, my people rode horses. Horses come in many colors, and a roan has red and white hairs all mixed together in its coat." He smiled a little and held her burning gaze. "My mother was Lakota. A red-skinned woman. My father was a white man, a teacher who has white skin. When I was born, my mother had this vision of a roan horse, whose skin is half red and half white, running down a lane beneath a thunderstorm, with lightning bolts dancing all around it. She decided to call me Roan because I was part Indian and part white. Red and white.''

Inca stared at him. She saw the vulnerable man in him. He was not afraid of her, nor was he afraid to be who he was in front of her. That impressed her. It made her heart feel warm and good, too, which was something she'd never experienced before. ''That is why you are not darker than you are,'' she said, pointing to his skin.

''I got my mother's nose, high cheekbones, black hair and most of her skin coloring. I got my father's blue eyes.''

''Your heart, your spirit, though, belongs to your mother's red-skinned people.''

''Yes,'' Roan agreed softly.

''Are you glad of this?''

''Yes.''

''And did you inherit the gift of healing?''

Roan laughed a little and held up his hands. ''No, I'm afraid it didn't rub off on me, much to my mother's unhappiness.''

Shrugging, Inca said, ''Do not be so sure, Roan Storm Walker. Do not be so sure....''

Chapter 4

Roan had excused himself and went to the opposite side of the tug from where she stood. Once he felt sure they were safely motoring down the Amazon, the shooters nowhere in sight. His adrenaline had finally ebbed after the firefight. He'd noticed her hands were shaking for a little while afterward, too. It was nice to know she was human. It was also nice to know she was one cool-headed customer in a crisis. Not too many people that he knew, men or women, would have been so efficient and clear thinking in that rain of hot lead.

Absently, he touched the medicine piece at his throat and found the blue stone was so hot it felt like it was burning his skin. It wasn't, but the energy emanating from it made it feel that way. The stone always throbbed, hot and burning, anytime he was in danger. Roan knew without a doubt, from a lot of past experience, that the mysterious blue stone was a powerful talisman. There had been so many times in the past when it had heated up and warned him of forthcoming danger. One of his biggest mistakes had been not listening to his intuition the day his wife, Sarah, had gone climbing and died. On that morning, before she left, Roan had had a powerful urge to take off his amulet and place it around her slender neck. He knew she would have accepted the gift, but he'd never, ever entertained the thought of giving the stone to anyone. It had been ingrained by his mother and the tradition of his mother's tribe that the medicine piece should remain with one person until near the time he or she was to die, and then be passed on to the next deserving recipient. Still, the urge to give Sarah the stone had been overpowering, but he'd fought it because of his ancestral tradition. He told himself that it was wrong to take the stone off and give it away prematurely. Sadly, he now knew why his cougar guardian had urged him through his intuition to give Sarah the necklace to wear that day. It *might* have saved her life. He would never know. Rubbing his chest, Roan frowned, the guilt eating at him even to this day.

When he'd grabbed a cab at the airport to head to the dock, the blue stone had begun to throb with heat and energy. Roan had thought the stone was warning him about Inca, but he'd been wrong. She wasn't the one to fear; it was the gang that followed him to the dock that had brought danger.

He wanted to ask Inca a hundred questions now that things were calming down, but he knew Indian protocol, so he had to forego his personal, selfish desire to get nosy. Still, being in her company was like being surrounded by an incredible light of joy and freedom.

Moving to the other side of the tug, he dug deeply into his canvas carry-on bag. Because he was Indian, and because it was only proper to introduce himself to the spirits of this new land, Roan pulled out a large, rainbow-colored abalone shell, a stick of sacred white sage and a red-tailed hawk feather fan. Native Americans did not presume that the spirits of the water, land or air would automatically welcome them into their midst. A simple ceremony of lighting sage and asking for acceptance was traditional.

Once the flame was doused, Roan placed the smoldering smudge stick in the shell. Picking it up, he faced the north direction, the place where Tatanka, the great white buffalo spirit, resided. Leaning down until the shell was near his feet, Roan used the fan to gently waft the thick, purling smoke upward around his body. The smoke was purifying and signaled his sincerity in honoring the spirits of this land. Fanning the smoke about his head, he then placed the shell back on the deck. Sitting down, his back against the cockpit, Roan closed his eyes and prayed. He mentally asked permission to be allowed to walk this land, to be welcomed to it.

As he said his prayers, his arms resting comfortably on his drawn-up knees, Roan felt a burst of joy wash over him. He smiled a little in thanks. That was the spirits of the river, the land and air welcoming him to their territory. He knew the sign well and was relieved. Roan didn't want to go anywhere he wasn't welcomed by the local spirits. It would have been a bad choice, and bad things would have befallen him as a result.

Opening his eyes, he dug into his tobacco bag, which he always carried on a loop on his belt. The beaded bag, made out of tanned elk hide and decorated with a pink flower against a blue background, was very old. It had been his mother's tobacco bag. Digging into it, he held the proffered gift of thanks upward to the sky, and then to the four directions, to Mother Earth, before bringing it to his heart and giving thanks. Then, opening his hand, he threw the fragrant tobacco outward. He watched the dark brown flakes fly through the air and hit the muddy water, then quickly disappeared.

To his surprise, four river dolphins, sleek and dark, leaped within ten feet of the tug, splashing the peeling wood of the deck. Stunned, Roan watched the playful foursome race alongside the tug.

"The river spirit has taken your prayers and gifts to heart," Inca said in a low, serious voice as she approached him from the left.

Surprised, Roan tried to hide his pleasure that she was coming to speak to him. He would never gain her trust if he kept going to her and plying her with endless questions; she'd slam the door to herself tighter than Fort Knox.

The dolphins leaped again, their high-pitched cries mingling with the sound of the foaming, bubbling water. They arced high and splashed back into the river.

Roan smiled a little. "Helluva welcome. I didn't expect it."

Inca stopped and gazed at him critically. He looked relaxed, his large, scarred hands resting on his narrow hips. His profile was Indian; there was no question. Only the lightness of his copper skin revealed his other heritage, through his father. "The dolphin people don't often give such a welcome to strangers to their land, to their river," she murmured. She saw and felt his amazement and gratitude. Maybe Michael was right after all: Roan stood apart from all other men she'd known before. He was more like a Jaguar Clan member, knitted into the fabric of Mother Earth and all her relations. Roan understood that all things were connected, that they were not separate and never had been. Her heart lifted with hope. It was a strange, wonderful feeling, and automatically, Inca touched that region of her chest. She studied the medicine piece that hung around his thickly corded neck. With her clairvoyant vision she could see the power emanating from around that beautiful sky-blue stone he wore.

"You said your mother was a healer, yes?"

Roan nodded and squatted down. "Yes, she was." He saw that the smudge of sage had burned out. Tossing it into the river as an added gift, he took the abalone shell and placed it back into his bag.

"And did she heal by laying her hands on others, as we do in the Jaguar Clan?"

Roan wrapped the feather fan gently back into the red cotton cloth and placed it back into the bag as well, and then zipped it shut. He craned his neck upward and met her half-closed eyes. There was a thoughtful look on Inca's face now. She was so incredibly beautiful. Did she know how attractive she was? Instantly, he saw her brows dip. Was she reading his mind again? Frustrated, Roan figured she was, as he eased to his full height once again.

"My mother was a Yuwipi medicine woman. Her assistants would tie her wrists behind her back and tie up her ankles and then roll her up into a rug and tie the rug up as well. The lights would be doused, the singers and drummers would begin. The ceremony takes hours, usually starting at nightfall and ending at dawn. My mother, with the help of her spirit guides, was released from her bonds. She then prayed for the person whom the ceremony was for. Usually, that person was there in the room. There could be five, ten or fifty people sitting in that room, taking part in the ceremony. Lights would dance through the place. Horns would sound. The spirits brushed the attending people with their paws, their wings or tails. All prayers from everyone were directed to the person who was ill."

Inca nodded. "A powerful ceremony. And did the person get well?"

He smiled a little and put his hands in the pockets of his jeans. "They always did when my mother conducted the ceremony. She was very famous. People came to her from around the world." He glanced at Inca's shoulder, where the splinter had wounded her. "And your clan heals with touch?"

Inca nodded. "You could say that."

"And healing is your calling? Your vision?"

"It is my life," she said simply. Lifting her hand, she watched as the dolphins sped away from the tug, finished with their play. "I took a medicine vow when I became a woman at age twelve. The jaguar priestess who was training me at that time inducted me into the service of our mother, the earth. She then prepared me to go to the clan's village for training, which began at age sixteen."

Roan shook his head. "It sounds like you were passed around a lot, from person to person. Did you ever find out who your parents were?" Instantly, he saw her close up. Her eyes grew opaque with pain and her lips compressed. Roan mentally kicked himself. He'd asked the wrong damn question. "Forget it," he said quickly. "You don't have to answer. That's too personal...."

Touched by his sensitivity, Inca found herself opening up at his roughly spoken words. She saw so much in his large eyes, in those glinting black pupils. Normally, if someone broached a question regarding her past, she'd shut down, get angry and stalk off. Not this time. Inca couldn't explain why her heart felt warm in her breast, or why her pulse quickened when he gave her that special, tender look. Always, she felt that blanket of security and warmth automatically surround her when Roan met and held her gaze. She was unsure of how to react, for she'd never met a man quite like this before. She wanted to be wary of him, to remain on guard, but his demeanor, and the fact that he was Indian like her, made her feel safe. Safe! No one had ever given her that sense before.

"No, I will answer your question." Inca sat down and leaned against the bulkhead. The last of the shakiness that always inhabited her after a confrontation left her. Being with Roan was soothing to her hard-wired nervous system, which was always on high alert. She crossed her legs, her hands resting on her thighs. Roan did the same, keeping a good six feet of space between them. Inca sighed. There was always something soothing about the gentle rocking of a boat in the arms of the Amazon River. "At times like this, I feel like a babe in my mother's arms," she confided throatily. "The rocking motion…somewhere in my memory, a long time ago, I recall being rocked in the arms of a woman. I remember fragments of a song she sang to me."

"One of the priestesses?"

"No." Inca picked at a frayed thread of the fabric on her knee. "I remember part of the song. I have gone back and asked each woman who helped to raise me if she sang it, and none of them did. I know it was my real mother…."

Roan heard the pain in her low voice. He saw her brows dip, and her gaze move to her long, slender, scarred hands. "I was abandoned in the rain forest to die. As I told you before, a mother jaguar found me. I was told that she picked me up in her mouth and carried me back to where she hid her two cubs. When the first jaguar priestess found me, I was a year old and suckling from the mother jaguar. I have some memories of that time. A few…but good ones. I remember being warm and hearing her purr moving like a vibrating drum through my body. Her milk was sweet and good. The woman who found me was from a nearby village. In a dream, she was told where to go look for me. When she arrived, the mother jaguar got up and left me."

Inca smiled softly. "I do not want you to think that the people who raised me from that time on did not love me. They did. Each of them is like a mother and father to me— at least, those who are still alive, and there are not many now…."

"You were on a medicine path, there is no doubt," Roan said.

"Yes." Inca brightened. "It is good to talk to someone who understands my journey."

"My mother set me on a path to become a medicine man, but I'm afraid I disappointed her." Roan laughed a little and held up his hands for a moment. "I didn't have her gift."

"Humph. You have a spirit cougar, a female, who is at

your side. Medicine people always have powerful spirit guides. Perhaps you will wait until middle age to pick up your medicine and practice it. That is common down here in Amazonia. Most men and women do not even begin their training until their mid-forties.''

''You were trained from birth, which means you brought in a lot of power and skills with you,'' Roan said. He saw Inca smile sadly.

''There are days when I wish…'' Her voice trailed off. Shaking her head, she muttered, ''To be hunted like an animal, with a price on my head…to be hated, feared and misunderstood.'' She glanced over at him. ''At least the Indians of the basin understand. They know of my vow, know I am here to help protect them. The white men who want to destroy our rain forests want my life. The gold miners would kill me if they saw me. The *gaucqueros,* the gem hunters, would do the same. Anyone who wants to rape our land, to take without giving to it something equal in return, wants me dead.''

Roan felt her sadness. Quietly, he said, ''It must be a heavy burden to carry. I hope you have friends with whom you can share your burdens and dreams.''

Rubbing her brow, Inca whispered, ''I am all but thrown out of the Jaguar Clan. Grandfather Adaire has sentenced me and told me never to return to the village where all clan members train. I—I miss going there. Grandmother Alaria…well, I love her as I've loved no one else among those who have raised me. She is so kind, so gentle, all the things I am not…. I am like a rough-cut emerald compared to her. She is so old that no one knows how old she is. I miss talking to her. I miss the time we spent together.''

''Then you're an outcast?'' Roan saw the incredible pain in every feature of Inca's face. In some part of his heart, he knew she was opening up to him in a way that she rarely did with anyone. The energy between them was tenuous…fragile, just like her. He found himself wanting to slide his arm across her proud shoulders, draw her into his arms and simply hold her. Hold her and comfort her against the awful weight of pain she carried. In that moment, she was more a hurting child to him than a warrior woman.

"No, not exactly an outcast… Oh, to be sure, some members have been cast permanently out of the clan." She gave him a pained, one-cornered smile, and then quickly looked away. "My sentence is an ongoing one. Grandfather Adaire says I am walking on the dark side with some choices I have made. And until I can walk in the light all the time, I am not allowed to return to the village as a full member of it."

Roan frowned. "Light and dark? Familiar words and themes to me." He opened his hands. "Where I come from, in our belief system, light does not exist without darkness, and vice versa. You can't have one without the other. And no human being is ever all one or the other." He glanced over at her. "Are they expecting you *not* to be human? Not to make mistakes?"

She laughed abruptly. "The Jaguar Clan is an honorable part of the Sisterhood of Light. There are rules that cannot be broken…and I broke one of them. It was a very serious thing. Life-and-death serious." Inca frowned and tugged at the frayed thread on her knee until it broke off in her fingers.

"Mike Houston said you saved his life," Roan said. He ached to reach out to her now. There were tears swimming in her eyes, although Inca's head was bowed and slightly turned away from his in an effort to hide them from him. In her softened tone he could hear the wrenching heartache she carried. She moved her hands restlessly.

"That is why I was asked to leave my own kind, my home…. Michael was dying. I knew it. And yes, I broke the rule and went into the light where the souls of all humans who are dying go. I pulled him back from the Threshold. I gave my life, my energy, my heart and love, and drew him back. If not for Grandmother Alaria, who revived me because I was practically dead after saving Michael, I would not be here today.''

"So, you saved a life? And Grandfather Adaire kicked you out of the clan for that?" Roan had a hard time understanding why.

"Do not be judgmental of Grandfather Adaire. He was only following the code of the clan. You see, we are trained in the art of life and death. Because we have the power, that means we must walk with it in strict accordance to the laws of the universe. I broke one of those laws. Michael had made his choice to die of his wound. I had been caring for him for a week, and for the first time in my life, I felt as if I had met my real brother. Oh, he was not, but that was the bond we had from the moment we met. It was wonderful...." She sighed unhappily. "I saw him slipping away daily. My heart cried. I cried alone, where no one could see me. I knew he would die. I did not want it to happen. I knew I had the power to stop it. And I knew it was wrong to intervene.'' Inca smiled sadly as she looked at the shore, which was a half a mile away on either side of the chugging tug.

"I wanted a brother just like Michael. I'd been searching so long for a family—I was so starved to have one—that I did it. I broke the law. And I did it knowingly." Gravely, Inca turned her head and met his dark blue eyes. "And that is why I was asked to leave. What I did was a 'dark side' decision. It was selfish and self-serving.''

Roan choked as she finished the story. He felt anger over it. "Didn't Grandfather Adaire realize that, because you were abandoned, family would mean so much more to you than it would to others?''

She hitched one shoulder upward and looked out at the muddy river. "That is an excuse. It is not acceptable to the clan. I broke a law. It does not matter *why* I broke it.''

"Seems a little one-sided and unfair to me," he groused.

"Well," Inca said with a laugh, "my saving Michael's life, in the long term, had its positive side. He asked to become my blood brother. And when he fell in love with Dr. Ann, and she had his baby, Catherine, I became a godmother to their child.'' The tears in her eyes burned. Inca looked away. She wanted to wipe them away, but she didn't want Roan to know of her tears. No one ever saw her cry. No one. Choking on the tears, she rasped, ''I have a family now. Michael and Ann love me. They accept me despite who I am, despite what I do for a living.'' She sniffed and reached for a pouch on her right side. ''Look…here…let me show you baby Catherine….''

Roan watched Inca eagerly fumble in the pouch. The joy mirrored in her face was like sunlight. She valiantly tried to force the tears out of her glimmering willow-green eyes as she handed him a frayed color photo.

''This is Mike and his family,'' he said.

''Yes,'' Inca replied, and she leaned forward, her shoulder nearly touching his as she pointed at the baby held between them. ''And this is Catherine…I call her Cat. She has a male jaguar spirit guide already! That is very special. She is special. Ann and Michael know it, too. Little Cat is my goddaughter.''

The pride was unmistakable in Inca's passionate voice. It took everything for Roan not to respond to her excitement. She was so close he could smell her. There was a wonderful, fragrant scent to Inca. It reminded him of the bright pink Oriental lilies that grew behind his cabin, where Sarah had planted them. Looking up, he smiled into Inca's glimmering eyes as he handed her the photo.

''You should be proud of Catherine. She's lucky to have you as a godmother. Very lucky.''

A sweet frisson of joy threaded through Inca's heart at his huskily spoken words. When she met and held his dark blue gaze, Inca's heart flew open. It caught her by surprise. A little breathless, she quickly put the photo back into the protective plastic and snapped the pouch shut.

''In my mind,'' she said, ''what I did to save Michael's

life was not wrong. It hurts to think I can never go home, but now my home is with him and his family, instead.''

The sweet bitterness of Inca's past moved Roan deeply. ''I don't know how you handle it all,'' he admitted. ''I'd be lost without my family, my parents.... I don't know what it's like to be an orphan.''

''Hard.''

He nodded and saw that she was frowning. ''I can't even begin to imagine....''

Inca found herself wanting to talk more to Roan. ''You are a strange man.''

He grinned. ''Oh?''

''I find myself jabbering to you, making my life an open book to you. Father Titus was such a talker. He would tell me everything of what lay in his heart and feelings. Being Indian, we are normally quiet and reserved about such things. But not him. He made me laugh many times. I always thought he was a strange old man with his bird's nest of white hair.''

''He was vulnerable and open with you.''

Sobering, Inca nodded, ''Yes, he was...and still is, even though I do not visit him as often as I would like because my duties are elsewhere.''

''So...'' Roan murmured, ''am I like Father Titus?''

''No, I am! I blather on to you. As if I have known you lifetimes. I bare my soul to you, my heart—and I do not ever do that with anyone.''

Wanting to reach out and touch her hand, Roan resisted. Instead he rasped, ''Inca, your heart, your soul, are safe with me. Always and forever.''

Regarding him gravely, Inca felt his words. She was afraid of him for some unknown reason, and yet, at the same time, drawn to him just as a moth is driven to dive into the open flame of a campfire. ''You are of two worlds, Roan Storm Walker. One foot stands in the white man's world, the other in the Indian world. Yet you are not a two-heart. Your heart belongs to Mother Earth and all her relations.''

''Judge me by my actions,'' he cautioned her. ''Not my skin color.''

Inca gazed at him raptly, before she suddenly felt the pull of the jaguar's warning.

Danger!

''Something is wrong.'' Inca was on her feet in an instant. When her spirit guide jaguar gave her such a warning, her life was in danger. ''Get up!'' she ordered Roan. Running around the stern of the tug, Inca grabbed her rifle.

Roan struggled to his feet. The soft, vulnerable Inca was gone in a heartbeat. Shaken by her sudden change, he stared at her. Secondarily, he felt the stinging, burning heat of the blue stone at the base of his neck throbbing in warning— only he hadn't felt it until now because he was so taken with Inca.

''What's wrong? What is it?''

''My guardian has warned me. We are in danger.''

Before Roan could say another word, he heard the heavy, whapping sounds of a helicopter approaching them at high speed. He turned on his heel. Coming up the river, directly at them, was an olive-green, unmarked helicopter. It flew low, maybe fifty feet off the water's surface. His eyes widened. This was no tourist helicopter like the one he'd seen plying the skies of Manaus earlier. No, this was a helicopter, heavily armed with machine guns and rockets. The lethal look of the dark, swiftly moving aircraft made his heart rate soar with fear.

''Captain Ernesto!'' Roan called. Before he could say anything, the blazing, winking lights on the guns carried by the military helicopter roared to life. Roan cursed. He saw two rows of bullets walking toward them like soldiers marching in parallel lines. The tug was right in the middle of the two rows.

''*Jump,* Ernesto!'' Roan roared.

Inca positioned herself against the cockpit. She aimed her rifle at the charging helicopter. The first bullets hit the tug, which shuddered like a wounded bull. Wood splinters exploded. Crashing, whining sounds filled the air. The thick thump, thump, thump of the blades blasted against her ears. Still she held her ground. Aiming carefully, she squeezed off a series of shots. To her dismay, she watched them hit the helicopter and ricochet off.

"Inca! Jump!"

At the urgency of his tone, she jerked a look toward Roan. Before she could say anything, he grabbed her by the arm and threw her into the water.

Choking, Inca went under. She was heavily weighted down with the bandoliers of ammunition she always carried. Panicked, she gripped her rifle. Wild, zinging, whining bullets screamed past her as she floundered, trying to kick her way back up to the surface. Impossible! She had to remain cool. She had to think. Think! If she could not focus, if she could not concentrate, she would drown and she knew it.

Kicking strongly, her booted feet also weighing her down, Inca felt the current grab her. The water was murky and opaque. She could see nothing. Bubbles streamed out her open mouth as she lunged toward the surface.

Where was Inca? Roan looked around as he treaded water. The helicopter was blasting the tug to bits. Ernesto had not gotten off in time. Roan suspected the man did not know how to swim, so he'd stayed with his tug. Jerking at his boots, Roan quickly got rid of them. Inca? Where was she? He saw some bubbles coming to the surface six feet away from him. Taking a deep breath, he dove, knowing she was in trouble. She was too weighted down by the ammo she wore and she'd drown. Damn! Striking out in long, hard strokes, he followed the line of bubbles. There! He saw Inca, a vague shape in the dim, murky water.

Lunging forward, his hand outstretched, Roan gripped her

flailing arm. Jerking her hard, he shoved her up past him to the surface.

Inca shot up out of the water, gasping for air, but still holding on to her rifle. Roan surfaced next to her and immediately wound his arm around her waist.

"Get rid of the boots!" he yelled, and he took the rifle from her.

Struggling, Inca did as he ordered. She saw the tug in the distance, a blazing wreck. The helicopter was mercilessly pummeling it with bullets.

"Now the ammo!"

"No!" she cried. "Not the ammo!"

"You'll drown!"

"No, I will not." Inca flailed and pushed his hand away. "Swim for shore," she gasped.

Roan wasn't going to argue. He kept the rifle and slung it over his shoulder. They struck out together. The Amazon River might look smooth on the surface, but the currents were hell. He kept his eye on the chopper.

"It's turning!" he yelled at Inca, who was ten feet ahead of him. "It's coming for us! Dive!"

Inca saw the military helicopter turning, its lethal guns trained on them. She heard Roan's order. Taking a huge breath into her lungs, she dived deeply and quickly. It was easy with the extra weight of the ammo around her upper body. At least twenty bullets zinged around her. Roan? What about him?

Worried, Inca halted her dive and turned around. Roan? Where was he? She could hear the helicopter's shattering sound just above them, the reverberation pulsating all around her. It was hovering over the water, very near to where she treaded. Roan was wounded! She felt it. No!

Anxiety shattered Inca. She kicked out violently and moved in the direction she knew Roan to be, even though she could not see him. The helicopter moved away, the dark shadow leaving the area. Concentrating, her lungs bursting for air, Inca kicked hard and struck out strongly. Roan? Where was he? How badly was he shot?

Her heart beat in triple time. Inca didn't want to lose Roan. She'd just found him! He was so much like her blood brother, Michael. Men like Roan were so rare. And she wanted—no, demanded of Mother Earth—that he be saved. She was lonely, and he filled that lonely space within her.

Yes, it was selfish, but she didn't care. Inca struck out savagely. She felt Roan nearby now. Well, selfishness had landed her in hot water with the clan before. Inca knew she was being tested again, but she didn't care if she failed this test, too. She would not let Roan die!

Blood and muddy water moved by her in thin, crimson and brown strips. She saw a shadow up ahead, striking toward the surface. Roan! Inca followed and, with her hand, pushed him upward. She could see blood oozing around his lower leg. He must have taken a bullet to the calf. Was his leg broken? Could he swim?

Unsure, Inca moved up, slid her arm around his massive torso and urged him upward.

They broke water together, like two bobbins coming to the surface. Water leaked into her eyes. She shook her head to clear them. The helicopter was moving back down the river, leaving them. Relief shuddered through Inca.

"Roan! Roan, are you all right?" She held on to him as he twisted around. His lips were drawn back from his clenched teeth. His face was frozen with pain.

"My leg…" he gasped, floundering.

"Can you use it to swim?" Inca cried. Their bodies touched and glided together. She kicked strongly to keep his head above water.

"Yeah…not broke. Just hurts like hell… And the blood. We've got piranhas in this water…."

Inca tugged at his arm. "Do not worry about them. Just head toward that shore. Hurry!" Mentally, Inca sent out her guardian and told him to keep the bloodthirsty little piranha schools at bay. Once they got the scent of blood in the water, fifty to a hundred of them would attack and shred both of them in a matter of minutes. That was not how Inca wanted to die. Nor did she want the man who relied heavily on her now to die, either.

"Kick! Kick your good leg," she ordered. "I will help you...."

It seemed like hours to Roan before they made it to the sandy red shore. Gasping for breath, he crawled halfway out of the water before his strength gave out. He was weakened from the loss of blood. Looking over his shoulder, he could see his bloody pant leg.

Inca hurried out of the water, threw off her ammo belts and ran back to him. She urged him to roll onto his back, and then hooked her hands beneath his arms. Grunting and huffing, she managed to haul him completely out of the water and onto the bank. Positioning him beneath some overhanging trees, she stopped for a moment, panting heavily. Dropping to her knees, she took out her knife and quickly slit open his pant leg to reveal the extent of his wound.

"H-how bad is it?" Roan gasped. He quelled the urge to sit up and grip the wounded leg. He felt Inca's hands moving quickly across his lower extremity, checking it out.

"Bad..." she murmured.

Roan forced himself to sit up. The bullet had torn through the fleshy, muscled part of his lower leg. Fortunately, it had missed the bones. Unfortunately, the wound was still spurting blood.

"An artery's been cut. Put pressure on it," he muttered. Dizzy, he fell back, and felt blackness encroaching on his vision. His gaze was pinned on Inca. Her hair was wet and stuck to the sides of her face. Her expression was intense, her eyes narrowed as she reached out and placed her hand across the jagged wound.

"Close your eyes," she snapped. "Do nothing but rest. Clear you mind. I will help you."

He didn't have much choice in the matter. Her hand, the moment it touched his feverish leg, was hot. Hot like a branding iron. Her fingers closed across his leg, strong and calming. Groaning, he stopped struggling and lay beneath the shade of the overhanging trees, breathing hard. His heart was pounding violently in his chest. Sounds meshed and collided. He was dumping. His blood pressure was going through the floor and he knew it. *Damn.* He was going to die. Darkness closed over his opened eyes. Yes, he would die.

Just as he drifted off into unconsciousness, Roan saw something startling. He saw Inca kneeling over him, her hand gripping his leg, and the blood spurting violently between her fingers. He saw the tight concentration on her face, her eyes gleaming as she focused all her attention on his wound. Roan saw darkness begin to form above her head. It appeared to be a jaguar materializing. Was he seeing things? Was he out of his mind? Was the loss of blood pressure making him delirious? Roan gasped repeatedly and fought to remain conscious. The head and shoulders of a jaguar appeared above Inca. And then it slid, much like a glove onto a hand, down across her head and shoulders. Blinking rapidly, Roan saw a jaguar where Inca had once been. Sweat ran into his eyes. Then he saw Inca, and not the jaguar.

Simultaneously, he felt raw, radiating heat in his lower leg. He cried out, the burning sensation so intense that it made the pain he'd felt before feel minor in comparison. Automatically, his hand shot out, but he was weak and he fell back. In the next instant, he spiraled into a darkness so deep that he knew he was dying and whirling toward the rainbow bridge where a spirit went after death.

Chapter 5

Roan awoke slowly. The howl of monkeys impinged on his consciousness first. Secondly, he heard the raucous screech of parrots as they shrieked at one another in a nearby rubber tree. And then—he was fatigued and it was an effort to sense much of anything—he felt warmth against his back. At first he thought it was Sarah snuggled up beside him, because she would always lay with her back against his in the chill of the early morning hours. The sensation in his heart expanded. No, he wasn't imagining this; it was real. Very real.

As he pried his eyes open, the events of the night before came tumbling back to him in bits and pieces until he put it all together. He'd been shot…he'd been bleeding heavily and he distinctly remembered dumping and preparing himself to die.

Wait… Inca…

His eyes opened fully. Roan pushed himself up on his elbow and twisted to look over his shoulder. In the gray dawn light, a vague yellowish-white glow illuminating to the cottony clouds suspended over the rain forest, he saw Inca. She was curled up on her side, one arm beneath her head, the other hand wrapped protectively around the barrel of the rifle that paralleled her body.

He'd been dying. Inca had leaned over him and placed her strong, firm hand over the spurting, bloody wound on his leg. He glanced down to see the pant leg torn up to his knee, revealing his dark, hairy calf. Sitting up and frowning, Roan slid his fingers along the area that had been chewed up by the bullet. Nothing. There was no sign of a wound. And he was alive.

"I'll be damned."

Twisting to look over his shoulder again, he stared hard at Inca. She had healed him with her mystical powers. Now he recalled the burning heat of her hand on his flesh. He'd thought he was getting third-degree burns. He'd fainted from loss of blood. Scowling, he touched his brow. Yes, he was feeling tired, but not as weak as yesterday, when he'd lost at least a couple pints of blood.

Looking down at her, Roan's heart expanded wildly. In sleep, Inca looked vulnerable and approachable. Her hair, once in a thick braid, was now loose and free about her shoulders and face. Black tendrils softened the angularity of her cheeks. Her thick, ebony lashes rested on her golden skin. His gaze moved to her lips, which were softly parted in sleep. Instantly, his body tightened with desire.

Grinning haphazardly, Roan forced himself to sit up and look around. Running his fingers through his sand-encrusted hair, he realized he needed to clean himself up. Testing the leg, he was surprised to discover it felt fine, as if nothing had happened to it. A flock of scarlet ibis, with long, scimitarlike beaks, flew over them. Their squawks awakened Inca. He watched, somewhat saddened because he'd wanted more time to simply absorb her wild, ephemeral beauty into his heart.

As Inca opened her eyes, she met the penetrating blue

gaze of Roan Storm Walker. Lying on the sandy bank, the warmth of it keeping her from being chilled in the dawn hour, Inca felt her chest expanding like an orchid opening. The look in the man's eyes was like a tender, burning flame devouring her. She was most vulnerable upon awakening. Normally, Inca would shove herself out of this mode quickly and efficiently. Nearby, Topazio lay and yawned widely. There was no danger or her spirit guardian would have growled and jolted her out of her wonderful sleep.

Inca drowned in the cobalt blue of Roan's large eyes. She saw a soft hint of a smile tugging at his mouth. What a wonderful mouth he had! She had never considered men beautiful, or bothered to look at them in that light before. With Roan, gazing at him was a sensuous pleasure, like eating a luscious, juicy fruit.

Inca found herself wanting to reach out and slide her fingers along his flat lower lip and explore the texture of him. She wanted to absorb that lazy smile of welcome. Simultaneously, she felt that incredible warmth of an invisible blanket embracing her once more. This time she didn't fight it. This time, she absorbed it and knew it came from Roan to her—as a gift. Inca accepted his gift in her sleep-ridden state. Nothing had ever felt so good to her. It made her feel secure and cared for. That particular feeling was so new to her that it jolted her even more awake. Her eyes widened slightly as she considered the feelings that wrapped gently around her like a lover's arms.

Always, it was Inca who cared for others, who protected them, and not the other way around. The last time she'd had this feeling of care and protection was as a child growing up. After being asked to leave the village of the Jaguar Clan at age eighteen, she'd never felt it again. Not until now, and this sensation was different, better. She felt like a thirsty jaguar absorbing every bit of it.

As she studied Roan's shadowed features, the soft dawn light revealing the harsh lines around his mouth, the deeply embedded wrinkles at the corners of his eyes, she realized he laughed a lot. Father Titus had similar lines in similar places on his round, pudgy face, and he was always laughing and finding pleasure in the world around him, despite the fact that he was as poor as the Indians he cared for.

"You laugh a lot," she murmured drowsily, continuing to lie on her back observing him.

Roan's smile broadened boyishly, then faded. "I used to. I lost the ability to find much to laugh about two years ago."

Placing one arm behind her head, she gazed up at the soft, grayish-yellow clouds that hung silently above them, barely touching the canopy of the rain forest. "Why did you stop laughing two years ago?"

Roan lost his smile completely. He felt the tenuous intimacy strung between them, and realized he was starving for such intimacy. He'd had it once before and he missed it so very much. Now it was a gift growing between himself and Inca, and Roan was humbled by it.

"Two years ago, my wife, Sarah, died in a climbing accident." Roan felt old pain moving through his chest. He pulled his knees upward and wrapped his arms around them. He looked out at the silently flowing Amazon that stretched endlessly in front of him.

"You'd have liked Sarah," he told Inca in a low, intimate tone. "She had red hair, cut short. She was an artist who drew the most incredible flowers and landscapes. She was a hellion. She knew no boundaries except the ones she wanted to create for herself. She was a world-class mountain climber. And she laughed at danger...." Roan closed his eyes. Why was he telling Inca all of this? It had sat in his heart like an undigested stone, rubbing and grinding on almost a daily basis. Yet, by him speaking to Inca, it was as if that stone was finally dissolving away and not hurting him as much.

"She was a warrior woman."

Nodding, Roan answered, "Yes. In all ways. She was a

part of nature. More animal than human at times.'' He smiled fondly in remembrance. ''We lived in a small cabin up in the Rocky Mountains in Montana. Hurt birds and animals would show up on our porch, and Sarah would care for them, feed them, tend their injuries, and when they were well enough, she'd free them. She'd always cry....'' He shook his head and smiled gently. ''Sarah was so attuned to nature, to life, to her own heart. One moment she'd be laughing and rolling on the floor with me, and the next, she'd read a newspaper or magazine and begin to cry over something sad she'd read.''

Inca digested his hoarsely spoken words. She realized he was allowing her entrance into the deepest part of his heart. She had no experience with such things, but she sensed that she needed to be careful. Just as she offered comfort when she held a sick baby in her arms for healing, Roan needed that comfort from her right now. Pushing her fingers through her hair, Inca whispered, ''How did she die?''

''On the Fourth of July, a holiday in our country. She was climbing a tough mountain made of granite to get ready for her big climb on El Capitan a week after that. She had friends that climbed that mountain every year. But this time Sarah was alone. I knew where she was, and what time she was to come home....'' Roan felt his gut knotting. ''I was out back of the cabin, fixing my truck, when I felt her fall. I could hear her scream in my head...and I knew...''

Wincing, Inca said, ''You were in touch with her spirit. People who touch one another's hearts have this direct way of talking to one another.''

Roan nodded. ''Yes, we had some telepathy between us.''

''What did you do then?''

''I jumped in the truck and drove like a madman to the rock wall where she'd been climbing.'' His voice turned ragged. ''I found her dead at the bottom. She'd died instantly of a skull fracture.'' And if he'd given her his medicine piece to wear, she might still be alive today. But he didn't voice his guilt over that issue.

"A clean death."

"Yes," Roan said, understanding Inca's words. "At least she didn't feel any pain. She was gone in a heartbeat. I'm glad she didn't suffer."

Wryly, Inca looked up at him. He was suffering and she wanted to reach out and console him. Shocked by that, she curled up her fingers. "But you have been suffering."

"Sure. When you love someone like I loved her…well…"

Inca sat up. Her hair fell around her back, shoulders and arms, the ebony strands reaching well below her breasts. She opened her hands. "I do not know what love is. I have seen it between Michael and Ann. I have seen a mother's love of her child, a father's love of his children."

Giving her a look of shock, Roan tried to hide his reaction. "But…you're twenty-five years old. Isn't there someone in your life—a man—you love?"

Scowling, she skimmed the hair through her fingers and separated it into three long swatches. Expertly, she began to braid it, her fingers flying through the silky length. "Love? No, I do not know love like that."

Trying not to stare at her like an idiot, Roan quickly put some facts together about Inca. "Don't your clan members ever marry among themselves?"

Shrugging impatiently, Inca said, "Almost always. Only we understand each other's special skills and talents. People outside the clan are afraid of us. They are afraid of what they do not understand about us. Sometimes, a jaguar clan member will marry outside of it. Michael married Ann. There is no law as to who you marry. Of course, we would like the blessing of the elders."

"And does the person marrying a member of the Jaguar Clan know about his or her special skills?"

"Eventually, perhaps. And sometimes, no. It just depends.

I know that Ann knows everything about Michael and his skills. She accepts them because she loves him.'' Inca took a thin strip of leather, tied off the end of her braid and tossed it across her shoulder. She saw the amazement on Roan's features. Why was he so surprised she did not have a lover? Did he not realize that in her business she had no time for such things? Life and death situations took precedence over selfish pleasures such as love...or so she told herself.

''Does Ann have problems coping with Michael's unusual abilities?''

Inca smiled. ''I think so, but she tries very hard to accept what she does not understand about metaphysics. And their daughter has her father's skills, as well. Clan blood is carried on, generation after generation. One day my godchild, little Catherine, will be going up to the village for years of training.'' She smiled, satisfaction in her tone. ''Until then, I get to see her from time to time, whenever I am near Mike and Ann's house.''

Inca's family. It was all she had, really. Roan was beginning to understand her loneliness, the lack of a man in her life who could love her, care for her and give her safe harbor from a world that wanted her dead at any cost. Frowning, he rubbed his face, the feeling of his beard spiky against his fingers.

''Do you have any children by Sarah?''

The question caught him off guard. Roan eased his hands from his face and met her inquiring gaze. ''No...and I wish I did, now.''

''She did not want children?''

''We both wanted them. We'd been married only two years and wanted to wait a couple more before we settled down to having a family.''

Inca rose slowly to her feet. She wriggled her bare toes in the red sand. ''That is very sad. My heart goes out to you. Sarah was a warrior. She died loving what she loved to do, and in that there is great honor.'' Inca looked up at the clouds that now had a golden cast because the sun was going to rise shortly. "But it was her time to pass over. She had accomplished all that she set out to do in this lifetime." Giving Roan a dark look, she added, "We all have a time when we will die. When whatever we wanted to accomplish is complete. And when that happens, we leave. We walk over the Threshold to the other worlds."

He slowly got to his feet. He felt a little weak, but not bad, considering what had almost happened. "Speaking of dying...I owe you my life, Inca. Thanks." He stuck out his hand to shake hers. "My mother could heal by touching a person, too, so I'm no stranger to what you did."

Inca stared at his hand and then slowly lifted hers. She slid her slender fingers into his roughened ones. Trying to tell herself she did not enjoy making such contact with this tall, stalwart warrior, she avoided the sincerity of his burning blue gaze and whispered unsteadily, "I did nothing. My spirit guide did it. You should thank him, not me."

Roan closed his fingers gently over Inca's proffered hand. Her fingers were strong and yet, even as she gripped his hand, he felt her softness, her womanliness just waiting like a ripe peach to be lovingly chosen by the right man—a man who would honor her as an incredible woman and human being. He found himself wanting to be that man. The thought shook him deeply as he watched her hang her head and avoid his gaze. In some ways, she was so childlike, her innocence blinding him and making his heart open when he'd thought it impossible that anything could make him feel like this again.

"Thank *you* and thank your guide," he murmured, and released her hand. He saw relief in her features as she snatched it back. Inca wasn't used to being touched. At least, not by a man who had heartfelt intentions toward her.

"It was not your time to die," Inca said briskly. She looked down at his bare feet. "Ernesto died in the attack,"

Inca said sadly. "He was a good friend and helped me often."

Roan frowned. "I'm sorry, Inca."

Nodding, her throat tight with grief, she whispered, "I will pray for him." Lifting her head, she said, "We must go. There is much to do. I know where to get shoes for both of us. I always hide gear at different villages in the Basin in case I need replacements." She frowned, dropped her hands on her hips and looked up the Amazon to where they'd nearly gotten killed the day before. "Who attacked us? Marcellino? He hates me. He blames me for his son's death when I had nothing to do with him dying."

Brushing off the seat of his pants, Roan said, "Marcellino gave his word he wouldn't try and kill you. Could it be drug runners?"

A wry smile cut across her face as she hoisted the bandoliers back into place on her shoulders. "That is always possible. Drug lords hate me. For once, the country's government and they agree on one thing." She slung the rifle across her shoulder and gave him an imperious look. "They agree that I need to be dead."

"They'll have to come through me, first."

His voice was a dark growl. Shocked, Inca realized Roan meant it. She saw his brows draw down, his eyes narrow. And she felt his protection wrapping around her. Laughing with embarrassment, Inca said, "You are the first man who has said that to me. Usually, it is the other way around—I protect men, women and children. They do not protect me."

"Even you need a safe harbor, some quiet, some down time," Roan reminded her. He looked around and then back at her. She had an odd look on her expressive features—one of pleasure mixed with shock. It was about time she got used to the fact that a man could care for her. Even though Roan honored her abilities, he knew that no human being was impervious to all the world's hurts. Sarah had taught him that. Inca was a woman. A beautiful, naive and innocent woman. And with each passing moment, Roan found himself wanting more and more to draw her into his arms and protect her from a world gone mad around her. She was too beautiful, too alive to die at the hands of some drug lord or crazed government soldier who wanted the considerable bounty on her head. No, as long as he was here, he'd make damn sure she was protected.

"Your feet," Inca said, pointing to them. "You lost your boots in the river. Where we need to go, you cannot travel. Your feet are soft." She held up one of her feet and pointed to the thick calluses on the bottom. "I can make it to the village, but you cannot."

"What if I cut off my pants to here—" he gestured with his index finger "—and wrap the cloth around them? Could I make it then?"

"Yes." Inca moved to the trees along the shore. She took out her knife and cut several long, thin, flexible vines from around one tree. She held them out to him. "Here, use my knife, and tie the cloth with these onto your feet."

Thanking her, Roan took her knife and the vines. In no time, his feet were protectively wrapped in the material. As he stood up and tried his new "shoes," she laughed deeply.

"My people will gawk at you when you enter their village. They will wonder what kind of strange man wears material on his feet."

Chuckling, Roan said, "Let them laugh. I'll laugh with them. How far is this village where you have supplies?"

Shrugging, Inca said, "By my pace, it is an hour from here." She eyed him. "But I do not think you will keep up with me, so it may take longer."

Grinning, Roan said, "Let's see, shall we?"

"Stop here," Inca said, and held up her hand. They halted near the edge of the rain forest. Before them was a Yanomami village of around fifty people. The huts were round in shape and thatched with dried palm leaves. In the center of the village were cooking pots hung on metal tripods. The men and women wore little clothing. Around their necks were seed and bead necklaces. Some wore feather necklaces from brilliant and colorful parrots. Their black hair was sleek and straight, cut in a bowl fashion around their heads. All the women wore brightly colored material around their waists, their upper bodies naked, save for the necklace adornments. Naked children of all ages were playing among the huts. Babies either sat on the yellow-and-red packed dirt, or hung on their mother's back as she worked over a cooking pot, stirring it with a stick.

Inca quickly divested herself of her bandoliers of ammunition, her knife and rifle. She laid them carefully beneath some bushes so that they were well hidden from prying eyes. She saw the question on Roan's face.

"I never enter any village with my weapons. I come in peace to my people. They see enough warfare waged against them, enough drug running soldiers brandishing weapons and knives. I do not want them to ever be afraid of me."

"I understand."

She pursed her lips. "Just watch. The Yanomami know very little Portuguese and no English. Say nothing. Be respectful."

Roan accepted her orders. She quickly moved out of the rain forest and onto the hard-packed dirt paths of the village. One of the first people to spot her was an old woman. Her black-and-gray hair was cut short, the red fabric of her skirt thin and worn around her crippled body. She gave a shrill cry in her own language, and instantly, villagers came hurrying toward where the old woman sat, hovering over her black kettle of bubbling monkey stew.

Roan stayed a good twenty paces behind Inca. The Yanomami looked at him, and then their expressions turned to adoration, their dark eyes glittering with joy as they threw open their arms, raised more cries of greeting and hurried toward Inca.

Every person in the village rushed forward until they surrounded Inca. Roan was startled by the change in her. No longer was she the defensive warrior. Instead, she was smiling warmly as she reached out and touched each of them— a pat on a person's head here, a gentle caress along a child's cheek there. Surrounding her, they began to chant, the people locking arms with one another and beginning to sway back and forth. Their faces were illuminated with unabashed joy over Inca's unexpected arrival.

Inca hailed them by name, laughed and smiled often. The Indians then ceased their welcoming chant in her honor, stepped away and made a large, respectful circle around Inca. Someone hurried forward with a rough-hewn, three-legged stool. They set it down and excitedly ask her to sit on it. As they brought her gifts—fruit and brightly colored parrot feathers—she complied.

A mother with a baby hurried forward. Her singsong voice was high-pitched, and tears were running down her tobacco brown face as she held her sickly infant toward Inca.

Inca murmured to the mother soothingly, and took the baby, who was no more than two months old, into her arms. The mother fell at Inca's feet, burying her head in her hands, bowing before her and begging her to heal her baby.

From where he stood, Roan could see that the infant was starving, his small rib cage pronounced. Did the mother not have enough milk to feed him? More than likely. Roan stood very still, knowing he was privy to something that few people would ever see. Even thirty feet away, he felt a shift and change in energy. It was Inca. He watched as she closed her eyes. Tenderly, she shifted the weak infant in her hands and gently placed him against her breast.

The mother's wailing and sobbing continued unabated and she gripped the hem of Inca's trousered leg. The pleading in her voice didn't need any translation for Roan. Narrowing his eyes, he saw darkness begin to gather around and above Inca. Blinking, he wondered if he was seeing things. No, it was real. A dark grayish-black smoke was coming out of the ethers above Inca's head. Then, quickly, the smoky mist began to take on a shape as it eased down across Inca's form. Roan stared hard. It was the jaguar! Roan recalled seeing it seconds before he'd lost consciousness the day before.

This time he steadied himself. He saw the jaguar apparition completely engulf Inca's upper body. It was superimposed upon her and he could see both simultaneously. Instead of Inca, he saw the jaguar's massive flat head, sun-gold eyes and tiny black, constricted pupils. A wave of energy hit Roan, and it reminded him of standing out in knee-high surf in the ocean and being struck by a large, far more powerful wave. He rocked back on his heels and felt another pulsating wave of energy hit him, and then another, as if the jaguar's intense and powerful energy was causing tidal fluctuations that rocked him rhythmically.

Roan tried to keep his concentration on the baby Inca held gently to her breast. Her head was tipped forward. At one point, she turned the child on his back and blew gently into his opened mouth. The sobs of the mother continued. Her face was streaked with tears, her eyes filled with agony as she begged Inca to save her dying baby.

Blinking, unsure of what all he was perceiving, Roan saw golden light coming out of Inca's and the jaguar's mouth simultaneously. He saw the golden threads move into the infant's slack mouth and fill his tiny form, which began to sparkle and throb with life. What was once a grayish, murky cocoon around the infant suddenly became clearer and more distinct. The grayness left, replaced by the white and golden light of life that now enveloped the baby.

As Inca raised her head, her eyes still closed, Roan saw the jaguar disappear. Instantly it was gone, as was the smoky cloud the animal had come out of. All Roan saw now was Inca and the baby. Holding his breath, along with the rest of the villagers, he realized he was watching a miracle take place. As Inca slowly opened her willow-green eyes, the infant in her hands moved and gave a weak cry. And then the baby's cry no longer wavered, but was strong and lusty.

The mother breathed the infant's name, leaped to her feet and stretched out her arms. Inca smiled softly, murmured reassuring words and carefully passed the baby back to her.

The woman held her child to her breast and bowed repeatedly to Inca, thanking her through her sobs. She looked at the baby, noting his animation and the fact that he was thriving and not sickly any longer. Face wet with tears, she knelt down before Inca.

Inca stood and drew her to her feet. She embraced the mother and held her for just a moment. Then releasing her, Inca asked who was next. Who wanted to be healed?

Roan stood there for a good hour, witnessing one healing after another. First to come were babies and mothers. After they were cared for, young boys and girls came forward. Sometimes Inca would simply lay her hand on a child's head. Sometimes she would ease youngsters onto her lap and hold them for a few moments. In nearly every case there was improvement, Roan noted. When it was finally time for the elderly, Inca went to them. Some were crippled. Others were so sick that they lay on pallets inside their makeshift huts.

Roan didn't mind waiting. A part of him wished that people like Colonel Marcellino could see this side of Inca. This was not the warrior; this was the healer. He began to understand what Mike Houston had said to him earlier. It was clear now why the Indians of the Amazon basin worshipped Inca as the jaguar goddess. No wonder. She had the power to heal. The power to snatch people from death's door and bring them back.

Her spirit guide did, Roan realized, mentally correcting himself. Inca was humble and lacked any egotism about her healing skills. That was typical of Indians. His own mother was one of the humblest souls he'd ever met. She never took credit for the energy that came through her and flowed into her patient. No, she gave thanks to the Great Spirit and to her spirit guides—just as Inca did.

Roan found a log to sit down on near the edge of the village. He was in no hurry today. As a matter of fact, being able to find out more about Inca and create a bond of trust with her was far more important than hurrying downriver to Marcellino's awaiting company. Roan hoped Inca would want to stay here overnight. He still felt weak, but was getting stronger and stronger as each hour slid by.

The peacefulness of the village was infectious. The laughter of the children, the barking of the dogs, the happiness on the faces of the people relaxed Roan. Above them, the clouds parted and sunlight lanced down through the triple canopy of the rain forest surrounding the village. A squadron of blue-and-yellow macaws winged overhead. They reminded him of rainbows in flight. Looking around, he saw that Inca was emerging from the last hut at the end of the village. He heard wails and cries coming from that hut. Inca looked tired. No wonder. She must have worked on fifteen people, nonstop.

Rising to his feet, he walked across the village to meet her. Without thinking, he reached out and slid his fingers around her upper arm. He saw turmoil in her eyes. The way her lips were set, as if against pain, touched him deeply.

"Come on," he urged her quietly, "come and sit down. You need to rest...."

Chapter 6

Jaime Marcellino stifled his anger toward his son. He had had only two children, but now only one was left. Julian was just a young, shavetail lieutenant straight out of the military academy, and Jaime wished mightily that he was more like his older brother, Rafael, had been: bold, brash and confident. As Jaime sat at his makeshift aluminum desk in the canvas tent, which was open at both ends to allow the humid air to sluggishly crawl through, he gripped his black-and-gold pen tighter. Julian stood at strict attention in front of him.

Oh, how young and cherubic his son's face was! At twenty-two, he looked more like a little boy than a man. Rafael had had Jaime's own sharply etched, proud and aris-tocratic features. Julian took after his mother, who was soft, plump and dimpled. Scowling as he scribbled his signature on some of the orders in front of him, Jaime jammed them into his attaché's awaiting hands. Around him, he could hear the company of soldiers preparing for the coming trek. They had just disembarked from a number of tug boats, and the men were setting up camp in the muggy afternoon heat.

"Lieutenant," he muttered, "your request to lead point with that—that woman is denied."

Julian's large, cinnamon-colored eyes widened. He opened his mouth to speak. His father's face was livid with rage. He could see it as well as feel it. The colonel's attaché, Captain Humberto Braga, blanched and stood stiffly at attention next to his father's chair.

"Sir, with all due respect—"

"Enough!" Jaime smashed his closed fist down on his table. Everything on it jumped. Snapping his head up, he glared at his son. "Permission denied. Point is the most dangerous position! I will not allow you to risk your life. You have a platoon to take care of, *Tenente,* Lieutenant. I suggest you do so. You have tents to set up, food to be distributed, and make sure that the men's rifles are clean and without rust. You have *plenty* to do. *Dismissed.*"

The attaché glared at Julian and jerked his head to the left, indicating that he should get out of the tent. Julian knew his father's rage well. He'd been cuffed many times as a child growing up, though after Rafael had been murdered, his father was less inclined to deride him and not take him seriously. Rafael had been a huge, heroic figure to Julian. He'd always looked up to his older brother. He'd gone to the military academy to follow in his big brother's footsteps, which he felt he could never possibly fill. Julian had labored and struggled mightily through four years of academy training. He'd barely gotten passing marks, where Rafael had gotten straight A's. Rafael had been captain of the soccer team, while Julian couldn't even make second string.

"Yes, sir," he murmured, and he did an about-face and stepped smartly out of the tent.

"Damn youngster," Jaime muttered glumly to his attaché after his son was out of earshot. He scribbled his signature hurriedly on another set of orders. He hated the paperwork.

He was a field officer, not a paper pusher. Oh, that kind of attitude had garnered him many enemies among the army ranks, that was for sure, but Jaime didn't care. He loved the outdoors. He reveled in missions such as the upcoming one. The only fly in the ointment was that the jaguar goddess was going to lead the company. And what the hell was wrong with Julian wanting, of all things, to work side-by-side with her? Had his youngest son gone *louco?* Crazy?

"I think he's trying to behave as Rafael might have in this situation, sir," the attaché ventured gently. "To do something heroic, to get your attention. My opinion, of course, sir." Humberto steeled himself for an explosion from his superior.

Grunting, Jaime looked up. He folded his hands restlessly. Looking out the side of the tent where the flap was thrown upward, he growled, "He'll *never* be Rafael. I wish he'd quit trying. Ever since he was murdered, Julian has been trying to make up for it." With a shake of his head, he muttered, "And he never will. Julian will never be what Rafael was."

"I think he knows that, sir," Humberto said, some pity in his tone.

"He's soft. Look at his hands! No calluses. His face is soft and round. I doubt he'll even be able to keep up with his men on this mission," Jaime fumed in a whisper so no one else would overhear. "Rafael was tough—hard as a rock. He was an incredible athlete. Julian has trouble making the mandatory runs and hikes." Snorting, Jaime looked up at the thirty-year-old career officer. Humberto Braga was a trusted individual who had come from the poverty of Rio de Janeiro and worked his way through college and eventually joined the army. Jaime admired anyone with that kind of courage and guts. Humberto was someone he could trust and confide in, too.

"Yes, sir, he's not Rafael in those respects," Humberto said, "but his men like him. They listen to him."

Raising his thick, black brows, Jaime nodded. "Yes, thank goodness for that."

"Perhaps this mission will be good for the boy, sir. He needs to show you he's capable."

Leaning back in the metal chair, Jaime pondered the younger man's reflection. "Asking to work with Inca is like asking to work with a bushmaster snake."

Humberto chuckled indulgently. Bushmaster snakes were well known to be one of the most poisonous in the Amazon. Not only that, but when the snake was disturbed, it would literally chase an unfortunate person down, bite him and kill him. Not many snakes were aggressive like the bushmaster, and it was to be feared. It had earned its reputation by leaving bodies of people in its wake over the centuries. The legends about the snake had grown, and Humberto knew most of them were true. "I hear you, sir."

Looking at his watch, Jaime muttered, "Where the hell is Storm Walker? He said they'd meet us here this morning. It's already noon." Again Jaime snorted and went back to the necessary paperwork. "And Morgan Trayhern said he was punctual. Bah."

Humberto was about to speak when he saw a tall man, an Anglo dressed in cutoff pants, a burgundy polo shirt and sandals, approach the tent. He'd seen a picture of Roan Storm Walker, so he knew it was him. Surprised, he stammered, "Colonel, Senhor Storm Walker is here...."

"Eh?" Jaime glanced up. Humberto was pointing toward the tent entrance. Jaime turned his head and met Roan's narrowed eyes. Storm Walker had a two-day growth of beard on his hard face and it made him look even more dangerous.

"It's about time," Jaime snapped. "Enter!"

Roan moved into the tent. He glanced at the thirty-year-old captain, who curtly nodded a greeting in his direction. "Colonel, I'm a little late."

Jaime glared up at him. "More than a little. I'm not impressed, Storm Walker."

Roan stood more or less at ease in front of the colonel, whose face had flushed a dull red. He saw the anger banked in the officer's eyes.

"I think you know why, too."

"What? What are you talking about?"

Roan studied him. The officer seemed genuinely surprised. "That unmarked helicopter that came out of nowhere and blasted the tug we were on to pieces? Does that ring a bell, Colonel?" Roan tried to keep the sarcasm out of his voice. Who else but Marcellino knew of their plans to meet, as well as the place and the time? No one.

Chagrined, Marcellino put down the pen and gave Roan a deadly look. "I haven't the faintest of what you are talking about, Storm Walker. What helicopter? And what tug?"

"We were attacked yesterday," Roan said tightly, "first by thugs in two cars. We barely made it onto the tug before they started firing at us with military rifles. There were six of them. And an hour later we were attacked by a green, unmarked military helicopter. It rocketed the tug. We jumped off it and dove as deep as we could." Roan decided not to tell of his wounding and of Inca's healing. He wanted to stick to the point with the colonel. "We had to swim to shore. And if it weren't for Inca knowing the lay of the land, I wouldn't be here now. We were twenty miles northwest of your landing area when the attack happened."

Marcellino slowly rose. "I know nothing of this attack," he protested strongly.

"You were the only one who knew our itinerary," Roan retorted, barely hanging on to his temper. He rarely got angry, but the colonel's innocent look and remarks stung him. He'd had a restless night's sleep, and hiking through the humid rain forest for fifteen miles this morning hadn't helped his mood at all.

"Are you accusing *me* of those attacks?" Marcellino struck his chest with a fist. Then he placed his hands flat on the table, leaned forward and glared up into the *norte-*

americano's livid features. "I had *nothing* to do with either attack!"

"You hate Inca," Roan declared. "You'd do anything to kill her because you mistakenly believe she killed Rafael, your eldest son."

Rearing back, Jaime put his hands on his hips in a defiant stance, despite the fact that he wasn't anywhere near Roan's height. "I gave my word to Senhor Trayhern that I would *not* lay a hand on her. And I have not!" His nostrils flared and quivered. "You are gravely mistaken, *senhor.*"

"Inca's angry. She has a right to be. She thinks *you* were behind the attack."

Jaime laughed explosively. "Oh, how I wish I were, Senhor Storm Walker." He lost his smile and glared at him. "But if I had of been, believe me, you two would not be alive today. I'd have hung that helicopter over the water and put a hundred bullets through her body when she came up to get air." He jabbed a finger toward Storm Walker. "Captain Braga!"

Humberto snapped to attention. "Yes, sir!"

"Take Senhor Storm Walker to our quartermaster. Get him a set of army fatigues, a decent pair of boots and other gear. And loan him a razor. He needs to shave."

Roan looked at the colonel. Was he lying? Was he telling the truth? Roan wasn't sure. The colonel's response seemed genuine; he'd looked surprised when he'd learned of the attacks. "As soon as I get cleaned up, I need a copy of the map you're using. Inca will look at it with me and I'll get back to you about the route we'll take tomorrow morning at dawn."

"Fine." Marcellino looked out of the tent. "Where is she?"

"Nowhere that you or your men will ever find her," Roan growled.

Shrugging, Jaime said, "Make sure she stays out of my

way. I have ordered my men *not* to fire at her, or to make any overture toward her that she may read as harm.''

Turning on his heel, Roan ducked beneath the canvas of the tent and followed Captain Braga out into the main encampment. The hundred and eighty men of Macellino's company were loosely strung out for half a mile along the shore of the Amazon. He could tell that the contingent wasn't used to rain forest conditions. Tents were going up. Men were smoking cigarettes and talking as they dug in for the evening hours ahead. The odor of food cooking caught his attention.

''Hungry?'' Humberto asked with a slight smile.

Roan looked over at the officer who accompanied him. Humberto Braga sported a thin, black mustache. His face was square and he was built like a bulldog. He wasn't aristocratic in bearing or facial features; he had more of a peasant demeanor. Roan couldn't dislike the soft-voiced officer. ''Yeah, just a little.''

''You hiked fifteen miles this morning?''

Roan gave him a cutting smile. ''Yeah.'' Inca had taken the lead and moved effortlessly, hour after hour, through the rain forest. He'd known she was in superb shape, but her ability to move at a continued trot without rest had stunned him. She'd only rested when he needed to take a break. As she had pointed out to him, he was wearing sandals that one of the Indians had given him, and sandals were not best for that kind of march.

Humberto pointed to the quartermaster's large tent. ''Here we are. I'll help you with getting all the equipment you will need.'' He eyed Roan again. ''Fifteen miles in how many hours?''

''Three.''

Sighing, Humberto said with a grin, ''And I wonder how fast we can push this company starting tomorrow morning.''

Roan halted. ''That's a good question, Captain, and not one I can answer right off the top of my head.'' He eyed the struggling company entrenching its position. A number of soldiers were heading out to predestined points several hundred yards ahead of the encampment, he saw. They would be forward observers—the eyes and ears of the company—to protect it from possible attack by drug runners.

"I think we will need two or three days to get—how do you say—the hang of it?"

Roan nodded. His mind and his heart were elsewhere—with Inca. She'd agreed to stay out of sight. Worried that the FOs might surprise her, he wanted to get done with the clothes exchange as soon as possible and get back to where she was hiding.

Julian Marcellino took off his helmet and wiped his sweaty brow with the back of his arm. He'd stumbled over some exposed roots and nearly fallen. Looking back, he grinned a silly grin. As usual, he wasn't watching where he was going. Rafael would never have tripped. He'd have seen the twisted roots sticking above the damp layer of leaves on the rain forest floor, and avoided them completely.

Halting, Julian heard the noise of the encampment far behind him. He had chosen men from each platoon to serve as forward observers, had picked out stations for them and ordered them to begin digging their foxholes, where they would remain for a four-hour watch before another two men took over for them. Then he'd made an excuse and gone off on his own.

He didn't like the cacophony of noise that was everpresent at the camp. No, in his heart he longed for the pristine silence of nature. As he looked up admiringly at the towering trees, the brightly colored orchids hanging off the darkened limbs, the sunlight sifting through the canopy, he sighed softly in appreciation. Tucking his helmet beneath his left arm, he wandered on into the rain forest, glad to be relieved of his responsibilities for just a little while. The leaves were damp and there was a wonderful musty, sweet scent from their decay. The screech of monkeys in the distance made him turn in their direction. The floor of the forest wasn't flat, but undulating. He climbed up and over a hill, and the noise from the company abated even more. That was good. He loved the silence.

Wiping his sweaty brow again, he moved quickly down the hill. At one point, he slid because of the dampness. Here in this humid country the rains would come and go, keeping the ground beneath the fallen leaves slick and muddy. Landing on his butt, he slid down to the bottom of the hill, where there was a small, clean pool of water. Laughing out loud over his lack of athleticism, Julian was very glad his father hadn't seen his awkward, unmanly descent. Or his men. Julian knew they tolerated him because his father was a colonel. He saw the amused and disdainful looks they traded when they thought he wasn't looking.

Remaining in a sitting position, Julian raised up enough to push his helmet beneath him. At least his butt would stay dry. Drawn to the beauty of the deep blue oval pool, of the orchids suspended above it on branches, he sighed again. Most of the noise of the company had faded in the distance. Here there was peace. A peace he craved. Placing his elbows on his thighs, he rested his jaw against his hands and simply drank in the beauty of the landscape. Being in Amazonia was turning out to be a wonderful, surprising gift to him.

Inca watched the soldier. She sat very still against a tree, hidden by the extended roots that stretched out like flying buttresses. When he'd appeared at the top of the hill, she had focused in on the soldier instantly. She had been eating her lunch, her back against one of the sturdy roots, when her guardian had warned her of his approach.

He was young looking. No threat to her. His face was babyish, his lips full. His eyes were wide with awe as he slowly absorbed the scene around him. The pistol he carried at his side indicated he was an officer, not an enlisted soldier. Snorting softly, she finished her mango and wiped her glistening lips with the back of her hand. Rolling over onto her hands and knees, she continued to watch the man. There was a bright red bromeliad on a dead log near where he sat. She watched as he reached out, his gesture graceful, the tips of his fingers barely grazing one of the many bright red bracts, which were really leaves and not petals. The way he touched the plant piqued Inca's interest. Most men would not even pay attention to it, much less touch it with such respect and reverence.

His hair was black, short and close cropped like Roan's. His ears were large and stuck out from the sides of his head, which was probably why he looked more like a boy growing through an awkward stage than a man. Inca smiled mirthlessly. She felt no threat from this young whelp. He looked out of place in a uniform. The way he touched the bromeliad again and again, and raptly studied it, made her decide to reveal her presence.

Julian heard a sound across the pool. It wasn't loud, just enough to snag his attention. As he lifted his chin, he gasped reflexively. There on the other side of the pond was a woman in military gear. Her willow-green eyes ruthlessly captured and held his gaze. She stood with her head high, a challenging look on her face, her hands resting arrogantly on her hips. And then, just as quickly, he realized *who* she was.

Inca laughed, the sound carrying around the pool. She felt the young man's shock when he realized who she was.

Lifting her hands, she said, "I am unarmed, *Tenente.* I come in peace. Do you?"

He saw the laughter in her willow-green eyes. He heard the derision and challenge in her sultry tone. Her hair was unbound and flowed freely across her proud shoulders and the bandoliers of ammunition she wore crisscrossed on her chest. Swallowing hard, he leaped to his feet. The heel of his boot caught and he slipped hard to the ground once more. Julian felt a rush of shame and humiliation. He expected her to deride him for floundering around like a fish out of water.

But she did not. Scrambling to his feet, he spread his boots far enough apart to give him some stability on the soft, damp leaves near the lip of the pond. Breathing hard, he stared across the hundred feet that separated them.

"Y-you're Inca...the jaguar goddess...." he croaked. "Aren't you?"

Julian had seen rough sketches of the woman on Wanted posters. She was supposed to have murdered his brother. He had never believed it. In person, she was shockingly beautiful. Just looking at her Indian features, the light shining in her eyes and the way she smiled at him, he rejected even more strongly the possibility that she had murdered Rafael. She had the face of an angel. Never had he seen anyone as beautiful as her! Even his fiancée, Elizabeth, who was truly lovely, could not match Inca's wild, natural beauty.

"I am," Inca purred. She removed her hands from her hips. "So, you are from the company that I am to lead?"

Gulping, his heart pounding, Julian stammered, "Er, y-yes...we are. I mean, I am...."

Laughing, Inca watched as his face flushed crimson. "Do not worry. I will not harm you, *Tenente.*" She held up her hands. "I was finishing my lunch. Would you care for a mango? I have one left."

Stunned by her pleasant demeanor, Julian found himself utterly tongue-tied. Maybe it was her beauty. Or maybe it was all the whispered legends about her filling his head in a jumble that made him cower before her obvious power and confident presence.

Inca leaned over, picked up the mango. "Here," she called, "catch!"

Julian's hands shot out. He caught the ripe mango.

"Good catch." Inca laughed. She watched the young officer roll the fruit nervously in his hands. "You are quick. That is good. We will need that kind of reaction where I am going to lead you."

"T-thank you, Inca...or do you want to be called jaguar goddess?"

Inca felt the shame and humiliation coming from him. Why? Her heart went out to this young man, who really didn't belong in the army. He belonged in a garden tending his vegetables. Or perhaps in a greenhouse tending beautiful orchids. That would make him happy. Still, Inca respected him. "Call me Inca. And you are?"

Holding the mango gently in his hands, he said, "Y-you may call me Julian." He hooked a thumb across his shoulder. "I'm a lieutenant with this company. I have a platoon that I'm responsible for. I was really looking forward to being here. I've never been out in the rain forest and I've always wanted to come...."

She smiled and said, "You are at home here."

Julian was dumbfounded. "Why, yes...yes, I am. But—how could you know?"

"I read minds when I want to."

Gulping, Julian nodded. "I believe you. I really do." His heart was pounding hard with the thrill of getting to see this legendary woman in person.

"And the other men," Inca called, "are they as friendly and unthreatening as you are toward me?" The corners of her mouth lifted in a barely disguised smile of sarcasm.

"Oh, them...well, they are all right, Inca. I mean...most of them have heard the legends about you. They are all hoping to see you, to get a glimpse of you—"

"Why? To put a bullet through my head?"

Wincing, Julian held up his hand. "Oh, no, no...not that. There's been so much speculation, even excitement, about you...the possibility of seeing you. That's all."

She moved slowly toward the edge of the pond and said, "What about Colonel Marcellino? Does he still want to see me dead?" Her voice was flat and hard.

Gulping, Julian raised his eyes. "That...my father has mixed feelings about you. I mean, it's understandable...I never believed you did it. Not ever. But he was so full of anguish and grief that he had to blame someone. I don't believe drug runners, and that is who said you killed Rafael.''

Inca froze. Her eyes narrowed to slits. The moment she heard Julian say "my father," her hand went to the pistol at her side. "Colonel Marcellino is *your* father?" she demanded.

"Y-yes, he is. I'm Julian Marcellino. I apologize. I should have told you my last name. It's just that…well, I'm a little shook up, afraid…." His voice drifted off.

Looking at him, Inca growled, "You do not believe I killed Rafael?"

Shaking his head adamantly, Julian said, "No…and now, seeing you in person, even more I do not believe you killed my older brother."

Inca knew that something greater was at play here. What were the chances of the brother of Rafael showing up where she was hiding? Very slim. She understood the karma of the situation. The soldier was white-faced now, and stood stiffly, the fruit clutched in his hands. Buffeted by his tumultuous feelings, Inca ruthlessly entered his mind to see if he was, indeed, telling her the truth.

Julian winced. He took a step back, as if he'd been physically struck.

"Sorry," Inca called. She moved more gently into his mind. Julian staggered and sat down unceremoniously. As she moved through his psyche, she saw and felt many things. That was the problem with telepathy—it wasn't just about getting information, it meant feeling all the damnable emotions that came along with the information. It was so hard on her that she rarely read minds. She didn't want to deal with many emotions.

In her mind, she saw Julian as a baby, a youngster, a teenager during his time spent in the military academy. As she withdrew her energy from him, he uttered a sigh of relief. Inca squatted down on her haunches and stared at him across the pond. "You are not a soldier at heart. This is not a job you love. You are doing this to please your father, not yourself."

Rubbing his head, Julian felt a slight headache. The power that Inca possessed stunned him. "Yes, well, my father wanted me to carry on in Rafael's place. How could I say no? He put such importance on me carrying on the family name and tradition. All the firstborn men went into the army and distinguished themselves. It is expected."

Laughing harshly, Inca said, "Better that you go tend a garden, my young friend." She knew now that Julian bore her no grudge. He wasn't a killer. Inca seriously wondered if he could even pull the trigger of a rifle pointed toward an enemy. No, he was a peaceful, serene person who was not faring well in the military world. At all.

"I like gardening," Julian said, slowly getting to his feet. He retrieved his helmet and settled it awkwardly on his head. "Is there anything I can do for you? Do you need supplies? Food?"

Touched by his thoughtfulness, Inca said, "No...thank you. I am waiting for Roan Storm Walker to return with the map."

"Oh, to see which direction we go tomorrow morning?" Julian smiled a little. "I'd give *anything* to be with you two as you take us into the rain forest."

The eagerness in his voice was genuine. Inca slowly relaxed. "Your father would never let you near me and you know it. Go back. Go back to your men and say nothing of our encounter. If your father finds out, he will be very upset about it."

"Yes, he would," Julian admitted ruefully. He smiled a little hesitantly. "Thank you for the fruit. That was very kind of you, Inca. And if there is anything I can do to help you, please let me know?"

She lifted her hand. "I will, *Tenente.* Go now."

Inca watched the soldier clamber awkwardly up the incline. Shaking her head, she realized that the entire company would struggle like that on this slick, leafy terrain. Turning, she went back to her hiding spot between the roomy wings of the tree roots, more than adequate to protect her from prying eyes. Sitting back down, she leaned against the smooth gray bark and closed her eyes.

Missing Roan, Inca wondered if he was all right. She felt a connection to him, like an umbilical cord strung invisibly between them. She sighed. The fifteen-mile hike this morning had been hard on both of them. Wanting to take a nap now, but not daring to do so, Inca felt her jaguar guardian move around. Instantly, she sat up, her eyes flying open.

There on the edge of the hill above the pool was Roan. He carried a map in his hand. She smiled and felt heat rush through her. How handsome he was in her eyes. And this time he was dressed in jungle fatigues and had a good pair of black leather boots on his feet instead of the sandals. Standing, she left the tree to meet him halfway down the hillside.

"You look different." She grinned and pointed to his face.

Rubbing his jaw, Roan absorbed her teasing expression. "Yeah, the colonel wanted me clean shaven. Now I know why I got out of the Marine Corps." He chuckled. Holding up the map, he said, "We've got work to do. Are you up to it?"

Inca nodded and fell into step beside him. There was something wonderful about his height, and that feeling of warmth and protection that always surrounded her when he was near. "Of course. Are *you?*"

Giving her an intimate look, Roan said, "Of course." He saw she had some mangos for him in the small cotton knapsack tied to her web belt. It was spring in Amazonia, and far too early for such fruit to be ripe. When she'd reached into it and brought out fruit and nuts earlier, during one of the rests they had taken on their march, Roan had considered asking about them.

"Where do you get this fruit? It's out of season," he said now, sitting down against the tree with her.

Inca picked out a mango and handed it to him. "I will it into being."

Opening the map before her, he glanced up. "What do you mean?"

"We are taught how to move and use energy in the Jaguar Clan village. If I will a mango into existence, it occurs. Or nuts." With a shrug, Inca said, "Our will, our intent is pushed and ruled by our emotions. If I am in alignment with my feelings and really desire something, I can manifest it on a good day." She grinned mirthlessly. "And on a bad day, when my concentration is not good, or I am emotionally shredded, I forage on the rain forest floor like all the rest of our relations to find enough food to stop my stomach from growling."

Taking the mango, Roan bit into it. "It's real."

"Of course it is!"

The flesh was juicy and sweet. He pointed to the map. "This is the army's best attempt at defining the trails through Amazonia. We're here—" he tapped his finger on the map "—and this is where we have to go. Now, you tell me—is there a better way to get there? I don't see any trail marked between here and there."

Studying the map, Inca grimaced. "This map is wrong. I expected as much." She tapped her head. "I know how to get us there."

"At least draw it on the map for me? The colonel will want something concrete. He's not a man who can go on a wing and a prayer like you or I do."

"Humph." Inca took the map and placed it across her lap, her thin brows knitting.

Roan absorbed her thoughtful expression. The moments of silence strung gently between them. Her hair was loose, and he had the urge to thread his fingers through that thick silken mass. There was such sculpted beauty in Inca, from her long, graceful neck to her fine, delicate collarbones, prominent beneath the T-shirt she wore, to the clean lines of her face.

"You will not guess who I just ran into minutes before you came."

Frowning, Roan asked, "Who?"

Lifting her head, she met and held his dark blue gaze. "Tenente Julian Marcellino."

Eyes narrowing, Roan rasped, "What?"

Chuckling, Inca told him the entire story. When she was done, she said, "He is a sweet little boy in a man's body. He is not a warrior. He does this for his father, to try and fill in for his missing big brother."

Sucking air between his teeth, Roan said worriedly, "That was a little too synchronistic."

Shrugging, Inca said, "We got along well. He believes me to be innocent of Rafael's murder. That is good."

Saying nothing, Roan allowed her to continue to study the map. After Inca had traced a route in pencil and handed it back to him, he said, "Marcellino swears he didn't try and bushwhack us with that helicopter, or those men on shore."

Inca eyed him. She slid her long fingers through her dark hair and pushed it off her shoulders. The afternoon humidity was building and it was getting hotter. "Do you believe him?"

"I don't know," Roan murmured, studying the route she'd indicated on the map. "He seemed genuinely surprised when I told him."

"If not him, then drug runners," Inca said flatly.

"Maybe. How could they get the info on where we'd be going and the time we'd be at the dock?"

"They have their ways," Inca said. "They are part of the Dark Brotherhood, and have people who can read minds just as I can. They can travel in the other dimensions, look at

information, maps, reports, and bring the information back
to the drug lords.''

''I didn't know that.''

One corner of Inca's mouth pulled inward. ''Do you think
I and my kind fight a battle only on this dimension you call
reality? No. The battles occur on many other levels, simultaneously. The Dark Brotherhood works to see chaos replace
the goodness of the Sisterhood of Light.'' She waved her
hand above her head. ''If you think for a moment that the
drug lords do not use every tool they can, think again.''

''Then…Colonel Marcellino could be telling the truth.''

She smiled a little at his thoughtful expression. The urge
to reach out, slide her hand across his cleanly shaved jaw
caught her by surprise. But then, Inca was finding that
around Roan, she was spontaneous in ways that she'd never
been with another man. Pulling her focus back from that
unexpected urge, Inca whispered, ''Yes, the colonel could
be telling the truth.''

Chapter 7

"Well?" Marcellino snapped, as he mopped his perspiring brow with his white, linen handkerchief, "what do you have for us, Storm Walker?"

Roan stood before the colonel, who had decided to leave his stifling tent and continue to make plans at a makeshift table beneath the tangled, grotesque limbs of a rubber tree fifty feet from the bank of the Amazon.

"I've talked to Inca," Roan said, spreading the map before the colonel, his captain and lieutenants, who stood in a semicircle around the metal table. Dusk was coming and shadows had deepened. When he'd arrived back in camp, all the tents were up, in neat order. The men had eaten and were now cleaning their rifles for the coming march, which would take place at 0600 tomorrow morning.

Moving his large hands across the map of the area, Roan traced the route with his index finger for the colonel. The lamp was suspended precariously above them on a limb and drawing its fair share of insects. "This is the route that Inca feels we should go."

Scowling, Jaime squinted his aging eyes. At fifty-three, he had to wear bifocals now. Grudgingly, he pulled them from his blouse pocket and settled them on the end of his nose. The light was poor, but he could see the penciled line on the map. Leaning down, he studied it for a number of minutes.

"This takes us through some of the worst terrain in the basin!" he muttered, as he lifted his head and straightened up. Perspiration trickled down his ribs. The long-sleeved fatigues, which everyone wore as protection from biting insects, did not breathe well. Jaime was gulping water like a camel to stay hydrated. Wiping his wrinkled brow, he saw his son, Julian, standing among the four lieutenants across the table from him. The boy's expression was eager as he studied the route.

"Sir," Julian said respectfully, "I see why Inca is doing it." He tapped his finger on the map. "We avoid the swamp to the south of us. To the north, there is a major river to cross, and we do not have the capabilities to span it. By tackling the steep terrain, we take the safest route. Swamps are well known for their diseases, piranhas, snakes and other vermin."

Many other soldiers were crowding around, at a distance, to eavesdrop. They had nothing else to do in the twilight, and Julian's soft voice made them trudge a few inches closer to hear his words.

"That's exactly why she chose the route," Roan intoned. He saw the colonel's narrow face flash with annoyance. The glare he gave his hesitant son made Roan angry. The young man was diplomatic, yet had the guts to take on his father, who everyone tiptoed around.

Captain Braga leaned down and studied the map. "The swamp is too large to try and march around, sir. But at this time of year, in spring, there is the chance of heavy rains, flooding, and that is lowland area. If we get too much rain, that swamp will rise five or ten feet in a hurry. Men could drown in such a scenario." He frowned and looked closely at the suggested route. "Yet I see why you don't like the other route, Colonel. It is very steep, hilly terrain."

"Exactly," Marcellino snapped. "It will increase our time to the valley by another week. Besides, men will fall, slip, and we'll have injuries—sprained ankles and perhaps broken legs." Marcellino looked down at the damp leaves beneath his shining boots. "This is slippery footage at best."

"Colonel, Inca strongly suggests you do not choose the swamp route," Roan said. "Even though spring signals the end of the wet season here, that doesn't guarantee it won't rain. If your men get out in the swamp and the river floods its banks, they could drown. We have no quick, sure way of rescuing a company that's stuck on one of the islands in that swamp. It's too far from any base, and helicopters, unless they refuel in flight, couldn't manage a rescue attempt."

"The swamp is the fastest route to the valley," Marcellino growled. "We can send point men ahead to test the terrain where we're going to march."

Julian compressed his lips. His father remained ramrod straight, his mouth thinned, hands resting imperiously on his hips. He was going to take the swamp route, Julian knew. He opened his mouth to say something when, from the back of the large group of men, there came a shout of surprise. And then another. And another. Because he was short, barely five foot ten inches tall, he stood on tiptoe to find out what all the excitement was about.

Roan turned on his heel when he heard a number of men calling loudly to one another and moving rapidly aside at the rear of the assemblage. It was Inca! She was striding toward them like she owned the place. Didn't she? Roan turned sharply and pinned the colonel with his eyes.

"It's Inca," he warned him tightly.

Instantly, Marcellino's hand went to the holster hanging at his right hip.

Roan nailed him with a glare. "Don't even think about it," he rasped.

Julian smiled in greeting as he saw Inca, who strode, tall and proud, up to the table. The crowd parted for her, the men's mouths hanging open in awe, their stares all trained on her. They gave Inca plenty of room. When she swung her cool, imperious gaze toward him, Julian bowed his head slightly in honor of her unexpected presence. She was, indeed, a goddess! Every man, with the exception of his father, looked up at her in admiration, respect and fear. She was afraid of no one and nothing. Marching bravely into their camp only made her more untouchable, in Julian's eyes.

Roan met and held Inca's laughter-filled eyes. The half smile on her mouth, the way she held herself as she halted at the table, opposite the frozen colonel, made him go on alert. Inca was in danger. Marcellino's face darkened like a savage thunderstorm approaching. His eyes flashed with hatred as he met and held her challenging look.

"If I were you, Colonel, I would listen to your son and your other officer, here." Inca flicked a hand lazily in Braga's direction, who stood staring at her in awe. "If you go the swamp route, you are guaranteeing the death of a number of your men. Is that what you want? A high body count before you even reach that valley where the Valentino Brothers hold my countrymen as slaves?" she demanded, her husky voice quieting the throng.

Roan moved to Inca's side, standing slightly behind her to protect her back. He trusted no one here. Marcellino had given his word that he and his men would not harm her, but he believed none of them. Cursing to himself, he wished Inca hadn't marched into camp like she owned the damn place. Keeping his eye on the men who were gawking like slobbering teenage boys at Inca, and the colonel, whose face was turning a dusky red with rage, Roan geared himself to take action.

"What you say has nothing to do with anything!" Marcellino hissed in a low, quavering tone. "You promised to stay out of my encampment."

Shrugging easily, Inca growled in return, "I am in the business of saving lives, Colonel, unlike you, who considers your soldiers nothing more than cannon fodder on the road to reaching your own objectives."

As she stared him down, beads of sweat popped out on the colonel's wrinkled brow. His hatred spilled over her, like tidal waves smashing against her. Because she was innocent, she did not connect emotionally into the colonel's rage, grief and loss. She had no compassion for the man whose fingers itched to pull the pistol at his hip out of that black, highly polished leather holster, and fire off round after round into her head and heart.

Marcellino cursed. "You bitch! You murdering bitch. Get out of here before I kill you!"

Roan stepped forward. "Colonel—"

It was too late. Marcellino unsnapped his holster, clawing at the pistol resting there.

Just as Roan moved to step in front of Inca to protect her, he felt the energy around her change drastically. It felt as if someone had sucker punched him with a lightning bolt. Roan staggered backward, off balance. Braga made a choking sound and backed away, too. Julian uttered a cry and fell back many feet. The energy sizzling around Inca was like an electric substation that had just been jolted with fifty thousand watts of electricity.

Roan heard Marcellino give a cry. Jerking his head around, he saw the colonel drop the pistol from his hand. Grabbing at his throat, he squawked and took two steps back, his face going white and then a gray-blue color. His eyeballs bulged from their sockets. His mouth contorted in a soundless scream.

"Do not presume you can kill me, Colonel," Inca snarled.

Roan blinked. Something invisible had the colonel by the throat, strangling him. He cried out and crashed to his knees, wrestling with the invisible force. He cried out again and began to choke.

Julian grabbed the tent pole to steady himself. When he saw what was happening, he leaped forward. "Papa!"

Roan turned, his back against Inca's. His narrowed gaze swept the men, who were now mesmerized and frightened by the unfolding spectacle. Automatically, he drew his pistol and held it in readiness, should any one of them try to shoot Inca.

Jaime choked. Slobber sputtered from the corners of his gaping mouth. He felt as if some large, powerful animal had gripped him by the throat with its invisible jaws. He was dying! Unable to draw in a breath of air, he fell, writhing, to the damp ground. All he saw were Inca's willow-green eyes, thoughtful and concentrated upon him. Devastated and shocked by her power, he kicked out. The table went flying.

Julian fell to his side, sobbing for breath. "Stop! Stop!" he begged Inca. "Don't kill him! He's my father!"

Inca lifted her chin slightly. She ordered her spirit guardian, Topazio, to release the white-faced colonel from his massive jaws. The army officer, now semiconscious, fell into his son's arms. "Very well, Julian. For you, I do this," she stated.

Marcellino gasped and then gagged. He rolled onto his side and vomited. Julian pulled out his handkerchief and cleaned around his father's mouth, then held him protectively in his arms.

Gripping his neck weakly, Jaime swore he could still feel the invisible force, though the sensation was dissipating rapidly. Head hanging down, he lay in his son's arms, breathing harshly. How good it felt to have air in his lungs again!

Julian's hand fluttered nervously over his shoulders. "Leave me!" he ordered his son hoarsely. "I'll be fine!" And Jaime forced himself to sit up on his own. Angrily, he shoved his son away from him, embarrassed that his men had seen him in such a compromising position.

Julian winced and staggered to his feet. Trying to hide his hurt over his father's rejection, he sought out and found Inca's gaze. "T-thank you...."

"Everyone stand down," Roan ordered, his voice carrying across the assemblage. "Inca came in peace and she's going to leave that way. If I see anyone lift a weapon, I'll fire first and ask questions later." He held up the pistol as a reminder.

Rage fueled Marcellino. He staggered to his hands and knees, and sat down unceremoniously, still dizzied. Spitting out the acid taste in his mouth, he twisted his head and glared up at the cool, collected woman warrior at whose boots he sat at like a pet dog.

"You promised not to hurt me," Inca reminded him in a dark tone. "You went back on your word. You are not to be trusted. I came here to help you."

"And you will," Jaime rasped as he staggered to his feet. Gripping the edge of the table with one hand, he wiped his other hand across his mouth. "The great Green Warrior will go back on her word, eh? So now you refuse to lead us?"

Inca smiled a deadly smile. "I will lead you, Colonel. My word is my bond. The only thing that will break it is death. But I am warning you—do not go through the swamp. It is too dangerous at this time of year as we move from wet to dry season."

"Inca, you'd better leave," Roan warned over his shoulder.

She smiled laconically and slid her fingers beneath the leather strap of her rifle, which rested on her right shoulder. "I am leaving now."

Julian rushed forward. He gripped Inca's arm.

Inca froze momentarily. She looked down at the lieutenant.

"Thank you," he whispered unsteadily, giving her arm an awkward pat. "For your compassion, your understanding..."

There was something heart-wrenchingly innocent and vulnerable about Julian. Inca reached over and placed her hand across his. "I did it for you, *Tenente*. Not for *him*." And she glared at the colonel. "Your son needs you as a father. I hope you realize that someday. You treat him like a mongrel dog come late to your family, and that is wrong."

Marcellino stared in shock at Inca as she turned on her booted feet and imperiously marched off the same way she'd come. He hated her. She had murdered Rafael. In the twilight, as she reached the rain forest beyond his gaping soldiers, Inca seemed to disappear into thin air. Rubbing his eyes angrily, Marcellino told himself it was the poor light of the coming dusk that tricked him. Gently touching his aching throat, he tried to explain away the pain that still throbbed where invisible hands—or jaws—had wrapped powerfully around his throat and damn near choked him to death.

"Pick up my pistol," he ordered Braga in a scratchy voice that warbled with fear. Irritated, humiliated in front of his men, Marcellino turned on all of them. They looked as if they'd seen a ghost. "All of you!" he roared, his voice breaking. "Get back to your quarters and your posts. We rise at 0500. Get some sleep!"

The men quickly departed. Marcellino saw Roan holster his pistol and come back to the table, his black brows drawn down with displeasure. Too bad. Grabbing the map, Marcellino threw it at his attaché.

"We go through the swamp, Captain."

Braga blanched, but took the map and gently folded it up. "Yes, sir, Colonel."

Roan stood there in shock. Was the man crazy? And then it dawned on him that whatever Inca said, Marcellino was going to do the exact opposite. Fuming, he turned away.

"I'll see you at 0600, Colonel."

Nodding brusquely, Marcellino turned and hurried back to his tent.

* * *

Roan moved back into the darkening rain forest. Very little light trickled down through the canopy as, with monkeys screaming and chattering, the cape of night was drawn across Amazonia. Being careful where he walked, he allowed his eyes to adjust to the gloom. What the hell had prompted Inca to make that kind of entrance? What was going through her mind? She was a proud woman. And she probably couldn't stand not being in on the planning of the march. In some ways, Roan didn't blame her.

He moved along the trail back to their hiding place. A sound—someone crying possibly—drifted into earshot. Halting, Roan keyed his hearing. Yes…there is was again: a soft, halting sobbing. Where? He turned and slowly allowed his ears to become his eyes. Turning off the trail, he moved quietly down a slight incline. Below were six silk-cotton trees, their winged roots splaying out around them. The grove looked like a darkened fortress in the twilight. The sound was coming from there.

Scowling, Roan lightened his step. It *was* someone crying. A woman weeping. Who? Frowning, he stepped down into the clearing among the trees. As he rounded one of the huge, winglike roots, he stopped. Shock jolted through him. It was Inca! Crouched there, her head bowed upon her arms, she was crying hard. Taken aback, Roan stood, unsure of what to do. He felt embarrassed for her, for coming upon her without her knowledge. Why was she weeping? Stymied, he cleared his throat on purpose to let her know he was there. Every particle of him wanted to rush over and embrace her and hold her. He felt her pain.

Sniffing, Inca jerked up her head. Roan stood no more than five feet away from her. Shaken and surprised, she quickly wiped her face free of tears. Why hadn't her guardian warned her that he was coming? Feeling broken and distraught, Inca knew emotionally she was out of balance with herself. When she was in this state, her guardian often had a tough time trying to get her attention. She was, after all, painfully human, and when she allowed her emotions to get the better of her, she was as vulnerable as any other person.

"What do you want?" she muttered, humiliated that he'd seen her crying.

"Stay where you are," Roan urged softly. Taking a chance, a helluva big one, he moved over to her. He slowly crouched down in front of her, their knees barely touching. "I don't care if you are the jaguar goddess," he whispered as he lifted his hand and reached out to her. His fingers grazed her head, the thick braid hanging across her left shoulder. Her hair felt crinkly from the high humidity.

Inca wasn't expecting Roan's gesture and she stiffened momentarily as his long, scarred fingers brushed the crown of her head. Warmth flowed down through Inca. She was shaken by his continued, soothing stroking of her hair. At first she wanted to jerk away, but the energy in his touch was something she desperately needed. Forcing herself to remain still, Inca leaned back against the trunk of the tree and closed her eyes. An unwilling sob rose in her. She swallowed hard and tried to ignore her tumultuous feelings.

Roan moved closer, sensing her capitulation to his grazing touches. He saw the suffering in her face, the way the corners of her mouth were pulled in with pain. "I'm glad to see you this way," he said wryly. "It's nice to know you are human, that you can cry, that you can let someone else help you...." And it was. Each time his fingers stroked her soft, thick hair, a burning fire scalded his lower body. Roan wanted to lean down and brush her parted lips with his, to soothe the trembling of her lower lip with the touch of his mouth. More tears squeezed from beneath her thick, black lashes.

"I cry for Julian," she managed to whisper hoarsely, in explanation of her tears. "I felt his pain so sharply. Julian adores his father, and yet his father does not even realize he exists.'' Sniffing, Inca wiped her nose with the back of her hand. She looked up at Roan's dark, heavy features. His eyes were tender as he leaned over her. She felt safe. Truly safe. It was such an unusual feeling for Inca. Her whole life was one of being on the run, being hunted, with no place to let down her guard. Yet she felt safe with Roan.

Smiling gently, Roan settled down next to Inca. It was a bold move, and yet he listened to his heart, not his head. He eased himself behind her, placing his legs on either side of her.

''You're crying for Julian. Tears for the boy who needs a father.'' Roan whispered. He allowed his fingers to caress the back of Inca's neck. Her muscles were tight. As he slowly began to massage her long, slender form, he felt her relax trustingly.

Everything was so tenuous. So fragile between them. As if an internal thunderstorm was ready to let loose within him, Roan felt driven to hold her, to comfort her, to be man to her woman.

Inca trembled. Roan's fingers worked a magic all their own on her tight, tense neck muscles. She leaned forward, her head bowed, resting her arms on her drawn-up knees so that he could continue to ease the tension from her.

More tears dribbled from her tightly shut eyes as he massaged her neck. ''Julian is sweet. He is innocent, like the children I try to help and heal. He tries so hard to please his father. Back there, I watched him. He was a man. More of a man than his father. And he is right about the path. I was surprised he accepted my route.''

Roan could smell her sweet, musky odor and inhaled it. She was like a rare, fragrant orchid in that moment. It would be so easy to pull her into an embrace, but his heart warned him that it would be rushing Inca and could destroy her growing trust in him. No, one small step at a time.

''If Julian knew you were crying for him, I think he would cry, too.''

Choking on a sob and laughter, Inca nodded. "I like him. He is a kind man. He reminds me of Father Titus, the old Catholic priest who raised me for a while."

"You don't see many of those kind of men down here, do you?" Roan moved his hand tentatively from her neck to her shoulders and began to ease the tension from them.

Inca moaned. "You have hands like no one else."

"Feel good?" He smiled a little, heartened by her unexpected response.

"Wonderful…"

"You let me know when you've had enough, okay?" Roan knew it was important for Inca to set her own emotional boundaries with him. She trusted him, if only a little. His heart soared wildly. He was close enough to press a warm, moist kiss on her exposed neck. What would her flesh feel like? Taste like? And how would she respond, being such a wild, natural woman?

Lifting her head, Inca gave him an apologetic look. "Much touches my heart."

"You just don't let others know that about you," Roan murmured as he moved his hand firmly against her shoulders. "Why?"

"Because the miners, those who steal the timber and those who put my people in bondage will think it is a sign of weakness." Inca wrinkled her nose. "What do you think Colonel Marcellino would do if he saw me crying over how he treated his devoted and loving son? He would put that pistol to my head faster than he tried to today."

"I can't argue with you," Roan said heavily. "How do your neck and shoulders feel now?" He gave her a slight smile as she turned sideways and regarded him from beneath tear-matted lashes.

"Better." Inca managed a broken, trembling smile. "Thank you…" She shyly reached out and slid her fingers across his large hand, which rested on his thigh. It was an exhilarating and bold move on her part and she could see

Roan invited her touch. She'd never had the urges she felt around him. And right now her heart was crying out for his continued touch, but she felt too shamed and embarrassed to ask him to do more.

"Anytime."

"Really?"

He grinned a little. "Really."

She lifted her hand from his, her fingertips tingling pleasantly from the contact. The back of his hand was hairy. She felt the inherent strength of him, as a man, in that hand. Yet he'd been so incredibly gentle with her that she felt like melting into the earth.

"I think you are a healer and do not know it yet."

Roan lifted his hands. "My mother wished that her medicine had moved through me, my blood, but it didn't. Sorry." Giving Inca a humorous look, he told her conspiratorially, "If I can ease a little of your pain, or massage away some tight muscles, then I'm a happy man."

She snorted softly and wiped the last of her tears from her cheeks. "It takes very little to make you happy, then, Storm Walker."

"I don't consider what we share as little or unimportant," he told her seriously. "I like touching you, helping you. You carry the weight of the world on those proud shoulders of yours. If I can ease a little of that load, then it does make me happy."

Inca considered his words, which fell like a warming blanket around her. She craved Roan's continued closeness. She liked the way his bulk fit next to her. In some ways, he was like a giant tree whose limbs stretched gently overhead, protecting her. She smiled brokenly at the thought. The warmth of his body was pleasant, too, with the humidity so high and the sun gone away for the night. The night hours were always chilly to her. What would Roan think if she moved just a few inches and leaned her back against his body? Frightened and unsure, Inca did nothing. But she wanted to.

"What is it about you that makes me feel as I do?" she demanded suddenly, her voice strong and challenging.

Eyebrows raising, Roan stared down at her. The way her petulant lips were set, the spark of challenge in her eyes, made him smile a little at her boldness. "What do you mean? Do I make you feel bad? Uncomfortable?"

"No…just the opposite. I like being close to you. You remind me of a big tree with large, spreading branches— arms that reach out and protect people."

"That's my nature," Roan said in a low tone. He saw her eyes narrow with confusion for a moment. Her tentative feelings for him were genuine and his heart soared wildly with that knowledge. Roan knew instinctively that Inca was an innocent. He realized she was a virgin, in more ways than one. Her relationship skills were not honed. Yet the honest way she had reached out to him touched his heart as nothing else ever could.

"You make me feel safe in my world—and in my world there is no safety." Inca's lips twisted wryly. "How can that be?"

"Sometimes," Roan told her gravely, "certain men and women can give one another that gift. It is about trust, too."

Inca sighed. "Oh, trust…yes, that. Grandfather Adaire said until I could trust someone else with my life, that I would never grow. That I was stuck." She frowned and leaned her head back, looking up at the silhouettes of the trees in the darkness surrounding them.

"And what did Grandmother Alaria say?"

Surprised, Inca twisted to look up at him. His eyes gleamed in the darkness, rich with irony and humor. "How do you know she said anything to me?"

"She's the leader of the village, isn't she? I'd think that she'd have something positive to say to you while you're working on the emotional blocks that were created by your being abandoned at birth."

His insight was startling. Inca found herself not feeling

alarmed about it as she normally would. Raising her hands, she said, "Grandmother Alaria said my heart wound was stopping me from trusting, but that, at some point when I was a little older, more mature, I would work on this blockage. She said she had faith in me to do it."

"Because you have a magnificent heart, Inca. That's why she said those words to you."

Deeply touched by his praise, she said, "I am a bad person, Roan. Grandfather Adaire has said that of me many times. A bad person trying to fulfill the Sisterhood of Light's plan to help all my relations here in Amazonia."

Reaching out, Roan captured some errant, crinkled strands of her hair and gently tucked them behind her ear. He saw her eyes mirror surprise and then pleasure. Good, she was beginning to see his touch as something positive in her life. Tonight Inca had opened her heart to him. The trust in him that inspired that made him feel like he was walking on air. The joy that thrummed through him was new and made him breathless.

"You're a good person, Inca. Don't listen to Grandfather Adaire. Good people make mistakes." He frowned and thought of how he hadn't given Sarah his medicine necklace to wear on that fateful climb. Why, oh why, hadn't he followed his instincts? "Guaranteed, they do. Sometimes really disastrous mistakes. But that doesn't make them bad." Just sorry for an eternity, but he didn't mouth those words to Inca. She was suffering enough and didn't need to know from what experience his words came.

Inca gave him a flat look, her mouth twitching. "Then what? If I am not bad, what am I?"

"Human. A terribly vulnerable and beautiful human being…just like me. Like the rest of us.…"

Chapter 8

"They are going to have many of their men injured or killed going through the swamp," Inca said the next morning as she stood beside Roan on a hill that overlooked the thin, straggling column of men a good half mile away. They were well camouflaged by the rain forest. Luckily, the floor of the forest was clear of a lot of thick bushes and ferns, due to the fact that the triple canopy overhead prevented sunlight from reaching the ground. It made marching faster and easier.

"The colonel is bullheaded," he said, turning and looking at her. This morning he felt a change in Inca. Oh, it was nothing obvious, but Roan felt that she was much more at ease with him. It was because of the trust he was building with her. "I wish he'd listen to his son."

Snorting, Inca adjusted the sling of the rifle on her right shoulder. "Julian has more intelligence than his father ever will."

"You like him, don't you?"

With a shrug, Inca said, "He is a gentle person in a ma-

chine of war. He does not fit in it. I like his energy. He is
a man of peace. My heart aches for him, for all he wants
from his father. The colonel is lucky to have Julian. But he
does not know that.''

''You don't find many men like that,'' Roan said, partly
teasing. ''The peaceful type, that is.''

''You are like that.''

''Yeah?'' He baited her with a growing grin. Just being
next to her was making him feel happier than he had a right
to be. Roan recalled that Sarah had made him feel that way,
too. There was something magical about Inca. She was completely naive to the fact that she was a beautiful young
woman. Not many of the men of the company had missed
her beauty. Roan had seen them staring openmouthed at her,
like wolves salivating after an innocent lamb.

Inca liked the warm smile he turned on her. ''Sometimes
I think you have been trained by the Jaguar Clan. You handle yourself, your energy, carefully. You do not give it away.
You conserve it. You know when to use it and when not
to.'' She found herself wanting to reach out and touch Roan.
That act was foreign to her, until now. He stood there in his
fatigues, the shirt dampened with sweat and emphasizing his
powerful chest and broad shoulders. Recalling his touch,
Inca felt warmth stir in her lower body like sunlight warming
the chill of the night. An ache centered in her heart as she
lifted her gaze to his mouth, which was crooked with that
slight, teasing smile. She liked the way Roan looked. His
face was strong and uncompromising, like him. When he'd
moved to her back and drawn his pistol to protect her from
possible harm by the soldiers as she confronted the colonel,
she'd been grateful. Not many men would stand their ground
like that. Though badly outnumbered, he'd been good at his
word; he had protected and cared for her when it counted.
He *could* be trusted.

She smiled a little as she watched the army column below.
The men were slipping and falling on the damp, leaf-strewn

rain forest floor. Inca wanted the colonel to make twenty miles a day, but the men of this company were too soft. They'd be lucky to make ten miles this first day.

"With the way they are crawling along, the Valentinos will be well prepared for them when we finally make it to that valley."

Roan nodded. "The troops aren't in good shape. It will take at least five days to toughen them up. We'll lose a lot of time doing that."

Inca's eyes flashed with anger. "And Colonel Marcellino said these were his *best* troops. Bah. My people would embarrass and shame them. The Indians are tough and have the kind of endurance it takes to move quickly through the forest."

"Well," Roan sighed, his gaze brushing her upturned features, "we'll just have to be patient with them. I'm more worried about what's going to happen when we hit the edge of that swamp two days from now."

Giving the column a look of derision, Inca growled, "Marcellino is going to have many of his men injured. The swamp is nothing but predators waiting for food."

Roan reached out and briefly touched her shoulder. Instantly, he saw her features soften. It was split seconds before she rearranged her face so that he could not see her true feelings. "Do you want to move ahead of the column?"

"Humph. They are many at the pace of a snail," Inca complained as she started gingerly down the slope. "I think I will move ahead to where I think they will straggle to a stop at dusk. We need meat. I will sing a snake song and ask one of the snakes to give its life for us as a meal tonight."

Roan nodded. "You'll find us, I'm sure."

She flashed him a grin as she trotted down the last stretch of slope to the forest floor below. "I will find you," she promised, and took off at a slow jog, weaving among the trees.

Roan smiled to himself. Inca moved with a bonelessness that defied description, her thick braid swinging between her shoulder blades. He thought he saw a black-and-gold jaguar for a moment, trotting near her side. When he blinked again, the image was gone, but Roan knew he wasn't seeing things. His mother had been clairvoyant and he'd managed to inherit some of that gift himself.

Moving along at a brisk walk, Roan opened the blouse of his fatigues, his chest shining with sweat. The humidity was high, and the cooling breeze felt good on his flesh. Planning on moving ahead and remaining with the point guards out in front of the column, he already missed Inca's considerable presence. Yes, he liked her. A lot. More than he should. His heart blossomed with such fierce longing that it caught him by surprise. Inca was like a drug to his system, an addiction. Roan had thought his heart had died when Sarah left him. But that wasn't so, he was discovering. And for the first time in two years, he felt hope. He felt like living once more, but squashed that feeling instantly. The thought of ever falling in love again terrified Roan. The fear of losing someone he loved held him in its icy clutches. He fought his feelings for Inca. He didn't dare fall for her. She lived her life moment to moment. Hers was not a world where one was guaranteed to live to a ripe old age. And compared to Sarah's love of climbing, Inca's career was even more dangerous.

Inca squatted down in front of the open fire. She had found Roan at dusk. He was in the midst of making sure the colonel's column was getting set up for the coming night. As he left the company, she met him near one of the mound-like hills and led him to her chosen hiding spot for the night, in a grove of towering kapok trees. It was easy to hide among the huge, six-to-eight-foot tall, winglike roots. There were smaller trees nearby, and she'd already hung out two hammocks for them to sleep in.

Just seeing Roan made her heart soar. Inca had found that

as she traveled the rest of the day without Roan at her side, she had missed him more than she should. His quiet, powerful presence somehow made her feel more stable. Protected. And that scared her. In her panic, she had left him with the troops instead of staying with him. She was afraid of herself more than him, of the new and uneasy feelings she was now experiencing. No man had made her feel like he did, and Inca simply didn't know what to do with that— or herself.

Inca had called a snake to give its life so that they could eat. It had come and she had killed it, and after praying for the release of the spirit, she had skinned it and placed it on a spit. As it cooked, she looked across the fire at Roan. The shadows carved out every hard line in his angular, narrow face. "I thought about you a lot today after we split up," she said. "It feels odd to me to work with someone." She squarely met his blue eyes, which were hooded and thoughtful looking after she tossed the bombastic comment his way.

"You're used to working alone," he agreed. "My job here is to be your partner." Roan lifted his chin and looked down at the clearing where the Brazilian Army continued to set up camp for the night. They could see the company, but the men there could not see them.

Snorting, Inca tried to ignore his deep, husky baritone voice. Fear ate at her. She decided to bluff him, to scare him off. "I told you before—I was abandoned to die at birth and I will die alone. I work alone. My path is one of being alone." But she knew, whether she liked it or not, she had felt a thrill race through her that Roan had chosen to be at her campsite and not remain with the colonel's company. Pursing her full lips, she concentrated on keeping the four-foot-long snake turning so it would not burn in the low flames. She liked the warmth of the fire against her body as she worked near it. "I do not need you. Go back to the company. That is where you belong, with the other men."

Roan swallowed his shock. Where was this coming from?

Until now, Inca had seemed happy with his presence. What had changed? Had he said something to her this morning? Roan wasn't sure. Seeing the fear in Inca's eyes, he realized she was pushing him away. If he didn't have the directive from Morgan Trayhern, he'd respect her request, but leaving her alone was not an option. Roan had given Mike Houston his word to protect Inca, and he sure couldn't do that if he was half a mile from her campsite at night. Clearing his throat, he said softly, "Everyone needs someone at some point in their life."

Inca scowled as she continued to deftly turn the meat over the fire. Her heart thudded with fear. Her bluff was not working. "That is not my experience. Jaguars, for the most part, live alone. The only time they see one of their own kind is during mating season, and they split shortly thereafter. The female jaguar goes through her pregnancy and birthing alone, and raises her cubs—alone." She lifted her head and glared across the fire at Roan. "I do not need a partner to do what I do here in Amazonia."

"Because?"

Anger riffled through Inca. The expression on Roan's face told her he wasn't going to budge on this issue. Her black brows dipped. "You have an annoying habit of asking too many questions."

"How else am I to know how you feel?" Roan decided to meet her head-on. He found himself unwilling to give up her hard-earned trust so easily.

"I am not used to showing my feelings to anyone." She raised her voice to a low, warning growl. Usually, such an action was enough to scare off even the bravest of men. Inca recalled vividly how Roan had found her weeping yesterday and how his touch had been soothing and healing to her. When she looked up again, she saw his blue eyes had softened with interest—in her. That set her back two paces and she felt panicky inside. Roan was not scared off like the male idiots she'd had the sorry misfortune to encounter thus far in her life. And maybe that was the problem: Roan Walker was *not* the usual male she was used to dealing with. That thought was highly unsettling.

"I'm not either, so I know how you feel," Roan murmured. "Sometimes, when we're in so much pain, we need another person there just to hold us, rock us and let us know that we're loved, anyway, despite how we're feeling." *Love?* Where had that word come from? Reaching out, Roan placed two more small sticks of wood on the fire. Light and shadows danced across her pain-filled face. A flash of annoyance and then fear laced with curiosity haunted her lovely willow-green eyes. He smiled to himself. Roan felt her powerful and intense curiosity in him as a man. He sensed her uneasiness around him and also her yearning.

More than anything, Roan needed to continue to cultivate her trust of him. Unless he could keep her trust, she would do as she damned well pleased and would leave him behind in an instant—which was exactly what Mike Houston and Morgan Trayhern didn't want to happen. Especially with that trigger-happy Brazilian colonel looking for Inca's head on a platter and the multimillion dollar reward he'd collect once he had it. And then the colonel would have his revenge for his eldest son's death at Inca's hands. No, it was important Roan be able to act as her shield—another set of eyes and ears to keep danger at bay, and Inca safe.

The snake meat began to sizzle and pop as the juices leaked out. With a swipe of her index finger, Inca quickly began to catch them before they fell into the fire. Each time she put her finger into her mouth and sucked on it, making a growling sound of pleasure.

"This is good...."

Roan smiled a little, enjoying her obvious enjoyment of such small but important things in her life. "So tell me," he began conversationally as he watched her sit back on her heels and continue to expertly turn the meat, "why do you distrust men so much?"

Inca laughed harshly. "Why *should* I trust them? Many of them are pigs. Brazilian men think they *own* their wives like slaves." She glared up at him. "No man owns a woman. No man has the right to slap or strike a woman or child, and yet they do it all the time in Brazil. A woman cannot speak up. If she risks it, her husband can strike her. If she so much as looks at another man, the husband, by law, has the right to murder her on the spot. Of course, any married man is allowed to have all the affairs he wants without any reprisal. To other men, he has machismo. Pah." Her voice deepened to a snarl. "I see nothing good in that kind of man. All they can do is dominate or destroy children and women. I will not be touched by them. I will not allow one to think that he can so much as lift a hand in my direction. I will not allow any man to dictate what I should or should not say. And if I want to look at a man, that is my right to do so, for the men here stare at women all the time."

"That's called a double standard in North American."

Curling her upper lip, she rasped, "Call it what you want. Men like that mean destruction. They manipulate others, and they want power *over* someone else. I see it all the time. I walk through one of my villages, and I see what drug dealers have done to those who will not bend to their threats and violence. I see children dead. I see women shot in the head because they refuse to give these men their bodies in payment for whatever they need."

"That's not right," Roan agreed quietly. He heard her stridency, saw the rage in her eyes. It was righteous rage, he acknowledged. And while he was a stranger to Brazil, he had heard of the laws condoning the shooting of a wife who looked at another man. And he'd also heard from Mike Houston that husbands here often had a mistress on the side, as a matter of course.

"Many men are not *right*." She pointed to her breasts beneath the thin olive-green tank top she wore. Earlier, she'd taken off her bandoliers and hung them on a low branch nearby. "All they can do is stare here—" she jabbed at her breasts "—and slobber like dogs in heat. You would think they had never seen a woman's breasts before! Their tongues hang out. It is disgusting! Yesterday, the soldiers stared at me when I walked into camp to challenge Colonel Marcellino."

Raising his brows, Roan nodded. With the bandoliers of ammo set aside, he had to admit that the thin cotton did outline her small, firm breasts beautifully.

"I have watched you," Inca said, slowly rising to her full height, the skewer in hand. "And not once have you stared at my breasts like they always do. Why not?"

Chuckling to himself, Roan reveled in Inca's naive honesty. He watched as she walked over to her pack. There was an old, beat-up tin plate beside it. She squatted down and, sliding the huge knife from its scabbard at her hip, cut the meat into segments and removed them from the skewer. Putting the skewer aside, she picked up the plate and stood up.

"Well?" she demanded as she walked back to him, "why do you not stare at me like they do?"

Roan nodded his thanks as she set the tin plate between them. Inca squatted nearby and quickly picked up a steaming hot chunk of meat with her fingers. There was such a natural grace to her. She was a wild thing, more animal than woman with that feral glint in her eyes.

Reaching for a piece of the roast white meat, he murmured, "Where I come from, it's impolite to stare at a woman like that."

"Impolite?" Inca exploded with laughter, her lips pulling away from her strong, white teeth. "Rude! Piglike! Even in nature—" she swept her arm dramatically around the jungle that enclosed them "—male pigs do not salivate like that over a female pig!"

Roan looked at her as he popped a piece of meat into his mouth. It tasted good, almost like chicken, he thought as he relaxed and watched the firelight lovingly caress her profile.

Her hair was frayed and it softened the angularity of her thin, high cheekbones. She was more sinew and bone than flesh. There was no fat whatsoever on Inca. She was slender like a willow, and each hand or finger movement she made reminded him of a ballet dancer.

"So the men from your tribe do not stare at a woman's breasts?"

He shook his head and took a second chunk of snake meat from the plate. "Let's just say that men of my nation consider women their equals in every way. They aren't..." he paused, searching for the right words "...sexual objects to be stared at, abused or hurt in any way."

She gave him a sizzling sidelong look. "Pity that you cannot teach these Brazilian soldiers a thing or two! I would just as soon put a boot between their legs when they stare and slobber like that, to remind them of the manners they do not possess."

"Try and refrain from that," Roan suggested dryly, hiding a grin desperately trying to tug at one corner of his mouth. "We need their cooperation. I can't have you injuring them like that. We wouldn't make twenty miles a day in this jungle if you did."

Throwing back her head, Inca laughed deeply, the juice of the meat glistening along her lower lip. With the back of her hand, she wiped her mouth clean. "These men, with kicks between their legs or not, will *never* make ten miles a day. They are out of shape. Unfit weaklings."

Roan didn't disagree. "You're right. We'll be lucky to make ten miles a day until they get their legs under them."

With a snort, Inca wiped her long fingers across her jungle fatigues. "They are city boys. They are not hard. They cannot take this hill climbing and humidity. They pant like old dogs with weak, trembling hind legs."

Chuckling, Roan motioned to the last piece of meat in the tin. "It's yours. Eat it."

Inca shook her head. "You have eaten too little today.

You are larger and heavier than me. If you are to keep up with me again tomorrow, this will give you strength.'' She jabbed with her finger. ''Eat it.'' Rising, she stretched fitfully. ''You were the only one to keep my pace.'' She eyed him with respect and acknowledged that although he towered over her, he was lean, tight and hard muscled. There was a litheness to him that reminded her of a jaguar fit for territorial combat. She liked the humor she saw glinting in his eyes as he took the last piece of meat and bit into it. Pleased that he would take directions from her, Inca walked slowly around the fire as she peered out into the darkness that now surrounded them.

''So how does your tribe see women, then? I am curious.''

Roan nearly choked on the meat as he looked up at her. She stood proudly, her shoulders thrown back, the thick braid lying across one shoulder, her chin lifted at an imperious, confident angle once again. Her green eyes glimmered as her gaze caught and held him captive. Her hands rested comfortably on her hips as she stared down at him waiting for him to answer. Swallowing the meat, he rasped, ''We see a woman like a fruit tree filled with gifts of beauty and bounty.''

''Fruit tree?'' Inca saw the sudden seriousness in his eyes and knew he was not joking with her. Why was he so different? And intriguing? Allowing her hands to slip gracefully from her hips, she moved back to where he remained in a squatting position. Taking a seat on a nearby log, she held her hands out toward the fire and savored the heat from it.

Wiping his hands on his fatigues, Roan twisted to look in Inca's direction. He saw that she was genuinely interested and that made him feel good. He hungered for deep, searching conversation with her and about her. ''All life comes from Mother Earth,'' he began, and he patted the damp, fallen leaves on the soil next to where he was crouching. ''We see women as a natural extension of Mother Earth.

They are the only ones who are fertile, who can carry and birth a baby. I was taught a long time ago that a fruit tree, which can bear blossoms, be impregnated by a honeybee and then bear fruit, is a good symbol for women. Women are the fruit of our earth. For me, as a man, a woman is a gift. I do not assume that a fruit tree or a woman wants to share her fruit with me. We always give a gift and then ask if the tree—or the woman—wants to share her bounty with us. If she or the tree says yes, then that's fine. If she says no, that's fine, also.''

Inca rested her chin on her closed hands. She planted her elbows on her thighs and pondered his explanation. ''Women and trees being one and the same...''

''Symbolically speaking, yes.'' Roan saw the pensive expression on her face, the pouting of her lower lip as she considered his words. The firelight danced and flickered across her smooth, golden features, highlighting her cheekbones and wrinkled brow. She was part child, part wise woman, part animal. And at any given moment, any one of those facets could emerge to speak with him. He found her exciting and had to contain the thrill he felt. But, Roan also felt her hatred and distrust of the Brazilian military, and he couldn't blame her at all for her defensive stance around them. After all, they had a high bounty on her head—dead or alive.

As she stared into the fire, lost in thought, Roan tore his gaze from Inca. She was too easy to savor, as if she were a priceless, rare flower. Too easy to emotionally gorge himself. If he took too much, it would destroy her pristine, one-of-a-kind beauty. Besides, he knew Inca did not like to be stared at; but then again, he didn't like it either. He wondered if it was their Indian blood that made them feel that their energy was being stolen when someone stared. Anglos certainly didn't get it, but he understood Inca's unhappiness. Still, she was incredibly beautiful and there wasn't a man in that military contingent that wasn't smitten by her drop-dead-gorgeous looks. Inca was as natural and wild as the rain forest that surrounded them with its humid embrace. Roan had seen more than a few looks of lust in those soldiers' eyes today as they marched and talked animatedly about her dramatic entrance to their camp the night before. And he knew Inca sensed their lust and was completely disgusted by it.

Inca's husky voice intruded upon his reverie.

"Then, if you see women as fruit trees—" she turned and stared at him fully "—how do you see their breasts?"

She asked the damnedest questions. Roan understood it was innocent curiosity, her obvious naïveté of men and the world outside this rain forest. Opening his hands, he said, "I can only speak for myself on this, Inca."

"Yes?" she demanded, goading him impatiently.

"A woman's breasts remind me of warm, sun-ripe peaches."

Her brows knitted. "Peaches? What is a peach? Do they grow here in South America?"

Shrugging, he said, "I don't know. They do where I live."

"Tell me about this peach. Describe it. Does it look like a breast?"

A slight smile curved his mouth. Staring into the fire in order not to make the mistake of looking at her too long, he murmured, "A peach is about the size of my palm," and he held it up for her to look at. "It's an incredible fruit. It's round in shape and when you lean close and smell it, well, it has the sweetest fragrance. When it's ripe, it's firm and has a soft fine fuzz all over it. The colors take your breath away. It's often a clear pinkish gold, but that graduates into red-orange, and orange, or to apricot or a bright sun-gold." He closed his eyes, picturing the fruit. "When I see a ripe, sun-warmed peach on the branch of a tree, all I want to do is reach out and cup my fingers around it, feel those soft, nubby hairs sliding against my fingertips. I want to test the firmness, the roundness and the heat of it as I continue to encircle it...."

Inca felt her breasts tighten and she sat up, surprised. What was going on? She gave him a disgruntled look. Roan sat there, his hands clasped between his opened thighs, his head lifted slightly and his eyes closed. What would it be like to feel him slide those long, large-knuckled, work-worn fingers around her breasts? Instantly, her skin tingled wildly. She felt her nipples harden and pucker beneath her shirt. A wonderful, molten ache began to pool through her lower body as she continued to stare at his hard, angular profile. It was as if her body had a life of its own! And worse, it was responding on its own to his husky, melting words, which seemed to reach out and caress her like a lover.

Scowling, Inca sat there. She'd never had a lover. She couldn't describe what having one was like. Yet his deep, rumbling words continued to touch her almost physically. Her breasts felt hot, felt achy, and she wanted Roan to reach out and caress them! The thought was so foreign to her that Inca gasped.

Roan opened his eyes and slowly turned his head in Inca's direction. He saw a pink stain on her cheeks. He saw her startled expression, and the way her lips parted provocatively, looking so very, very damn kissable. What would it be like to kiss that wild, untamed mouth of hers? How would she feel beneath his mouth? Hot? Strong? Fierce? Hungry? Or starving, like he felt for her? As Inca turned to meet and hold his gaze, Roan sensed her chagrin, her embarrassment and—something else he couldn't quite put his finger on. If he wasn't mistaken, the gold flecks in her willow-green eyes hinted of desire—for him. The impression he received from her was that she wanted him to reach out with his fingers, touch the sides of her breasts, caress them and... With a shake of his head, he wondered what the hell was happening.

It was as if he was reading Inca's thoughts and feelings in her wide, vulnerable-looking eyes during that fragile moment. He saw that her nipples were pressed urgently against the material of her shirt and he could see the outline of the proud, firm breasts that he ached to encircle, tease and then suckle until she twisted with utterly, wanton pleasure in his arms. Roan wanted to be the man to introduce Inca to the realm of love. It was a molten thought. She had never been touched by any man, he knew. A virgin in her mid-twenties, she was a wild woman who would never entertain the touch of a mere mortal, that was for sure.

Inca tore her gaze from Roan's dark, hooded stare. She felt a lush, provocative heat radiating from him toward her. Because she was of the Jaguar Clan, her six senses were acutely honed. For a moment, she'd allowed her mind and heart to touch his. When it had, she'd seen the flare of surprise and then his smoldering, very male look in return. Inca understood in that split second that Roan could touch her in a way she'd never before experienced…and the sensation was galvanizing, aching, filled with promise—yet it scared her.

Heart palpitating wildly in her chest, Inca stared, disgruntled, into the fire. Suddenly breathless beneath that glittering look in his blue eyes—one that reminded her of lightning striking the earth—she was at a loss for words. Her skin tightened deliciously around her breasts. She felt needy. She felt hungry for *his* touch. A man's touch. Of all things! Inca could not reconcile that within herself. Her mind railed against it. Her heart was wide-open, crying out for the intimate touch he promised her in that one look, in that one touch with his mind and heart. Closing her eyes, she hid her face in her hands momentarily.

"I am tired," she muttered. "I must sleep now." Getting up quickly, she moved around the massive root to where she had placed her hammock.

Roan heard the turmoil in her tone. He sat very still because she appeared to be poised like a wild horse ready to spook and hightail it. What had happened? He swore he'd felt her very real presence inside his head—and even more so, in his expanding heart. For an instant, Inca had been *in* him, somehow—attached to or connected to his thoughts and feelings as if… Stymied, Roan wished he could talk to Houston about this experience.

Something had happened, because when Inca had lifted her face and her hands fell away, he'd seen the fear in her eyes. Fear and…did he dare put the name desire to it, also? Was that smoldering, banked desire in her cloudy gaze aimed at him? Very unsure, Roan muttered, "Yeah, we both need to turn in and get some sleep. Tomorrow is going to be a rough day."

In more ways than one, he thought as he rose to his feet. *In more ways than one…*

Chapter 9

Inca halted in her tracks and gulped. It was the third morning of the march into the swamp, and she had gone down a hill to wash herself before the day's activities began. Only, Roan had beat her to the enchanting place. He stood out in the middle of a shallow pool that had been created by the seasonal winter rains. Though the pool was small now, it was just large enough for a person to be able to grasp the white sand surrounding it, and scrub his flesh clean before rinsing off in the knee-deep waters. Hiding behind a tree, her hand resting tentatively against the smooth, gray bark, Inca found herself unable to resist watching Roan's magnificent nakedness as he bathed. Surprise and then pleasurable, molten heat flowed through her.

Inca was torn. She *should* leave. Oh, she knew what men looked like, but an unbidden curiosity and something else was tempting her to remain hidden and devour Roan with her eyes. His clothes were hung on the limb of a nearby rubber tree. He was sluicing the clear, cooling water across his thick, broad shoulders and well-sprung chest, which was covered with a dark carpet of black hair. Gulping unsteadily, she dropped her gaze lower…and lower…then just as quickly, Inca looked away. Disgusted with herself, she spun around and placed her back against the tree, her arms wrapped tightly across against her chest. Nostrils flaring, she told herself she shouldn't be doing this.

Heart pounding, Inca felt that warm, uncoiling sensation deep in her body. It was a wonderful, new feeling that seemed to blossom within her when she was around Roan. She had not been able to bully or scare him off. He'd stayed at her side like a faithful dog would its master, and Inca had grudgingly given up on trying to get him to go back to the company of men. The last two days had cemented their relationship to the point where Inca felt the last of her defenses toward him dissolving. Oh, it was nothing he did directly, just those smoldering looks he gave her from time to time, that crooked smile that heated her spirit and made it fly, his sense of humor and ability to laugh.

She heard him singing, his voice an engaging baritone. The forest around the pool area absorbed most of the sound as he chanted in a language that was foreign to her. Understanding it was a ceremonial song of his people, to greet the rising sun, she slowly turned around and peeked from behind the tree. Both hands on the trunk to steady herself, Inca watched as he leaned down, grabbed some sand from the bottom of the pool and briskly began to scrub his chest. There was something vulnerable and boyish about Roan in that molten moment. Gulping hard, Inca found herself wondering what it would be like to slide her fingers through that dark hair splayed out across his broad, well-developed chest. Or to allow her hands to range downward in exploration.…

Making a strangled sound, Inca jerked away and dug the toe of her boot into the soft, muddy earth. She had to get out of here! Hurrying silently up the hill in a line that would hide her from his view, she wiped her lips with the back of her hand. Her whole world was crumbling because of Roan.

She could not keep him at bay. She melted a little more each time he shared an intimate glance with her, or smiled at her.... So many little things were unraveling her mighty defenses!

Panicked by all that she was feeling, because she'd never felt it before, Inca had no one to turn to to ask what was going on inside her. She wished one of the Jaguar Clan mothers who had raised her were still alive. They'd been old women when they nursed her from babyhood to girlhood. They were all gone now, having long ago walked across the Threshold to the other worlds. Again the biting reminder that she was alone, abandoned by everyone, sank into her.

Back in their makeshift camp, Inca hurriedly removed her dark green nylon hammock from between two trees and stuffed it in the bag she would carry across her shoulders. If only she hadn't been banished from the Jaguar Clan village. Inca yearned to talk to Grandmother Alaria. Yes, Grandmother Alaria would understand what was going on inside her. Grandfather Adaire, however, would block her entrance to the village and tell her to leave—or else deliver the worst punishment of all: ban her forever not just from the village but from the Jaguar Clan. Inca couldn't tolerate the thought of being forced to give up the one thing that she'd been raised to do all her life—work as a healer for her people.

"Your turn."

Inca gasped. She dropped the hammock and spun around, caught off guard. Roan stood behind her, dressed in his fatigues, his upper chest naked, the towel draped over his head as he casually dried his dark hair. She saw the sparkle in his blue eyes. Gulping, she realized he knew she'd seen him bathing. Heat rolled up her neck and into her face. She avoided his tender look. There was no laughter, no censure in his eyes. Indeed, he seemed to understand what she'd done and why. Inca wished she did.

"I—it was an accident," she stammered, nervously picking up her hammock and rapidly jamming it into her small canvas pack.

"Of course," Roan murmured. The rosy flush in her cheeks made Inca unbearably beautiful to him. He saw the surprise, the shame and humiliation in her darkening eyes. "Accidents happen. I wasn't upset."

Lifting her head, she twisted to look in his direction. "You weren't?" She would be.

Wiping his brow dry, Roan hung the small, dark green towel on a branch to dry. Not that it would dry much in this humidity. Shrugging on his fatigue blouse, he rolled up the arms on each sleeve to his elbow. "No."

"I would not like someone coming upon me as I washed."

"That's different." He smiled as she straightened. Inca was not the confident warrior now. Instead she was a young woman, unsure of herself, of her relationship to him, and possibly, Roan ruminated, of what she was feeling toward him. He knew, without question, that Inca was drawn to him like a bee to sweet honey. And he was no less smitten with her even though he was trying desperately to ignore his feelings toward her. Constantly, Roan had to harshly remind himself that they had a mission to complete. He refused to fall in love with another woman. He would not indulge in his growing, powerful feelings for her. Having to cap them, sit on them and ignore them was becoming a daily hell for him. It was a sweet hell, however. Inca was precious to him in all ways—from the smallest gesture to her great unselfishness toward others who were less fortunate than her.

"Humph," Inca said as she grabbed her towel and moved quickly toward the pool. "I will return."

Buttoning his shirt, Roan grinned to himself. When he heard the snap and crackle of boots crushing small sticks that had fallen from the canopy above, he knew someone was coming. Moving out from behind a tree, he saw it was

Julian. The young officer's face was flushed and he had a worried look.

"Good morning," Roan greeted him, placing the towel on top of his pack.

"*Bom dia,* good morning," Julian said, breathing hard. "I just wanted to tell Inca that she was right. Coming into this swamp is creating a disaster of unexpected proportions." He stopped, removed his cap and wiped his brow with his arm. Looking back toward where the company was preparing to march, he continued. "I tried to talk to my father this morning. We have ten men down with malaria symptoms. We have another five with dysentery. And six from yesterday that have assorted sprained ankles or knees from falling and slipping." He shook his head. "I don't know what to do.…"

Roan patted the shorter man on the shoulder. "There isn't much you can do, Julian. We're halfway through the swamp." Looking up, he saw a patch of bright blue sky. It looked as if the weather was going to be sunny. That meant it would be very hot today, and with the humidity around ninety-five percent at all times, the stress on the men would be great. "How about heat exhaustion? How many cases?"

"My *médico,* Sargento Salvador, says we have fifteen men who are down. We need to get a helicopter in here, but we are too far into the jungle for them to land. One of the other officers is taking all the injured and sick back to the edge of the swamp. From there, they will march to the river, where the helicopters will fly in and take them to the nearest hospital, which is located in Manaus."

"A lot of technical problems," Roan agreed somberly. He reached down and removed his tin cup, which had coffee in it that had been warming over the last of the coals of their morning campfire. He offered some to Julian, who shook his head.

"Does Inca know any *quick* way out of this swamp? Is there any way we can get out of it now?"

Roan shrugged and sipped his coffee. "She said there is none. That was the problem. Once you committed to this route, there was no way out except back or straight ahead."

"Damn," Julian rasped. "Very well. I am lead point with my squad today. We will be working with you and Inca." He smiled a little, his eyes dark with worry. "I'm afraid we'll lose many more men today to this heat. There's no cloud cover...."

"Just keep them drinking a lot of water, with frequent rests," Roan advised solemnly.

"My father wants out of the swamp. He's pushing the men beyond their physical limits. I can try, but he's in command...."

Roan nodded grimly. "Then we will just have to do the best we can to get through this."

Inca moved silently. It was dusk and she was watching the weary soldiers of the company erect their tents and reluctantly dig in for the coming night. Perspiration covered her. It had been a hot, humid, brutal day. She saw Colonel Marcellino in the distance. He was shouting at Julian, who stood stiffly at attention. Her heart broke for the young officer. She liked Julian. Why did his father have to treat him so cruelly? Did he not realize how fragile life was? They could all die in a minute in this deadly swamp.

She felt Roan coming, and leaned against a tree trunk and waited for him. The day had been hard on everyone. Even he, with his athleticism and strength, looked fatigued tonight. She nodded to him as he saw her. When he gave her a tired smile in return, her heart opened. Crossing her arms, she leaned languidly against the tree. Roan halted about a foot away from her, his hands coming to rest on his hips.

"They look pretty exhausted," he muttered.

"They are. How many men went down today?"

"Twenty more to various things—malaria, dysentery and heat exhaustion."

"Humph." Brows knitting, Inca watched as Julian was dismissed. He disappeared quickly between the tents that were being raised. "The colonel is an old man and a fool. He will lose as many tomorrow, before we get out of this place."

Scratching his head, Roan studied her in the soft dusk light. She had discarded her bandoliers and her rifle back at their recently made camp. Tendrils of hair stuck to her temples, and her long, thick braid was badly frayed by the high humidity. The soft pout of her lips, her half-closed eyes, made Roan want her as he'd never wanted another woman. He hoped she wasn't reading his mind. Inca had told him she rarely read other people's thoughts because it took much energy and focus. Most people's thoughts were garbage anyway, she told him wryly. Roan sighed. Well, Inca was tired, there was no doubt. There were faint shadows beneath her large eyes. The heat had been brutal even on her, and she lived here year-round.

There was a sudden scream, and then a hail of gunfire within the camp. A number of men were running around, screaming, yelling and brandishing their weapons. More shots were fired.

Inca stood up, suddenly on guard. "What…?"

Roan moved protectively close, his hand on her shoulder, his eyes narrowed. The company of men looked like a disturbed beehive. There were more screams. More shouts. More gunfire. "I don't know…."

Keying her hearing, Inca heard someone shout, *"Médico! Médico!"*

"Someone is hurt," Inca said, her voice rising with concern. "Who, I do not know. There are no drug runners around, so what is going on?"

Before Roan could speak, he saw one of the point soldiers they'd worked with today, Ramone, come racing toward them. The point patrol always knew where they had their camp for the night. The look of terror etched on his young face made Roan grip Inca a little more securely. "Let's see what's going on."

Inca agreed. She liked the touch of his hand on her shoulder. He stood like a protective guard, his body close and warm, and she hungrily absorbed his nearness.

Both of them stepped out into the path of the running, panting soldier. He cried out their names.

"Inca! We need you! Tenente Marcellino! A bushmaster snake bit him! Hurry! He will die!"

Stunned, Inca tore from beneath Roan's hand. She knew she wasn't supposed to enter the colonel's camp. She was unarmed, and risking her own life because the colonel was capable of killing her.

"Inca!" Too late. Roan cursed. He saw her sprint down the trail, heading directly for where the men were running around and shouting. *Damn.* Roan gripped the soldier by the arm. "Let's go. Show me where he's lying." Roan was a paramedic, but he didn't have antivenin in his medical pack. He wasn't even sure there was antivenin for the poison of a bushmaster. As he ran with Ramone, who was stumbling badly, he mentally went over the procedure for snakebite. This particular snake was deadly, he knew. No one survived a bite. No one. He saw Inca disappear between two tents. Digging in his toes, Roan plunged past the faltering and gasping soldier.

Julian Marcellino was lying on the ground near his tent, next to the brackish water of the swamp, and gripping his thigh. Blood oozed from between his white fingers. No more than three feet away lay a dead bushmaster snake that he'd killed with his pistol. Julian's eyes were glazing over as Inca leaned over him. The *médico*, Sargento Salvador, had tears in his eyes as he knelt on the other side of the semiconscious officer.

"I can't save him!" Salvador cried as Inca dropped to her knees opposite him.

"Be quiet!" Inca snarled. Out of the corner of her eye,

she saw Roan running up to her at the same time Jaime Marcellino did. "Move away!" she shouted. "Give me room. Be quiet! All of you!"

The men quickly hushed and made a wide semicircle around Julian. All eyes riveted upon Inca, who studied the two fang punctures as she gently removed Julian's hand from his thigh.

"Uhh," Julian gasped. His eyes rolled in his head. He saw darkness approaching. Inca was watching him intently through her slitted gaze. Her mouth was compressed. "I—I'm going to die...." he told her in a rasping tone.

"Julian," Inca growled, "be still! Close your eyes. Whatever you do, do *not* cross the Threshold! Do you understand me? It is important not to walk across it."

"Stop!" Jaime screamed as he ran toward them. "Do not touch my son!" He saw Inca place one hand over Julian's heart and the other on the top of his head. His son lay prostrate and unmoving. His flesh, once golden, was now leached out like the color of bones found in the high desert of Peru.

Roan jerked the colonel's arm back as he reached out to haul Inca away from where she knelt over Julian.

"No, Colonel! Let Inca try and help him," Roan ordered tightly.

Glaring, the colonel fought to free himself from Roan's grip. "Let me go, damn you! She'll murder him, too! She's a murderer!" His voice carried in the sudden eerie calm of the camp as the men stood watching the exchange.

Breathing hard, Roan pulled the pistol from his holster and pressed the barrel against the colonel's sweaty temple. "Damn you, stand still or I'll take you down here and now. Inca isn't going to kill Julian. If anything, she's the only thing standing between him and death right now. Let her try and heal him!"

Jaime felt the cold metal pressed against his temple. He saw Storm Walker's eyes narrow with deadly earnestness.

Yes, this man would shoot him. Sobbing, he looked down at Julian, who was unconscious now, his mouth slack, his eyes rolled back in his head.

Roan looked around. "No one move!" he roared. "Let Inca do her work."

Taking a deep, steadying breath, Inca leaned close to Julian. With one hand on his heart, the other on top of his head, she silently asked her guardian to come over her. She felt the incredible power of her guide as he did so. The moment he was in place, much like a glove fitting over a hand, she could see through his eyes. A powerful, whirling motion took place, and she felt herself being sucked down counterclockwise into a vortex of energy. In seconds, she stood in the tunnel of light. They were at the Threshold. Breathing hard and trying to hold her focus and not allow outside sounds to disrupt her necessary concentration, Inca saw Julian standing nearby. Two light beings, his guardians, were on the other side of the Threshold. Moving to them directly, she asked, "May I bring him back?"

Under Jaguar Clan laws, if the light beings said no, then she must allow his spirit to cross over, and he would die, physically. Inca had only once in her life made the mistake of disobeying that directive when she'd brought Michael Houston back from this place. He should have died. But she'd decided to take things into her own hands. And because she was young and only partly trained, she had died physically doing it. Only Grandmother Alaria's power and persuasion had brought her back to life that fateful day so long ago.

Inca waited patiently. She saw the light beings convene. Julian was looking at them. She saw the yearning on his face to walk across that golden area that served as the border between the dimensions.

"If you decide to bring him back to your world," one of the light beings warned, "you may die in the process. He is full of poison. You must run it quickly through your own body, or you will die. Do you understand?"

Inca nodded. "Yes, I do." In her business as a healer, she had to take on the symptoms, in this case, the deadly snake venom, and run it through her own body in order to get rid of it. She would certainly perish if not for the power of her jaguar guardian, who would assist her with his energy in the process, draining it back into Mother Earth, who could absorb it. If it was done fast enough, she might survive.

"Then ask him to return. His tasks are not yet complete."

Inca held out her hand to Julian. "Come, Julian. I will bring you home. You have work to do, my young friend."

"I don't want to return."

Inca saw the tears in the young officer's eyes. "I know," she quavered unsteadily. "It is because of your father."

"He doesn't love me!" Julian cried out, the tears splattering down his face. "I am so distraught. I drew the snake to me, to bite me. I can't stand the pain any longer!"

Inca knew that when things in life were very tough on a person, they sometimes drew an accident to them in order to break the pattern, the energy block they were wrestling with. By creating an accident, the gridlock was released and the person was allowed to work, in a new way, on the problem they'd chosen to learn from and work through. "I understand," she told Julian in a soothing voice. Stretching out her fingertips, Inca moved slowly toward him. "Come, Julian, take my hand. I will bring you back. Your father loves you."

"No, he doesn't!" Julian sobbed. He turned toward the light beings on the other side. "I want to go. I want to cross. He's never loved me! He only loved Rafael. I tried so hard, Inca…so hard to have him love me. To say he loved me, or to show me he cares just a fraction of how he cared for Rafael. But he treats me as if I'm not there. That is why I want to leave."

Inca took another, deliberate step forward. "You cannot.

You *must* come back with me, Julian. Now." Once he touched her outstretched fingers, he had committed to coming back. Julian didn't know that, but Inca did. It was a cosmic law. Halfheartedly, he took her hand.

"I don't know…" he sobbed.

"I do." And Inca forced the darkness she saw inhabiting his body to funnel up through her hand and into her body. She was literally willing the snake venom into herself. Instantly, she groaned. She felt the deadly power of the poison. Losing sight of Julian, of the light, Inca felt as if someone had smashed into her chest with a huge fist. Gasping, she tightened her grip around Julian's hand. She knew if she lost him at this critical phase, that his spirit would wander the earth plane forever without a physical body. *Hold on!*

Roan heard Inca groan. She sagged against Julian, her head resting on his chest, her eyes tightly shut. Her mouth was contorted in a soundless cry. Worriedly, he sensed something was wrong. Marcellino moved, and Roan tightened his grip on the officer's arm. "Stay right where you are," he snarled, the pistol still cocked at his temple.

"My son!" Jaime suddenly cried, hope in his voice. He reached out toward Julian. "Look! Look! My God! Color is returning to his face! It is a *miracle!*"

Roan shot a glance toward Julian. Yes, it was true. Color was flooding back into Julian's once pasty face. The men whispered. They collectively made a sound of awe as Julian's lashes fluttered and he opened his eyes slightly.

But something else was wrong. Terribly wrong. Inca was limp against Julian. Her skin tone went from gold to an alarming white, pasty color. Roan felt a tremendous shift in energy—a wrenching sensation that was almost palpable, as if a lightning bolt had struck them. The soldiers blanched and reacted to the mighty wave of invisible energy.

As Julian weakly lifted his arm, opened up his mouth and croaked, "Father…" Inca moaned and fell unconscious to the ground beside him.

Roan released the colonel. Jamming the pistol into the holster, he went to Inca's side. She lay with one arm above her head, the other beside her still body. Was she breathing? Anxiously, he dropped to his knees, all of his paramedic abilities coming to the forefront.

"Salvador! Get me a stethoscope! A blood pressure cuff!"

The *médico* leaped to his feet.

Jaime fell to Julian's side, crying out his name over and over again. He gripped his son by the shoulders and shook him gently.

"Julian! Julian? Are you all right? My son, speak to me! Oh, please, speak to me!" And he pulled him up and into his arms.

A sob tore from Jaime as he crushed his son against him. He looked down to see that Julian's color was almost normal. His lashes fluttered. When he opened his eyes again, Jaime saw that they were clear once more.

"Father?"

Jaime reacted as if struck by a thunderclap. A sob tore from him and he clasped his son tightly to him. "Thank God, you are alive. I could not bear losing you, too."

Roan cursed under his breath. He took Inca's blood pressure. It was dumping. She was dying. Heart pounding with anxiety, he threw the blood pressure cuff down and held her limp, clammy wrist. He could barely discern a pulse.

The men crowded closer, in awe. In terror. They all watched without a sound.

"Inca, don't die on me, dammit!" Roan rasped as he slid his arm beneath her neck. He understood what she had done: used her own body to run the venom through. That was the nature of healing. Could she get rid of it soon enough? Could her jaguar spirit guide help her do it? Roan wasn't sure, and he felt his heart bursting with anguish so devastating that all he could do was take her in his arms and hold her.

As he pressed her limp body against his, and held her tightly, he blocked out Jaime's sobs and Julian's stammered words. He blocked out everything. Intuitively, Roan knew that if he held Inca, if he willed his life energy, his heart, his love, into her, that it would help her survive this terrible tragedy. He'd seen his mother do this countless times— gather the one who was ill into her arms. She had told him what she was doing, and he now utilized that knowledge.

The instant Roan pressed her hard against him, her heart against his heart, his world shattered. It took every ounce of strength he'd ever had to withstand the energy exploding violently through him. Eyes closed, his brow against her cheek, he felt her limpness, felt her life slipping away.

No! It can't happen! Breathing hard, Roan tried to take deep, steadying breaths of air into his lungs as he held her. Behind his eyes, he saw murky, turgid green and yellow colors. Out of the murkiness came his cougar. He'd seen her many times before in his dreams and in the vision quest he took yearly upon his mother's reservation. The cougar ran toward him full tilt in huge striding leaps. Roan didn't understand what she was doing. He thought she would slam into him. Instead, as she took a mighty leap directly at him, he felt her warm, powerful body hit and absorb into his. The effect was so surprising that Roan felt himself tremble violently from it.

The yellowish-green colors began to fade. He felt the cougar in him, around him, covering him. It was the oddest sensation he'd ever experienced. He felt the cougar's incredible endurance and energy. It was as if fifty thousand volts of electricity were coursing through him, vibrating him and flowing out of him and into Inca. Dizzy, Roan felt himself sit down unceremoniously on the damp ground with Inca in his arms. He heard the concerned murmurs of soldier's voices. But his concentration, his focus, belonged inside his head, inside this inner world where the drama between life and death was taking place.

Instinctively, Roan held Inca with all his strength. He saw and felt the cougar's energy moving vibrantly into Inca. He saw the gold color, rich and clean, moving like an energy transfusion into her body. The murky colors disappeared and in their place came darkness. But it wasn't a frightening darkness, rather, one of warmth and nurturance. Roan knew only to hold Inca. That in holding her, he was somehow helping her to live, not die.

When Inca moaned softly, Roan felt himself torn out of the drama of the inner worlds. His eyes flew open. Anxiously, he looked down at the woman in his arms. Her flesh had returning color. And when her lashes fluttered weakly to reveal drowsy willow-green eyes, his heart soared with the knowledge that she was not going to die. Hot tears funneled through him and he rapidly blinked them away.

He felt Salvador's hand on his shoulder. "How can we help?" he asked.

Slightly weakened, Roan roused himself and looked up. "Just let me sit here with her. She's going to be okay...." he rasped to the soldiers who stood near, their faces filled with genuine concern.

Looking down at Inca, Roan gave her a broken smile. "Welcome back to the land of the living, sweetheart."

Though incredible weakness stalked Inca, she heard Roan's huskily spoken words and they touched her pounding heart. She was too tired to even try to lift her hand and touch his face. How wonderful it felt to be held by him! Inca had wanted to experience this, but not like this.

"Roan...take me home...out of here. I need rest...." Her voice was a whisper. Gone was her husky, confident tone. She felt like she was a drifting cloud, at the whim of the winds.

"I'll take you home," he promised.

Roan eased Inca into a sitting position. Many hands, the hands of the soldiers who had witnessed this drama, came to help. Inca sat with her head down on her knees. She was very weak and incapable of walking anywhere on her own. Getting to his feet, Roan felt the last of the dizziness leave him. Looking over, he saw Julian sitting up, too, his father's arm around his shoulder. And he saw Jaime's face covered with tears, his once hard eyes now soft with love for his son.

Several of the soldiers lifted Inca into Roan's awaiting arms. He reassured them all that she would be fine, that all she needed now was a little rest. Julian looked up, his eyes still dull from the event. Roan nodded to him and turned and left. Right now, all he wanted to do was get Inca to their camp to tend to her needs.

The soup tasted salty and life-giving to Inca as she sat propped up against a tree at their camp, and accepted another spoonful from Roan. He had opened up a packet of soup and made it for her and the chicken broth was revitalizing. He stood up and moved to the fire to place more wood on it, the flames dancing gaily and highlighting his hard, carved face. Inca was covered with only a thin blanket and was chilled to the bone. Though the soup warmed her, she wished, more than anything, that Roan would come and sit next to her, embrace her and warm her with his powerful body.

"More soup?" Roan asked as he came back to her and knelt down beside her.

"No…thank you…." Inca sighed deeply.

"You almost died," Roan said as he sat down.

Inca avoided his hooded look. She felt terribly vulnerable right now. "Yes. Thanks to you and your spirit guide, I will live."

IIis heart told him to move closer and take her into his arms. After almost losing her, he no longer tried to shield himself from Inca. Roan wasn't sure when his guard had come down, only that the crisis earlier had slammed that fact home to him. "Come here," he murmured, and eased her against him. She came without a fight, relieved that he was going to hold her. Her flesh was goose pimpled. As Roan settled his bulk against the tree with Inca at his side, her head resting wearily on his shoulder, he'd never felt happier.

"Okay?" he asked, his lips pressed to her long, flowing hair. She felt good in his arms, fitting against him perfectly, as if they had always been matched puzzle pieces just waiting to be put together.

Sighing softly, Inca nuzzled her face into the crook of his neck. "Yes…" And she closed her eyes. Risking everything, she lifted her hand and placed it on his chest. The moment was so warm, so full of life. She could hear the insects singing around them, the howl of some monkeys in the distance. All that mattered right now was Roan.

"You are so brave," she whispered unsteadily. "I needed help and you knew it. I was told before I took Julian's hand to help him return that it might kill me."

Roan frowned. "And you did it anyway?"

Barely opening her eyes, she absorbed Roan's warmth, felt his hand moving gently across her shoulders. "What choice did I have? He had not finished his life's mission on this side. He had to come back. He drew the snake to him to create a crisis that would overcome his father's reserve."

"Well," Roan muttered, "that certainly did the trick. The man was crying like a baby when Julian returned."

"Good," Inca purred. She nuzzled against his shoulder and jaw, a soft smile on her lips. She felt the caress of Roan's fingers along her neck and across her cheek and temple. How wonderful it felt to be touched by him! All these years, Inca had been missing something. She couldn't verbalize it. She hadn't known what it was until now. It was the natural intimacy that Roan had effortlessly established with her. The warmth, the love she felt pouring from him brought tears to her eyes. Was this what love felt like? Inca had no way of knowing for sure. She'd read many books by famous authors and many poems about love. To read it was one thing. To experience it was something new to her.

"Do you often get into this kind of a predicament with someone you're going to heal?"

Inca shook her head. "No."

"Good."

She smiled a little. Roan's fingers settled over the hand she had pressed to his heart. She could feel the thudding, drumlike pounding of it beneath her sensitive palm. "Someday you must go with me to the Jaguar Clan village. I would like you to meet the elders. I think you have powerful medicine. All you need is some training to understand it and work with it more clearly."

Roan nodded. He lay there in the darkness, near the dancing fire, and told her what he'd felt and seen when he'd taken her into his arms. When he was done, he felt Inca reach up, her fingertips trailing along his jaw.

"You are a very brave warrior," she told him. Lifting her head so that she could look up at him, she saw the smoldering longing in his eyes—for her. Because she was weak and feeling defenseless, or perhaps because she'd nearly died and she was more vulnerable than usual, Inca leaned up…up to press her lips to his. It wasn't something she thought about first, for she was completely instinctual, in touch with her primal urges. As her lips grazed the hard line of his mouth, she saw his eyes turn predatory. Something hot and swift moved through her, stirring her, and she yearned for a more complete union with the softening line of his mouth.

Surprised at first, Roan felt her tentative, searching lips touching his like a butterfly. Her actions were completely unexpected. It took precious seconds for him to respond—appropriately. Primally, his lower body hardened instantly. He wanted to take her savagely and mate with her and claim and brand her. But his heart cautioned him not to, and instead of devouring her with a searing kiss, Roan hauled back on his white-hot desires.

If anything, he needed to be gentle with Inca. As her lips tentatively grazed his once more, he felt the tenuousness of her exploration of him, as a man to her woman. He understood on a very deep level that people did odd things after they almost died. Making love was one of them. It confirmed life over death. All those thoughts collided within his whirling mind as her lips slid softly across his. She did not know how to kiss.

The simple reminder of her virginal innocence forced Roan to tightly control his violent male reaction. Instead, he lifted his hands and gently framed her face. He saw her eyes go wide at first, and then grow drowsy with desire—for him. That discovery just tightened the knot of pain in his lower body even more so. Swallowing a groan, Roan repositioned her face slightly, leaned over and captured her parted lips. The pleasure of just feeling her full mouth beneath his sent shock waves of heat cascading through him. He felt her gasp a little, her hands wrapping around his thick, hairy wrists. Easing back, Roan tried to read Inca and what her reaction meant.

He saw her eyes turn golden-green. The heat in them burned him. She trembled violently as he leaned down and once more tasted her lips. This time, he captured her firmly beneath his mouth. He felt her hesitantly return his kiss. Smiling to himself, he broke it off and moved his tongue slowly across her lower lip. Again, surprise and pleasure shone in her half-closed eyes. Smiling tenderly, he leaned over and moved his mouth against hers once more. This time her lips blossomed strongly beneath his. She caught on fast.

Inca purred with pleasure as Roan's mouth settled against hers. This was a kiss. The type she'd seen other people give to one another. And now she understood the beauty and sensual pleasure of it, too. Now she knew why people kissed one another so often. A flood of heat flowed through her.

She felt the caresses of his mouth upon her lips, the gliding heat created by their touching one another. Her heart was skipping beats. Lightning settled in her lower body, and like a hot, uncoiling snake, she felt a burning, scalding sensation flowing through her. The feeling was startling. Intensely pleasurable.

Shocked by all that she was feeling, Inca tore her mouth from his. She blinked. Breath ragged, she whispered, "Enough... I feel as if I will explode...."

He gave her a lazy, knowing smile. Brushing several strands of hair from her cheek, he rasped, "That's good. A kiss should make you feel that way." Indeed, the flush in Inca's cheeks, the golden light dancing in her widening eyes told Roan just how much she'd enjoyed their first, tentative kiss. Exploration with her was going to be hell on earth for him. He felt tied in painful knots. Inca could not know that, however. She was a child in the adult world of hot love-making and boiling desire. It would be up to him to be her teacher and not a selfish pig, taking her in lust. If nothing else, today had taught Roan that he felt far more toward Inca than lust, but because of his past, he had denied it. He told himself their relationship was only temporary, that when the mission was over, their torrid longing for one another would come to an end.

Inca shyly looked up at him, and then looked away. Her lips were throbbing in pleasure. She touched them in awe. "I did not know a kiss could do all this. Now I know why people kiss so much...."

Laughter rolled through Roan's chest. He embraced her a little more tightly and then released her. "I'm not laughing at you, Inca. I agree with your observation."

She smiled a little tentatively. Touching her lips once more, she looked up at him. "I liked it."

He grinned. "So did I."

"The feelings..." she sighed and touched her heart and

her abdomen with her hand "…are so different, so wonderful…as if a fire is bursting to life within me."

"Oh," Roan said wryly, "it is. But it's a fire of a different kind."

"And it will not burn me?"

He shook his head solemnly. He would burn in the fires of hell while she explored her sensual nature, but he was more than willing to sacrifice himself for her. "No, it won't hurt you. It will feel good. Better than anything you can imagine."

Stymied, Inca lay content in his arms. "Being like this with you is natural," she whispered. "It feels good to me. Does it for you?"

"You feel good in my arms," Roan told her, pressing a small kiss to her hair. "Like you've always belonged here…." And she did as far as he was concerned. He was old enough, experienced enough to realize that Inca owed him nothing. He was her first man, and he understood that it didn't mean she would stay with him. No, he expected nothing from her in that regard. Inca was the kind of wild spirit no man could capture and keep to himself. She had to be free to come and go as her wild heart bade her. Selfishly, he wanted to keep her forever. But Inca's life was a day-by-day affair. And in his own philosophy of life, Roan tried to live in the moment, not in the past and not trying to see what the future might bring him.

Inca nuzzled beneath his hard jaw. She closed her eyes. "You saved my life today. And you gave me life tonight. I do not know how to thank you."

Grazing her shoulder, Roan whispered, "Just keep being who you are, sweetheart. That's more than enough of a gift to me."

Chapter 10

"Inca…you've come…." Julian weakly raised up on the pallet where he lay. Shortly, two soldiers were going to carry him out of the swamp and back to the Amazon, where a helicopter would take him to a hospital in Manaus for recovery. He smiled shyly and lifted his hand to her as she drew near.

Inca ignored the soldiers who stood agape as she approached the *tenente*'s litter. There was admiration and wariness in their eyes. They didn't know what to make of her, and that was fine; she liked keeping people off balance where she was concerned. She'd known intuitively that Julian would be gone as the sun rose this morning, and she wanted to say goodbye to him. In her usual garb, she removed the rifle from her shoulder and knelt down beside the young officer, who was still looking pale. Inca knew that the colonel didn't want her in camp with weapons, but that was too bad.

"*Bom dia,* good day," she said, reaching out and gripping his fingers. "You are better, eh?"

Julian's mouth moved with emotion. His lower lip trembled. The strength in Inca's hand surprised him. He held her hand as if it were a cherished gift. "Yes, much... I owe you everything, Inca." His eyes grew soft with gratefulness. "I understand from talking to the men earlier that you risked your life to save mine. I don't recall much...just bits and pieces. I was so shocked when I walked out of my tent. The snake was waiting for me at the flap. I never saw him until it was too late. After he sank his fangs into my leg, I screamed. I remember pulling my pistol and firing off a lot of shots at it. And then...I fell. I don't remember much more." His eyes narrowed on hers. "But I do remember being in the light, and you were there." His voice lowered. "And so was your jaguar. I saw him."

Julian glanced about, wanting to make sure the men of his platoon couldn't hear his whispered words. "I felt myself on the brink, Inca. I wanted to leave, and you brought me back." He squeezed her hand gently and closed his eyes. "I'm glad you did. Don't think for a moment that I wasn't glad to open my eyes and find myself in my father's arms." He looked at her, the words filled with emotion. "He was holding me, Inca. Me. And I owe it all to you, to your strength and goodness."

She saw the tears well up in his eyes. Touched to the point of tears herself, she whispered, "Yours was a life worth saving, my friend."

Julian pressed a soft kiss to the back of her scarred hand and then reluctantly released her strong fingers. Sighing, he self-consciously wiped the tears from the corners of his eyes. "I shouldn't be crying. I feel very emotional right now."

Inca nodded. "That always happens after a near death event. Let your tears fall." She smiled a little. "I see you and your father have connected again?"

Julian's eyes grew watery. "Yes...and again, I have you to thank."

Shaking her head, Inca sensed the crush of soldiers who

had begun to crowd around to get a closer look at her and to try and hear what they were talking about. "No, Julian, I had nothing to do with that. I am glad that it happened, though."

Julian kept his voice down. "Yes, we are really talking to one another for the first time since Rafael's death." Choking up, he rasped, "Last night, my father told me he loved me. It's the first time I can recall him saying that to me. It's a miracle, Inca."

Smiling tenderly, Inca nodded. "That is wonderful. And so, you go to Manaus to recover, my friend?"

Nodding, Julian said unhappily, "Yes. I want to stay…. I want to lead my men into that valley, but my father says I must go." With a wry movement of his mouth, he said, "I shouldn't complain. He cares openly for me, and he wants to see me safe. He told me that I was their only son and now it is my turn to carry the family's honor and heritage forward."

"A wise man," she murmured. Patting Julian's hand, she rose. "I wish you an uneventful journey, Julian. Because where we go, it will be dangerous and interesting."

Julian's gaze clung to hers. "I'll never forget you, Inca. The legend about you being the jaguar goddess is true. I'll speak your name with blessings. People will know of your goodness. Your generous heart…"

She felt heat tunnel up her neck and into her face. Praise was something she could never get used to. "Just keep what you have with your father alive and well. That is all the thanks I need. Family is important. More than most people realize. Goodbye…" She lifted her hand.

The men parted automatically for her exit. Inca looked at them with disdain as she strode through the crowd toward Roan, who stood waiting for her at the rear of the crowd. Her heart pounded briefly beneath the smoldering look of welcome he gave her. When his gaze moved to her mouth, her lips parted in memory of that scorching, life-changing kiss they'd shared last night. She had left camp early this morning to bathe and then find Julian. At that time, Roan had still been asleep in his hammock as she moved silently around their camp.

The warm connection between her heart and his was so strong and beautiful. Inca felt as if she were not walking on Mother Earth but rather on air. Just the way he looked at her made her joyful. A slight smile curved her lips as she drew near.

"I see what you are thinking," she teased in a husky voice meant for his ears only.

Roan's mouth moved wryly upward. He slid his hand around her shoulder and turned her in another direction. "And feeling," he murmured. His gesture was not missed by the soldiers, for they watched Inca as if mesmerized by her presence and power. "Come on, Colonel Marcellino wants to see you—personally and privately."

Instantly, Inca was on guard. She resisted his hand.

Roan felt her go rigid. He saw the distrust in her eyes, and the wariness. "It's not what you think, Inca. The man has changed since yesterday. What you did for Julian has made the difference. He's no longer out to kill you."

"Humph, we will see." She shouldered the rifle and moved with Roan through the stirring camp. There were a hundred and twenty men left in the company, thanks to the colonel's poor judgment in taking them through this infested swamp. Inca was angry about that. Julian would not have been bitten by the bushmaster had they gone around the swamp.

Inca tried to steady her pounding heart as they approached the opened tent, where Colonel Marcellino sat at his make-shift desk. His attaché, Captain Braga, bowed his head in greeting to Inca.

"Colonel Marcellino would speak privately with you," he said with great deference, and he lifted his hand to indicate she was to step forward. Inca looked over at Roan, a question in her eyes.

"I'm staying here."

"Coward."

Roan grinned. "This isn't what you think it is. Trust me."

Flashing a disdainful look at him, Inca muttered, "I will. And I will see where it leads me."

Chuckling, Roan touched her proud shoulder. "Sweetheart, this isn't going to be painful. It's not that bad."

Inca thrilled to the endearment that rolled off his tongue. She liked the way it made her feel, as if physically embraced. Roan was not aware of his power at all, but she was, and Inca indulged herself in allowing the wonderful feelings that came with that word to wrap around her softly beating heart.

Turning, she scowled and pushed forward. Might as well get this confrontation with the colonel out of the way so they could get out of this dreaded swamp today.

Jaime Marcellino looked up. He felt Inca's considerable presence long before she ducked beneath the open tent flaps to face him. She stood expectantly, her hands tense on her hips, her chin lifted with pride and her eyes narrowed with distrust.

"You wanted to see me?" Inca demanded in a dark voice. She steeled herself, for she knew Marcellino was her enemy.

With great deliberation, Jaime placed the gold pen aside, folded his hands in front of him and looked up at her. "Yes, I asked for you to come so that we may talk." Flexing his thin mouth, he said with great effort, "Most important, I need to thank you for saving my son's life. I saw firsthand what you did. I cannot explain *how* you saved him. I only know that you did."

Inca held herself at rigid attention. She did not trust the colonel. Yet she saw the older man's face, which was gray this morning and much older looking, lose some of its authoritarian expression. His dark brown eyes were watery with tears, and she heard him choking them back. It had to be hard for him to thank her, since he accused her of murdering his eldest son.

Her flat look of surprise cut through him. Her facial expression was one of continued distrust. Jaime wanted to reach inside that hard armor she wore. What could he expect? He'd treated her badly. Lifting his hands in a gesture of peace and understanding, he whispered, "I wish to table my earlier words to you, my earlier accusations that you murdered my eldest son. Because of what has happened here, I intend, when this mission is over, to go back to Brasilia and interrogate the drug runner who accused you of shooting Rafael. And I will use a lie detector test on him to see if indeed he is telling the truth or not." His brows drew downward and he held Inca's surprised gaze.

"I owe you that much," he said unsteadily. "My logic says that if you saved Julian, why would you have murdered my firstborn? All that I hear about you, from the gossip of my soldiers, as well as the villagers we have passed on this march, is that you heal, you do not kill."

Inca slid her fingers along the smooth leather sling of her rifle. "Oh, I kill, Colonel," she whispered rawly. "But I do it in self-defense. It is a law of my clan that we never attack. We only defend. Do you really think I *enjoy* killing? No. Does it make me feel good? Never. I see these men's faces in my sleep."

"You are a warrior as I am," he replied. "Killing is not a pleasure for any of us. It is a duty. A terrible, terrible duty. Our sleep is not peaceful, is it?" He cleared his throat nervously. "I have heard legends surrounding you, of the lives you have taken." Jaime rose, his fingers barely touching the table in front of him. "And judging from what I've seen, you do *not* enjoy killing, any more than I do."

Inca's nostrils flared. Her voice quavered. "What sane human being would?" She waved her hand toward the encampment. "Do any of us *enjoy* killing another human being? Only if you are insane, Colonel. And believe me, I have paid dearly…and will continue paying for the rest of my life, for each person's life I have taken. Do you not see those you have killed in your sleep at night? Do you not hear their last, choking cries as blood rushes up their throat to suffocate them?'' Eyes turning hard, Inca felt the rage of injustice move strongly through her. ''Even the idea that I would murder anyone in cold blood is beyond my comprehension. Yet you believed it of me.'' She jabbed her finger at him. ''I told you I did not kill your other son, Rafael. Father Titus has an affidavit, which is in your possession, that tells you I was nowhere near that part of Brasil on that day.''

The colonel hung his head and moved a soiled and damp sheet of paper to the center of his desk. ''Yes…I have it here.…''

''Since when did you think priests of your own faith would lie about such a thing?''

Wincing, Jaime rasped, ''You are right, Inca.…'' He touched the crinkled, creased paper that held Father Titus's trembling signature. ''I have much to do to clear your name of my eldest son's death. And I give you my word, as an officer and a gentleman, that once I return home, I will do exactly that.''

Inca felt her rage dissolving. Before her stood an old man worn down by grief and years of hatred aimed wrongly at her. ''I will take your words with me. Is that all?''

Nodding, Jaime said wearily, ''Yes, that is all. And I also want to let you know that you were right about this swamp. I'm afraid my arrogance, my anger toward you, got the better of me. From now on I will listen to you. You know this land, I do not. Fair enough?''

Inca hesitated at the tent opening, her fingers clenching the strap of the rifle on her shoulder. ''Yes, Colonel. Fair enough. In five more days we will reach the valley, if we follow my route through the jungle.''

* * *

Inca lay on her belly, the dampness feeling good against her flesh in the midday heat as she studied the valley below. Roan lay beside her, and his elbow brushed hers as he took the binoculars from her and swept the narrow, steeply walled valley.

"Do you see the factory?"

Roan kept his voice low. "Yes, I see it."

Inca watched as the colonel's company spread out in a long, thin line along the rim of the valley. They had a hundred men ready to march against the Valentino Brothers' factory, which was half a mile away, nestled at one end of the valley. The factory was large, the tin roof painted dark green and tan so that it would not be easily spotted from the air. They had positioned it beneath the jungle canopy to further hide its whereabouts from prying satellite cameras.

Eyes narrowing, Inca watched as her Indian friends moved ceaselessly in and out of the opened doors of the huge factory. A dirt road led out of the area and down the center of the valley, more than likely to a well-hidden villa up the steep valley slopes. They carried bushel baskets of coca leaves, which would be boiled down to extract the cocaine. Other Indians were carrying large white blocks wrapped in plastic to awaiting trucks just outside the gates. That was the processed cocaine, ready for worldwide distribution. Guards would yell at any Indians who moved too slowly for them. She saw one guard lift his boot and kick out savagely at a young boy. Her rage soared at the bondage of her people.

"It looks like an airplane hangar," Roan muttered, adjusting the sights on the binoculars. "Big enough to house a C-130 Hercules cargo plane."

"I estimate there are over a hundred Indians in chains down there," she said, anger tinging her quavering tone.

"There's a lot of guards with military weapons watching every move they make," Roan stated. "A high fence, maybe ten feet tall, with concertina wire on top to discourage any of them from trying to escape.''

''At night, the Indians are forced to live within the fence. Sebastian and Faro Valentino are down there. Look near that black Mercedes at the gate.'' She jabbed her index finger down at them. ''That is them.''

Roan saw two short men, one with a potbelly and the other looking like a trim, fit athlete. Both were dressed in short-sleeved white shirts and dark blue trousers, and they were talking with someone in charge of the guards, a man in military jungle fatigues. ''Got 'em.''

''They look pitifully harmless,'' Inca growled. ''But they are murderers of my people—hundreds of them over the last four years. The one with the pig's belly is Sebastian. Faro is the thin one, a pilot. His helicopter is over there.'' She pointed to the machine sitting off in the grass near the compound. ''He has a fleet of military helicopters that he bought from foreign countries, and he uses them to ferry the cocaine out of the area. He has also used his helicopters to shoot down Brazilian Air Force helicopters that have tried to penetrate this area. He is dangerous. He is here to pick up a load of cocaine and fly it to Peru. The Indians are carrying it to the machine right now.''

Roan heard the grating in her voice. Faro had a military helicopter, dark green in color and without markings. ''I've read up on these two. Sebastian is the lazy one of the family. He stays put in Brazil, which is his territory. He's satisfied with doing business from here. Faro has his own military air force, with choppers in nearly every South American country. He wants to dominate not only all of South America, but eventually Central America, as well. We're lucky to catch the brothers together. I was hoping we'd get Sebastian.'' His voice lowered with feeling. ''I'd like to take 'em both down.''

''Do not be fooled by the piglike expressions on their faces. They are as smart as jaguars.''

"And you think the best time to attack is at night?"

"Yes, under cover of darkness. The guards go inside the factory at night to package the cocaine into blocks and wrap them, while the Indians sleep outside. I will go down, contact the chief who leads all the people there, and they will spread the word quickly and quietly as to the coming attack. I will break open the chain around the gate and open it. They will run. That is when the colonel will attack."

Roan nodded and counted the guards. "I see twenty guards."

"There are more inside the factory. Perhaps an equal number."

"Forty men total. Against our hundred."

Snorting, Inca gave him a cutting glance. "Do not think forty men cannot kill all of us, because they can." She glared at the line of Brazilian soldiers hunkering down on their bellies along the rim to observe their coming target of attack. "While these soldiers have gotten stronger over the last ten days, no one says that they are battle hardened or can think in the middle of bullets flying around them. The Valentinos' men are cold, ruthless killers. Nothing distracts them from the shots they want to take. Nothing."

"I understand," Roan said. He reached out and touched Inca's cheek. Time was at a premium between them. And as much as he wanted to kiss her, he knew that she had to come to him. Inca had shyly kissed him two more times. The enjoyment was mutual. He could almost feel what she was thinking now, as if that invisible connection between them was working with amazing accuracy. Inca had told him that because a bond of trust was forged between them, he would easily pick up on her thoughts and feelings—just as she would his.

Roan watched her eyes close slightly as he touched her cheek. "I worry about you. You're the one taking all the chances. What if the guards spot you at the fence?"

Inca captured his large hand and boldly pressed a kiss

into the palm of it. Smiling widely, she watched his eyes turn a dark, smoky blue, which indicated he liked what she had done. The last five days had been a wonderful exploration for her. She felt safe enough, trusting enough of Roan to experiment, to test her newfound feminine instincts. He made her happy. Deliriously so.

"Do not worry. They will not see me coming. I will use the cover of my spirit guide to reach the fence. Only then will I unveil myself." She released his hand and turned over on her back, her gaze drifting up through the canopy. Above her, a flock of red-and-yellow parrots skittered among the limbs of the trees. "You worry too much, man of my heart."

Roan gave her a careless smile in return. He lay on his back, slid his arm beneath her neck and moved closer to her. When she pressed her cheek against him, he knew she enjoyed his touch. "I like where we're going, Inca," he told her quietly as they enjoyed one of the few private moments they'd been able to steal during the march. "I don't know where that is, but it doesn't matter."

Inca laughed softly. She closed her eyes and fiercely enjoyed his closeness, the way he nurtured her with his touch, with his hard, protective body. "I do not know, either, but I want to find out."

A sweet happiness flowed through Roan. "So do I." And he did. In the last five days they had bonded so closely. Despite his fear, Inca had somehow surmounted that wall within him. Roan was scared. But he was more frightened of losing Inca to the danger of her livelihood. Did she love him? Was there hope for their love? There were many obstacles in their path. Was what she felt for him puppy love? A first love rather than a lasting love built upon a foundation of friendship and mutual respect? Roan wasn't sure, and he knew the only way to find out was to surrender his heart over to her, to the gift Inca had given to him alone.

Inca opened her eyes and looked at Roan, a playful smile on her face. "You are the first man to open my heart. I do not know how you did it, only that it has happened." She lightly touched the area between her breasts where the bandoliers of ammo met and crossed.

More serious, Roan held her softened willow-green eyes. "What we have…I hope, Inca…is something lasting. That's what I want—what I hope for out of this."

"Mmm, like Grandfather Adaire and Grandmother Alaria have? You know, there is gossip that they are a thousand years old, that they fell in love on an island off the coast of England. They were druids on the Isle of Mona, where they were charged with keeping the knowledge of druid culture alive for the next generation. When the Romans came and set fire to the island, destroying the druid temples and thousands of scrolls that had their people's knowledge recorded on them, they fled. It is said they came by boat over here, to Peru, and helped to create the Village of the Clouds."

"And they're husband and wife?"

Chuckling, Inca said, "Oh, yes. But Grandmother Alaria is the head elder of the village. Grandfather Adaire is one of eight other elders who comprise the counsel that makes decisions on how to teach jaguar medicine and train students from around the world."

"A thousand years," Roan murmured. "That's a long time. How could they live so long?"

Inca shrugged and gazed up through the trees. "I do not know. It is said that when humans have a pure heart, they may live forever or until such time that they desire to leave their earthly body." She laughed sharply. "I do not have a pure heart. I will die much, much sooner!"

Roan moved onto his side, his body touching hers. He placed his hand on her waist and looked deeply into her eyes. "You have the purest heart I've ever seen," he rasped. Reaching out, he brushed several strands of hair away from her brow. "The unselfish love you have for your people, the way you share with others…if that isn't pure of heart, I don't know what is.''

Just the touch of his fingers made her skin tingle pleasantly. Reaching up, Inca caressed his unshaved jaw. "Roan Storm Walker, you hold my heart in your hands, as I hold yours. You think only good of me. Those of the Jaguar Clan are charged with seeing us without such feelings in the way.'' She smiled gently.

Leaning down, he whispered, "Yes, you hold my heart in your hands, my woman—''

"Excuse me….''

Roan heard the apologetic voice just moments before he was going to kiss Inca. Instead, he lifted his head and sat up. Captain Braga stood uncertainly before them, clearly embarrassed for intruding upon their private moment. "Yes?''

Clearing his throat, Captain Braga said, "A thousand pardons to you both.''

Inca felt heat in her face as she sat up. She picked several tiny leaves out of her braid. "What is it?'' she demanded. More than anything, she'd wanted Roan's kiss, that commanding, wonderfully male mouth settling against her hungry lips.

"The colonel…he asks you to come and help him with the attack plans. Er, can you?''

Inca was on her feet first. She held out her hand to Roan, who took it, and she pulled him to his feet. "Yes, we will come….''

Roan tried to quell his fear for Inca's safety. He'd followed her down the steep, slippery wall of the narrow valley in the darkness, but Inca had disdained his offer of a flak jacket and headphone gear. Roan adjusted the microphone near his mouth. He was in contact with the officers of the company, who also wore communication gear. He wished Inca had agreed to the headset and protective vest. She had told him it would hamper her abilities to shape-shift and he'd reluctantly given in. The one thing he did do, however, was take off his medicine necklace and give it to her—for protection. The urge to give it to her had overwhelmed him, and this time he'd followed the demand.

Inca's eyes had filled with tears as he'd hung it around her neck, the beautiful blue stone resting at the bottom of her slender throat. She'd smiled, kissed his hand, knowing instinctively the importance of his gesture.

The clouds were thick and a recent shower made the leaves gleam. The rain had muffled their approach to their target which was fortunate. The factory was less than two hundred yards away. The road to it was deeply rutted, and now muddy. Trees had been cleared from the edge of the road, but otherwise the valley was thickly covered by rain forest. Faro's helicopter sat tethered near the factory. He and his brother had disappeared inside the main facility hours earlier.

Roan's heart beat painfully in his chest for Inca as he followed her, for her raw courage under such dangerous circumstances. She didn't seem fazed by her duties, and if she felt fear, he didn't see it in her eyes or gestures. How brave she was in the name of her people.

Inca carefully removed her bandoliers and put her rifle aside. She took off the web belt. There was a guard outside the gate, his military weapon on his shoulder as he walked back and forth in front of it. Hidden in the forest above and around the factory were the Brazilian soldiers, who had crept carefully into position. The attack would take place in a U-shaped area. The only escape for the Indians would be down the road. Inca would urge them to run and then take cover in the rain forest. There was a squad of Brazilian soldiers half a mile from the front gate, their machine gun set up to stop any guards from driving away from the factory once the battle began.

Roan said nothing. His heart hammered with worry and anxiety for her. What was Inca going to do? Just walk up to the guard and knock him out? The guard would see her coming. Though his mouth was dry, Roan wiped it with the back of his hand. She slowly stood up, only a foot away from him.

"It is time," she said. Looking up at him, her mouth pulled slightly upward. "Now you and all of them will see why they call me the jaguar goddess."

Roan reached out and gripped her hand. "Don't do anything foolish. I'm here. I can help you...."

She squeezed his fingers. "You just gave me the greatest gift of all, my man." She gently touched the medicine necklace. "Your heart, your care, will keep me safe." Stepping forward, she followed her wild instincts. Her mouth fitted hotly against his. She slid her fingers through his damp hair, and hungrily met and matched his returning ardor. Pulling away, her heart pounding, Inca whispered, "I will return. You have captured my heart...." Then she quickly moved down the last stretch of slope to a position near the road.

Roan's lips tingled hotly from her swift, unexpected kiss. He watched through the lazy light filtering through the clouds from the moon above them. Inca's form seemed to melt into the surrounding grayness. For a moment, Roan lost sight of her. And then his heart thudded. Farther down, something else moved. Not a human...what, then?

Eyes slitting, he lifted the light-sensitive binoculars to try and pinpoint the dark, shadowy movement. He was looking for Inca's tall, proud form. It was nowhere to be found. *There!* Roan scowled. His hands wrapped more strongly around the binoculars. He saw the shadowy outline of a jaguar moving stealthily toward the guard in the distance. His black-and-gold coat blended perfectly into the shadows and darkness surrounding him. Was that Inca? The jaguar was trotting steadily now toward his intended target—the guard walking past the gate. She had told him of her shape-shifting ability, of being able to allow her jaguar spirit guardian to envelope her so that she appeared in his shape and form.

Roan didn't know how it was done, exactly, but he recalled his own experience with his cougar recently. Among his own people, there were medicine men and women who were known to change shape into a cat or wolf. In this altered form, Inca had told him, she possessed all the jaguar's powerful abilities, including sneaking up on her intended target without ever being noticed.

Roan's breath hitched. The guard had turned and was coming back toward the corner of the fence closest to the jungle. Compressing his lips, Roan hunted anxiously for the cat. Where was it? It seemed to have disappeared. Instead, he watched the guard, who was lazily smoking a cigarette, a bored look on his face. Just as the guard reached the corner and was going to turn around, something caught his attention. Startled, he dropped the cigarette from his lips, jerked his rifle off his shoulder and started to raise it to fire.

Out of the darkness of the rain forest, a jaguar leaped toward the man. In an instant, the stunned guard was knocked on his back, the rifle flying out of his hand. In seconds, the cat had strangled the soldier by grabbing hold of his neck in his jaws and suffocating him into unconsciousness, not death though that was how a jaguar killed.

Roan stood, the binoculars dropping to his chest. He picked up his rifle and moved rapidly down the hill. In the distance, he could barely see the soldier lying motionless on the ground. A number of Indians had run to that area of the fence. All hell was going to break loose in a few seconds. Running hard, Roan hit the muddy road and sprinted toward the front gate. The other guards would be making their rounds. Inca would have only moments to open that front gate and release her people.

Inca moved soundlessly. It took precious seconds for her spirit guardian to release her. Shaking off the dizziness that always occurred afterward, she blinked several times to clear her head. Then, breathing hard, she picked up the machete the soldier had strapped to his belt.

The Indian factory workers pressed their faces to the fence, clenching the wire. Their expressions were filled with joy as they whispered, "the jaguar goddess." Inca hissed to them in their language to be silent. Digging her feet into the muddy red soil, she lunged toward the gates. Gripping the handle of the deadly three-foot-long machete, Inca raced to where a chain and padlock kept the two gates locked together.

The Indians followed her, as if understanding exactly what she was going to do to free them. Men, women and children all ran toward her without a sound, without any talking. They knew the danger they were all in. Their collective gazes were fixed on the woman they called the jaguar goddess. The thin crescent moon on her left shoulder blade—the mark of the jaguar—was visible as her sleeveless top moved to reveal it. There was no question in their eyes that she was going to save them. She was going to free them!

Breathing hard, perspiration running down the sides of her face, Inca skidded to a halt in the slimy clay. She aimed the machete carefully at the thick iron links that held the Indians enslaved. Fierce, white-hot anger roared through her. She heard a sound. *There!* To her left, she saw a guard saunter lazily to the end of his prescribed beat. He'd seen her! His eyes widened in disbelief.

Lifting the machete, Inca brought it down not only with all her own strength, but with that of her guardian as well, the combined power fueled by the outrage that her people were slaves instead of free human beings. Sparks leaped skyward as the thick blade bit savagely into the chain. There was a sharp, grating sound. The chains swung apart.

Yes! Inca threw the machete down and jerked opened the gates. She saw the guard snap out of his stupor at seeing her.

"Come!" she commanded, jerking her arm toward the Indians. "Run! Run down the road! Hurry! Go into the forest and hide there!"

They needed no more urging. Inca leaped aside and allowed them to run to freedom. She jerked her head to the left and remained on the outside perimeter of the fence. The soldier was croaking out an alarm, fumbling with his rifle. Yanking at it with shaky hands, he managed to get it off his shoulder. He raised his rifle—at her. With a snarling growl, Inca spun around on her heels and ran directly at the drug runner guard. It was the last thing he would expect her to do, and she wagered on her surprising move to slow his reaction time.

The man was shocked by her attack; he had expected her to run away. He yelped in surprise, his eyes widening enormously as Inca leaped at him. She knocked the rifle back against his jaw, and there was a loud, cracking sound. As the guard fell backward, unconscious, Inca tumbled and landed on all fours. Breathing hard, she saw the soldier crumple into a heap. Grinning savagely, she scrambled to her feet, grabbed his rifle and sprinted down the fence to find the third guard. By now there was pandemonium. Gunfire began to erupt here and there.

Breathless, Inca slid to a halt in the mud near the corner of the compound. She nearly collided with another guard, who was barreling down the fence from the opposite direction after hearing his compatriot's shout of warning. This man was big, over two hundred pounds of muscle and flab. He saw Inca and jerked to a stop. And then his lips lifted in a snarl as he pulled his rifle to his shoulder and aimed it at her. As he moved to solidify his position, one foot slipped in the mud. The first bullet whined near her head, but missed.

Firing from the hip, Inca got off two shots. The bullets tore into the legs of the guard. He screamed, dropped his rifle and crumpled like a rag doll into the mud. Writhing and screaming, he clawed wildly at his bleeding legs.

Inca leaped past him and began her hunt for the fourth and last guard outside the gate. If she could render him harmless, the colonel's men would have less to worry about. Jogging through the slippery mud, she ran down the fence line. Glancing to her left, she saw that the Indians had all escaped. *Good!* Her heart soared with elation. She heard the Brazilian soldiers coming down the slopes of the valley. They were good men, with good intent, but nowhere physically fit for such a battle.

Turning the corner, Inca spotted the last soldier outside the gate. She shouted to him and raised her rifle. He turned, surprised. Rage filled his shadowed face as he saw her. Lifting his own weapon, he fired several shots at her.

Inca knew to stand very still and draw a bead on the man who fired wildly in her direction. She heard the bullets whine and sing very close by her head. Most men in the heat of battle fired thoughtlessly and without concentration. Inca harnessed her adrenaline, took aim at the man's knee and fired. Instantly, he went down like a felled ox. His screams joined the many others. From the corner of her eye, she saw a shadow. Who?

Twisting to face the shadow that moved from behind the building inside the fence, Inca sensed trouble. When the figure emerged, his pistol aimed directly at her head, her eyes narrowed. It was Faro Valentino. His small, piggish eyes were alive with hatred—toward her. He was grinning confidently.

At the same instant, through a flash of light in the darkness, she saw Roan. He shouted a warning at her and raised his rifle at Valentino.

Her boots slipped in the mud as she spun around to get off a shot at the murderer of so many of her people. And just as she did, she saw the pistol he carried buck. She saw the flicker of the shot being fired. She heard Roan roar her name above the loud noise of gunfire. And in the next second, Inca felt her head explode. White-hot pain and a burst of light went off within her. She was knocked off her feet. Darkness swallowed her.

Chapter 11

"**S**he's down! Inca's down!" Roan cried into the microphone. Scrambling, he leaped down the slope to the muddy ground near the compound. "I need a *médico!* Now!" He slipped badly. Throwing out his hands, he caught his balance. *Run! Run!* his mind screamed, *she needs you! Inca needs you!*

No! No! This can't be happening! Roan cried out Inca's name again. He ran hard down the fence line toward her. He fired off shots in the direction of Faro Valentino, who was standing there smiling, a pleased expression on his face he eyed Inca's prone, motionless form. The drug runner scowled suddenly and jerked his attention to Roan's swift approach. He took careful aim and fired once, the pistol bucking in his hand.

Roan threw himself to the ground just in time. The bullet screamed past his head, missing him by inches. Mud splashed up, splattering him.

Faro cursed loudly. He turned on his heel and hightailed

it down the fence to where his helicopter was revving up for takeoff.

Cursing, Roan realized he faced a decision: he could either go after Faro or go to Inca's side. It was an easy choice to make. Getting awkwardly to his feet, he sprinted the last hundred yards to her.

Roan sank into the mud next to where Inca lay on her back, her arms flung outward. "Inca!" His voice cracked with terror.

The gunfire was intense between drug runners and soldiers as the Brazilian army closed in around the compound. Several nearby explosions—from grenades—blew skyward and rocked him. The drug dealers were putting up a fierce fight. Faro's helicopter took off, the air vibrating heavily from the whapping blades in the high humidity. He was getting away! Hands trembling badly, Roan dropped the rifle at his side.

"Inca. Can you hear me?"

His heart pounded with dread. Automatically, because he was a paramedic, Roan began to examine her from head to toe with shaking hands. It was so dark! He needed light! Light to see with. *Where is she wounded? Where?* Gasps tore from his mouth. In the flashes of nearby explosions, he saw how pale Inca was. *Is she dead? Oh, Great Spirit, No! No, she can't be! She can't! I love her. I've just found her....* His hands moved carefully along the back of her head in careful examination.

Roan froze. His fingers encountered a mass of warm, sticky blood. After precious seconds, his worst fears were realized. Inca had taken a bullet to the back of her skull. *Oh, no. No!* He could feel where the base of her skull protruded outward slightly, indicating the bones had been broken. Lifting his fingers from beneath her neck, he screamed into the mouthpiece, "*Médico! Médico!* Dammit, I need a doctor!"

Médico Salvador came charging up to him moments later.

Panting, he slid awkwardly to a halt. Mud splattered everywhere. His eyes widened in disbelief.

"*Deus!* No!" he whispered, dropping to his knees opposite Roan. "Not Inca!"

"It's a basal skull fracture," Roan rasped. Sweat stung his eyes. He crouched as gunfire whined very close to where they knelt over Inca. Automatically, he kept his body close to hers to shield her.

Salvador gasped. "Oh, *Deus*…" He tore into his medical pack like a wild man. "Here! Help me! Put a dressing on her wound. *Rápido!*"

Roan took the dressing, tore open the sterilized paper packet, pulled the thick gauze out and placed it gently beneath Inca's neck and head. He took her pulse. It was barely perceptible. Roan shut his eyes and fought back tears.

"Pulse?" Salvador demanded hoarsely, jerking out gauze with which to wrap the dressing tightly about her head.

"Thready."

"Get the blood pressure cuff…."

More bullets whined nearby. Both men cringed, but kept on working feverishly over Inca.

Roan went through the motions like a robot. He was numb with shock. Inca was badly wounded. She could die…. He knew her work was dangerous. Somehow, her larger-than-life confidence made him believe she wasn't mortal. Could he hold her as he did before? Could he heal her? Another grenade exploded nearby, and flattening himself across Inca's inert form, Roan cursed. She *was* mortal. Terribly so. The battle raged, hot and heavy around them, but his mind, his heart, centered on her. *Great Spirit, don't let Inca die…don't let her die. Oh, no… I love her. She can't die— not now. She's too precious to you…to all of us….*

Salvador cursed richly as he pumped up the blood pressure cuff. "This is bad—90 over 60. Damn! We have no way to get her to a hospital for emergency surgery." He gave Roan a sad, frustrated look.

Just then, Roan heard another noise. *No! How could it be?* Lifting his head to the dark heavens, he held his breath. Did he dare believe what he heard? "Do you hear that?" he rasped thickly to Salvador.

The Brazilian blinked, then twisted in the direction of the noise, a roaring sound coming from the end of the valley. Within moments, it turned deafening and blotted out the gunfire around them. "*Deus,* it's helicopters! But…how? They cannot travel this far without refueling. Colonel Marcellino said none were available. Is it Faro coming back with reinforcements? We saw him take off earlier. He's got a chopper loaded with ordnance. What if it's him?" Frightened, Salvador searched the ebony heavens, which seemed heavy with humidity—rain that would fall at any moment.

Out of the night sky, to Roan's surprise, at least three black, unmarked gunships sank below the low cloud cover and came racing up the narrow valley toward them. He croaked, "No, it isn't Faro. They're Apache helicopters! At least two of them are, from what I can make out from here. They must be friendlies! I'll be damned!" Roan had no idea how they'd gotten here. Or who they were. There was still a chance they were drug runners. He knew from Morgan's top-secret files that Faro Valentino had a fleet of military helicopters stationed in Peru. And according to their best intelligence from satellites, there were no enemy helicopters in this immediate area. So who were these people? Brazilian Air Force? Roan wasn't sure. Even if they were, they would have had to have refueled midair to penetrate this deeply into the Amazon basin. Colonel Marcellino had never said anything about possible air support. Roan was positive he would have told his officers if it was an option. Besides, the Valentinos were known to have refuelling capabilities to get in and out of areas like this one.

"Captain Braga!" Roan yelled into his microphone. "Are these approaching Apaches ours? Over!"

Roan waited impatiently, his eyes wary slits as he watched

the aircraft rapidly draw near. If the copters were the enemy, they were all dead. Apaches could wreak hell on earth in five minutes flat. Roan's heart thudded with anxiety. He jerked a look down at Inca. Her mouth was slack, her flesh white as death. Her skin felt cool to his probing touch. Looking up, he saw Salvador's awed expression, his gaze locked to the sky. Flares were fired. The sky lit up like daylight as the helicopters approached the compound area.

Roan scowled. Of the three helos, two were Apache and one was a Vietnam era Cobra gunship. Surprised, he didn't know *what* to make of that. The valley echoed and reechoed with the heavy, flat drumming of their turning blades. Who the hell were they? Friend or enemy? Roan was almost ready to yell for Braga again when Braga's winded voice came over his headset.

"We don't know *whose* they are! They're not Brazilian! They're not drug runners. Colonel Marcellino is making a call to headquarters to try and find out more. Stand by! Over."

"Roger, I copy," Roan rasped. Blinking away the perspiration, he saw the Cobra flying hell-bent-for-leather between the two heavily armed Apaches. There was a fifty-caliber machine gun located at the opened door. He saw the gunner firing—at the drug runners!

"They're friendly!" Salvador shouted. *"Amigos!"*

The gunships all had blinking red and green lights on them. The two Apache helicopters suddenly peeled off from the Cobra; one went to the right side of the valley, the other to the left side. The Cobra barreled in toward the compound, low and fast, obviously attempting to land. The valley shook beneath their combined buffeting.

Roan suddenly put it all together. Whoever they were, they were here to help turn the tide against the savagely fighting drug runners! The Cobra began hovering a hundred feet above them, an indication that it was going to land very close to the compound. Sliding his hands beneath Inca, Roan growled to Salvador, ''Come on! That chopper is going to land right in front of this factory. We can get Inca outta here! She has a chance if we can get her to the hospital in Manaus. Let's move!'' Inca weighed next to nothing in his arms as Roan lifted her gently and pressed her against him. He made sure her head was secure against his neck and jaw. Every second counted. Every one.

The sound of powerful Apache gunships attacking began in the distance. Hellfire missiles were released, lighting up the entire valley. The missiles arced out of the sky toward the main concentration of drug runners, many of whom began to flee down the road toward the other end of the valley. Brutal noise, like that of a violent thunderstorm, pounded savagely against Roan's eardrums.

Salvador jerked up his medical pack and ran, slipping and stumbling, after Roan as he hurried in a long, striding walk to the compound entrance. The rain forest was alive with shouts from excited Brazilian soldiers. Hand-to-hand combat ensued. Out of the corner of his eye, Roan saw Captain Braga running down the slope with a squad of men. In the flashes of light, he saw triumph etched across the captain's sweaty, strained face.

Gripping Inca more tightly, Roan rounded the corner of the compound fence, heading directly to the Cobra, which had just landed just outside the gates. Neither he nor Salvador had weapons. Salvador was a medic and they never carried armament. Roan had left his rifle behind in order to carry Inca. Out of the darkness came two drug runners, weapons up and aimed directly at them.

Roan croaked out a cry of warning. ''Salvador! Look out!'' He started to turn, prepared to take the bullets he knew were coming, in order to protect Inca, who sagged limply in his arms.

Just then another figure, dressed in body-fitting black flight suit and flak jacket, helmet on his head, appeared almost as if by magic behind the drug runners who had Roan in their gunsites. The black helmet and visor covered the upper half of his face, but his pursed lips and the way he halted, spread his booted feet and lifted his arms, told Roan he was there for a reason.

Roan stared in horror and amazement as whoever it was— the pilot of the landed Cobra helicopter?—lifted his pistol in both hands and coolly fired off four shots. All four hit the drug runners, who crumpled to the muddy earth. The man then gestured for Roan and Salvador to make a run for it. He stood tensely and kept looking around for more enemy fire.

"Come on!" Roan roared, and he dug his boots into the mud. He saw the pilot turn and yell at him, his voice drowned out by the machine gun fire of the nearby Cobra. The pilot lifted his arm in hard, chopping motions, urging them to hightail it.

Roan's breath came in huge, gulping sobs as he steadied himself in the mud. *Hurry! Hurry!*

Salvador slipped. He cried out and smashed headlong into the ground and onto his belly. His medical pack went flying.

Roan jerked a look in his direction.

"Go on!" Salvador screamed. "*Corra!* Run! Get to the chopper! Don't worry about me!"

Roan hesitated only fractionally. He surged forward. Barely able to see the six-foot-tall pilot except in flashes of gunfire, Roan saw him reach toward him. The grip of his hand on his arm was steadying.

"Stay close!" the pilot yelled, his voice muffled by the shelling.

Roan's only protection for Inca as he ran along the compound fence was the wary pilot, who moved like a jaguar, lithe and boneless, the gun held ready in his gloved hand. Roan followed him toward the front corner of the barbed-wire barrier.

As Roan rounded the corner, he saw the helicopter, an antique Huey Cobra gunship from the Vietnam War, sitting on high idle waiting for them, its blades whirling. Roan followed the swiftly moving pilot back to the opening where the machine gunner was continuing to fire at drug runners. More than once, the pilot fired on the run, to the left, to the right, to protect them. Bullets whined past Roan's head like angry hornets. Slugs were smattering and striking all around them. Mud popped up in two-foot geysers around his feet. Roan saw the copilot in the aircraft making sharp gestures out the opened window, urging them to hurry up and get on board. The gunfire increased. The drug runners were going to try and kill them all so they couldn't take off.

Hurry! Roan's muscles strained. They screamed out in pain as he ran, holding Inca tightly against him. Only a hundred feet more! The pilot dived through the helicopter's open door, landed flat on his belly on the aluminum deck and quickly scrambled to his knees and lunged forward into the cockpit. The gunner at the door stopped firing. He stood crouched in the doorway, arms opened wide, yelling at Roan to hurry. All of them were dressed in black flight suits, with no insignias on their uniforms. Their helmets were black, the visors drawn down so Roan couldn't make out their faces. They looked brown skinned. Indians? Brazilians? He wasn't sure. Roan thought they must be from some secret government agency. The real military always wore patches and insignias identifying their country and squadron.

The blast of the rotor wash just about knocked him off his feet. His arms tightened around Inca. The pilot was powering up for a swift takeoff. The violent rush of air slapped and slammed Roam repeatedly as he ducked low to avoid getting hit by the whirling blades. The gunner held on to the frame of the door, the other hand stretched outward toward them. He was screaming at Roan to get on board. An explosion on the hill rocked him from behind. Fire and flame shot up a hundred feet into the air. One of the attack choppers must have found an ammo dump! Thunder rolled through the narrow valley, blotting out every other sound for moments.

By the time Roan made it to the doorway, his arms were burning weights. The gunner wrapped a strong hand under his biceps and hefted him upward, then moved aside and made a sharp gesture for Roan to place Inca on an awaiting litter right behind him in the rear of the small helicopter. Wind whipped through the craft. As Roan gently lay Inca on the stretcher and quickly shoved several protective, warm covers over her, the gunner placed a pair of earphones across Roan's head so he could have immediate contact with everyone else in the helicopter.

"Get us to the nearest hospital!" he gasped to the pilot as he knelt over Inca. "She's got a basal skull fracture. Time's something we don't have. She's gonna die if we can't get her stabilized. Let's get the hell outta here! Lift off! Lift off!"

The gunner went back to his station, and in seconds, the machine gun was firing with deep, throaty sounds once again. Red-and-yellow muzzle light flashed across the cabin with each round fired. Roan heard bullets striking the helo's thin skin as the craft wrenched off from the ground and shot skyward like a pogo stick out of control. He bracketed Inca with his own body, the gravity and power of the takeoff a surprise. This old machine had a lot more juice in it than he'd thought. The ride was violent and choppy. Everyone got bounced around. The pilot took evasive maneuvers, steering the aircraft in sharp zigzag turns until they could get out of the range of gunfire from below, moving swiftly up the valley, to gain altitude and head for Manaus.

The instant they were out of rifle range, the gunner stopped firing. He slid shut the doors on each side of the Cobra so that the wind ceased blasting through the aircraft. The helicopter shook and shuddered as it strained to gain altitude in the black abyss surrounding them. Before Roan could ask, a small, dull light illuminated the rear cabin where they were sitting on the bare metal deck, allowing him to see in order to take care of Inca. Quickly, he tied the green nylon straps of the litter snugly around her blanketed form so she couldn't be tossed about by the motion of the chopper.

"Give him the medical supplies," came the husky order from the pilot over his earphones.

Roan was in such shock over Inca's condition that it took him precious seconds to realize the ragged voice he heard was a woman's—not a man's. Surprised, he jerked a look toward the cockpit. He saw the pilot, the one who had shot the two drug runners and saved their lives, twist around in her seat and look at him for a moment. She pushed the visor up with her black glove and gazed directly at him and then down at Inca, the expression on her face one of raw emotion. Her eyes were alive with anger and worry as she stared at Inca.

His mouth dropped open. Even with the helmet and military gear, Roan swore she was nearly a carbon copy of Inca! How could that be? The light was bad and her sweaty face deeply shadowed, so he couldn't be sure. The shape of her face was more square than Inca's, but their nose and eyes looked the same. The pilot's expression was fierce. Her eyes were slitted. There were tears running down the sides of her cheeks. She was breathing heavily, her chest heaving beneath the flak jacket she wore.

"How's Inca doing?"

Roan blinked. Clearly this woman knew Inca. His mind tilted. He opened his mouth. "Not good. She's stable for now, but she could dump at any time."

Nodding, the woman wiped her eyes free of the tears. "She couldn't be in better hands right now."

Stymied, Roan saw the depth of emotion in her teary eyes. Tears? Why? The stress of combat? Possibly.

"I know you have a lot of questions, Senhor Storm Walker. In time, they'll be answered. Welcome aboard the black jaguar express.'' She made a poor attempt to smile. ''I'm Captain Maya Stevenson. My copilot is Lieutenant Klein. Take care of my sister, Inca, will you? We're heading for Manaus. My copilot's already in touch with the nearest hospital. There'll be an emergency team waiting for us once we land. We brought some help along.'' She jerked a thumb in the direction of her door gunner. ''Sergeant Angel Paredes has a lot of other skills you can use. We call her the Angel of Death. She pulls our people from death's door.'' Her lips lifted, showing strong white teeth. ''Get to work.'' She turned back to her duties.

''Here,'' the door gunner said, ''IV with glucose solution.'' She pushed up the visor into her helmet, her round Indian face in full view beneath the low lighting.

Stunned, Roan looked at her. Paredes grinned a little. ''This is a woman's flight, *senhor*. Tell me what else you need for Inca.'' She gestured toward a large medical bag nearby. ''I'm a paramedic also. How may I assist you?''

Shaking his head in stunned shock, Roan had a hundred questions. But nothing mattered right now except Inca and her deteriorating condition. ''Put the IV in her right arm,'' he rasped. Leaning out, he pulled the IV bag over to him and hung it on a hook so that the fluid would drip steadily into her arm. ''You got ice on board?''

Paredes nodded as she knelt down and wiped Inca's arm with an alcohol swab. ''Yes, sir.'' She pointed to it with her black, gloved hand, then took off her gloves and dropped them to the deck. ''In there, *senhor*. In that thick plastic container.'' She skillfully prepped Inca's arm to insert the IV needle.

Roan found the containers and jammed his hand into the pack. This was no ordinary paramedic's pack, he realized. No, it was like a well-stocked ambulance pack. It had everything he could ever want to help save Inca's life. The helicopter shook around him. His ears popped. He heard constant, tense exchanges between the pilot and copilot.

Both women's voices. A three-woman air crew. What country were they from? He picked up the plastic bag of ice and struck it hard against his thigh, then waited a moment before gently placing it beneath Inca's neck. It was an instant ice pack, which, when struck, mixed chemicals that created coolness. The door gunner handed him some wide, thick gauze.

"To hold the ice pack in place," she instructed.

Nodding his thanks, Roan began to feel his adrenaline letdown make him shaky. Inca lay beneath the warming blankets, her beautiful golden skin washed out and gray looking. Reaching for the blood pressure cuff, he took a reading on Inca. To his relief, her pressure was holding steady. Ordinarily, on a wound like this, the person dumped and died within minutes because the brain had been bruised by the broken skull plates and began to swell at a swift rate. So far, her blood pressure was remaining steady, and that was a small sign of hope.

"How's Inca doing?" Stevenson demanded.

Roan glanced forward. The captain was flying the helicopter as if the hounds of hell were on her tail. They needed all the speed this old chopper could give them. Time was of the essence, and she seemed to share his sense of haste. The aircraft shook and vibrated wildly as the pilot pushed it to maximum acceleration, tunneling through the clouds.

"Stable," he croaked. "She's remaining stable. That's a good sign."

"I could use some good news," Stevenson growled.

And then Roan noticed that the helicopter was following another one, at less than one rotor length. Stymied, Roan saw the red and green, flashing lights on the underbelly of the copter in front of them.

"What's that chopper doing so close?" he demanded, terror in his tone.

Stevenson gave a bark of laughter. "This old bag of bones doesn't have any IFR, instrument flight rules, equipment on board to get us through the clouds or for night flight, Senhor Storm Walker. The chopper ahead of us is a state-of-the-art Apache gunship. She's equipped with everything we need to get the hell out of here and get Inca to Manaus. I'm following it. If I lose visual contact with it, we're all screwed. I'll lose my sense of direction in this soup and we'll crash.''

Roan's eyes narrowed. She was doing more than following it, for there was barely a hundred feet between them. One wrong move and they'd crash into one another. That kind of flying took incredible skill and bravery. No wonder the Cobra was shaking like this; it was in direct line of the rotor wash of the far more powerful Apache. Yet he knew the gunship was a two-seater and had no room for passengers.

''Shove this old crone into the redline range,'' the pilot ordered the copilot. ''Tell them to put the peddle to the metal up there. Squeeze *every* ounce of power outta her.''

''Roger.''

Roan shook his head disbelievingly. He looked down at Inca. Her face was covered on one side with mud. Taking a dressing, he tried to clean her up a little. He loved her. He didn't want her to die. Moving his hand over Inca's limp one, he felt the coolness of her flesh.

''Pray for her, *senhor*. Prayer by those who love someone is the most powerful,'' the door gunner said as she got up and crawled forward toward the cockpit.

Roan touched Inca's unmarred brow with trembling fingertips. She looked so beautiful. So untouched. And yet a bullet had found her. Why hadn't he realized she was vulnerable just like any other human being? Why hadn't her spirit guide protected her? Squeezing his eyes shut, Roan ruthlessly berated himself. Why hadn't he shot first before Faro Valentino had fired at her? His heart ached with guilt. With unanswered questions. Again he stroked Inca's cheek and felt her softness. Gone was her bright animation. Inca's spirit hung between worlds right now. Roan didn't fool himself. She could die. The chances of it happening were almost guaranteed.

"Another hour, Senhor Walker," the pilot murmured. "We'll be there in an hour…."

How could *that* be? Roan twisted to look toward the gunner, who was crouched in a kneeling position, her hands gripping the metal beams on either side of her as she hung between the seats of the two pilots. They were a helluva lot farther from Manaus than an hour! What was going on? Roan felt dizzy. He felt out of sync with everything that was going on around him. He realized he was in shock over Inca's being wounded. He was unraveling and everything felt like a nightmare.

"An hour?" he rasped. "That can't be."

The pilot laughed. "In our business, *anything* is possible, Senhor Walker. Just keep tending Inca. Be with her. I'll take care of my part in this deal. Okay?"

Who are these women? The question begged to be asked. Roan watched through the cockpit Plexiglas as they rose higher and higher. Suddenly they broke through the soup of thick clouds. He gasped. The Apache gunship was just ahead of them, and he felt the hard, jarring movement from being in the air pockets and rotor wash behind it. Captain Stevenson was within inches of the Apache's rotors. Marveling at her flying skills, Roan turned away. He couldn't watch; he thought they'd crash into one another for sure. The woman was certifiable, in his opinion. She had to be crazy to fly like this.

His world was torn apart and tumbling out of his control. Roan felt stripped and helpless. He leaned close to Inca and placed a kiss on her cool cheek. All he could do now was monitor her blood pressure, her pulse, and simply be with her. And pray hard to the Great Spirit to save her life. She was too young to die. Too vital. Too important to Amazonia. Oh, why hadn't he taken out that drug runner first? Roan hung his head, and hot tears squeezed beneath his tightly shut lids.

He felt a hand on his shoulder. "You did all you could, *senhor*," Paredes said gently. "Don't be hard on yourself. Some things are meant to be…and all we can do is be there to pick up the pieces afterward. Just hang in there. Manaus is nearby…."

Roan couldn't look up. All he could do was remain sitting next to Inca, his bulk buttressing the litter against the rear wall of the aircraft so that she had a somewhat stable and stationary ride. He felt Paredes remove her hand from his shoulder.

His world revolved around Inca. Never had he loved someone as he loved her. And now their collective worlds were shattered. All the secret hopes and dreams he'd begun to harbor were now smashed. Closing his eyes, Roan took Inca's hand between his and prayed as he'd never prayed before. If only they could be at Manaus right away. If only they could get her into emergency surgery. If only…

Roan sat tensely in the waiting room on the surgery floor of the hospital in Manaus. There was nothing else he could do while Inca was being operated on. Forlornly, he looked around at the red plastic sofas and chairs. The place was deserted. It was one in the morning. The antiseptic smells were familiar to him, almost soothing to his razor-blade tenseness. An emergency team had been waiting for them when the woman pilot landed the Cobra on the roof of the Angel of Mercy Hospital. And just as soon as Inca was disembarked by the swift-moving surgery team, Captain Stevenson had taken off, her Cobra absorbed into the night sky once again. He hadn't even had time to thank her or her brave crew. Instead, Roan's attention had been centered on Inca, and on the team who rushed her on a wheeled gurney into the hospital. He gave the information on Inca's condition to the woman neurosurgeon who was to do the surgery.

Her team hurried Inca into the prepping room, while he was asked to go and wait in the lobby area.

Reluctantly, Roan had agreed. He'd paced for nearly two hours, alone and overwhelmed with grief and anger. Life wasn't fair, that he knew. But to take Inca's life, a woman whose energy supported so many, who held the threadbare fabric of the old Amazonia together, was too unfair. Rubbing his smarting, reddened eyes, Roan had finally sat down, feeling the fingers of exhaustion creeping through him. He was filthy with mud that had encrusted and dried on his uniform. Inca's blood was smeared across it as well. He didn't care. He stank. He could smell his own fear sweat. The fear of losing Inca.

Nothing mattered except Inca, her survival. He heard a sound at the doorway and snapped up his head. The neurosurgeon, Dr. Louisa Sanchez, appeared in her green medical garb. Her expression was serious.

"Inca?" Roan voice rang hollowly in the lobby. He stood up and held his breath as the somber surgeon approached.

"Senhor Storm Walker," she began in a low tone, "Inca is stable. I've repaired the fracture. The bullet did not impact her brain, which is the good news. It ricocheted off the skull and broke the bone, instead. What we must worry about now is her brain swelling because of the trauma of the bone fracture. It is very bad, *senhor*."

Roan blinked. He felt hot tears jam into his eyes. "You've packed her skull in ice?"

"Yes, she is ice packed right now."

"And put an anti-inflammatory in her IV to reduce the swelling of her brain tissue?"

Dr. Sanchez nodded grimly. "*Sim.* I've given her the highest amount possible, *senhor*. If I give her any more, it will kill her." The surgeon reached out. "I'm sorry. We must wait. Right now, she's being wheeled into a special room that is outside of ICU. She will be monitored by all the latest equipment, but it is not glass-enclosed. It is a private room.''

Roan felt his world tilting. He understood all too well what the doctor was saying without saying it. The private room was reserved for those who were going to die, anyway. This just gave the family of the person the privacy they needed to say their goodbyes and to weep without the world watching them.

''I—see....'' he croaked.

Sadly, Dr. Sanchez whispered, ''She's in the hands of God, now, *senhor*. We've done all we could. I anticipate that in the next forty-eight hours her fate will be decided.... I suggest you get cleaned up. And then you can stay with her, yes?''

The doctor's kindness was more than Roan had expected. Inca was going to die. Blinking back the tears, he rasped unsteadily, ''No, I want to stay with her, Doctor. Thank you....''

The beeps and sighs of ICU equipment filled the white room where Inca lay. Normally, Roan felt a sense of security with all these machines. Inca was breathing on her own, which was good. As he stood at her bedside, he saw how pale she had become. Her head was swathed in a white dressing and bandage. The ice packs were changed hourly. And every hour, her blood pressure was moving downward, a sign of impending death. Miserably, Roan stood at her bedside, her cool hand clutched within his. Dawn was peeking through the venetian blinds. The pale rose color did not even register with him, only as a reminder that Inca would enjoy seeing the beauty of the colors that washed the dawn sky. So many conversations with her played back to him. Each one twinged his aching heart. He had tried to heal her as he had once before, but it didn't work. He was too exhausted, too emotionally torn to gather the necessary amount of laser-like concentration. Never had he felt so helpless.

Leaning down, Roan pressed his lips to her forehead. Easing back a little, he studied Inca's peaceful face. She looked as if she were asleep, that was all; not fighting a losing battle for her life. Roan knew that the brain could continue to swell despite whatever efforts doctors made, and that if it swelled too much, it would block the necessary messages to the rest of the body and she'd stop breathing. Her blood pressure dropping was a bad sign that her brain was continuing to swell despite everything. A very bad sign.

"I love you, Inca. Do you hear me, sweetheart?" His voice broke the stillness of the room. His tone was deep and unsteady. Hot tears spilled from his eyes. "Do you hear me? I love you. I don't know when it happened, it just did." He brushed the soft skin of her cheek. "At first, I was afraid to fall for you, Inca. But now I'm glad I did. I want you to fight, Inca. Fight to come back to me. To what we might have. This isn't fair. None of it. I've just found you...loved you.... Please—" he squeezed her fingers gently "—fight back. Fight for our love, fight for yourself, because there are so many people who need you. Who rely on you..."

The door quietly opened and closed. Roan choked back a sob, straightened up and twisted to look in that direction. He'd expected the nurse, who would take Inca's vitals and replace the old ice pack for a new one. His eyes widened. It was Captain Stevenson. She was still dressed in the clinging black nylon uniform, her flak jacket open. Beneath her left arm was her helmet. His gaze ranged upward to her face. His heart pounded hard. She looked drawn and exhausted as she stepped into the room.

He met her slightly tilted emerald-green eyes as they locked on his. Blinking, Roan again saw the powerful resemblance between her and Inca. They almost looked like—twins! But how could that be? His mind spun. She had her black hair, tightly gathered in a chignon at the nape of her long neck. The pride and confidence in her square face was unmistakable. But there was grief in her eyes, and her full lips twisted slightly in greeting.

She moved soundlessly to the other side of Inca's bed. Glancing down at Inca, she quietly placed her helmet on the bedstand. "You're right, Senhor Storm Walker. I *am* her twin." She smiled tenderly down at Inca and ran her fingers along her arm. "Fraternal twin."

"But…how…? Inca never told me about you."

Maya shrugged. Her expression softened more as she leaned down and placed a kiss on Inca's damp brow. Straightening, her voice hoarse, she said, "Inca never knew I existed. So she couldn't tell you about me. I was told of her being my sister a year ago by the elders of the Jaguar Clan. Once I knew, I was told I would meet her." She grimaced. "They didn't tell me how I would meet her until a week ago. That's why I'm here…."

Stunned into silence, Roan stared at the woman. She was a warrior, no doubt. She was as tall as Inca, and he could see the black leather holster on her thigh.

"My poor sister," Maya whispered in a choked tone as she continued to stroke Inca's hair in a gentle motion. "Our fate has been one made in darkness. I'm so sorry this happened. I wished I could've stopped it, but I couldn't. You have one more bridge to cross, my loving sister. Just one…" And Maya straightened and looked directly at Roan.

"She's going to die," Maya told him in a low tone.

Roan rocked back. He gripped Inca's hand and tried to deal with the truth.

Maya sighed as the pain moved through her heart. She held Inca's other hand in hers.

"I tried to save her like I did once before," he told Maya.

She shook her head. "You don't have the kind of training it takes to be able to heal in the middle of a battle." She gave him an understanding look. "It takes years of training to do it, so don't blame yourself."

"It worked once…I hoped…wanted it to work again…."

"You're lucky it happened once. There's a huge difference between a snake bite and a firefight. You just didn't have the emotional composure to pull it off when she got shot."

Roan stared at her. "Earlier you said 'black jaguar express.' I thought you were kidding. But if you're Inca's sister, then you're from the Jaguar Clan, too?"

She smiled tightly. "The *Black* Jaguar Clan, *senhor.* Very few know about us. Let's just say we do the dirty work for the Sisterhood of Light. The Jaguar Clan you know of, Inca's people, work in good, positive ways. The Black Jaguar Clan…well, let's just put it this way—someone has to clean up the ugliness in life." Her mouth was grim. There was a glitter in her eyes that said she was committed to what her life was about.

"You—work for the Brazilian government, then?" His mind spun. His heart ached. Inca was going to die.

Maya shook her head and gave a low growl as she continued to devote her attention to Inca. "What an insult. We work for a much higher power than that. But enough of this. You need to listen to me carefully, *senhor.* Inca has one shot at living. That's why I'm here. I've been told that she can have her life back. There's only one possibility for her to live, however."

Eagerly, Roan listened. "How? What can I do?"

Maya studied him fiercely. "You are a credit to the human race, *senhor.* Yes, you can help." She pointed toward the ceiling. "In the laws of the Sisterhood of Light, it's said that if a person willingly gives up her or his life for another, the one who is dying may survive. But—" Maya gave him a hard, uncompromising look "—in order for that to occur, that person must *willingly* give her or his life in exchange. It must be someone who loves the dying person unselfishly."

The silence swirled between them.

Roan looked down at Inca. He would have to die in order

for her to live. His hand tightened around hers. He felt Maya's stare cutting straight through him. It was clear she possessed a power equal to Inca's, and then some.

Inca's life for his own. His heart shattered with the finality of the her words.

"You know," Roan whispered in a broken tone, "I've been a lucky man. I never thought I'd know what love was in this lifetime until I met Sarah. And then she was torn from me. After that—" he looked up at Maya, tears in his eyes "—I never expected to fall in love again, until Inca crashed into my life. I'd given up hope. I was just surviving, not living life, until she came along." Gently, he brushed Inca's arm with his fingertips. "My life for hers. There's no question of who's more important here. She is."

Roan lifted his chin and met and held Maya's hard emerald gaze. Her expression was uncompromising as she stood there, the silence deepening in the room.

"Yes. Take my life for hers. Inca is far more important than me. I love her...."

Maya regarded him gravely. "In order for this exchange to occur, you must love her enough to not be afraid of dying."

Shaking his head, Roan rasped, "There's no question of my love for Inca. If you're as powerful metaphysically as she is, then you already know that. You knew the answer before coming here, didn't you?"

Giving him a mirthless smile, Maya whispered, "Yes, I knew. But you see, my brave friend, there's always free will in such matters." She glided her hand across Inca's unbound hair. "If I could give my life for hers, I'd do it in a heartbeat. But the laws state that I can't; we're twin souls, and therefore, it's unacceptable."

Roan looked at one monitor. He saw Inca's blood pressure dipping steeply. "She's dumping," he growled, and pointed at the screen. "She's dying. Just do it. Get it over with. Just tell her when she wakes up that I loved her with all my heart and soul.''

Maya took a deep breath and gave him a warm, sad look. ''Yes, I promise she'll know. And…thank you. You've given me my sister, whom I've never been allowed to approach or to know. Now we'll have the time we need to get to know one another…and *be* sisters.…''

Roan nodded. ''More than anything, she wanted a family, Maya. I'm glad she has one. I know she's going to be happy to see you when she wakes up.''

Blinking hard, Maya whispered, ''Place your hand over her heart and your other hand over the top of her head. Keep your knees slightly bent and flexed. It will allow the energy to run more smoothly. If you lock your knees, you'll block it and cause problems. And whatever happens, keep your eyes closed and keep a hold on her. Me and my black jaguar spirit guide will do the rest.''

Roan leaned down. One last kiss. A goodbye kiss. His mouth touched and glided against Inca's, whose lips were slightly parted. Her lips were chapped and cool beneath his. He kissed her tenderly, and with all the love that he felt for her. He breathed his breath into her mouth—one last parting gift. His breath, his life entering into her body, into her soul. As he eased away, he whispered, ''I'll see you on the other side, sweetheart. I love you.…''

''Prepare!'' Maya growled. ''She's leaving us!''

Roan did exactly as Maya asked. He stood at Inca's bedside and braced himself against the metal railing for support. He had no idea what would happen next. Well, he'd had one hell of a life. He'd been privileged to love two extraordinary women—two more than he deserved. The moment his hands were in place, he felt Maya's strong, warm hands move over his. It felt like a lightning bolt had struck him. He groaned. The darkness behind his lids exploded into what could only be described as sparks and explosions of color and light. In seconds, Roan was whirling and spinning as if caught in a tornado's grip. He lost all sense of time, direction and of being in his body.

And then he lost consciousness as he spun into a darkened void. The only thing he felt, the last thing he remembered, was his undying, tender love for Inca....

Chapter 12

An intense, gutting pain ripped through Roan and made him groan out loud. His voice reverberated around him like a drum sounding. Was he dead? He felt out of breath, gasps tearing raggedly from of his mouth, as if he'd run ten miles without resting. Everything was dark. His body felt as if a steel weight was resting on him. It was impossible to move.

"Lie still, lie still, and soon the pressure will lift. Be patient, my son...."

Roan didn't know the woman, but her voice was remarkably soothing to his panicked state. Had he died? Struggling to see, he groaned.

"Shh, my son, just relax. No, you are not dead. You've just been teleported from Manaus to here. In a few moments your eyes will open."

He felt her hand on his shoulder, warm and anchoring. His head hurt like hell, a hot, throbbing sensation. What of Inca? What had happened to her? He opened his mouth to speak, but only a croak came out of it.

He heard the woman chuckle. She patted his shoulder.

"Young people are so impatient. Try to take a deep breath, Roan. Just one."

Struggling to do as the woman asked, he concentrated hard on taking a breath. His mind was scattered; he felt like he was in five or six major pieces, floating out of body in a dark vacuum.

"Good," she praised. "And again…"

Roan was able to take the second breath even more deeply into his chest. He was hyperventilating, but by honing in on her voice, he was able to slow his breathing down considerably.

"Excellent. My name is Alaria. When you open your eyes, you will find yourself in a large hut here at the Village of the Clouds. You and Inca are welcome here."

Roan felt a surge of electricity move from her hand into his shoulder. The jolt was warm and mild, but he was very aware of the energy moving quickly through him. "My son, when Inca returns from the Threshold, she will want to see your face first…." He felt the gentle pat of Grandmother Alaria's hand on his shoulder.

And then, almost without effort, he lifted his lids. Bright light made him squint, and he turned his head briefly to one side to avoid it. Shafts of sunlight lanced through an open window. Blinking several times, Roan managed to roll onto his side and then slowly sit up. Dizziness assailed him. All the while, Alaria's hand remained on his arm to steady him. That electrical charge was still flowing out of her hand and into him. Shaking his head, he rubbed his face wearily.

"Take your time. You've been through a great deal," she said quietly. "Inca is fine. She is lying next to you, there." She pointed to the other side of the mat where he sat. "Inca will recover fully, so do not fret. I need you to come back, into your body, and become grounded. Then the dizziness will leave and you will no longer feel as if you're in pieces, floating around in space."

Next to him, on a soft, comfortable pallet on the hard dirt

floor, was Inca, who was asleep or unconscious. She lay beneath several blankets. Her skin tone was normal and no longer washed out. Most of all, the peaceful look on her unmarred features made Roan's fast-beating heart soar with hope. Looking up, he saw the woman named Alaria for the first time. Relief flooded him that Inca was here and she was all right. He didn't know *how* she could be; but having been around Inca, he knew that miracles were everyday occurrences in the life of Jaguar Clan members.

And perhaps a miracle had just occurred for both of them. He felt better just looking into Alaria's aged but beautiful face. Her eyes sparkled with tenderness, her hand firm and steady on his shoulder. She had her silver hair plaited into two thick braids, which hung over her shoulders, and she was dressed in a pale pink blouse and a dark brown cotton skirt, her feet bare and thickly callused. His mind spun. With her parchmentlike hands, she continued to send him stabilizing energy, reassuring him that he wasn't dead.

"I know you have many questions," Alaria soothed. "Just rest. You are still coming out of the teleport state that Maya initiated with our help. All questions will be answered once Inca has returned to us." She brushed his dampened hair with aged fingers. "You are a courageous and unselfish warrior, Roan Storm Walker. We have been watching you for some time. Be at peace. There is safety here in the Village of the Clouds for you and Inca." Pouring some liquid into a carved wooden cup, she handed it to him. "Drink this warm tea. It contains a healing herb."

He was thirsty. His mouth was dry. Eagerly, he drank the contents of the mug. There was a slightly sweet and astringent taste to the tea. Roan opened his mouth to speak, then closed it. He watched Alaria slowly get to her feet. She straightened and gave him a grandmotherly smile.

"Inca will be awakening soon, and she will be disoriented and dizzy just like you for a while. Be with her. We are monitoring her energy levels at all times. Her wound has been healed. There is no more swelling of her brain.'' A slight smile crossed her lips. ''And you are not dead. You are both alive. I'll return later. Give Inca the herbal drink when she's ready for it.''

''T-thank you,'' Roan said, his voice sounding like sandpaper.

Alaria nodded, folded her thin hands and moved serenely out of the roomy thatched hut. Outside, thunder caromed in the distance, and he saw an arc of lightning brighten the turbulent blue-and-black sky. It was going to rain shortly. The beam of sunlight that had blinded him earlier was gone, snuffed out by the approaching cumulus clouds, which were dark and pregnant with water.

Turning his attention to Inca, Roan moved his trembling fingers along her right arm. She wasn't dead. She was alive. Her flesh was warm, not cool and deathlike as before. Dizziness assailed him once more, and he shut his eyes tightly and clung to her hand. He still felt fragmented. He felt as if pieces of him were still spinning wildly here and there in space. It was an uncomfortable sensation, one he'd never experienced before.

Opening his eyes, Roan studied Inca's soft, peaceful features. Her lips, once chapped, were now softly parted and had regained their natural pomegranate color. Her hair was combed and free flowing, an ebony halo about her head and shoulders. And his medicine piece now lay around her neck, resting on her fine, thin collarbones. The last thing he remembered was placing the amulet between their hands—a last gift, a prayer for her, for her life. Someone must have put the necklace back in place around Inca's neck, but he didn't know who had done it. Roan gently touched the opalescent blue stone which felt warm and looked as if it was glowing.

So much had happened. Roan couldn't explain any of it. One moment he was in the hospital room in Manaus, following Maya's orders to save Inca's life. And the next, it felt as if fifty thousand volts of lightning had struck him squarely. Roan remembered spinning down into a dark abyss, but that was all. And then he'd groggily regained consciousness here, in this hut.

Frowning, he felt a wave of emotion. Inca was here with him. He loved her. His heart swelled fiercely with such feeling that tears automatically wet his lashes. Not caring if anyone saw him cry, Roan didn't try to stop the tears that were now moving down his unshaved face.

"Come back, sweetheart. They said you would live...." he rasped thickly, as he moved his fingers up her arm in a comforting motion. She should have had needle imprints and a little bruising around where the IVs had been placed in her arms, but there was no sign of them on her beautiful, soft flesh. And when he examined the back of her head, the wound was gone. Gone! Her skull bone no longer protruded. There was no tissue swelling. It was as if the injury had never occurred.

How could this be? Roan couldn't stop touching Inca. His heart was wide-open and pounding with anguish one second, giddy with joy the next. Her skin was warm and firm. Her thick, black lashes rested across her golden, high cheekbones. Moving his fingers through her lush, silky hair, he marveled at her wild, untamed beauty.

The rain began, pelting softly at first on the thatched roof. Lightning shattered across the area and illuminated the rain forest at the edge of the village, its power shaking the hut. Thunder caromed like a hundred kettledrums being struck simultaneously. Cringing slightly, Roan waited tensely.

Inca stirred.

His hand tightened around hers. He held his breath. Did he dare hope? Was she coming out of the coma? Would she be whole or brain damaged? Would she have amnesia and not recognize him? Roan leaned down, his eyes narrowing, his heart pounding wildly.

"Inca? Sweetheart? It's me, Roan. You're not dying.

You're alive. Open your eyes. You're here with me. You're safe. Do you hear me?'' His fingers tightened again about hers. Once more her lashes fluttered. And then her parted lips compressed. One corner of her mouth pulled inward, as if she were in pain. Was she? Anxiety tunneled through him. Roan wished mightily for Alaria to be here right now. He had no idea what to expect, what to do in case Inca was in pain. It was his nature, as a paramedic, to relieve suffering, and right now he felt damned useless.

''Inca?''

Roan felt her fingers twitch, then curve around his. He smiled a little. ''That's it, come on out of it. You're coming back from a long journey, my woman. You're my heart, Inca. I don't know if you can hear me or understand me, but I love you.…'' He choked on a sob. Roan watched in amazement as color began to flood back into her face. He felt a powerful shift of energy around her and himself. Her cheeks took on a rosy hue. Life was flowing back into her.

A second bolt of lightning slammed into the earth, far too close to the hut. Roan cringed as the power and tumult of the flash shook the ground. Rain was now slashing down, the wind howling unabated. The wide, sloping roof kept the pummeling rain from coming into the open windows. Instead, cooling and soothing breezes drifted throughout the clean, airy hut.

Inca's brows moved downward. Roan's breath caught in this throat as her lashes swept upward and he saw her drowsy looking, willow-green eyes. Anxiously, he searched them. Her pupils were huge and black as she gazed up at him. Was she seeing him? Or was she still caught in the coma? Roan knew that it took days and sometimes weeks or even months for a person who was in a coma to come out of it and be coherent. She stared up at him. Her pupils constricted and became more focused. His heart pounded with anxiety.

''Inca? It's Roan. I'm here.'' He lifted her hand and

pressed it against his heart. Leaning down, he caressed her cheek. "I love you. Do you hear me? I'm never going to leave you. You're coming out of a coma. Everything's all right. You're safe…and you're here with me…." He managed a wobbling smile of hope for both of them.

A third bolt of lightning struck, even closer to the hut than the last one, it seemed. This strike made the hut shudder like a wounded beast. Automatically, Roan leaned forward, his body providing protection for Inca. As the thunder rolled mightily around them, Roan eased back. It was then that he recalled that Inca had been born in an eclipse of the moon and during a raging thunderstorm. Sitting up, he watched her eyes become less sleepy looking and more alive, as if her spirit were moving back inside her physical form and flooding her with life once again. The symbolism of the storm was not lost on him. Mike Houston had told him she'd been born in a storm it would make sense that her rebirth would take place during another storm.

He smiled a little, heartened by that knowledge. Indians saw the world as a latticework of symbols and cosmology that were all intertwined. As he gently pressed her hand against his heart, he saw her lashes lift even more. Inca's eyes were now clearer and far more focused. Her gaze clung to his. Roan felt her returning; with each heartbeat, he felt Inca coming home, to him, to what he prayed would be a lifetime with her if the Great Spirit so ordained it.

"Where…?" Inca croaked, her voice rough from disuse.

"You're here at the Village of the Clouds, sweetheart. With me. Alaria said we were teleported by her from the hospital in Manaus." Roan didn't care if his voice wobbled with tears. With joy. Inca was here. And she was alive! He reached down and tenderly caressed her cheek. Her pupils changed in diameter, so he knew she was seeing him and that her brain was not damaged as he feared.

"Welcome back," he rasped. "You're home, with me…where you belong…."

The words fell like a soft, warm blanket around Inca. The sensation of vertigo was slowly leaving her. She felt her spirit sliding fully and locking powerfully into her physical body. Roan's large, scarred hand held hers. She closed her eyes, took in a deep, shaky breath and whispered, "I can feel your heartbeat in my hand...." And she could. Inca opened her eyes and drowned in his dark, smoky-blue gaze. There was no question that she loved him. None. Just that little-boy smile lurking hesitantly at the corner of his mouth, and the hope and love burning in his eyes, made a powerful river of joy flow through her opening heart.

"Are you thirsty? Alaria said you should drink this herbal tea. It will help you."

As Inca became more aware of her surroundings, she frowned. Alaria? Yes, Roan had mentioned Grandmother Alaria. Inca's heart bounded with hope. She had been here with her? Could it be they were *really* at the Village of the Clouds? Her head spun. She had been banned from her real home. So why was she here now? Nothing made sense to Inca. Her hope soared. "Y-yes..."

Roan reached for a pitcher and poured some of the contents into a mug carved out of a coconut shell. "Hold on," he murmured, "and I'll help you sit up enough to drink this."

Inca heard the wind howling around them. It was a powerful storm. She felt it in her bones, felt it stirring her spirit back to life within her body. As a metaphysician, she had experienced many strange sensations, but this one was new to her. She'd teleported once or twice before and was familiar with the process. But this was different. When Roan leaned over and slid his thick arm behind her neck and shoulders and gently lifted her into his arms, Inca became alarmed at how weak she was.

"Don't fight," he soothed as he angled her carefully, cradling her against his body. He watched as Inca tried to lift her hand. It fell limply back to her side. Seeing the surprise in her eyes, he raised the mug to her lips.

"Drink all you want," he urged. "Alaria said you would be weak coming out of the teleportation journey."

He held her like he might hold a newborn infant. The sense of protection, of love, overwhelmed Inca, and she drank thirstily. The warm herbal tea tasted sweet and energizing to her. She was a lot thirstier than she'd first realized. She drank from the mug four times more before her thirst was sated.

The medicinal tea brought renewed strength to her. This time when she forced her arm to move it moved. As Roan placed the mug on the mat beside him, Inca looked up at him with pleading eyes. "Just hold me? I need you...." And she weakly placed her hand against his thick biceps. Roan was dressed in his fatigues, spattered with dried mud, with blackish-red blood stains on his left shoulder. She realized it was *her* blood. From her wound. And yet she felt whole, not wounded. So much had happened. Inca was unable to sort it out. Later, she knew, the memories would trickle back to her.

Roan smiled down at her. "Anytime you want, sweetheart, I'll hold you." And he slid his other arm around her and brought her close to him. A ragged sigh issued from her lips as she rested her head against his shoulder, her brow against his hard, sandpapery jaw.

Closing her eyes, Inca whispered, "I almost died, didn't I? I feel as if I've just returned from the Threshold. You saved me, Roan. You gave your life willingly for me—I remember that. But that's all. I recall nothing more...."

Rocking her gently in his arms, he took one of the blankets from the pallet and eased it around Inca's shoulders and back to ensure her continued warmth. The fierce thunderstorm was dropping the temperature and there was a slight chill in the hut now. He smiled, closed his eyes and gave her a very gentle squeeze.

"Between the two of us, Inca, you're the one that should've had the chance to live, not me." She felt so good in his arms—weak and in need of his protection. That was something he could give her right now, and it made him feel good and strong. Gone was the fierce woman warrior. Right now, Inca was completely vulnerable, open and accessible to him, and it was such a gift. Roan knew that when a person had a near death experience, he or she came back changed—forever. Sliding his arm across her blanketed back, he caressed her.

"I love you. I never told you that before you were shot and went into a coma."

Inca lifted her head and met his stormy blue gaze. She saw the anguish in his eyes and felt it radiating out from him. Roan's love for her was so strong and pure that it rocked her returning senses. "I did not think anyone would find me worth loving," she whispered brokenly. Lifting her hand, Inca added hoarsely, "I am not a good person. I have a dark heart. That is why I was told to leave the village and never return."

"Well," Roan said in a fierce whisper, "I think all that's changed, sweetheart." He caressed her loose, flowing hair. "And your heart is one of the purest and finest I've ever seen. So stop believing that about yourself."

A sad smile pulled at her mouth. "I am so tired, Roan. I want to sleep...."

Roan eased Inca to the pallet. "Go ahead. Sleep will be healing for you. I'm going to close the windows. There's too much breeze coming in on you." He got to his feet, groping for the wall of the hut to support himself. The dizziness was gone and his legs felt pretty solid beneath him. He shut the windows to stop the wind from filtering into the hut. Turning, he saw Inca watching him from half-closed eyes. She opened her hand.

"Will you sleep with me? I need you near...."

Touched, Roan nodded. "There's nothing I'd like better."

He expected nothing from Inca. He had shared his love with her. Even if she never loved him, she would know the truth of what lay in his heart. As he knelt down upon his pallet, which was next to hers, he heard the storm receding. The pounding rain was lessening now. Father Sky had loved Mother Earth. That was how Indians saw the dance of the storms that moved across the heavens—as a way of the sky people and spirits caressing and loving their mother, the earth.

Inca sighed, her lashes feeling like weights. Her heart was throbbing with so much emotion, feelings she'd never experienced before. Just the way Roan cared for her told her of his love for her, and quenched and soothed her thirsty heart. She could no longer say she did not know what love was for she had experienced it with him—on the highest and most refined level. He had given his life so that she could return and continue her work in Amazonia. And through whatever mechanism and for whatever reasons, Roan's life had been spared. Joy filtered through her sleepy state. Inca knew she was still weak from having nearly died. It would take days for her to recover fully. The fact they were here in the Village of the Clouds surprised her, but she was too exhausted, and too in need of Roan's steady and loving presence to find out why.

Inca nuzzled Roan unconsciously as she awoke from the wings of sleep. She felt his large, strong body next to hers. She had one leg woven between his, and his arms were around her, holding her close to him. The masculine odor of him drifted into her flaring nostrils. The scent was heady, like an aphrodisiac to her awakening senses as a woman. Automatically, she began to feel heat purl languidly between her legs. Her belly felt warm and soft and hungry—for him. All these sensations were new to her and she reveled in them. Around her, she heard the screech of monkeys, the sharp calls of parrots in nearby trees, and the pleasant, gurgling sound of a nearby creek behind the hut.

She was alive…and Roan loved her. Stretching like a cat, Inca gloried in the movement of her strong, firm body against his. One of her arms was trapped between them, the other wrapped behind his thick neck. Savoring their closeness, Inca sighed, leaned forward and pressed a small kiss on his roughened jaw. How good it felt to be alive! And how dizzying and glorious to know that someone loved her—despite her darkness. Roan loved her as a woman—not as a goddess to be worshipped, as her Indian friends did, but as an ordinary human being. Opening her eyes, Inca absorbed the sight of Roan's sleeping features. His breath was like a warm caress against her cheek and neck. Wondering at all the small, beautiful things that a man and woman could share, Inca welcomed this new world of love he'd opened to her. No wonder being in love was written about so much throughout literature. Now she knew why.

Roan stirred. He felt Inca move. Automatically, his arm tightened and his eyes groggily opened. He felt her pull away, to sit up. Drowsily, he watched as her dark, shining hair cascaded about her shoulders. She wore a soft cotton shift of the palest pink color. As she eased her fingers through her hair, he watched in sheer enjoyment of her femininity. Her profile, that proud nose and chin, and her soft lips, grazed his pounding heart. Today was a new day. A better day, he realized.

Rousing himself, he eased into a sitting position beside Inca. The covers fell away. Through the open doorway, Roan saw a bright patch of sunlight slanting into their hut. Moving his gaze back to Inca, he smiled tenderly at her.

"You look more like your old self. How are you feeling?"

She brushed her hair back and drowned in his sleepy blue gaze. "I feel human again." She leaned forward and placed her hand on his shoulder. He had taken off the soiled shirt and was bare chested. Moving her fingers through the dark hair there, Inca murmured, "I feel alive, Roan, and I know it is because of you...because of your heart and mine being one...." And she pressed herself against him and placed her lips against his mouth.

Pleasantly shocked by her boldness and honesty, he felt her small, ripe breasts grazing his chest, the surgery gown a thin barrier between them. Roan knew Inca's innocence of the world of love and respected it. She was reaching out to him as never before, and he gratefully accepted her bold approach as normal and primal. Sliding his hands upward, he framed her face and looked deeply into her shining willow-green eyes, which seem to absorb him to his very soul. Her pupils were huge and dark, filled with sparkling life once more. And with returning love for him. Oh, she'd never said the words, but that didn't matter to Roan as he smiled deeply into her eyes. The fierce, proud warrior woman had now shifted to her soft and vulnerable side with him. It was an unparalleled gift for Roan. He thanked the Great Spirit for her love, for her courage in reaching out boldly to him despite her own abandonment.

He wasn't about to destroy the new, tenuous love strung delicately between them. Inca needed to explore him at her own pace. As her lips grazed his curiously, he kissed her gently and warmly. She growled pleasantly over his actions, her arms moving sinuously up across his and folding behind his neck as she pressed herself more insistently against his upper body. Roan smiled to himself. He loved her boldness. She tasted sweet and innocent to him as her lips glided tentatively against his. Rocking her lips open, he took her more deeply, his hands firm against her face. He felt her purr, the sound trembling throughout her. Her fingers slid provocatively along his neck and tunneled sinuously into his hair and across his skull. Fire exploded deep within Roan. She was sharing herself with wild abandon, not realizing how powerfully her presence, her innocence, was affecting him.

It didn't matter, he told himself savagely. Inca needed the room to explore him and what they had in her own timing. Roan wanted to ignite the deep fires of her as a woman, passions she was just being introduced to through his love for her.

"Ahem…excuse me, children. Might I have a moment with you?"

Roan tore his mouth from Inca's. Grandmother Alaria stood in the doorway of their room, her face alight with humor. In her hands was a tray filled with steaming hot cereal, fresh fruit, a pitcher and two glasses.

Inca gasped. "Grandmother!" She blushed deeply and avoided the older woman's shining eyes, which were filled with understanding and kindness.

"Welcome home, my child," Alaria murmured. With a sprightly air, she moved into the large room and said, "I felt you awaken. You are both weak from your experiences. I thought that a good hot cereal would bring you back to life." She grinned as she placed the tray across Roan's lap. "But I see that life has returned of its own accord to both of you in another way, and I'm joyful."

Inca stared up at the old woman, who was dressed in a long-sleeved white blouse and dark blue skirt that fell to her thin ankles. "But—how—how did I get here?" she stammered.

"Tut, tut, child. Come eat. Eat. Both of you. I'll just make myself at home on this stool here in the corner. While you eat, I'll talk. Fair enough?" Her eyes glimmered as she slowly settled herself on the rough-hewn stool in the corner.

Shaken, Inca looked at Roan, who had a silly, pleased smile on his face. He, too, was blushing. She touched her cheek in embarrassment. It felt like fire. And then she stole a look at the village elder. Alaria had the same kind of silly grin on her mouth that Roan had. What did they know that she did not? Roan handed her a bowl made of red clay pottery, and a hand-carved wooden spoon. The cereal looked nourishing and good. The tempting nutlike flavor drifted up to her nostrils.

"I took the liberty of putting some honey in it for you," Alaria told Inca. "This was always your favorite meal when you were with us."

Inca thanked Roan and held the bowl in her hands. Much of her weakness was gone, but she was still not back to her old self. "Thank you, Grandmother." As always, she prayed over her food before she consumed it. The spirits who had given their lives so that she might live needed such thanks. Lifting the wooden spoon, she dug hungrily into the fare. Her heart was still pounding with desire, her senses flooded from the swift, hot kiss Roan had given her. Her body felt like lightning, energized and unsettled. She wanted something, but could not name what it was.

Alaria nodded approvingly as they both began to eat. "Food for your spirits," she murmured, "and a gift to your physical body." She lifted her hands from her lap. "I know you both have many questions. Let me try to answer them in part. Some other answers will come later, when you are prepared properly for them."

Inca discovered she was starving, and gratefully spooned more of the thick, warm cereal into her mouth. Grandmother Alaria had doted upon her when she was at the village in training. At one time she had been a favorite of Alaria's and Adaire's. Once, Alaria had admitted that Inca was like the child they'd always wished to have, but never did. In some ways she'd been like a daughter to them, until she'd gravely disappointed them by breaking the laws of the clan.

"I do not understand why you have allowed me to come back here," Inca said, waving the spoon at the ceiling of the hut.

"I know," Alaria whispered gently, her face changing to one of compassion. "There was a meeting of the elder council after you were wounded and dying."

Inca frowned. "A meeting? What for?"

Roan looked at her. "You don't have a memory of Faro Valentino shooting you, do you?"

Inca solemnly shook her head. "All I remember is that I was dying, Roan, and you traded your life for mine. That is all."

"She will recall it," Alaria counseled. "All things will come back to you in time, my child, as your heart and emotions can handle the experiences."

"I was wounded by Faro Valentino?" She looked down at the cereal bowl in her hand, deep in thought. She aggressively tried to recall it, but could not. Frustration ate at her.

"In the valley…" Roan began awkwardly. He knew that victims of brain trauma often wouldn't remember much of anything for weeks, months or years after the experience. "We were with Colonel Marcellino's company. You had freed the Indians who were slaves in the cocaine compound of the Valentino Brothers. You were working your way around the outside of the compound, getting rid of the guards, so that Marcellino's men wouldn't be in such danger when they attacked from the walls of the valley." He looked to Alaria, who nodded for him to continue the explanation. "One drug runner—"

"Faro Valentino," Alaria interjected unhappily.

Roan nodded, trying to handle his anger toward the man. "Yes, him."

Gravely, Alaria said, "He has murder in his heart. He is one of the darkest members of the Brotherhood of Darkness." She turned to Inca. "Faro shot at you before you could turn and get a shot at him. Roan was behind you, and shouted at you, but you slipped in the mud, and that is what doomed you. At the angle Roan was standing, he couldn't get a bead on Faro to stop him before he fired at you. A bullet grazed the back of your head, my child, and broke your skull, and you dropped unconscious to the ground." Alaria gestured toward Roan, tears in her eyes. "He saved you later, by giving permission to give his life so that you might return from the Threshold to us. There are few men of Roan's courage and heart on the face of Mother Earth. Without his unselfish surrendering, you would not be with us today.''

Inca lost her appetite. She set the bowl aside and looked deeply into Roan's eyes. ''I remember only part of being on the Threshold. I remember him calling me back…. That is when I knew I was dying.''

''And you took his hand, which you had to do in order to decide to stay here instead of moving on to the other dimensions in spirit form.'' Alaria smiled gently and wiped the tears from the corners of her eyes. ''His unselfish act of love did more than just save your life, my child.''

Inca reached out and threaded her fingers through Roan's. He squeezed gently and smiled at her. ''What else did it do?'' Inca asked.

Alaria looked at her for a long time, the silence thickening in the hut. She placed her hands on her thighs. Her mouth turned inward, as if in pain. ''You were told not to come back to the Village of the Clouds because you broke a cardinal rule of the Jaguar Clan.''

''Yes,'' Inca said haltingly. ''I did.''

''And when a clan member knowingly breaks a rule, the council must act on it. You were told to leave and never return.''

Hanging her head, Inca closed her eyes. She felt all those awful feelings of the day she'd been asked to leave. Roan held her hand a little more tightly and tried to assuage some of her grief. Choking, Inca whispered, ''I had been abandoned once without choice. By coming to Michael's rescue, I knowingly gave up my family, and it was my choice. I have no one to blame for my actions but me. I knew better, but I did it anyhow.''

''Yes,'' Alaria murmured sadly. ''But we, the council, have been watching you the last seven years since you left us. We have watched you grow, and become less selfish, living more in accordance with the laws of the Sisterhood of Light.'' She gestured toward the rain forest behind the village. ''For seven years you have followed every law. We have watched and noted this, Inca. You have turned into a wonderful healer for the sick and the aging. This is part of your blood, your heritage. But it is also part of your life to protect and defend the people of Amazonia. And this you have done willingly, without any help from us at any time. You have been completely on your own. You could have gone over to the Brotherhood of Darkness, but you did not. You struggled, grew and transformed all on your own into a proud member of the Jaguar Clan.''

Inca blinked. ''But I am not of the clan. I stand in the in-between world, neither dark nor light. That is what you said at my judgment.''

''That was then.'' Alaria spoke quietly. She held Inca's unsure and fearful gaze, feeling the pain of her abandonment and loss. ''You came to us without family. Without relatives. We loved you like the daughter we never had. Adaire and I cherished you. We tried to give you what you had been denied all those years, without a true mother and father.''

Hot tears moved into Inca's eyes. She felt emotionally vulnerable because of all that she'd just experienced, and could not hide how she felt, or hold back the tears that now ran down her cheeks. ''And I hurt both of you so very much. I am sorry for that—sorrier than you will ever know. Grandfather Adaire and you loved me. You gave me so much of what I was hungry for and never had before I came here.'' Self-consciously, Inca wiped her cheeks. ''And I ruined it. I did not respect the love that you gave to me. I abused the privilege. I will be forever sorry for the hurt I have caused you, Grandmother. You *must* believe me on that.''

''We know how sorry you are, Inca. We have always loved you, child. That never changed throughout the years while you were away.'' Alaria's face grew tender. ''Inca, you could have chosen so many other ways to lead your life when you left the village. No one but Adaire and I had hope that you would turn out to be the wonderful human being you are now. You care for the poor, you protect them, you heal them when it is within the laws, and you think nothing of yourself, your pain or your suffering. You have put others before yourself. This is one of the great lessons a clan member must learn and embrace. And you have done that.''

Inca sniffed and wiped her eyes. "T-thank you, Grandmother.''

"You're more than welcome, child. But here is the best news yet. The council has decided, unanimously, that you are to be allowed back into the Jaguar Clan with full privileges and support.'' She smiled as she saw the shock of their community decision register fully on Inca's face. She gasped. Roan placed his arm around her and gave her a hug of joy. He was grinning broadly.

Alaria held up her hand. "Not only that, Inca, but when you are fully recovered, the council wants to publicly commend and honor you for what you have accomplished in Amazonia, thus far. *That* is why you are here, child. Your banishment is over. You have earned the right to be among us once again.'' She smiled a little, her eyes glimmering with tears. "And I hope this time that you honor the laws and never break any of them ever again.''

Inca sobbed. She threw her arms around Roan and clung to him as she buried her face against his shoulder.

Roan felt tears in his own eyes. He understood what this meant to Inca. Moving his hand through her thick, dark hair, he rasped against her ear, "You have your family back, sweetheart. You're home…you're really home…''

Chapter 13

Roan found Inca wandering in a field near the village. Since it was nearly noon, he had made them lunch. Swinging the white cotton cloth that held their meal in his left hand, he stepped out into the field. It was alive with wildflowers, the colors vibrant against the soft green of the grasses, which were ankle- to knee-high. The meadow was bordered on three sides by old, magnificent kapok trees, their buttressing roots looking like welcoming arms to Roan.

Above him, as always, were the large, slowly rolling clouds that seemed to always surround the village. He'd been here seven days and he had more questions than answers about this very special place. All his focus, however, was on Inca and her continued rehabilitation from her near death experience. From the day that Grandmother Alaria had told her she was part of the Jaguar Clan once more, Inca had become more solemn, more introspective. She was holding a lot of feelings inside her; Roan could sense it. He saw his part in her adjustment as simply being on hand if she wanted to talk about it and a needed, sympathetic ear, a shoulder to lean on. So far she hadn't, and he honored her own sense of healing. At some point, he knew, Inca would talk with him at length. All he had to do was be patient. Fortunately, his Native American heritage gave him that gift. The other good news was that the mission led by Colonel Marcellino had been successful.

As he crossed the field, the sunlight was warm and pleasant. The village seemed to be climate controlled at a balmy seventy-five degrees during the day and sixty-five degrees at night—neither too hot nor too cold. Even the temperature reflected the harmony and peace that infused the village and its transient inhabitants. The white-and-gray clouds that slowly churned in mighty, unending circles around the village had something to do with it, he suspected. He could see the steep, sharp granite peaks of the Andes in the distance. On the other side of the village the rain forest spread out in a living green blanket. They were literally living between the icy cold of the mountains and the hot, humid air arising from the rain forest below. No wonder there were always clouds present around the village, hiding it from prying, outsiders' eyes like a snug, protective blanket.

Inca was bending over a flower and smelling it, not yet aware of his presence. Since her accident, she seemed much more at ease, not jumpy and tense like before. As Grandfather Adaire had told him, this was a place of complete safety. Nothing could harm the inhabitants who lived and studied in the village. Maybe that was why he was seeing her relaxed for the first time. The change was startling and telling for Roan. Here Inca wore soft cotton, pastel shifts and went barefoot, her hair loose and free about her proud shoulders. Gone was the warrior and her military garb. There were no weapons of any kind allowed in the village. All the people Roan saw—and there were many from around the world—were dressed in loose fitting clothing made of natural fibers.

Inca lifted her head in his direction, her eyes narrowing.

Roan smiled as he felt her warm welcome embrace him, an invisible "hug" he knew came from Inca. The serious look on her face changed to one of joy upon seeing him. This morning he'd gone with Grandfather Adaire on an exploratory trip around the village. The elder had shown him many of the new and interesting sites that surrounded them. No wonder Inca had loved living and studying here. Roan understood more than ever how devastating it had been when she was told to leave. The way she had sobbed that morning when Grandmother Alaria told her she was welcomed back had been telling, pulled from the depths of her hurting, wounded soul. Roan had held her, rocked her and let her cry out all her past hurt and abandonment, the relief that she was once more welcomed back to her spiritual family. And they had told him not to mention anything about Maya to her yet. Inca was still reeling emotionally and Grandmother Alaria said that at the right time, Inca would meet her sister. Roan could hardly wait for that to happen. He knew how much Inca needed her real family.

Waving his hand, he quickened his stride toward her. The breeze lifted strands of her shining ebony hair. How soft and vulnerable Inca appeared as she stood expectantly waiting for him. In her hand were several wildflowers that she'd picked. He grinned. Gone, indeed, was the warrior. In her place was the woman who had resided deeply in Inca until she could be released in the safety of such a place as the village. Roan liked the change, but he also honored her ability to use her masculine energy as a warrior. Every woman had a warrior within her, whether she knew it or not. He was at ease with a woman who could use all the strength within herself.

Every woman had to deal with the myriad of issues life threw at them. They were far stronger emotionally and mentally than men, and Roan had no problem acknowledging that fact. He'd seen too many women squash that latent primal warrior, that survival ability within themselves, never tap into it because society said it was wrong for a woman to be strong and powerful. At least Inca had not allowed that to happen to her. She had carried her warrior side to an extreme, but her life mission asked that of her. Still, it was good that she had the village to come to, to rest up. To let go of that role she played.

Lifting the cloth bag with a grin, he called out, "Lunchtime. Interested?" His heart seemed to burst open as he heard her light, lilting laughter bubbling up through her long, slender throat. The gold flecks dancing in her willow-green eyes made him ache to love Inca fully and completely.

"I'm starving!" she called, and eagerly moved toward him, the hem of her dress catching now and then on taller flowers and grass blades.

How Roan loved her! A fierce need swept through him, and as Inca leaped forward, her hair flying behind her shoulders like a dark banner, he laughed deeply and appreciatively. Suddenly, life was good. Better than he could ever recall. Sarah, his wife, would always have a part of his heart. But Inca owned the rest of it.

Every day, Inca surrendered a little more to her own curiosity and feminine instincts to touch him, kiss him. Someday, he hoped, she would ask him to love her fully and completely. Right now, Roan knew she was processing a lot of old emotions and traumas, and working through them. Her heart was shifting constantly between healing herself and reaching out to him, woman to his man. He was more than content to wait, although it was wreaking havoc on him physically.

Inca reached him and threw her arms around his neck.

Laughing, Roan caught her in midair and pressed her body warmly against his. Her arms tightened around his neck. He saw the mischievous glint in her eye and dipped his head to take her offered, smiling mouth.

Her lips tasted of sunlight and warmth. Staggering backward from her spontaneous leap into his arms, he caught himself, stopped and then held her tightly against him. She had such a young, strong, supple body. Like a bow curved just right, Roan thought as he held her against him.

"Mmm…this is my dessert," Inca purred wickedly as she eased her lips from his. Looking up into Roan's eyes, she saw his hunger for her. She felt it through every yearning cell in her body, and in every beat of her giddy heart. How handsome Roan looked to her. That scowl he'd perpetually worn in Brazil was gone here in the village, which lay within Peru's border. Today he dressed in a pair of cream-colored cotton trousers, sandals on his huge feet, and a loose, pale blue shirt, the sleeves rolled up to his elbows. The warrior in both of them had been left behind when they came to the village.

Chuckling, Roan eased her to the ground. "Still hungry, or do I finish off this feast by myself?" he teased. Sliding his arm around her waist, Roan led her to the edge of the meadow. Sitting down in the shade of a towering tree, his back against one of the buttressing roots, he pulled Inca down beside him. She nestled between his legs, her back curved against him.

"No, I am hungry. Starved like a jaguar…." And Inca quickly opened the cloth bag.

Roan leaned back, content to have her within his loose embrace. He heard her gasp in delight.

"Pineapple with rice!" She grinned with triumph. "You must have begged Grandmother Alaria to make this for us. It is my favorite recipe. She used to make this for me when I was training here in the village."

Tunneling his fingers through her dark hair, Roan watched the breeze catch it as it sifted softly down upon her shoulders. "Yep, I bribed her."

"Oh!" Inca held up a container, her face alight with surprise. "Cocoa pudding!"

"Your second favorite, Grandmother said. I asked her to

make you something special, and she said you used to hang around her hut every day and beg her to make it for you.''

Inca gloated as she tore the lid off and grabbed a spoon. ''Hah! And more times than not, Grandmother gave in to my pleadings.''

''Hey, that's dessert! You're suppose to eat your other food first.''

Inca twisted around and gave him a crooked grin of triumph. ''Who said so?'' She pointed to her belly. ''It is all going to the same place. It does not care what comes first, second or third!'' And she laughed gaily.

Watching her spoon the still-warm pudding into her mouth, Roan picked up a sandwich of cheese and lettuce liberally sprinkled with hot chilies. ''Now I know why you like this place so much. You can do exactly what you want to do here.''

Chuckling indulgently, Inca leaned back and quickly consumed half of the pudding with gusto. When she'd finished, she set the container aside. ''Your half,'' she instructed him primly.

''That's big of you. I thought you were going to wolf the whole thing down in one gulp.''

''Jaguars do such things,'' she agreed wryly, meeting his smiling eyes as she picked up the other cheese sandwich. Munching on it, she announced, ''Today, I feel magnanimous in spirit. I will share with you my favorite dessert.''

''I like it when you can smile and tease. Here you have a sense of humor and you're playful. I never saw that side of you in Brazil. It's nice.''

Inca nodded and eagerly finished off the sandwich. The bread, too, was still warm from the oven. Licking her fingers one at a time, she murmured, ''Here I do not have to be anything but myself. I do not have to be a warrior constantly. I can relax.''

Sobering, Roan wiped his hands on another cloth and reached for the bowl of chocolate pudding. ''I'm glad you have this place to return to, Inca. You were worn down. You needed someplace to heal." He gazed around. In the distance he saw a great blue heron flying toward what he knew was the waterfall area. The day was incredibly beautiful. But every day in this village was like being in a secret, hidden Shangri-La.

Inca turned around and crossed her bare legs beneath the thin fabric of her dress. Taking one of the mangoes, she began to methodically peel it with her long, slender fingers. "I feel better today than ever before, Roan. More…" she searched for the right word "…whole."

"Yes," he murmured. "You've had a long, hard journey for seven years, sweetheart. You've more than earned this place, this down time." He looked fondly toward the village. "All of it."

"I have my family back," Inca said as she bit into the ripe mango.

Roan nodded, understanding the implications of her softly spoken, emotion-filled words. There was so much more he wanted to say, but he was under strict orders by Grandmother Alaria to say nothing of Maya, who had helped to save Inca's life. A part of him chaffed under that stern order. He wanted to share his discovery of Maya, and the fact she was Inca's twin sister, but Alaria had warned him sufficiently that he backed off from saying anything. Inca needed time and space to heal. She would know the truth when Maya chose to appear and break the news to her, Alaria had told him.

Roan watched Inca through half-closed eyes, the afternoon heat, the good food and her company all conspiring to make him feel regally satisfied in ways he'd never experienced.

Wiping her hands on the damp cloth, Inca looked at him. "You look like a fat, old happy jaguar who has just eaten more than his fill and is going to go sleep it off."

His mouth lifted. "That's exactly how I feel." Roan

reached out and grazed her cheek. "Only I have my jaguar mate here with me. That's what makes this special."

"I put you to sleep?" Inca demanded archly, unmercifully teasing him.

The fire in her eyes, the indignation, wasn't real, and Roan chuckled. "You would put no man to sleep, believe me," he rasped as he eased her around so that her back fit beautifully against him once more. "Come here, wild woman. My woman…"

Sighing contentedly, Inca settled against Roan. He took her hands in his, and they rested against her slightly rounded abdomen. A small but warming thought of someday carrying his child in her belly moved through Inca's mind. As she laid her head back on his broad, capable shoulder and closed her eyes, she sighed languidly. "I have never been happier, Roan. I did not know that love could make me feel this way." She felt the warmth of the breeze gently caressing her as she lay in his arms, his massive thighs like riverbanks on either side of her slender form. "You make me feel safe when I have never felt safe before. Did you know that?" She opened her eyes slightly and looked up at him, and felt him chuckle, the sound rolling like a drumbeat through his massive chest.

"I know," he replied as he moved his fingers in a stroking motion down her slim, golden arm. He saw many old scars here and there across her firm flesh. It hurt him to think of her being in pain, for Inca had lived with not only physical pain, but the sorrowful loss of her family, from the time she was born. In a way, it had made her stronger and self-reliant. She was able to move mountains, literally, because of the strength this one event had given her in life. Roan tangled his fingers with hers. "I love you, my woman," he whispered next to her ear. Her hair was soft against his lips. "Just know that you own my heart forever."

Her fingers tightened around his. Nuzzling his jaw, she whispered huskily, "And you hold my heart in your hands.

You did from the beginning, even if I was not aware of it at first.''

"When I saw you," Roan said in a low, deep tone as he caressed her hair, "I fell in love with you on the spot."

"Is that possible?"

"Sure. Why not?"

Inca shrugged. "When I first saw you, I felt safe. Safe in a way I never had before. I knew you would protect me."

"That's a part of love," Roan said, smiling lazily.

"I do not know much of what all love is about," she began, frowning. "This is new to me." She touched her heart. "I see others who are married. I see them touch one another, as we touch one another now. I see them kiss." She pulled away and met his hooded eyes. "I think our kisses are more active than others I have seen. Yes?"

Grinning, Roan said, "*Passionate* is the word I think you're searching for."

"Mmm, yes... And I see married couples touch each other's hands and hold them...and we do that, too."

"Loving a person, Inca, means loving them in many ways. There's no one way to tell that special person that you love them. You love them in many, many ways every day."

"And you brought me flowers that morning after Grandmother Alaria told me I was a member of the clan once again." Inca smiled up at him. "I was deeply touched. I did not expect such a gift from you."

"I wish I could have done more. I know what it meant to you, to be allowed to come home." Roan caught several dark strands of hair that moved with the breeze across her cheek, and tucked them behind her ear.

"I must understand more of this love that we hold for one another. I try to learn by watching what others do." Her eyes lit up with laughter. "And then I try it out on you to see if it works or not."

He chuckled. "No one can accuse you of not being an astute observer," he said dryly. "I like discovering love with you. Just give yourself time and permission to explore when it feels right to you, Inca.''

Sliding her hand across his dark, hairy one, she said, ''My body is on fire sometimes. I ache. I want something...but I do not know what it is, how to get it, how to satisfy that burning within me.''

''I do.''

''Yes?''

''Yes.'' Roan looked down at her animated features.

''Will you show me? I feel as if I will explode at times when you kiss me, or touch me, or graze my breasts with your hand. I ache. I feel...unfulfilled, as if needing something and I do not know what it is. I feel frustrated. I know something is missing...but what?''

Roan kept his face serious. Caressing her cheek, he said, ''All you have to do is ask me, Inca, and I'll show you. It's something I can teach you. Something that is beautiful and intimate, to be shared only by those who love one another.''

Nodding, she sighed. ''Yes. I'd like that.''

''A woman should always be in control of her own body, her own feelings,'' he told her seriously, and pressed a kiss to her hair near her ear. ''You tell me what you want, next time you feel like that—where you want me to touch you, where you want my hand placed. Making love to another person is one of the most sacred acts there is between human beings.''

''It is more than the mating frenzy,'' Inca said. ''I have watched many animals couple. It is because they want to make babies. I understand that. But...'' She hesitated. ''This is different, yes? Between people? Do they always want to make a baby when they couple?''

He felt her searching. Having lived her life in a rain forest, without any education about her own sexuality, about how a man and woman pursued intimacy, Inca was truly innocent. Gently, Roan took her hands into his. ''Maybe we're lucky, sweetheart. Humans don't have to couple for the express purpose of having a baby. We can do it because it feels right, and it feels good for both of us. It's the ultimate way to tell the other person how you feel about them.''

Inca smiled and closed her eyes. ''Grandmother Alaria said I should go to the Pool of Life and bathe there. She said I need the healing water to help me. Right now I want to have a nap with you. After I wake up, it feels right for me to do that.''

Roan held her gently. Closing his eyes, he murmured, ''Go to sleep, my woman. When you wake, go to the pool.''

Inca lay in the soft grass beside the Pool of Life, where she had bathed and swum for nearly an hour. Now she understood as never before the healing qualities of the sparkling, clear water. The glade sheltering the oval pool was filled with flowering bushes and trees. As she lay on her back, arms behind her head, watching the lazy, late afternoon clouds move across the deep blue sky, she sighed. Never had she felt so whole or so much in balance. Her errant thoughts centered on Roan and how much he meant to her. She loved him. Yes, she knew now as never before that she loved him. When she left this wonderful place, she would search him out and tell him that to his face. A tender smile pulled at her lips as she lay there, enjoying the fragrance of the wildflowers and the warmth of the sun.

Dressed once again in her pale pink shift, her skin still damp from the pool, Inca dug her toes joyfully into the grass that tickled the soles of her feet. Birds were singing, and she could hear monkeys screaming and chattering in the distance. Life had never felt as good as it did now.

Inca suddenly sat up, alert and on guard. She felt a vibration—something powerful that distinctly reminded her of someone teleporting in to see her. Who? The energy was very different, like none she was familiar with. Turning, Inca looked toward where the energy seemed to be originating. She saw a woman—a stranger—standing near the bushes, no more than twenty feet away from her. She was dressed in a black military flight suit and black, polished boots. As her gaze flew upward, Inca gasped. Instantly, she was on her feet in a crouched position, her hands opened, as if prepared for an attack by the unexpected intruder to her reverie.

Shock bolted through her, made her freeze. Her eyes widened enormously as she met and held the dark emerald gaze of the intruder. Her gasp echoed around the flowery glade. The woman looked almost exactly like her! Head spinning, Inca slowly came out of her crouched position. All her primal senses were switched on and operational—those instinctual senses that had saved her life so many times before. The woman who stood relaxed before her had black hair, just as she had. Only it was caught and tamed in a chignon at the base of her slender neck.

Breathing hard, Inca shouted, "State your name!"

The woman gave her a slight smile and lifted her hand. She took off her black flight gloves. "Be at ease, Inca. I'm Captain Maya Stevenson. And I come in peace." Her smile disappeared and she took a step forward. "I'm unarmed and I'm not an enemy. I'm here to fulfill a prophecy...." Tears glittered in her narrowed eyes.

Gulping, her heart pounding, Inca was assimilating all kinds of mixed messages from this tall, darkly clad woman warrior whose face was filled with emotion. "Y-you look like me! Almost..." She took a step back, not understanding what was going on. Her pulse continued to race wildly and she had to gasp for air. She felt like crying as a sharp, jolting joy ripped though her heart. Inca understood none of these wild, untrammeled feelings as the woman walked slowly down the slope toward her, and halted less than six feet away

Searching her face, Inca saw that there were minute differences between them. This woman—Maya—had a square face. Though her eyes were slightly tilted like Inca's, Maya's were a different color—emerald and not willow-green. Her mouth was full and her cheekbones high, but her face was broader. Her bone structure was different, too; while Inca was slender, Maya was of a larger, heavier build, and more curved than she. Still, the woman in black warrior garb stood equally tall, with that same look of confidence, her shoulders thrown back with unconscious pride.

"I—I do not understand this. You look like me. A mirror image. What is going on? What prophecy?"

Maya wiped her eyes. She tucked the gloves, out of habit, into the belt of her flight suit. "I think you'd better sit down, Inca. What I have to tell you might make you faint, anyway." And she gestured to the ground.

"No. Whatever you have to say I will take standing."

"Okay…have it your way. You always did have one helluva stubborn streak. Me? I need to sit down to say this to you." Maya grinned a little and sat down in front of her. She pulled her knees up and placed her arms around them, hooking her fingers together. "Of course, your stubbornness also gave you the guts to survive and flourish."

Breathing hard, Inca stared down at Maya. "What do you speak of? Who *are* you?"

Maya looked up, her emerald eyes dark and thoughtful. Her voice lowered, soft and strained. "I'm your fraternal twin sister, Inca. Our mother birthed us minutes apart. I came out first, and you, followed. We're sisters, you and I. I was finally given permission by the elder counsel to come and meet you, face-to-face, to initiate contact with you." She shook her head sadly. "And I've waited a long time for this day to come…."

Inca staggered backward. Her eyes flared and her lips parted. When she felt her knees go wobbly, she dropped to the grass on her hands and knees. Staring at Maya, who sat calmly watching her, she could not believe her ears. She saw the compassion in Maya's strong face, the tears running freely down her cheeks. In the next moment, Inca felt a shift of energy taking place between them, and she swallowed, unable to speak. Indeed, Maya was almost a carbon copy of her. Shaking her head, Inca clenched her fist.

"I do not understand!" she cried in desperation. "How can you be my sister? I was abandoned by my parents at birth! I was left for dead until a jaguar mother came and carried me back to her den to raise me." Inca's nostrils flared. Her breathing was chaotic. Her heart was bursting with pain and anguish.

Maya leaned forward, her hand extended. Gently, she said, "I'm sorry you had to suffer so much, Inca. You were so alone for so long. And for that, I'm sorry. We agreed to this plan long before we ever entered human forms. We each did," she stated with a grimace. Looking up, she took a deep breath and held Inca's anguished gaze. "I have a story to tell you. Listen to me not only with your ears, but with your heart. Sit down, close your eyes and let me show you what happened—and why. Please?"

Unable to catch her breath, Inca sat down and faced Maya. She had a sister? *She* was her sister? Maya looked so much like her. How could this be? Tears escaped from Inca's eyes. "Is this a trick? A horrible trick you have come to play on me?"

"No, my loving sister," Maya said in a choked tone, tears filling her eyes again, "it isn't. Please…try to gather yourself. Close your eyes. Take some deep breaths…that's it. Let me tell you telepathically what happened to us.…"

Inca rocked slightly as she felt the energy from Maya encircle and embrace her. It was a loving, warm sensation and it soothed some of the ragged feelings bursting out of her hurting heart. Transferring her full focus to her brow, between her eyes, Inca began to see the darkness shift and change. Like all clairvoyants, Inca could literally see or perceive with her third eye. Her brow became a movie screen, in color. What she saw now made her cry out.

She saw her mother and father for the first time. Her mother was breathing in gasps, squatting on the ground, her hands gripping two small trees on either side of her to stay upright. She saw her father, a very tall, golden-skinned man with black hair, kneeling at her side, talking in a soothing, calming tone to her. His hands opened to receive the baby that slid from his wife's swollen body. Within moments, the child was wrapped snuggly in a black blanket made of soft alpaca wool. To Inca's shock, she saw a second baby being delivered shortly thereafter. The infant was wrapped in a gold blanket with black spots woven into it. Inca knew at once that it was she—the second baby born from her mother's body. Twins…she had a twin! And she'd never known it before this moment.

Heart pounding, Inca zeroed in on her mother's gleaming face as she slowly sat down on another blanket with the help of her husband, and then reached out for her babies. She had a broad, square face and her eyes were the deep green color of tourmaline gemstones. Her hair was long, black and slightly curly as it hung around her shoulders. She was smiling through her tears as her husband knelt and placed each baby into her awaiting arms. Both parents were crying for joy over the births of their children. The exultation that enveloped Inca made her injured heart burst open with such fierceness that she cried out sharply, pressing her hand against her chest. She felt her heart breaking.

For so long she'd thought her parents did not want her, did not love her. That that was why they had abandoned her, to die alone.

But she was not alone! No, she had an older sister! Inca watched with anxious anticipation as her father, whom she most closely resembled, put his arm around his wife and his babies. He held them all, crying with joy, kissing his wife's hair, her cheek, and finally, her smiling mouth. It was a birth filled with joy, an incredible celebration. That realization flowed like a healing wave of warmth through Inca's pounding heart. She was loved! She was wanted! And she had a sister!

Staggered by all the information, Inca could no longer stand the rush of powerful emotions that overwhelmed her. She opened her eyes, her gaze fixed on Maya's serious, dark features.

"Enough!" she whispered raggedly. "It is so much…too much…." And she held up her hand in protest.

Maya nodded and stopped sending the telepathic information. She threw her shoulders back, as if to shake herself out of the trancelike state. When she looked up, she saw Inca's face contorted with so many conflicting emotions that she whispered, "I'm sorry it had to be revealed to you like this. You've been through a helluva lot…almost dying…but they said you needed this information now, not later."

Staring at Maya, Inca whispered unsteadily, "Who are 'they'?"

Smiling a little, Maya lifted her hand. "The Black Jaguar Clan. The clan I come from."

More shock thrummed through Inca. She sat there feeling dizzy, as if a bomb had exploded right next to her. She'd heard talk of this mysterious clan, and of those who volunteered their lives to work on the dark side knowingly, in the service of the Sisterhood of Light. Blinking, she looked strangely at Maya. Hundreds of memories came cascading through her mind. For several minutes, she sat there trying to absorb them all. Finally, Inca rasped, "I remember you now…. You saved my life, didn't you? I was shot in the back of the head and Roan was carrying me to your helicopter. You came around the end of the compound fence and shot two drug runners who were taking aim at us."

With a slight nod of her head, Maya said, "Your memories of that night are coming back. Yes, that's right. I couldn't let them kill my little sister, could I?"

Maya's teasing threaded through Inca's continuing shock. The rest of her rescue avalanched upon her, the memories engulfing her one after another. She saw the helicopter she was flying in, with Maya at the controls. She felt the urgency of Maya, her worry for her life as it slowly slipped away. And then she saw Maya standing at her bedside, opposite Roan. "Y-you saved me...."

Maya shook her head. "No, I can't take credit for that one, Inca. Roan saved you. I was under orders to tell him that he had to give up his life in order to save yours. Of course, that was a lie. It was really a test for him. And you know how tough our tests are." Her mouth pulled downward in a grimace. "He didn't know it was a test, of course, but in order to get you back, it had to be played that way. Those were the rules of the Sisterhood of Light. I told him the truth—that he had to love you enough to surrender his life. The elders of this village set up the conditions for him, not me or my clan. If Roan could pass this test, they knew he was worthy of being trained here, at the village. Of course, he willingly said yes. I had him place his hands on your heart and the top of your head, just as we do when we transmit a catalytic healing energy into a patient with the help of our jaguar spirit guide."

Her smile was gentle. "He did it. It was his love for you that brought you back. All I did was facilitate it by sending him to the Threshold to retrieve you. Then I teleported all of us here, to the Village of the Clouds. Helluva job, I gotta say. I did good work." She flexed her fist, pleased with her efforts. "I don't have many metaphysical talents, unlike you. But I'm a damn good teleporter when I set my mind—and heart—to it."

Maya shrugged, her eyes brimming with tears. "In my business, I work in the underbelly of darkness. It was something else to see Roan's pure, undiluted love for you pull you back from the Threshold. He doesn't have memory of this—yet. He will when it's right for him to know. Right now, *you* need to know that I'm your sister and that our parents loved us—fiercely. They surrendered their lives for us, so that we could come into being, to help a lot of other people. Our destiny was ordained long before our births. We agreed to come, to fight for the light, to fight for the under-dogs and protect them. And we both do this in our own way.''

Gulping back tears, Inca whispered, ''Tell me more about our parents. I *have* to know, Maya…please.…''

Wiping her eyes, Maya said, ''Our parents knew who we were, spiritually speaking, and why we were coming into a body for this lifetime. Our mother was a member of the Jaguar Clan. Our father, a member of the Black Jaguar Clan. They met, fell in love and married. The elders who married them here, at the village, twenty-seven years ago, told them of their destiny—that they were to give each of us up. To trust the Great Mother Goddess and surrender their two children over to her. They were told they would then be killed by drug runners shortly after our births.'' Maya frowned. ''They accepted their fate, as we all do as clan members. We know we're here for a reason. They knew ahead of time what those reasons were. They had two wonderful years to-gether, before we came. They were very happy, Inca. Very. After we were born, they kissed us goodbye, and our mother took you and went east. My father took me and went off in a westerly direction. They were told where to leave each of us.''

Shaken, Inca moved a little closer. Close enough to reach out and touch Maya, if she chose. ''Who killed them?'' she rasped thickly. ''I want to know.''

''Juan Valentino. The father of the two Valentino sons, Sebastian and Faro. And Faro damn near added you to his coup belt,'' Maya said grimly. ''We're in a death spiral dance with the Valentinos, Inca. They murdered our parents. And now Sebastian has been captured and faces a life in prison in Brazil. That's one down, and one bastard to go. Faro nearly took your life.'' She flexed her fist again, her voice grim with revenge. ''And shortly, I'll move into a death spiral dance with him. He's fled to Peru in his gunship. He thinks he's safe there. But now the bastard's on *my* territory…and I promise you, dear sister of my heart, I'll find him and avenge what he did to you…."

Staring disbelievingly at Maya, Inca whispered, "This is all too much. Too much…" She dropped her head in her hands.

Gently, Maya reached out and slid her strong fingers along the curve of Inca's shaking shoulders. She was crying, too. "I know," she said in a choked voice. "You don't know how long I've waited to finally get to meet you in person. To tell you that you weren't ever alone, Inca. That you weren't really abandoned. That you were loved by our parents—and by me…." Smoothing the cotton material across Inca's shoulders, Maya inched a little closer to her. Sniffing, she whispered brokenly, "And how long I've dreamed of this day, of being here with you…with my own blood sister…."

Inca heard the pain in Maya's husky voice. Turning, she allowed her hands to drop to her sides. Tears ran freely down her cheeks as she stared into the marred darkness of Maya's gaze. "You really *are* my sister, aren't you?"

Maya nodded almost shyly. "Yes…yes, I am, Inca. We came from our mother's body. Greatly loved. Given over to a destiny that needed us for a higher calling." Reaching out, she slid her hands once more over Inca's shoulders. "And all I want to do right now is hug the hell out of you. I want to hold my sister. It's been so long a time in coming…."

Inca moved forward into her twin's arms. The moment they embraced, her heart rocked open as never before. When Maya tightened her arms around her, Inca understood for the first time in her life what family connection truly meant. She wept unashamedly on her sister's shoulder, and so did Maya. They cried together at the Pool of Life, locked in one another's embrace, saying hello for the first time since they had been separated at birth.

Chapter 14

Inca gripped Maya's hand after her tears abated. She felt that if she released her, Maya would disappear into thin air and she'd never see her again. Oh, that was foolish, Inca realized, but her heart was so raw from learning she had *real* family that she couldn't stand the thought of Maya being ripped away from her again.

Squeezing her fingers in a gesture meant to comfort Inca and allay her worries, Maya said, "Listen, from now on you'll see so much of me you'll be sick of me." And she gave a wobbly smile as she brushed the last of her tears from her cheeks. The clouds parted for just a moment and sent golden, dappling sunlight glinting upon the quiet surface of the pool at their feet.

Inca laughed a little, embarrassed by her sudden clinginess, and released Maya's hand. "I know my response is not logical. And I will *never* tire of seeing you, Maya. Not ever."

Maya reached out and patted Inca's arm. "Well, you're stuck with me, little sister. And I only found out about you and our past a year ago. Grandmother Alaria told me. I wanted to see you right then, but she said no, that you had the last of your karma to work through.'' Maya frowned. ''She said you must experience death, but that I could be there to help save you. That's why we were waiting at a nearby secret base we use. I didn't know how your life might be threatened. When the time drew near, Grandmother Alaria told me when to go and where to fly in order to help you through all this.''

''It must have been very hard for you to wait and say nothing,'' Inca whispered painfully.

Maya sighed and held her compassionate gaze. ''I gotta tell you, Inca, it was hell. Pure torture. I wasn't sure I could abide by the rules of the clan and stay away from you.''

''You are stronger than I am,'' Inca acknowledged.

''Not by much.'' And Maya smiled a little.

She turned and looked over her shoulder. ''Hey, I think Grandmother Alaria and Roan are coming our way. I know Grandmother had more to tell us after we got over our introductions. Are you ready for them?''

Inca realized that she was so torn up emotionally—in shock, in fact—that she hadn't even felt their energy approaching the secluded glen. Her jaguar guardian had manifested and was lying near the pool, his head on his paws, asleep. She looked up. ''Roan is coming?'' Her heart beat harder. With love. With the anticipation of sharing her joy over her newfound sister. A sister!

Grinning, Maya said, ''And Grandmother Alaria, too.'' She reached out and playfully ruffled Inca's hair. ''I can tell you're head over heels in love with that hunk of man.'' She smiled knowingly. ''Wish that I could get so lucky. All I know is Neanderthal types from the last Ice Age who are out to squash me under their thumb because I'm a woman. I envy you, but you deserve someone like Roan. I like him a *lot*. He definitely has my seal of approval.'' She winked wickedly. "Not that you need my okay on anything. You've got excellent taste, Inca!"

Blushing fiercely, Inca absorbed her sister's playful touch and teasing. It felt so good! Almost as good as having Roan in her life. As Inca impatiently waited for him to appear on the well-worn dirt path that led to the pool, she realized that there were different kinds of love—what she felt for her sister, what she felt for Roan. And for Grandmother Alaria. All were different, yet vitally important to her.

Grandmother Alaria appeared first. There was a soft smile on her face and tears sparkled in her eyes. Roan appeared next, an unsure expression on his face. He hung back at the entrance to the grove.

"Come on in," Maya invited with a wave of her hand. "You're supposed to be here, too, for this confab."

Roan looked over at Inca. Her eyes were red and she'd been crying. Not wanting to assume anything with her, he looked to her for permission to join them. Even though Grandmother Alaria had coaxed him into coming with her, he felt like an outsider to this group of powerful women.

"Sit by me?" Inca asked, and she stretched out her hand toward him.

Roan nodded and held her tender willow-green gaze. He felt such incredible love encircling him and knew it was Inca's invisible embrace surrounding him. Carefully moving around the group, he sat down next to her. She smiled raggedly at him.

"I have a sister, Roan. A sister! Maya, meet Roan. He holds my heart in his hands."

Maya grinned broadly. She reached across the small circle they had made as they all sat cross-legged on the earth. "Yes, we've met. But official introductions are in order. Hi, Roan. It's good to meet you—again." And she gripped his proffered hand strongly, shook it and released it.

"Same here," he said. "I never got to thank you for saving our lives when those two drug runners had a bead on us. Nice shooting.'' He liked Maya's easygoing nature. She was very different in personality from Inca.

Maya nodded and grimaced. "We knew there was going to be danger for you two. I'm just glad I got there in time."

Grandmother Alaria settled her voluminous cotton skirt across her knees. "Children," she remonstrated, "let me pick up the threads of why you are here. Inca, I've come to tell you all that happened, and why. I know some memories are returning to you, my child."

Inca felt Roan's arm go around her shoulders, and she leaned against his strong, stalwart body. "I have many questions," she said.

Inca listened as the elder told her everything, from beginning to end, about that night she'd nearly died. Alaria smiled kindly as she finished. "It was Maya who was able to teleport you, herself and Roan here, from that hospital in Manaus. Members of the Black Jaguar Clan are the most powerful spiritual beings among our kind. She had our permission to transport." Alaria gave Roan a gentle look. "And it could not have been accomplished without Roan. His heart is large and open. Maya needed to tell him to give his life for yours, Inca, because it required that kind of surrendering of his energy, his being, in order to try and affect this transport. If the heart is not engaged in such an activity, teleportation will not work for all concerned."

Maya laughed softly. "And I've gotta tell you, folks, it wasn't easy. Oh, I've teleported when I managed to get my ducks in a row, but nothing like this…not when it was my *sister* involved. I've never had to overcome so many fears as I did that day, Inca. I was crying inside. I was afraid of losing you. Roan here helped keep the stability of the energy pattern, whether he knew it or not. His love for you was so pure, so untainted, that it held this paper bag on wheels together so I could affect the transfer."

Inca nodded and felt his arm tighten slightly around her

waist. "His heart is pure," she whispered, and she gave him a tender look. "I was saved by people who love me."

"I thought I was going to die," Roan admitted quietly. "I was ready to give up my life for Inca. She was far more important than I was. The things she was doing in the Amazon far outweighed anything I'd ever done in my life."

Grandmother Alaria looked at him for a long moment, the silence warming. "My son, you are far more powerful than you know. Your mother was a great and well-known medicine woman among us."

Roan gave her a startled look. "What do you mean?"

Alaria reached out and touched his arm in a kindly manner. "She was a member of the northern clan, the Cougar Clan, which is related to the Jaguar Clan here in South America. When she died, she sent her chief spirit guide, a female cougar, to you. What you did not know was that this cougar was in constant contact with us." She patted his arm in a motherly fashion. "We were watching, waiting and hoping that you would make the right decisions to come down here, to meet Inca and, hopefully, fall in love with her, as she is beloved by us."

Inca nodded, overwhelmed. "When I met Roan, I knew it was not an accident, Grandmother. I knew it was important. I just did not know *how* important."

"We're faced with many, many freewill choices," Alaria told them gravely. "Roan could have chosen not to come down here. He could have hardened his heart, because of the loss of his wife, and not given his love to you. You also had choices, Inca."

"I know," Inca whispered, and she looked down pensively at the green grass before her. "From the moment I met Roan I felt this powerful attraction between us. It scared me—badly. I did not know what love was then."

"You do now," Maya said gently, and she gave them a proud look. "You made all the right moves, Inca. Believe me, it was hell on me waiting, hoping, praying and watching you from afar.''

Inca looked over at her. ''You knew all along that if I made the right choices, I would be wounded out there in that valley that night, did you not?''

Glumly, Maya nodded, then gave Grandmother Alaria a pained look. ''Yeah, I knew. And it was hell on me. I didn't want you hurt. I was told that you would have to go through a life-death crisis. I didn't know the details. I was able to get permission from both clans to fly my helos into the area and be ready to help you when it happened. I was told when I could fly into the valley, and that was shortly after you were shot by Faro Valentino. It took all my training, all my belief and trust and faith, to stand back and let it happen. It was one of those times when I seriously considered breaking a clan law. I didn't *want* to have you go through all that stuff.'' She managed a crooked smile. ''But I was told in no uncertain terms that if I didn't abide by the laws in your karma, I'd *never* get to see you, and that's something I didn't want to happen.'' Maya reached out and gripped Inca's fingers briefly, tears glimmering in her eyes.

Inca gave her a sad look. ''I know how you feel. I have been placed in such a position before—and failed.''

Maya made a strangled sound. ''Well, I damn near did, too, with you. It's different when it's someone you love. It's real easy to let a stranger go through whatever they need to experience, but it's a whole 'nother stripe of the tiger when it's your family involved.'' Maya shook her head and gave Grandmother Alaria a rueful look. ''I hope I *never* have to go through this kind of thing again with Inca.''

''You will not, my child.''

Roan frowned. ''What I want to know is how you got those helicopters into that valley. Did you teleport in? There's no known airport or military facility close enough to give you the fuel you needed to reach us.''

Maya laughed and slapped her knee in delight. ''Hey,

teleporting *one* person, much less three, is a helluva big deal. But a bunch of helicopters? No way. I don't know of anyone who can facilitate that kind of energy change. No, we knew ahead of time what could possibly happen, so we flew in days earlier. Trust me, there are hundreds of small bases of operation that we've laid out all over South America. We've been fighting the drug trade in all these countries for a long, long time on our own—long before any governments got involved, or the U.S. started providing training support for the troops and air forces.''

Roan nodded. ''Colonel Marcellino mentioned that he's seen unmarked, black helicopters from time to time. And he said he didn't know where they were from, or who they represented.''

''Not the druggies, that's for sure,'' Maya chuckled derisively. Humor danced in her emerald eyes. ''Like I said before, the Black Jaguar Clan is the underbelly, the dark side of the Sisterhood of Light. We aren't constrained by certain laws and protocols that Inca and her people are. We're out there on the front lines doing battle with the bad guys— what Inca knows as the Brotherhood of Darkness—no matter what dimension they are in. To answer your question, we have a base near that valley. We were simply waiting.'' Maya lost her humor and reached out and gripped Inca's hand momentarily. ''And I'm sorry as hell it had to happen to you, but in nearly dying and being saved with Roan's love, you were able to spiritually transcend your past and move to a higher level of ability. It gave you the second chance you wanted so badly. When I was told by the elders what could happen to help you, I stood back. Before that, I was more than prepared to interfere to save you from being hurt, law or no laws.''

''I understand,'' Inca whispered. ''Sometimes it takes a near death experience to break open the door to the next level on our path.'' She gave Roan a wry look. ''And thanks to you, I made it.''

Roan shrugged, embarrassed. He looked around the circle at the three women. "I think," he told her huskily, "that this happened because of a lot of people who love you."

"Yes," Grandmother Alaria said, "you are correct. Anytime people of one mind, one heart, gather together, miracles will happen. It's inevitable." She turned her attention to Inca. "And we've got a wonderful gift to give you, my child, because of all that's happened." She smiled knowingly over at Roan and then met Inca's curious gaze. "The elders have voted to have you remain at the village for the next year for advanced spiritual training. And—" she looked at Roan, a pleased expression on her features "—we are also extending an invitation to you, Roan Storm Walker, as your mother once was invited, to come and study with us. You may stay to perfect your heritage—the abilities that pulse in your veins because of your mother's blood."

Gasping, Inca gripped Roan's hand. "Yes! Oh, yes, Grandmother, I would be honored to remain here! Roan?"

Stunned, he looked down at Inca. "Well…sure. But I'm not a trained medicine person, Grandmother. I don't know what I can offer you."

Chuckling indulgently, Alaria slowly got to her feet. Her knee joints popped and cracked as she stretched to her full height. She slowly smoothed her skirt with her wrinkled hands. "My son, people are invited to come here to the Village of the Clouds and they haven't a clue of their own heritage or traditions—or the innate skills that they may access for the betterment of all life here on Mother Earth." She gave him an amused look and gestured toward the village. "You see every nationality represented in our community, don't you?"

"Well, yes…" There were people from Africa, from Mongolia, Russia, the European countries and from North America, as well. Roan thought he was at a United Nations meeting; every skin color, every nationality seemed to be represented at the Village of the Clouds. It was one huge training facility to teach people how to use their intuition, healing and psychic abilities positively for all of humanity, as well as for Mother Earth and her other children.

"Our normal way of contacting an individual is through the dream state. We appear and offer them an invitation, and if they want to come, they are led here through a series of synchronistic circumstances. We talk to them, educate them about themselves and their potential. It is then up to them if they want to walk the path of the Jaguar Clan or not." She smiled softly. "Do you want to walk it?"

Roan felt the strong grip of Inca's fingers around his own. He looked over and saw the pleading in her eyes. "I'll give it a try, Grandmother. I still don't understand what you see in me, though...."

Maya cackled and stood up, dusting off her black flight suit. "Men! Love or hate 'em. I don't know which I'd rather do at times. The Neanderthals I know would be telling the elders they *deserved* to be here, and then there's guys like you, who are harder to find than hen's teeth—and you wonder why you're here." Maya threw up her hands and rolled her eyes. "Great Mother Goddess, let me find a man like you, Roan!" And she chuckled.

Inca frowned. "Do not worry about this, Roan. I came to this village when I was sixteen without knowing anything. They will teach you and show you. You will be taught certain exercises to develop what you already have within you."

"And," Alaria said, "it is always heart-centered work, Roan. The people who are invited to come here have good hearts. They are terribly human. They have made many mistakes, but above all, they have the courage to keep trying, and they treat people as they would like to be treated. Two of the biggest things we demand are that people have compassion for all life and respect for one another. You have both those qualities. That is not something you find often. You are either born with it or you are not. One's spirit must have grown into the heart, developed compassion for all our relations, in order to train here with us. And you are such a person. We'd be honored to have you stay with us.''

Roan felt heat in his cheeks and knew he was blushing. Giving the elder a humorous look, he said, ''I'll give it a go, Grandmother. Thanks for the invitation.'' He saw Inca's eyes light up with joy over his decision. She pressed her brow against his shoulder in thanks.

''I have to go, Inca,'' Maya said reluctantly as she looked at her military watch on her left wrist. She glanced apologetically over at Grandmother Alaria. ''Duty calls. My women are telling me it's time to saddle up.'' She hooked her thumb across her shoulder. ''I've got my squadron of black helicopters winding up outside the gates of the village back in real time. We've got a drug factory to bust.''

Scrambling to her feet, Inca threw her arms around her sister. ''Be safe?''

Maya hugged her fiercely and then released her. ''Don't worry. I watch my six, Inca. Six is a military term that means we watch behind our backs. The bad guys are the ones who are in trouble when I and my force of women are around. In our business, I'm known to hang ten over the surfboard of life. I scare my copilots to death when I fly, but I guarantee you that drug runner is going to be out of business when I get done with him.'' She chuckled indulgently. Reaching over, Maya gripped Roan's hand. ''Take care of my little sister? She's all the family I've got, and now that we have each other, I don't want to lose her a second time.''

Roan gripped her strong hand. ''That's a promise, Maya. Be safe.''

Inca stood with Roan's arm around her waist as Maya hurried up the path and disappeared behind the wall of ferns and bushes. ''She is so different from me in some ways, and yet so much like me.''

Grandmother Alaria moved to Inca and gently embraced her. ''You and Maya have twenty-five years to catch up on.

She was raised very differently from you. Now you have time to explore one another's lives. Don't be in a rush, Inca. Right now, Maya is entering a death spiral dance with Faro Valentino. She will not get to see you very much until her own fate can be decided.''

Roan frowned. ''A death spiral dance? What's that?''

''Faro tried to kill Inca. Maya had freewill choice in this karmic situation, Roan. She promised that if Faro decided to try and kill Inca, she would take it upon herself to even out the karma of his actions toward her sister. She will be his judge and jury in this, provided all things work the way she desires.'' Alaria shrugged her thin shoulders and looked up at Inca. ''You know from your own death spiral dance that things often do not go as planned. And many times, both parties die in the process.''

''I wish she had not taken the challenge against Faro,'' Inca whispered. ''I do not want to lose Maya.''

Alaria held up her hand. ''Child, your sister knew what she was getting into when she promised revenge against Faro Valentino. Right now, she and her squadron of helicopters are working to free the Indians at those five other factories that Colonel Marcellino never got to in Brazil. Be at ease. She and her women warriors know what they're doing. Maya is highly trained for military warfare. But more about that at another time. You need to trust your sister in the choices she's made. And not worry so much.''

Roan squeezed Inca's tense shoulders. ''I think it's only natural, Grandmother,'' he murmured.

''Of course it is,'' the elder replied as she moved up the path. ''Come, it's time for siesta. I know you're both tired. You need to sleep and continue your own, individual healing processes.''

As they followed her out of the glade, Roan asked, ''You said Maya is going to free the Indians at those other factories we had targeted?''

''Yes.'' Alaria turned and stopped on the trail back to the

village. "Colonel Marcellino was completely successful in his attack on the first compound. His men captured forty drug runners who worked with the Valentino Brothers. Sebastian was captured, too. They marched them back to the Amazon River, where Brazilian military helicopters took the company and the prisoners back to Brasilia. Of course, the colonel was worried about his young son, Julian, so he called off the rest of the attack. And he didn't have Inca to lead him or his men."

"I see...." Roan murmured, relieved. At least one of the Valentino Brothers was out of commission.

"Does he know that Maya and her helicopter squadron are going to take over the assaults?"

"Of course not. In our business, Roan, we are like jaguars—you see us only when we *want* you to see us." She smiled mischievously. "Maya is going to continue to clean up Inca's territory for her. That way, Inca won't have to worry about drug runners putting her people into bondage during the year she's with us. By the time you're both done with your education here, you'll return to the Amazon to live out your lives. You'll be caretakers of the basin, and of its people and relations. The difference is, this time you'll have our help and intervention, when asked for. Previously, when Inca was banished, she had no support from us whatsoever." Alaria eyed Inca. "Now it's different, and I think the drug barons are going to find it much harder to carry on business as usual in Brazil."

Roan moved down the path that led to the rainbow waterfalls, a small cloth in his right hand. The morning was beautiful, with cobbled apricot-colored clouds strewn like corn rows in the sky above. Inca had left much earlier to go down and wash her jaguar, Topazio, in the pool below the waterfalls. It was a particularly beautiful place, one of Roan's personal favorites. As he stepped gingerly down the well-trodden path, away from the busy village, his heart expanded with anticipation. With hope.

He knew that time at the village was not really based upon twenty-four-hour days, as it was in the rest of the world. Still, it had been three months, by his reckoning, since they'd arrived here. And today, he felt, was the day. Inca knew nothing of the surprise he had for her.

As he moved along the narrow, red clay path, he watched as a squadron of blue-yellow-and-white parrots winged above him. The lingering, honeyed fragrance of orchids filled the air. Early mornings were his favorite time because the air was pregnant with wonderful scents. What would Inca say? His heart skittered over the possibility that she'd turn him down. How could she? They had drawn even closer together over the months. And although it was a personal, daily hell for Roan, he patiently waited for Inca to ask him to love her fully. Completely. They had time, he told himself. But he had long waited for the day he could physically love her, fulfill her and please her in all ways.

More than once, Roan had talked to Grandmother Alaria about the situation, and she'd counseled time and patience.

"Don't forget," the elder would remonstrate, "that Inca was a wild, primal child without parental guidance or direction. She was loved and cared for by the priests and priestesses who raised her, but she never experienced love between a man and woman before you stepped into her life. Let her initiate. Let her curiosity overwhelm her hesitancy. I know it's challenging for you, but you are older, and therefore responsible for your actions toward her. Wait, and her heart will open to you, I promise."

Today was the day. Roan could feel it in his heart. His soul. As the path opened up and he left the ferns and bushes, he spotted Inca down at the pool. Her male jaguar was standing knee-deep in water and she was sluicing the cooling liquid lazily across his back. Her laughter, deep and husky, melted into the musical sounds of the waterfall splashing behind them. Because of the sun's angle, a rainbow formed and arced across the pool. Yes, Inca was his rainbow woman, and made his life deliriously happy.

"Roan!"

He smiled and halted at the edge of the water. "Hi. Looks like Topazio is getting a good washing."

Laughing, Inca pushed several strands of damp hair behind her shoulder. "We have been playing." She straightened and gestured to her wet clothes, which clung to her slender, straight form. "Can you tell?"

Roan grinned. Inca was dressed in an apricot-colored blouse and loose, white cotton slacks that revealed her golden skin beneath them. "Yes, I can. When you want to come out, I have something for you."

Instantly, Inca's brows lifted. "A gift? For me?" She was already turning and wading out of the clear depths of the pool.

Roan laughed heartily. "Yes, something just for you, sweetheart." Inca had changed so much in the last three months. She was no longer guarded, with that hard, warriorlike shield raised to protect herself. No, now she was part playful child, part sensuous woman and all his…he hoped.

As she hurried up the sandy bank, Roan gestured for her to join him on a flat, triangular rock. It was their favorite place to come and sit in one another's arms, and talk for hours. Often they shared a lunch at the waterfall on this rock, as their guardians leaped and played in the water. Of course, her jaguar loved the water, and Roan's cougar did not; but she would run back and forth on the bank as the jaguar leaped and played in the shallows.

Breathing hard, Inca approached and sat down next to him. She spied a red cotton cloth in his hands. Reaching out, she said, "Is that for me?"

Chuckling, Roan avoided her outstretched hand and said, "Yes, it is. But first, you have to hear me out, okay?"

Pouting playfully, Inca caressed his recently shaved cheek. Because the weather was warm and humid, all he wore was a set of dark blue cotton slacks. He went barefoot, choosing to no longer wear sandals. His feet were becoming hard and callused. Sifting her fingers through the dark hair on his powerful chest, she teased, "Can I not open it first and then hear what you say?"

As he sat on the rock, his legs spread across it, Inca sat facing him, her legs draped casually across his. "No," he chided playfully. He warded off her hand as she reached for the gift lying in his palm. "It's not a speech, so be patient, my woman."

A wonderful sense of love overwhelmed Inca as he called her "my woman." It always did when that husky endearment rolled off his tongue. Sitting back, she folded her hands in her lap. "Very well. I will behave—for a little while."

Smiling, he met and held her gaze. "I love that you are a big kid at heart. Don't ever lose that precious quality, Inca. Anyway—" Roan cleared his throat nervously "—I've been thinking…for a long time, actually…that I want to complete what we share. With your permission." He saw her eyes darken a little. His heart skittered in terror. "Among my people, when we love another person, Inca, we give them a gift of something to show our love for them. In my nation, if we love someone, we want to make a home with them. We want to live with them—forever. And if it's agreed on by both the man and the woman, children may follow."

She tilted her head. "Yes?"

Fear choked him. Roan knew she could turn him down. "In the old days of my people, a warrior would bring horses to the family of the woman he loved. The more horses, the more he loved her. The horses were a gift to the family, to show the warrior's intent of honoring the daughter he'd fallen in love with, wanted to marry and keep a home and family with for the rest of his life."

"I see...." Inca murmured, feeling the seriousness of his words.

Clearing his throat again, Roan said, "I don't have horses to give your parents, Inca. But if I could, I would. I have to shift to a white man's way of asking for your hand in marriage." He opened his fingers and gave her the neatly tied red cloth. "Open it," he told her thickly. "It's for you—a symbol of what I hope for between us...."

Roan held his breath as Inca gently set the cloth down between them and quickly untied it. As the folds fell away, they revealed a slender gold ring set with seven cabochon gemstones.

Gasping, Inca picked up the ring and marveled at it. "Oh, Roan, the stones are the color of my eyes!" She touched the ring with her fingertips, watching it sparkle in the sunlight. "It is beautiful!" She sent him a brilliant smile. "And this is a gift to me?"

"Yes." He tried to steady his voice. He saw the surprise and pleasure in Inca's expression, the way her lips curved in joy as she held up the ring. "It symbolizes our engagement to one another. An agreement that you will marry me...become my wife and I'll be your husband...." His throat became choked. He saw Inca's eyes flare as she cradled the ring in her palm.

"You are my beloved," she whispered softly, reaching out and gently touching his cheek. "You have always held my heart...."

"Is that a yes?"

Inca looked down at the ring, her eyes welling with tears. "For so long, I thought no one loved me. That I was too dark, too bad of a person, to love," she said brokenly. "You came along—so strong and proud, so confident and caring of me that I began to think I was not as bad as I thought I was, or as others have said of me...." Sniffing, Inca wiped the tears from her eyes and looked up at Roan. She saw the anguish, the unsureness, in his eyes, but she also felt his love blanketing her just as the sun embraced Mother Earth. "I understand what love is now...and I have had these months to take it into my heart." She pressed her hand against her chest.

"You were never a bad person, Inca. Not ever. Enemies will always say you're bad—but that's to be expected. You shouldn't listen to them. And I know you thought you were bad because you were banished from the village."

Inca hung her head and closed her eyes. "Yes," she admitted hoarsely. Reaching out, she gripped his hand, which was resting on her knee. "But you showed me I was a good person. That I was worthy of care, of protection, of being loved." Opening her hand, Inca stared down at the ring through blurry eyes. Tears splashed onto her palm and across the delicately wrought ring.

"If I accept this gift from you, it means you will be my husband? That you love me enough to want me as your partner?"

Tenderly, Roan framed Inca's face with his hands, marveling in her beauty. Tears beaded on her thick, black lashes. He saw the joy and suffering in her eyes. "Yes, my woman. Yes, I want you as my partner and wife. You're my best friend, too. And if the Great Spirit blesses us, I want the children you'll grow with love in your belly."

Sniffing, Inca placed her hands over his. "I love you so much, Roan.... You have always held my heart safely in your hands. I want to be your wife. I want Grandmother Alaria to marry us."

Gently, he leaned down and placed a soft, searching kiss on her lips. He tasted the salt of her tears. He felt her hands fall away from his and glide across his shoulders. Her mouth was hot with promise, sliding slickly across his. She moved to her knees and pressed her body against his in an artless gesture that spoke of her need for him.

Slowly, Roan eased his mouth from hers. He took the ring from her hand. "Here," he whispered roughly, "let me put it on your finger to make it official." His heart soared with such joy that Roan wondered if he was going to die of a heart attack at that moment. Inca was smiling through her tears and extending her long, slender fingers toward him. How easy it was to slip that small gold ring onto her hand. She wanted to marry him! She was willing to be his partner for life....

Sighing, Inca admired the ring. "What are the stones in the ring?" She marveled at their yellow-green, translucent beauty.

"They're called peridot," Roan said. "And they came from a mine on an Apache reservation in North America."

Murmuring with pleasure, Inca ran her finger across them. "Indian. That is good. It comes from their land, their heart."

"You like it?"

She nodded. "I like it, yes." Lifting her head, she looked at him through her lashes. "But I love the man who gave it to me even more...."

Chapter 15

The time was ripe. Inca sighed as Roan pulled her into his arms after he'd moved off the large, flat rock.

"There's a special place I found," he rasped as he lifted her easily. "I want to share it with you. It was made for us...."

"Yes...show me?" Inca pressed a kiss to his bristly jaw. The ferns gently swatted against her bare feet and legs as he carried her away from the waterfall and deep into the rain forest. Eventually the path opened up into a small, sunlit meadow ringed with trees. Bromeliads and orchids of many colors clustered in their gnarled limbs.

There was a shaded area beneath one rubber tree, and Inca smiled as Roan set her down upon the dark green grass. Looking up into his stormy eyes, she whispered, "Teach me how to love you. I *want* to love you, Roan, in all the ways a woman can love her man."

Nodding, he squeezed her hands and released them. She sat there, chin lifted, her innocence touching his heart as never before. "We'll teach one another," he told her as he

began to unbutton his pants. "But you'll take the lead, Inca.
You tell me what you want me to do. Where you want me
to place my hands on you. I want you to enjoy this, not be
in pain or discomfort."

Nodding, she watched as he eased out of his pants and
dropped them to one side. He stood naked before her, and
she thrilled at seeing him this way. There was no fat on him
anywhere. His body was tightly muscled. The dark hair on
his chest funneled down across his hard, flat stomach, and
she gulped. Unable to tear her gaze from him, she felt her
mouth go a dry. Oh, she'd seen animals mate, but this was
different. This was a sacred moment, holding a promise of
such beauty and wonder. Her mind dissolved and her feelings rushed like powerful ocean waves throughout her.

Just looking at Roan in the power of his nakedness as he
knelt in front of her, his knee brushing hers, made her smile
uncertainly. "I am shaking, Roan," she whispered. "But not
from fear…"

Roan smiled in turn as he eased the buttons of her blouse
open. "Yes, that's the way it should feel," he told her in a
low, roughened tone. "Anticipation, wanting…needing one
another."

Inca felt the material brush her sensitized breasts, her nipples hardening as the cloth was pulled away to expose them.
She felt no shame in her nakedness with Roan. As he eased
the blouse off her shoulders, she gloried in the primal look
in his narrowed eyes as he absorbed the sight of her. His
hands were trembling, too. Elated that he wanted her as
badly as she wanted him, Inca stood. In moments, she'd
followed his lead and divested herself of her damp cotton
slacks. Standing naked in front of him, she felt a sense of
her power as a woman. The darkening, hooded look in his
eyes stirred her, making her bold and very sure of herself.
She took his hand and knelt down opposite him. Acting on
instinct, she lifted her hands and drew Roan's head down
between her breasts.

Closing her eyes as their skin met and melded, Inca sighed and swayed unsurely as his hands, large and scarred, moved around her hips to draw her between his opened thighs and press her fully against him. The feel of his warm, hard flesh was exciting. The wiry hair on his chest made her breasts tingle, the nipples tighten, and she felt dampness collecting between her legs. Inca uttered another sigh of pleasure at the sensual delights assaulting her. The sounds of the rain forest were like music to her ears, the waterfall in the distance only heightening her reeling emotions, which clamored for more of Roan's touch.

As he lifted his head away, his hands ranged upward from her hips to graze the rounded curve of her breasts. A gasp of pleasure tore from her and she shut her eyes. Moaning, she guided his hands so that her breasts were resting in his large palms. Her skin tingled, grew even more tight and heated.

"Feel good?" he rasped.

Inca could not speak, she was so caught up in delicious sensations as his thumbs lazily circled her hard, expectant nipples. Oh! She wanted something…and she moaned and dug her fingers into his thick, muscular shoulders.

Understanding what she needed, Roan leaned over and licked one hardened, awaiting peak.

Uttering a cry of surprise, of pleasure, Inca dug her fingers more deeply into his flesh. She tipped her head back, her slender throat gleaming.

Seeing the deep rose flush across her cheeks, her lips parted in a soundless cry of pleasure, Roan captured the other erect nipple between his lips and suckled her. Inca moaned wildly, her hands opening and closing spasmodically against his shoulders. Trembling and breathing in ragged gasps, she moved sinuously in his embrace as he lavished the second nipple equally. A sheen of perspiration made her body gleam like gold in the dappled shade and sunlight beneath the tree where they knelt.

Inca collapsed against him, her head pressed against his, her soft, ragged breath caressing him. Roan was glad for the experience he had, so he could lead Inca to the precipice of desire. When the right moment came, she would gladly step off the ledge with him, he had no doubt. Gathering her into his arms, he moved to a grassy hummock, a few feet away from the tree and sat down, leaning his back against the firm, sloping earth. He smiled darkly up at Inca as he guided her so that she straddled him with her long, curved thighs. His hands settled on her hips and he gently positioned her above his hard, throbbing flesh.

Inca's eyes widened as she opened her legs to move across him. Never had she been close to a man like this! But she trusted Roan. Besides, her mind was so much mush that she could no longer think coherently. He lifted her into place, and her hands came to rest on his thick, massive shoulders. And as he slowly lowered her against his hard, warm length, she gasped, but it was a cry of utter surprise and growing pleasure. Her own feminine dampness connected and slid provocatively against him. She heard and felt him groan, as if a drum thrummed deeply in his body. A tremble went through him as if a bolt of lightning had connected them invisibly to one another.

The utter pleasure of sliding against him, the delightful heat purling between her legs made her shudder and grip him more surely with her thighs. What wonderful sensations! Inca wanted more and she wasn't disappointed. As if sensing her needs, Roan tightened his grip around her hips and dragged her forward across his rigid, pressing form. A little cry escaped her. More sensations shot jaggedly up through her boiling, womanly core as he slid partially into her throbbing confines. Her belly felt like a bed of burning, glowing coals. Her hands moved spasmodically against his chest. Her breath was coming in gasps.

Lost in the building heat as he moved her slowly back and forth against him, Inca felt him tremble each time. There was something timeless, something rhythmic and wild about this, and she wanted more, much more. Leaning forward, she brushed her breasts against his chest. Capturing his mouth, she kissed him with fierce abandon. He gently teethed her lower lip in the exchange, and she felt him lift and reposition her slightly. The sensation of something hot, hard and large pressed more deeply into her feminine core. The pressure remained, and heat swirled deeply within her and between her tensed thighs.

Gasping, Inca pressed downward and drew him more deeply into herself. Instantly, she heard Roan growl. Oh, yes, she recognized that growl. She'd heard it many times when two jaguars were in the throes of mating. He felt large and throbbing as she eased herself fully down upon him. The pleasure doubled. Then tripled as she slowly sat up, her hands tentatively resting against his hard abdomen. He was guiding her, monitoring her exploratory movements. Eyes closed, Inca marveled at all the exploding feelings, the wildness pumping through her bloodstream, and her heart pounded with a fierce, singular love for the man with whom she was coupling—for the first time in her life.

Moving her hips, she moaned and eased forward, then back. The oldest rhythm in the world took over within her. She was moving with the waves that pummeled the shore of her being, a movement so pure and necessary to life that she gripped his arms and pushed more deeply against him. Again he groaned. His body was tense, like a bow drawn too tightly. She could hear him breathing raggedly. His hands were tight around her hips, guiding her, helping her to establish that harmony, that wild rhythm between them.

Somewhere deep within Inca, something primal exploded. The savagery, the vibrant, throbbing pleasure, rolled scaldingly through her. She gripped Roan hard with her thighs and pushed rhythmically against him. The moment he lifted his hips to meet and match her hot, liquid stride, another powerful explosion rocked her, catching her off guard and tearing her breath from her lungs. For a long, amazing moment Inca sat frozen upon him, her hands lifting, her fingers flexing in a pleasure she had never before experienced. She could not move, the shower of hot ecstasy was so intense within her. When Roan eased her forward, the sensation was intensified tenfold. Inca threw her head back as a growl, as deep as her unfettered spirit, rolled up and out of her parted lips.

Roan could no longer control himself. As Inca moved wildly against him, lost in the throes of pleasure pulsing through her slender, damp form, he found his own pleasure explode in turn. Thrusting his hips upward, Roan took her deeply and continuously. White-hot heat mushroomed within him, and he groaned raggedly. He gripped her hips. Tensing, he felt himself spilling into her sacred confines.

Unable to move after the intensity of his release, he lay there panting for endless moments, his eyes open barely. Instinctively, Inca moved her hips in order to prolong the incredible sensations for him. A fierce love for her overtook him, and Roan lifted his hands and placed them on her shoulders.

Drawing her down upon him, their bodies slick against one another, Roan eased Inca off him and to his side. The grass welcomed them, cool against their hot flesh as he slid one arm beneath her neck and rolled her to her back. Pushing up on one elbow, he raised himself above her, their body's touching from hip to feet. Beads of sweat trickled down the sides of his face. His heart was beating erratically in his chest as he smoothed several dark, damp strands from her brow and temple. Inca's mouth was soft and parted, her lips well kissed and her eyes closed. Breathing raggedly, Roan studied her intently. It had been wonderful for both of them and he was thankful.

Her hands were still restless, wanting to touch him, feel him and absorb him. Her flesh was like a hot iron against him as her fingers tunneled through the damp hair on his chest. Inca dragged open her eyes. Her body vibrated with such joy and pleasure that she could only stare up through her lashes at Roan in wonder. His mouth was crooked with pride. She could feel his pleasure, his love for her and she sighed, then gulped to try and steady her breathing.

"I—I never knew…never imagined it felt like *this!* Why did we wait so long if it felt like this?"

Leaning over, Roan slid his mouth against her lips. She was soft and available. Although he knew the warrior side of her was still within her, he was privileged to meet, love and hold the woman within her, too. Lifting his mouth from her wet lips, he rasped, "There's a time for all things, sweet woman of mine. And it will get better every time we do it."

Gasping, Inca whispered, "I do not know how I can stand it, then." She slid her fingers across his damp face and into his thick black hair. "I feel like I am floating! As if the storm gods have come into my body." She gestured to her belly. "I still feel small lightning bolts of pleasure within me, even now. This is wonderful to share with you."

"Good," Roan whispered raggedly. Lying down, he drew Inca against him once more. She rested her head wearily in the crook of his shoulder, her arm languidly draped across his chest. The warmth of the day, the slight breeze, all conspired to slowly cool them off. Closing his eyes, Roan murmured, "I love you, Inca. I will until the day I die, and after that…."

Touched, Inca tightened her arm around his chest. Lying next to Roan was the most natural place in the world for her to be. "Our love created this," she whispered unsteadily. "How I feel now, in my heart, is because of you—your patience and understanding of me." She lifted her head and gazed deeply into his half-opened eyes. There was such peace in Roan's features now. Gone was that tension she'd always seen around his mouth. "I understand what love is, at last. You have shown me the way."

As her fingertips trailed across his lower lip, he smiled

lazily up at her. Her hair was slightly disheveled, a beautiful ebony frame around her flushed face and widening, beautiful eyes. There was such awe and love shining in her gaze. It made him feel good and strong in ways he'd never felt before.

"Love is a two-way street, sweetheart. It takes two to make it work. We love one another and so the rest of easy." He trailed his fingers across the high slope of her cheek. "And best of all, you're going to be my partner, my wife. It doesn't get any better than that...."

Inca nodded and playfully leaned over and gave him a swift kiss, feeling bold and more confident about herself as a woman. "I never thought I would have anyone, Roan. I thought I was born into this life alone, and that I would die alone."

"No," he said thickly, catching her hand and placing a kiss into her palm, "you changed that, remember? You made a mistake, but you proved to everyone after making it that you were cut from a piece of good cloth. You worked long, hard years alone, to show the elders you were worthy of reconsideration." Using his tongue, he traced a slow, wet circle across her open palm. She moaned and shut her eyes for an instant. How easy it was going to be to give Inca all the pleasure he knew how to share with her. She was wide-open and vulnerable to him. She'd given the gift of herself to him, her innocence, and he cherished her for that. He hoped he would never hurt her in the coming weeks or months—that he would always honor the sacredness of the wild, primal woman she was.

"My jaguar woman," he teased gently. "I just hope I can keep up with you." As he moved his hand across her left shoulder, he felt the small crescent of jaguar fur that would always remind him she was uniquely different from most human beings. But that didn't mean she wasn't human, because she was.

Laughing delightedly, Inca said, "You are of the Cougar

Clan! Why should you not be my equal? The cougar is the symbol of the north, just as the jaguar is of the south. One is not stronger or better than the other.''

Roan sat up and took Inca into his arms. It felt damned good to be naked against one another. She threw her arms around his neck and kissed him spontaneously on the cheek.

''Let us go to the Pool of Life,'' she whispered excitedly. ''I will wash you, my beloved. And you will wash me.''

Grinning, Roan said, ''I like your take-charge attitude, Inca.'' He helped her to her feet and then holding her hand, gathered up her clothes and his.

''Let's go, sweetheart.''

Inca was standing beneath a rubber tree near their hut, at the round table where they took their meals, when she felt a disturbance in the energy around her. She was preparing lunch for her and Roan when it happened. Roan was out in the field with the rest of the men, tending their large, beautiful vegetable gardens beyond the meadow in the distance. Soon he would arrive, and she wanted to have a meal prepared for him.

Looking around, she saw that other inhabitants of the village were going about their noontime business. Shaking her head, she wondered what she'd felt. It was vaguely familiar, but nothing she could put her finger on right away. Sunlight glanced off the peridot ring on her left hand. Holding it up, she smiled happily. How had three months flown by? Grandmother Alaria had married them shortly after they had loved one another in that wonderful, private glade near the Pool of Life. Inca had never known what happiness was until now. She had been slogging through life alone, and suddenly life had taken on wonderful shades and hues of joy—ever since Roan entered her world. Yes, love made the difference. That and the fact she had family now.

Placing bowls on the table, Inca straightened. Maya, her sister…she had seen her only four times in the last three months, and only for an hour or two at the most. Maya was busier than Inca was. Yet they utilized every scrap of every moment to talk, share and search one another's separate lives, to understand how life had shaped them and made them into what they were today.

Inca always marveled at how alike they were. It was a joy to connect telepathically with her sister, to share, openly all her emotions with Maya. To have a sister was as great a gift as having Roan as her husband. And after talking it over with Roan, she had gifted Maya with the medicine necklace that Roan had bestowed on her. Somehow, Inca knew that the blue stone in the center of it was a great protection. How or why, she couldn't explain, but that didn't matter.

Roan had approved of her giving Maya the very ancient and powerful amulet. And Maya had received it with tears of thanks in her eyes. She told them that, as a pilot, she wasn't supposed to wear any jewelry when flying her daily, dangerous missions against the drug runners. Maya had tucked it gently beneath her flight suit, a grin of pride playing on her wide mouth. She thanked both of them for it, for she knew it had originally come from Roan's family and that sacred articles were always passed down through family.

Yes, Inca was truly blessed. She knew now that she had been in a dark tunnel for the last twenty-five years. She was out of that tunnel now, and in the light. It felt good. Very good. And Maya was now protected with the mysterious necklace that held that incredible blue, opalescent stone. That made Inca sleep better at night, knowing that the stone's amazing powers were supporting her sister's best interests.

"How are you today, child?"

Inca turned and saw Grandmother Alaria moving slowly toward her. She wore her hair in thick braids, her shift a dark pink color and her feet bare and thick with calluses. The gentle smile on her face made Inca smile in turn and eagerly pull out one of the rough-hewn stools for the old woman to sit upon.

"I have coffee perking. Would you like some, Grandmother?"

Sighing, Alaria nodded. "Yes, that sounds perfect, thank you." Settling down carefully on the stool beneath the shade of the rubber tree, Alaria painstakingly arranged the shift over her crossed legs. "The day is beautiful," she mused as Inca handed her a mug with steaming black coffee in it. "Thank you, child. Come, sit down near me."

Inca sensed the change in the air. Over the months, as she'd gone into training with her, she knew when Alaria had something of importance to say to her. Taking the other stool, she sat opposite her. Today she wore a sleeveless, white cotton tunic and dark red slacks that barely reached her slender ankles.

"Something is going on, is it not?" Inca asked.

Alaria sipped the coffee. "Yes. I have asked Roan to come in early from the fields. He'll be here shortly."

Frowning, Inca sensed that all was not well. She knew better than to ask, because if she was to know, Grandmother Alaria would tell her at the appropriate time.

"Did you sense a shift in the force field around the village?"

Raising her brows, Inca said, "Was that what it was? I sensed something but I could not identify it directly."

"Your sister just landed her helicopter outside the village. That is what you felt."

Gasping with joy, Inca said, "Oh! Maya's coming?"

Smiling, Alaria said, "Yes, and she's bringing Michael Houston with her."

"Really?" Inca clapped her hands in joy. She shot off the stool and craned her neck to look down the path toward where the clouds met the earth. That was one of two entrances in and out of the highly protected village. She saw no one—yet.

"Yes, you will have much of your family here in a few minutes," Alaria told her with a soft smile.

Unable to sit in her excitement, Inca saw Roan coming across the meadow. He had a rake propped on his shoulder as he walked in sure, steady strides toward the village center.

Joy thrummed briefly through Inca. She stopped her restless pacing and looked down at the elder, who sipped her coffee with obvious relish. "This is unusual, for Michael to be here, yes?"

"Yes."

"Are Ann and the baby coming, also?"

Alaria shook her head. "No, my child. I'm afraid this is a business visit."

A warning flickered though Inca's gut. She halted and scowled. Placing her hand against her stomach, where she felt the fear, she whispered, "Business?"

Setting the coffee on the table, Alaria nodded. "I'm afraid so."

Inca's heart pounded briefly with dread. She didn't want her perfect world shattered. She knew it was a childish reaction and not mature at all. Still, her love with Roan was so new, so wonderful and expanding, that she wanted nothing to taint what they had. Knowing that the grandmother could easily read her thoughts and emotions, Inca glumly sat down, all her joy snuffed out like a candle in a brisk breeze.

"I feel fear."

Reaching out, Alaria patted Inca's sloped shoulder. "Take courage, my child. You are of the Jaguar Clan. We face and work through our fears—together."

Just as Roan put his rake up against the hut and arrived at the table, Inca saw Maya and Mike Houston appear out of the gauzy, white cloud wall and walk toward them. Inca gave Roan a quick hug of hello, turned on her heel and ran through the center of the village toward them, her arms open, her hair flying behind her like a banner.

Roan chuckled, poured himself some coffee and sat down next to Alaria. "Looks like family week around here for Inca."

"It is," Alaria said, returning his smile and greeting.

Resting his elbows on the table, Roan watched with undisguised pleasure as Inca threw her arms first around her sister, who was dressed in her black flight suit, and then Mike Houston, giving him a puppylike smooch on his cheek. Then, nestled between the two, she slid her arms around their waists and walked with them. Roan couldn't hear their animated words, but the laughter and joking among the three of them made him grin. He was so happy for Inca. She had family now. People who loved her, who wanted her in their lives. He shifted a glance to Alaria, who was also watching them, with kindness in her eyes.

"She deserves this," he told the old woman in a low tone.

"Yes, she does, my son."

"All I want to do is keep that smile on her face, Grandmother. Inca's been deprived of so much for so long."

Patting his sun-darkened hand, Alaria said, "All you need do is continue to love her and allow her to grow into all of what she can become. I will warn you that Maya and Mike coming today is not good news. Inca will be distraught."

"Forewarned is forearmed. I'll take care of her afterward." Roan was grateful for the warning. At least he could hold Inca, console her, and be there for her. It was more than she'd had before, and Roan wanted to serve in that capacity. Being married meant being many things, wearing different hats at different times for his partner, and it was something he could do well. The years he'd spent with Sarah had prepared him for Inca. And he was grateful.

After everyone had shaken hands or embraced, they sat around the table. Coffee was poured and Inca brought out a dish of fresh fruit and cheese, plus a warm loaf of wheat bread and butter. Then she sat close to Roan, anxiety written in her features. Maya sat across from her. She'd placed her helmet on the table and thrown her black gloves into it. Her hair, as usual, was drawn back into a chignon at the base of her neck. Mike Houston was in military fatigues, his face grave. Inca threaded her fingers under the table nervously.

Alaria spoke quietly. "Inca, your sister is going to be working directly with Michael for the government of Peru. As you know, Maya and her band of pilots and mechanics have hidden bases in every country here in South America. When we want them to lend their considerable support in a situation, they fly in and help. Maya's main staging area is a Black Jaguar base near the Machu Pichu reserve in Peru. The Peruvian government has requested aid from Morgan Trayhern, and he's asked Michael to coordinate a plan to do so. Michael has spent most of his life in Peru, and he knows the land and its people well."

Inca nodded. She felt her mouth going dry. "This has to do with the death spiral dance between Maya and Faro Valentino, does it not?" The words came out low, filled with concern and trepidation. Seeing her sister's green eyes narrow slightly, Inca glanced back at Grandmother Alaria, for she was the authority at the table.

"It does, my child."

Inca's heart dropped, then froze with fear. She stared at Maya, who sat looking completely unconcerned about it all. Oh, perhaps there was a time in Inca's past that she'd behaved similarly, but not now. Not in the last three months. Compressing her lips, she struggled to keep quiet and let the elder do the talking. It was so hard, because Inca's love for Maya was just taking root. She'd just met her. They'd had so little time together. Inca acknowledged her selfishness, but still she wanted more. Much more. And a death spiral dance meant that only one of the two people involved would come out alive—with luck. Too many times, Inca had seen both people die as they circled one another like wary jaguars fighting over turf and territory. Fights to the death in the spiral dance were common—the death of both protagonists.

Dipping her head, Inca shut her eyes tightly, the tears feeling hot behind her lids. "I—I see...." The words came out brokenly. When Roan's hand moved gently across her drooping shoulders, Inca felt his concern and love. It stopped some of the fierce anguish and pain from assaulting her wide-open heart.

"Inca," Maya pleaded gently, "don't worry so much about me. This isn't any different from what I do out there every day. I'm always in the line of fire. And I *want* to take down Faro Valentino, more than anything."

Inca lifted her head and opened her eyes. She saw the fury burning in Maya's narrowed gaze. "I do not want you in a death spiral dance on my behalf, Maya. I want you alive. I—need you...."

Reaching across the table, Maya gripped Inca's proffered hand. "Silly goose. You have me. Don't worry, okay? I've been around this block many, many times. Mike will tell you that."

Mike leaned forward, his voice low and cajoling. "Inca, I've worked off and on with Maya for years. Now, I didn't know who she was, or what her relationship was to you. We called those black helicopters the 'ghosts of the rain forest.' Sometimes, during a hot firefight, when I and my men were tangling with drug runners or a drug lord, she and her colleagues would show up out of the blue. Many times, they made the difference between us living or dying, the battle moving in our favor and not the enemies. I never got to meet Maya personally to thank her. I had no idea it was a woman-run operation, or that they were part of the Black Jaguar Clan. Not until recently."

Inca saw the challenging sparkle in Maya's eyes as she released her hand and straightened up. There was no doubt that Maya was a leader in every sense of the word. It was clear in her defiant and confident expression; in the way she walked with military precision, her shoulders thrown back;

in that sense of absolute power and authority exuding from her.

"Inca," Maya pleaded, "we have a chance to not only get Faro, but close down his main factories in Peru in this sweep. Mike is going to coordinate the whole thing from Lima. He'll be buying us new Boeing D model Apaches to compete with Valentino's Kamov gunships. He's our contact. Morgan Trayhern is assigning people from Fort Rucker, Alabama—Apache helicopter instructors—to teach us the characteristics of the D model. I haven't met them yet, but Mike says Morgan is borrowing the best instructors from the U.S. Army, and they're considered the cream of the crop. The best! So you see, you have nothing to worry about. I'm in the best of hands." She flashed a triumphant grin.

Alaria looked from one sister to the other. "Inca can feel many possible outcomes of this death spiral dance," she stated quietly.

Maya lost her smile. "I'm prepared to die, little sister, if that's what it takes." Shrugging, she said, "I was born to die. We all were. My life is lived in the now, the present. That is how the Jaguar Clan operates, as you know." And then she eased the blue medicine piece from the neck of her flight suit. "See? I wear it twenty-four hours a day. It keeps me safe."

Nodding, Inca whispered brokenly, "Yes, yes, I know all that." She lifted her hand, searching Maya's grave features. "Suddenly, taking revenge on Faro does not feel right to me. Not if it puts you at risk, Maya." She looked pleadingly at Alaria. "Must the Jaguar Clan always even each score against it? Is there not another, better way?"

"My child, each member of the clan must walk through this lesson. Yes, it is much better not to seek revenge for hurt against one you love. Each of us learns this truth individually, however. One day, you and Maya will come to realize that surrendering over the hurt to a higher authority is better than trying to settle the score directly. Inca, you are at that place where you can see and understand this. Maya is not." Alaria held up her hands. "You can't stop Maya. Nor should you. I suggest you pray daily for her, for her life. That is all you can do. Just because you love someone does not mean that love protects them always."

Roan slid his arm around Inca. He could feel her tensing up with fear and anxiety, see it written clearly across her face. He wished he had the words to soothe her, to quell her anxiety, but he didn't.

Mike sighed and gave Inca a half smile. "Listen to me. Maya is in the best of hands. These army instructors will be the best— They will be there to make the difference, to give her and her squadron even more of an edge. We've got some incredible technology for the gunship she flies. That will help her in finding and locating the drug runners and their facilities in northern Peru. So stop worrying so much."

"Are these other instructors members of the Jaguar Clan?"

Maya shook her head. "No…they don't know a thing about us, our skills and other talents. They're walking into this cold. I don't intend for them to know about our closet abilities, either." She flexed her hands. "Besides, compared to you, I'm nothing. The only thing I can do is teleport when I'm in a good mood." Maya grinned. "You, on the other hand, can heal, teleport, read minds…the list goes on. I'm blind, deaf and dumb compared to you." She laughed good-naturedly and reached over and gripped her sister's hand again. "Whoever these pilot instructors are, I'm not about to tell them about us, either. So far as they know, we're a spook ops comprised of women pilots who are crazy enough to fly the best damned helicopter gunships in the world where they aren't supposed to be able to go."

Inca nodded. "I see.…"

"Anyway," Maya said with a quick grin, "I'm starving to death! Inca, I'm gonna help myself to this bread you just made.'' And she reached for a thick slice of it. Rising from the stool, she grabbed a knife. ''Mind if I dig in?''

Everyone chuckled.

''Just like a black jaguar,'' Mike intoned, trying not to smile. ''Take no prisoners…''

Alaria cackled. ''Black jaguars aren't known for their diplomacy or subtleties. Did you notice?''

Inca snapped out of her self-pity. She should savor the time she had with her family, not wallow in worry over their unknown futures. Live today for today. Expect nothing; receive everything. Those were Jaguar Clan Maxims. Well, she had to continue to learn how to do that. Rising, she reached out and gripped her sister's arm.

''Manners, please. Sit down. I will serve all of you.''

Mike chuckled. He pulled a wrapped gift out of a duffel bag he'd brought with him. ''Hey, Inca, this is for you— from Ann, the baby and me.''

How quickly the energy shifted, Roan thought as he saw Inca rally. She snapped out of her funk and her expression brightened. How much he loved her. She was at such a precarious point in her growth. Finding her sister, being allowed back into the clan and getting married all in three months was asking a lot of anyone. But especially someone with her background.

''What is it?'' Inca gasped, as she reached out for the bright red foil wrapped gift topped with a yellow ribbon.

''Open it,'' Mike said with a laugh. ''You'll see….''

Like a child, she eagerly pulled the paper from around it. ''Oh! Smoked salmon!''

Pleased, Mike winked at Roan. ''In case you don't know, she's a real jaguar when it comes to fish.''

Roan grinned. ''Jaguars eat fish. At least, that's what she told me.''

''Humph,'' Maya growled, sinking her teeth into the warm, buttered bread, ''they'll eat *anything* that isn't moving.''

"And even if it is moving, we'll freeze it, jump it and make it our own," Mike added, grinning broadly. Jaguars killed their quarry by freezing its movement. What few knew outside of those in metaphysics was that the jaguar pulled the spirit out of the body of its victim. Without the spirit, the victim cannot move.

Again, laughter filled the air. Roan watched as Inca quickly opened up the package and placed the salmon on the table so that everyone could partake. A fierce appreciation of her natural generosity rolled through him. He saw Inca trying to release her fear about Maya's coming mission. As always, she was putting others ahead of herself.

Rising, Alaria bestowed a warm smile upon them all. "Enjoy your lunch together, my children. I've already eaten and I'm being called to a counsel meeting. Blessings upon you…" And she turned and slowly walked away.

Mike dug into his bag again. "Hey, I brought something else for us, too." He grinned and lifted a bottle of champagne up for all to see.

Maya clapped her hands. "Yes! Perfect! What else have you got in that bag of tricks of yours, Houston?"

"Oh," he crowed coyly, "some other things." And he shifted the bag to the other side of his stool, out of Maya's reach—just in case.

Laughing, Inca quickly set wooden plates on the table and passed around the large platter of fresh fruit. Roan got up and handed everyone a mug so that the champagne could be uncorked and passed around. He then went to work on slicing the cheese.

Maya took the dark green bottle and, with her thumbs, popped the cork. It made a loud sound. The cork went sailing past Roan, struck the wall of the hut and bounced harmlessly to the ground. "One of the few times I've missed my intended target!" she exclaimed.

"You have to do better than that," Roan told her dryly. "I duck fast."

Laughing deeply, Maya stood and poured champagne into each cup. As Inca placed the sliced cheese on a large plate, she passed the first cup to her.

"Here, little sister, taste this stuff. You're gonna like it. You're a greenhorn when it comes to modern society, and this is one of the nice things about it. Go on, try it."

Sniffing the champagne cautiously, Inca sat down next to Roan. As the others began to reach for the sliced bread, fruit and cheese, she pulled her cup away and rubbed her nose. "It tickles!"

"You've been out in the bush too long," Maya said with a giggle. "That's champagne. It's supposed to bubble and fizz. Here, lift your mug in a toast with us." Maya raised her mug over the center of the small, circular table. "Here's to my sister, Inca, who I'm proud as hell of. For her guts, her moxie and never giving up—this toast is to her!"

Everyone shouted and raised their mugs. Inca hesitantly lifted hers. "This is a strange custom, Sister."

Roaring with laughter, Maya said, "Just wait. You've been sequestered in a rain forest all your life. I wasn't. So, each time I visit you, from now on, I'm gonna share a little of my partying life-style with you."

Inca watched as everyone grinned and took a drink of the champagne. Unsure, she sniffed it again. Lifting the mug to her lips, she tasted it. "Ugh!"

Roan smiled when Inca's upper lip curled in distaste. Brushing her cheek with a finger, he said, "Champagne is an acquired taste. The more you drink it, the more you like it over time."

"I do not think so." Inca frowned and set the mug on the table.

Giggling, Maya said, "Jungle girl! You've been too long out in the boonies, Inca. Come on, take another little sip. It will taste better the second time around. Go ahead.…"

Giving Maya a dark, distrustful look, Inca did as she was

bid. To her surprise, Maya was right. Staring down at the mug, Inca muttered, "It tastes sweeter this time...."

"Yep. After a couple more sips, you'll see why we like it so much." Maya reached for the champagne bottle, which sat in the middle of the table. "Come on, Houston, drink up. I'm not polishing this bottle off by myself." She wiggled her eyebrows comically. "Of course, I *have* been known to do that—but not this time."

Inca sat back and laughed, the mug between her hands. She couldn't believe that Maya could drink a whole bottle by herself! Her sister was so funny, so playful and joking compared to her. Inca looked forward to Maya's visits so she could absorb every tiny detail of her sister's life. Compared to her, Inca felt as though she had been raised in a bubble.

Inca shared a loving look with Roan. Warming beneath his tender gaze, she felt a lot of her worry dissolving. Maya was a woman of the world. She knew and understood life outside the rain forest and how it worked, while Inca did not. Perhaps Maya *would* be safe. Inca prayed that would be true. With Michael working with her sister, Inca felt some assurance of that. However, she also knew that no Jaguar Clan member was impervious to death. They died just as quickly and easily as any other human being if the circumstances were right. She knew that from her own dire experience.

Epilogue

Inca sighed, nestling deeply into Roan's arms. They had just settled down for the night in their own hut, which to her delight was situated near the bubbling creek. Inhaling Roan's scent, she gloried in it as she moved her fingers languidly across his chest. Feeling his arms clasp her in a tender embrace, she closed her eyes.

"Each day, I become more happy," she confessed.

Smiling in the darkness, his eyes shut, Roan savored Inca's warm naked body pressed against his. He lay on his back, the pallet soft and comfortable beneath them. A cool breeze moved through the windows and brought down the temperature to a pleasant range for sleeping.

"I never thought I would have the kind of happiness I have now," he murmured near her ear. Sliding a strand of her soft, recently washed hair through his fingers, he pressed a kiss to the silky mass.

Snuggling more deeply into his arms, Inca lay there a long time, her eyes partly open, just staring into the darkness.

"What is it?" Roan asked as he trailed his hand across

her shoulder. "You're worrying. About Maya? Her mission?"

"I cannot keep my thoughts from you, can I?"

Chuckling indulgently, Roan said, "No."

"I am glad you allowed me to give her the necklace you gifted me with. Did you see Maya's eyes light up when she saw that blue stone?"

"Mmm, yes I did. She seemed to know a lot about that rock. One day, when the time's right, maybe she'll tell us about it. At least we know it comes from one seam in a copper mine north of Lima."

"And she held it as if it were precious beyond life."

Nodding, Roan continued to move his fingers down the supple curve of Inca's spine. Gradually, he felt the fine tension in her body dissolving beneath his touch. Love could do that. And he loved her with a fierceness and passion he'd never known before. "That stone has been passed down through my family for untold generations. My mother gave it to me after my vision quest at age fourteen—at the ceremony when I turned into a man. She told me then that it came from the south. I thought she might have meant the southwest—perhaps Arizona or New Mexico. Now I realize she meant South America, and specifically, Peru. It's had an amazing journey, and now it seems like it's come home to where it started so long ago."

Sliding her hand across his massive chest, Inca absorbed his warmth and strength. How wonderful it felt to be able to touch him whenever she pleased. It was a heady gift. "Maya said there is only one mine in the world that has a seam of this stone. It is so rare. She said men kill to steal it from miners who look for it."

"Yes, and that it possesses certain powers." He smiled a little. "I'd sure like to know more about what they are."

"I think Maya knows, but sometimes, because we are in the clan, information is given only when it is appropriate. Otherwise, we are not told."

Roan nodded and quirked the corner of his mouth. "Still, I'm curious. I'm beginning to think that maybe one of my ancestors was South American, but I have no way to prove it. Our people pass on traditions verbally, so nothing's written on paper to verify it one way or another."

Pressing a kiss against the thick column of his neck, Inca murmured, "I believe you are right. Why else would you have come back? Our spiritual path always makes a circle of completion. Perhaps one of your ancestors walked north and met and fell in love with one of your Lakota relatives, and remained and lived there. That would explain your twin path between the two Americas, yes?"

It made a lot of sense to Roan. "I like the idea of living in the Amazon basin with you and helping the Indian people to keep their land as the hordes flee the cities of Brazil. I'm looking forward to making a life for us there."

"I am content that our people are safe without us being there."

Roan knew Inca had worried about that. She was driven and responsible in the care and protection of the Indians in Amazonia. Maya's reassurances that they had reduced the number of cocaine-producing factories and, therefore, the ability of drug lords to enslave the Indians, lessened her anxiety about it.

"I want to use this next nine months here in the village as a well-deserved rest for you," Roan said, turning onto his side and pressing her gently against him. He felt Inca make that deep-throated purr that moved through him like promising, provocative fingers of heat. "See this as a vacation."

Laughing throatily, Inca eased back and looked up into his dark, carved features. She melted beneath his smoldering blue eyes, which regarded her through dark, spiky lashes. Mouth drawing upward, she whispered, "We are here for training. And the elders are pleased with your progress."

"I think they're pleased with both of us," he said, tracing

the outline of her broad, smooth forehead with his fingertips. "And I also think they're very glad you're back home here, with them. You're a powerful person, Inca. They need warriors with hearts like yours. People like you don't grow on trees, and they know that. Best of all, Grandfather Adaire has made amends to you. He's no longer the enemy you thought he was, and I'm glad to see that rift between you healed."

She nodded, her eyes softening. "He has always been the father I did not have, and now he is that again for me." Inca caught Roan's hand and placed a soft, searching kiss into his palm. She felt him tense. Lifting her head, she said, "In our business, there are not always happy endings, Roan. I was glad to hear of Julian, and his father, Colonel Marcellino, from Michael."

"Yes," Roan murmured, "the colonel embraced Julian and finally came to realize that his second son is just as worthy of all the praise and attention his first son had received. I'm sure it's made a difference in their family dynamic."

"So perhaps getting bitten by the bushmaster was a good thing." Inca sighed. "So often I see bad things happen to good people. At the time, I know they think they are being cursed, but it is often a blessing. They just do not realize it yet."

"No argument there," Roan said as he leaned down and nibbled on her bare shoulder. She tasted clean, of mango soap with a glycerin base that someone in the village had made days earlier. "I had a lot of bad things happen to me, and look now. Look who is in my arms and who loves me, warts and all." And he chuckled.

Laughter filled the hut, then Inca said petulantly, "You are not a frog! You have no warts, my husband."

"It's slang," he assured her, grinning at her impertinence. "In time, I'll have you talking just like Maya does."

"Humph. Maya was educated in North America. She

picked up all those funny words and sayings there. Many times, I do not understand what she talks about.''

"Slang is a language of its own," he agreed, absorbing Inca's pensive features. Her eyes were half closed, shining with love—for him. "But next time Maya visits us, you'll be able to understand her better. I'll teach you American slang.''

"Good, because half of what she says, I do not grasp.''

"Like?''

"Well," Inca said, frustrated, "words such as *fire bird*.''

"That's slang for an Apache helicopter gunship. They're called fire birds because of all the firepower they pack on board. They've got rockets, machine guns and look-down, shoot-down capabilities. A fire bird is one awesome piece of machinery. And in the right hands, it's a deadly adversary.''

"Oh. I thought she meant a bird that had caught its tail on fire.''

Roan swallowed a chuckle. "What other slang?''

Rolling her eyes toward the darkened ceiling, she thought. The chirping of crickets and croaking of frogs was a musical chorus against the gurgling creek. "Herks.''

"That's a C-130 Hercules—a cargo plane. I think she's referring to the Herks that provide her helicopters with fuel in midair. The Apache can be refueled in flight to extend its range of operation. The Herk carries aviation fuel in special bladders within the cargo bay.'' He lifted his hand above her to illustrate his point. "The Herk plays out a long fuel line from its fuselage, like a rope, and the helicopter has a long, extended pipe on its nose. There's a cone at the end of the fuel line, and when the helo connects with that, gas is pumped on board, so the helo can continue to fly and do surveillance to find the bad guys.''

"I see....'' Inca sighed. "Her world is so different from mine. She was adopted and taken north and educated there. She is a pilot. She flies like a bird.'' Inca shook her head.

"I am on the ground, like a four-legged, and she is the winged one."

"Both of you carry very heavy responsibilities in the jobs you've agreed to take on," Roan reminded her. "Maya's role might appear more glamorous to outsiders, but the ground pounder—the person in the trenches, doing what you do every day—is of equal importance. Winning sky battles is only part of it. If people such as yourself were not on the ground doing the rest of the work, the air war would be futile."

"She has told me of the sky fights she's had with drug lords. She said they have helicopters that can shoot her out of the air." Inca frowned up at him. "Is this so?"

Groaning, Roan gathered her up and held her tightly to him. "My little worrywart," he murmured, pressing small kisses against her wrinkled brow. "Over the next few months, I'll try to outline what Maya does for a living. Mike Houston told me a lot about her background and education. I think once you know and understand more about her, you'll stop worrying so much. Maya is considered the best Apache helicopter pilot in this hemisphere. That's why the army is sending their best instructor pilots here. The army's hoping to map out a long-term strategy to eradicate drug lords from the highland villages, destroy all the little, hidden airports so that they can't ship their drugs out so easily. Maya's been trained for this, Inca. She's just as good at what she does as you are."

Satisfied, Inca sighed and surrendered to the warmth and strength of his arms. Lifting her hand, she looked at the two rings glittering on her finger. One of the gifts Michael had brought with him in that sack of his was a plain gold wedding band. Unknown to her, Roan had asked the major to furnish him with one to compliment her peridot engagement ring. Roan had given her the second ring when they were alone in their hut that very evening. Its beauty and symbolism touched her heart and soul deeply.

"I love you, man of my heart...." she said softly near his ear.

Roan smiled tenderly and stroked her hair. "And I'll love you forever, Inca. Forever..."

* * * * *

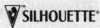
SILHOUETTE®

THE MACGREGORS

4 BOOKS ON THIS WELL-LOVED FAMILY

BY

NORA ROBERTS

Book 1 - Serena and Caine - September 2000

Book 2 - Alan and Grant - December 2000

Book 3 - Daniel and Ian - May 2001

Book 4 - Rebellion - August 2001

Don't miss these four fantastic books by Silhouette's top author

The romance you'd want

Escape into

Silhouette

DESIRE ®

Intense, sensual love stories.

Desire™ are short, fast and sexy romances featuring alpha males and beautiful women. They can be intense and they can be fun, but they always feature a happy ending.

The romance you'd want

Escape into

Silhouette

SPECIAL EDITION®

Vivid, satisfying romances, full of family, life and love

Special Editions are romances between attractive men and women. Family is central to the plot. The novels are warm upbeat dramas grounded in reality with a guaranteed happy ending.

GEN/23/RTL

The romance you'd want

Escape into

Silhouette

SENSATION®

Passionate, dramatic, thrilling romances

Sensation™ are sexy, exciting, dramatic and thrilling romances, featuring dangerous men and women strong enough to handle them.

GEN/18/RTL3